LINES

OF

BLOOD

BOOK ONE OF THE BLOOD SCION SAGA

Birth

By Stephen Fenech

Stephen Fenech

© Copyright 2022

Portfolio Visions Books
ISBN 9780995261167
Toronto Canada

For Ian Barret: Sensei, Friend, Hero

Stephen Fenech

Starbond

When the Circled River's flowing red
And the Ancient Lines of Blood have bled
When seethes Eternals' crimson gale
Vein or Siphon will prevail

Octagon

Four opposed to Four opposed
First Circle's fire: First Circle's wrath
Where spiral balance will compose
The stellar dance or stellar death
To make or break the final path.

Starbond

-Excerpt from *The Kusp of the Testament*
Songs of the Kusp: Revelations and Prophecies

Stephen Fenech

CHAPTERS

PROLOGUE I
1056 C.E.

Lord Shirdron stood alone atop the summit of Spires' Mast, gazing with dead eyes upon the desecration he had wrought. Tremors continued beneath his sandaled feet. The wind held its breath. But the air vibrated with dark magic as the sky faltered.

He should have gained a suit of armour, along with a shield, helm, and sword. Yet despite his sorcery, Shirdron remained naked and divested. Resounding proof that the end of all things had come. The limitless power he had once commanded surrendered no tools from the ether—and no answers.

Except one.

His efforts had proven premature: all his magic stripped away, leaving him powerless. The staff Shirdron used to trigger these events had broken. The Octagon and double-crucifix emblem he had etched into the mountain stone erased before his eyes, burned away by some intruding presence.

And the omnipotent Kalibah Crystal, which once adorned the headpiece of his sceptre, had exploded. The blast scattered the shards of the lodestone to the four winds. And with them fled the Kalibah's life-healing power.

Now, Shirdron would never reach the First Circle of Creation to repair the damage he had caused.

Damnation, he had abdicated his throne, set aside everything—for this? His frustration mounted. The prophecy had evinced a lie! All the immense might he commanded of the crystal had been for naught.

Branded a heretic by his royal peers, Shirdron thought he would curtail the Dragon Wars, put an end to the wanton bloodshed by removing its sole perpetrator and Areth's most vile nemesis: Deathwrought—the Darkest One.

Only now did the Lord realize that he had been falsely lured to this moment, manipulated by the very same foe he sought to vanquish. This had been Deathwrought's ploy all along.

And he had played right into the Darkest One's hands.

Shirdron's misconceptions and arrogance had betrayed him. Now, at the end, did the wilderen magic show its true face—forged like a double-edged sword—leaving him no choice, but to fall on it.

By his own hand, Shirdron had struck mortal wounds against the very thing he strived his entire life to protect. Betrayed the trust of those he swore to guard—and damned them all forever. Not only the subjects of his former realm, but all of Creation would pay for his folly.

Shirdron had single-handedly aberrated time and disrupted events from their intended course—events long-heralded by the Time Wardens. The Blood Scions would birth in stillness, trapped by the Darkest One's cunning and his own recklessness. There would be no balance, for Shirdron had tampered with and broken the Law of the Octagon.

As long as voices endured to cry out and ears to hear their lament, the freeborn would curse his name with their dying breaths before they themselves met annihilation. His name would remain synonymous with genocide—pariah fouler than the Darkest One.

For though Shirdron knew he harboured no evil, he had done greater despoliation than any twisted by Deathwrought.

Chest seizing with overwhelming guilt, Lord Shirdron buried his face in his trembling hands. "What have I done?"

The earth responded.

It bucked and cracked and parted in an ear-shattering cacophony. The spread of the infliction gathered strength and momentum, escalating towards final eradication.

Body wracked with exhaustion, the tormented lord straightened and braced stiff legs against the quivering ground, knowing his final doom at hand. He reached out with his inner eye and saw the devastation grip his world.

Tidal waves drowned distant shores across the Main and beyond. Volcanoes erupted, blasting lava above the clouds, raining fiery death on the dragons and great geese, even as they fought.

The firestorm cremated all the lesser raptors as well, before falling across the steppe, incinerating great tracts of forest and the creatures trapped within. Bleeding mountains calved and collapsed on top of thousands of people as they fled. Deserts lost their consistency and became fluidic, drowning every caravan in their endless sands.

Shirdron bore witness to every razed city, every scene of ruin.

It all came back to him.

But at *Her* behest. She had insisted, it was the only way.

The gutrock far below Spires' Mast split into a yawning gulf, tearing a fatal lesion into Areth from horizon to horizon and wrenching Shirdron off his feet. He nearly toppled off the vertiginous height but somehow managed to hold on.

High above the clouds, upon that pinnacle of rock, he crawled on hands and knees to the shaking edge of the outcrop. There, he could only watch the drop in sickening horror as the tear in the earth ripped wider, deeper, wider.

"Creator!" Shirdron wailed as the cataclysms intensified across his world and the heavens beyond. "How can you let this happen? First Father, why have you forsaken your children?"

The Starbond had begun. And it was False. Now oblivion would claim all of Creation.

A blinding white light seared reality and in his final moments before the deepest sleep took him, Lord Shirdron could hear Deathwrought laughing triumphantly over him.

PROLOGUE II
2028 C.E.

The capricious waves rolled past like endless hills of grey lead. They rattled the *Tide Turner*'s hull, making the small yacht rock left and right. Outside, the rain fell in lashing torrents and the gusts howled like ghosts from the scary movies. They seemed so angry.

Zzzzzzzzz-PANG!

Eight-year-old Zach gasped as the thunder struck right on the heels of the lightning flash. Trapped in the boat's pilothouse, he clung white-knuckled to the high swivel chair's armrests—and prayed for land.

Wide-eyed, the boy focused on the ghosting green line that swept a circular course around the radar screen.

"Shit," Dad cursed, drawing Zach's attention.

Dad spun the chromed wheel with one hand, his other locked on the throttle.

The boat's diesel motor screamed like a panicked orca.

Zzzzzzzzz-PANG! Lightning split the black sky. Closer.

Zach cried out, tears beginning to stream down his face.

"We'll make it, Zach," Dad soothed over his shoulder. "Don't you worry. We're through the worst of it. Just three more miles and we'll be safe and sound back in the harbour."

"Tristan, hurry!" Mom urged as she made her way up the steps, her raincoat dripping, matted hair strung like seaweed to her face.

"I'm red-lining as it is, honey," Dad replied in a quavering voice.

Mom pursed her lips and studied his face for an anxious moment. Then she crouched and wrapped her arm around Zach, checking his lifejacket. And kissed his cheek. "Dad's got this under control."

She glanced up at her husband. "I'm terrified."

Dad gave her a long look. "That makes two of us, Belle."

Zach gulped and sobbed, his hand clutching the pendant around his neck.

Zzzzzzzzz-PANG!

Dad faced forward again and spun the wheel hard to the left. "Two miles, Gang. I'm gonna try and move us closer to shore. Maybe find a lee to shelter us the rest of the way."

The radar blipped.

And blipped again, louder.

The overcast sky took on a greenish tinge.

Mom's regard swung back to Zach, eyes searching, encouraging. She brushed his hair back and offered a thin smile. "We're gonna make it, kiddo. You'll—"

The engines died.

"Holy-good-Christ!" Dad exclaimed. He leaned over the wheel and peered out of the rain-streaked window.

Mom inhaled sharply.

The green aura encompassed the boat.

Shaking uncontrollably, Zach followed their stares.

And saw… Him.

Not thirty feet beyond the bow, a cloaked figure floated *above* the swell. Pointed at the boat.

And blasted it with emerald fire.

The windscreen shattered. Chattel detonated all around Zach. And the yacht listed hard to the right.

Ears ringing, blinded in a haze of smoke, a concussed Zach suddenly found himself completely alone.

Through the ether, another green bolt struck the *Tide Turner*, peeling the roof back and casting Zach into the sea.

Stephen Fenech

BOOK 1: Birth
1000 years following the False Starbond

1: Cleft Augury
Sonart

It is a *Sword.* Even before the artifact fully materializes within the abyss, Sonart confirms his suspicion: the blade also functions as a magical emblem.

Odder still, the Sword mirrors Sonart's motion as he drifts alongside, suspended in the same expanse of luminous cloud.

At least that's what his inner eye tells him when he entered *the State*—a visceral iteration of reality, where the mind separates from the body, leaving it free to wander and envision this faraway plane.

Currently, Sonart's corporeal form lies elsewhere: prostrate on the floor of his prison cell within the Dunge. The State removes the dwarven's fetters for a time, allowing him to see, feel, hear, and touch, outside his trapped body.

But if the Sword truly is a charmed weapon, it does not match any he is familiar with, like the flaming broadswords the monstrous Colossals wield. Dark powers infused those blades, their flats spanning wider than a dwarven's head and near twice one's body length.

Stars, it isn't even a large sword, akin to those wrought in the fire pools of Bulkforge, the weapons Proclaimers brandished to administer the Darkest One's justice. No, this foil would only serve as a small trinket—an ironock-monger's castaway.

But perhaps… that is its trick: the mask of its metallic canvas. Magic has made the blade a powerful talisman. A cognizant entity? Seems so.

Sonart feels its energy without touching it. No one holds the weapon as it dances. It seems to defy nature with an arcane will of its own, naked at pommel, hilt, guard, and point, devoid of any grasp.

Again, and again, the weapon slices the ether between itself and him. Descending and ascending upon an unseen mark, the blade moves like a wisp on a current of air. And yet, determined in both stroke and pause.

Sonart has proven the only one among the caged dwarven to get this far. And he will likely go further this time—much further. He knows this for a certainty, senses it like the air in his lungs, the survival instinct in his gut.

If only he could understand the eldritch energy that made the Sword.

Chromatic flares of intense blue light begin to shift across its flat and radiate outward. The blade's speed and light whisper ghosting copies of itself like visual echoes.

Now, the blade's power flows freely, coruscating in every direction to augment the vaporous aura.

And the nimbus reciprocates, feeding back its lambent energy to the Sword, bonding the weapon's sweep with—the movement of Sonart's eyes.

But unlike the emblem, the ether has a pattern, a counterpoint to the Sword's chaos. Together they produce a kind of disjointed harmony, like contrasting notes in the orchestration of... *music*.

The more Sonart studies the image, the stronger it becomes, lifting the weight in his heart. His sorrow diminishes in the presence of the Sword, more than it ever had in the aura alone.

Sonart covets this miraculous sensation. It washes his soul clean and cloaks his mind from the harsh reality of his existence. Perhaps through it, he might find a permanent way from suffering.

This is not the first time Sonart has come to this place. But the Sword... it marks a new element—a usurper. He strives to stay in tandem with the bewitching totem—use himself as a conduit to channel the healing energy of its Song. Where aura and blade form harmony, Sonart might provide the melody connecting the two, composing an opus to redeem his people.

Sonart grasps a veiled design in the Sword's movement. Chaos held in check? Or merely how he perceives the conundrum? What uncanny truth does the weapon hold? What implications? Why a sword at all?

The revelation seems too much, too soon. Sonart treads dangerous ground. His efforts for answers only further his confusion, making him lose his link to the weapon. He discerns greater, vaster voids opening beyond his world—or tearing a rent.

The dwarven ignores what it might mean. If he loses focus now, he will squander his first real chance at redemption. It will be too late to begin again.

He has crossed a line. Passed the point of no return.

Sonart strains against his dilemma, his impetus flares anew—brighter. He forces his thoughts back into alignment. Unsure, the dwarven surrenders his hold. Relaxes enough to observe the blade's path without letting go completely.

The Sword solidifies once more.

Relieved, Sonart guides it back to him.

If only his connection to the emblem wasn't so fragile, so ephemeral.

Sonart shifts tack. Concentrating on the aura itself, he maps its contours, forming a similar vacuum in his mind. The Song grows louder, its notes more resolute.

Next, Sonart ponders the matter of the blade. The metal that gives it form will provide his solution. He suddenly knows this on an intrinsic level—and how to bridge with it. No sooner does he make the revelation than he recalls a voice from his distant past, 'All you must do is survive.'

Presently, another voice sounds in his head, a voice not his own. "Careful," it warns. "The key to the Augury only works for those aligned to its need."

Its need? The Augury's or that of the key? Sonart does not understand the warning, or who has spoken it—Malrik? Most like.

Regardless, Sonart takes the caution to heart and centres on the very definition of 'need.' To him, that would scabbard the greatest motive of all: preventing the downward spiral of his people—a key to that, drives him to THIS—!

The Sword halts, as though acknowledging Sonart's presence for the first time. The point of the blade turns toward him.

And springs.

Before Sonart can react, the weapon plunges into his chest. But stars eclipse, no pain lances him. He feels instead a wash of understanding. The Sword *is* the key—to the Augury.

The emblem nudges him forward. Pulls him with more insistence and greater swiftness. It impels him into uncharted warrens, opens gates of pure light and draws him through glowing tunnels, deeper into a stranger, airier plane.

Energy courses into Sonart's flesh and marrow. His head throbs under the sensation of motion. As if the incandescent surroundings move around the scope of his vision while he remains stationary.

The short journey ends within an inner sanctum, an alienage remarkably brighter than the hinterplane beyond. It pervades Sonart with a purity and terror of purpose. The light in this place conjures an image that feels true: the ethereal domain where his ancestors transcended, the haven where all who served the Kusp found their ultimate resting place—the reward that trauma in the Cradle bought.

The Afterworld?

No, stars align, Sonart has reached the Cleft Augury.

But something isn't right.

It cannot be the same place. A strange awareness creeps over him, an instinctive premonition of urgency. Apprehension renews his despair. Moments later he understands why.

He is not alone.

Something foreign to the place fast approaches from the opening void he felt tear earlier—something vile corrupts the aura. Scars the nimbus with its rouse.

The strange voice that told him to be careful resounds, anxiety plain as it shouts, "Flee, flee!"

But the heft of gloom confuses and paralyses Sonart. He misconstrues his course of action.

The aura begins to spin around him, using his carriage as its axis.

Closer and closer, the obscure presence looms.

Stricken with indecision, Sonart panics. His muscles tense into tourniquets. Tears well and flood his vision. His thoughts snag into tangled brambles.

The Sword erupts out of his body.

Its loss diminishes him. Pulsating with azure flashes, the weapon accelerates and resumes its erratic sweep, reflecting Sonart's turmoil. A blur in a craze, the emblem appears to struggle. As though trying to escape the sanctum and save itself from the alien, from Sonart.

Or both.

Sonart desperately needs the Sword. He must re-establish his link to the icon: the hinge between clarity and ignorance. But also, to escape the Augury himself. The key brought him here. It is his only way out.

The dwarven lunges wildly at the spinning blade. He bats his arms, digits scrabbling, clawing through the mist.

To no avail. The weapon evades his reach.

Frustration mounts with every failed attempt.

The Sword ebbs away.

"Hooks and Dunge, come!" Sonart grates between clenched teeth. Heart pounding to the point of bursting, his veins bulge, arms cabling in a maniacal effort to retrieve the emblem.

But the dwarven's last strength saps. Utter fatigue steals over him.

The Sword winks out. And does not return.

BAM!

A wall of raw power ploughs into Sonart, wrenching him into motion and ejecting him out of the sanctum. He hurls backwards, pitchpoling head over heels. The light gates slam shut as soon as he shoots past them. The luminous tunnels collapse in the ungodly torrent the dwarven leaves in his wake. He flushes out from all light and into consummate darkness.

Even as the sudden murk obliviates everything, its peace shatters, devoured by an unholy roar.

khhh-RRRAAAUUUGGGHHHhhhh
khhh-RAAAUUUGGGHHHhhhhhhh

It echoes across the black penumbra in a series of waves that escalate in measure, until the caterwaul reaches a torturous crescendo, drowning Sonart in its bedlam.

The terror is nowhere, and everywhere. It turns Sonart's marrow to ice. The onyx limbo makes enduring its harrowing screams much worse.

The entity rears, an inky blackness looming within the black.

And attacks.

With abrasive insistence, a multitude of tendrils seizes Sonart. They burn, sting, incise and lacerate every inch of his flesh. Voracious fingers smother, eviscerate, and incinerate him.

Clinging to the fragment of his soul which persists, Sonart struggles against his bonds for any surcease, including death.

He cries out his last.

A lone word in a language he has never heard before screams past his ravaged lips.

And hurls into the void.

The pain vanishes. So does the abomination inflicting it.

But Sonart's cry of anguish lingers, as he topples up from the depths.

Back into his real body, where he projects the last of his torment against the stone ceiling of his prison cell.

Lungs about to burst, Sonart sucks in dank, stale air. His panting subsides, but his mind races on as he lies there, heart trip-hammering like a Kworn's doom-drum.

A pair of dwarven arms reach under Sonart's sweat-soaked armpits and gently lift him into a sitting position. When the hands release him, he scooches back and feels the clammy mortar of the prison wall.

Sonart squints and blinks to clear the mix of soot and saltwater congealed in his eyes, glazing their corners and preventing his vision from sharpening.

But his ears still hone and perk, fine and good.

Out of the aural obscurity, the *thrump-thrump thrump-thrump* of marching boots arises.

"Sonart," Malrik's voice whispers urgently beside him, "they are coming."

Stephen Fenech

2: Dunge
Sonart

One of the three Kworn beastmen that guarded the prison level trudged away from his peers. The sentry chose the closest cell, occupied by a pair of unconscious dwarven, to relieve himself. He pressed up to the bars and grasped the gangly pillar between his legs.

Without warning, an invisible power wrenched him into the air. Slammed him against the far wall, then drove him to the stone floor with bone-crushing force.

Again! Again! Again!

His ironock armour dinted further with every blow until it cracked.

Suddenly maniacal, the guard squealed and flailed his arms and legs. Blood frothed from his viridian eyes and gaping mouth. In the space of three heartbeats, the sentry was pulverised. A final shudder and his paroxysms stilled.

The two surviving Kworn guards yowled and gesticulated misshapen arms, stumbling back as fast as they could. In their haste, they collided with the jagged corners of an adjoining tunnel and fell. Lantern orbs bulged in terror, intensifying the green glow they cast upon their dead cohort.

His remains darkened to an opaque black, before vanishing from the stone floor. Only a carbonized imprint of the victim's body remained.

Fresh beads of sweat trickled down Sonart's back. Breath laboured, his clothes sodden, he felt every muscle nag at him, turning his body into one giant bruise.

The pale-skinned dwarven winced as he raised a hand to remove debris from his dishevelled hair and beard. Strands that should've been auburn had been rendered charcoal with grime.

His short stature, stout limbs, large forehead, prominent eyebrows, and semi-cavernous eye-sockets marked a lighter version of his race's common traits but he bore a different kind of light, an inner light that he kept hidden for his protection as well as that of his peers.

Through a turbid haze, Sonart tethered all his hurts and used them to gain a toehold on his dire reality. His jail cell marked but one among a thousand such cages, crudely erected to house the incarcerated dwarven—dregs the Proclaimers deemed a threat to the Cradle.

A long tongue of flame lit the twelve-by-eight-foot pen. That torch sat caged as well, in a sconce bolted to the wall across the passageway beyond the cell bars. It made the shadows dance.

Sonart's study drifted languidly to the ceiling. The cubicle seemed a paradox of a room—closed to the point of suffocation, yet so empty of anything that might mend the rupture left in his disassociated mind.

Apart from Malrik, his brown-bearded cellmate, the only faces Sonart regularly saw belonged to the Kworn guards who patrolled the lost caverns and warrens that made up the Dunge.

While his heartbeat slowed, Sonart's awareness hitched on Malrik, pensively regarding him now—and his companion's grim revelation from a moment before.

Though the boots clopping down the distant corridor were not coming for him, if the ruckus and caterwauling Kworn gave any indication, something terrible had happened. And Sonart held little doubt that he was connected—the prized insect in the spider's web.

As if to affirm his conviction, a fist-sized arachnid appeared on the far wall, tracing a diagonal path down the mortar.

Sonart followed the hairy spider's descent from ceiling to floor, where a body lay heaped near the bars of the cell.

The dwarven blinked.

Facedown, the mottled figure's awkward position of torso and head suggested death. But the congregation of rats assured it. They suckled the corpse and pinched holes through the jerkin to claim bits of flesh while chittering to one another.

Sonart frowned. Down here in the Dunge, he'd seen his share of grizzly fates, hundreds of bodies consumed in this manner, but the height of the victim vexed him. This was no dwarven, no Kworn either. The corpse looked as though a dwarven had been elongated by some nefarious device. Yet managed to stay intact. Tall, wiry.

The Dunge contained torture facilities to render all manner of corruption in the deeper, fouler depths, far below this level. For certain, the further one went down, the larger and more heinous, the spiders.

Sonart had only descended so far, his knowledge scant, but rumours among the prisoners proliferated. Any dwarven with a semi-intimate knowledge of those cellars had already succumbed. The Dunge was after all a place of death. But stars be fucked, what brought that corpse into his locked cell?

Sonart's taciturn stare found Malrik.

"My stars eclipse, Sonart," a distressed Malrik blustered. "It happened so fast. I was focused on you."

"What did you see?" Sonart croaked, his words sounding scratchy to his ears.

"A Colossal—I believe. He must know. You've doomed us for certain this time."

"Malrik!" Sonart blazed through his parched throat. "Calm yourself."

His sudden ire made Malrik flinch, but it also steadied the brownbeard. He released a rush of air and dipped his beard.

"Now slowly, tell me all you witnessed," Sonart pressed.

Malrik splayed his hands. "Hooks and Dunge, I don't remember."

Sonart tightened his jaw. "Try."

"Everything seemed as before," Malrik explained in a small voice, "the other times you entered the State. Then, it—appeared." He indicated the corpse with a flick of his chin. "The Dunge itself shuddered—a blinding explosion— seared my vision. The discharge bashed me against the wall." He paused and presented his arm and shoulder, riddled with burns, bruises, and scrapes. "My back fared worse."

When Sonart inclined his head, his companion continued. "After my sight cleared of flash ghosts, I found that one—lying there—dead."

Sonart threaded fingers through his hair. "That may have been the very one that attacked me in the State."

Malrik's eyebrows sprang high. "Attacked—?"

"Did you examine the body?" Sonart asked.

Malrik looked down at his feet. "No, I wasn't sure it had passed. By the time I found my courage, you began convulsing. I shook you vigorously, but you refused to wake. Your face reddened, racked in torment, but no cry emerged from your lips."

Malrik checked himself. "No—wait. You murmured something—a single word, but I didn't catch it. A moment later, your seizures stopped. You grew moribund. I thought the deepest sleep had claimed you, but then you awoke of your own volition, screaming as if seared by a molten brand."

Despite his sore and stricken limbs, Sonart took his cellmate's hand in his and squeezed. "Forgive me, Malrik."

The dwarven gulped past his nod. "What happened to you?"

Sonart drew a deep breath and regaled Malrik with a vague account of his experience and encounter in the State. He carefully censored his words for his companion's sake. "I cannot begin to guess how I made such progress." *Or that Sword.* He cocked his head towards the dead body. "Or that."

"I'll check it now," Malrik offered dutifully. As the dwarven stood and shifted over to the corpse, the rats scattered, filtering past the cell bars.

With slow caution, Malrik crouched, reached for the far shoulder, and pulled. After some resistance, he lifted and turned the corpse.

When it flopped onto its back, Malrik recoiled. "Hooks and—" he shutter-gasped, "It has no face."

"Come quickly," Sonart urged. "We haven't much time."

When Malrik hunkered down before Sonart, he continued. "You said you believe a Colossal did this?"

Malrik hesitated. "Well, I can't be certain of course, but it's the only explanation for the light, especially here. No ordinary flame could create such intense brisance... and leave such a faceless carcass in its wake. I fear the Worst. He knows."

Sonart understood what Malrik meant by *He* and *Worst*—every damn dwarven did—the maleficent lord who held them all in thrall.

The Lightdimmer—Deathwrought—the Darkest One.

"You remained in the State longer than ever before," Malrik went on. "And everything fell apart out here." His voice guttered as a large rat scampered up to the dead body, claimed another morsel, and scurried out between the bars.

Malrik dry-swallowed. "I fear after this, He'll settle the Proclaimers' account with all dwarven—the Cradle over."

Sonart flashed with anger but held his tongue. The Dunge had crumbled his friend's resolve into detritus. The brownbeard's nerves, strung tight on tenuous chords, supported a husk of his former self.

The prison was a bane hanging over every dwarven head, those still fortunate enough to exist above the ground. It had once functioned as an ironock mine. But that had been long ago before the quarry exhausted its treasured ore. Stripped clean, it had since been retrofitted with bars forged from the mine's own deposits. And for any dwarven singled out as a dissident and 'proclaimed' Dunge-bound, it meant a one-way trip.

Barred at its entrance and guarded every turn of the dial, the giant labyrinth scalloped the foothills of the Innereach Mountains. The den teemed with droppings left by rodents in their relentless pursuit of any morsel that might pass as food, including each other. All sustenance, which might prolong their meagre animation for another *drear*—the dwarven day.

The rats' success could be measured by the number of vermin skeletons in the enclosure and the winding corridor beyond.

But dwarven and rodents aside, the vileness of the Dunge did propagate existence for the clandestine. Spiders proved the true masters of these dark pits, spinning webs on the ceilings and inaccessible cracks to avoid the maws of the rats, still virile enough to catch them.

When the moment ripened, the spiders would strike, sucking blood from all the prison's denizens: unlucky insects, dead or dying rats, and unconscious or emaciated dwarven. The arachnids would scuttle down the walls or slip hastily along their spun threads, clawing their way in and out of the cracks and crevices.

"Listen to me, Malrik. Do not fear any tribunal for the dwarven, or yourself. The only sod in the State was me. Neither you nor any other gleaned my vision, and I intend to keep it that way. I alone made this trespass." *But I am not alone. Others have had the same vision. This isn't isolated—it's a movement.*

Malrik's mouth opened but then his crow's feet lost their edge. "Strong you are, and resolute," he said, tone firming. "And I understand. Do not give me any details, but tell me—"

"Even a simple yea or nay I'll not impart," Sonart sidestepped. "Otherwise, you may be held accountable by association. Now, no more questions. We must be silent." His voice dropped to a whisper. "I fear the walls have grown ears."

"Of course," Malrik said with a brusque nod, his cheeks flushing red. Pity imbued Sonart, softening his rigidity as he studied his cellmate. The depraved brownbeard attempted a show of courage they both knew he no longer possessed.

With a curt bow, Sonart feigned an encouraging smile. And said no more.

Prefaced by the sound of marching boots, a cadre of five Kworn guards arrived. The emerald glow of their lantern eyes bathed the walls and floor of the tunnel, cutting through the perpetual darkness of the Dunge's warrens.

Standing between five and six feet, two heads taller than the average dwarven and near twice as wide, the barrel-shaped Kworn drew up to Sonart's cell. The hideous frowns marring their impassive faces etched their greyish-green skin—an inherent trait to their ilk.

Savage they were, with burly disjointed arms. They had no necks to speak of. Conic heads sat on extended shoulders that hunched like hillocks above the furrowed crowns they framed. Myriad veins networked their obtuse carriages. Clumpy tufts of coarse hair sprouted all over their bodies like sawgrass.

Swathed in grease, their skin generated a foul stench of rotten meat. The oily secretions spilt onto their rusted armour, most of which had been permanently grafted into their flesh—more as a symbol of status than any viable functionality. The beastmen's rivet-lined breastplates, gorgets, and grieves appeared superficial, easily split by a well-placed axe blade.

Heavy irregular rasps filled the cell as their chieftain pulled out a set of keys—only chiefs and castellans carried them—and wrestled with the lock. It clicked open with a sharp metallic thunk.

The ironock door screeched in protest as the Kworn forced its hinges to grind around their corrugated pins. One by one, they entered, choking off what little space remained. Fangs gnashed when Sonart and Malrik scuttled back against the wall.

Sonart had long anticipated a reckoning for his risky ventures. Hewn of ironock, the dwarven's gall and willpower galvanized his resolve. But he wouldn't delude himself into believing it would be enough.

One of the guards closed in on Malrik. With abrupt swiftness he served the dwarven's head a backhand blow with his gauntleted arm, sending him sprawling to the floor.

Sonart had just enough time to see his companion crumple and lay still before the same lightning cracked against the back of his skull, hurling him into blackness.

3: Brooke

BOOM!

The explosion rocked the darkened streets of the city. In the next instant, fire turned night into day.

BOOM-BOOM-BOOM! Multiple blasts sprang everywhere. Flaming coruscations flashed, sprouted, built. And ignited again. Countless founts detonated in the endless overture, each heralding a bouquet of blazing stone.

BOOM!

Flurries of panicked men and women ran in every direction. Pandemonium reigned. Voices roared, trying in vain to carry over the fierce din generated by a thousand conflagrations. The flames feverishly licked all the fractured redoubts, warrens, and ramparts. They rendered the city surrounding Pathguard Castle a collection of charred and smouldering ruins.

Out of the cacophony, the thunder of hooves rang sharply off the walls. A regiment of twenty king's guardsmen astride massive destriers filled the cobblestone square.

Armoured in full plate and chainmail hauberks, grieves, and helms with nasal bars, the company glowed orange in the firelight as they pulled their mounts up and beckoned the hapless throng. Twenty warhorses whinnied in shrill chorus.

The wide-eyed commoners rushed in, pleading for deliverance as they converged on the horsemen and their red-caped leader.

Commander Aviry Brooke stood in the stirrups. A glance told him where their greatest danger lay. Many among the citizenry had been scorched by the incessant waves of heat, but alive they remained, thank the gods.

Bearing dark hair, larger alert eyes, a lean proportional nose, plump lips, and a well-defined jawline, the commander had been told by his peers that his was a face of authority. He could only hope it counted for something here and now, offering a firm but friendly anchor to help settle the panicked populace.

BOOM! Brooke flinched as a watchtower bracing one corner of the bailey ignited near its base. A sparking blossom of stone blocks rained down on the heads of the fleeing people. Most avoided the blast, but it smote the closest. Two unlucky souls caught fire as they fled.

A second later, the crown of the tower toppled as its stem caved in on itself in a mushroom of smoke. Stricken people ran in confused circles, seeking a refuge that could not be found. Cut off on all sides, they cowered before the encroaching flames.

In the distance, the air cracked several times as more explosions ignited.

Fire engulfed another of the city's residential districts as the incendiary strikes laid waste to homes and flats. Noxious fumes choked the air all around them, making them gag.

To his troops, Brooke commanded, "Form a phalanx, shield the people from the advancing fires—the flames carry on slicks of oil!" Then he addressed the terrorized crowd. "All of you, quick, follow us through the south causeway."

"It's shut," cried an old man, his hands splayed.

"Looks worse than it is," Brooke shouted back. He squared his jaw. "And it's the only safe route."

A thick cloud of smoke wafted past, making them all cough. Some civilians hacked up phlegm. A few bent forward and retched.

When the black skein passed, Brooke blinked the worst of the soot from his watering eyes and cleared his throat. "Linger, and you will die. Now, stay close behind our mounts. To me!"

He spun his horse, Maxan, to face his lieutenant. "The entire bloody quadrant's doomed."

Brooke unsheathed his sword and pointed it towards his intended route. The insignia on his breastplate distinguished his rank, but the temerity in his voice and his severe comportment seemed to have restored a measure of calm. Searching gazes and brisk nods abounded as the press flocked within the soldiers' phalanx like lost children reunited with their parents.

For these people, at this moment, Brooke's direction became the spoken Kusp doctrine to them—and his guards. If only he could take stock in it as well.

The procession, two hundred strong, surged south out of the fray. A moment later, several fire-ridden edifices collapsed right behind them. When they reached the next courtyard beyond an interconnecting causeway, a lone rider galloped up to the regiment's arrowhead.

"Commander Brooke!" The soldier hailed as he reined in his mount and sidled up beside Maxan.

Brooke cocked his chin at the scout. "Report."

"A safer route lies towards the left-wing of the West Ward—in District Six."

Brooke nodded, then turned to address the civilians under his care. "My men will escor—"

A blast of light discharged throughout the only shadowy quadrant of the kingdom. Seconds later, a concussive echo reached them. It made every flame-tongue jitter, rattled every structure and body.

A two-hundred-foot wall of flame plumed a moment after that. Fires now burned high beyond all sides of the arcade. The ambient heat intensified.

Commander and scout shared a curse.

Brooke's voice vaulted over the common folk's panicked ruckus as it arose once more. Feigning humour, the commander laughed, "Appears District Six has—*cough-cough*—other plans. The West Ward is no longer an option."

Stuck in the crux of a cataclysm, Brooke's station demanded he quell his surmounting frustration and set the example. Any indecision or dalliance henceforth carried a verdict of incineration.

The commander swept his scrutiny past the expectant faces, across the fire-ridden courtyard. The arched porticoes at either end of the enclosed plaza—scorched and burning red-hot—taunted him like the open maws of dragons. They had effectively boxed in the soldiers and civilians alike. And set them upon a pyre.

"Stars blacken!" one of his guardsmen gasped, causing him to cough violently.

At his wit's end, Brooke tilted his head to the night sky—to plead some mercy of the Starsmith. As he did, something caught his notice. Past the undulating columns of smoke ran a viaduct.

Brooke followed the ponte to its closest juncture with the courtyard before it curved away to another quadrant. The viaduct fed the aqueduct. And the vertical pipe connecting the flyover to that canal system lay just beyond *this* arcade's closest building.

An idea struck Brooke and he cornered it. "Quick! Everyone, follow me!" He kicked Maxan's flanks and charged towards the building in line with that stone tower.

The edifice looked nothing more than an open-faced wagon repair shop, but a narrow warren right beside it revealed a five-foot-wide civil works access corridor. A locked wooden gate barred the entrance.

No time for finesse.

With a hard touch of spur, the commander impelled Maxan to rear up on his hindquarters. In an expert move, the destrier kicked at the lock. It splintered off its housing with his first kick. The gate blasted back wide with the second.

"Into the canal," Brooke yelled over his shoulder. "It's our only chance."

Eyebrows raised and mouths formed large O's, but no one questioned the commander. They all fell in after him as Maxan raced into the tight entryway. Forty feet later, the horse angled down a short slope into the coolness of the kingdom's water routing system.

Only six feet deep, the water splashed up and surged away from the cavalry as the company drove their horses in, their hooves knocking unsteadily on the canal's stone bottom.

As Brooke's mount half-swam half-walked in the direction they had just come, the commander greedily sucked in an untainted breath. The smoke skeins had not yet penetrated the duct—a benison to be sure. But he knew what a slim chance the canal offered.

Despite its slow current and shallow depth, several commoners could drown or be smothered in the confined aqueduct. But by taking this route, most would have a feasible way out, relatively free from the worst of the fiery scourge above.

The falling debris proved considerably less along the banks of the aqueduct. Luckily, the current flowed with them and not against. It made it easier for the horseless civilians, speeding them along as they trod water or hopped along.

The waterway passed through a series of tunnels and culverts that ran under the bridges and buildings above. During those times, it grew too dark to make out more than the closest faces. A glance back confirmed that at least the entourage still swam or drifted behind his men. No cries of pain at Brooke's backside and no further obstacles ahead. But to what end would he take them?

When the artery opened into a wide reservoir, lit ochre by the fires still raging on all sides, the commander got his answer. Towards the far end of the basin, a solid bridge traversed the pool, providing a beacon of hope. Beyond the span, the pool narrowed again to feed the city's main trunk.

As the train of bodies pushed towards the bridge, chunks of fiery rubble rained down like flaming potshots. Amidst the chorus of whistling detritus, the first mortal cry went up as one of the larger blocks hit an ill-fated man among the swimmers.

Once they reached the comparative safety beneath the bridge, the commander guided Maxan to one side of the construct.

The destrier splashed, then coursed up the sloped embankment in an echoing *thabulup thabulup* of hooves. Brooke brought Maxan to a halt on the level portion of the rampart directly below the parapet. This would serve as a haven where they could all wait out the calamity. Used as a floodgate for overflow during the rainy season, it would keep them safe with any luck.

Luck had led Brooke through most campaigns, audacity saw him safely past the rest. Both halves to the whole. Both sorely needed to weather this disaster—a disaster that could have easily been avoided had cooler heads prevailed in the debate.

He spun his mount around and waited, allowing space for the rest of his charges to egress. The sound of knocking hooves and splashing feet reverberated beneath the bridge as the congregation of haggard faces spilled up onto the levee. The men-at-arms alighted.

Within minutes, the lot of sodden, winded townspeople joined the military conclave, trudging or wavering drunkenly up the slope, helped by the more able soldiers.

Other men-at-arms from Brooke's regiment hobbled the excited horses together. Within minutes the mounts stood leg to leg in a row, atop the rampart and away from the growing press.

One by one, the survivors gathered tightly outside the circle of soldiers that formed around Brooke, still astride Maxan. The vantage made it possible to survey the destruction on either side of the bridge, lit by the rippling dance of amber and red against the water of the reservoir.

Brooke dismounted.

Distant flareups continued to rock the city everywhere, sending tremors under the commander's boots and up his spine.

But the devastation had peaked. The explosions sounded softer, less frequent, and further away with every passing moment.

Brooke waited in grim silence, pupils trained on the distant barrage of fiery ignitions. When no more detonations sounded, he let his taut shoulders sag. Sombreness and expectancy reigned amongst the near two hundred faces pinioned to his. They would wait here. They would survive.

"The worst of the fire's rampage seems past," Brooke announced. "You will all remain safe here, under our guard and protection."

Relief washed over the common folk's expectant faces. Palms pressed to hearts, gradually all of them slumped to the ground.

"Stars chase the shadows, there's nothing left to burn," the commander added under his breath.

His nearest troops nodded firmly. Jaws set, they seemed to steel their resolve.

Within moments, the smoke in the immediate warren dissipated. Some minutes more and the coughs, heaves, and gagging of the survivors also ebbed.

No doubt, the fires would continue to blaze past the witching hour and unto dawn. Then, the citywide demolition would be complete.

Brooke handed Maxan's bridle to one of his men. As the soldier led him away to the others, the commander sat down on the stone slope. He used a fold of his drenched cape to wipe the worst of the ash and soot from his face, then rested his arms and head on lifted knees.

Smoke continued to rise in the further quadrants, curling columns of black and grey against dawn's pink and purple blush.

One of his officers sat down beside him. "Commander?"

Brooke lifted weary eyes. "Aye?"

"All due respect, Sir, how could this have happened?" The soldier swallowed, looked over either shoulder, and bit his lip. "Was it the sprites—as His Grace feared?"

"Nay," Brooke replied. He picked up a small stone and lobbed it into the canal. It plopped and sank. "For a certainty, this is *his* work—Targin, of the Nightwolves."

4: Cradle
Sonart

Dead calm. It meant something. Meant something bad approached. An ill portent always foreshadowed a dead calm, like the hush before a Proclaimer's verdict or the pausing front of a razor storm—the worst expression of the Scourge's wrath.

A javelin of pain speared Sonart's head, jarring him back into consciousness. The pommel of a Kworn's sword had laid him out cold. His skull throbbed like a fractured boulder, losing purchase on a barren slope.

Sonart grew aware of guttural breathing, running feet, and the pervasive smell of musk. He tasted mud on his tongue and spat it out.

A chill breeze roused the stale air. It hissed louder and more persistent, further detangling his mind. The hurt from his contusion lessened.

Wind could mean only one thing: stars, he was *outside* the Dunge. No dwarven that still drew air ever left the Dunge.

Umph! Another ache announced itself: his abdomen made tender by a series of dull blows. When he rolled his eyes open, shock from the unexpected brightness careened through them like a thousand tiny pins. Pupils swimming through salty tears, his vision cleared.

He was being carried up a mountain, hefted like a sack of grain over the malformed shoulder of a Kworn—the first in a party of five. Undoubtedly, the same cadre that invaded his cell. If so, what of Malrik?

Between his dangling arms, the ragged legs of his captor ran full-tilt up a muddy slope. To evade a fresh wave of clay rivulets kicked up by the beastman, Sonart hoisted his head to face the defiled path behind the trailing brutes.

Flanked and riddled with rock fragments, the rutted trail wound up stark foothills. They overlooked the brown barren plain of the Steppe, stretching far below.

Even after two star-cycles, locked and buried in the Dunge, Sonart quickly gleaned what the guards feverishly scaled. A twist of his neck confirmed the Thorned Spikes rising before the advancing host.

Jagged to a saw's serrated edge, the four central mountain peaks defined the Innereach. As seen from the dwarven villages along the fringe of the Lobe, the immense sentinels of black rock resembled prongs of an obsidian crown.

Dread seized Sonart. Like every dwarven, he knew what lay within that circlet, what king.

Up one shattered slope, down another, the Kworn band moved like parts of the same beast, nothing but determination in the gallop of their heels. Every higher pinnacle and plateau the beastmen summited, the more dismal the vista became, unfolding the ravaged tundra that defined Sonart's world.

The Cradle.

To say one stood in the shadows of the Innereach was a misnomer, for apart from the Darkest One Himself and the shadows that danced to lamp and torch, no natural shadows in the Cradle existed: the sky was eternally overcast, eternally scorched. Only the degree of shade could be discerned.

Above the howl of the wind, a distant rumble sounded in the Spikes' upper reaches. The five Kworn let out nervous grunts, one a curt wail, before doubling their pace. The creatures' trepidation stemmed from storm fear—something Sonart had not contended with since his imprisonment. Now it came back to him in a rush.

Another razor storm brewed, a machination of the Scourge. The roiling fester of louring clouds had already crowded in and grew heavy over the Steppe. Thunder rolled in the distance. By the wind's piercing yowl and the coppery taste on his tongue, it would be potent.

The weather throughout the Cradle was severe, but a razor storm proved something else entirely, exacerbated by the eldritch energies of the Scourge—One of the Four Siphons—archdemons in service to their only master, the Darkest One. Together, they formed a sinister quintet of evil.

Razor storms kept the dwarven underfoot, 'safely in their homes when an unknown posed a potential threat to the Cradle'—or so the Proclaimers preached. The Scourge's squall became an effective tool of fear and control long before Sonart took his first breath. It herded the dwarven people into confinement and compartment—as if they hadn't already had their backs broken by thraldom and depravity.

Small wonder all crops in the Cradle were root crops. Similarly, every last tree started as a gnarled mass of ironbark at the surface, but rather than grow up from the earth, they tunnelled down into the soil, reaching for nutrients and groundwater. A marvel that they grew at all in such a hammered land.

The dwarven undercastes' entire existence had been one of subsistence and servitude. The storms merely added one more baleful reminder of how lost their plight had become.

Hewn of stone and reinforced with *ironock*, the same implacable ore they mined, dwarven shelters provided their only defence against the harrowing tempests. As the hardest element in the Cradle, ironock also armoured the structure of the Winged Ones' bastion. The metal formed Kworn blades, Zürshuck spears, and dwarven tools.

But so fierce the wind of a razor storm, it didn't merely unhinge the upper regolith but stripped tiny shards of bedrock to sandblast the air with bladed particles.

Anyone unlucky enough to get caught outside during a razor storm had their flesh stripped from their bones. When such a tempest finally passed, the Cradle might be littered with smashed skeletons, their shards abrasive to the touch without a pinch of flesh revealing to whom the bones belonged.

The most severe storms grated the bones into fine sand. Scattered the grainy remains far afield, to mingle with a different kind of sand: that found throughout the Lobe—the furthest extent of Sonart's reality. Beyond the blighted desert loomed a ring of mountains known as the Outereach.

The Cradle was a natural fortress, based on a series of concentric rings. The Outereach Mountains formed the furthermost cordon, protecting all existence from the Void of Obliteration beyond. Barely visible on the clearest drear, the mountain belt lay shrouded in mystery—save rumours that the land's deadliest perils filled its heights. Not that any could verify such claims—venturing across the Lobe to the Cradle's perimeter was forbidden and punishable by death.

The Lobe marked the vastest of all the Cradle's ringed tracts. It was in effect *cradled* by the Outereach foothills, which bottled the desert's dunes. Devoid of verve, the Lobe contained enough traps and pitfalls of its own that could just as easily swallow any trespasser. Its sands would also consume the Steppe it encased—if it could.

But a steep two-hundred-foot-tall scarp lifted the plateau from the desert—ensnared it like a granite manacle. A relatively narrow band of arid but habitable table, the Steppe provided sustenance that welled from the earth, or rather within it, making existence possible. Across the flat, dwarven cloistered in villages scattered amongst the mines they worked.

The dead mist which usually hung over the craters and hills came alive now. It stirred, confirming a razor storm loomed and would soon scour the earth. The Kworn party had scant time before the savage cleanse of Sonart's world would begin.

He suspected the torrent would be much worse at these yawning heights. But who's to say? He had no experience up here—as far as he knew, no dwarven had. Without shelter, the small company would never stand a chance. Yet despite their predicament, the Kworn pushed on, ever upward.

Why risk a dawdling climb in such conditions at all? Sonart could've easily been brought before their master by some other means—he'd witnessed instantaneous transport before. Even the Winged Ones would have expedited the precarious journey.

Some imperative hung over the Kworn, impelling them to risk it. Their madness could only mean they feared something more if they didn't. Some unparalleled development above Sonart's Augury trespass, no doubt.

The path abruptly veered towards the easternmost of the Thorned Spikes. Because of the band's proximity to the mount, Sonart could not see the other three peaks, but he envisioned them all the same. A cirque joined the four granite sentinels like a crown's rim clasped together by four saddles at great elevation.

The outside lips of the adjoining cirques fell away, forming a natural redoubt with a sheer thousand-foot drop to the broken plains of the Steppe.

The Innereach guarded the Darkest One's tower within. Atop each of the Four Spikes stood an obsidian holdfast, guarded by an onyx-scaled dragon and its black rider.

Four sordid mountain peaks, four bastions, four dragons, and four devils—the Four Siphons of Fire—as the archdemons eventually came to be known. Their collective title was later shortened to 'the Four.'

Four, four, four, to fuck us craven whores—or so the dwarven mining chant went.

Thunder rattled closer. And the first drops of rain touched Sonart's skin as the Kworn attacked the eastern mount. Its scree-laden slope curved at a much steeper grade until the path met the sheer face of an ebony cliff. Through a series of switchbacks carved into the face, they continued to ascend. Their way grew narrower, forcing them to run single file.

The quarter-league that followed exposed the party to an unprecedented gale. It echoed in Sonart's ears, amplified by the cavernous drop, rising and falling like the demented warble of a lost soul.

Lightning forked. With a simultaneous thunderclap, it struck a short distance above the heads of the guards, igniting an explosion of stone fragments. The mountain shook under the assault, its gutrock cracking with clamorous protests.

The Kworn carrying Sonart pitched forward and stumbled to the ground, but managed to keep a firm clasp on his burden. As the sound of the aftershock roared across the slope, sections of rock calved away from the cliff face. The granite avalanche crashed down upon the company.

Behind Sonart, a pair of the beastmen squealed. His eyes shot up, just as the falling rubble took out the two Kworn bringing up the rear. They tumbled off the precipice, disappearing into the rushing air. Unprecedented indeed.

The raining detritus tapered but no one dared move. Until the pelting lash of the shower bestirred them. First to stagger to his feet, Sonart's captor barked at the other survivors. They rose and hastened on.

When the rain began falling in droves, the ebbing visibility forced the Kworn to hold fast to the mountainside's crevices and fractures as they slogged on, putting one misshapen leg in front of the other.

The sheer amount of water hampered every step the troupe took. In a relentless gush, it streamed down or flared off the sheer wall, spraying directly into their faces.

A vertical wave splashed and flattened them against the cliff face. When it subsided, Sonart could only detect a small section of pathway, cliff, and abyss—an unbalanced spot without beginning or end.

Above the drone of the wind, a granular scratching sound arose as sand began scouring the rock face. With abrasive impunity, the razor part of the Scourge's storm reared. Kworn and charge would soon be shredded into powder.

Sonart tensed. Braced himself for a horrific death... when the torrent's vehemence abruptly muted—? The wind's wail diminished.

Head and body numbed by the storm's lash, he managed to bat a watery eye to see how.

The Kworn had entered a wedge. It cut into the face of the cliff and formed two barricades, the outer shielding them from the drop. Now numbering four, the party and their charge achieved a modicum of shelter from the worst of the elements. The confined fissure continued along the saw-toothed escarpment before it plunged deeper into a tapering crevice. Its slick walls rose on either side of them, close to eighty feet straight up. High above, a gap still opened to the tumultuous sky, but the Kworn had effectively crossed the threshold from death to survival.

Rain still fell, creating a swift stream about their feet. The storm's lament lingered beyond, but its sound grew fainter and fainter from one splashing stride to the next.

Without respite, the huffing Kworn marched on as the grade levelled off and curved further inward in a supine arc. The crack of light above narrowed until the two walls converged and clamped flush into an overhanging cavern.

Stars align, they were going *through* the mountain.

Shakespeare once said, 'All the world's a stage,' but in Sinathor's case, and closer to the point, it meant worlds—plural. An infinity's worth as far as the blond singer was concerned. But it centred on two in particular: tangent worlds locked and knotted in a kind of yin and yang.

Question was which would prove the real one? Earth, where he performed innumerable times in front of his band's loyal fans, or the realm he glimpsed in his dreams? Areth—the World in Chaos?

Both fronted storms on the singer's horizon.

But Sin often pondered, if he headed into the tempests—would he face some natural occurrence, or something unnatural, waiting to swallow him? Would the storms happen because of him? Or would he bring the storms?

The voices never answered his countless queries. They spoke in riddles.

The riddles inspired thoughts. The thoughts guided his pen to lyrics for songs—the songs he sang up there, night after night in the spotlight, *on* the world's stage. The tunes made the band famous, rich. And in demand.

Sin's dreams seemed so real, like visions of a future foretelling. The faces reoccurred and he remembered them. Like his most recent dream of the deadly storm hectoring the captive dwarf. All part of some fantasy film blockbuster Hollywood could have had a field day with.

But Sin had been plagued by nightmares as well. That archdemon, that... *Siphon.* The same devil of the singer's childhood visions who sought to steal him away. *Mine Eyes are Your Eyes.* Would take him away, make a slave of him one day, or so it promised.

Another tried that already. A—sorcerer. But the luminous beings intervened. What was real? What was not? The definitions blurred, since the boating accident, maybe *because* of the accident.

Sin locked the memory away, his closest brush with death. The night he lost both parents.

A light knock at his dressing room door brought him back to the moment. He straightened in his chair, ears perking.

"Sin, five minutes to showtime."

"Got it, Bear," he croaked over his shoulder. Then he stared at his reflection in the makeup mirror. Framed by his long mane of silver-blond tresses, an angelically bladed but blank visage stared back.

Another time. His dark contemplations would have to wait.

5: Cele
Brooke

Brooke crouched, helping an alchlemage brace the broken leg of a middle-aged man. The sound of knocking hooves lifted his eyes.

A company of five mounted soldiers filtered past huddles of common folk, who shifted and shied away to let the small cavalcade pass under the bridge.

Brooke remained fixed, too worn to stand or acknowledge their leader—a captain by the insignia on his breastplate. He dismounted and strode towards the commander. The determined set of his jaw suggested he'd been appointed some important charge. But his diffident eyes indicated he bore a message he did not relish delivering.

Brooke expected as much as he dropped his attention back to the makeshift splint. Since he didn't relish answering, why make it easier?

The captain's boots rapped against the flagstones of the rampart as he drew up. "Commander Brooke?"

"What is it?"

The captain hesitated.

Brooke didn't have time for this. "Out with it, man."

"Much has been lost, Sir," the soldier stammered. "Explosives targeted His Majesty's Royal Arsenals."

"You mean, his royal arse," Brooke corrected as he tied the last knot of the injured man's splint. Several of his men looked away and stifled laughs.

Brooke stood and faced the captain, not bothering to hide his irritation. "That would explain the larger detonations, wouldn't you say?"

The captain's face turned red. "The King deemed it fit to distribute his caches throughout the city. Claimed they'd be safer from espionage."

"Safer for the weapon stores, Captain—not for the people who lived in their midst, unaware—people King Cele swore an oath to protect. Any tally of the casualties?"

"Difficult to say, Commander. But judging by the gathering crowds, it could have been much worse."

Brooke sighed and raised his eyes to the heavens. "Some good news. Where's the largest congregation?"

"By the Sixteenth Gate, North Quadrant," the captain said. "A field hospice has been set up there."

"Then we'll go there at once," said Brooke. He turned to his troops. "The healers have the wounded here well in hand. Muster your mounts—all haste to Gate Sixteen."

Maxan nickered as one of the soldiers led him up by the bridle and handed the reins to Brooke.

The captain coughed behind him. "Um, Commander?"

Brooke put his foot in the stirrup and swung up into the saddle. "Something more to report?" Pupils focused on Maxan's tack, he braced his ears for the forthcoming collection notice.

"King Cele summons all commanders of the homeguard to assemble for an emergency meeting at once. His Grace was quite clear—and quite cross—on that last point."

Brooke swore under his breath. "I see," he grated past tight lips.

The commander would keep a civil tongue, at least until he knew for certain how his wife and children fared. He was dutybound to his charges, and though he'd sent a scout to check on his family, of yet, he'd received no news. This unwanted diversion only multiplied his worry and frustration.

After some instructions to one of his subordinates, Brooke gave Maxan a touch of spur. The horse sprang into motion, galloping out from the charred embankment and through the remnants of what had hours before been a wide magnificent esplanade.

The ride did little to quell Brooke's vexation over his king's foolishness, at how easily the destruction and loss of life could have been prevented.

Tyrant dotard, you should've listened to me.

The warnings had come, but King Cele stubbornly refused to heed them, insisting the invasion continue as planned. And now, on what would've marked the first day of the war campaign, Pathguard's citizens mourned the dead within their own savaged walls.

Brooke's anger escalated when he beheld the collateral: the road lined with corpses, some eviscerated, heaps more burned beyond recognition, and a few carbonized in bass relief against the decimated walls. The detonations may have wrought the carnage, but the casualties could be laid at the feet of one brash monarch.

Taking great gulps of air, Brooke repressed the urge to kick his steed's flanks harder. He needed a vent for his bitterness to quell his mounting anxiety. *Master yourself before you master the situation.* A lunatic though His Grace might be, Cele was not one to trifle with.

Riding a storm of ash dust amid a hard song of clicking hooves, Maxan charged into the castle's bailey. Heads spun as he shot past. Heartbeats later, the destrier drew up to a marshalling station where a series of tethers awaited. The commander swung off Maxan's back and quickly spied a young stable boy trudging past, arms wrapped about a square bale of hay near his height.

"Hold there, lad," Brooke called.

The copper-haired freckle-faced boy skidded to a halt and cocked his chin up, eyes bright and attentive.

"See to my horse. He needs water posthaste. An added kindness if you can manage some oats and feed."

"Yes, Milord, at once," said the boy. He dropped the bale where he stood and raced to take Maxan's reins.

The commander surrendered the leather straps and a brief smile. "Treat him well and an added coin goes home in your purse upon my return."

The boy bowed courteously. "Thank you, Milord."

Brooke marched up a cobblestone ramp to the main artery, which led to the castle proper. Through the closest portcullis and along a warren to its upper terminus, he trod.

Following several corridors that connected at T-junctions, Brooke emerged into the wider halls within the keep.

Ancient tapestries still adorned the great arcades of the citadel. Perhaps Targin fancied himself a patron of the arts, Brooke mused. His smile faded when he realized the entire stronghold had been left intact—like as not done by design. The palace looked a lone flower sprouting up in the centre of a burned field. At every stage of his hasty march, nothing appeared out of the ordinary—with the structure. Every warren and great hall seemed deserted.

Not two days prior, the corridors bustled with activity, teaming with soldiers, common folk, and highborn. The commander had to sally past servants running errands. He'd stopped on many occasions to exchange affable words with patrolling city watch.

A loud din of conversations had prevailed then. They ranged from court gossip to commerce barter between buyers and merchants to the pleasant songs of street musicians, the grovel of preachers, and the odd convivial row of spectators pressed tight to watch a puppeteers' show.

The savoury smells of mead dispensaries, freshly baked bread and greasy pork sausage sizzling over flaming grills never far—in essence, the sounds and smells of the kingdom's lifeblood.

But today that blood had been drained.

The commander encountered few people: mostly retainers, squires, Home and Highguard—the latter appeared in greater numbers as he closed the distance to Cele's council chamber.

Another thought furthered Brooke's anger—why hadn't Cele opened the palace doors to shelter the people? Such a vast space with its trove of medical supplies could've easily served as a hospice instead of a pavilion. Lives could have been saved.

Two of the king's White Capes stood guard outside the entrance, flanking a set of massive golden doors. Impressive longswords at their side, the elite sentries were clad in gilded boots, gorgets, helms with closed visors, chainmail hauberks, and thick ivory mantles and britches.

At Brooke's approach, each clasped a filigreed door handle, turned, and pushed it back. The doors swung silently inward on well-oiled hinges.

Brooke paid the White Capes a perfunctory glance as he strode between them and into the high-domed chamber. Around a twenty-foot-long oaken table, retinues worked, filling cups with water and dusting off chairs with feather brushes. Beyond them, some thirty commanders, arrayed in silver armour partially covered in crimson capes, stood in three separate circles.

His own cloak soiled, torn, and still damp, small clothes chafing beneath, Brooke felt like a haggard scullion among his peers. The men spoke in low grave voices, which trailed to silence when the doors clanked closed behind the commander. All heads turned.

The back of a scribe in finespun livery blocked the raised throne beyond, a long scroll dangling in one hand. But as the servant leaned in, it became apparent King Cele sat in attendance, pale hands gesturing feistily atop his elevated seat.

"Highness," the scribe announced, "Commander Brooke has come."

From behind the retainer, Cele's familiar voice rasped, "Stars burn him, at last." The royal's arm brusquely swept the scribe out of the way and he tethered Brooke with a red glare. "We've waited an *eon* for your arrival."

Cele's crow's feet danced, his chin sharpened as he curled his lower lip. But his voice sounded relieved when Brooke stepped forward. "In sooth, that you return at all bespeaks a small mercy. This vicious attack on the Throne claimed Heashe and Miel. We shall toast to your survival." He pointed a finger at one of the servants. "You. Bring wine!"

"Hold," Brooke interceded, drawing the servant's attention, and reclaiming his regent's scowl. "With all due respect, Your Grace, Pathguard remains in crisis. The death toll notwithstanding, we cannot afford indulges to dull our senses—and the treasury. We must ascertain the full extent of the damage the warlord has wrought."

"Careful," the king warned under his breath.

A full six feet two inches tall, Brooke towered over Cele, but he learned early not to judge the frail monarch by his age or physical shortcomings. Behind Cele's wrinkled face, the suspicious eyes of a ferret stared back. Shrewd orbs that might observe treachery where none hid—sentence his commander to prison. Or make him disappear.

After the uncomfortable moment, the king shifted his cold steel blues to the assembled quorum. In a louder voice, he declared, "All be seated. We hold council at once."

Thirty men converged on the table. Brooke claimed a vacant seat, taking notice of his peers' burns and facial scars as he did. A few bore bandages on their cheeks and noses.

He waited as the scuffling sounds ebbed to silence. For several moments no one moved or breathed a word. Their unblinking king stared trancelike down the length of the table. Would he fall asleep?

No, predictable as ever, Cele awaited his prized lickspittle and crutch.

Moments later, the sound of careful footsteps bestirred the king. He looked up and brightened. Without turning, Brooke knew who had joined their congress: Cele's Grand Vizier and Haft of the King, Necatar.

The thin sallow-faced chamberlain strutted into view wearing an embroidered purple robe cinched tight about the waist with a large belt lined with citrine cabochons. Ivory bracelets encircled his wrists and gold rings bejewelled his hands. An amber-encrusted sachet crossed his chest like a farmer's seed bag.

Sharp birdlike movements marked his every step, pointed gesture, and glance. Hooked forward like a raptor's beak, his spiky rimless hat matched his nose and the colour of his glaring robe. Beneath it, oily black hair crept out and bristled like a field left to fallow.

Necatar plied a careful gait past the table, leaving a rancid trail of lime perfume in his wake. Noses bunched and snorted. It smelled as though the steward had gone and sprayed himself with embalming fluid.

The Haft's bony form hunched before an expectant Cele and kissed the king's hand. Then he turned and faced the assemblage, a grim custodian guarding his simpleton child.

Fond of neither man, Brooke held a special brand of disdain for Necatar. King Cele had always been high-strung—his cords of late, stretched fishing-line thin. But his worm of a Haft conducted a fouler business—the baiting fisherman jigging the royal line. Necatar exhaled accusation and underhandedness into every discussion. The king may voice the decree, but it didn't take a seer to know the Haft gave the order.

When the other retainers left, closing the gilded doors behind them with nary a whisper, the king raised his sceptre. He brought it down on the marble floor with a dull thud. "Council is now in session. Today we meet under the gravest of circumstances. Instead of riding out to vanquish our enemies, we sit with heavy hearts and bewail our precious dead. Pathguard lies in ruins. We *cannot* let such despicable acts against our sovereignty go uncontested."

Brooke held his tongue, heart veering into cavernous gloom.

"It is your King's wish to continue our campaign as planned," Cele snarled. "I only allow enough time to regroup and rethink our strategy. Vamsah as my witness, this setback will be short-lived—and serve to double our retaliation."

Brooke clenched his teeth. He had to look down to hide his distress and ire. But his fingers, hidden by the edge of the table, gouged slivers of wood from the chair's armrest.

"Long have the sprites of the Three Mountains hid within their lofty drop, infiltrated and subverted the realms across the Main, from the Sisters to the Spires, the Chain to the Spikes. They now stand poised to deliver a hammer blow ahead of our march to protect Areth. To end it before it begins.

On the blackest, fiercest winds, the prophesized Starbond approaches. The sprites pose too great a threat—as this unprovoked assault demonstrates. But no more."

Cele shook a shrivelled fist. "They, and those who serve them, will *pay* for their crimes against the men of the North."

Brooke adjusted his posture. Everything the king had said sounded misplaced or nonsensically wrong.

"Necatar assures me, we can muster considerable weaponry from our garrisons in Ganex," Cele rambled on. "Then, we take the fight to them, rout their vile ilk wherever they hole up."

The regent propped his sceptre against the table's edge, lowered his head and clasped his hands together as though in prayer. "Alas, their deceit spreads like pestilence, turns former allies against us."

Cele lifted his gaze. "Betrayal looms where we least expected it." He stood and reclaimed his staff, eyes burning like twin firestorms. They scoured every face in the room. "It wounds me to reveal, the elven of the Three Cities colluded with the sprites in their sinister plot against Pathguard."

Thirty variations of gasp, harrumph, and rude noise shared one alarm at the monarch's accusation. Several officers shifted in their chairs as dissent moved up and down the table like echoes in a cistern.

More precipitous, more preposterous than declaring against the sprites, the news shocked Brooke as well. His Grace blaming the elven for conspiring against Pathguard—a stretch, even for the mad king.

But Brooke would strive to keep silent in the matter, most certainly in this arena. If Cele wished to drag the elven into his arrow's sight, there was nothing for it.

With renewed fervour, the king slammed his staff down on the floor, causing its metal to spark as it chipped stone. Several of the seated men flinched. "And that accursed Hidden Kingdom! It dares harbour those other rats, instead of thwarting them—they must also pay!"

Brooke rolled his eyes at the monarch's tirade but took great care to cover them with his hand. In as many breaths, Cele had expanded his war declaration to include two more neutral fronts.

"I'll not suffer Johlarin's slights and intrigues any longer," the king raged, his voice pitching to high, half-crazed octaves. "And that *witch-wife* he beds to spawn his dark seed and dark purpose—*she* put him up to it. But I will tear them both down. Call the banners of our allies, Grimsford and Spirespoint. They'll help us bring Serenthia's jackanapes ruler to his knees."

Cele became so lost in his anger that he confused his enemies, their apparent wrongdoings, and their motives. Serenthia, the Three Cities, Etern's Drop and the Nightwolves had somehow meshed into a single foe. "We will rout the dogs who roam our borders at Johlarin's behest. Bring down the very gates of Etern's Drop. Send the sprites' holdfast over that infernal abyss—them with it!"

Like an infant having a tantrum, the regent brandished his sceptre high and slammed its headpiece down on the table, hard enough to split the wood.

As the heavy thud finished reverberating, Brooke chanced a look at Necatar. The Haft's expressionless face revealed nothing but something slithered behind his serpent orbs. Amusement?

Commander Conby cleared his throat. "Your Grace? Pathguard's entire arsenal has been wiped out. And the weapons we hold in Ganex offer but a token cache—they will not suffice to launch any offensive." He hesitated. "There is discord also—our men fear because the banes have proven true."

"Yes, yes, yes," the king retorted impatiently. "That is precisely why we must attack as planned—don't you see? We cannot let intimidation fester our soldiers' hearts. We must let them avenge the dead." He swept his arm in a circle at the assembly. "Pathguard is beleaguered on all fronts. If we sit on our hands and idly wait, next time... stars, there won't be a next time."

"Your Grace," Brooke quietly cut in. "The slaughter that instigated this mess—we've never confirmed it to be the work of the sprites, or the Nigh—" he checked himself. "—the others for that matter."

Cele's cheeks coloured and he let out a sound, half-moan, half-growl.

"But the evidence," Necatar interrupted with a sharp lilt, "points directly to them." Thirty heads turned as the Haft entered the debate. He raised a manicured finger. "The reek of their magics—*and* that of elven loremasters—lingers at the crime scenes, affirmed by His Excellency's alchlemage."

Brooke did not rise to the Haft's comment. Eyes firmly fixed on his king, he implored, "Please, Majesty, the warnings came not from the nymphs. Stars chase the shadows, they are merely magical creatures who helped shape and steward the land and its people. The rook's message was signed by our true nemesis, the brigand himself."

Bells trilled just outside the chamber, making Brooke pause and extend an ear—likely the king's fool being turned away by the guards.

When the jingling petered, Brooke faced the council and continued. "A sprite has not been seen in our parts of the Northland for more than a decade. I beg you, treat with them, seek parley and fully determine the truth of matters. Before we send our men to war, based solely on presumptions made from evidence that is dubious at best." Brooke directed his last comment at Necatar.

"Commander," the Haft countered. "Unlike you, King Cele has the wisdom to see such actions for what they are—folly. The slaughters and the banes and the destruction of Pathguard clearly indicate the sprites. The dog only signed them to deflect suspicion."

"And you would know of such deflection, Necatar!" Brooke flared before he could stop himself. "The commanders do well to steer clear of your counsel, lest they raze the shaken morale of their troops completely."

Then, turning back to the king, Brooke recovered his calm, "My King, the cautionary served you, came from none other than the outlaw, Targin, and his band of Nightwolf marauders. They alone are responsible for this attack on our city."

A hushed silence ensued. Except for Necatar and Cele, everyone's face held some semblance of relief mixed with terror at Brooke's mention of the warlord's name—a name Cele had explicitly banned from utterance in his presence. The regent's eyes shot daggers at him.

Necatar broke the quiet with a mirthless laugh and a toss of his head. "That is absurd. The gates have been sealed and enchanted with my own powerful wards. No wolf tracks seen within leagues of the city. Only sprites can penetrate such enchantments."

"As-we-all-know," Brooke retorted, no less trenchant, "Targin has sworn allegiance to the sprites. If you choose to include them in this farce, that would be their only offence—association, accepting the Nightwolf's fealty."

Brooke paused to mute his remonstrance and collect his wits. In a calmer tone, he added, "Perhaps the sprites had to concede some part of their lore in the bargain, and the warlord used it to get past our defences—the only plausible explanation that fits." He splayed his hands. "Twas the Nightwolf who said we would not ride this day—and, stars burn us all to ash, is it not so?"

"Continue to bander at your peril, Commander," Cele seethed. "The Night-dog's nothing more than a nefarious butcher. I have put a price on his head of one million gold crowns. The savage will be dealt with in due time, but his crimes stand unrelated to what has befallen Pathguard."

"Sooth, Your Grace," Necatar extolled over a fervent nod. "The war dog's pack has left several of our realm's villages thrashed in their wake, murdering indiscriminately. Savages, as you say. Nothing more."

Cele dipped his chin. "Aye, more the reason, the nymphs must be brought to justice for their part in this."

When no one responded, the king's wrath ignited anew, his scrutiny searing the faces around the table to embers. "Is there not a commander among you who will raise your voice in solidarity—prevent my wounded army's back from being broken completely?"

"Your Grace," Brooke said evenly, "Your army will march under any commander seated here, but knowing they tread in an unclear and accursed campaign will not break the back of their resolve—it will kill them. Targin knows our Northland tract, and our tact. Combined—"

Necatar cut him off with a dismissive wave of his hand. "Ever you persist in laying guilt for the act at the feet of a lowly barbarian." His weasel orbs swung back to the king. "Majesty, this war dog knows nothing of such policies. A heathen rogue he remains, running naked through the woods sodomizing wolves and men, more to appease his darkling nature than to curry favour with Deathwrought. He condones all manner of vile acts. His very being, a blasphemy against the Kusp, Vamsah, and all His First."

The Haft paused and stared off into the distance. "My Liege, the savage could not have wrought such destruction so quickly upon Pathguard undetected. We'd have ensnared at least one of his cutthroats—as I did in Clawvale."

"That's how King Foram thought," Brooke pointed out, "before he tested Targin's threat. And what of King Dalin, pray tell, or Iet, or Vakk? Why did their actions procure the same result? The reason is simple. Reciprocity. He has reaped from us what we ourselves plotted to sow."

The commander's words drew mixed reactions: dour nods and murmurs of assent from his peers, a firm headshake from Necatar, and a scowl basted in pure acid from Cele. But they all knew the names and the decimated kingdoms the titles represented.

"All those attacks reeked of the sprites," Necatar grated. He spread his arms towards Cele.

"Necatar," Brooke derided to his back. "Do not be more the usurper than you are the fool, frivolously gambling with lives not your own."

The Haft whipped around so fast, he nearly dislodged his hideous hat. Lips squished as though pressed in a vice, he slanted forward like a tower about to topple. The commander braced: his mouth forming a taut bowstring aimed at said tower. Pound for pound, he must mirror his opponent's glower and the choler that fuelled it.

No words were exchanged in the vacuous standstill, but ill thoughts screamed like a thousand trumpets over the parapets.

With a tsk, Brooke shifted his attention to the king. "Your Grace, the sprites never meddle in a kingdom's affairs, unless its rulers prove false, imposing upon their concerns first—exactly as Iet and Vakk attempted. Where are they now? What has become of their rule?"

Cele swallowed and his pupils lost their hardness. Stars align, was the monarch prepared to listen at last? But something else breached the surface of that look—an ironock fetter beleaguering the king's resolve.

Encouraged nonetheless, Brooke exhaled and walked around the table. "Were we not about to tread the same path as the fallen kingdoms, visiting harm upon the sprites? Do they not reserve the right to defend themselves?"

Silence.

"If we assail them—or their allies," Brooke pressed, "do we not provoke further retaliation and widen the confrontation?" He spoke in a soft measured voice, hoping to advocate reason. "If we declare against Serenthia and the elven," he added, "this precarious course Necatar sets us upon will only self-fulfil. We must pause to breathe. Don't allow this rash warmonger to spur Pathguard's ruin. And with it, your undoing?"

Necatar's eyebrows sprang to the brim of his hat, lips folding back to discharge a sneer.

The grating of wood on stone stopped him. One of the other officers named Krane pushed back his chair and stood. His cold stare held Necatar. "You will let Commander Brooke speak, without further interruption."

Krane shifted his focus to Brooke. "He's the only one among us with the courage to apprise His Grace with the hard, necessary truth." His incisive tone kept the Grand Vizier silent.

Brooke gave Krane an appreciative nod as the other sat back down. If he could rally the other commanders with his arguments, that would make thirty voices to sway Cele into reconsidering.

"Powerful as the sprites may be," Brooke went on, "history has shown they will always sue for peace, not war, if given the chance. As evinced in the Rennen, machinations that impel peaceful states into warfare can solely be placed at the feet of the Darkest One. Ever has it been men who seek to bolster their dominion with a magical edge—men interfering in the sprites' affairs to sap their wilderen strengths. If we continue as we are, we render ourselves vulnerable to invasion from foreign powers—and in all likelihood, darker, fouler threats."

Brooke did not need to elaborate. Every soldier in the room drew forward, having had firsthand experience with such banes.

But he did so regardless.

"Several of my own patrols have had to deal with trolls, goblins, dark elven. Witnesses have come forward—survivors who lived to tell the tale. They share accounts of other horrors the like of which have never been seen in the Main. Every day the minions draw nearer to our gates."

Cele rested his head on the bridge of his arm that still held his sceptre. "What would you have me do?" he croaked in a defeated tone.

Brooke arched an eyebrow, not daring to believe his chance fortune. "Heed the warnings, My King, and the signs of the Starbond. Allay this madness and seek the sprites under a banner of truce. I cannot say it en—"

"Then do not say it at all," Necatar blazed, striding towards Brooke, a shaking finger held before him like an arrow waiting to be loosed. "Dare accuse me of mongering war when you seem equally intent on conjuring fear, dissent, misdirection, where none need exist?" He pressed his palms on the table and angled closer to Cele. The move wrenched the king's gaze away from Brooke. "And subversion, deigning to ask His Majesty to bend a knee to them—and weaken his great kingdom."

"If I do not speak my mind now, and loudly," Brooke yelled, "you needn't worry about my propagating fear and despair. Vamsah save us, it shall run rampant throughout the Main as it does now in this forsaken realm. Only, our people will suffer more than they already have." He slanted his efforts back to Cele. "For pity's sake, they are your people. You have sworn an oath to defend them."

A dangerous silence fell over the gathering. Well past the point of no return, Brooke quietly accepted it. "Next time we meet, perhaps the number of our quorum will not be sufficient to even hold council." He dropped his arms to his side and stepped back from the table. "The Starbond is nigh. We may never meet again."

"Enough!" the King thundered from out of his clouded trance. "Your words are treason, Commander! Thrice over, you've forgotten your place. And openly defied my edict four times in this council. I forbid you from uttering his name a fifth. Quell that tongue, or so help me, I'll cut it out myself, and flog you with it."

Cele's glower shackled the other commanders. He balled two quivering fists. "That goes for you lot as well, disrespecting the high office My Haft wields. You insult your King!" Through flaring nostrils, he huffed a blast of heated air to make a dragonling envious. "Damn you all. We have not gathered to discuss if the campaign will continue—but when!"

Brooke gritted his teeth but stayed silent. *So much for reason.* This had proven nothing more than a hand puppet show for halfwit children. Cele's sudden umbrage dashed any hope for a binding armistice with the sprites or their associates.

The king's grimace deepened, cheeks turning purple. His voice scaled higher as he ranted, "Quick, quick, quick, we must be. Delegate tasks and prepare for war. The rooks have already flown. Necatar has drawn up an initial plan for you rabble. Carry out my decrees. Or be carried off—to my dungeons."

The King stabbed his sceptre at Brooke as though preparing to bludgeon him with it. "You, ride to Cillinox on the morrow for supplies and men. In light of recent events, Bathurian will fluster more than his usual, so remind that feisty varmint of our treaty—by whatever means."

Brooke cursed inwardly but he forced a nod, recognizing the troubling depth of Cele's vehemence. To gainsay the episodic regent here would almost certainly earn him that flogging.

"Commander Frazer, I need you in the North Quadrant. Set up what pavilions we still have available. Address the inevitable food shortages—we'll need to feed our people, aye, but see that dispensation is given to our troops first—they take all precedence."

As the king snapped assigned duties, Brooke's mind drifted relentlessly like a bulrush caught in the clout, roll, and tug of a crosswind's changing grasp. If the commander ever had control of this tragic situation, he had lost it to such a gust.

Why did his wayward sovereign so loathe and fear the sprites? Why was he bent on making enemies of the coastal elven? Of Serenthia?

And who in blazes was this big bastard, Targin—to bring not one, but several kingdoms to their knees? Make Pathguard's regent detest him so much that the mere mention of his name could send the king into such explosive fits of rage? Questions on top of questions and traps within traps.

The answer lay with the sprites. Or with Targin. Nothing else could be gained here, except more shame, woe, and miscarriage of justice. The debate, a long-vanished cause.

Brooke desperately needed to focus on something else to cool his ire. His thoughts turned to his family. By centring on them, he endured the agonizing minutes of the fools' mockery until, Vamsah be blessed, the departing sun adjourned the meeting for him.

The commander strode from the chamber, ragged cape billowing behind him.

6: Hive
Sonart

Sonart found it near impossible to discern much in the meandering passage. If not for the emerald light emanating from the Kworn's eyes, the company would be moving in utter darkness. The beastmen's shadows made a lengthened mockery of their vile carriages, projected against the tunnel's floor and walls.

Though his hurts had all but vanished, dread and exhaustion joined battle inside him. Sonart kept both at bay. Such coping ruled his existence in the Cradle, every drear measured in strife.

An extra weight pressed his heart. At best, the dwarven race made reality tolerable, but their future seemed bleak: bodies pulled from the mines daily. Plague claimed many, the Dunge claimed more. Suicide ran rampant.

Why?

Because nothing lay beyond the Cradle; beyond the circle of mountains that formed the Outereach. The chain separated Sonart's world from the Void of Obliteration—a mass of nothingness, which surrounded and continually threatened the Cradle.

The Kusp professed as much—the *Kusp of the Testament*. That sacred book contained the ancient lore of the dwarven and their present laws of society. Sonart's people widely believed the tome's prophecy that one drear, the Outereach would fall, allowing the Void to devour the Cradle. Their cruel haven would cease to exist, taking them with it.

Less than an hour passed when a red glow began to infuse the walls of the tunnel. It quickly overpowered the green penumbra the Kworn emanated. A deep rumbling din accompanied the increasing light and a sulphuric smell invaded Sonart's nose.

His brooding deepened.

A wall of heat rushed past as the party emerged from the opposite side of the mountain. The guard carrying Sonart stopped and twisted his stance. He slid the dwarven off his crooked shoulder and set him down upon his feet.

Sonart craned his head up. His jaw moved in the opposite direction.

Mouth agape, he could only stare.

A soaring black tower stared right back.

The Hive.

Deathwrought's unholy bastion loomed through a shifting veil of smoke, struck by cherry-orange skeins of fire-rain. A quarter-league at its base, the obsidian monolith rose out of a bleeding moat of lava at the bottom of the vast chasm. The spire soared more than two thousand feet from the burning hearth to a mattress of murky clouds that swallowed the rest. As such, Sonart could not gauge its true height—though if the elders' tales held true, it topped five thousand.

The Hive mounted the very hub of the Cradle, guarded by the inner walls of the cirque that formed the Innereach. Between its molten floor, granite cordon, and cloud ceiling, the domain resembled a titan's massive enclosure, supported by an onyx pillar at its centre.

Here, in the middle of all the Cradle's concentric rings, the Darkest One had built his church.

Giant thorn-like protrusions laced the tower's length. Jets of flame shot out a hundred feet from the largest flanges before arcing upward, giving way to roiling ebony plumes. They spiralled up until the clouds absorbed them.

The scale and appearance of the tower branded Sonart's soul—a vision of grandeur most terrible. He never thought he'd lay eyes on the finished edifice. The deepest sleep had long claimed all the dwarven forced to construct it.

For his entire existence, it had been a place forbidden to his brethren. So, it remained a mystery, hidden within the crown of the Innereach. No one of sound mind and any sense of self-preservation would hazard venturing here.

Before his incarceration, Sonart heard rumours of its countenance from the oldest, frailest elders, whose grandsires had been among the builders. They only whispered such tales when in their cups—until murmurs grew to brazen debates in the taverns of his village.

But now, daunted by the sight of it, Sonart almost forgot why he'd been brought here. He also failed to notice the razor storm's absence on this side of the mountains.

Undoubtedly, the tempest still raged on, outside the circular barrier. The Scourge would not be done sating his vehemence any time soon.

As if in answer to Sonart's thoughts, sheet lightning ignited the clouds and strobed across both monolith and mountainside, making his lids flutter. A wave of acrid air drew his attention to the fiery moat encircling the Hive. It bubbled with lava two hundred feet below, launching geysers of molten rock high into the air.

The hazardous showers cascaded the moat's myriad channels and splattered across the blackened flats while glowing columns of auburn and crimson fume rode the updrafts. The fount served as the source of the River Seething.

A lattice of tubular stone bridges traversed the chasm at different heights, connecting the lower third of the Hive to various plateaus on the far side of the lava plain. The carbonized traverses curved organically like the exposed roots of a burned tree.

Sonart's company stood on one of the ledges now, until a grunt and shove from behind impelled him forward.

They hadn't covered half the distance to the first bridge when the dense air erupted in a flurry of swarming silhouettes. Hundreds of black-winged creatures poured out of the Hive's smaller thorn openings and took wing. They filled the sky, partially blotting out the clouds above them like a horde of insects.

Sonart recognized the foul demons. Zürshuck—the Winged Ones. But in such numbers, they seemed countless.

The immense pillar was their Hive, aye, but it doubled as the fortress and central locus of Deathwrought—whom the hellspawn worshipped.

Sonart had never seen so many amass at one time, not since his childhood—not since the Ritual. *Stars blacken, the direst portent if they've multiplied so.*

As far as Sonart could see, the multitudes flew, a group of three here, a V-formation of ten higher up. In and out of the holes they spread their veined parts and sailed out across the gulf. The harrowing sound of so many beating wings orchestrated a discordant clamour.

Yet, he detected a certain order to their chaos, as though assembling for some purpose. Could he be the reason for such a response?

At their full height, Zürshuck stood seven feet tall, with razor-sharp bat wings, elongated torsos, arms that extended to claws and back-jointed legs that dropped to large talons. They bore the heads of devils with fierce snouts and a jagged array of fangs and double-pointed ears.

On closer inspection, their charcoal bodies betrayed an olive sheen. Like the Kworn, a green fire burned in the demons' eyes, but that marked their only commonality. In the Cradle's hierarchy, the Zürshuck presided over the Kworn, who in turn kept the dwarven caste underfoot.

Presently, a pair of the winged creatures glided in close and slowed, wings aflutter as they inspected Sonart and his Kworn escorts. Sneers stretched lips over fangs. Lantern eyes narrowed with unmistakable contempt before they veered away towards their bastion.

Unlike the other side of the mountain, the way here seemed much easier. But as the company neared the parapet of the closest bridge, Sonart grew sullen, physically and mentally oppressed by the dramatic rise in temperature.

The searing air from the furnace below grew stifling. Sonart coughed when the rising smoke and ash plumes found his lungs. As the company reached the apex of the bridge, the river's heat grew unbearable. Drained already, Sonart felt as though his skin was melting while his muscles cooked.

One of the Kworn guards began convulsing. The depraved creature collapsed where he stood, fell still, and did not move again. The two remaining beastmen did not stop.

Three Kworn had now died to deliver Sonart here, and the prevailing two swayed unsteadily and panted ragged breaths.

But still, the leader pushed on towards the bastion, using his burly arm to prod Sonart forward with every step. Towards his trial and final reckoning.

Plight sealed, Sonart must answer for his crime to the Darkest One.

The Kworn guards quickened their pace, their exhalations sounding more laboured. He couldn't blame them; they looked moments away from expiring themselves. But their deadly charge would soon be fulfilled. If they survived, they'd be given leave to flee this cursed domain.

Sonart could not say the same. Despite surviving all, his reward for seeking something to lift the weight landed him in a web, a fly awaiting the fangs of its weaver. His end approached fast.

7: Warning
Brooke

Once in the courtyard, Brooke strode with a dogged purpose to get to his steed as quickly as possible. His cheeks firestorm hot, scrutiny ablaze, the musculature of his legs corded and pumping.

Out of an adjacent warren, thirty paces in front of him, a jester emerged—a hunched and hulking ox of one, that is—drabbed in garish pink and emerald motley, laden with silver tinker bells that rang in quiet chorus.

Behind him, the fool dragged an ill-suited cart, painted loud orange with a wobbly left wheel that made rattling protests at regular intervals.

Rather big and burly for an entertainer. But give the sod a change of wardrobe, and a bath perhaps, the mummer would fit in nicely with that farce of a council, if not lead it. At least the fool bespoke an authenticity of sorts.

Barring a quick nod, neither Brooke nor the jester paid the other any mind as they crossed paths. Through the emptier concourse, the commander continued, retracing his bitter path to the stables.

When he reached the splayed door of the horse barn, Brooke found the bright-eyed stable boy and an equally lively Maxan awaiting him. He exchanged a silver for a smile with the lad and took the refreshed destrier's reins from him.

Brooke prepared to mount when a stout knight approached. The paladin wore a jerkin of boiled black leather and the telltale insignia that marked his rank and office as one of the City Watch. Brooke recognized the dark eyes, big lips, and square jaw: his wife's brother, Solan Racine.

"Commander Racine," he greeted formally.

"Commander Brooke," Racine returned with equal gravity. "A word if you please—in private." He gave the stable boy a pointed look. The young lad took his cue, hefted two buckets of feed, and hastened away.

"What is it, Solan?" Brooke asked when they were alone.

Racine glanced over either shoulder before meeting Brooke's regard. "Aviry, I've come to warn you."

Brooke frowned and drew back his head. "Warn me?"

"Something I've heard—something troubling. You must needs be made aware."

Brooke swallowed. "I'm listening."

Another look past Brooke, then Racine leaned in and whispered in his ear, "Two of my men—loyal they are. I trust them implicitly."

"As I trust you," Brooke said. He dipped his chin. "Go on."

Racine pulled back and locked gazes once more. "Three nights past, during the black hour it would be. Whilst on patrol along the eastern ramparts, they overheard a loose tongue in the shadows below. A voice relayed instructions to a few ears. Other voices answered."

The knight bit his lip and studied Brooke's measure. "There may be treachery within the guard—a dark plot hatched from the highest levels. Brooke, your name came up more than once. Other words found their way up the wall: murder, besmirched, necromage. Due to the intervening crisis, my men only came to me with their news today."

Racine gulped. "I made all haste to find you."

Brooke rubbed his temple as he made some quick calculations. If Racine's men had gleaned a scheme three nights ago, the plot had been hashed antecedent to his council meeting—which meant, it would not have mattered what case he made in that fool's forum.

Or would it have?

"I see," Brooke said evenly. "If you glean any more news, I trust it will be forthcoming?"

"Aye," Racine answered, his eyebrow lifting slightly. "You are my joined blood."

"And you, mine." Brooke asserted. He clasped Racine's arm above the elbow and offered a thin smile. "Of all weapons, fear cuts the deepest. But I thank you, Solan. I will remain on my guard."

Racine nodded solemnly. "The Starbond draws nigh, Brother. Extra vigilance is needed."

"Sooth you speak," Brooke agreed. "Many a fray, we've watched each other's backs. This is one of those times. May the stars align for us both—Pathguard's turmoil and the greater chaos worming through the Northland notwithstanding."

The knight bowed his head. "Words unto deeds."

With that, Brooke turned his attention to Maxan. Racine took two steps back as the commander mounted, gripped the saddle horn, and tightened one hand around the steed's reins. Then nudged his chin at his brother-in-law and peer. "Any message for your sister?"

Racine grinned broadly. "Give Dayanthi my love. And to the boys."

Brooke leaned over his destrier's opposite flank, pretending to adjust the stirrup to hide his grimace. *Vamsah guard them—that I may relay the message.*

"I will," Brooke promised.

With that, he wheeled Maxan around and headed out the way he'd come.

Outside the courtyard, the warhorse accelerated from canter to full gallop, leaving a trail of hoofprints in the ash and soot-covered cobblestones. Once again, Brooke faced the blackened ramparts and buildings, which had borne the costly brunt of Cele's foolishness.

His path led him across districts undamaged by the scourge of fire. And others simply devastated by it.

So, Brooke took it as a good omen when he found his home unscathed, with only a smear of carbon scores discolouring the front façade. The two-storey dwelling lay inset, fifty yards from the rest of the flats on the street.

An extensive swatch of grass and the two trees framing the path to his home had not been spared: stripped of their foliage, trunks and branches charred black.

Wisps of smoke still rose from the left tree. The undulating columns caught the last rays of the descending sun, filtering through it.

Brooke surveyed the scene, transfixed by its unexpected beauty.

Until the sun disappeared over the tops of the closest houses, leaving the courtyard in morose gloom.

Snapped back into the moment, Brooke dismounted and tethered Maxan to his post by the front gate. Then he moved quickly towards his domicile.

Steps later he froze. The front door was ajar.

Suddenly heartsick, the commander closed the distance at a full sprint, drawing his sword as he raced inside. Instinct bade him not to call out for his family.

Silent as a cat, he bounded up the staircase, taking the steps three at a time. When he reached the top landing, he dropped to a crouch. Ears and eyes perked.

Brooke gauged the immediate area, alert to sound or sight, ready to dart at the slightest disturbance.

Apart from his pounding heart, silence rang.

The house seemed intact. Other than the lingering smell of smoke, no sign of fire damage did he see. But Brooke discerned another kind of harm—looters' destruction and the clear signs of a struggle. Torn clothing lay scattered amidst all the chipped and overturned furniture.

He looked down and narrowed his eyes. A trail of blood led into his bedchamber.

Dread seized him.

Keeping low, Brooke quietly stole into the room. He found a study in havoc: the flipped bed ripped asunder, mirrors shattered, their shards strewn everywhere atop heaps of clothes and smashed sundries.

In the centre of it all, five large forms lay inert, splayed in a puddle of dark congealed blood.

Brooke moved over to the corpses—too brutish to be any member of his household. But why in seven fucks were they in his home? And where were his wife and children?

Thugs? They all had ogrish faces, with harsh jaws, bulbous noses, and sideburns. Cavernous orbs stared fixedly at the ceiling, their expressions frozen in sudden surprise, their swords still seated in their scabbards.

These men had taken the deepest sleep, unaware—at the hands of professional assassins. The insignias on their cloaks identified them as Royal Guard—trained well to reach that elite echelon. Though not well enough.

Senses piqued, Brooke retraced his steps, checked and rechecked every corner of the residence, but still found no sign of his family, or the guards' killers. He might have thought the soldiers slain, trying to protect his family—if not for Racine's warning.

Or… was he himself the target, and the assassins still here?

A tingling sensation settled at the base of his spine.

The air exploded as dark forms plunged from the ceiling. Before Brooke could bring his sword to bear, they forced him to the floor, flattened and pinned him. Deft hands and legs rendered him helpless under their weight and perfect stance.

Blinded by their raiment, Brooke could not tell how many of them had detained him. They pressed him down just hard enough to immobilize him, but still allowed his lungs to draw air.

When he inhaled, a different scent of wood fume and musk filled his nose.

The gloved hand stretching across his mouth prevented him from calling out for help. Not that any would hear. He could not even twitch a muscle to that effect. Professionals.

Still, Brooke reflected, if they had wanted to kill him, he'd already be dead. So, he relaxed and waited.

His attackers sensed his desistance, for the pressure against his body ebbed. Hands flipped him onto his back with a minimum of force. One hand still gagged him and he tasted leather in his mouth. But he could see again.

Two lithe but powerful forms, dressed head to toe in black, held his arms and legs captive. Their garb also concealed their faces.

He would have sworn that at least four men had ambushed him. No thieves or thugs, but expertly-trained and experienced assassins of the highest order.

Fear gave way to curiosity.

After exchanging glances with each other, one of them lowered his gaze again. He whispered in a measured tone, "As you've rightly guessed, Commander Aviry Brooke, we did not come to harm you—unlike the lot in your bed-chamber. We relieved them of their charge."

The other masked assassin spoke. "We will release you momentarily, but we must have your word that you will not attack us or call for help."

When Brooke nodded with his eyelids, his captor removed his gloved hand.

The commander found his voice and whispered back, "How can you trust me?"

"We know enough of you to offer this promise," the first one replied. "Your word shall decide us—will you give it?"

Brooke cleared his throat and took two deep breaths "I take it, you neutralized me and whisper out of a need for continued stealth. So, agreed, you have my word, and no doubt my sword as well."

The enigmatic figure let out a quiet laugh, "Stars, of course, but only until you let us untangle a few knotted truths for you."

"You can begin by telling me where my family is," Brooke said, trying to remain calm on that one haunting point.

Brooke's assailants alighted and let him stand. As the commander rubbed his sore elbows, the first speaker said in an appraising tone, "True to your word—unlike the tyrant you name king."

"And, that is precisely why we have come," the second masked man explained.

Brooke raised an eyebrow. "To crucify me?"

"To spare you crucifixion," Second answered.

"I care not for my own safety, following a campaign that will only lead us into the Darkest One's embrace, if not the claws of the butcher, Targin."

The two men chuckled at his comment, which left Brooke nonplussed. Failing to see anything remotely humorous about his accusation, he sharpened. "But I do care about the safety of my family."

"I warrant you do," First said. "We would think you less a man to treat matters otherwise. Your plight is their plight."

The commander blanched. "Are they—?"

"No, they still live," the first speaker assured. "But if your king's Haft has his way, I assure you, they will soon be dead. They've been kidnapped. The evidence planted here, and where the cohorts took them, will implicate the sprites. And you."

"Why?" Brooke stutter-gasped.

"Another ploy of that villain, Necatar, to assert his false case to your regent—who already limps precariously close to his own tipping point. And to discredit your command, by assuring you wind up charged with their murder."

Murder? Brooke scowled, immediately suspicious. But they echoed Racine's warning. "H-how?" His voice faltered. "How do you know this?"

"We have ears throughout Pathguard, in very high places. Trust our tale. You would've been ensnared by those five and placed under a *demonica* spell—as Cele is now."

Brooke swallowed at the revelation. "Continue."

"Townspeople would have witnessed your act—something harrowing like publicly hacking your wife and children to death. They would've ruined you—a fate worse than death or disappearance."

"Stars, man, I would gladly take my leave and disappear forever from this madness, provided I could bring my family with me," Brooke amended.

"That is something which absolutely must not happen," First said.

"Why?" Brooke demanded, feeling his hackles rise.

"Because of your profound importance, Commander," Second said. "Your removal would not only have far-reaching effects in the hearts of Pathguard's soldiers still loyal to your command but many *others* as well."

Although the masked man's riddlesome inflections and choice of words troubled Brooke, his tone brooked no argument, resonating a certain logic and truth to what he said. Such a move would cripple morale among his men, who looked to him for guidance.

Still dubious, Brooke cocked his head to one side. "What you tell me could be the ruse. How do I know what you reveal is true?"

"You won't—at least not until we liberate your family," Second said.

Brooke swore under his breath. "Where are they?"

"Three days ride from here on the fringe of the Northern Forest, held under guard within a derelict farmstead. There is still time. We will save them together."

In his moment of crisis, Brooke found solace in the conviction spurring the other's tone. He clung to it like a life-saving branch on a cliff.

When the mysterious First handed Brooke his sword back, rather than quell the commander's doubt, it amplified it.

Brooke sheathed the blade in its scabbard and squared his carriage towards Second. "What do you gain by helping me?"

"Well, *you* of course. Namely, your allegiance. We require your knowledge and skillset—our chief covets both, implicitly."

"We...?" Brooke flinched. "Wait, who are you, and who is your chief?"

The two figures removed their masks, revealing handsome weather-worn faces framed by matted manes of identical flaxen hair.

"I am Scrit," the first speaker said. "And my companion—also my blood, two years my senior—is named Cras. Our chief goes by the name Targin. And we serve as sworn brothers in his band of Nightwolves."

Brooke gaped, vacillating between dread, doubt, and deliverance. He took a deeper sniff and finally recognized the two new scents imbuing the pair's leathers: campfire and canine—of course.

He allowed himself a trace of a grin. "For savages, intent solely on rapine, you seem quite informed, resourceful, and organized."

Both men chuckled. When the moment passed, Scrit placed his palm on Brooke's arm. "You're a good man, Commander, just wrongly placed." His jaw firmed, crow's feet crinkling. "Join us."

Brooke stopped smiling. He felt the circles under his eyes deepen as he measured the earnestness in that look. "I'll consider such a radical shift only when I know for certain that my family is safe. And that can only happen once I am reunited with them. Then, you'll have earned my trust—enough for me to contemplate your proposal."

"Well said," Cras extolled before adding, "And you need never fear us again."

The Nightwolves removed their gloves and extended their hands. Brooke clasped them each in turn. "And now?"

Scrit flicked his chin as he met the commander's unblinking stare. "And now, we rescue your family."

8: Darkest One
Sonart

Fear consumed Sonart as the lone Zürshuck extended its talons and clasped him firmly about his midsection. The demon lifted him away from the Kworn party with such a lurch, it left his stomach behind. Across the fiery chasm, the Winged One sailed before shooting into one of the Hive's wider apertures.

Sonart suppressed the sudden urge to retch as he laid eyes on what resembled the shadowy innards of a bleeding carcass. It reeked of it too.

But this blood glowed—with the flowing magma that fuelled the blasts of flame outside the tower.

Hundreds of Zürshuck milled about the extensive hollow. They flew in every direction or hung upside down from bone-like perches, wings folded, eyes shut. Several of the devils turned and observed Sonart as his escort slew past.

Thankfully, he did not have long to endure the sights, stink, and scrutiny. Wings pounding, his demon flew its dwarven cargo up to the ribcaged ceiling where the maw of a sinewy shaft opened, awaiting to swallow the pair.

Into the vertical, thirty-foot-wide shaft, the Zürshuck rose. After some time, it breached an orifice framed by an ironock hatchway. Judging by the time the demon took to reach the landing, the level must lay just beneath if not astride the tower's crown.

As the Zürshuck alighted atop the lofty stage, it released Sonart from its biting grip and shoved him forward.

Sonart went down in a heap as the Winged One dropped back through the trap door. The lid slammed shut behind it, releasing a hollow thud that echoed in the dwarven's ears. Locked inside, he would face Deathwrought's judgement alone.

Despite his anxiety, Sonart took some relief when he picked himself up and looked around. Though stark and empty, the slate grey enclosure contrasted sharply with the tangled tunnels, irregular spaces, and jagged openings beneath the hatch. Stranger still, none of the Zürshuck hordes filled the antechamber.

Symmetry prevailed on this level, set in a simple economy of space. Clean linear angles defined the corridor and naught else. A giant rounded hallway curved away in a wide circle, two hundred feet to either side of Sonart, withdrawing from view as it did. Somewhat of a paradox, the empty enclosure hinted at freedom.

But in another way, the circular hall seemed more menacing than the organic twists of the colony it crowned: an architectural mask veiling a fouler purpose. His inner voice cautioned him to keep up his guard.

Sonart turned his attention to the corridor's outer wall. Open windows, barred with corrugated ironock rods, lined the outside perimeter and gradually disappeared from view with the curvature of the wall's arc. The Cradle was based on rings—its core proved no different.

When he noticed wisps of vapour creeping into the passage from every window, Sonart moved to the closest one and peered outside. Swirling grey mist filled its frame. His uncanny sense of direction had proven accurate: he now stood upon the highest tier of the Hive, within the clouds.

The mist dampened his face and beard as flowing skeins found their way into his nostrils. They carried a strange heady redolence. The scent strengthened, enough that Sonart could taste it as he rolled his tongue over his chapped lips.

Salt.

But not like that of the flats; this briny aroma elicited some distant recall. Though the memory eluded him, Sonart had savoured this smell before. When he filled his lungs, it carried him away to some faraway place. His shoulders slackened and his thoughts grew lucid.

As Sonart strove for detachment, staring into the netherworld beyond the window, the fragrance befouled with some new stench. His nose bunched, recognizing the obtrusive reek at once: brimstone—*deathbreath* as the dwarven called it. Such a toxic fume nimbused all others. It came from somewhere behind him.

Sonart glanced back, and flinched. The entire inner wall of the corridor had vanished, exposing a sunken chamber within. Spanning near the full diameter of the Hive, the magnificent amphitheatre had eight definitive finely crafted sides—obviously dwarven hewn.

But stars eclipse, of all places, why here?

Far across the chasm, the same barred windows lined the opposite side of the encircling corridor, its ring girdling the nested sanctum like a halo.

The stairs surrounding the border led down, following the same concentric octagonal pattern—a smaller octagon sunken within an octagon—until the stairs terminated upon a raised pediment some two hundred feet below.

Atop the plinth sat a diminutive dais constrained by the same eight-sided shape as the entire shrine. On this pulpit, an identical set of eight triangular windows inlaid the obsidian stone floor. Capped with panes of clear crystalline glass, the triangular windows formed yet another octagon as they converged on the podium's centrepoint.

Even from this height, the glass triangles revealed a conduit beneath them. Proportionate to the circumference of the dais, it plunged like a stone drainpipe sealed with an embedded glass lid.

Sonart tried to gauge the shaft's depth, but it appeared unfathomable, falling away to a vanishing point. Greyish-green smoke eddied inside the encased sluice and obscured his keen eyes. It might very well run down the entire length of the Hive.

Besides the windows, etched canals furrowed the stone of the dais. At each point where the lines intersected, either a long blade of fire arose two feet from the floor or a large crystal shard protruded like an upturned dagger.

Strangely, the curling smoke plumes produced by the flames did not dissipate as they rose. Rather, they capriciously fed a single mass that coalesced like a vaporous ornament floating a hundred feet over the dais. Above this aggregate, the ceiling of the chamber remained hidden, its upper recesses lost in shadows.

Sonart's doubt mirrored its gloom. The hairs on his nape stood at attention. Though overwhelmed by the sight, he surmised by the way the chamber appeared, he must descend the steps to the dais. No point in delaying his inevitable trial, only to add to the sum. Best to get it over with.

He started down.

Foreboding crawled up and down Sonart's spine as he neared the chamber's base. When the shadows deepened, a glimpse back confirmed the walls to the corridor above had reclosed, sealing him inside.

The deathbreath taint became overpowering as Sonart scaled the pediment and stepped onto the dais. A queer oscillation commenced as soon as he crossed the outermost markings etched in the floor. His footfalls had triggered the response.

The flames at the various junctures of the podium dimmed, their smoke dying to trickles as the opaque cloud above him descended, its mass sinking lower until it hovered just over the dais.

The ethereal shroud thrummed and the crystals in the floor flared brighter. Streaks of a preternatural *un-light* ignited from out of the gems, transforming into glowing tendrils of emerald. The fronds traced narrow paths along the thin channels carved into the stage.

The weight in Sonart's heart increased tenfold. His knees buckled and he collapsed heavily. The invisible burden pressed down harder, forcing Sonart to prostrate. Rolling onto his back, he lay supine on the cold stone—like a sacrifice.

A corona of the same green aura strobed like sheet lightning from the cloud above, imbuing the entire chamber. The mist began to gyrate around the centre of the podium. Sonart detected forms dancing within the cloud. The silhouettes looked two-dimensional, as though reflected in an angled mirror. Flat, inhuman wafers sailed swiftly around like leaves whipped by a whirlwind. They loomed closer and became corporeal, taking on the snouted forms of hellspawn. Savage were their fenced sneers, maws open wide.

Other abominations joined them, dragged up from some ethereal plane. Living refuse, repulsive marionettes in thrall to the demon horde, one step away from the deepest sleep.

Paralysed by dread, Sonart had seen their like before, in a harrowing vision: the ilk of the Darkest One's cruellest machinations. Repugnant carcasses riven from the bowels of the Dunge and reanimated into a true demonic form. The other hellions had tooled them, to gratify their sick lusts.

But this was no vision.

Sonart registered as much—when they attacked.

The demons and their spawn took turns at him, with claws, fangs, and stingers. They exposed, pummelled, rent, and violated him. Pain masticated Sonart as they brought him to the final brink of the deepest sleep. But the hellions denied him leave to cross death's final threshold, repairing the damage they caused only to drag him back for recourse.

Abruptly, they abandoned Sonart and the agony stopped. He had weathered all unharmed. The demons continued their macabre dance above him for a while longer but something quelled their violence, a new arrival, something they held in veneration, leery of, if not terrified.

A giant reptilian head materialized out of the ether above them. It seemed to draw substance from the demons, subsuming the swarm's essence as it solidified. The forty-foot-wide face leered down at Sonart, orbs burning white fire and purest hate.

The Darkest One had come.

Some eighty horns and tendrils flowered out of Deathwrought's monstrous head like ebony plants forced to grow abnormally fast. On the tip of each snaking stem the bulbous head of a demon writhed. The multitude of devil faces drifted back and forth like fleshy beads tied to thick strands of hair. Each countenance mirrored the vehemence in the colossus' venomous glower.

Through fang-laden maws, the dark choir hissed a collective droll, filled with loathing and despite, "*Penancesss, penancesss, penancesss.*"

Mouth gaping wide, the giant head plunged. Before Sonart could scream, it sucked him up from the dais and swallowed him whole.

An instant later, the smaller demon heads manifested inside the Darkest One's mouth, the emerald glow of their eyes lighting the cavity. The press still seethed, but their overture quieted, as though judging Sonart in baleful silence.

His trial had begun.

Somewhere in the disorientating wilderness, the Darkest One's caustic voice scorned, "Wretched mortal. Wretched and accursed."

Every word stabbed Sonart like a crucifixion, every syllable, a spike, parroted by the congregation of nested heads, fading with each repetition, "*wretched, wretched, wretched...*"

"Dare tamper with the Cleft Augury? The very firmament which keepeth the Void of Obliteration at bay? A treacherous act too heinous to warrant mere subjugation to the lowest pits of the Dunge. As Shirdron attempted and failed to do, you have meddled in matters and places that will doom your foul breed. Now, a certainty, for the Starbond true draws nigh."

The demanding voice sprayed Sonart with pure vitriol, "Did you find what you pilfered for, knave? Speak, before the power I wield plucks your soul from all existence."

Dispelled by the power of the phantasm's imperative, a numbed Sonart could not find the strength to reply.

"Lo Vein, thou shalt bleed your fire yet, but for my cause. Now, come hither to my bidding. SPEAK, I command," the black deity railed. "Speak or forever vanquish your kith and kin."

"*speakss, speakss, speakss,*" the demon heads chorused.

'*I——cannot!*' Sonart screamed in his mind.

"At last," the omnipotent voice mused, "You may beseech an adjournment, but whether I stay my verdict depends upon a great many things. What will you confess of your trespass in the most sacrosanct of all places? Knowledge of a being, a theft of power perhaps? Do I bestir a memory? Now SPEAK, cur!"

Sonart's eyes went wide as Deathwrought jolted him into understanding. A will not his own seeped into his mind, infiltrating it as easily as opening a book. There, it attached itself like a parasite. His attempt to repel it met with pain, which only allowed it to core deeper.

Riven by the ambivalence of what he could divulge and what he most certainly should not, Sonart hesitated. The floor shuddered and bucked in retort. Flames scorched him.

When they dithered, the Darkest One rasped, "Have you forgotten what I am? Do not pause to sift your answer, speak sooth, or I will know it—and pain serves as a dutiful reminder if you deign test my wrath. Your essence was there, craven, within the Cleft, whilst your corporeal form lay in the Dunge. Dwarven forefathers and brethren alike will rue the bitch that brought you screaming into this world, for screaming they will depart it, cursing your name as they burn for your atonement."

To Sonart's horror, the Darkest One could hear and see his thoughts. Even in the State, the deity had reconnoitred. There could be no lies or half-truths. But maybe...

"Think you that I have not prepared for this meeting?" Deathwrought derided. "For every conceivable eventuality? I have waited and watched the Cleft Augury for eons before I ever permitted your feeble forebears to coexist with the favoured of my realm. Deny me what was given you within the Cleft and you will spend all of eternity in the throes of the Dance."

"*The dance, the dance, the dance,*" the eighty demon faces brayed. "*We only tasted the Scion's blood. We hanker. Grant us the Vein's succour for eternity, Master. Pleasssssess. Pleassssess. Pleassssess.*"

Sonart shrank back in sudden understanding. By the *Dance*, he meant the demons' unending torture of his mind and soul.

The dwarven fumbled for a riposte, "I received nothing," he blurted, before amending, "nothing, but a vision." *Many in the Dunge have, if not the Cradle whole.* "I only—acted upon it."

Without warning, Deathwrought spat Sonart out. He landed on the dais with a crunch that jerked his bones. The Darkest One's gargantuan orbs pinned him with new percipience. "Tell me of this—act."

"A sword *bit* me. The blade flew of its own volition. Pulled me into the sanctum. I heard a voice and detected a monstrous presence—it ejected me and brought horrible agony. That is all I remember," Sonart stammered, grappling to affirm the recollection to mollify his judge and tormentor. Convinced that he'd thrown his words off a cliff, the dwarven believed they would prove his last.

They did not. A loud silence filled the chamber and the tongues of fire on the stage brightened momentarily.

The Darkest One said more to himself than to his captive, "So, tis in motion as I have foreseen. The Starbond is indeed at hand." Demeanour calming, his nefarious scowl shifted away for the first time. "Solemn, this turn of events, Son of Farkshone. He who styles himself 'First Father' presents a bane to us all. He tried once with Shirdron, and failed. Now, he repeats his folly, making the gravest of errors to impart a wretch like you with the forbidden knowledge of the Cleft—knowledge never meant for you."

Deathwrought stabbed each syllable like the point of a dirk. "This dark seed Vamsah has elected to plant in you must not take root as he intends. It must flourish in the soils of my favour. The tree's roots must need drink from my devices and mine alone. If not, the sapling will still bear its one fruit, but of poisoned flesh it shall prove. Then, the First Father—our mutual enemy—will have already won."

Sonart wore his confusion like a chain around his neck. What First Father? What error? What knowledge? What cursed tree? Each question formed another link, but the more he tried to tear the fetter from his neck, the greater its press and the more violent the vortex of the deity's malice.

"I don't understand!" Sonart wailed. "I hold no knowledge! This— conflict—lies beyond me. What role could I possibly have in it? I am of no consequence!"

A fulsome laugh burst from the giant head, "Ah, but you are, my fractured votive. I'll warrant your ignorance has been planned thus by the First Father—clever of my nemesis to do so. Tis only fitting. But, Worm, you are utterly mistaken about your role in Vamsah's sinister plan. He considers you instrumental, sowing the tree of which I speak. An expedient against me! Unless…"

Sonart croaked past the ironock nugget lodged in his throat, "Unless?"

"You may harbour the prohibited knowledge in the gloom of ignorance yet, but when you do grasp its import—and you will—you must hearken to my edict, not his. I must stem the fruit's poison. And reap its power, when the nexus of the Starbond draws near. Can you not hear the storm winds build? I have, and when they reach gale strength, left unchecked, existence shall cease. All will be lost to the conniving machinations of the First Father, as will your reality before you begin."

Sonart became plaintive. "What have I done to merit this brand?" His mind flashed back to Malrik's amnesty and his own efforts to distance the other dwarven from his plight. He had taken sole ownership of their fate, but even that was a feigned convention. Sonart knew better. *I am not alone. Others have had the same vision. This isn't isolated—tis a movement.*

"Precisely, Blood Scion—Vein!" the Darkest One bellowed. "You state your part henceforth and the reason why you will serve me and the Cradle, and the very *divinations* of the Kusp: existence."

Incredulity dropped Sonart in a maze, scrambling to understand. "The Kusp of the Testament? How can I possibly be linked to the sacred tome?"

"You will see—when you go back among your people. Hunt down those who have shared your vision of the Augury—and destroy them."

The outrageous mandate struck Sonart dumb. *Stars blacken—as if.*

But in his mind, he repeated Deathwrought's demand like a mantra, his inner fires blazing to combat the new turmoil roiling in his gut. Sizzling currents lanced through him before he could utter a sound to that effect.

"No choice!" the Darkest One berated. "You are to blame for the current situation: your tampering in the Cleft has left the Cradle more vulnerable than ever before. You have invited desecration as Shirdron once did—indeed expedited the collapse. It falls on you to remedy it."

Who in all hells was this Shirdron?

The overlord glowered as the demon heads danced and jerked to the point of rapture. "You say that you sensed a presence in the Cleft: that presence is the heralding wraith of Obliteration's Void. Ever does it seek to annihilate the sanctuary I have provided for your breed. The Void works at Vamsah's behest to exterminate the Cradle's denizens."

"*Denizens, denizens, denizens,*" the tethered hellions sang.

"Those who share your vision exacerbate an already dire situation. If not quelled, the pariahs will bring it to fruition all the quicker. They must be dealt with in the only way possible, and because you can sense their presence, you must do it. It will spell genocide upon all of your brethren if you do not rout this small quarry and put an end to their mischief."

The air vibrated under the strain of so much magical power.

"The Void had been shut in the Cleft, but you broke it out, freed it from its wards and manacles. When the Augury evicted you, did you not glean the wake of the wraith's escape? Ere long, the Outereach will be unable to withstand the Void. Our last line of defence will crumble and fall as that very same presence gains sway and power over the Cradle. Do you understand?"

Sonart's beard jigged as he bobbed his head like a redeemed child.

"Do this, dwarven, and you may yet redeem your trespass. A suture upon the grievous wound Shirdron inflicted. You will at least postpone the fulfilment of the Kusp's prophecy. With the ancient tome as your guide, you might still circumvent the Starbond's rampage when it strikes. As Shirdron learned too late, either way, the blade will cut. You must decide the direction, how soon, and how deep."

Sonart's will bound itself to every word spoken by Deathwrought, succumbing even as the shadow lord uttered them. A wave of compliance forced open the innermost refuge of his mind. It gathered momentum, scraping away every last stitch of Sonart's resistance.

"Eternal cataclysm for all, or the removal of a mere handful—the choice is simple. It must be done. But you needn't dwell on your own destruction for a while yet, now that you serve as the harbinger of my imperative."

Sonart faded into a ghost of his former self, but fed by the power of the dark god, found a voice to speak aloud. "How will I recognize those who have shared my vision?" He did know how: of late, an awareness had manifested—of those who'd shared even some small glimpse of his visions.

"You are the cynosure of the Endstorm. As such, they will be drawn to you like moths to the lantern. But when they do, heed my warning; do not entertain any notion of betraying me or shirking any part of my purpose. Remember, with your eyes, I doth see exactly what you see. I will learn exactly what you learn. Think on what I say, Blood Scion, and let that dishearten you into compliance."

Aghast at his fate, Sonart rose to his hands and knees and crawled off the dais. But before he reached the next landing, an invisible force hauled him to his feet like a reclaimed puppet.

"Wait! I am not finished. One more thing I will have you oblige me before you set out to execute my justice."

The impaling crystals flared anew with greater brisance. Forks of lightning shot out and struck Sonart in delicate places. His inner soul retreated, making more room for the Darkest One to fully ingrain his essence. And fuse with it.

More than ever, Deathwrought had become a part of him. From that moment, Sonart felt lost to the hilt of his being.

Somewhere in the horrible storm, he became cognizant of his master's voice once more. To his shock, he himself uttered the unnatural words, "I cannot risk igniting any offspring like some goat in rut. This is war. Dismantled, I go forth to vaunt the lore of the Kusp. 'He who suffers most endures all.'"

Having demonstrated how deep his mastery had ingrained itself, Deathwrought's speech issued from the giant head once again. "Beware, thane, dwarven Proclaimers and my favoured keep watch. But also, my Four Siphons. You have already seen that mine eyes doth dwell in your eyes. *Mine eyes are your eyes*. Now begone knave, go forth and carry out the decree of Carnalahfardum Farill. Go damn the damned."

The appalling countenance dissipated, relinquishing its hold as it faded back into the swivelling mass from whence it came. The incursive presence within Sonart vanished with it.

Before he could collapse, a pair of ragged claws seized his midriff and hoisted him into the air, sending his heart plunging into his stomach. A Zürshuck had come to take him back. With a swish of air and a thrump of mighty wings, the Winged One bore him away from the arena.

Stephen Fenech

9: Warang
Brooke

Except for the lamplight spilling from the windows of the buildings unaffected by the attack, the streets remained relatively dark and empty. Brooke rode alone from his home, past makeshift squatter camps erected in various squares, to the closest stronghold gate.

His two new companions had gone on ahead to avoid raising suspicions. As matters stood, the late hour itself might warrant unwanted attention. Thankfully, he only had a relatively short journey to test the notion.

The Nightwolves promised to ward his passage and ensure he reached the gate with his skin. If all went according to plan, they would intercept him further up the road. As to how they would get past the entryway, they did not say, but their earlier demonstrations left little to doubt.

When Maxan drew up to the ruined vestiges of the southwest gate, one of the two sentries stationed there stopped him. The young soldier, no more than a boy, stood outside the torch-lit gatehouse flanked by four pole-mounted sconces and a row of stanchions on either side of the portcullis. Lamp flames chased all shadows within, turning the entire portal into a giant stone lantern.

By his lifting eyebrows, the soldiers recognized Brooke at once. He saluted. "Commander."

From atop his horse, Brooke gave the guards cursory nods. "Greetings."

The younger soldier looked down at a scroll splayed on a wooden podium beside the gatehouse. He frowned, then swallowed. "Beg pardon, Commander, says here your departure isn't scheduled until the morrow."

"Plans change," Brooke said a little tersely before adding, "but you do well to challenge me. I'll sign off on your manifest—and put in a good word to your captain upon my return. Now, give it here."

The sentry chewed his lip and glanced uncertainly at his peer, who only shrugged. Returning his eyes to Brooke, he handed him the scroll and lapis.

"Shall I send word to the King?" the sentry asked while Brooke wrote.

"As you wish," the commander replied, handing back the guard's effects. "Perhaps, His Grace won't mind the late interruption to his sleep with information he already has."

The guard hesitated a moment longer before briskly saluting. His fellow sentry followed suit. "Stars light your way, Commander."

"Safe journey, Sir," the other guard added.

Brooke dipped his chin to both before nudging Maxan forward at a trot.

The guards appeared green to the post, but Brooke wouldn't take any chances. Better to intimidate than to appear intimidated.

Certain that he was being watched by more than two sets of eyes, some friendly, others not, Brooke didn't glance back to check. He looked up. The night sky was crowded with stars, but the waxing moon would soon occlude them.

The commander followed the Eastwest Road for near two leagues before bringing Maxan to a stop within a small clearing, forty feet in from the thoroughfare and surrounded by a thicket of trees. The copse would shield him from unwelcome attention, full circle and bird's sight.

Brooke dismounted and loosely tethered his steed to the closest tree. A brief survey revealed wild scruff berries hanging from some nearby bushes. More to pass the time while he awaited his cohorts, he plucked one of the purple-blue fruits and popped it into his mouth. As he nibbled the tiny berry, amidst a din of chirping crickets, it brought him back to a happier time.

Brooke first met his wife as she picked these same berries. While ranging the Northern Forest—just a novice scout, younger than the two sentries he left by the gate—he stumbled upon Dayanthi. The tall raven-haired beauty froze him in his tracks and tangled his tongue. Until she pressed him to sample a few of the forest fruits she'd gathered.

So taken in by her warm brown eyes and charming smile, a few berries became a bushel's worth. And before he knew it, he had a cramped belly and a sore throat from talking up a storm. She stuck with him as he hunched over and retched a scruffy purple mess over the ground.

Dayanthi encouraged him, patting his back while innocently laughing at his misfortune. But it proved a benison, worth every purple spew, for it had allowed their first contact. And brought them together.

She accompanied him back to his outpost, inspiring him to appreciate nature and the simpler things in life. Brooke knew right then and there that he'd found his soulmate. That walk marked their first steps together, towards a long and loving courtship, which eventually led them up a chapel's red carpet and into a solid bond of matrimony.

Her face and those of their two boys, six-year-old Ferin and eight-year-old Hue, haunted his thoughts now. If and when he liberated them, he would have to ensure their continued protection. War was upon them for certain, but something far more diabolical brewed beneath the surface. The sooner he accepted the latter, the better he could brace for it. Alas, his family's fate had irrevocably twined with this darker intrigue.

Maxan let out a nervous snort, which stung Brooke back into sharpness.

He drew his sword, eyes darting left then right. With his teeth, the warhorse untethered himself from the branch but stood his ground.

Moments later, a large animal's guttural breathing rose above the crickets' serenade. Horse and commander turned as one to face the disturbance. Brooke held his air and listened closer.

It sounded like a bear—no, two bears. He couldn't see them, but he knew they padded nearer, steps away. At last, he discerned a pair of massive shadows flanking him—stars, larger than bears.

Brooke's blade shot up. Maxan neighed again and pawed a shallow trench in the grass with a hoof. The destrier had long been battle-hardened and not without his defences. His ironshod hooves could deliver death with impunity, as many a hobgoblin and lessrtrol had discovered too late.

Two more silhouettes detached themselves from the deeper shadows of the underbrush, making four in total. But these belonged to men.

"We have come, Commander," Scrit's familiar voice hailed. Brooke's shoulders sagged and he let out a breath. He also reseated his sword back in its scabbard.

Beyond the approaching men, the two massive beasts sat back on their haunches and stayed put.

"What are those creatures?" Brooke asked, unable to hide his incredulity. "Stars, they look too large for bears, let alone wolves."

Cras glanced over his shoulder. "What—our rides?"

Brooke almost choked on his own spittle as he harrumphed. "You—*ride* those things?"

Both men threw their heads back and laughed.

"Indeed, we do," Cras said after the moment passed. "They are canines true, not unlike the wolves that roam the Northlands up in the barren tracts of the Matted Spikes, and their whiter cousins that tramp the Ice Wastes. But their true line comes from a much more distant shore. Sprite lore has further hardened them. They 'bear' sentience, sharper, fiercer, and more cunning than the lesser wolves of their kind."

The massive canines rose and slowly moved closer. Under the moon's argent light, Brooke gauged exactly how large: heads, two feet from ear to ear stood five feet from the ground. How fierce: three-inch fangs protruded from their jaws, which thankfully remained shut.

Large ice-blue eyes regarded him dispassionately. The fur of one midnight-black, the other grey-brown. Both coats grizzled thick, their sheen flaunting an impressive musculature beneath.

"Proud, noble, ferocious," Scrit added as he ran a hand under each of the wolves' muzzles. "Steeds of the pathless path, the giant canines can commune with men and the lesser of their kind, even at great distances. They rally timber and snow wolves, hearkening multiple packs to our cause at need."

Brooke swallowed, unable to take his focus off the great beasts. "What do you call them?"

"This one here is Yggn." Cras gave the grey-brown wolf a firm pat on his flanks. "Scrit's Black is named Drasil."

"We call their kind Warangs," Scrit vaunted. "And they name us Wrayns, which in the Noirlunen tongue means—" He flicked his chin at the hilt of the longsword slung across his back. "Wolves that Sting."

"Wolf and man together bear the pack's collective name: Nightwolves," Cras put in.

The commander nodded absently, suddenly feeling very small.

Scrit drew back and studied Brooke. "You didn't think Night-*wolf* merely some fancy title?"

Brooke surrendered a bemused smile.

"As brethren, the Warangs share our path. We treat and tread beside them as peers," Scrit went on. "Recognised brothers in battle, they merit not only a place in our band but the highest regard therein."

The commander arched a brow when the Warangs tossed their enormous heads. They growled low. Three-inch claws, curved like a row of scimitars, pawed the earth, gouging furrows three times deeper than Maxan had dug.

"Seems there is much I must learn of your ways," Brooke admitted.

"We'll have the opportunity to teach you," Cras said. "As we ride."

10: Spiders and Webs
Deathwrought

The lone Zürshuck issued from the tower's highest portcullis. It pitched into the air, the Son of Farkshone firmly clasped in its talons. They fell swiftly into skeins of rising fume until a heat-charged updraft filled the demon's wings. With a loud *thrump,* it levelled off and sailed across the chasm.

Deathwrought watched it unfold through the dwarven Vein's eyes.

As soon as the Winged One made its exit, the walls of the inner sanctum closed, sealing off the flow of grey light trickling in from the windows beyond. The Darkest One released his possession over the dwarven and came back into his current form: a giant head hovering over the altar of his holy sept. A moment later, he ghosted back into the ether.

From the upper reaches of the chamber, a deeper gloom emerged, penetrating the shadows as it sifted down upon the dais. Torchlight extinguished before the invader's opaqueness.

From proscenium to floor, the entity swallowed the air like a vacuum. It coalesced and split into two forms, both hulking demons, ten feet tall, hooded and cloaked. They faced one another across the dais. One a Siphon. The other, the archdemon's master.

"Reechabah Saween," droned the Darkest One in his black tongue.

"Carnalahfardum Farill," came the icy response. The Siphon's rasp carried like a whisper but held immeasurable violence in check. "Why have you summoned me?"

The Darkest One exploded with sudden fury. "Someone or something has infiltrated Grendamaul! A *man's* corpse was found in the Dunge, translated there. And for that to happen, here of all places, he needed an accomplice. One or more insurgents remain at large, hidden in our very midst. Find them."

Reechabah stared. "We currently probe all levels of the Cradle. The Kworn herd the dwarven cattle while the Proclaimers infiltrate the masses. The Colossals guard the translation points; our dragons patrol the skies across the Lobe. My siblings and I ward against any incursive magics—from this plane to the Perpetual."

The archdemon dropped to one knee. "But we will double our efforts and discover any concealed foes. You shall know when I know."

"We must tread this path with delicacy," Deathwrought cautioned. His gaze fell upon the canals etching the platform. The intricate pattern depicted an octagon, inlaid with a double-crucifix. Together they formed eight sides and eight points.

He took in Reechabah's kneeling form. "Rise."

The archdemon rose.

"Nothing can be forfeit—or unheeded," said Deathwrought. "Ever vigilant you and your three brethren must remain. Our wait draws to an end: the Starbond true has come at last." He raised his hands and drummed his ebony digits together. "And now, I have placed all Four Veins."

Reechabah started at the revelation. "The dwarven—he is the Vein we have sought? One of the Four?"

"He has uttered the Word of Vamsah—the watchword."

In the dimness, the archdemon frowned. "But—Chosen? I harbour doubts. It may have been falsely planted—a ruse, like the Chosen at the last Kworn ritual."

Deathwrought stifled an urge to seize Reechabah by the throat and wring his neck. The Siphon's bold mention of the incident forced him to recall the greater knave's false lure. The Kworn decoy had cast a shadow over the god's designs, compelling him to rethink his strategies. *Does he do so again*?

Oblivious to his master's internal rage, Reechabah went on, "The prophecy warrants a deity among archangels."

"He is the Vein we have sought," Deathwrought maintained.

"Then, Master, let *me* bring Maudlin's opponent to heel," the Siphon pressed. "I would relish such a charge, extracting the knowledge you seek. The Law of the Octagon—in that, he is my sibling too, let him serve as my thrall as well, before I kill him."

"You forget your place among the Eight, Reechabah," Deathwrought said. "Like the dwarven Vein, you also must abide by the Law—and you know why."

Reechabah bowed low, his great horns tilting forward until their tips pointed at his lord. "Balance."

The Darkest One studied his highest disciple. "I control this dwarven cur, tooling his wilderen to suit my scheme. Isolated, bereft of seed, he now stands broken and alone against us. As an indentured servant, the Son of Farkshone can be quelled easily enough when that time comes. But now is not it. The Blood Scion's worth will be far greater, having him unwittingly tip the Starbalance permanently in our favour."

Reechabah lifted his eyes. "But a millennium ago, Shirdron failed to derange it permanently, bifurcating the Kusp's foretellings—and availing Vamsah in the process."

"This time will be different," Deathwrought assured. "Shirdron came near enough for me to glean where the flaw occurred. Twas the Watchers' Law that intervened, then."

Reechabah's wings fanned out from behind his cloak. After a moment he folded them back in. "You seem certain."

"Witnessed my interrogation?" Deathwrought asked.

The Siphon dipped his chin towards his barrel chest.

"My favoured would have crushed the most iron-willed mortal of the lot, yet he survived their tests of pain. For this alone, I command you and your brothers to wait. And watch."

The Darkest One fixed the other with a cold stare, "Now, what of the Tendril your Sibling summoned to ward the Cleft?"

"That—was no Tendril, Master, but the hyperdemon from beyond the hells of Infern. I felt its extreme power—as it devoured the Tendril."

"Truly?" Deathwrought was impressed. His unbidden guest was proving its worth tenfold. He brought his spectral hands together as though in prayer. "All well and good."

Begot of oblivion itself, the hyperdemon will illicit my windfall. Unbridled chaos rules it—the crucial aberration I seek. If played correctly, an element birthed outside Creation's cosom will pave my route, burn all prophecies of the Kusp, sway the Observers, and decide the fate of the Starbond. The alien will break the final path.

"And it did not manifest at the Scourge's bidding," Reechabah said, interrupting his lord's pondering. "But the necromage from the Main. Seems the hyperdemon will only answer to him."

For now. "Relthi—yes," Deathwrought said as he gripped his chin thoughtfully. "Souleater helped me attaint a Vein already. It will do so again."

"I remember," Reechabah said. "The necromage summoned and set it to dispatch the intruder. It slew his corporeal form as the translation completed—but the insurgent's soul slipped past. The hyperdemon feasted on the torment of some useless Kworn instead."

"Because of this infiltration, I had the dwarven delivered here on foot, instead of a quicker translation," said Deathwrought, his anger rising again. "The trespasser got to the dwarven—spoke to him within such a transitive state. Tis why I directed the Scourge to whip up a razor storm: to lock down the lands outside the Innereach."

Reechabah's orbs dropped to the dais. "So, the dwarven presents no danger while suppressed by the gloss of ignorance."

"But tis that which we cannot see that hazards us," Deathwrought reminded him.

"Other than what we effort to quell it, is there anything more you would have us do?"

"That will depend upon what unravels between the Vein and any surviving intruders. Look only to your own antithesis—and we will triumph over the Kazir as well. Have our revenge upon his master, the conniving Impostor who stole my crown."

"Vamsah," Reechabah spat the title with pure venom. "You were here long before any of his children and their fey descendants walked the soils of Areth or Earth, long before his cursed sprites."

"—and Highprites." Deathwrought supplied as he observed his partisan. "That includes you." He tilted his head up towards the ceiling high above. "But you are right to say. We only take back what is duly ours, before His doomsday conjuring tore my reality asunder and left us with this disorder. There is a better way. I must show the freeborn, but also the Watchers. Alas, that can only happen once the truth of the Imposter's Creation is revealed—at the time of the Starbond."

"What is that master?"

"That Creation is flawed. It embodies Chaos. I must erase his manifestation before I can remake it to my own *original* designs and strictures. Balance the whole so it exists in uniformity and order for all life—no more disparity between gods and mortals. All should share their suffering equally and know a measure of what I have endured."

"To that effect, how will you use your newfound Vein?" Reechabah asked.

"The dwarven Scion will lure the other Three, as a river finds confluence—mingling tainted waters to poison them as well. The Son of Farkshone must be allowed to return to the Augury. He will in time, for he's drawn there like a flame to dry kindling."

"Words unto deeds," Reechabah answered in a low deferential tone. The archdemon traced the nails of one claw down the length of his horn. It grated like metal on stone.

"Regardless of the Kusp's prophecy, and the skews therein, the Law of the Octagon ordains the Veins' Merger take place before the Starbond. Regrettably, that is something to which we must also adhere, lest we match Shirdron's Folly and negate the boon that cur inadvertently laid at our feet."

Reechabah's eyes blazed like twin suns. "Then, you have found a way around the irksome Law?"

Deathwrought nodded. "Rest assured, the balance will soon shift past the tipping point—in our favour. I've planted seedlings ahead of the First Father's reap. When his Four Scions flourish, we strike! With impunity and vengeance."

"All Four Veins lost before they begin," Reechabah mused. His glowing red pupils flared to infernos. A wicked sneer pulled his lips back over his fangs.

"Unbeknownst to them, their very joining will mark their undoing. The Starbond hastens now with greater alacrity—let it. I want all Four of you to return to your bastions. I have instructions for each of you."

"Befoulen, Goodakh, and Maudlin await my summons atop their Spikes. Do you wish a moot?"

"Not yet. Have one of your Colossals brought before me. A small chore must needs be done—before I take my leave."

"At once, Master," Reechabah said. "Where will you go?"

Deathwrought paused in contemplation. "Much time has passed since I last met Relthi's hyperdemon. I must posture the sycophant necromage and put his pet in its rightful place. For now, continue your investigations, keep watch. And remain wary."

Reechabah hammered a fist against his chest. "Eyes out, wilderen unblinking, as only we can." He bowed and made for the translation point of the dais. Steps away, he paused and turned. "Master?"

"Yes?"

"What of—*Otherworld?* It still poses a threat, and I hear rumours amongst the dark elven that One of the Scions has birthed there."

"Yes, I know," the Darkest One replied with a lilt of impatience. He waved his hand dismissively. "As I told you, all Four, including the outlier, have been placed. Long have I taken covert measures there. Otherworld hastens to its own demise, even if left to its own moribund devices. The sprites of Earth have already lost—they simply do not know it yet."

Deathwrought fell quiet and measured Reechabah's compliance. Satisfied, his voice took on an almost avuncular tone. "I have piqued your curiosity—as insatiable as your lust for rapine and obliteration. Come then, My Shadow, let me indulge you with a glimpse of our grand scheme."

Deity and demon dissipated from the chamber, coalescing in another part of the Hive a moment later. Deathwrought led his disciple to a recessed dais where a pair of altars stood, separated by a distance of thirty feet.

On one table, sat a shallow ebony bowl, its inside completely embedded with web strands converging on a hairy black spider the size of a large fist. It stared coldly up at its two observers, multiple eyes reflecting the crimson glow of theirs.

The spider braced, ready to pounce. But when Deathwrought lowered a bony finger and prodded the large arachnid it did not attempt to flee or bite the digit. Stinger and fangs poised, it sat still and cowed.

Before Reechabah could form a question, Deathwrought took his hand away and gestured towards the dais.

A shaft of emerald light sprang from the altar's surface to form a glowing halo. It intensified and rose until the nimbus completely permeated bowl and spider. From the luminescent ring, a beam arced to the second altar, imbibing the two onlookers. Within a blossoming aura on the adjacent slab, another bowl materialized—identical to the first.

Abruptly, the light rings and arch winked out.

Reechabah's snout pinched. "The arachnid looks unchanged."

Deathwrought tilted his cowled head towards the second altar. Master and servant glided there. In the middle of the newly manifested bowl, another spider scuttled across its weave—indistinguishable from the first.

Reechabah looked up from the bowl to his master.

"This is how I stifle the threat of Otherworld," Deathwrought exalted, "how I will conquer that realm's denizens and crush the heart of her Gaia."

The Darkest One scrutinized his pupil's measure. "Why *does* your master deem translation worthy of your audience?"

The creases of Reechabah's visage opened and closed in clear confusion.

"No mere translation, my friend," Deathwrought explained, "but propagation. Two spiders now exist, independent of each other, but cognizant of the same purpose, and akin to it."

The Siphon's fangs chewed air. Lantern eyes dimmed as they dropped to the closest spider, then flitted towards the first altar. "Is it your intent to send a plague of arachnids to subvert Earth?"

Deathwrought threw back his cowl and let out a dry roar. "Earth *and* our own insufferable prison world." He spread his arms and rotated his torso, sweeping the full length of the enclosure like a bird of prey about to take wing.

"Nay, my friend," he vaunted, knowing his certitude would slam Reechabah's doubt back into his scabbard. "Spiders have their place. But I will propagate something—somewhat larger."

Sonart awoke from his catatonic state just as the lone Kworn hefted him past the entrance gate of the Dunge. Down they marched into the depths of the prison's misshapen throat. As they neared his cell, the dwarven sharpened his wits and bunched up his nose. The sulphuric taint of deathbreath and burned fat overpowered the jail's usual dank stench.

The Kworn lowered him to the floor with surprising care and left. He did not slam the door but closed and locked it quietly.

Sonart sniffed again. Something felt wrong.

His pulse quickened. When his eyes adjusted, his heart howled.

On the far side of the cell, in a pond of congealing blood, lay Malrik, his head split open like a splayed book. By the stunned stare on his frozen face, death had come for the dwarven suddenly and unexpected. There would have been little or no pain. Judging by the cauterized edges of the massive cleave, a Colossal's flaming broadsword had ended his companion.

Gasps escaped Sonart's lungs as he drowned in a mire of angst. He beat his fists in a lobby against the mortar. "Stars burn you. Why?"

"Because!"

Sonart wheeled and faced his dead companion. Malrik's corpse became animate, the expression transformed into a corrupted grin filled with malice.

"You, not your decoys, possess that which I desire!" the corpse laughed, both sections moving simultaneously.

"Sonart, tis the Way of the Kusp," said Malrik in his former voice.

Sonart blinked. "Malrik, is that you? Does your spirit endure beyond the deepest sleep?"

A fiendish cackle answered him. "*Mine eyes are your eyes.*"

"No, no, NO!" raged the dwarven.

"You should be content, thrall," the corpse spat. "I spared you part of your charge, dispatching all in the Dunge who possessed a semblance of your vision. You need only focus on the hidden rebels outside of it. Consider this, your liberation—granted. You will be freed on the morrow."

Up until that point, the eyes of Malrik's corpse moved independently of each other, but now they both fixed Sonart with a penetrating stare. "Already we have pushed back the hands of the dial from your annihilation, strengthening the Outereach against Vamsah's Void."

Malrik's voice trailed into silence. The corpse fell still and did not move again. The puppeteer controlling the deceased dwarven had tired of his bewitchment and abandoned him.

Alone with his dead, Sonart collapsed. He wept into his arm until exhaustion numbed him past despair's terminator into unconsciousness.

Not for the first time, he dreamt of suicide—and a horizon of water.

Sin awoke screaming in his bed. He bolted up into a seated position, startling the young blonde woman, naked at his side. His sweat dripped off his forehead and dampened the sheets while he sucked in air, trying to bring his heart rate down. The sheet beneath his legs and ass had soaked through.

The woman reached for his clammy hand. "Sin, you okay?"

Gooseflesh bristling, he turned and gaped at her concerned eyes. For a long moment, he didn't respond as he finally brought his respirations under control. "Bad dream," he croaked. "I'm okay."

With a heavy purge of air, he leaned back down, drew her lithe form to his side, and nestled his face in a wealth of her lavender-scented hair.

She kissed his chest and enveloped him, wrapping one leg over him. The feel of her warm body married to his comforted the musician. He relaxed tensed muscles and stared up at the coffered ceiling of the suite.

The visions were getting stronger. More forceful and clear. First, they centred on him, then the two cloaked and cowled figures, on a long journey aboard some kind of sailing ship made from shells. And the floating child—but in some kind of furry costume with floppy puppy ears.

Now, this dwarf entered his thoughts for the second time. Who was the little guy? Sin could not make out his face, any of their faces—that part blurred. And yet, something seemed so familiar about him, about all of them. But in the midget's case, it touched him deeper, intrinsic like a TV character the viewer could relate to. Like a déjà vu doppelganger, fast-forwarded into the future. Some friend or brother Sin hadn't yet met, but soon would.

The tortured dwarf was in serious trouble, made to suffer in the most heinous fashion at the hands of devils. They tore him apart and sewed him back together, though not entirely. They had polluted him.

Sin knew it in his gut like the stench of sour milk. Could witnessing the dwarf's fate indicate a sign of things to come—a dark fantasy horror come to life? The dwarf's murky cell would make any banana republic prison seem like a palace. All those rats and spiders! Jesus, the two dead guys.

And those monstrous pig-faced guards. Holy shit, it all felt so real, as though Sin had already been there.

He had glimpsed it many times before. But not like this. The visions began after his accident, now twenty-one years on. The night he lost his parents.

Sin, an eight-year-old Zach Thornbury then, had concussed when the green bolt struck the boat and cast him into the sea. He remembered looking up as the boat split in two and sank. Between the relentless flashes of sheet lightning, he espied a wraith, tattered black cloak fluttering in the gale, hands raised, without any flesh, skeletal. The wraith floated in the air thirty feet above the violent seas.

As Zach bobbed in the swell, frozen to his core, his parents drowned moments before, the sorcerer hovered above the trough of the waves. His nefarious lamp eyes glowed scarlet as they fixed Zach with consummate evil. The wraith had caused the sinking—through *blood magic*—whatever the fuck that was.

The voices in Sin's head assured he would learn all of it, quite soon. When he returned to Areth. But he doubted it, dismissing it all as the product of panic: another post-traumatic coping mechanism.

And yet, he could never shirk the memory of the sorcerer. Sin dreamt often of him, long after that one and only encounter. Was he real or just another figment of the troubled singer's imagination? Was any of it real? His life on Earth, the dream?

Part of him suspected he didn't belong here anymore—if ever. All he knew for certain was that the same blurred faces reappeared whenever he slept. Some friendly, some hideous, all familiar. They filled the cinema of his brain with voices, and caterwauls.

11: Dayanthi
Brooke

"Two more fucking days to wait in this rotten cabin," Shick lamented. He pulled a green glob from his bulbous nose and inspected it. "I'm bored."

The sellsword regretted many things in his sorry life—a ladder of mistakes that began with his failure as a royal guard, when he panicked during a village demonstration and killed two innocent whelps. Stripped of office and imprisoned, he'd still be locked in the dungeon, if not for Necatar. The Grand Vizier had him freed—with one caveat. By selling his sword to the Haft, Shick had also sold his soul.

Lit by the flames of their small hearth, Ub, his boil-faced companion smirked. "Forest keeps us hid good—n' we got diversions. Why not take her now?" Mounted too close to a twice-broken nose, his eyes grew excited as he rubbed his palms together. "Make some sport of her, eh?"

Unshaven and reeking of barn and sweat, Shick took a long swig from his ale horn. The burlier of the two guards, he kneaded his potbelly and studied his weaselly peer. "She's buggered anyway. Be a shame to let such a precious thing go to waste fore she takes the deepest sleep."

"Sweetmeat indeed," Ub agreed with a fervent nod. "Been craving a haunch since I done laid eyes on her."

Shick burped. "Fuck being teased—I want my cock appeased. Full-on, full-in. Aye, let's do her."

Ub chortled. "Haven't had me a wench in so long, times I forget I got me a prick." His grin straightened. "But this ain't one of them."

"Just be careful. Leave her unscathed for the espousal show—else be us facin' the gibbet, or worse windin' up in Necatar's lab."

A cheerless laugh answered the man's slur. "True that."

The unkempt pair gloated at their prize. Through the open door of the adjacent room, three sets of eyes stared back. Bound and gagged, Brooke's raven-haired whore and her two whelps lay prostrate on the dirty floor, firelight dancing against their stricken features.

Ub clambered to his feet, his gaunt form swaying as he grappled with his trousers. And grappled.

Shick grew restless and scoffed, "You bumbling foolhead sot." He rose, knocking his scrawny cohort aside as he pushed past. "*I* go first. Since you obviously can't handle the Haft's grog, you can watch; handle your piece awhile instead."

Ub backed up against the table while Shick made for the bitch, wetting his chops in drunken anticipation. He stopped short when the wench rolled to the wall.

The fat man studied her lithe form with fascination as she struggled into a seated position. Back pressed against the wall, the woman shimmied up until she stood on bound legs. Her brown eyes harboured a fierceness like that of a cornered wolverine.

The harlot clearly wouldn't submit so easily as the others. But brazened by drink, he'd snuff her defiance and gain a more gratifying notch. The prospect heightened his lewd desire for her.

"More the challenge, sweeter the release," Ub cackled. The sound of eager stroking ensued behind Shick.

With a snort, the pear-shaped guard started forward. He moved slowly, savouring the swell between his legs.

Around their gags, the runts' muffled protests filled the space—giving Shick the perfect card to play. He sneered at them before lifting his hungry gaze to their mother. "Please, resist me, whore; give me sport and reward. Fail to satisfy... we'll run your cubs through as you watch. Even skewered on my blade they'll stand for our little farce." He massaged the press of his rigid member against the front of his trousers. "Either way, I'll run you through—with a different kind of sword. Wager, you'll enjoy that a tad more."

Venom hissed past her muzzle. *"Infr-al bea-sths!"*

Shick turned back to his peer. A slash of a grin spread across Ub's scarecrow face as his cock finally stirred.

With a snigger, Shick wheeled on the woman and drew a dirk from his belt sheathe. Using brute force, he cut the gag from her mouth, tore her dress, and ripped the underclothes from her body.

The woman flinched but never cried out.

Through the grog's bleary lens, Shick's prize met his thirsty stance with ice. "Enjoy your glimmer, you fucking coward—it will be your craven last." Something else shone in her eyes, which unsettled the guard. But it was too late to back down now, not after two insults to his manliness.

Rheumy pupils drinking in her pretty browns, Shick cooed. "What's wrong, Wolfy?" He unbuttoned his trousers with one hand and let his rod point to his goal. "Just sheered your fur. And fuck—is precisely what I'm gonna do. So, make it nice for me and I'll be nice to you."

Shick called over his shoulder. "Stop pettin' that scraggy worm and draw your blade—case she tries anything."

Metal sang and swished the air as Ub obliged. Footfalls sounded as his twig-pole partner advanced. Shick seized a handful of the slut's hair and yanked her head back, making her lips part. Then, he stuck his tongue in her mouth, holding his knife quivering under her neck.

She gagged as his spittle ran down her cheek, but the fire filling the woman's glare made the rogue soldier cringe. He'd break her, he would, quell that insolent fury in her glower. And yet, not once did she resist him.

Or couldn't—he had superior strength—least in body.

Encouraged, he dropped his knife and pawed her exposed breasts with calloused hands. Her skin, so soft. His cock stiffened into an ironock spike.

The cubs struggled against their bonds, trying to stop him. He kicked them away. But the woman relaxed and shifted her position. She spread her legs, making it easier for him. Ah yes, a mother's love for her children, how touching. He never thought she'd submit so soon—disappointing that, but he too relaxed.

Dayanthi bit down hard on Shick's tongue. He shrank back and howled in pain as the coppery taste of blood filled his mouth. With all his strength, he wound back his arm and struck her across the face.

The blow sent her sprawling to the floor.

"That's it, bitch," Shick roared. "Kill 'em both Ub! The she-wolf can watch'em take the deepest sleep." Red sputtered from his mouth as he added, "You'll still be the star of my play's climax."

Ub did not reply.

"Ub, you fucking sot, I said slay the weasels or I'll—" *Shripppp.*

A blade tip pierced the front of Shick's pudding gut. A gloved hand grappled his shoulder and spun him about. The face before him did not belong to Ub. It belonged to Commander Brooke. Ub hunkered on his knees, minus a head.

***

"Play's cancelled, you dickless filth!" Teeth gritted, Brooke pulled a dagger from his belt. He wrenched it up in a lightning thrust that severed the man's rod. The swollen member dropped to the floor with a thud. Then he twisted Shick around to face Dayanthi and kicked his legs from under him. The henchman fell to his knees.

Brooke pocketed the small blade and held the sellsword fast, one hand clamped like a manacle about the fiend's neck.

As the soldier's head rolled back, Brooke loomed over him, making sure the hellish torrent in his eyes would be the last thing the cretin saw before his vision dimmed forever.

Only when Shick had taken the deepest sleep did the commander's fury ebb. He released the corpse, letting it flop forward, the frozen face colliding against his own severed penis.

The wooden floor let out an imperious clug.

After removing his blade and wiping it on the back of the knave's trousers, Brooke sheathed both weapon and wrath. He tore off his cape and rushed to his wife. Cut the bonds coiled around her feet with Shick's fallen dirk and helped her up. Then he gingerly wrapped the shawl around her.

Dayanthi buried her head in his embrace as Scrit and Cras emerged from the shadows to free the two boys. Brooke's children scampered to their feet and hastened to join their parents, letting out their own emotional deluge.

"My rock!" Dayanthi bawled. "Vamsah be praised, Aviry. I thought you dead. Hope vanquished."

"No more tears, beloved. No more fear." Brooke kissed her gently on the lips. "These bastards—small fish though they may be in the rising tide—have paid my price for their sins. Nothing more would have been gained with a thorough interrogation; the fiends interrogated themselves ahead of my arrival. And my cohorts knew full well their motives and allegiances. But the bigger fish still roams the ocean depths, still owes. And I swear by all the holy stars that share Vamsah's light, I will see the traitor pay the full tally. I swear to you, wife, others will be brought to justice for this treachery."

"Why did they *do* this—especially now?" Her sobs ebbed and her brows slanted inward. "Was the army not to ride against the sprites at this time? And how did you know where to find us?"

Brooke arched an eyebrow as realization dawned. "Of course, you are unaware of what has unfolded: Pathguard lies in ruins."

Dayanthi gasped. "Ruins?" When Brooke inclined his head, her frown drifted to her two wide-eyed sons. A purple welt had swollen Hue's cheek where Shick's boot had connected.

Dayanthi lifted Hue's chin and inspected the wound closely. "Stars align, no lasting trauma, my brave and valiant knight. Your mother is relieved and grateful."

She offered him a tired smile before seeking Brooke's regard. "Are the sprites responsible, or was it the Nightwolves as you suspected?"

Brooke exhaled. "Regarding Pathguard's fall, let's just say, I remain suspicious." He gave his wife a bemused smile. "As to your rescue—the latter for a certainty." He indicated his two companions with a flick of his chin.

Dayanthi bit her lip, eyes flitting warily to the Wrayns. Brooke's grin slackened as he dropped to one knee and ardently hugged his boys. "Ferin, Hue, how fares my two warriors? Your father is so proud of you—honourable cavaliers of the highest order, I dub you—warding your mother until I returned. You are rightly my children."

When Brooke withdrew, they beamed at his praise. He ruffled their hair and stood. No longer was he a commander in the King's Guard, but the humble father he so desperately wanted to be.

Brooke's work had taken him much too long and far afield to succeed at that. Still, being reunited, if only for a brief time, helped steady him. Now, the commander could get his bearing, and rationalize his new allegiance.

After a time, steps sounded at his back.

"I am forever in your debt," Brooke said over his shoulder. "Truly." Not only had the Nightwolves saved the lives of his most precious, but redeemed Brooke's soul in the bargain. On the brink of war, for a few moments at least, he felt a flicker of holy peace towards his world.

When the moment passed, Brooke turned.

The two Wrayns regarded him, unmasked and unblinking.

"Coast is clear I take it, and you've come to remind me of my side of the bargain," Brooke supplied.

Cras cleared his throat. "If we are to make our rendezvous, we should be off soon—for your family's sake. You have some time while we ready the Warangs to seat the extra passengers." With that, the two Wrayns left the cottage, closing the door behind them.

Dayanthi knitted her brows. "Bargain?"

"That warrants some explanation," Brooke said.

Before he could shed light on his contract with his black-garbed companions, Dayanthi gripped him tightly about the back of his head and pressed a desperate kiss upon his lips. Husband and wife entwined into a single entity for a wondrous minute.

Only when Brooke detected the small hands of his two lads pulling at his britches, did he remember their dire need for haste.

The chamber's candles flickered, their crimson light dancing against the rounded mortar walls of the high tower laboratory. From beneath his cowl, Necatar peered into the swirling depths of his seeing device—watched with grim orbs as Brooke's cadre stole away into the night. When the misty image within the contraption's glass circlet dimmed, the necromage remained still. Hunched and scowling over his tool, he contemplated the ramifications of this unforeseen development.

Necatar expunged a hollow breath and spoke to the dank air. "That is what you think, my ill-begotten friends."

The sound of whimpering broke the Haft's quiet satisfaction and furthered his dragonish appetite. He turned to face its source. On a heavy wooden rack besmirched with greyish-green bits of pungent rot, the naked form of Commander Racine lay, strewn. The ropes that secured him chaffed his wrists and ankles. A gag fastened his mouth.

Past other devices of torture, some of which still bore human corpses in varying degrees of decay, the spindly mage approached the man.

"The time has come for you to pay for your transgression, Little Bird." Necatar projected his voice like a funeral dirge—its harrowing effect on his captive: simply delicious. He could feel Racine's pulse doubling. His skin crawled with gooseflesh, his eyes widened and his breaths came in shallow huffs. "Brooke was not to learn of my designs. By aiding the turncape, your true allegiance was revealed to me." He nodded. "Yes, I know of your other secret liaison. The tune of your deeper espionage disrupted Pathguard's salvation—but by no means quelled it."

Necatar placed his palm against Racine's cheek and gave it a quick pat. "No matter. It will not serve my purpose to simply kill you. I have found a way for you to redeem yourself and fulfil my requisite contrition. Alas, I must use your soul to bait the one I truly require. Together, you will join forces to do my bidding."

He wagged a skeletal finger at the man. The digit elongated to twice its natural length. "Remember, Little Bird, when the Sorgon comes for you this eventide, you must welcome it into your body. Serve as an accommodating host, embrace your guest with courtesy and your end will go, less painful. Dwell on that and be dismayed."

Necatar turned to go but something in his prisoner's panicked gaze stopped him. Stirred him. The mage licked his lips as he produced a dagger from the folds of his purple cassock and drifted back to Racine's side.

The mage stuck out his tongue and slid it across his captive's face. Then he whispered in his ear, "No need in wasting such a savoury specimen before that time. Little Bird, I want you to sing a song for me before I go."

Necatar thrust his blade into Racine's abdomen. Eyes bulging, the man wailed past the gag in his mouth.

"Yes! That's the tune I crave. Sing, sing!" the mage chorused in escalating tones as he pressed against his captive. Necatar stiffened as rapture took hold. "Sing, Little Bird, *sing*!" he cried in falsetto as delight swept the dark mage over euphoria's edge.

When Racine's body slackened, Necatar drew back and studied the wound he inflicted. "I'll leave that dagger in your sheath. Its blood magic will keep you alive—just long enough." The mage wiped sweat from his brow and exhaled as his gaze lifted to the man's face. "I will say this, Little Bird, you did not disappoint. My demon is in for a treat."

With that, Necatar spun on gratified heels and strode out of his tower lab. He must summon his obsequious puppet-king—make the highborn fool dance harder on his jerking strings.

12: Let Loose
Sonart

Ghoulish screams, children laughing: the sounds meshed together like tightly strung wires singing in the wind. Voices barely audible at first grew to a din in the darkness.

Save us, Vein. Do not destroy the desecrated. Save us from our corruption. Save us from the land. Save us from ourselves. Save us. They cried in a chorus of taint-riven pleas. The voices wavered to a steady drone, only to return, louder, protracted. The ululations diminished a second time.

On the third crescendo, they sounded different—soothing to the ear.

Sonart did not know where he was. Could neither see nor feel, but he recalled this new voice. It stirred a memory long buried. Had he taken the deepest sleep?

No, he decided. This voice expressed softness and encouragement. Not a hint of malice. Hands caressed him, gentle frail digits.

The two senses wed, offering greater clarity, but Sonart focused on the comforting speech—high-octave, female. Although he could not understand what she said, her words had an urgent quality to them. He pursued her voice, if only to assuage its need, and return to his earlier numbness.

His efforts only made the woman sound more resolute. Her breath escalated. Shelving any notion of retreat, Sonart returned her touch as she fussed over him.

Her voice sang with jubilance—enough to sting his ears.

"Pray stop," Sonart croaked, barely a whisper. "Mercy, please."

The woman, whoever she was, stopped and laughed. Laughter full of *mirth*, another forgotten sound. When her elation simmered, Sonart understood the discomfort she'd caused bespoke something good, familiar.

"By the Stars, Auckland, come quick! He's returned from the dead!"

The scuffling of running boots followed, an abrupt one-two stomp, then a long throaty exhalation. "Aye, Mila, his face escapes the grey of the deepest sleep. Colour's returning even as I say so."

Auckland, Mila—Sonart recognized the names—they buoyed fond memories. Their flame had long ebbed in the pyre, but their embers glowed yet. Mila took him in and cared for him after his father's disappearance. The other voice, deeper, wizened, august, belonged to Auckland, Mila's husband—and Sonart's uncle.

"Lad, speak to me," Auckland said in a scratchy tenor.

"Please, Sonart," Mila added her voice scaling higher.

Vision swimming, Sonart worked moisture past the bile in his mouth. He coughed through a parched throat. "Cannot see—yet—but I'm all right."

His guardians broke out in delighted merriment. Sharing such open jollity was something Sonart had not done since his incarceration, something he thought he would never do again.

When his sight cleared, it revealed a husband and wife embracing as their radiant faces beamed down at him. And though he could not bring himself to join in their gaiety, their benevolence diminished the weight of his recent ordeals.

"Let him rest, woman," Auckland said in a soothing tone. "On the morrow, with the light of the drear, we'll stir him again. Assuredly, the worst is behind."

Grateful for Auckland's intervention, Sonart allowed a wan smile to stretch his lips as he drifted out of consciousness again. He took his leave without voicing it. And without burden. *All you must do is survive.*

When Sonart's lids fluttered open the next morning, tears welled up. Blinking rapidly, the dwarven cleared his vision and beheld the wrinkled whey-faced countenance of Mila. She stooped over him, grey eyes shining beneath brows furrowed with concern.

"Mila," Sonart whispered. "I've come home."

The creases on her face eased and her cheeks glowed with generous warmth. Above her bent form stood Auckland, who gently squeezed his wife's shoulder, piercing deep-set blues glistening as they regarded Sonart.

The elder dwarven compressed his lips into a tight line, across a jaw set in a forge of strength. The years had weathered his uncle's face. Auckland's grizzled beard had blanched white with the star-cycles, but he retained the vitality of youth in his stern countenance, square shoulders, and straight back.

Sonart took in the details of the room. Somehow, someone or some thing had delivered him to his kin. He recognized the sandstone walls, the ironock lattice. A shallow bed of deep orange coals filled a small hearth to one side of the enclosure. The embers' warmth still lingered from yester's evening fire, enough to permeate the air with the faint smell of wood smoke.

An earthenware cup of water on the bedside table reminded Sonart how depleted he was. Mila followed his gaze and immediately jumped up to help her husband prop him into a sitting position. She raised the vessel to Sonart's mouth and slowly tipped it forward.

Some of the water dribbled down his chin and soaked his beard, but enough trickled into his throat. Cool, clean, refreshing, it revitalized his body and spirit, washing away, if only symbolically, the taint he'd been forced to endure for so long.

"Can I get you anything else, love?" Mila asked. Her rough-edged voice lifted Sonart and made the sombre room seem cheerier. "Water's just to get yer gears turnin'. You'll be needin' some proper food in that belly—soon by the look of ya."

"I'll see to it," Auckland offered.

"Don't ya go payin' it no never-mind, Auckland. Keep yer nephew company. Leave the grub to the expert."

With that, Mila left, hobbling out the door and into the kitchen.

A racket ensued in the other room as cupboards opened and closed and metal pots clanged.

Auckland angled back from the door to face Sonart. "Don't say too much, or anything if you can help it. We'll have words later."

Sonart dipped his beard.

When Mila returned, she held in her stout arms a tray containing a plate of bread and a steaming bowl of greenish-brown stew. Yellow noodles and a medley of deep orange vegetables with dark green flecks floated on its surface.

Sonart's nose perked up as its arboreal aroma filled the room. His stomach grumbled aloud.

"Nothin' like a bowl of Mila's hogsweed to set ya right. I spiced it up special for ya—to speed up yer recovery. Something this good could bring anyone round, I reckon," the old woman chided.

She placed the tray on Sonart's lap and touched his forehead. "Still a bit of fever, but a vast improvement, I dare say."

As Sonart swallowed the broth, the tension in his muscles eased. Verve bolstered him with every spoonful, and he soon felt better than he had in the last two star-cycles.

Astute as ever, Mila gave him an encouraging grin. "Ya don't know how happy we are havin' ya back with us, son, and whole at that. We thought ya lost forever the drear the buggers took ya—that you'd been killed. N' yet, after all 'em moon-cycles down there, here you are."

"Indeed." Auckland shot his wife a sideways look as he interjected. "You were but a corpse when we found you outside our door, two drears following that last razor storm—close to a fortnight ago. How you survived the Dunge and the Scourge's rampage, I'll never know—and frankly, I don't care. All that matters is that you are here now, breathing."

Sonart managed a half-smile. "Thank you, Uncle." He tore off a chunk of bread and sank it into the stew. "I mean it."

"Stars, no," Auckland replied. "Thank—you, on two counts: proving two old fools wrong and lessening the weight and madness gripping the Cradle."

Sonart raised an eyebrow at that.

Auckland took a step towards the door. "We'll talk more, later. I must away to the mines. Damned if I miss the wagon. Doubly so if they let me come away early, these drears—as I said, madness."

The elder dwarven gripped Sonart's shoulder. "Be well, and stars burn you if you move from this bed before I return from work."

"You forget the mettle of the woman you took for wife," Mila protested.

Auckland threw back his head and laughed. "That I did—and she's worth every punch she's laid on me since. Sooth you speak on that score, Blossom." He gave Sonart his attention again. "Till I return then, my boy."

Sonart gave Auckland a curt nod.

When his uncle left, he turned to Mila. "What madness?"

Mila hesitated. "Me stars eclipse in the Cradle's affairs—that hasn't changed, not since those bastards took ya. And I'm sure as my stew that Auckie 'll want-tell any of that himself first. Y' know my mate. He'll regale everythin' ya need to know."

Sonart put down his bowl and let out a long breath. "Dearest Auntie, 'a need to know' implies sieves. Precisely why I press you now. Tell me only what you're comfortable with. Give me a better idea of the right questions to ask my uncle."

Mila wavered, her eyebrows knitting a few anxious moments before she met his gaze. "The Kworn still invade the villages, abductin' our men and boys. And them traitorous dwarven fanatics roam everywhere, proclaimin' this one and that one an enemy of Kusp and Cradle. Too many of late face the Hooks before the deepest sleep takes 'em. Then there's them Afflicted Ones."

Sonart frowned. "Afflicted?"

Mila pursed her lips and nodded. "Sorry sods, the lot: the spread of their pestilence grows rampant. Sonart, if ya must know, things be worse than ever before."

Sonart bobbed his head but remained quiet. Mila had painted a dismal picture, but he'd expected as much. She went on to answer many of his other questions. Except one. She evaded that like a traverse of the Lobe.

"Leave matters be, fer now," Mila finished. "Gettin' better should be yer first concern."

"Stars align, I promise," Sonart lied as he lowered his face and reached for his spoon. His unsated inquiry disturbed him, but as he sank the ladle into the broth, he resigned to let it rest.

He *would* resolve the dark riddles of his plight, as soon as he was able—from others, should his hosts opt to keep the truth from him.

13: Sending
Brooke

Eight days later, Brooke found himself having to let go of what mattered most to him. He wouldn't have done it at all had the elderly couple not engendered so much trust.

From the moment they greeted his party by the edge of the Northern Forest, Brooke found them kindly, wise, and endearing, especially towards Ferin and Hue. During the two-day journey they shared, the old man had the boys sit with him in the driver's box of his horse-drawn carriage.

As they rode east along the forest road, he kept them entertained with endless tales and sleight-of-hand tricks, which left them gasping in delight.

The old man's wife wore a bonnet and had the warmest eyes and manner. They drew one in like the smell of baked bread.

She quickly bonded with Dayanthi, taking Brooke's spouse under her wing as her own daughter. That the senior husband and wife happened to be Cras and Scrit's grandparents quelled the commander's last doubt.

The plan had been prearranged by the Nightwolves' chief. Aboard the couple's wagon, Brooke's family would be taken deep into the forest to a temporary hermitage, near thirty leagues further east. From there, they would go to ground in earnest, absconding to a secret haven to which only the grandparents had been made privy.

Not only would it remove his family from the looming paths of war, but also the more immediate threat. Brooke's enemies could no longer use them as gamepieces to be played against him.

In the interest of his family's continued safety, Targin bade the couple not to divulge any further details, save it being a wilderen-protected refuge.

"Targin's secret bears an Orbical's mark," Cras had said.

"Aye," Scrit agreed. "That being the case, Commander, we can vouch that your family will remain safe and clandestine."

Brooke had to trust his two companions. Forsooth, he hadn't stopped trusting them since they kept true to their word, safely reuniting him with his wife and children.

The night before, at the same backwoods crossroad, while the boys shared one of two travellers' cabins with the Wrayns, and the grandparents slept in their coach, Brooke took Dayanthi into the other cottage. There, he bedded his wife and their lovemaking proved ravenous, desperate.

Beneath the joy and promise of their coupling, shame harangued Brooke, knowing he would abandon her again come morning. He still hadn't convinced himself that it was the lesser of his horrible choices.

Despite Dayanthi's constant assurances that she understood his reasons, Brooke couldn't shirk his conviction that she felt forsaken—but too caring to cause him more duress.

The poor woman: dragged around these savage lands like chattel. Caged away while he put everything they'd built at stake to join a rebel band.

With a soldier's burdened heart, Brooke embraced his family, not knowing whether he would ever see them again. Pushing aside his grim thoughts, the commander swung up into Maxan's saddle and gave his wife and children the most confident smile he could muster.

Dayanthi's glowing countenance mirrored his efforts. Their sons too sought to appear valiant as they grinned back, eyes beaming.

"Don't worry Papa," Hue said. "We'll take care of Mama."

"Me too, Papa!" blurted Ferin. "Like bwave War-ans."

"Then Mama has no finer knights to ward her!" Brooke laughed.

"I love you, Husband," Dayanthi called.

"And I, you, Wife, May Vamsah continue to watch over you until our reunion." Brooke turned his mount away so they would not chance see him grimace. His two cloaked companions saw it, offering consolatory looks, as Maxan fell into stride with their Warangs.

Together the small clave headed off the trail and into the deeper folds of the Northern Forest, piercing the green shroud of its veil. Within moments, the travellers' cabins disappeared.

Silent and sombre, Brooke followed the Nightwolves through the musky woods. The trees here looked ancient, cloaked in moss and underscored by swathes of ferns; their weighty branches drooped close to the underbrush, like his heartstrings.

Cras and his brother began a quiet conversation but directed it at Brooke. "Targin may be his own greatest hero," Cras japed, "but when the game is afoot…"

"You want the Chief on your team rather than against it," Scrit finished.

Grateful for the distraction, Brooke's mood lightened as he listened to their myriad tales, most of which concerned their leader's trials and travails. Brooke's ordeals soon paled as the men carried on over the Warangs' rumbling breath and the odd snort and nicker from Maxan.

"When they come of age, your boys would make fine pups for our band," said Cras. "Most children run terrified from our mounts at first sight. But your lads displayed rare courage. I dare say a fascination."

"They've never seen such creatures," Brooke chuckled. "Neither have I until recently." His smile faded. "How much longer, Cras?"

"Vamsah willing, tonight we'll sleep among our brethren—in Targin's camp."

Brooke's innards twitched at the prospect of coming face-to-face with the warlord. How could a man be so revered by his followers and yet so scorned by civilized folk? He pondered this and a host of other questions as the shadows lengthened and the small company rode on.

By late afternoon, they began a slow descent into a deep ravine. The sun filtered through the giant overgrowth with limited penetration, and soon the day wore down to a pale dusk.

Almost immediately, dampness enveloped Brooke, clinging to his skin and raiment like the dewy webs of a spider. The sounds of forest animals and birds diminished as the murk darkened. The air grew thick and still as the party rode further down into the widening fissure.

Strung along by his inner thoughts, Brooke didn't notice Maxan's distress, until the horse's quivering penetrated his leather saddle.

As his rump trembled, the commander glanced at the Warangs. Ears folded back, their heads darted in tandem to the left, paused, sniffed, then whipped to the right. They moved carefully, their footfalls measured as if stalking a creature, or trying to evade one.

"I think—" Brooke's observation died in his throat when Cras lifted a finger to his lips, gesturing him to silence.

By a small creek at the base of the valley, the canopy opened some, but despite the gap, the space seemed to close in. Scrit stopped the company and both Wrayns dismounted.

The stream gurgled softly as it trickled past, but in the hushed quiet, it sounded like a torrent. The advancing gloom rendered the water's colour a red froth, like blood.

Despite Maxan's constitution, forged through fierce battle, Brooke's mount let out short jumpy huffs. He stamped a forehoof.

"From the west," Cras said calmly. "It approaches."

Both Warangs raised their heads and growled in that direction.

Brooke stared at the Nightwolf. "What approaches?"

"A demon of Infern," Scrit announced as though telling a tavern owner his choice of fare. He raised his chin, parted his lips, and extended his tongue like a clairvoyant tasting the air for some sign of rain. When it retracted, Scrit faced Brooke again. "The sprites call it a Sorgon in their language—*Sending*, in the common tongue."

Brooke furrowed his brows. A blackfly bit him and he slapped it away. "How can you be certain?"

"Communion. Through Areth's Gaia, the creatures of the forest speak to the Warangs. They have seen the demon pass. They relayed their message until our canines received it. The wolves in turn communed with us."

Cras inclined his head. "My brother gleans the truth of it. The demon comes to eliminate us, but in all likelihood, you're its true target."

Brooke's chest tightened. "How big are we talking?"

"Big enough to make the ground tremble in its wake," Cras answered.

Brooke felt the blood drain from his face as he adjusted his clammy grip on Maxan's reins. And swatted another fly.

Do they jest to make mock? But no humour in their faces did Brooke detect. He swallowed. "How much time do we have?"

"Half a turn—at most," a solemn Scrit replied.

"Only thirty minutes?" Brooke stood in his stirrups and looked around, taking in the vale's full lay before shifting his focus back to the Wrayns. "Shouldn't we flee at once?"

His companions shook their heads.

Brooke tautened his jaw and reseated himself in Maxan's saddle. "This demon stalks us—stalks me. If not flee, what do we do?"

Scrit shrugged. "No point trying to avoid it. The Sorgon will not stop until it kills you, or we kill it. Upon its singular purpose, the demon is bent, so, the only thing we can do—is wait."

"Wait?" Dread and disbelief coiled and stretched Brooke's nerves like a rope in a tug of war. "How can we? Why—how is this happening?"

"Your friend, Necatar, no doubt," Cras said. "He's the necromage that conjured it—through blood magic. Wouldn't be the first time. Someone familiar to you has been sacrificed recently. That's how a Sorgon functions, the forfeit soul will ferret you out."

Brooke's mouth fell open. "Necatar's capable of *that*?"

"And more," Scrit said. "Much more. You too sensed something out of place in his presence, Commander—correct?"

"Aye, but…" Brooke paused as something dawned on him. "I thought you said he wanted me ruined, not dead."

Scrit lifted his shoulders again. "Like as not, our intervention forced his hand to more desperate measures. Wouldn't be the first time for that either."

"I always suspected that centipede delved in dark disciplines." Brooke shifted his weight in the saddle. "But no one could ever verify it."

"Aye, Necatar's grown powerful," Scrit agreed. "He's infiltrated other kingdoms, leading them to similar ruin. The necromage kneels before the Lightbringer's antithesis."

"The Darkest One—Deathwrought?"

Scrit dipped his chin.

Suddenly angry at his companions, Brooke snapped. "If you knew this, stars burn you, why haven't you sent assassins to dispatch him, instead of razing entire kingdoms, inciting so many wars of attrition?"

"Lost close to a hundred Wrayns and half as many Warangs, trying to do just that," Scrit said without emotion. "Fucker's too damn protected, by more than guards. Black wards, enchantments, and demon ilk—like the one he sends our way."

"Our efforts to circumvent his geas or quell his poison directly have only met with disaster," Cras piped in. "So, we focus our attacks on what we can do. Disable his machinations of war: a realm's supply chains, weapon stores, possessed rulers."

Brooke expunged stifled air. "Cele's always been a fool, but a ruthless tyrant turned passive?" He looked off into the middle distance. "Doesn't take an Orbical to see that Necatar sank his hooks in the king's mind."

"That hold is the demonica," Scrit said, "the same fate he designed for you. It's irreversible."

"Cele's days are numbered," Cras added. "Eventually, it will kill him. In your case though, the necromage wanted you publicly ruined before you took the deepest sleep."

"Why?" Brooke demanded.

Cras raised a hand. "Something better explained by our Chief."

Brooke's tone sharpened. "Necatar's a villain." He squeezed Maxan's saddlehorn. "We must stop that parasite."

"We will do as we must," Scrit said evenly. "Targin knows exactly what's at stake, what must be done. Take heart, Commander, all will be answered and set aright in time."

"Perhaps, you're right," Brooke resigned, running a hand through his hair. "Madness plays out whenever the King's council meets in session. But of late more than ever, Cele seems determined to declare against all freeborn." With a weary sigh, he dismounted his destrier. "For now, we have a more pressing threat to quell."

Brooke led Maxan across the stream to the scrim of trees sidling the opposite slope of the ravine. He gave the warhorse a firm slap on his hindquarters, sending him bolting up the grade.

Maxan would linger in the immediate area, awaiting Brooke's whistle to return. But the commander wouldn't blame the destrier if he kept going. Stars, would that he could do the same.

When Brooke returned, his companions explained their Nightwolf strategy. Legs braced, the three men formed a triangle with their backs. The Warangs took higher positions atop flanking ledges. There, the canines crouched and hid in a thicker copse to either side of the rift.

Their vigil began.

Brooke didn't have to wait long before the air shivered.

Gplah-screeeeeesh! *Gplah-screeeeeesh!* Echoing ululations filled the ravine.

Mind rattled and stung into sharpness, Brooke bit his lip and tightened his grip on his sword hilt.

The forest floor quaked in heftier, more strident measures.

Tree limbs snapped in the distance, then not as far.

Closer.

Louder.

Brooke caught sight of the Sorgon's serpent body as it stabbed violently through the trees, sl— th— er—ing erratically towards them. His breath left him.

It was huge. Endless.

The ground bucked as its reptilian head, six feet wide, barged into the clearing.

More branches snapped over Brooke's shoulder. He twisted, just in time to see the abomination's tail rush towards him.

Up shot his blade. "Behind us!"

The Sorgon had trapped them like a tightening noose.

Brooke glanced at his companions. Swords raised high, they fanned out, enlarging their triangle.

Purpose burned in the yellow cluster of eyes inundating the demon's head *and* tail. Both sets flitted independently of one another, tracking each of the three defenders.

The Sorgon's onyx head reared up.

Its mouth gaped, revealing a circular array of scimitar fangs pointed inward around a parasol of black flesh. Putrid mustard-coloured ooze squeezed between its pointed teeth as they flexed outward.

The demon lunged at Cras. And scalloped earth as the Wrayn danced away. It stabbed long towards Scrit. Found air as the Nightwolf feinted.

Scrit answered with a lightning thrust and slash.

Ironock carved flesh.

And the blood dance began.

The Sorgon recoiled.

Loomed again

Time stopped.

Twilight shimmered as the Warangs launched themselves from the treetops. Claws extended, canine jaws wide, they seized the giant snake like living grapnels, shredding their way down the demon's flanks before it could meet them.

Scrit and Cras sprang. They buried their swords in the Sorgon's underbelly and sliced. The demon backed away, freeing their blades.

Brooke wheeled and rushed the creature's tail segment. Sword ablur, he swiped and thrust, gorging the bulbous tip and bursting several eyes in the process.

Gplah-SCREEEEEESH! The demon's squeal rent Brooke's ears as its squelching tail hastened back into the thicket.

Brooke spun and raced to join the others.

The demon's jaws gnashed, yawning wide like a flower with thorns embedded in its ebony petals.

Blades, fangs, and claws ripped into the Sorgon. The multisided attacks confused it and kept its formidable maw at bay.

But then to Brooke's horror, every fresh wound his party tore open, closed again. The ooze the demon bled sutured and sealed every gash and perforation. Stars blacken, such a defence made it implacable.

The five fighters renewed their frenzy, but with every passing moment, their fatigue weighed more heavily. Brooke's sword arm strained, muscles burning. Sweat stung his eyes and his strikes grew sluggish.

Too wearied to fight, he was forced to go on the defensive. Tricked into exhaustion, they would all die.

The tail lanced forward again.

Blade tip up, Brooke darted aside.

As he parried, he noticed one small boon. Unlike the creature's flesh, its eyes did not heal. They sat there like punctured egg yolks, dripping glowing yellow fluid.

Brooke focused his attack on those, managing to take out three more. And another two. Before the tail scurried back again and disappeared into the underbrush.

But even as Brooke swivelled, the tail sprang from a different gap. It landed a blow to Drasil. Scrit's wolf yelped as the impact sent him sprawling into a tangle of gnarled roots lining the creek. The giant canine did not rise again.

Gplah-screeeeeesh! *Gplah-screeeeeesh*!

"Aim for its eyes!" Brooke cried as he swung, voice lifting over the demon's high-pitched mewling. "Don't fight—together—so fierce—sap us quicker!"

"Too evenly matched," Cras yelled back, sword arm whirling in a slashing frenzy. "Can't retreat." *Swing—stab—cut*! "We *must* stand."

They all seemed to know. And apparently, the Sorgon did too, that the brutal melee had come to a standstill, evenly balanced but futile. Only a matter of time—its pendulum nudging closer to the demon's victory.

Yggn let out a fierce howl and threw himself at the Sorgon, powerful jaws clamping down on the demon's throat. Thrashing his head violently, the grey-brown Warang tore chunks from the demon like a living meat grinder. A momentary elation buoyed Brooke when Drasil reappeared to add his jaws to the assault.

But the battle grew desperate as the four Nightwolves kept the creature's precarious chops occupied.

Muscles leaden, Brooke hacked and dodged, while their foe did the same—to the commander's resolve.

Brooke's hope crumbled under the demon's tenacious barrage.

The Sorgon ignored the Warangs even as they gouged crisscrossing fissures in its flesh.

The demon broke off its exchange with Scrit and Cras and surged towards Brooke. He raised his sword in time as the maw snapped shut.

Crack!

Brooke's blade wedged between two of the Sorgon's fangs.

The demon tossed its head back, tearing the weapon from his grasp.

Brooke's shoulder popped. Wincing, he backstepped in an off-balance scramble.

The Wrayns darted to his defence.

Like a sprung trebuchet, the creature's tail swept low and batted their legs from under them, hurling both men into the creek. Their bodies skipped the surface like swiftly cast stones.

Even as they ploughed onto the stream's far bank, the Sorgon twisted back and renewed its pursuit of Brooke. Head and tail now ensnared the commander like pincers.

He dove to the ground, tucked, and rolled atop an errant tree limb.

It moved with him—felled earlier by the Sorgon's rampage.

Brooke twisted, found purchase, and hefted the branch just as the monster pounced.

Part of the limb shattered in a splintering wrench between the demon's upper row of fangs. The rest of the limb buried itself hilt-deep in its mouth, absorbing the full impact.

But the sheer weight of the attack pounded Brooke into the sodden earth, pinning him. Pain needled every nerve, but it assured that he yet lived.

Again, the Sorgon reared. Freed itself of the impaling branch with a shake of its head.

In a shower of wood splinters, the limb pitchpoled out of sight.

Brooke cringed as the demon readied its killing stroke.

Something twitched against the darkening sky. High above the Sorgon's crown, a shadowy form detached itself from the canopy: a humanoid juggernaut armoured in a tangle of muscle.

Blurred by the speed of his attack, he flew at the Sorgon. Straddled its backside and braced knees to its flanks like a tourney rider atop a bucking horse.

Prostrate and half-buried, Brooke could only stare up as the giant newcomer produced a broadsword—the largest the commander had ever seen.

The blade flashed once.

Twice.

Thrice!

A primal squeal escaped the Sorgon's maw. It rang off the trees, stuffing the natural enclosure with anguish that bespoke a fatal wound.

Brooke scrambled away and climbed to his feet as the giant rode the demon's head to the ground.

The Sorgon writhed for several pounding seconds before slumping to its side with an imperious shudder. The tail careered side to side twenty feet behind Brooke. It thumped uselessly, breaking off arbitrary tree branches close enough to its tip. At both ends, the buttery glow from the Sorgon's surviving eyes dimmed.

Heart ready to burst, Brooke peered closer. Just before the demon's lantern orbs darkened completely, something appeared in them that froze his spine and made his soul jitter to its core.

For a fleeting moment, within the cluster of dying lights, the spectral face of his wife's brother, Solan Racine appeared.

Lips atremble, Brooke moved to join his giant saviour as he dismounted the Sorgon further back.

The barbarian stood with legs braced, the rising moon behind silhouetting his face. But his stance and carriage exuded an air of calm, poised like a finely wrought sculpture of a titan.

A mountain of corded muscle and sinew, cut by rivers of sweat, the man towered over Brooke by more than a head. An even seven feet, he stood barefoot and naked, except for a pair of calf-length britches cinched with a leather sword belt that allowed for his enormous scabbard.

A splashing commotion lifted Brooke from his trance. He swivelled as Cras and Scrit forded the thigh-deep stream towards him, their faces cut and bruised.

Another disturbance from behind made him spin back. Both Warangs padded up, similarly wounded. The midnight wolf's eyes had been swollen shut and he dripped blood from his ear. The other had a painful-looking abrasion where his fur had been stripped from his flank.

Brooke had forgotten his own hurts until then. Though none of them won free unscathed, Vamsah be praised, they had all survived. Relief flooded through him, easing some of the strain and hurt in his muscles and jarred corners. The coppery taste of blood found his tongue.

When the giant angled his chin towards the approaching Wrayns, his face caught the moonlight. A crop of curly dark hair dropped past his ears but fell short of his brawny shoulders. It framed a square jaw, deep-set green-grey eyes and chiselled cheekbones. A titan's face as well.

"Anything broken?" Scrit called to Brooke as the pair clambered up the riverbank.

"I don't think so but stars, the pain is livid," Brooke confessed as the Wrayn drew up, Cras limping close behind.

"Better livid and living than lucid in the deepest lay," the mysterious hulk pointed out, his tenor stern but jocular. "These two Warangs would bark as much."

Yggn and Drasil lifted their snouts. And barked.

Brooke surrendered a wan nod. "I thought it would finish us."

"By Vamsah's holy scrotum, I'm glad to prove you wrong!"

The giant stooped and threaded his magnificent blade through a tuft of grass, removing the worst of the demon's viscera. "Sorgons can be tricky bastards to dispatch—if you don't know how to deal with them."

He cantered down to the creek and let the flow rinse away the rest of the weapon's bloodstain. "Fortunately for you, I do. This makes my third after the pair sent my way, not two moon-cycles past."

"Pair?" Brooke harrumphed, unable to mask his shock. "How did you kill them? We barely hampered the one."

"The trick, Commander Brooke, is to ignore the parts of the Sorgon that stem from the original demon. You must attack its host and *only* its host. That said, you did hamper the beast, I see, by taking out its eyes—some of them in any case." He returned to the party, drying his broadsword across the front of his trousers as he did. "But even if you blinded the fucker, it'd still be able to sniff you out—by your soul."

Brooke coughed past the lump in his throat. When the Warangs whimpered in their canine speech, Scrit and Cras moved to address their wolves' injuries.

The giant exhaled a destrier's winded breath. "When that vassal is slain, the demon cannot maintain its toehold in this plane. Alas, in this one's case, twas your peer and kinsman, Commander Racine, a good man in his own right. He tipped me off on numerous occasions, including the plot against you. I too saw his face—aye."

"You—killed him then—Racine?" Brooke asked, though he already knew the answer. Dayanthi's brother—was dead, because of him. And now he had no way of telling his wife the tragic news. His eyes suddenly felt like lead balls.

The giant sheathed his blade and faced him. "Had to be done, sadly. But in so doing, I freed his soul. Racine will find peace with Vamsah now, rather than torment in the hellish bowels of Infern—whence its summoner recruited this monster. If it's any consolation, the demon will never return to its ilk. I destroyed it utterly—which is more than the fucker deserved."

The giant gave the dead Sorgon a swift kick, cracking the demon's bones like brittle sticks. "*Worm*, you almost disrupted my designs on Commander Brooke!" His yelling drew snickers from the two brothers. "I still have need of him before he takes the deepest sleep."

The gregarious barbarian threw his head back and let out a raucous laugh that made Brooke flinch. The Wrayns shook their heads slowly as they chuckled. And the Warangs yammered.

As the ogre-sized man let out an ogre-calibre bellow, Brooke swore he could hear the man's heartbeat through his chest like a distant war tocsin.

"Hear the song in my heart, do you?" he observed. "Come, Brooke, listen closer. You needn't fear me, or my stinger. The giant unsheathed his broadsword again, pointed its tip to the ground, and leaned the hilt towards the commander. "Fang is its name—a relic of the Dragon Wars, the last of its kind on the Main, if not the Whole of Areth."

Brooke approached the man, grimacing from his dislocated shoulder and lingering aches, courtesy of the Sorgon's final blow.

A grin stretched across the giant's face as Brooke's fingers purchased the pommel and touched the flat. The metal felt cold against his skin.

With lightning speed, the giant cast his blade aside, grasped the spent commander about the waist, and hoisted him into the air like a mother with her infant child. He then lowered him until their eyes met level. Brooke's boots remained suspended above the ground.

Does the big bastard mean to kill me?

"You've triggered too many hassles to eliminate you without just cause," the giant laughed.

Brooke's eyebrows sprang high. "You—can read my thoughts?"

"Aye." his saviour-turned-captor winked. "Allegiance with my little sprite friends has its share of benisons. Such as hearing the forest creatures warning of your plight—which hastened me to your aid. And my charmed blade—a handy weapon to expedite a horror's departure."

The muscled mountain gave the demon's flank another kick, before cocking his head towards his discarded broadsword. "Alas, a blade that large also has its curse. I am the only one strong enough to wield such a weapon, so horrors have become a regular part of my job. Even if I am branded an outlaw by those I protect. What was it Cele called me? Nefarious butcher?"

"Your—job?" Brooke narrowed his eyes. Then he gasp-croaked as realization dawned. "You are—him!"

"Aye, *Targin* is my name. Say it. You'll feel—better," he joked.

"Targin," Brooke managed, surprised at his own calm. "I'll feel better—once you put me down. These heights make me dizzy."

That sent Targin into another fit of mirth. But he did set Brooke on his feet again and stepped back. The commander had never been so relieved to feel solid earth beneath his soles. Thank the stars, none of his Pathguard peers or subordinates witnessed the lift—he'd have been ruined for sure.

"None of my initiates would speak to me as boldly as you have," Targin reflected. "You have the heart of a Nightwolf, Commander. The sprites made the right choice with you."

"They, *chose* me?" A wave of trepidation stole over Brooke. "For what?"

"You enter a larger world, my good man—to help save it. I don't expect you to grasp my import this very second. But rest assured, you'll come to know all of it in good time."

With a heavy sigh, Targin exchanged a look with Scrit and Cras, then shifted his attention to the sky. "Your horse is near. Call to him so we may be free of this cursed snare and rejoin the pack. Shan't take long. They've drawn close to intercept us and make camp as we speak."

Targin's eyes turned south. "No more than an hour's ride will see us surrounded by friends and well-rested, belly and mind full to your satisfaction. And mine."

14: Words unto Deeds
Sonart

When darkness fell later that dimming, Auckland returned, shoulders hunched and covered head to toe in rock powder and soot from the mines.

Mila shifted her gaze from her spouse to Sonart. "Well, now that husband's home, my turn to get off me arse. Must be off m'self—too many errands, too little time."

The old woman stood. "Make sure Auckie sees to yer needs n' takes good care of ya. Else I'll string him up by his beard and whoop him." She ran a hand down Sonart's cheek and offered him a smile before making her exit.

When the door closed behind her, Sonart faced Auckland. Beneath the caked layer of dust, the elder dwarven's countenance shone, eyes bright as they studied Sonart.

"Stars, Uncle, what is it? You seem at one with the Kusp."

"Maybe I am," Auckland admitted as he removed his cloak and hung it on a peg. "Having you back and on the mend inspires the routine. My weight lessens."

If you only knew. Part of Sonart wanted to illustrate the irony of Auckland's words but decided it best that his uncle not know the full depth of his situation. He needed information, free of screens and bias.

Sonart tilted his head to one side. "Auckland, you are no more the fool than I to believe that my jailers set me free, delivered to your very doorstep out of the kindness in their hearts."

The elder dwarven let slip a half-grin. "Aye—they're watching you. I also know the risk I take by keeping you under my roof."

Sonart drew his chin back. "And yet you still choose to involve yourself?"

Auckland's smile didn't waver. "You are my brother's son. We share the blood of our line. And in the game of prophecy, to feign ignorance of its rules and roles does not make them go away. I'll not bury my face in the sands of the Lobe."

Auckland pulled up a chair and sat down. "We would be foolish—aye, but no more than those who think they have fooled us. And yes, I speak of the Darkest One. The usurper's no dullard: your freedom bespeaks a special dispensation. Perhaps immunity from the Proclaimers. We must play our part as is our part, and for me, that means seeing to your recovery and setting you upon your path —dare I say, with Deathwrought's blessing?"

Sonart swallowed around a smirk he could not prevent. His uncle had said it plainly, giving him room to vent what he chose to reveal and not a word more. As the elder brother of Farkshone, Sonart's father, Auckland proved equally perceptive.

Sonart picked his words carefully. "Tell me news of the dwarven's plight in my absence. Mila waffled vaguely, but I must know its full effigy."

Auckland shook his head. "Stars eclipse, there's nothing I'd trouble you with now, as you lay—"

"—abed?" Sonart cut him off and threw back his sheets.

Before Auckland could protest, Sonart swung his legs off the mattress and stood, clad only in his small clothes. "The Dunge has honed one improvement in me: an uncanny ability to *not* die. I heal much quicker than before they buried me down there."

When Sonart brought his face within inches of Auckland's, his uncle raised his hands and made a placating gesture. "I assured you, lad, we'd have words. But I cannot deny the eerie root that grows within you."

Sonart wrinkled his nose. "What do you mean, pray?"

"In good time… but if you must know the broad strokes, greater weight and more sacrifice plague us. A phantom of doom spreads across the Cradle like never before."

Auckland lifted a finger. "Though, it does not hold sway—not yet. I've no doubt you can manage yourself. But it is our people you must need consider. Remember what your father told you. Their survival of late has been tested to the brink. It depends upon your survival. A tempest brews. This storm of storms will break soon—already it simmers with latent power—feel it in my bones, I do, worsening."

"No doubt," Sonart muttered. "I sense your *meaning* will be neither succinct nor unfiltered."

"Then our stars do align, though not for the best reasons," the elder dwarven confessed. "I'll not lie. You form part of the malignancy—though not its full sum."

Sonart tightened. "Then perhaps the time has come to cleanse the tumour, sue for a way *from* the Kusp."

Auckland's eyebrows sprang high. "Do not blaspheme, Nephew. I'm no Proclaimer but speak such of the Holy Testament and you only invite more trouble—if they should hear." He looked over his shoulder at the entrance.

"Let the traitors hear," Sonart scoffed towards his uncle's back. Past fear, he would not hide his bitterness, especially now that his role had vaulted him above their authority.

"The jackanapeses are what they are," Auckland said as he observed Sonart again. The crinkles of his crow's feet converged. "But the wise dwarven is the quiet dwarven. A smuggler does not advertise. Let those sleeping hounds lie."

His gaze dropped to Sonart's waist. "As to your cleansing, in that, you'll have ten blessings, as soon as you cleanse your person. Stars, you stink of a Kworn's dung heap—one left to ferment," he added with a chuckle.

"Feel like one too," a smirking Sonart agreed.

He followed Auckland into the bathing chamber.

Sunken in the plain room's stone floor, a natural pool of steaming water awaited, heated from the fire earth far below and fed from a bubbling spring close to Farkshone Village.

Stacks of wooden shelves laden with towels framed one wall and a long bench lay close to the bath. On the wooden plank sat a metal tray with a thick bar of freckled beige soap and a neat pile of clothes. It included a pair of roughspun dark britches, grey tunic, woollen hood, light-brown shirt, belt, hose, and a set of black leather boots.

"They'll be a bit big at the waist and snug at the shoulder," Auckland said. "But I think the jerkin and trousers will fit. If not, Mila can rip and rethread them. Oh, and they smell a ghost of the mines, but that won't do you any harm either, unlike the rags you turned up in—Mila burned those."

Sonart arched an eyebrow. "That bad, hmm?"

Auckland nodded. "She didn't dare risk a more thorough scrub of your hide, lest she hindered your recovery. Stars, you looked that frail, but now..." the elder dwarven paused and checked himself. "Well, I'll leave you to it. Holler if you need anything."

Sonart inclined his beard. "I will. Cheers."

When Auckland departed, Sonart removed his token bit of clothing and slowly entered the pool, easing his carriage into the water.

Despite the heat of the liquid, he shivered.

Water—something troubled him about its very notion, inextricably linked to the truth hidden beneath all the vexing layers of his dilemma.

A thought occurred to him. Could it be, as Rusic once promised, that the answer might be actively seeking him? For whether Sonart wished it or not, events seemed to hasten. And if water held the answer, well, it just found him.

Sonart let the liquid's heat penetrate his bones and loosen the knots in his muscles, sinew, and mind—to a joyous degree he'd all but forgotten.

What would he do now that he'd been freed? He'd spend his drears well, though forever shadowed by guilt and a spectre of doubt, knowing the Darkest One had emblazoned such a horrific imperative upon him. What could one dwarven do to oppose such mastery, such omnipotence?

Not for the first time, Sonart closed his eyes and prayed to his dead sire. *Wretched and damned, afraid of what I'll do, or not do—with what I know. You sent me this curse, Father. Send me the cure to lift it—I beg.* What twist of fate could have set him on this obscure road, reducing him to a pariah among his people? To what end?

His father knew what end. And took that unsolved puzzle with him to the grave.

Once more, against the proclamations of the Kusp, Sonart considered destroying himself. That'd leave the Darkest One without His coveted vassal. Sonart should already be dead already like Malrik and Rusic. Like his father. He might've wept then as sorrow and futility entangled. Could he kill himself? But in so doing would he not also forsake his brethren to their doom?

Footsteps in the other room decided Sonart. He drowned the thought as he temporarily drowned his head, letting it sink beneath the surface of the soupy pool. Eyes open, he watched the slow procession of bubbles escape his chafed lips. They rose, gurgling to the surface, where they broke in a series of pops.

Sonart believed Auckland's warning, but beyond his uncle's words, an inner voice assured that his people's only chance hinged on his continued existence.

Sonart's head breached the surface and he drew a deep breath. As the hot liquid cascaded down his red hair and beard, he rubbed his eyes, peered down.

And flinched.

The water had turned inky black, not the deep grey from coal residue, which left the body after a drear's mining, but opaque as ironock. The lower half of his carriage disappeared beneath the waterline. *What new devilry is this?*

An image of a cottage manifested in the ebony liquid. It looked familiar, set back from a cluster of village dwellings in an abandoned cul de sac. The stone cabin lay in seclusion, unlit and deserted. Sonart squinted at the vision, shimmering on the water's surface. He could make out a sword floating in the home's only window.

Sonart recognized the small house—his childhood home. And the weapon—the blade that ushered him into the Cleft Augury. He entered the frame, stood outside the dwelling, beyond the window's glass pane and extended his hand towards the sword. It drew closer—

A white aura danced in the dwarven's periphery. He whipped his head around, beard flinging a cascade of droplets across the floor. Only to find an empty room.

When he peered back down, the image had vanished, the opaqueness gone, just a normal grey film in its place. Sonart shook the bizarre vision from his mind as he reached for the bar of soap.

When he'd finished bathing, he left the pool, dressed, and exited the chamber.

15: Stew
Sonart

"Hogsweed Stew," Auckland announced. "Mila makes the best damn batch of it this side of the Cradle."

"And that ain't no lie neither," Mila agreed, grinning with her wizened eyes.

Sonart and Auckland ladled the stew into their bowls and then waited for Mila to do the same. Clasping hands around the table, the three sat facing the centre where an oil lantern burned, its light casting their faces in a warm glow.

"The Cradle that guards also gives," Auckland incanted, his voice low and solemn. "Little is better than none. Thus says the Kusp. It is the Way."

In unison, the other two responded, "It is the Way."

After a spoonful, Sonart turned to Auckland. "This *is* the best hogsweed. Contents the palate and strengthens the body." He grabbed a piece of bread and ripped into it with his teeth. Crumbs sprinkled his beard and the table. "So much so, should think I'll be ready to walk among my brethren on the morrow."

An awkward moment passed over the lantern's flicker. At length, Auckland sighed. "If that is your wish. Mila and I do not suffer any great hardship, thank the stars, but much has changed since they abducted you. Two full star-cycles have elapsed—they did not pass lightly. Darker times followed."

"Darker?" Sonart snorted. "How is that even possible?"

"The drear they rounded you up marked the beginning," his uncle said. "Every village was sacked, some homes razed to the ground. Many dwarven never left their domiciles, believing the psalms of the Kusp would shelter and protect them."

Sonart stopped chewing. "And?"

"They were vanquished." Auckland blew out his cheeks. "Thought the scar would heal in time, but then our foodstuffs spoiled. Already stricken by the attacks, countless younglings perished. Kworn forced us to surrender our livestock—believed to be the source of the malady. They slaughtered and burned every animal. Not only Farkshone Village, mind you, but all dwarven settlements the Cradle over."

With a splash and clang, Sonart let his spoon drop into his bowl.

"Aye, lad," Mila confirmed, lips pressing into a tight line. "Haven't had no meat in our bellies goin' on eighteen moon-cycles, give or take."

"Farkshone Village fared better than most," Auckland supplied before lowering his voice. "But then the radicals rose in prominence."

"Proclaimers," Sonart cursed. "Turncapes."

"As if the situation wasn't bad enough." Auckland balled a fist, his jaw turning to stone. "The traitorous lot call themselves 'Proclaimers of the Kusp,' but they're nothing more than lickspittles and madmen—mad fucking people for mad fucking times."

The elder unfurled his fist and dropped his hand again. "Under a veil of religious fanaticism, the reprobates sow distrust and fear everywhere they go. All they really are—" his voice faltered.

"Spies, in service to the Darkest One," Sonart spat. "The bastards betrayed their own kind to Deathwrought."

Mila placed her hands on the table and leaned forward. "Lad, tis an ill omen, mentionin' His name in our home. You too, Auckie. Still yer waggin' tongue on that point."

Auckland's eyes lost their fire. He placed a calloused hand on his wife's shoulder and gently kneaded it. "Forgive me, Dearest. I will."

He shifted his regard back to Sonart. "It is unsafe to speak outside this house. The Proclaimers' webs are sometimes impossible to see until they ensnare you."

"Caught I have been," Sonart said. "But not by any Proclaimer or Kworn."

Auckland frowned. "Then whom?"

Sonart hesitated, glancing at Mila before locking gazes with his uncle. "Zürshuck. There's been a resurgence."

Mila flinched. "Winged Ones—again?"

Sonart dipped his chin. "Lest my mind deceived me, they've grown legion—tens of thousands."

Auckland peered into the middle distance. "Twas long before my time, but the Elders claim that the Zürshuck numbered a mere handful when they first cast their shadows upon the Cradle—before the sky's perpetual grey."

Sonart nodded. He too recalled the Elders' tales of how the Winged Ones flew across the Void of Obliteration to heed the summons of the Darkest One. The demons quickly established their place in the Cradle's hierarchy.

"We are where we are because of them," Auckland said. "The Zürshuck pressed us and the Kworn into subservience."

Sonart bowed. Everyone knew how lethal a Zürshuck's razor-edged wings could be. "Dwarven ancestors fought a bloody campaign, to no avail. When it was over, the Cradle's gullies ran red with Kworn and dwarven blood."

"My brother taught you well," Auckland observed. "Construction of the Hive galvanized the pact between the Zürshuck and De*h*—the Darkest One. That bastion serves both."

"N' we be the sorry ones who done built it," Mila put in.

Sonart's beard bobbed lower in agreement. Prior to his arrest, he'd spent most of his existence toiling in the mines towards that goal, as did his father and grandfather before him.

"Erecting the Hive reduced us and the Kworn to a hapless lot," Auckland added. "Meanwhile, the Zürshuck proliferated. Secured their place just beneath the Colossals' yoke and that of the Siphons."

Rather hastily, Mila picked up a small tankard filled with mead and poured measures into each cup. Her jerky movements bespoke discomfort.

"The Hive mocks every dwarven who helped build it," Sonart grated.

"Not every dwarven, Sonart," Auckland corrected. "One drear, as the tower neared completion, those who left their homes to work on the monolith, never returned. Though I reckon the access tunnels endure still, the way to the core has been shut to every dwarven this side of the Innereach."

"Not every dwarven, uncle," Sonart echoed.

Mila's lips parted but she made no sound.

Auckland narrowed his eyes into slits. "You've *been* to the black tower?"

"Recently," Sonart admitted. "Seen, entered, and survived the Hive. The bastion is complete, but it bears no resemblance to any dwarven construct. Attainted, misshapen like an elongated wasp nest—one made of ironock and mortar. It bleeds fire and exhales smoke."

Mila's hand shot to her mouth. Auckland gulped but received the news with gravitas. "Corruption at work, that is, fashioned by dragonfire, or demon lore, like as not both. Guess something needed to be done to make it impervious to the firewater surrounding it."

Sonart inclined his head. "Aye, the Circled River is that terrible."

"Like the River Seething, on the far side of Bulkforge?" Mila asked.

"Hotter, more violent," Sonart answered, forced to remember the Kworn that had perished atop the bridge. He retrieved his utensil and lifted another spoonful to his lips.

"What infernal source wrought that moat remains unclear," Auckland said. "Elders bander opinions with no consensus."

Around the ladle at her mouth, Mila laughed. "Part of the problem, see, be the Elders themselves. Most be addled—*slurrrpp*—some, completely lost, accused of bein' Afflicted for their bullheadedness."

"Confusion and debate always reign whenever the dwarven hold counsel," said Auckland.

Again, Sonart released his spoon loudly into his bowl. "They still do?"

"Aye," his uncle confirmed. He took a long pull of mead. "Although, the gatherings occur too infrequently to be of any benefit." He wiped the froth that clung to his beard with his sleeve. "On occasion, the meetings turn into a cabal of discontent and suspicion. No solidarity or progress, no direction."

"Unless they be raided by Kworn," Mila said. She wielded her empty spoon like an upturned dagger and waved it in front of her. "Then those idiots pull together n' find direction—which direction to run!" She let out a sardonic chuckle Sonart found infectious.

But the woman's smile quickly faded; the wrinkles above her lips constricted. "Me mother told me sometin' once—jist fore she passed."

Sonart and Auckland adjusted their posture and gave her their eyes.

A distant look came over Mila's visage and her voice pitched low. "All the shite we suffer wouldn't last forever. Sometin's comin'—sometin' *real* big. Gonna fix everything." With her free hand, she patted her chest lightly. "If we keep it in our hearts."

Mila's gaze drifted back. "Less I miss me guess, Ma called it star-bang—bonny." Mouth working side to side, she glanced up at the ceiling. "Maybe twas bird she done said."

The old woman parked her spoon back in the bowl and flicked her mottled hand dismissively. "Ah, sometin' like that—name's not the point, Sonart. The point be the point—pay that yer mind."

Sonart sent his spoon diving into his stew while his brows arched up. *The Starbond—is a movement.* He needed to keep her talking. "Pardon, Auntie?"

Mila lifted her shoulders and tipped back her ale. Her lips shrugged. "Y'all have ter fergive me bumpkin way o' speakin'. Don't never talk good, but me heart knows m' mind well enough—both honed sharp as a blade."

She cocked her head at Auckland. "Yer uncle's the one blessed with the smarts, especially when it comes to talkin'."

Auckland gave his wife a bittersweet smile. "My love, I've never judged you by your country accent, except for it being music to my ears. You were raised on a farm and I, in the city. You may not use the same words, but I understand your beautiful mind and heart the same."

Auckland's cheekbones lifted, hoisting his beard. "And when it comes to wits and wisdom—*smarts* as you say—tis I who look to you for counsel. Stars, you should lead the damn quorum—maybe they'd accomplish something for a change."

Mila reached over and rested both palms on Auckland's forearm. "Sweet of you to say, Auckie. Sometin' else Ma said—I made the right choice marryin' you."

"Ah, so that's where your sagely wisdom comes from," Auckland chortled. Across the table, Mila blew her husband an affectionate kiss.

The sight eased the tension in Sonart's chest. Perhaps such fealty and devotion would serve the Cradle what it needed most to survive.

Auckland's attention swivelled back to him. "But it's true, what Mila says about the council. Troupes of Kworn have been sent in to disrupt any collusion. They crash down doors, overwhelm entire villages, killing indiscriminately. Gatherings must now be held in utmost secrecy, and only among a chosen few."

"Pressed flat," Mila chimed in. "Reduced to slaves. And it all comes from them cursed Winged Ones. Now you say they've come back?"

"Even the Zürshuck get their marching orders," Auckland pointed out in a calm voice. His pupils floated to Sonart. "Tell me, nephew, what know you of the Four Siphons?"

By his guarded tone and choice of words, Sonart detected more in his uncle's meaning. He drained his cup and let out a weary breath. "They attend the Darkest One and Him alone. The archdemons earned their common tongue names through their brand of malevolence."

Mila cleared her throat. "The Shrill done petrify victims with that devil-holler. Shard preys on their minds too. Scourge wields the weather. And the Shadow does all three and then some—hear tell. Parasites, the lot."

She glowered at the door. "The Scourge's last razor storm was insane. After the tempest gone done its worst, they found ground-up remains of eleven souls here abouts Farkshone."

"Eleven sandblasted in the immediate vicinity, Dearest," Auckland reminded her. "Multiply that number by the twenty-four settlements that still exist across the Steppe..."

Sonart poured himself another cup of mead. "The Shadow *is* the worst of the Four—his malice, cunning and power second only to the Darkest One."

As if on cue, an anguished cry sounded in the distance. Auckland's eyes flitted to the window. When the caterwaul ebbed, he exhaled. "They're above us right now—the Four. Atop the parapets crowning the Spikes. On their black thrones, they scorn unblinking over every compass point of the Lobe."

Mila downed her cup and looked at Sonart. "Ever watchful, with lidless orbs they pierce the clouds shroudin' the Cradle from the Inner to the fuckin' Outer." Her lungs heaved. "When drear's clear enough, ceilin' high n' good, even me tired ol' peepers kin see the closest fort. N' if that ain't enough, them dragons—four of 'em—sailin' overhead, ready to scorch our butts to ash. And have done a few, I've heard tell. As to their screechin'—hears that any turn of the dial."

"But for all our woe, the dial still turns," Auckland said.

Mila picked up the stew ladle and tapped a rhythm against the table's edge. "Sixty clicks to one sordid turn, two dozen turns to every drear, spinnin' outta control." The dipper's wooden beat stopped. 'Time's up. Chance the Void, a lot of sods do." She shook her head. "Folly."

Sonart meshed his fingers together as he pondered Mila's import. The most desperate dwarven sought the Void. They'd set out to cast themselves into obliteration beyond the Outereach. The misguided clods convinced themselves death alone could not cleanse them of suffering—that it would continue in the Great Beyond. They needed the unequivocal permanence only the Void could provide.

The Darkest One forbade it, decreeing it a violation of the Kusp's edicts. Proclaimers discovered most before they set out. The ones that did embark faced a worse fate. If the Lobe did not claim the deserters, it brought the wrath of the Colossals and Winged Ones. Either way, it ultimately incurred His wrath.

In Sonart's thirty-two star-cycles, scores of dwarven made the attempt. All failed. All paid: some eviscerated by the Winged Ones, others swallowed by the desert itself. The unluckiest were brought back.

Sonart trembled, remembering two of his closest peers. Bordu and Piskin were too young for the mines to have taken a toll upon them. The Zürshuck captured and dragged them back to face the Hooks.

Atop the town's stockade, the dwarven were strung up on hooks, barbs dug deep to catch bone and bear their weight. Drears later, when carrion birds had sated their fill, the pair were cut down and flushed into the bowels of the Dunge—to meet their end in the prison's crypt. Sonart learned of this from the Proclaimers' verdict posted on the square's belfry. The memory burned like acid on his soul.

What was the Cradle but a crucible to forge despair? Unless… "If the Council still functions," Sonart said evenly. "Then I must attend."

Auckland studied him as though weighing several replies. "It's perilous to leave the house after darkness falls, cravens who resort to violent crimes notwithstanding. Did you not hear the chilling scream just now, or earlier when you lay abed?"

Sonart bit his lip. "I recall a chorus of shrill voices when I first awoke— thought them the songs of children." *Save us Vein.*

Another tormented wail sounded, closer than the first.

And another.

Auckland shook his head slowly, his long white beard swaying in time. "Nay, Sonart, you heard the wails of the Afflicted Ones."

"Mila told me they suffer from some sort of pestilence," Sonart said.

Auckland topped up Sonart and Mila's cup. "Aye, but tis a condition aggravated by devilment of a sort."

The elder drained the last drops into his own vessel. "Harrows the mind, then advances through the body. The cries belong to the critically inflicted. We heard the first one tonight—earlier than usual. It's still unknown how it spreads, but the plague's effects seem irreversible. Fortunately, Mila and I possess enough coin to afford vials of a potion sold by racketeers—one rung above Proclaimers. Guards against the strange magics conjured by the malady."

"There were sickened dwarven before they clapped me in irons," Sonart protested. "Though few and none contagious."

"Yes, I know," Auckland said. "But as a people, we grow weaker the closer the Endstorm approaches. Sunken to dregs, the dwarven cannot survive this much longer."

Sonart steeled his jaw. "Then please, give me a measure of this potion and let me strike out to make my own choice."

Auckland raised his hands in a calming gesture. "Mila drops it into her hogsweed whenever we sup. Even though you've consumed it, I'm concerned you might still be susceptible if you go out now, due to your weakened state."

Aghast, Sonart stared back. "Stars burn me, Uncle. This isn't merely 'bad'—it's bloody chaos." He moved his head from side to side, feeling the weight double upon his heart. "Freed from the Dunge, I've only stumbled into something a far cry worse."

Auckland swallowed hard and made a brave face. "Let's not dwell on such dire tales. By the stars, lad, you arise a hero true, survived and set free from the Dunge!"

Sonart blinked. Set free, or set *loose?*

"Unprecedented," Auckland extolled. "None before you have emerged from that foul pit, and in such good stead... mayhap, others will follow."

Sonart regarded him before exhaling slowly. "Dunge or no, seems we've all suffered the same—our drears passing as a woman giving birth. Though in my case, stuck in that cell, if not for the sound of the doom-drums, I wouldn't have been able to tell drear from dimming."

Auckland's nose crinkled. "That is odd. The drums have kept silent throughout the Cradle as far as I knew, ever since..." his voice trailed off and he gulped. "Ever since the Incident."

Sonart grimaced. The watchword stung his heart, sending it veering over a scarp with an avalanche of regret and distress behind it.

But he opened his mind to the horrific memory nonetheless. Allowed it to take hold: the last ill-fated Kworn Ritual.

For that dimming marked the last time he ever saw his father.

Stephen Fenech

16: Nightwolves
Brooke

A horse, two Warangs, and a half-naked warlord raced through the underbrush, streaking past a procession of trees, gowned in sage-coloured moss. To Brooke's amazement, the Nightwolf chief ran barefoot alongside the Warangs at a pace he could not dream possible for any man to match.

Who was this rogue? Stars, *what* was he?

Shortly after the commander had beckoned Maxan with a whistle, his horse trotted in. By his nervous snorts and hesitant gait, Brooke's mount had feared to approach the Sorgon's mammoth corpse. Or maybe Targin had given the destrier pause.

The latter seemed closer to the mark when Maxan fell back and maintained a berth of twenty equestrian paces behind. Were it not for his steadfast loyalty, the horse would've surely bolted. If only Brooke could flee with him.

But as they entered the Nightwolves' encampment, that option sank into the mud behind Maxan's hooves. Anxiety burned through Brooke's heart, his stomach aflutter, as the procession slowed. He contemplated what answers awaited. His gut assured him he'd detest them all.

Some two hundred men and women and as many if not more canines gathered about a series of bonfires, set in a concentric pattern around a larger central firepit. Wolves howled and barked and yammered contentedly, answering the boisterous laughter of the black-garbed Wrayns. Their collective voices filled the forest with a carnival-like atmosphere.

Rabbits, wild boar, and fowl impaled spits suspended over a blanket of coals, glowing orange in the main hearth. The herbed smell of the roasting meats reminded the commander how ravenous his appetite. While his mouth watered from hunger, his eyes watered from woodsmoke.

The surprises continued when no one appeared to take any notice of Brooke's entrance—or that of their leader. Not until they drew up before the camp's busiest locus did a crowd gather around.

A tall Nightwolf strode forward as Brooke, Scrit, and Cras dismounted. "Targin, so good to see you safely returned to the fold."

"Aye, Alghan—warrant it is," Targin said with a wide grin. He did not even seem winded by his exertion—the better part of two leagues. "Let's share mead and meat. Slaying yet another one of that bastard's Sorgons has sent me a voracious hunger."

"If you hadn't shown up when you did," Brooke chimed in. "I would have sated *its* hunger."

Targin raised an eyebrow. "Humour too—that's good. You'll definitely fit in with this lot." The Nightwolf exhaled. "But true what you say of the nastier demon breed—though far from Infern's foulest that assist the Four."

Brooke knitted his brows. "The Four? You refer to the Four Siphons mentioned in the Kusp?"

"Mentioned, feared, despised. Yes, I refer to the Darkest One's vicars. The sprites entrusted this broadsword to me for that reason." Targin grasped the pommel of his blade but did not unsheathe it. "Would that I could sink my precious Fang into one of them." Targin shifted his regard to the fire. "For now, I must sink my teeth, into something more immediate, and if my nose discerns correctly, a lot tastier. Come, Brooke, sup with me this night."

He led Brooke to a large log strewn before the fire. The commander sat down on the vacant limb and stretched his legs.

"Heard your appraisal of my band's indifference when we first arrived," Targin said as he lowered his carriage beside him.

Blood rushed to Brooke's ears but he nodded.

"Put simply, we consider Warangs and Wrayns as equals. Though our noble wolves humble themselves to carry us, we never consider them beasts of burden. So, in address, one will not welcome the rider until after his or her feet touch the ground."

"Then, there is much I must learn," Brooke admitted.

"Indeed, my friend, and you'll learn all of it." Targin's smile straightened. Every trace of humour left his face. "My need for you, Commander, reflects the sprite's need—Areth's need—a requisite far greater than you can possibly imagine."

Scalp prickling at the sound of that, Brooke changed the subject. "Scrit explained the wolf-part of your band's name, but why this other distinction, *night*—wolf? Wouldn't wolf suffice?"

Targin leaned forward and raised his index finger. "*Night* is the preface that defines our purpose. We await the coming of the Night without Dawn. As a lesser wolf stalks its quarry, we hunt *the* Night—the Starbond. You've undoubtedly read about it in the last chapters of the Kusp. You know—the scary parts?"

Brooke snorted. "Stars, it's all scary."

"True enough," Targin allowed as he tilted his head up to the inky sky. "Willing or not, we hasten to the prophecy's fulfilment. Though, the Nightwolves seek something more."

"More?"

"Revenge for a long-standing crime against our ancestors: the first Wrayns who migrated from their lost lands on the far side of the Sancean and across the Ice Wastes. This blood debt defines the Nightwolves—when

Deathwrought forced our hand. At the behest of the sprites, we follow the pathless path."

Brooke wrinkled his nose. "The pathless path?"

Targin's fierce pupils left the fire and sought Brooke. "It underlines the Code of the Nightwolves. We roam the land, taking the random unexpected course toward our goals, following three simple principles: the Quick, the Creed, and the Code."

Targin's gaze shifted to the tall one who first greeted them. "Alghan here fancies himself a scholar of sorts. He knows all of our lore—in nauseating detail, but is well versed in our history and coven."

Brooke bowed his head towards the Wrayn.

"Alghan is a true blood," Targin went on, "directly descended from the First Wrayns who took the Dire March over Areth's frozen crown and south into the Main proper. Most of the Warangs gathered here come of the true line as well."

Targin reached over and tapped Brooke's arm, a sly grin tethering his ears like a suspension bridge. "But don't let him make that distinction with you."

"Lord Targin, I wouldn't think of it," Alghan protested, a wounded look on his face.

Targin let out a chuckle before turning back to Brooke. "As for the reason that spurred that march, look no further than our bookish wolf here. The other Wrayns will teach you what you must need learn of the Quick, specifically *combart*."

Once again Brooke's eyebrows pulled together in the firelight. "Ever you speak in unfamiliar terms."

"It defines our art-of-combat," the giant clarified, "the Nightwolf fighting style unique to us. Far more adroit to the reckless methods you Northerners employ."

Targin paused and pointed a thick finger at Brooke. "But of all weapons our foes may use against us, Commander, fear cuts the deepest. *You*—won't let it."

Sweat trickled down the nape of Brooke's neck. Had someone piled more fuel on the fire? Targin had made a statement—not posed a question.

As he stared at the warlord's grave countenance, Brooke sensed a deeper exchange taking place—as though he'd just sworn the greatest oath ever uttered, bending the knee to all Creation. Or maybe sheer exhaustion pressed his thoughts, enough to hunker down with bears and hibernate until spring.

A pair of large hands reached over Brooke's shoulders and placed a metal tray on the ground, interrupting the awkward moment. On it, sat two large plates filled with strips of steaming meat, a scallop of greens, and a loaf of bread.

"At last, our food," Targin announced, rubbing his hands together. He reached down and claimed one of the plates. Still bent over, he handed the other to Brooke.

Mouth watering, Brooke accepted the dish and balanced it on his knees. If not for the crackle and pop of the fire, his host surely would have heard the grumbling protests of the commander's stomach.

While Targin tore off a haunch and chewed noisily, Brooke lifted his face to the server who'd delivered the tray.

And flinched.

No mere camp scullion. Barring a few inches in height, he looked no less the warrior than Targin himself—who dwarfed everyone. Clad in full battle armour of boiled black leather and spikes, gauntlets and grieves, the sable-haired man regarded Brooke in silence, severe and dour. This man knew his business.

"Val!" Targin exclaimed past his full mouth. Eyes perked, neck craned, the chief dropped his plate to the ground and bolted to his feet. He clasped the man's arms and drew him into a gruff embrace.

But where Targin came off as engaging and full of mirth, the other stood counterpoint: reserved and noncommittal.

After a moment, Targin reseated himself and picked up his dish. "Come Val, don't just stand there," he growled. "Break bread with us—and a smile if you can. Here now, sit opposite us. Meet our latest recruit."

Val remained standing.

Targin slanted towards Brooke, a lopsided grin playing on his face. "Val is my Second, staunch, formidable, unpredictable." With his arm, he gestured back and forth between Val and Brooke. "There, I've acquainted you. Greet each other as brothers."

Brooke shifted his plate to one hand and extended the other. Reluctantly Val clasped it.

The Second's grip, fierce and cold like a vice, made Brooke wince.

"You do well to sit with Targin, on your first night," Val said with stiff courtesy. He released Brooke's hand, but his stare did not follow suit, frigid orbs crushing the commander.

Brooke looked to Targin, busy gorging another haunch of meat and gnawing it off the bone with sloppy vigour.

Mouth full, Targin belched. "Damn it, Val, this is good."

Despite Brooke's unease at Val's hostility, Targin's blunt mannerisms amused him. Strangely, it made the man seem honest, more authentic. But beneath his comic exterior rested an implacable fighter. He could deliver death in an instant if crossed. The chief's short work with the Sorgon exhibited that well enough.

Val's grapnel clasp notwithstanding, his snub mired Brooke with festering doubt. Obviously not intended to flatter, closer to a warning. Brooke had crossed into a larger world joining this rebel band—one far more dangerous.

At least his family was safe.

"They will remain so," Targin answered aloud. "But this is not the time for hesitation. Before you sleep tonight, our gathering will see you furnished with the truth, in all matters. All plans."

Targin lifted his eyes to Val. And took aim. "Sit."

When Val complied, Targin called over his shoulder. "Mead or wine will not do on such a momentous occasion. Have the pups crack open a keg of the good stuff. Let's drown Brooke's anxieties—and Val's—with a healthy measure of spritewater."

Val narrowed his eyes and stared at his chief. Targin took his Second's measure, his smile tight. And Brooke scrutinized both.

With a brusque nod, Val upped, turned on his heel and strode out of the firelight.

"What was that all about?" Brooke asked.

Targin made a dismissive gesture with his hand. "Worry not. The matter's settled." His attention lowered to his supper.

Despite the lingering ache nagging his shoulder—thankfully reset by Cras before they set out—Brooke savoured the well-done roast.

Val returned just as the pair had finished their meals. He placed a small keg and three metal cups in front of Targin. The warlord snatched two of the vessels and, holding both in his enormous palm, tipped the spout of the barrel to fill them. He handed one to Brooke and the other to Val. Then, ignoring the third cup, raised the remnants of the barrel and tipped it back, throat working in silence.

Brooke found the taste of the grog akin to the strongest stout but with a cinnamon aftertaste—a good combination and potent enough to sooth his nerves. "You carry casks of this spirit with you?"

Targin lowered the keg to his lap and wiped his lips with the back of his hand. "Very observant. No, its weight would hamper us. Show him, Val."

The Wrayn put his cup down and unfastened a leather pouch from his belt. He loosened its drawstrings and poured a small measure of white crystalline powder onto his palm.

"The sprites produce it to bolster our constitution. But nothing quite satisfies like fresh game, spritewater in smaller doses will sustain us when carrying out our covert activities. All that's needed is water to mix it with.

Two pinches in a three-gallon barrel—" Targin curled his fingers then splayed them, palm up. "Poof, instant spritewater."

The chief pushed an errant flop of curls from his forehead. "But when you really need to slacken the nerves, as we do tonight, you triple the mix— guaranteed to make your cock not grow."

Everyone within earshot broke into laughter. Brooke decided he could use some more of the brew—though not to vouch-true Targin's guarantee. More than anything, he needed steady nerves for what surely would come next.

As Targin refilled Brooke's cup, he warned, "One must be careful not to overindulge. The elixir relaxes for a certainty, with no jim-jams come morning. But its strength may make you impotent—with both heads. Look what happened to Jaak here." He cocked his head to a middle-aged man with a receding grey crown, shoulder-length at the sides, and a leather patch covering one eye. "Though in his case, that might be just age."

"Balls of the lamest hound to you too, Targin," Jaak rumbled good-naturedly. "I've mired and sired thrice over, and my old shaft can steel to the deed yet—ask the wife."

"If and when an opportunity presents herself," a much younger Wrayn put in. "I'd like to determine such a feat. With any luck, before I take the deepest sleep," he added with a chortle.

Targin joined him in his mirth. "Aye, Gauley, I've got a woman in a man's skin for you to test your mettle, and your metal. Fuck that hector-made-flesh, Necatar."

"We all need to fuck that villain," a bald bulldog-faced man added as he entered their circle. Stern orbs, a slightly hooked nose and heavy jowls sculpted his weathered visage. White whiskers dotted his chin. His voice sounded like the scraping of cloth against bark. "Fuck him to death, with a hundred arrows through his black heart."

"Gnor." Targin bowed both head and voice to the wizened man, his deference plain. "How fares your pup's pup?" The chief glanced around. "Where is the lad?"

"Gnolin's here somewhere. And fares well, learning more every day. He'll soon be a warrior to make his father—Vamsah watch over his soul— proud."

"No doubt," Targin agreed. "Please, my friend, join us."

Gnor took a place in the innermost circle and poured himself some grog from a fresh barrel. Brooke liked the way the stout newcomer comported himself. Despite his rough and tough exterior, this Gnor sounded august, reminding the commander of his own noble father—now close to five years in the grave.

As for Targin, his band seemed drawn to his presence, his largesse, like acolytes to a meister.

Targin interrupted his thoughts, "Does it ail you, Commander, to hear us speak so savagely about your friend?"

Brooke felt his smile wither as he drew back. "Friend? Cele's Haft is no friend of mine. I'd not place word and worm in the same book, let alone have them share a sentence—unless I can sentence 'my friend' to a fitting execution."

"That—is why we honour you—with my presence this eventide," Targin chided.

"Then may your presence honour its promise to my ears," Brooke gave back. "You owe me an explanation. And my ears await to be sated as my hunger and thirst have so finely been."

"Well said," Targin acknowledged with a raised chin. The Nightwolf took another long draught from the keg in his lap.

When his eyes found Brooke again, they firmed with conviction. "You need to know what's really going on. Pathguard will fall very soon now, but not by my hand. Necatar's behind every incident which befell the Northern Kingdoms, including the raids on the villages and the demonica Cele suffers. Glib of tongue, he plays the powers against each other, sowing distrust and hostility. Your king's vehemence towards the sprites, towards me for that matter, emerged from that sorcerer's manoeuvring."

Targin had said that all in one breath. He tipped back the keg for three swallows. "And still your kingdom's demise marks but a grain of sand lost to the Sancean expanse. We face the destruction of Areth, and more."

Brooke waited. "What do you mean, Targin?"

The giant put down the cask and levelled his gaze at him. "I mean, Commander, what the counsel of the sprites means—what the prophecies long writ in the Kusp mean. Henceforth, what we do, or not do, will have far-reaching repercussions. Cele's Haft wishes to alienate the sprites so that the freeborn will not look to them as the Endstorm breaks. He wants the kingdoms of the Main to fight each other so when the real threat raises its ugly head, we'll find ourselves disorganized, divided, lost."

"Again, you reference the Starbond," said Brooke. "The Haft is tied to that?"

"Aye, the real shitstorm." Targin steepled his hands and hunched over to examine them. "More than a parasite of court, intent on undermining a kingdom by overthrowing a monarch's mind and mongering war on false pretence, Necatar's not after any throne. He positions his pieces to ensure victory when the twilight falls. Delves into the darkest arts, has special dispensation from the demons of Infern, including longevity. He is an ancient, known by many false names throughout history—Relthi for instance—all guises of his true form."

Targin lowered the small barrel to the ground and slapped his knees. With a sigh, he faced the pyre. Its orange nimbus danced across his features.

"Scrit and Cras told me the Haft bows before the Darkest One."

"Could there be any doubt?" Targin's nod came fierce. "A disciple of Deathwrought he is. The only throne Necatar covets is the seat of the Darkest One Himself."

"If Necatar's bent on such lofty—or lowly—ambitions, Deathwrought must surely be wise to his designs," Brooke piped in. "Wouldn't he simply do away with him?"

Alghan coughed and raised a finger. "A mystery indeed—to embolden the necromage no doubt, handing him power without reckoning, independent of His Four."

"Necatar represents a different ilk of demon," said Targin. "Guised in the skin of a man who sheds his cloak of flesh from time to time, venturing between worlds. He recently became the cynosure of a great war which engulfed Areth's sister, Otherworld."

Brooke drove his eyebrows down. "The fabled world—through the Eye?"

Gnor cleared his throat. "No fable, Commander. And neither is this. We stand at the precipice of the war to end all wars, and Cele's Haft has found a place in the centre of it, pulling countless strings of subterfuge to make his puppets dance. He had sought to add you to that collection. But he'll get his due for the pain he has wrought."

The Bulldog's expression tightened into a mask of death and when he spoke his voice seethed acid, "When that time comes, he will learn that he too is a puppet, one with its strings cut."

"Vamsah willing," Targin put in before taking another drink. "Though Necatar poses a greater, more immediate threat, he forms but the sniffing snout on the monster's head."

"And Deathwrought, the monster," Brooke guessed as he took another swallow of grog.

The Chief shook his head. "Nay, I speak of another ancient malevolence, not yet allied with the Darkest One."

Brooke arched a brow. "How do you know this? Could be more of that shyster's devious horseshit, to spread fear."

"That's what I thought. But no, the sprites and my own mentor confirm the existence of this *hyperdemon*. A breed of evil unlike any that walks the Whole of Areth, or wallows in the pits of Infern. An entity whose domain lies beyond the Void, alien to all the conflicts either Gaia has known since the Starbirth."

"If I were to guess, the only reason the Darkest One suffers Necatar is his connection to this hyperdemon," Alghan put in. "The Stardimmer covets its full allegiance. The necromage functions as an intermediary."

"Aye," Targin concurred. The fire popped loud enough to rival a thunderclap. Several Warangs howled in chorus. When their canine protests ebbed, the chief continued. "The sprites say it exists apart from any divination writ in the Kusp, inherently evil, ubiquitous, harbouring a fury beyond the Darkest One." He swallowed. "This black-within-black horror haunts my dreams. I have heard its harrowing warble."

Brooke wasn't certain but the warlord may have shivered in the firelight.

"As to Necatar's slipshod nature," Targin recounted, "he has infiltrated several of Areth's kingdoms and more in Otherworld. All will fall ere the Starbond. And that is merely the beginning."

The beginning? Brooke expected Targin's band to crack smiles at the preposterous revelations, but they only dipped their chins. The Wrayns' expressions remained grave and unsmiling. In the distance, a raptor shrieked.

"Among the fawning accolades he's placed at my feet, Cele labelled me 'savage' and 'outlaw.' My true role takes on a somewhat more prophetic nature." Targin released a heavy breath. "I wouldn't fault you your doubt at what I am about to tell you. But promise to prove it before the night's through."

"Though my stars dim to your import, you have my ear," said Brooke as he lifted the cup to his mouth.

"Born to Areth as its protector and champion, I heed a Blood Scion's calling, descended from the ancient Lines of Blood. I am—a Vein of Fire."

Brooke harrumphed, spraying spritewater in the process. "*You?* One of the Four?" He understood the reference to the divination, but *this* man? He waited for Targin to reveal his farce and throw back his head in a raucous bout. But the commander missed the mark a second time.

Targin's mouth never wavered from level, mirroring every face in his band. "Like you and many here, I came into the world in the immediate aftermath following the Great War. I grew up an orphan, tormented by visions: some uncanny, others terrifying. The sprites, through the words of a wizard, opened my eyes. He told me all I need hear, confirming my special place as One of the Four emblem bearers."

Brooke sized up the giant, curious exactly how this barbarian would evince what he claimed, let alone tell the commander what he expected of him. "I'm confused. You ward the sprites?"

Targin shook his head. "Nay, their cause. The sprites conjured the vision which aligned my stars thus. I'm to forge a reciprocal bond with the other three Veins. We form Vamsah's Four in the Octagon Equation."

Brooke bit his lip. "The Law of the Octagon."

Targin surrendered a half-smile. "Aye, Deathwrought's Four Siphons mark the other half. And through the sprites' instrumentality, ascribing the Four Veins with the Creator's limitless power, together we protect—Creation."

"A tall order," Brooke said. His scepticism deepened, hearing this lawbreaker trying to sound like a prophet. Like Shirdron.

But no turning back now. For better or worse, Brooke had committed to join this rabble, an out-of-work sellsword taking up with a circus.

"Very soon, I'll fulfil my true role and purpose," Targin said, "to guard the other three Veins." He drained the last drops from the keg, reached back, and seated the drum behind the log.

"All fates face the Starbond," Alghan quoted. "All souls mirror the Stellar Dance."

Head spinning, Brooke could not contain his quandary any longer. "You said the sprites chose me—how do I fit into this prophecy? Am I...?"

"Nay, Commander, you are not a Vein of Fire," Targin disclosed. He leaned back and blew out his cheeks. "Consider that a blessing. But your role here bears equal importance. In time, you'll understand my motives for attacking Pathguard."

Brooke drew a breath. "Then I was right about you. Pathguard's destruction can be laid solely at your feet, not the sprites. I'd long-suspected as much since I read your warning to His Grace."

Targin made a quick study of the other Nightwolves. He raised his broad shoulders and surrendered a snicker. "I should think that much was evident. Painted brigands, guilty as charged. Your fool king left me no choice. I gave the order. But I swear, what we did served only to equalize the balance of power in these lands. I sent the rooks to make all the subjects under Cele's rule aware of the stakes. Give them a chance to dissent or evacuate, possibly turn up allies like your peer, Racine. Like you."

Targin hesitated and pondered. "Though in your case, I suspect it was preordained. You too shall champion the sprites' cause."

A lump formed in Brooke's throat. "You're mistaken, Targin." He gave his head a firm shake. "I am a com—former commander, turned rogue, like as not with a price on my head. Having abandoned a destitute army on its way to ruin, the only thing I'll champion is a spike outside Pathguard's bailey."

Targin dismissed him with a swipe of his hand. "The title of commander you'll retain—addressed as such by me and mine. We require your skills in combat and court. In return, you needn't pledge fealty to me. Swear an oath to your family. Trust me, our stars will align, you and I."

"Only the stars can be certain of that," Val mumbled.

Targin's jaw tightened at his Second. He inhaled fiercely and held it as he glared. When Val looked away, a harsh gust cleared Targin's nose.

Brooke took in all the stern faces surrounding the fire and bit his lip. "But even this many insurgents do not seem enough to set an entire city ablaze. The city guard would have noticed before you cast the first torch."

Targin smirked with his eyes. Then bellowed over his shoulder, "Spifer! Show yourself!"

Somewhere beyond the firelight, a loud belch answered the chief. A chorus of laughter followed everywhere else.

Moments later, a lean man with canine features, dishevelled hair, and several scars staggered into view. He grinned savagely from ear to ear.

"Allo," he slurred before punctuating his greeting with another belch, longer than the first. The overpowering smell of grog emanating from the man invaded Brooke's nostrils, making him bunch up his nose.

The tankard in Spifer's grip danced, sloshing and dripping spirit onto his black garb. Little doubt, the Wrayn had increased his spritewater recipe by a factor of ten, clearly at his cups a while.

Targin regarded him with an expression somewhere between reprimand and amusement. Without taking his eyes off the inebriated Nightwolf, the chief growled, "When the sot's not-so-pickled, Spifer's the tinder beneath my flames." He angled his chin at the Wrayn. "And why is that, Spifer?"

"Because good sirs, I knows how to burn," the pyromancer drawled. "I can scorch anything I want—and do it right. Chaos be my lovely whore, and fire, the seed I sow between her legs."

Spifer's torso swerved to the left, then angled to the right. "I sets water to ash if I so chose. When M' Lordship Targin says burn Pathguard, Ize up and do it right, strategic-like. Yup, me birthin' name may be Spifer, but every one of these dogs knows me as Spit-fire."

"Tell him why!" one of the Nightwolves shouted from the crowd.

"Cuz I'm a goddam dragon!" Spifer bellowed before turning to face Brooke again. "N' now, am at your service." The unsteady man tried to finish with a bow, tripped himself, and promptly fell on top of the fire. His mead spilt over the flames, singing as steam bloomed in the darkness, filling the tract with the smell of baked cinnamon bread.

Spifer rolled off an instant later, arm charred black with soot, hair singed, and his sleeve aflame. He hooted hysterically at his own folly. Once he snuffed out the burning cuff, the scene erupted in similar bouts of hilarity.

When the rollicking press simmered down some, Targin said, "And in true form—reckless as ever. We should call you Spill-fire."

Another detonation of merriment ensued.

"I take it, that's how you earned those scars," Brooke observed.

Spifer beamed, running a hand across his charred scalp. "Well, Milord, is like this, fire, see, pure chaos, like a harlot who wants to be a lady." His eyebrows squished together. "Or maybe it be the other way round? No Matter. You got to know how to handle them to get your pleasure is all—cause get it wrong, they grow volly-tile, blow up in your face, they will. Like I say, I knows how to burn anything—including me-self apparently."

Brooke allowed a thin smile but felt this man a little too precipitous. The collateral damage to Pathguard proved as much. But within his coven at least, Spifer meant well and he had definitely mastered his profession, managing to make short work of Cele's arsenals in such swift surgical strikes, it left an army crippled and a city in pandemonium.

Best to keep such opinions silent in this circle. Again, if Targin had caught wind of Brooke's mind, he did not stir to its murmur.

"You've learned the first rule of communion," the giant said a few moments later.

"Communion? I thought that happened between Wrayns and their Warangs—and forest animals."

Targin shook his head. "I can read thoughts heedlessly cast—like your less-than-fawning comment about my circus," he added with a wink. "Otherwise, they stay yours to safeguard. This is how we remain in concert when in the field to coordinate our efforts. Problem being, the minions of the Darkest One share this ability. So, we must be careful."

Another plate filled with steaming meat was placed before Brooke, but he declined. Targin took a fowl thigh from the proffered dish. He stuffed it in his mouth and continued to speak as he chewed. "Soon, you'll know all the Wolves. You've already shared a fight with Scrit and Cras so you've gleaned a measure of their skills. Many in the band have unique talents."

Targin swallowed, burped, and threw the stripped bone into the fire. He looked up. "Take pretty Gauley here for instance, a charmer with the ladies. Has a way of exacting secrets from highborn birds, all too willing to impart them while their legs are spread. They sing at the expense of their despot husbands. But don't let that fool you. He lives for the fight, and if the odds do not totally stack against him, does not consider it a challenge."

"Just want to take the deepest sleep same way my old man cashed in," Gauley said, flashing a wolfish smirk. "A glorious death worthy of the Kusp—that was Pops." He turned his eyes skyward.

"Admires all acts of gall and recklessness, including those of the enemy," Targin laughed. "That's why the men just call him Gall. I think

Spifer's his greatest hero."

"I worship no man," Gauley countered. "Save my sire. Char's the one in love with the pyro."

A burly Nightwolf with a set jaw and angry eyes scowled. "Both are careless. Mongrel fire makers, the pair—liabilities."

"Which Warang pissed in your mead, Lonus?" Targin sniggered before pointing to another Wrayn. "Onis knows his way around poultices and potions. He's patched me up more times than I can count."

"From spare parts," Onis chortled.

Targin shrugged. "There's Cash, Rish, Bhom, Tretak, Craw, Rurk, Quiver, Gard, Gormel, Quarin, Curls, Wornin, Tallicah, Ahn: not every Wrayn come from true blood, some are mixed mongrels, some the products of past banes. But fierce warriors all, they join as true hearts and contribute something to the cause. No dead weight in these ranks."

"What about my contribution?" Brooke pressed. "My function?

"I'll get to that in a moment," Targin said absently. "We operate as a pack, which makes us implacable. Even with our reckless dragon here."

"But what Spifer did?" Brooke chewed the inside of his cheek. "Still seems impossible for one man. How?"

"Save the question for later," Spifer slurred, "when I've sobered a tad. Oh, time to piss." He swaggered away out of the firelight.

Still addressing Targin, Brooke asked, "How did you learn enough of Necatar's ploys to execute your campaigns to such an effect—right under his snout?"

"Ah, I wondered when you'd ask about that. Alghan?"

The tall Nightwolf handed Targin a small roughspun sack. He reached inside and drew out a set of jingles and a gaudy fool's costume.

The chief shook the noisy chimes in his hand. "Ring a bell?"

Brooke widened his eyes. "The jester I passed when I left the council session in the castle—no wait, you stood right outside the king's chamber."

Targin shifted forward and winked. "Infiltrated many of Cele's council meetings. Learned his intent in that mummer's sham and what I would effort to stop."

Brooke could only gawk at Targin's grin. When the moment passed, the Nightwolf's face turned to stone, orbs steadfast in their solemn cast. "Even if you began on the wrong side, changing allegiances will feel disconcerting—shows your assertiveness, does you credit, and I like you more for it."

"Thank you—I think," Brooke said, a bemused smile stretching his cheeks.

"I know you'll have many doubts long after this eve falls behind you, but at those times trust that it is ultimately Vamsah's will that you and I have united. The sprites didn't pick you in haste from some herder's flock."

Targin twirled a lock of his dark curls around his index finger. "The same holds true with me. Despite what you've heard, I've never had any direct quarrel with the realms my fold has unfolded. And the sprites were never to blame for what befell your villages."

"But witnesses have come forward," Brooke pointed out. "They swear under oath, and alchlemage trance, to have espied nymphs at the scenes of the rampages—magical signatures of their spent power left behind."

"I'll wager they did," Targin said, rubbing the back of his thick neck. "But have you considered the sprites came to quell a more grievous attack perpetrated by the real nemeses?"

Brooke matched the Vein's stance. "Is that why you've sworn fealty to them?"

"Their plight mirrors our plight," Targin replied. "The sprites are essential to the survival of the Universe since the Highprites—Vamsah's First—proved fallible. Deathwrought evinced that much: a Highprite turned just about as wrong as one can, becoming the very vessel of Morgrand."

Brooke blinked.

"No, I don't expect you to grasp this concept," Targin said. "But you will understand that once hope's vanquished, we'll look to the battlefield with dead eyes. For your family, you can never let that happen to you, Commander. Or those you lead will falter. Can you embrace my meaning?"

"Embrace it, Targin?" Brooke replied evenly. "Hope is the fuel which keeps the fire of my hearth going—the undying blaze of a father's love and care for his children, a husband's devotion to his endearing wife. Dayanthi is my heart."

The lines around the warlord's countenance lost their terseness and he gave Brooke a sad smile. "At the core of my own heart, I feel for one the same."

Brooke drew back and stuttered. "You've someone in your life?"

Targin nodded. "I have neither sired, nor been wed, but I stand betrothed. A wildflower and untamed she-wolf, both, Tasmin is. Her kisses are tender and her fangs sharp but yes, I do love her with all that—"

A sudden gust of wind and the sound of creaking branches high in the canopy made Targin pause and glance up. Brooke followed the Nightwolf's surveillance but discerned nothing. After a moment, Targin lowered his gaze and faced the commander. Brooke noted something new in the giant's hard eyes, a bittersweet memory perhaps.

Targin stood to his full seven feet and sucked back a forge's bellow of air. "Wolf Brothers and Sisters, on the morrow you will strike camp and head out. The moment I've prepared you for draws ever nigh. We've rattled the sabre enough. Be on your guard—for the response will come swift and ere long. We'll live to regale each other with heroic deeds and epic tales. Toast in final victory over the Night. Stay the purpose!"

"To the Purpose!" the chorus shouted back. The Warangs tossed their canine heads and howled.

When the wolven hubbub petered, a still-seated Brooke raised a hand and gently tapped Targin's arm. "After so many revelations, you have piqued my curiosity beyond measure. Please Targin, tell me *my* purpose?"

Targin studied Brooke for several heartbeats before raising his chin. "Ah, your purpose, we come to it at last." He raised his voice and swept the faces of his band. "The War of Night darkens across the Main. As much as I wish to lead the final charge of my Wolves, with regret, I cannot. The sprites have set me on a different path. The Path of the Four."

Targin raised a fist and punched it into his catching palm. "The key to our success lay not in strength of arms but the stronger strategy, positioning the strands of many entwined fates—not just friends and allies, but our enemies as well. I would heed both calls if possible. Alas, it is not."

His eyes found Brooke again. "You, Commander, shall replace me as leader of the Nightwolves."

Stephen Fenech

17: Ritual
Sonart

The three dwarven fell into a solemn silence, heads lowering, gazes focused on their bowls of hogsweed. As he ate, Sonart reflected upon his adroit father, and the incident from his distant past, which stole Farkshone away.

Sonart had witnessed only one enactment of the Kworn ritual, with the eyes of a youthling who bore naught but a smear of rust for a beard.

His sire led twelve dwarven, risking discovery and punishment, to observe the ceremony and 'grasp their own plight.'

Or so Farkshone claimed. Even then, Sonart suspected more to his father's motives, as well as his adamance that his son attend.

Now, long after that dimming's perilous incursion, any answers had been scoured away by time, abandonment, and death. Stripped to fine dust and scattered by a razor storm. Yet the memory remained, as though it had happened only yester-drear...

Farkshone trusted the twelve who accompanied them that eventide. Unlike the majority, the small cadre secretly refused the dogma of the Kusp. They followed the wisdom and guidance of Sonart's father alone. He avowed that one drear, the dwarven would rise again and take back their lands.

Under cover of darkness, the dimming before the ritual would take place, the dwarven party advanced—Auckland not among them. Within the crags and folds of the Northern Spike's foothills, they took up covert positions overlooking the Kworn's proving ground.

There, shoulder to shoulder with Farkshone's closest friend, Rusic, and his son, Seolad, Sonart waited, anticipation making his hands clammy.

Twas a vicious rite of passage that the Kworn had conceived, centring on a single Chosen—a sacrificial emblem of the entire tribe.

Come mid-morning, a contingent of their brethren joined the throngs already gathered in the barren valley. The Chosen entered a roughly burrowed arena, walled by tightly packed ranks of Kworn.

Stripped of the usual armour the creatures wore grafted to their skin, the revered Chosen sat in a chair atop a wooden plinth in the middle of the makeshift pitch. The square platform, thirty feet by thirty, rested on ten-foot-tall stilts and accessed by a ladder. Beneath it, the beastmen stockpiled lengths of timber and stuffed wads of dry brush between.

The sound of giant doom-drums—eight feet in diameter—rose from out of the encampment, signalling the first stage of the ritual. Drummers beat their fists against the tocsins like war hammer peens, creating a powerful cadence that shook the ground. The pounding *one-two*, *one-two* rhythm hailed the arrival of a few selected team members.

Sonart's pulse quickened. He felt a lightness in his chest as he watched, rapt with fascination. A glance at the other dwarven revealed pressed lips, focused eyes trained forward, and faces solemn as statues.

Eyelids half-shut, chin resting on an upturned palm, Seolad looked bored—and confirmed it with a yawn.

In full armour, groups numbering five to ten entered the arena bearing serrated blades and heavy cudgels. All drear long, the teams challenged one other. They raved supremacy, barking in their guttural tongue as they demonstrated feats of strength and virility. Throughout the build-up to the main ritual, the drummers pummelled their massive drums, *one-two*, *one-two,* fists raw, arms corded thick.

When dusk fell, the Chosen uprooted himself and climbed down the ladder. He took a nearby torch that burned on a pole-mounted sconce and cast it atop the woodpile. Flames quickly licked up the mound, engulfing the entire construct.

Dimming coruscated into drear.

"The main ritual begins," Rusic said.

Back to the inferno, the Chosen braced his legs and balled his fists, face and torso twisting in lockstep. He danced left then right, in response to his opponents as they fanned out, death shining in the viridian glow of their eyes.

"He must remain leery to hold back his glorious end for as long as he can," Farkshone whispered in Sonart's ear.

"Why?" asked Sonart, pupils never straying from the Chosen.

"Their belief is simple," his sire answered. "The longer the Chosen Kworn endures, the greater the tribe's constitution for the next five star-cycles. The team members represent the Darkest One's malice—a malady afflicting every last Kworn."

The Elders held that the Kworn served Deathwrought by force and not out of any reverence. As an already conquered race, they loathed him, but their time to rise up had long passed. The Zürshuck saw to that.

Traditionally, if luck favoured the Chosen, he might survive an entire team before meeting his poignant doom.

But after two turns of the dial, when the deepest sleep would be late to embrace any previous Chosen, this Kworn not only stood unscathed, he had turned the tables. The tumult he incited erupted up and down the crush of Kworn spectators. Superstition drove their elation beyond madness as the teams sought to hem the lone champion in.

By the third turn of the dial, the crowd beat each other senseless to vent their excitement.

One-Two-Two, One-Two-Two, the doom-drums cracked louder.

Quicker.

They matched tempo with the congregation's soaring jubilation.

From his distant hiding place, young Sonart could feel the ground shake under the spectacle's turmoil while the air throbbed in his ears.

Whenever the Chosen felled an opponent, cheers went up.

And Sonart's heart imploded from the crowd's thunderous uproar. Despite the ritual's raw savagery, he found himself caught up in its fervour. His eyes fixed on the lone Kworn, who sidestepped his adversaries with unnatural ease and endurance.

Three full teams, four, five, stalked and pursued, only to collapse, furious with failure. They entered the ring, brimming with zeal. They left it exhausted, wounded, or dead.

The cunning and resilience of the Chosen demonstrated a prowess too much for them. He singled out his would-be executioners, using their numbers against them. A cudgel's lunge at his head wound up dashing the skull of another opponent rushing in from behind.

In a frenzied move too quick to follow, the Chosen relieved a hapless foe of his sword as he sailed past. With a weapon of his own, the Chosen moved on the offensive.

Ironock bit flesh and his opponents dropped in greater numbers, while the unflagging champion persisted, showing no visible signs of fatigue. He stripped the spiked gauntlets from a corpse and donned them even as he held back the remnants of the latest team.

By the fourth turn of the dial, such a wave of insanity swept through the press, Sonart had to clap his hands over his ringing ears.

As he did, he stole a glance at his father.

And froze.

Beneath brows woven into tight hogsweed sacks, Farkshone's orbs stared out from a mask of dread. His knotted beard trembled.

"Something is wrong," Farkshone shouted over the din. Of all those present, dwarven and Kworn alike, only Sonart's father sensed something out of place.

But what? Sonart drew a blank.

Beguiled by the orgy of death, the Kworn masses hadn't even noticed the strangeness with which the Chosen acted. They followed each of his killing sprees with the trust and naiveté of dwarven younglings.

The drums thundered on at mercurial speed. Sonart's heart pounded one beat faster. The combatant fatalities had reduced the teams to broken factions of their original numbers.

Until the last squad members went down under the bite of the Chosen's purloined sword.

A long vacuous pause followed.

Sonart held his breath as the Chosen tossed the red-stained blade to the ground and craned his head to the ebony sky. He lifted two bloody arms above his head, making claws of his hands.

And let out a roar of triumph that reverberated off the hills.

The firelight of the burning pyres gave the champion a sinister cast like some berserker demon in mid-apotheosis. If Sonart didn't know any better, the Chosen's display bespoke defiance—a challenge?

Regardless, the crowd's lunacy became infectious.

As did Farkshone's anxiety.

The violent throng joined the Chosen's wail in solidarity. They bellowed with one voice, shaking the very firmament of the Cradle. At that moment, they had exalted their Chosen to an echelon above god.

So focused on the mania's cynosure, no one, Sonart included, caught sight of the two bat-like forms swooping down from the blackness above...

Almost perfunctorily, the Zürshuck pair smothered the Chosen, wings enwrapping him as though in veneration.

The cheers suddenly died.

Like wildfire to dry bracken, a murmur of dissent swept over the bestial hordes as the two Zürshuck obstructed their view. When the Winged Ones revealed their bewitchment, disquiet burst into outrage.

Two ironock spears impaled the Chosen, forming an X through his torso. He collapsed on bent knees like a discarded puppet. The demons had crucified and held him fast to the ground. His lantern eyes glazed over; their emerald glow guttered and went dark.

The air hummed with disquiet.

Before death transformed the Chosen into a statue, one of the Zürshuck lopped his head off clean with a forward thrust of its wingtip.

His decapitated head tumbled to the ground and rolled away.

The Kworn crowd surged forward, wrath impelling them headlong. Like the wind of a razor storm, their feet ripped the ground as they launched themselves at the winged intruders.

Swift as the Zürshuck were, they could not flee the sudden torrent of hulking bodies. The closer demon grappled the first Kworn by the neck, drawing him close enough to kiss.

Jaws clamped shut, snapping the beastman's spine.

But the Winged One could not meet the second bout.

The Zürshuck went down, trampled under the mob's frenzied avalanche.

The Kworn converged on the second demon as it bounded along the ground, wings beating furiously in a desperate bid to gain the inky skies. After several failed attempts, the Zürshuck took wing.

A hurled gauntlet blasted out of the closing ranks.

It caught the Zürshuck at the shoulder joint and shattered the bone.

The demon plummeted twenty feet to the Steppe, a moment before the ravenous tide of Kworn drowned it. They tore the Zürshuck's frame, riving it into the earth.

"Stars blacken," Farkshone gasped. "Our worst fears realized."

Far above the cabal, a hysteria of lightning forks seized the darkness, blasting across the sky and down upon the Kworn.

Bedrock convulsed, bucked and burned.

The explosive strikes ripped the closest Kworn apart, flung them to the ground, and incinerated them. Howling terror in place of rage, any survivors abandoned the carcasses and fled.

But then, the headless Chosen arose before them, and ignited. Dead flesh sluffed off, uncovering a mass of searing onyx light in silhouette of the body that housed it moments before.

Despair strangled Sonart as he caught his first harrowing glimpse of the Darkest One. Had Deathwrought possessed the Chosen, enchanting him to succeed?

The god's baleful laugh stormed the dale, hurling thunderous vehemence in all directions. "Filth, expect forbearance for such an affront? Such sacrilege? The Zürshuck and I are legion. To raise arms against them is to sin against me. You must all serve penance. My favoured will serve it to you!"

With the light of the central pyre's soaring flames and the burning islands ignited from the multiple lightning strikes, the sky's ceiling appeared to collapse. Spears hurled down like rain upon the Kworn.

A host of Zürshuck dropped behind them. Several of the beastmen collapsed, perforated by the bolts. The rest routed like panicked sheep ahead of the slaughter. With their projectiles and sheer numbers, the Zürshuck quickly laid waste to the Kworn as they fled the bedlam.

Farkshone hauled Sonart to his feet and whipped around to the others. "Disband. Regroup at Bulkforge." He spun on Rusic. "See our sons away. The upper path behind us—all haste. We'll guard your retreat. Go!"

With the curtest nod, Rusic impelled Seolad forward before grabbing Sonart by the arm. As the carnage drew closer to their hiding spot, the three dwarven disappeared around an outcropping of rock directly behind the small clave.

Sonart did not look back.

Like thieves in the night, they ran alongside the steep boulder-ridden foothills. Guided by the surefootedness of Rusic, they stole across a sheltered plateau and down a crevice that spilled out into a great divide. Urgency fuelled their strides as they gained access to a well-trodden path.

With the first grey blush of dawn less than a turn away, the three dwarven safely arrived in the town of Bulkforge.

Sonart questioned a despondent Rusic about his father, but he only shook his head. By the gaunt look in his eyes and the inward curl of lips, Rusic had scoped the unsaid depth of Farkshone's imperative but said no more.

Turning to Seolad garnered no answers either. Rusic's short-tempered son glowered and muttered some stretched curse under his breath.

They did not regroup in Bulkforge later that drear, or the next.

Or ever.

Sonart yearned for his father's return, but each new drear bore no tidings. Only tears, shed in silence and solitude. His heart emptied as youth suddenly ebbed.

Sonart eventually forced himself to accept that his sire would never come home—that he had taken the deepest sleep. No news came because no witnesses survived to bring it.

Worst fears realized—what had his father guessed that none of the dozen in their party could fully comprehend? Why did Farkshone not flee with them? And what dire fate befell him?

Before Auckland caught wind of his younger brother's disappearance, and Sonart's fate therein, the drears held only questions and longing. With no siblings, and his mother, Evangel, gone to the grave shortly after his birth, Sonart found himself utterly alone.

One dimming, near a moon-cycle after the incident, Rusic came to Sonart's home. He deposited a small coin purse in the youthling's hands 'to help out.' Sonart had monies of his own but until he could earn for himself, matters would be tight. So, he accepted the charity with sincere thanks.

Sitting Sonart down at the kitchen table, Rusic told him first of the Kworn decimation. The Zürshuck's retaliation expanded to include the nonpartisan Kworn, bending their ilk into further submission. Throughout the Cradle, the demons killed several of the beastmen at random.

Rusic had chanced return to the scene and discovered dwarven bodies flattened in the Kworn stampede, but of Sonart's father, no trace did he find. Nothing to unravel Farkshone's vanishing, save the scorched ground.

"I do not fully grasp the import behind Farkshone's bane," Rusic avowed. "But your father stayed behind for a higher purpose, other than your immediate safety." He raised a finger. "Though that indeed formed a fair part of it, there's the greater good to consider. Trust me, lad, your innocence at this juncture bodes you well."

Rusic paused and checked himself, his attention drifting to a side table where a stack of old books resided. His brows lifted slightly. "Your sire bade me deliver a message he deemed very dangerous."

"Dangerous?" Sonart started, blood draining from his neck. "To me?"

"To all dwarven," Rusic answered as he sought Sonart's attention once more. "Do you recall what happened, specifically the way of it?"

Sonart inclined his head.

"What I am about to tell you, lock it deep inside and never speak openly to any other, for it is forbidden knowledge." He tugged at his beard and studied Sonart for a moment. "This token will not make sense to you now. But one drear, with any luck, it will."

Sonart gulped, trying to steady his courage. He tightened his jaw and bowed in acquiescence.

"Before the incident," Rusic said, "your father bequeathed a phrase to me should something befall him—made me recite it repeatedly, so I could relay it exactly as he intended your ears to hear."

Sonart leaned in. "Go on."

Rusic chewed his lip for a moment before clearing his throat. "They are all in your keeping now. Only your hands can shape the path of those to follow. You are bound to your doom by a vast conundrum and destiny therein, beyond the lore of any testament. Within the chaos you will find the true path to structure, and deliverance for us all."

Sonart frowned, puzzling over the strange edict.

Rusic took a slow draw of air. "One other thing your father made me swear to tell you, lad." He tilted his head to the side. "Admittedly, I found it rather odd, being such a common psalm phrase. But riddle or no, Farkshone remained quite adamant."

"What?" Sonart croaked.

"Be at one with the Kusp."

Sonart knitted his brows.

Rusic exhaled and placed his hands on his knees. A bead of sweat trickled down his forehead. Then another.

Shoulders sagging, he looked unburdened but tired. Was it relief in his sunken eyes, having fulfilled his vow to his lost friend?

Sonart peered deeper. Guilt and helplessness creased the elder dwarven's face.

Rusic stood and made for the door, but stopped at the threshold. "I—apologize for laying such troubling enigmas at your feet—to add to your grief." He turned back. "Know that I miss him like my own kin. But, for what it's worth, nothing Farkshone said or did was frivolous. Ever he sought to change our narrative. I'm willing to bet he found a way. So, attend his words to the letter. Your father meant for you to hear his message exactly as you have."

"I've committed it to memory," Sonart said with some effort. "It's all I have left now."

Rusic grimaced and let out a breath. "Come see me, should you choose. If I can offer you any counsel or further assistance within my means, I will. That said, my first bit of advice would be this: do not seek an answer. If I know your father the way I know your father, the answer will seek you. The answer will find you. All you must do is survive." With that, he curved away and left.

Sonart never laid eyes on him again.

Of course, when Rusic brought word of Farkshone's death to Auckland, Sonart's uncle immediately reached out, insisting that his nephew come stay with him and his wife. They had no children of their own and welcomed him with open arms.

Sonart kept Rusic's strange revelation to himself, not wanting to burden his selfless hosts with disturbing riddles.

Despite his young age and his guardians' protests, Sonart took up early work in the mines. He wanted to earn his keep and take his mind off his bereavement and uncertainty.

But in the moon-cycles that followed, the questions continued to burn in his heart, cinders of doubt refusing to die until he could endure their burning nag no longer.

One drear, free from the tunnels, Sonart decided to seek Rusic out—have him make good on his promise.

From Auckland's home in Farkshone—an eponymous village that had taken his father's own namesake, Sonart made for Rusic's parish, Split Rock, less than a drear's journey across the Steppe by mule and cart.

But when he arrived, Rusic was gone. Seolad, his scowling blunt-as-a-hammer son, confirmed that his sire had disappeared prior to a recent countermanding, not three weeks before Sonart's arrival.

Curiosity unrequited, Sonart left the obtrusive Seolad to his grumbling. He never saw that dwarven again either, or any other who'd witnessed that hellish dimming.

From that point on, Sonart's existence in the Cradle diminished to one of alarm and loathing. Auckland and Mila's assurances could only carry him so far. If not for his father's words, Sonart would have crumpled, possibly even tempting the fate of the Lobe and Void, as Bordu and Piskin had done.

The answer will find you.

Despite everyone's belief about the Kusp's promise of 'salvation through suffering,' the daily melees, the dependence on vices like drink and flesh and violence, bound every drear with confusion and consternation. It elicited the only truth: there would be no redemption.

Unlike his peers, Sonart had been cursed that eventide, his existence forever changed—the weight in his heart grew heavier, not lighter. All the other dwarven accepted their plight, acknowledging the psalms of the Kusp and their proclamations.

But he could not. His father's message resounded like a splinter in his mind, one that would always set him apart. He must prevail to believe it, although he did not parse its meaning.

As Rusic urged, Sonart trudged on while the suffering of his people all around him worsened. Pestilence spread like a brush fire through the villages, taking the very young and very old.

And then the visions came. Three score and six drears following his thirtieth star-cycle in existence—his fourteenth in the mines.

The visions allowed Sonart to escape his lot, entering another world beyond. It released him from the dread of reality and lifted the weight, allowing him to revisit his father's words with greater acceptance.

And the first spark of understanding. His destiny crystallized, linked to the doom of his people, but he alone had an escape the masses did not. Or so he thought.

Other dwarven spoke freely of strange foretellings they'd witnessed. Sonart listened in as they toiled in the mines, blasting ironock and carting it away. He fell back into misery, having his newborn purpose so quickly expunged. Sonart waited for another solution, but in beginning a new vigil, every click of the dial felt an eternity.

Those who did not share the insight scoffed, declaring the visionaries' thinking flawed—a falsehood conjured by dullards to fill their empty longing.

People spoke.

Others listened.

And the answer came in the form of a decree. That changed everything.

The beginning of the end.

The Kworn pillaged Sonart's village, leaving many dead in their wake as they rampaged every warren, farmstead, and home. Many among those spared were arrested. Along with Malrik and several others, the beastmen herded Sonart into that pen.

The Kworn bound the dwarven in manacles, hobbled them together with chains, and carted the train to the Dunge. The reason for their incarceration soon became apparent: sharing the vision. For that crime alone their suffering would also be shared.

It took some time for Sonart's command of the dreams to flourish, for he resisted his ability after learning of the others, sure that it would only lead to more sorrow.

But the vision took hold of him, nonetheless, accelerated his clairvoyance far above the rest. He learned that he could map out directions in what they'd come to call *the State*, travel outside his body, with naught but his freed mind.

The heightening disparity between him and his peers became its own truth.

Might it be that his brethren had been imprisoned en mass because the Darkest One could not tell which of them, would prove the true infiltrator? Sonart wagered on his cloak of subterfuge and worked to ultimately penetrate the Cleft Augury.

And now, when the dwarven finally reached his goal, Deathwrought had found him out—a fly caught in the web, stifled, sapped—and retasked.

Head hung forward, Sonart stared through a fog at the stew remnants staining his empty bowl. The hollow space mirrored the confines of the Cradle and his own dire plight.

Deathwrought charged Sonart to correct the terrible wrong he had inadvertently set into motion. The son of Farkshone had betrayed his father and his people, becoming the very evil he sought to vanquish.

Oh, the answer has found me Rusic—stars curse you. It has found me indeed.

18: Schism
Sonart

"*Nephew!*"

Auckland's voice cut through Sonart's dark meandering. He flinched, jerking his hand and spilling some of his ale. Head down, he'd been staring at an empty bowl—by the dry veneer of stew bits, for some time.

Remembering himself, Sonart lifted his chin. "Sorry, Uncle. Your mention of the incident surpassed my recall of the Dunge, put me of a mind, lamenting the last time I'd had words with my sire."

The circles under Auckland's eyes deepened but the orbs they cradled softened. "I can understand that, lad. Tis I who must beg forgiveness, reopening such a grievous wound. The loss of my brother hammered me like a cudgel to the heart. I have buried my grief but will never forget the man, a hero of the people. In shared sorrow, we keep the memory of your father with us. And all for which he stood—champion that."

"Auckland," Mila cut in sternly. "I think that's enough advice n' tales fer one dimming."

"No, it's quite all right," Sonart said quietly. He filled his lungs and exhaled to shore up his grief. "I do not wish to speak of my father or the incident, but I will share-tell of the Dunge."

The gaps between Mila's crow's feet drew close together and she gave him a long look. "It's yer choice, of course."

Sonart fanned back an errant lock of hair that had drooped past his cheek. "As you can well imagine, drear in, drear out, the Dunge taxed me. On the sixth drear of my captivity, shortly after the doom-drum's heralded mid-death, a Colossal appeared."

Auckland and Mila's eyes widened at the mention of the abominations, created by and indentured to the Shadow. Wielding flaming broadswords, the eight-foot-tall drones served as extensions of the Siphon himself, beings perpetually aflame with black fire. As vassals of the Shadow, the Colossals could enforce the archdemon's edicts to the full extent of his malice and violence.

Sonart dropped his voice to a whisper. "The Colossal shifted through the bars of our cell as though they weren't even there. The sheer energy it exuded— stars. Onyx flames licked its body and charged the very air with an acrid fume. I thought it had come to incinerate us."

Mila covered her mouth with her hand. "Hooks and Dunge."

147

Auckland removed a stone pipe from his tunic pocket. "What happened?"

"The Colossal pointed its flaming sword at Malrik and me," Sonart said. "Its length reached a full six feet from guard to tip. They have no faces, these beings, yet somehow it spoke." *The Ancient Lines will bleed again. If you be of that Line, come forward now before the doom of your people is complete. Else all falters to oblivion. The Starbond's already begun. We watch all of you.*

Auckland began stuffing weed into his pipe. "What did it say?"

Sonart scratched the top of his crown as he met Auckland's frown. "Its import befuddled me—and Malrik. Suffice to say it sounded like dire tidings." He took a long pull from his cup, evading the scrutiny of his uncle and aunt.

Auckland picked up a thin strand of kindling from a crate beside his chair and extended it into the lantern's flame. When it caught, he used the burning tip to light his pipe. The weed's pleasant musky smell filled the space and allowed Sonart to relax.

"One boon to the Colossal's appearance," Sonart let out a fulsome laugh. "Its furnace singed the pen's rank. For the better part of a moon-cycle, nary a rat or spider hectored us."

Auckland mumbled something as he drew smoke, slanted his chin down, and pushed his empty bowl away. Another demented cry sounded in the distance, filling the awkward silence.

"Seems a mob's worth afoot this dimming," Mila rumbled. She faced Auckland.

"Door's locked," he confirmed.

It stirred an echo in Sonart's mind: 'all in your hands... bound by destiny.' He may not know his father's words or reasons, but now that he'd been set loose, Sonart would not squander his chance as he had before they locked him up. Stars burn Rusic, he would search for and uncover his higher purpose.

"In the last two moon-cycles of my—my—" Sonart's voice caught in his throat. His jaw fell open midsentence as a sinister thought paid him a glancing blow—a thought that did not belong to him.

Mine eyes are your eyes.

Mila broke the tense quiet. "Nephew?"

Sonart tried desperately to rid his mind of the invading vertigo—the same possession that stole over him in the Hive. Sweat beaded down his forehead and ran down the small of his back. Shivers spidered up from his extremities and blood fled his arteries.

Suddenly flustered, Mila pushed back her chair, face blanching.

Pipe gritted between his teeth, Auckland reached across the table and grabbed Sonart by the shoulders, spilling the pitcher of mead across the counter as he shook him. A deluge of ale streamed to the floor. "Sonart, come back to us!"

The dark seizure vanished. And the colour returned to Auckland's visage.

In the wake of his swift terror, Sonart felt more himself again. Stronger. "I—I don't know what came over me. I had a waking flash of—an emblem."

Mila used a towel to sponge up the mead that had splashed the floor. Auckland righted the overturned carafe and handed Sonart a sideways look. "A weapon?" His ambivalent tone implied he already knew the answer.

"No, some kind of totem, like a sceptre." Sonart lied. He went on to describe his journey to the Hive and his harrowing encounter with the Darkest One. When he'd finished, he squared his shoulders. "Tomorrow, I must leave you—and begin my search for clues. Unravel the quandary."

"But, yer *plainly* still recoverin,'" Mila protested. "N' haven't ya been listenin' t'wat Auckland done said?"

"All too well, Auntie," Sonart replied evenly. "Precisely why I must go. Fret not, I've survived the Dunge *and* the Hive. If I am truly cursed, that which you deem so dangerous will flee in terror before me. Believe you me, Afflicted Ones and Proclaimers will be the least of my worries."

Mila stood abruptly and took the soaked towel to the bucket beside the wall. Its splash as she rang out the cloth sounded like vomit. When she came back to the table, her movements seemed wooden. Lips compressed into a thin line, she shifted her regard to Auckland.

Sonart's uncle snatched his napkin and busied himself sopping up the yellow pond of mead still on the table. His attention fixed on the effort, pipe stem working between his teeth and farting small puffs of smoke.

Mila let out a timorous sigh and sank back into her chair, her resignation plain.

Auckland cleared his throat. "The best place for you to begin any search will be your own home, Sonart. Passed that way recently. The cottage still stands, though certainly not well—left to the blight of countless razor storms, coupled with time and neglect. A derelict to be sure, but not completely razed. I'd suggest you go there first."

Sonart looked at the elder dwarven with new eyes. Auckland shouldered the weight of his long years, but he had ironock in his mettle. Sonart did his best to match it. "Good counsel that is. Admittedly, I'd not considered it. Thank you, Uncle."

Auckland took the cob from his mouth and emptied its ashes into his vacant bowl. "If you were not the son of my brother, I'd say you'd already succumbed to the first stage of the pestilence. But you know yourself and, like your father, you carry your burdens well. Farkshone would've been proud. I'll not dissuade you."

The elder dwarven slapped his hands on his knees and raised his mass with a groan. "Pitcher's empty. Listening to such tales has sent me an added thirst. Up for another pint?"

"Gone without ale for so long, my tongue's lost its memory. And I sorely want to remember the effect of a second pint, like as not a third."

Auckland threw his head back and laughed. "Spoken like my brother. The blood of the line flows strong yet." Retrieving Sonart's cup and his own, he filled them directly from a wooden barrel set against one wall.

"If serious drinkin's in your plan," Mila said with mock disapproval, "I'll leave you two sots to your cups." A faint grin found its way to her cracked lips. "I'm off to bed, but don't be too long, husband. Mustn't miss the mine wagon."

"Have I ever?"

"True, Dearest, but seein' ya got company, there's always a first time."

"And that would be my last," Auckland snorted. "We'll be fine, Love."

Mila nodded and offered Sonart an easy grin. "Just leave yer plates where they be. I'll take care of 'em come mornin'. You'll be awright then, lad?" she asked, bending her neck forward to inspect Sonart's eyes.

"I'm in good hands," answered Sonart as he rose and gave her a firm hug. "The best actually."

Mila left the dimly lit room, taking her warmth with her. When the noise of her footfalls subsided, Auckland grabbed his cup and downed its full contents. He observed Sonart for a time in silence.

"Auckland?"

"Hooks and Dunge, boy, I don't know how to say it any other way so I'll give it to you straight. Words said can mislead, whoever utters them. If your father is connected to all this, he'll have sought a way to see you through the worst of it. But other voices—born of malice or desperation—can taint words and poison their meaning. Trust no one, you hear?"

Sonart flicked his chin up at his uncle. "Stars align, I swear."

"My brother was the bravest and wisest among dwarven, righteous, august, kingly, a considerate sibling, a staunch friend. But matters cloud and skew paths. Even the Elders overlook, misinterpret, or ignore at their peril. With unrivalled acumen, your father embraced these aberrations, meddled in great intrigues, he did. Made sacrilege against the Kusp, twisting the connotations of our ancient lore."

Sonart dipped his face towards his cup to hide his surprise.

"He frightened me," Auckland confessed, expunging a breath. "And I wilfully shut him out when he spoke of such things or acted upon them, but-"

Auckland paused as though chewing his next sentence. "Fore my ears completely deafen to the knell of danger, I recall him mentioning some puzzle. Said, not long after the Darkest One walks among us, a dwarven would emerge from the Dunge, unscathed. But the survivor would mark a 'start of sorrows and the end of morrows', as he put it. Tainted by the Darkest One, heralding an epoch of calamity."

Auckland sought Sonart's regard and studied his measure. "I ask you solemnly, and tell me true, boy, are you that one?"

"You think I am *that*?"

A blustery gust escaped Auckland's nostrils. "My stars eclipse in the matter. Troubled times, these are, worsening of late, but as I said, truths obscure. The opposite may hold true. But only your father would have known forsooth."

Auckland shook his head, which made his beard wag in the lantern light. "Nay, Sonart, my heart tells me you have a vital part to play. Perhaps you merely symbolize the dimming that precedes the drear. You are my blood, the only son of Farkshone, and to whatever end that may avail us, I place my fullest trust in all my brother intended."

A hint of doubt still cloaked Auckland's words. Sonart undressed it immediately. "Uncle, I'll not admit or deny any belief you may harbour. In truth, I've fallen victim to my own ignorance, and the oath I took... could place you and Mila at great risk."

Auckland hoisted his mug and stood, refilled it at the keg, and downed half. When he settled back in his chair, Sonart reached for his arm and squeezed it. "My goal *will* benefit our people, provided I don't speak with a loose tongue. I do not know how or why, but I promise you this: my father spoke of many mysterious things and half-shaven revelations—you said it yourself. His words bent the bough of prophesy writ, but held back before it snapped. You must— be at one with the Kusp, as earlier today. Do not stray. Promise our stars align in this."

Sonart's allusion to the most commonly repeated and pointless axiom of scripture worked.

"Words unto Deeds," Auckland replied dully, using the same ceremonial vernacular.

Then he rose and made for the door. As he reached it, he stopped and curved back. "When you first arrived, Sonart, I spoke truly when I said you lessened the weight. Trust in that."

"I trust everything you say, Uncle," Sonart replied, offering him the warmest smile he could muster. "Sleep well."

Auckland returned his grin, nodded briskly, and left the room. Sonart continued to drink in solitude. After pondering his plans for the next drear he retreated to his room and stretched out on the cot, falling asleep in seconds.

Later that dimming, in the lost hours immediately following mid-death, an unbidden vision came to Auckland's unconscious mind. In it, he travelled down ethereal tunnels, past opening gates, until he reached an aura of light.

It revealed the backlit silhouette of a sword.

19: Roles
Brooke

All the air left Brooke's throat as conversations hushed to silence. Val's eyes burgeoned at Targin's announcement but he said nothing, maintaining his icy scrutiny of the commander.

Brooke froze solid without it, except for his knees, which chose the moment to wobble.

The creaking branches continued in the upper canopy and Brooke thought he heard the flapping of feathers, though that might've been his own fluttering heart. *Replacement?*

Targin took a long breath and locked gazes with Brooke. "The Darkest One has tipped the scale, shoving us into jeopardy. Despite any misgivings you may harbour about my intent, I plan to stop that from happening. I've been accorded a pivotal role in determining the outcome of this cosmic dichotomy. As have you."

Apart from a sore neck, staring up at the Nightwolf, Brooke 'determined' he could no longer sit. Neither could he act the quiet spectator while the giant went on with outlandish disclosures like some daft mystic.

The commander bolted to his feet and squared his carriage to the warlord. He only wanted one question answered: why in eight points of fuck make him steward?

Targin raised a hand in a calming gesture before Brooke could baulk. "I must convince you of my claim. And my reason why you must also tread the pathless path."

Targin seized Brooke's wrists—and with them, his mind. He married the commander's thoughts to his own.

Brooke resisted the incursion until Targin's voice communed, '*Desist and be enlightened—by the bane lurking in our future.*'

With great reluctance, Brooke acquiesced.

Then, his inner eye bulged.

Voiceless despair seized Brooke as a glimpse of Targin's future played out. A firestorm of flying demons and dragons filled the sky—ignited it. The gentle lay of Areth's plains and forests turned into a battleground, blighted and burning—calamity beyond the commander's worst imaginings of Infern.

Freeborn armies spanned the horizon, succumbing before an unreal tempest. Men and women and children taken and desecrated into abominations or slaughtered by the thousands.

And then, the land itself heaved and tore, rent into chasms filled with lava as Areth's Gaia bled and began to die. Brooke could feel her anguish in his soul as if drawn and quartered himself. The harrowing devastation grew by orders of magnitude as countless worlds hammered apart, torn asunder. Stars exploded and vanished before a swathe of utter blackness engulfed all.

When Targin released him, Brooke doubled over and vomited. Cold sweat soaked him as he coughed, tapping the last of his strength to shirk the horrendous revelation. His spine trembled and he swallowed excessively, until a thick hand touched his shoulder. A cup of water was thrust before him.

Brooke wiped his mouth with his sleeve and accepted the vessel. After draining it, he staggered upright and gaped at Targin. "Gods be merciful, that—is too—*much*," he rasped between pants. "Pray, a false vision." He shook his head in disbelief. "Must—can't—be true, it's incomprehensible."

Targin inclined his head and pressed his lips together. "I too thought it apocryphal, the first time."

Brooke grimaced, fumbling for expression. "It's... obliviation." But even as the right word escaped his parched mouth, his gut assured him Targin hadn't conjured some spell to tether his mind. The Vein had exposed the truth: a vision of the Kusp's direst prophecy.

"I only revealed parts of my vision," Targin said solemnly, "to make you appreciate the doom of the astral plane. And Creation's full plight."

Brooke lifted his hands and rubbed his temple, trying to erase the nightmare from his mind, but he could not un-see it. "How did you *do* that?"

"To fight sorcery, one must glean the roots of its art—I didn't guess at how to dispatch a Sorgon," said Targin astride a chuckle. "Though my little sprite friends had a substantial hand in my wilderen tutelage, I must attribute that gift to one of my mentors, the Kazir wizard, Gjengaegungen, whom I mentioned, and the Orbical, Brapin. Perhaps you've heard of them, if only by reputation."

Brooke sucked in a lungful of air and slowly exhaled. Steadying his nerves, he dropped his hands and met Targin's regard. "I do recall the wizard, Gaegungen, and his acolyte—Laethan, I think him named." His heart rate slowed further. "They came to meet with Cele, some five star-cycles ago, but the king's retinues turned them away. We never exchanged words. As for the other, I've never met an Orbical."

"But he's met you." Targin stared off into the woods and sighed. "Gaegungen is also a Vein. The other two, whom I've never met, hail from other places. But both are male: one, a dwarven of Grendamaul and the other, an elven of—well, I'm not entirely sure where the dandy might come from— like as not some Arborian brothel for homosexual halfwits."

That drew a mix of sniggers from his band.

Brooke raised an eyebrow. "I take it you're not overly fond of elven, Targin."

"Let's just say I—no, not one bit," he amended in a flat tone.

"Regardless, our phalanx must conjoin ahead of the Endstorm, symbiont counterparts to oppose the Four Siphons."

"You speak of the Merger," Brooke ventured. "Of the Four—the penultimate chapter of the Kusp before the Starbond itself."

Targin's eyes narrowed. "If you've summited that conviction, let us dispense with dire tidings and get to my proper point."

His features softened, enough to lose some of their cutting edge. "I'd like to tell you not to fear, but you know better. What you do in the face of such fear will decide the fate of many."

Targin raked his fingers through his hair. "Trust me, Brooke, I've watched you for some time. Seen you demonstrate your mettle on the battlefield, your grit in court. The sprites, Gaegungen, and Brapin have cast their dice on you. And I wholeheartedly agree that you'll rise to meet this challenge. Lead my Wolves in a victory toast ere long. Before that time, you and I will meet again."

A loud silence ensued. The commander did not need any special power to see how awkward the situation had become. Wrayns exchanged dubious glances, shook their heads or gaped at their feet. A few studied Brooke or Targin, blank expressions on their faces.

Still shaken by Targin's apocalyptic foretelling, Brooke could only stare back.

Alghan cleared his throat. "My Lord, surely Val or Gnor would be better suited to lead us into the Night. His eyes flew to Brooke. "No offence, Commander, I mean no disrespect."

"None taken," Brooke supplied. "I couldn't agree with you more."

Alghan bowed slightly and shifted his attention to Targin. "Simple experience in the ways of the pack will profit—"

Targin spun on him. "Do not query my choice in this matter, Wrayn. If experience is simple as you say, educate him *simply*, so he gets some. My decision stands."

Alghan dipped his chin. "Words unto deeds."

Brooke began to protest but Targin quieted him with a brisk wave of his hand. "You'll learn my motives when the pack arrives safely within the walls of Serenthia—my father-in-law's keep."

Gnor's eyebrows dove down. "Then, we do not travel west to Cillinox? Or north to the sprite's domain as planned?"

"No. And there is no more *we*," Targin said. "You will away to the southeast. At dawn, ride with Brooke at your head." He turned to the commander. "Give your steed as much feed as he can stomach from our stores. He'll need it to keep up with the Warangs."

Targin looked down and inspected his arms and chest as if realizing his near nakedness for the first time. A grin spread across his face. "As for me, I'll need a commoner's garb and boots—can't very well enter a village in nothing but my skin." His hulking torso curved towards a passing scullion. "You there, pup."

The boy skidded to a halt, face flushed from running. "Aye, Milord?"

"Be a good lad and fetch my tunic and boots from my tent. Just toss them in a sack. I'll take them with me and dress when I arrive."

The boy bobbed his head and hastened away.

Targin's pupils sought Brooke. "Seems you and I must reverse roles for a time. I become the civilian and you, the savage."

Brooke cringed inwardly as the chief bellowed. This bargain sounded worse with every syllable. What had he gotten himself into with this crew?

"You won't ride with us, not even part of the way?" Brooke asked.

Targin moved his head from side to side. When he spoke again, his words lost their dry mirth and bite. "Forces muster and I must depart at once, ahead of our vanguard. A rook arrived yester morn. I've been summoned by another ally. We'll meet soon enough within the walls of the Strong Helm."

Targin's focus swivelled across the press of faces, all cast in stone, like monuments in a forested cemetery. Their granite expressions flickered in the orange firelight.

The Vein raised his voice above the hushed deliberations of those further back. "May the pathless path guide you—to the Purpose."

Two hundred voices cried in chorus, "To the Purpose!"

Clearly inspired by the Wrayns' uproar, the Warangs added their howls. A smirking Targin nodded when the young adjutant returned and handed him the sack.

As the din ebbed, the giant lowered the bag to the ground and touched Brooke's shoulder. "Concerning the sprites' anointment, time will reveal better than any words or visions of mine how significant you are. For the moment, I need you to make this leap of faith. I've already made mine."

Targin winked before lifting his arms wide towards the congregation. "Nightwolves, I take my leave."

Hefting the bag over his shoulder like a rucksack, and holding its drawstrings between clamped teeth, Targin sprang up the trunk of the closest tree. He scurried up its length with the quick efficiency of a wildcat. In two breaths the leaves of the lowest branches swallowed him.

Head tilted up, Brooke could only stare at the waving foliage. A few heartbeats later, a heavy *thrump thrump thrump* of monstrous wings sounded in the upper canopy. Then, that too diminished, the steady crack and fizz of the bonfire holding sway once more.

"Prone to theatrics, Chief's always been," a stout-faced Gnor said to the air.

Brooke reflected on the bizarre fool in King Cele's court as he met the Wrayn's eyes. "So I have seen, Gnor. So I have seen."

Above the Northern Forest, the blur of a giant avian shadow, cast by argent moonlight, streaked over the treetops less than fifty feet below. The shadow bore a rider.

Targin admired the sight's tranquillity even as he dwelt on his newest recruit and the heavy charge he placed at the conscript's feet. Could he trust a man extracted from his enemy's ranks? The sprites, the Orbical *and* the wizard thought so, but the Nightwolf found himself not so easily swayed— or painfully convinced.

It remained a wonder that he and Brooke had survived long enough to make it to their divined juncture. Undoubtedly, the next confluence would test the Vein even more, but the Merger had also been preordained in the Kusp. Targin should be more at ease, would've been, if not for the prophecy's skew that plagued him so. *The hyperdemon comes...*

With an effort, he dismissed its implications, keeping his mind focused on the journey ahead and the more immediate task at hand. He might glean an added clue from the old one. Then again, he might not. For certain, twas a meeting of hard truths the Nightwolf sorely did *not* relish.

Wraith-like, the avian dove into a narrow gap splitting the forest canopy. Wings aflutter, he sped between the tree trunks, into the dead of night. The warbird proved an enigma of the forest, flying faster than any charmed wind-sprint its rider might've mustered at need.

A few hours later, in the night's witching hour, bird and passenger arrived at the secret haven, just shy of the frontier village of Riverside.

Keeping to the greater swathe of moon shadows, Targin dismounted and led his avian steed into a hidden cavern, set back from a stable adjoining the yard of the village pub.

Inside the cave's wooden pen, he removed his effects from the raptor's saddlebags, including the sack containing the morrow's wardrobe. Next, he unfastened the saddle and tack, slid them both off the avian's back, and heaped them against one wall of the enclosure.

Targin saw to his mount's needs, laying down fresh hay and filling a feed trough and water basin. That done, he quenched his own thirst from a crude tap, sought the closest hay bed, and collapsed onto it.

It had proved a very long day. But his gut guaranteed the next would be longer.

Stephen Fenech

20: The Beginning of the End
Sonart

Gloom oozed down the mud-caked roads of Farkshone Village. It appeared deserted when Sonart stepped out of Auckland and Mila's front door, but he knew better. Adjusting the straps of his rucksack, he started forward.

The homely industrial feel of the village seemed as tangible as death, its mood equally hushed. Yet some distant sounds stirred—a few dwarven miners going out to catch the wagon to their designated mine shafts, their children trailing to see their fathers off.

Most of the able-bodied men would already be toiling in the mines about now, alongside a few unable ones: the very old or invalid.

By the wider footprints in the mud, several Kworn had passed recently. A drear's rain would have erased anything before that.

Sonart bent an ear to the wind's glean, pitch and sigh. At a very early age, forecasting its blow accurately became second nature and could mean the difference between survival and the deepest sleep. The wind behaved but something else carried on the breeze. To his right, voices: women and children.

He trod in their direction.

Around the corner, dwarven younglings milled about the rutted tracks, chasing one another and throwing stones.

"Just passing through," Sonart hailed. They answered with a shower of pebbles, two shying just past his forehead.

When he bluffed a charge, they took flight and giggled as they scattered. Mothers interceded. As they herded their children away, a few glanced over their shoulders at Sonart. The women's frowns bespoke puzzlement and anxiety.

He mirrored their sentiment, disturbed by the appearance of their children. Eyes sunken, faces gaunt and ashen from malnutrition, they looked emaciated—husks of the vitality Sonart remembered before his abduction.

Aye, the children played, but what children did not? Mila and Auckland had not exaggerated one bit. Some of the younglings resembled skin-on-bones stick figures with swollen bellies, giving them a monstrous complexion. Too soon for those who barely glimpsed the Cradle's harsh reality.

Cursing inwardly, Sonart walked on, his path slanting upwards. The battering of previous razor storms carved gullies and fissures across the sloped road. Homes to either side of the artery showed greater signs of weathering than the ones further below. Cracks and divots pockmarked every dwelling and the wooden fences appeared flimsy, one swift kick from toppling.

Further ahead, a sight stopped the dwarven in his tracks. An entire block of the village had been reduced to charred rubble, likely razed by one of the Siphon's dragons. Higher up the hill, the sorry vista only got worse, revealing the full expanse of Farkshone below.

Hundreds of stone cottages lay in tatters and ruin, swathes of the village reduced to hillocks of debris. Roads abruptly ended in some massive crater or landslide, engulfing five to ten dwellings at a time. Fire and smoke consumed smaller patches to complete the scene of devastation.

Sonart swallowed, recalling Auckland's words: *Farkshone Village fared better than most.* He clenched. The destruction here jammed the plateau on which the village sat.

But in the main square, visible from this lofty height, the ironock stockade still rose unmolested. The tower ignited columns of inky smoke, spiralling up until they blended with the grey ceiling of clouds, thousands of feet above the Steppe.

Judging by the amount of drearlight present, the time drew close to mid-drear. He adjusted his pack straps again and quickened his pace.

Past the next shambled crossroads, the path fell away to the left on a twisted downward slope. It wound its way between crevices and over a crumbling stone rampart that traversed a shallow creek.

After a few turns through a maze of crashed boulders, the path abruptly ended and his destination hove into view. The beaten dwelling that had been his childhood home stood alone and long-deserted, ever since Auckland and Mila had taken him under their wing.

Coarse brush engulfed the structure from pediment to sagging rooftop. The building appeared half-collapsed, folded under a wall of creepers and bracken, seeking to strangle and penetrate it. The limbs beneath the green foliage resembled claws dragging the derelict into the ground.

With a heavy breath, Sonart reached behind and unsheathed a serrated knife from a side-harness. Auckland had given it to him for this very purpose.

Dagger in hand, Sonart slashed and sawed the bracken, cutting a path into the house.

The act served as his first statement.

Much to Sonart's surprise, the inside had survived intact. He used the blade to pull down cobwebs, coiling them about its metal flat. The webs had long-veiled the drab walls and chattel. A quick inspection revealed no eight-legged masters. Abandoned by their weavers, the strands had collected a thick coat of dust from countless razor storms.

After Sonart had cleared the webs, he tasked himself with restoring the domicile, if only perchance to uncover some clue behind the riddles. But in so doing would Deathwrought not glean what he might learn? *Mine eyes are your eyes.*

Fuck it.

Doubt and denial cast deeper shadows over Sonart's efforts, but it would avail him nothing to let either steer him.

So, after he dropped his pack to the floor, he worked perfunctorily.

Next came the windows: they presented the greatest trouble with all the accumulated water and mud from so many storms. Dirt, inches thick in some places, caked the glass. Again, with the short blade, he managed to pry the more stubborn clumps away. They dropped to the floor with a dull thud.

Sonart removed a bundle of rags, soap, simple tools, and utensils. He filled a bucket with water from the well, thankfully full, and by its smell, still potable.

The cottage looked like a tomb when he first entered it, dust sprawling everywhere, but roughly three turns of the dial past mid-drear his efforts began to tell, and the place appeared semi-habitable. His washing and scrubbing went on for the better part of two more turns before exhaustion and the waning drear bade him rest for a time.

When darkness descended, Sonart struck an oil lamp Mila had given him. Setting it alight with scratch and flint, he resumed his work into the dimming.

Satisfied and empowered by his excellent progress, Sonart stopped to address his stomach's protests. He removed all the rations from his pack and laid them out on the table—enough for two, perhaps three drears.

Sonart reached for a loaf of bread and tore off a piece. Sitting himself down on an available chair, he ate in solitude while the waving flame of the lamp made his shadow dance against the stone wall beside him.

Hunger sated, Sonart took out a bedroll—another of Mila's insistences— and made ready for bed. He lay on his back, folded his arms behind his head, and stared up at the dark ceiling. His well-honed ears waited for the sound of rodent activity, but only a loud silence filled them. This dimming, even the rats seemed at peace.

Boom-boom, Boom-boom, Boom-boom, Boom-boom

With a start Sonart awoke, eyelids fluttering open to the distant resonance of—doom-drums. In the darkened common room of his father's home, he lay still. But the tocsins sounded all the same. Perhaps the Kworn had been instructed to pound the skins again, as they had done in the past to mark the mid-death and mid-drear turn of the dial. Perhaps not… *Boom, boom*

As the last faint echoes of the drums hushed to silence, another closer sound arose out of the gloom. Sonart flinched and sat up. Several unsteady footsteps approached the cottage.

Sonart sprang to his feet, Auckland's dagger in hand. He crept to the closest window and peered out.

Honed by his time in the Dunge, Sonart's vision had sharpened to see in near pitch-black. Under cover of the dimming, several dwarven silhouettes trudged languidly past, mere feet beyond the building.

But—were they truly? Their unsteady gait cast a doubt, until a chorus of shrill cries rang out from their midst.

Afflicted Ones.

Up close their shrieks sounded more harrowing, like the primal wailing of mortally sick children.

Sonart tiptoed back to the kitchen table and popped the cork off the vial of potion Mila had given him. She promised it would keep him safe from their plague. He tipped back a swallow and reseated the vial's stopper.

The Afflicted's uneven steps denoted a mindless direction. Above their warble, hollow thuds sounded as they collided with the cottage walls and with each other. Every impact beat against Sonart's heart. So hapless the plight of this forsaken lot, it stung him with pity.

Mercifully, they moved on, their haunting mewls diminishing. A while later, the gnawing effect on Sonart's soul ebbed. He gave some thanks for the darkness, which kept the extent of their malady, hidden.

'*Go damn, and be damned*,' a voice chimed in his head.

Hell-fuck-fire! The seizure set upon him with no warning. He would soon lose his will, and with it, his mind. How long before he surrendered both completely? And what would happen then?

Sonart knew the answer to that question, but loathed to admit the true horror of it: he would become an agent of evil.

Dawn eased Sonart's apprehension some, but his long night had been a silent battle against an unseen foe. He'd spent the entire dimming trying to convince himself that he remained in control. But the intrusions came and went as though testing the *water*. There came that word again.

With a bitter sigh, Sonart threw back his bedding and rose. He dragged his feet to the window and looked outside. Stars, twas past mid-drear. He needed to get a feel for the greater lay before he lost its light. Once he determined to go, Sonart hoisted his empty rucksack and left, making for Farkshone's central square.

At the arcade, vendors in ramshackle kiosks busied themselves packing up their goods, readying to leave their stands. Sonart quickened his pace. If memory served, this was the best time to trade, for the merchants would be apt to make a brisk sale and get indoors before dimming blanketed the Cradle.

The first seller Sonart passed scowled as he drew up, obviously wanting no further dealings. The second had nothing he needed. At the third vendor's stall, the dwarven thought he might quell both dilemmas.

"You there," Sonart called, "If your prices ring fair, I may be able to relieve you of a few wares."

When the merchant looked up, he squinted his eyes and pressed his lips flat. "Who are you?"

The icy reply made Sonart cringe inwardly, but he set his jaw. "My name matters not. I need food, which you have. You need coin, which I have. But if you prefer conflict over commerce, I can accommodate you."

The merchant raised his hand. "Nay, stay your wrath, stranger. You present a new face to me is all and Proclaimers ever seek to usurp simple men of merchantry. I just wanted to measure who I was dealing with before I trade. It can be dangerous for you too—to tread freely when shortages exist—of able-bodied dwarven in the mines. Dealing with you could invite notice and add trouble to my already crippled state."

The vendor shot Sonart a sideways glance. "But, if you got the coin as you say, I'll run that risk."

Sonart produced a small oilcloth purse and jingled it. The coins belonged to him, earned before his arrest and kept safely by Auckland. The money would keep him in good stead for some time.

The rest of his barter with the aged man went amicably enough. Sonart pointed to what he needed. The vendor filled his order and tallied it.

Sonart handed him the promised money before depositing the goods in his empty sack.

About to take his leave, the merchant stopped Sonart with a subtle hand gesture. "Have a care, Redbeard. Think of it as a bit of free advice from an old rock—for being such a good customer. Those Proclaimers—a churlish lot and they spy at all turns of the dial. You best be pretending to have some sort of limp as you walk away from here—preventing you from the mines."

His eyes darted left and right before settling on Sonart. "Chances favour they scout us now and may follow where you go. Trust me, they're trouble you don't want to know—not in these times."

"I don't fear them, or their Kusp," Sonart said in an even tone.

"What do you mean?" the vendor asked, his caution written in his furrowed brows.

"We attend the same master."

The merchant inhaled fiercely, orbs widening.

"Allay your fears old man, I am no Proclaimer. But let's say, I am unique and tramp with... special allowances. Tis they who'll fear me."

The shopkeep swallowed, nodded, and said no more.

Sonart strode back to the cottage, in better spirits with the replenished rations stuffed neatly in his pack. His dealings with the merchant counted as his second statement.

Not wanting to get ahead of himself, Sonart kept his head low all the same. And avoided any passer-by he encountered. As he rounded the last cleft to his hermitage, the grey masses overhead deepened in shade as evening encroached.

Once inside, Sonart busied himself stocking shelves.

A sharp rap at the door startled him.

His breath caught.

The knocking became more adamant. Could it be the Proclaimers as the old merchant had warned? Or worse?

A gruff voice hailed him. "No use hiding. Open up or I'll break the fucking door down. You—shortly after."

Dagger in hand, Sonart approached the entrance.

"What do you want?" he asked guardedly.

"Open first," the gruff voice insisted. "I have to make sure it's you and not some impostor, or Proclaiming cunt."

"Who am I supposed to be?"

"Currently, an annoying door. Don't toy with me, Sonart of Farkshone, or stars burn me, I'll carve you a new asshole with this door I'm about to smash down. Then you can be whoever you like. There'll be Afflicted passing these parts shortly, and I prefer to keep my guts inside my skin."

Although disarmed by the dwarven's hostility, he spoke with earnestness.

Sonart lowered the dagger and unlatched the bolt.

It swung outward forcefully and a scowling dwarven stomped in before Sonart could protest. The darkness made the intruder's countenance sinister, but the tight-faced dwarven kept his distance as he sized Sonart up.

"What?" the stranger complained. "You don't recognize me?"

Sonart shook his head. Truthfully, he did not. This dwarven, black of beard and dark of face, looked more or less the same age as himself but weathered beyond his years a further ten star-cycles. He comported himself with the terseness and shrewd defiance of an old man, long-set in his ways.

The blackbeard's face crumpled into a glower and he clicked his tongue. "You cannot shirk your duty any longer."

"Duty?" Sonart unhinged his jaw and parted his lips. He must have looked as bewildered as he felt, for the stranger's face reddened, his moustache quivering.

"The *mines*, knave, a hundred of the Big Bastard's curses on you. Like the rest of us, you're dutybound to our brethren toiling in the Cradle's sour belly. Thousands more will take the deepest sleep, while you hide in a rut of self-pity, skulking under the skirts of the past."

Sonart's ears went hot. "Proclaimer!"

The blackbeard twisted his face into an uncomfortable knot. "Hooks and Dunge, if I served as one of those curs, I would proclaim you an idiot! I call the Darkest One a bastard and you put me in the same privy as the sycophant worms that suck his cock?" He threw his hands up. "Guess I am a Proclaimer. And you—are an idiot."

Sonart hid his relief under a guise of umbrage. "Enough insults. I don't know who you are, trespasser—yet you know my name. Give me yours and, by the stars, how you've come by mine and my whereabouts."

The dwarven's face flushed a shade of crimson Sonart had not thought possible. It seemed to preface a detonation. Indeed, the blackbeard let out a litany of rude noises, half-consonants and whole curses—enough to make a demon lord blush and duck for cover.

Rage and frustration clearly stifled, the firebrand dwarven let out a bellow's worth of heated air and answered in a simmering tone. "All right, Thick-one. I am Seolad of Rusic, stars burn you, the only other dwarven to witness and survive the Incident. Now, balls of a Kworn, do you recall? Or shall I mine it out of your Dunge-tainted skull?"

"Seolad—you say?" Sonart pondered. "I remember the name—aye, and the belligerence. And how could I forget that dimming?" He narrowed his eyes. "But you expect me to remember your face—even without your permanent glower? Convince me you are who you say? And that your little diatribe about the mines isn't some ruse to gain my trust. How can I be sure that you do not hearken to the Kusp's Proclaimers?"

"Baugh," Seolad spat. "Had I been one of those gutless fiends, the mines would be the least of your worries—you'd be dead by now. The turncapes are craven, sold their souls to Deathwrought, they have."

He arched an eyebrow and cleared his throat. "But tis true: you do dally and need to get moving to the mines. You'll need that, cover."

The way Seolad said *cover* meant more, stretched past the word itself. "We'll require all that ironock to be at 'one with the sodding Kusp.' Perilous times have come, filled with false prophets, saviours, pariahs, Afflicted, Proclaimers, His Four lickspittles and, stars lantern my ass through the Void of Obliteration, mustn't forget the big malignant boil himself."

Seolad shot Sonart a sideways glance and pointed to his dagger. "Nice trinket that, but ironock needs be forged into bigger things, broadswords, *shields*—you would know a bit about that too, I reckon."

He paused and studied Sonart's measure. "By the look of you, wager you need some forging too—reforging, truth is. That said, the dwarven people need a monger, not a fucking mummer."

Sonart started. There it was again. Seolad's hard inflexions were not lost on him: the blackbeard veiled his meaning with his words. Hoping to deliver a subtler, all-the-more vital message that could not be said aloud.

Sonart gleaned the secret missive, but not its full import. And he'd be a fool not to assemble the cautioned truth therein. He bit his lip and listened with more than his ears.

Seolad kept talking, and yet his pupils said something entirely different— for Sonart's safety, or his own? Like as not, both.

And Sonart must play along.

The blackbeard made a prodding gesture with his index finger. "Maybe we should see which one you are. See what kind of blood flows in your veins."

Veins—? ——!

Something triggered inside Sonart. He flinched involuntarily. Then shuddered harder.

'*Suffer words of sacrilege for your vision, against my possession pro——CLAIM!*'

An evil wave crashed over Sonart's mind and smothered it. All at once, he lost control. Could only witness the black power coursing through his blood, and out from hexed orbs. The inner fire of his will fled before an avalanche of dark purpose.

Dagger in hand, he lunged at Seolad.

The blackbeard dodged the attack easily, drawing his sword as he sidestepped Sonart's assault.

With a backhand thrust, Seolad swung his blade.

It arced down and across Sonart's nape as he surged past.

The stroke should have clove him. But it only glanced off the possessed dwarven, as though he'd been hewn of solid ironock.

The impact staggered Seolad too: an explosive recoil that flung the dwarven to the far wall, ripped the blade from his grasp, and into the hands of an indentured Sonart.

But Seolad demonstrated an uncanny quickness as he rebounded with the efficiency of a cornered predator. Ebony shanks and beard askew, he coiled on the balls of his feet and dove through the open doorway just as Sonart fired the sword. End over end, it flew like a throwing axe.

By nary a foot, the blade missed his intended target, ironock biting into the wooden window sill beyond.

There, it lodged and quivered.

Sonart's trapped voice wanted to rejoice at the crusty dwarven's escape, but a wave of vehemence quashed his elation. The Darkest One howled frustration through Sonart's mouth. "Mine Eyes—are Your Eyes!"

The possession gushing within Sonart abruptly guttered like a candle flame snuffed by a powerful squall.

Shame thickened the hollowed-out dwarven. He wanted to shed a million tears, but his emotions clenched so tight, he could not even dampen his ducts to form a single bead. Immured, he tried to grasp some semblance of normalcy and cohesion.

Working the rigid muscles of his arms and neck, Sonart staggered to the door and closed it with the celerity of a mindless thing.

He was losing control, his fits worsening.

After a long disconsolate numbness, Sonart steeled his courage and with it, a possible solution surfaced: the Elders. Quarrelsome or not, they were all well-versed in the ancient lore of the Kusp. But with Proclaimers afoot, would they deign to speak with him? Had he become one of the turncapes?

"Nonsense," he reprimanded aloud.

Still, the stories might fly. That meddlesome Seolad could bring others. But even if the blackbeard did report him, fear might serve as Sonart's ally— and keep them away.

Least for a time.

Sonart's attention stumbled back towards the sword he'd forced Seolad to abandon. The hilt still swayed slowly in his general direction as if trying to track him. It reminded him of another foil.

When the weapon finally stopped, its pommel pointed towards his chest like an accusation.

Or an invitation.

21: Steward
Brooke

Brooke awoke to sunbeams filtering through the opening in his tent. His eyes flitted outside to the mist-shrouded trees crowding the forest tract. The rays made the underbrush glisten with filaments of gold that created shifting steps of light and shadow.

He shivered in the early morning dampness, which had managed to seep under the covers of his bedroll during the night's loneliest hours.

Clammy, sore, and still exhausted from his exertions the previous day, Brooke needed a few moments to gather his thoughts. And wrap his mind around the bizarre charge handed to him by the chief of the Nightwolves. Such drastic change in such a short period—had it been a dream? Was he still dreaming?

Not only had Brooke changed sides, to be forever branded a turncape by his former regime, he had vaulted to the steward's office of the same outlaws he'd sworn to rout. A touch of Vamsah-wrought irony to say the least. He sat up. Stars eclipse, what insanity compelled him to this precarious juncture.

Then in a rush, it came back to him. Love. Devotion to his family and their survival—a continuance no longer possible within Pathguard's city walls. He lamented leaving his family behind, but also his troops and fellow officers. Their fates were now tethered to the downward spiral of their mad king and his attainted kingdom.

Brooke reflected on Targin's last instructions *...make this leap of faith ...time will reveal better than any words or visions of mine how important you are.* What did he mean?

Steam hissed, wolves barked, and metal clanged. The overture silenced the commander's contemplations. He ducked his head out of the canvas. Several Wrayns busied themselves striking tents, piling pegs, and rolling up groundsheets, while many wolves sauntered past.

Most of the cookfires had been put out, but one still sang, its flames licking a jumble of half-blackened sticks nested in a bed of ochre coals. Smoke rose in an undulating column between the tree trunks, creating havoc with the sunlight. The effect made Brooke think of the impending war Targin had mentioned—and the mayhem it promised to unleash.

"Ho there, Commander! Still on all fours, I see."

Brooke's gaze moved alongside the front of his tent to the tall Nightwolf he met the night before.

The commander frowned. "Alghan? Did I get it right?"

The corners of the tall man's mouth curved up as he approached. "Stars align, aye. Breakfast been laid out for you at the table by the main fire. When you are ready, we make for the Strong Helm."

Alghan seemed to sense Brooke's puzzlement. "Serenthia, the Hidden Kingdom—um—where Targin went," he laughed. "You needn't worry. No one expects you to take the reins at once. Besides, every Nightwolf knows the way home. We'll escort you and, along the way, teach you whatever you wish to learn until you feel comfortable enough to fill Targin's boots."

Brooke smiled wanly, relieved that he could ease into his new role. He climbed to his feet. "I'm not sure I'll ever find that comfort, but thank you, Alghan. I'll likely seek your counsel a great deal in the days ahead."

"Then, I am at your service," Alghan said with an easy bow. He sighed. "Right then. We'll away after you break your fast."

Stretching stiff muscles, Brooke stepped into a wide ribbon of orange light. It made him pause and relax as it warmed him. He surveyed the camp and the surrounding area: a bright and pristine valley with a shallow creek running through it. Wildflowers adorned the forest floor, spearing the thick bed of fermented leaves from seasons past. They gave off a pungent but pleasant arboreal scent.

The Northern Forest appeared untouched by the Nightwolves' presence. Unlike the scourge that marred the blackened countryside near Pathguard, this tract seemed a holy refuge from the tumultuous world beyond.

Brooke filled his lungs, letting the refreshing air revive his mind with renewed purpose. Yes, he had stepped into a larger world the moment he accepted Targin's charge, reawakening as a truly free man.

The commander donned his outer garments and fastened his weapons before making his way to the fire. As he passed the Wrayns, busy with their decamping preparations, they greeted him with gruff courtesies, curt bows, waves, and grins. Twas as though he'd been among them for years.

Brooke found a covered metal pan waiting for him on the makeshift wooden table. A fork and knife sat atop.

He seated himself, took both utensils in one hand, and uncovered the lid, amazed to find a hearty assortment of toasted bread, fried eggs, potatoes, and bacon steaming before him.

A young cheery-faced boy with dimples and short-cropped dark hair strode up. He gestured to the kettle in his hand. "Kofei?"

Brooke softened his eyes. "Aye, please." His charge had definitely started on the right foot. "And you are?"

"Gnolin," the lad replied as he tipped the kettle's spout into the cup beside Brooke's plate. Steaming black liquid poured in a steady cascade, suffusing the forest air with a welcome aroma. "Gramps said he met you last night. I'm training to be a full-mark Wrayn. All apprentices are assigned camp duties, including cooking for the band. That's why I was asleep when you arrived and didn't meet you."

"How many star-cycles have you, Gnolin?"

"My first star shone near fourteen years ago—shy two months. All pups train back at Serenthia until they reach their twelfth year. After that, they move with the band and look after camp, including the young Warangs who've also come of age—that's my favourite duty. I love all animals, but most especially wolves."

Brooke sipped the kofei and reached for his plate, listening as the boy carried on. "The new Warangs guard the base camp against any intruders. When they grow up, they accompany the Wrayns on their missions. Till then, they patrol and keep us informed. I haven't mastered communion with them—I'm not as good as Weet. But he's convinced I'm close," Gnolin said proudly. "In a couple of years, I'll be a Nightwolf proper, like my pops, Gnail, and his sire—my Gramps, Gnor."

"I've no doubt you will," Brooke said amicably. "We are well met, Gnolin, for you've already taught me something important about your customs. Sure to require more instruction, can I look forward to your continued tutelage?"

"Absolutely." The boy beamed and nodded. "Weet will be so envious."

"Who's Weet?" Brooke asked.

"Oh, my pup-brother—not blood, mind you. Weet's an orphan but partly of the true wolf bloodline. He can already commune. We're the same age, shy a moon-cycle—best friends. Gramps took him in after he found him, eight years back." He shrugged his shoulders. "When I set out from Serenthia with the Wolves, so did he."

Brooke smiled. "I see." He stuffed a piece of bacon in his mouth, took a bite of toast, and began cutting up one of the eggs. "Maybe the pair of you will assist me—in learning your ways," he said between mouthfuls.

A shadow crept over Gnolin's features. "I could ask but he's—" the boy hesitated, "timid—with everyone except me. But I'll ask," he finished.

"In any case, I'd like you to squire for me if you'll suffer the task."

Gnolin's face shone. "Stars align, Commander, aye."

"Good. Stay close as we ride to the Hidden Kingdom."

The boy bobbed his head emphatically before taking his leave. Brooke watched him go, thinking about his own two sons. As he finished his breakfast, he also reflected on the countless misconceptions Pathguard held as Kusp concerning this band. 'Savages,' Cele had branded them. Brooke allowed a smirk to stretch across his face. What would the despot do when he learned exactly who had taken charge of them?

By the time Brooke drained his cup, the Warangs had formed up, waiting patiently as Wrayns adjusted their saddles and mounted their backs.

Alghan stood among them, an apologetic grin on his face, one hand clasping the bridle of Brooke's horse behind him.

The commander swallowed as he approached, certain some perfunctory address in order before they mobilized. He took Maxan's reins from Alghan and led his horse back.

"Nightwolves," he hailed. "I do not feign to know why your leader placed such a formidable charge before me, nor do I presume to guide your pathless path. You know the way a far cry better than me. You deserve stronger leadership than a surrogate can provide."

Not a one agreed or disagreed. Brooke may as well have been addressing the trees. "I can only strive to justify Targin's choice in your eyes. I swear this on the lives of my family, whose plight I consider inextricably connected to yours. My coven with them brought us together. Ergo, I extend that vow unto you."

A nicker from his horse and a few chuffs and snorts from the Warangs answered him. *So far so good.* "You have my sword, and my oath—that I will stick to the Purpose."

"To the Purpose!" two hundred voices shouted back. Then, a din of baying Warangs. Maxan let out a sharp whinny.

Grateful for their endorsement, or rather, the absence of gainsay, Brooke mounted his loyal horse. With a touch of heel, the commander nudged him forward. Maxan fell into stride with the ranks of the giant canines and their black-garbed riders. They formed a train as they filed out of the shallow valley, heads turned towards Serenthia.

The company moved at a steady pace, maintaining a relatively narrow column three abreast. A few of the riderless Warangs shot away in pairs, fanning out to scout the flanks of the main pack. Other Warangs stayed back to patrol the rear.

The outriding canines could then give the main host warning of possible threats, travelling in twos in case one of them got killed before they communed an alert.

Seemed a callous but efficient system that had proven itself in combat and surveillance situations, like the antennae of an insect.

Brooke learned much and more, discussing at length the ways of the Wolves with young Gnolin, who rode a fledgling Warang beside Maxan. A limitless repository of knowledge, the pup filled Brooke's first day with endless tales and enlightenment.

Gnolin's father, and Gnor's son, Gnail, had perished in one of the Nightwolves' campaigns against the Kingdom of Weybanan. Beset by dark elven and a host of hobgoblins. His father had taken a poisonous arrow—one intended for Targin.

The Nightwolf Chief managed to get Gnolin's father to safety, but the poison had penetrated too quickly and too deep. Before he took the deepest sleep, Gnail bequeathed that Targin ensure his son followed the pathless path, so Gnolin could take his father's place.

The pup admitted he'd never really known his father, but resolute Gnor sought to instil his lost son's ideals upon his grandson. Gnor had succeeded, but Brooke sensed Gnolin's pride tempered by sorrow and regret over the circumstances of his career path.

The boy's upbringing must've been hard, living under the shadow of a dead father while trying to live up to the expectations of a bereaved grandfather.

"After burying my Da," Gnolin said, "Targin flew his hawkrike in pursuit of the hobgoblins who took my father's life, and the dark elven who commanded them. Chief caught up with them close to the borders of their northern realm. And slew the whole company—with Fang."

"His sprite-wrought blade," Brooke supplied.

Before Gnolin could answer, his Warang twisted his neck, bright green eyes looking up at his young master.

Returning the wolf's smile, Gnolin leaned forward and scratched the canine's furry crown behind his raised ears. The Warang whimpered contentedly as the lad explained, "A few of the Wrayns, Targin included, say it's a sprite weapon used in the Dragon Wars. But who really forged it, no one knows."

When his wolf faced forward again, Gnolin shifted his gaze back to Brooke. "Gramps said, Targin finished the lot of them—twenty in all. As a warning to the dark elven, he mounted their heads on wooden spikes and set them in a row to face the gates of their forest lairs."

"That Fang seems a formidable blade," Brooke said. "He dispatched a Sorgon with it. I've not seen its like anywhere across the Main."

"You wouldn't," the boy said. "It's the only one known to have survived the War of the Elementals. But truth be told, tales of its origin conflict. I think Targin's father gave it to him when he got to my age. Though it was way too big for him, then. Gramps told me the sword had been used to kill dragons—could even repel their fire. I've never seen it in action," Gnolin confessed with a quick chuckle. "Cept when the Chief cleans or sharpens it."

Brooke's cheekbones rose, quite taken with the lad. Gnolin gestured here and there, tireless in his regale, displaying a courage, humility, and wisdom well beyond his years. Death and loss in his life seemed to have strengthened his character, not diminished it.

Gnolin went on to describe in great detail the stories of many different Warangs and Wrayns, some of whom had taken the deepest sleep and some who still ran with the pack.

"Bor and Ethor, they are named," Gnolin chattered on, "large for Warangs, though not as big as Yerik—the chief of the Warangs. Oh, here they come now!"

Gnolin pointed to three riderless wolves as they raced past, tearing up the underbrush. "The wolf pups became orphaned after their mother was killed in a campaign. Liina, another she-wolf saved them and became their surrogate mother, nursing them as her own. Now that she's getting on in years, they ward her tirelessly, fiercely. You'll never see her without one or the other at her side. Most times, like just now, both. Liina is precious to them."

Gnolin spoke of the Warangs with reverence and at great length about their characters and laughable nuances. He observed everything about them, it seemed.

Of the Wrayns, the astute boy talked up a storm about Jaak and his wry sense of humour. "Always quick with a jest, Jaak is, no matter the situation. He cusses a lot—even for a Nightwolf. He's missing an eye, but that's his only injury. Gramps swears he's the product of pure experience.

"There's Onis, who's amazing at tending the worst injuries—had some training as an alchlemage before he joined the band. Spifer you've met, but, stars, you should see his apprentice. Char worships the ground Spifer walks on, when his master's sober that is," Gnolin said over a giggle. "Oh, and Bhom is a barrel of laughs."

"Bhom *is* a barrel," Brooke chided. Gnolin's mirth joined his.

"What about Val?" the commander asked.

Gnolin's smile straightened. His jollity seemed to fade as he ran his tongue over his teeth. "Val's powerful but, always so serious. He's been through much the same as Jaak, but from what Gramps said, it was hard and painful. He's an outrider, keeps to himself almost as much as Weet. Nobody except the Chief ever jokes with Val. 'Humour's wasted on him,' Jaak told me once."

Gnolin took a deep breath and shifted the wolf's reins to his other hand. "Lonus is the one you need to watch out for: he's one of the fiercest warriors here, and means well, but always plays a true-blood card whenever a debate arises among the wolves."

"I take it many debates arise among the wolves," Brooke said.

Gnolin nodded. "Except for Targin, Lonus regards any non-true Wrayns as mongrels but he's loath to trust Val for other reasons—they have a history. So, Lonus won't take orders from him when he's in command. Gramps says there's never been any love between them. That's why Targin keeps them separated when he's around. But when he's not—"

The boy blushed red and looked away, clearly uncomfortable. Brooke changed the subject. "I hear Targin is betrothed. What is she like?"

Gnolin brightened and opened his mouth to elaborate. A guttural harrumph stopped him. "I can answer that, Commander."

Brooke spun and faced a Wrayn of medium build with sly angular features, yet his mischievous grin seemed at odds with his large earnest eyes. At a glance, he could pass as a younger, scarless brother to Spifer.

"Greetings by the way. I'm Char," he declared in a throaty voice.

Despite Char's discourtesy, interrupting the pup, Brooke gave the Nightwolf his eyes. "And to you, Char... So?"

Char licked his lips, obviously relishing the subject. "Targin's woman is worthy a Vein of Fire—because she is fire, Tasmin is—aye, a pretty one. If beauty could be called fierce, that woman embodies it. Perfect really, in a blazing, sultry, angry yet innocent and thoughtful way."

"Stars, that's some comparison," Brooke said. "Do you speak of a woman, or take note of one of Spifer's explosions?"

"Not much difference," Char laughed.

Brooke's interest piqued even more. "How so?"

"I know I want to pitch a tent with the sturdiest pole whenever she passes my way."

"Maybe that's why she never passes your way," Jaak called from behind. His comment caused raucous outbursts from everyone within earshot.

"Don't doubt it," Char ceded gruffly. "Nay, Commander, she's that beautiful—enough to give a eunuch a stiff one!"

This time they all broke into hysterics at the crude image, including Brooke, who couldn't help but surrender a few chuckles. The banter continued back and forth and before long dusk had descended. At length, the company halted under Alghan's direction and made camp. Fires were lit, and patrols exchanged, rosters coming and going around the main encampment.

His chores done, Gnolin kept company with the boy he named Weet. Gnolin's peer looked of the same height as the pup but with a much darker complexion. If Brooke had to guess, Weet bore a southerner's features, with black hair, onyx eyes, full lips and thick brows, perhaps a fishmonger's son hailing from Seawatch or the Pebblereach Islands.

Brooke relaxed his posture as he studied them. Arms gesticulating, an animated Gnolin entertained Weet, telling him some comedic account, while his stoic companion listened attentively but without expression. Of relatively the same age, half the average of those gathered, the two appeared inseparable.

At various stages of the second night, several faces, new and old came to keep company with their new steward. Brooke engaged all of them. As the night wore on, he noticed that since Targin's departure, he had not seen hide or hair of Val anywhere.

After they had supped, Brooke whispered to Alghan, who had not left his side the entire evening. "I am told Val led your band in Targin's absence before I came."

Alghan let out a breath and poked the fire with a stick. "You could call it that. Val has the might and stealth to match the years he spent with the band, but he carries a wound so deep and so guarded, many see him as a liability in the impending storm. A few have sought to penetrate the shroud of his mind only to meet a redoubt of scorn, if not hostility."

The tall Nightwolf placed a hand on Brooke's shoulder. "Do not fear him though. He carries a grudge but does so quietly—unless you challenge his introversion. When certain moral issues arise, he's but piss and wind. As a warrior, he can organize the band well enough, but to truly lead I fear he's too rash and extreme—prone to vehemence when others cannot match him. In his case, better to let the sleeping wolf lie. Eclipsed by all the stars, that outlier is."

Brooke grimaced and drained the last of his spritewater. "Then I came along and supplanted him." He exhaled wearily. "If I'm to lead this band as Targin intends, I must attempt to gain Val's confidence."

"Confidence!" Alghan sputter-coughed. "I'd agree if you spoke about a rational man. Val is not a rational man. Continue to address the band in general audience. He'll follow your orders—if you do not give them directly to him. Ask any Wrayn how you'd fare trying direct reason with Val. Stars, the two mix like ice and fire."

Brooke rubbed the back of his neck. "Will he follow my decisions, when they really count?"

Alghan pondered the question for a moment. "Val will follow the Code. Then he'll decide if your stewardship weds to it."

"I see." Brooke sighed, disheartened by Alghan's reply, but he didn't become commander of Pathguard's main garrison by neglecting the human factor. He resolved that the bookish Nightwolf was wrong. Whatever demons possessed Val, Brooke would confront—and deal with them.

"Alghan," Brooke ventured, "Targin said you would tell me more of this Code. Explain it to me, if it pleases."

The Nightwolf grinned and looked down at the cup of mead nestled in his lap. "Stars, where do I begin?"

22: Shayla
Sonart

As dawn's light filtered through the windows, the menacing incident of the prior dimming faded. Sonart dwelt on Seolad's words and the unvoiced truth they implied. He repeated the watchwords like a mantra.

The word *Vein* resonated the loudest, invoking many possibilities and associations. It was the key, but how the term connected to him remained a mystery, as did the rest of the blackbeard's veiled message. The name had given Sonart a jolt, though more so, his possessor.

Then it came to him. Stars, of course, the Darkest One had called him that, in his chantry atop the Hive, 'Lo Vein, you shall bleed your fire for me.' The demon ilk had chorused the title as well, 'Grant us the Vein for eternity.' And more recently the Afflicted themselves—*save us, Vein.*

Yet only when Seolad had uttered the word did the hint lodge in Sonart's recollect like a sliver under his fingernail.

Vein? Singular. What fucking vein? A vein of ore? Sonart knitted his brows as he looked down and pondered the blue tubes embossing the skin of his forearm. The body's veins brought blood back to the heart. Could the name carry some similar meaning about his purpose? Symbolic? Or utter nonsense: the conjuring of an Afflicted's compromised thoughts?

If he dawdled too long in fruitless contemplation, darkness would descend again over the Cradle. Over him. He must solve this mystery before then.

Scathing though Seolad had been, Sonart could've used more of his clever guidance. But this *Vein* had gone and scared the other away for good. Sonart feared what Deathwrought might do through him if he ever laid eyes on Rusic's ill-tempered son again.

Sonart had no time to gnaw implications. He had retreated to his father's house for a specific reason, not merely to distance himself from Auckland and Mila for their safety, though that indeed formed part of it. A vision led him here and, stars be damned, it wasn't to cower and hide as Seolad had reprimanded.

He had come to begin his search.

With renewed resolve, Sonart set to the task, sifting through all of his home's abandoned shelves and drawers. Whatever had goaded him back to this dwelling, the Darkest One allowed it. Clue enough? The answer *was* here—Sonart knew it in his bones—but so did Deathwrought.

Caught in the excitement of the search, Sonart jogged from one room to the next. For the rest of that drear and into the evening, his search turned up nothing. But he kept at it, apart from short breaks to eat and drink. When he finished, he started again at the beginning.

Darkness fell.

A turn of the dial into his second pass, another sharp rapping assaulted his door. Sonart halted midstride. Seolad returned? Heart clenching, he quickly checked his blade and peered out his window.

Unless Seolad had sprouted breasts, it most certainly was not Rusic's son.

The shadows of her cowl hid most of the trembling woman's face as she regarded him through the glass. But Sonart recognized the fear burgeoning in her eyes. They glinted in the lamplight spilling from his home.

"Let me in," she shrilled. "Please!"

Sonart hesitated. "What do you want?"

"Sanctuary—from the Afflicted."

In the distance, ghoulish mewls grew louder.

Cursing inwardly, Sonart wrenched the bolt free, threw the door open, and pulled the terrified woman inside.

The door shuddered as he slammed it behind her stumbling form.

Sonart locked the door, turned, and bit his lower lip.

Body hunched, the woman's chest heaved as she sobbed. Nervous moments passed before her respiration slowed and she straightened.

When the maiden removed her hood, big blue orbs locked onto his and stole his breath. High cheekbones chiselled her round face, surrounded by a mane of chestnut hair, matted and damp. For a moment Sonart forgot his own predicament.

After an awkward pause, he found his voice and with it his ire. "Fool woman, what possessed you to venture into these abandoned warrens? Have you lost your way, or your wits?"

Her attention darted to the window, then the wall. She ran her fingers along its crevices, like as not to measure the barricade's solidity. "Neither," she said as her gaze returned to Sonart. "And forgive me. I was being pursued—by Proclaimers, I believe."

"Proclaimers?" Now Sonart's turn came to scan the window. He narrowed his eyes as he took her in again. "Who are you?"

"I am Shayla—of—an orphaned line. But my foster father is named Wroughn." She brushed her arms. "And I am not lost."

"Well, Shayla of Wroughn, you've certainly lost direction in my mind.

"I came to seek you out."

Sonart flinched. *Not again.* His blood soured. "Why?"

"To bring you to a Gathering."

"Gathering? What *kind* of Gathering?"

"You know what kind, dwarven," she responded.

"Stars burn you, woman." Sonart flashed. "You should not have come. Leave, at once."

Shayla's face blanched as Sonart shifted to the door. "But—"

"Afflicted and Proclaimers will be the least of your worries."

"You—can't."

"Trust me: I pose the graver danger."

"The request comes from my surrogate father—an Elder," Shayla said as if she didn't hear his warning. "He sounded most adamant."

"How did you find me?" Deeper suspicion mired Sonart's tone. "How do you even know me?"

"Your uncle sought my father out. Told him you needed to consult with the Council. My sire's old and frail. He sent me to bring you before them in his stead."

Hooks and Dunge, should never have told Auckland a word of my intentions. "Then, I am the one you seek—curses and damnation. But I warn you again: I have been marked and attainted by—"

"The Darkest One," Shayla finished for him. "A dire combination of that which agitates the Afflicted and impels the Proclaimers—my sire told me. And your uncle told him."

"You do not understand," Sonart fumbled. "At any mo—"

"Deathwrought may seize control of you—his slave and minion." Shayla raised her hands in a calming gesture. "For that very reason, my father sent me, Sonart of Farkshone. I am a clairvoyant, warded against such outbursts, and my sire is a learned alchlemage with a sharp mind of magic, science and—"

Her gaze locked onto his. "Healing. He knows much of your dilemma, but more importantly how it intertwines with the plight of all dwarven. My father wants to free you of your curse."

Sonart pinched the bridge of his nose. "How do I know you are not a Proclaimer yourself?"

Shayla's orbs darkened. "You cannot. But I am here at your behest. Did you not express a wish to seek the Elders' quorum out? Or will you deny such a plan existed in your heart? Spur me if you will. Throw me out your door to certain death." Her voice sharpened to a dirk's point. "But lost in doubt you'll remain."

She made for the door. "If that is what you prefer, then stars burn you back, I'll go. Forsooth, you'll never suffer me again."

Sonart reached for her hand as it lifted to the bolt and stopped her. "Wait."

Shayla turned and faced him. Sonart observed her quivering lips. When they steadied, she took his other hand in hers and gently squeezed both. He didn't resist, resolve melting under the warmth of her touch and the tender feel of her soft skin.

Locking eyes with his, she whispered, "You need not stand alone in this doom."

Bump—b-bump.

Something collided against the side of the house.

They both spun.

A series of bangs and thuds and groans of the Afflicted followed.

Their interruption made Shayla start. She let go of his hands.

Sonart let out a resigned breath, already missing her contact. He moved to the table, pulled out a chair, and gestured to it. "Sit. You look like you could use a cup of tea—more so, wine."

"Thank you. Wine, if it pleases." She meekly seated herself in the proffered chair while Sonart poured them both a measure of red from a decanter.

He placed one of the two goblets before Shayla and took the seat opposite her. "Since my father disappeared, I've trod my pathless journey alone. But I'll not deny that any offer of help is welcome. I only ask for some assurance—for your safety as much as mine."

Shayla took a sip from her cup and nodded. "No great mystery ordained in the Kusp. Auckland has a tongue. But I understand. Given your circumstances, trust must be earned. So, my father bade me tell you this: 'Only your hands can shape the path of those to follow. Within the chaos you will find the true path to structure, and deliverance for us all."

Before he realized what he'd done, Sonart pushed his chair back from the table, its legs grating against the floorboards. How could they have exacted the last words spoken by Rusic, unless they bore some connection?

"Beware, lass," Sonart cautioned, "the Darkest One hears all." He lifted a finger and tapped the crow's feet above his right cheek. "Sees too."

Shayla blossomed with melodious laughter. Sonart found it disconcerting as he focused on her disarming smile. She made him more nervous: he couldn't help but wonder how her lips would taste. A wave of sadness fell over him.

When Shayla's mirth subsided, she handed him an earnest look. "You speak sooth, but if I hold tangent with the Kusp, I promote His will—not so?"

Blood rose to Sonart's cheeks. "Twisting testament, you may regret your words, Milady, and your actions."

With the memory of Seolad fresh in his mind, Sonart braced for another black episode. But it did not come. Perhaps Shayla's claim about her wards *would* prove true. That steadfast look in her emboldened eyes: special percipience, or a fool's blind confidence?

Shayla sniffled. "As I mentioned, they hold a secret council session. The Elders will meet on your behalf. They come from all points, the Cradle over, to Farkshone Village. Because your fate intertwines with their own, they wish to learn as much as they can. Help you lift your burden. Make no mistake, you compel them."

Sonart blew out his cheeks. "I was afraid of that."

180

"News of your emergence has spread far and wide to the other side of the Steppe. How could it not? You mark the first dwarven released from the Dunge. The Elders sense that some vital knowledge has been imparted to you."

"Knowledge?" Sonart growled. "What sodding knowledge? I've had some dreams, but their significance evades me."

"You need only recount what you saw," Shayla soothed. "The Elders will glean their import, and what to do about it. That is why you must come with me."

Sonart studied her evenly before giving her a curt nod. "You have fared better than the dwarven I met last eve—I'll grant you. If the Darkest One has not claimed my mind in your presence, perhaps you do hold sufficient armour: a protected wardeness as you say or a talisman of some weird strength."

Shayla gave him a slight bow. "Just so—on both counts."

"But, I have felt the extent of Deathwrought's malice in the Dunge and the Hive," Sonart added, sharper than he intended. Before Shayla could corner him with another point, he raised a hand. "I will continue to fear in your presence, for both our sakes. That will not change. His machinations and invasions work quickly, and yet—He seems late in your case, or has misstepped altogether."

Shayla pursed her lips. "This, other dwarven of whom you speak—did you know him?"

"No," Sonart lied.

"What did he want?" she asked with casual indifference.

Sonart lifted his shoulders. "Saw me in the market. Said I'd better report to the mines or he'd report me."

"Oh," she said and took another drink of wine. "What happened?"

"Deathwrought stole my mind and I drove him out."

Shayla's lids closed and she shivered. "There are many who would sell out their own mothers to curry favour with the Proclaimers—varlets, the lot. As for the Darkest One's intervention, have you considered that maybe the evil forces consider you equally vital? And wish you to come to no lasting harm either?"

Bump—b-bump.

More Afflicted collided with the house, their moaning lament creating a din outside.

Sonart shrugged again and faced the table lamp. He would need to refill its vat soon. "Time will tell."

Shayla released a zephyr from her purple lips. "At my sire's behest, the Council charged me to bring you to this assembly—that is the extent of it. Between the Proclaimers and the Afflicted, the dwarven drears are numbered. Since we have precious little left—" she jutted her chin. "I refuse to fear Him."

Her response did not satisfy Sonart, but he did not voice it, captivated by the sincerity, and the haunting beauty in her eyes. She seemed to sense his thoughts and abruptly their pupils married.

Heat rushed to Sonart's ears and he looked away, embarrassed and awkward. But then, Shayla extended her arm across the table and stroked his elbow lightly. Another more strident tremor ran through him at her touch. He strove to keep his attention averted from her probing.

"Sonart," she said thoughtfully, "a strange name. Does it bear some meaning?"

"My father named me. When I was a child, he told me that in the ancient tongue of our forebears, it means, *psalm of justice*."

Shayla removed her hand. "We could use some of that. As a clairvoyant, I speak with some heft to my foretellings. So, you may take stock in what I say. Your deeds will validate your worthy namesake."

Sonart swallowed and regarded his wine cup through a filter of scepticism.

"The Gathering will lessen the weight for you, if only to share your burden with those who just might be able to do something about it," Shayla went on. "You seek answers. The Council can offer them."

Sonart's breath caught as recognition took hold. *The answer will find you.* He met her gaze. "When is this Gathering?"

"Morrow's eve, they will convene two turns before the chime of mid-death."

23: Noirlunen
Brooke

A din of crickets infiltrated the copse as Alghan considered the subject. For a long moment he remained silent, making a steeple of his hands and studying them.

"The Code," he began, "forms a complex coven we follow. As do all of Areth's kingdoms, we subscribe to our own edict: the law of our purpose. *True blood* refers to our forebears, the *Noirlunen*. They came from lost lands so remote and distant that none alive today have set foot there. Not that any can."

Brooke leaned in. "Why is that?"

"It's cut off," Alghan replied. "Noirland—as it was called—lies on the other side of the Sancean, heading east, or due north across Areth's polar Ice Wastes, and then south, so far-flung, not even a map of Areth has charted it."

"The reason?"

"Because Commander, any living cartographer with half a mind knows it would mean the deepest sleep to venture back there," Gnor supplied. "A northern traverse across a frozen hell and the Land of Fire, or worse across the Sea of Sand—which the Guile has claimed."

Brooke frowned in the firelight. "Guile?"

"Know you, the Clysm, indentured to the merekin?" Gnor asked.

"The entity that roams Areth's seas—I've heard mariners' tales," Brooke answered.

"Same brood—arcane wraiths with immeasurable power," the elder Wrayn said. "Though the Guile hearkens to no one."

"One of Penthor's fairy tales from Cornerstone," Lonus laughed.

Gnor tightened but maintained a calm voice. "That fairy tale has sunk an armada's worth of desert skiffs. And don't speak of my King as some dotard, or we'll settle this with ironock."

Alghan raised his hands in a calming gesture. "Peace, Gnor. He meant no disrespect."

Gnor shot the tall Nightwolf a dubious look but let the matter slide.

Alghan turned his attention back to Brooke. "Noirland was utterly lost during the worldwide scourges of the Eclipsed War, but before that time it endured desecration under the wrath of dragons. As told in the Kusp, Shirdron's Folly eclipsed the Dragon Wars."

"The two names are interchangeable," Brooke said.

Alghan tapped his finger against the side of his temple. "Precisely. Our ancestral lands were torn asunder, but not so the blood of my people. Every true blood today vaunts the memory of our origins—of what they lost when Deathwrought blighted their realm, rendering it uninhabitable. For the sake of survival, they embarked on a perilous migration northward, into and across the polar Wastes, until they came south unto the Main."

Gnor coughed and took up the tale. "The Noirlunen proved a hard, iron-willed lot. Their prowess with weapons made any one of them deadlier than ten from the Main. Hence, the reason Deathwrought sought their allegiance. Through a translation portal, the Darkest One came to their shores, cloaked as a Kazir wizard. He cited the precursors of the Starbond—threats that would ultimately destroy their lands."

The Bulldog paused and scratched the top of his bald crown, glistening in the firelight. "He presented himself as a victim of the war's maleficence, one that would eventually spread to and despoil Noirland—if they did not join him in stemming the raging storm. In return, Deathwrought offered them protective wonders beyond count."

"Twas a bargain with tethers," Alghan said. "Though the Noirlunen's meisters could authenticate his claim about the Endstorm, our shrewd ancestors grew wise to his manoeuvring. Ultimately, they refuted him."

The tall Nightwolf set his stick down, reached for his cup of mead, and took a long draught. "So, he sent the dragons. The ravage of the firedrakes came swift and brutal—red venom-spitters and black fire-breathers."

Alghan ran his foot back and forth in the dirt. "But not all dracos align with evil. Jabberwockies put their wicked peers to rout and defeated them—at least on Noirland. Twas after all a war betwixt dragonkind. And the resolve of our ancestors too stood strong, holding Deathwrought's serpent flock in check with crossbows, ballistae, cunning, and willpower."

"Ever have dragons been used as pawns," Onis added with a shake of his head. The soft-spoken Nightwolf healer had since joined the circle and stood staring at the flames, its orange light dancing in his green eyes. "By both sides. The Dragon Wars were in fact proxy wars—firestorms set by arsonists to usurp the peoples of Areth."

Their shared tale drew in everyone within earshot. Brooke took in the unblinking faces around the fire before his eyes settled again on the healer. "It worked, Onis, for it incited the War of the Rennen."

"Whether immediately or a millennium later," Gnor pointed out, "war breeds more war, Commander. Peace?" He scoffed. "Only an illusion."

Brooke gave the Nightwolf a slight bow. Apart from the hiss and crackle of the fire, and the stray bark of a Warang, silence reigned.

Until Alghan hefted the story where he'd left off. "When done, all the dragons dead or gone, even after the False Starbond's upheaval, the Noirlunen set about repairing the damage. Alas, the Darkest One hadn't finished with them. He cast one final hex, from which they could not survive."

Alghan's voice petered and he looked off into the middle distance. "Two large islands marked the Noirlunen realm, rich in boreal forest and farmable steppe. Temperate seas teeming with fish surrounded them. Deathwrought's curse did not rear immediately, but with each passing season, the weather grew steadily colder. The Ice Wastes encroached south, forming an ice cap that penetrated down to the ocean bottom, freezing water and fish alike."

Just then, Gnolin walked past and took a seat on the ground at Gnor's feet. When the stout Nightwolf reached a hand and ruffled his hair, the pup smiled up at his grandfather.

"The decline eventually affected the islands themselves," Onis said. "Plants no longer flourished as a new malady took hold. The soil became a poison. Livestock perished. And fishing was no longer an option as the seas froze to our northern shores. All life in it or dependent upon it died."

"What about your other shores?" Brooke asked.

"They fared worse," said Gnor. "The southern waters didn't freeze or shrink back. They filled up—with fluidic sand. It became the Sancean—*the Sea of Sand*, which now dominates a full third of Areth, beyond what had once been the eastern coast of the Main."

Brooke scrunched up his face. "Fluidic sand?"

"Sand you cannot stand upon," Gnor clarified. "You would sink and choke on its grains, if the sand-eels didn't swallow you first. The Eastern Kingdoms have fashioned the desert skiffs I mentioned—vessels equipped with runners and sails that ply the sand-ocean to expedite passage up and down Cornerstone's former seaboard. But even they do not venture far from the coast as the further one draws away from the firmament of the mainland, the more hazardous the Sancean becomes."

"Maps of Areth show the Sancean," Brooke remarked. "But I always thought of it as a desert."

Gnor shook his head slowly. "It is no desert. But a syrupy sediment, devoid of most life except the parasitic eels I spoke of—and the Guile."

The Bulldog cast a covert eye at Lonus, but the brawny Wrayn held his tongue. "The eels are mindless serpents of enormous girth, but they usually live deep within the sand, sifting the lower reaches for dead matter to consume—unless something disturbs the surface."

"The passage of sailing vessels?" ventured Brooke.

Palms out, Gnor extended his arms towards the pyre. "Aye, if pressed, the eels can be killed with the right skiff crew, and some sprite lore." He threaded his fingers together and cracked his knuckles. "But the Guile is implacable and always deadly, swallowing skiffs whole. The primeval

Stephen Fenech

wraith's the true reason why the Sancean separates Noirland from the continent forever."

"Unless you're a dragon, or an Ahzarim," one of the Wrayns pointed out with a mild chuckle. Brooke turned to face the speaker. He had a hard but handsome countenance framed by a loose mane of russet hair. His calm orbs bespoke a quiet strength.

Gaze downcast, he seemed content to sit on the ground and inspect the small bundle of arrows beside him. Since supper, the bowman had been at it. He lifted them one at a time, touched the edge of each arrowhead, and ran a hand down the length of its wooden shaft. Then with two fingers, pulled and fanned every fletching.

Gnor nodded in his direction. "Right you are, Quiver."

"For the best," Alghan blurted with a note of finality. "You would find naught but desecration there. The rape and ataintment of our ancestral homeland have lasted to this day—the islands' fate, irreversible."

The tall Nightwolf stretched his lanky arms and poured more mead into his cup. "My ancestors vowed to take the fight to the Darkest One. They came to the Main to destroy he who set the dragons upon them, who forever ruined their lands."

Alghan took a sip of his mead and straightened. "Thus, began the Dire March. With their dogs, they set out north across the Ice Wastes instead of breathing their last in a doomed land."

Brooke considered this for a moment. "How did they know where to find Him?"

"Visions—shared visions, some of which the Darkest One himself revealed, and some gleaned from... other sources," Alghan said in a puzzling tone.

The commander furrowed his brows. "Where *did* they find him?"

Alghan shrugged. "They didn't. The Noirlunen who survived the Wastes trudged all the way to the blight north of Mount Marwolaeth—Mount Death in the common tongue."

"Aye, the Death volcano is known to me, by its sprite name as well," Brooke said. "It marked the site of the Darkest One's stronghold at the time."

"Exactly right," Alghan said. "But as the Noirlunen descended to more temperate lands, their *path* became strangely diverted by some hundred leagues. They found themselves among the Ghost Spires, above the Ruin, in the vicinity of ancient Stormhearth."

"That's where they met the sprites," Gnolin piped up.

Alghan inclined his head. "Believing the sprites minions of the Darkest One, falsely luring them into a trap, the Wrayns formed a vanguard and charged. But the Warangs hesitated."

"At that moment, communion between wolf and man faltered for the first and last time," Onis said. "Something stronger, deeper, took root in the wolves. They lay down like contented farm dogs before the sprite host."

Brooke tried to imagine one of the wolven monsters as some farmer's pet. And failed.

"Only then did the Noirlunen realize no evil ruled the tiny nymphs," Alghan went on. "That they'd been responsible for sending our forebears the other visions. The egalitarian sprites did not meet them in battle. They knelt and bayed with the wolves, matching their canine tongue."

As if on cue, a few of the Warangs whimpered to each other nearby. Gnolin stood and went to join them.

Brooke watched him go until Alghan resumed his tale. "In the tempest of shared howls, the Wrayns heard truth and empathy—a poultice to hearts rent asunder by suffering and bereavement. The sprites gave Warang and Wrayn alike a vent to fully purge their pain. They all broke down in tears. And the sprites joined them."

The tall Nightwolf's face constricted with fervour as if reliving the moment firsthand. "The sprites proved to my ancestors that if they charged headlong against the Darkest One's citadel, it would aid their foe's purpose. The only ruin the Noirlunen would visit would be upon themselves."

"The Darkest One had laid a cordon of pitfalls and traps," said Gnor, "throughout the Land of Fire surrounding Mount Marwolaeth. He set an army of lavatrols to guard and patrol the fire-mountain's bastion. And if the Noirlunen had managed to penetrate all his defences, breach the walls of his stronghold and cavalier, it would still have been in vain."

"Why?" Brooke asked.

"He was no longer there," Alghan said. "He had long since abandoned it, shifting his fortress to Grendamaul—the Cradle."

"Brapin—Targin's mentor—remains adamant that the Darkest One disappeared long before," Gnor put in.

Alghan gave the bulldog-faced man a thin smile before shifting his focus back to the commander. "The sprites showed the Noirlunen a purpose much greater than they thought possible. If they would but align themselves to a three-fold purpose, they could achieve the solace their hearts longed for."

"We learn our greatest lessons when we pay the heaviest price," Gnor said. All heads bowed at the stout Wrayn's comment.

Alghan looked across his shoulder, the profile of his face distant and unreadable. After a moment he spoke again. "With their lore, the sprites increased the lifespan of the Warangs to match and in some cases surpass that of the Wrayns. Yerik is the only wolf still alive to have crossed the

Wastes from Noirland."

Brooke could not believe his ears. "By the—stars!" he exclaimed. "That would make him...?"

"More than a thousand years old," Alghan confirmed. "The sprites also fortified the entire pack's constitution, instincts, fierceness, strength of mind, and power of body. We call it the *Quick* and it forms the third part of our Purpose. The other two parts are the Code—the coven with the sprites, and the Creed—the remembrance of our heritage and the vow to secure full recompense from the Darkest One for our lost home and every life he stole since."

"Ever since we swore fealty to the sprites," Gnor said, "we've served as Vamsah's fist, awaiting the Starbond."

"But, the Darkest One also waits," Brooke pointed out. "He too moves his pieces—like the Four, and Necatar—with trickery and subterfuge."

"True," Alghan allowed. "Yet in the small part the Wolves play, balance is maintained."

A Warang howled in the distance. Alghan's hard eyes fixed on the fire. "At the behest of the sprites, we allowed others not of true Noirlunen blood to join our band. As matters stood, we needed to replenish our ranks after the Dire March. So, the pack you now see blends a mix of true blood and *true heart*. But all are considered wolf-brothers and sisters—part of the pack under one Nightwolf banner."

A wave of scepticism pressed Brooke's heart flat. "Will this have any bearing on the true bloods following my commands?"

Gnor sniggered. "Targin is not a true blood—and neither was his sire before him—Tragmar, the First Nightwolf. Nor am I."

"Gnor—you are," Jaak laughed, inciting a brief bout of chuckles from his peers.

The commander arched an eyebrow and faced the bonfire. He juggled implications and doubts and options. Over them all, one question smothered the rest: *What was I thinking?* The magnitude of his charge threatened to bury him.

As one of Pathguard's high officers, he had faced many struggles on countless battlefronts, boosted morale, navigated the affairs of the court, liaised between political and military hierarchies. Yet all of it paled before what brewed here.

"Alghan?" Brooke whispered, his mouth suddenly parched. "I'll not shirk from what I've sworn to do. But I am one man—stars chase the shadows—born of no ancient line—with no special power or magic." *I've no right to lead your people through a blood feud, let alone a long-foretold world war.* "How am I expected to turn the wheels of your pathless path when I have no path of my own to follow?" *Except that which awaits any turncape in Pathguard—a path to the stockade or the gallows. But I'm part of this venture now—I own the bloody thing.* "How can I lead these men in their purpose when it was never mine to begin with?"

The fire popped as Brooke braced for a verbal hammer fall. But when he met Alghan's gaze, no rebuttal did he see in the tall man's eyes.

On the contrary, they softened with what looked like pity and understanding.

"The point is moot," Alghan said. "Several here share your beginnings. They may not be of the true ancestry, but have demonstrated a fierceness to surpass those of our lines of blood."

"You form but one leaf on the Gaia tree, Commander," Gnor added grimly. He looked around. "But we are all leaves along its branches, connected to her trunk, receiving life and returning it. If we are all removed, the tree will perish. Equally, if the tree dies, so do we."

Brooke gulped. "We are all connected, but—"

"Courage," the Bulldog overrode, "and honour—that is how we'll recognize you—the common ground that bonds all wolf-brothers and sisters. It forms the ironock foundation of the Code, the keystone of the Creed, the unrelenting fuel of the Quick."

Alghan placed his palm on Brooke's shoulder and gave it a firm squeeze. "You would be a fool not to feel dread. How you rise above your fear determines your measure. Courage will pull you through and keep those you lead going when hope seems lost."

"Alghan's right," Gnor agreed. "For what it's worth, Commander, the sprites did not choose you on some whim, like some scapegoat or placeholder. But for crucial reasons—at the joint bidding of a king, an Orbical, and a wizard. What does that tell you?"

I'm fucked, Brooke wanted to reply. He inhaled fiercely, his heartbeat quickening. "Point taken."

The tall Nightwolf lifted the decanter at his feet and refilled Brooke's cup with spritewater. "As Gnor pointed out, Targin—our Chief Wrayn—is not a true blood, enlisted just the same, recognized for what he would rise to become, by none other than the Chief Warang himself, Yerik."

Brooke harrumphed, eyebrows leaping towards his hairline. "A *wolf* recruited him?"

"He did indeed," Alghan chuckled. "Ask Gnor or Jaak—they were there."

Gnor lifted his chin when Brooke faced the elder Wrayn. "It is true."

"I can attest to that too—*with* two," Jaak added. "Young enough that I saw it happen with both eyes."

189

"Likewise," Alghan went on, "Targin recognized the same quality in others." He studied the commander. "The Chief saw this eminence in you. This is our time. And yours."

Brooke glanced at the others. With all eyes trained on him, he tried to form some verbal rally to the tall man's assurances. But it only made him feel awkward, vapid, and more uncertain.

A smoking pipe interrupted Brooke's pondering. His nose lifted, following the arm that held the cob to a smiling Quiver. "Untried waters take time, Commander," the Wrayn said without pretence. "A bit of green weed might help you organize your green thoughts."

Brooke gave the bowman an appreciative look as he accepted the pipe. "It would. Thank you, Quiver."

Quiver returned Brooke's gratitude with the briefest of nods. The commander put the pipe to his lips and drew the smoke deep. The leaf inside the chamber crackled and glowed as it burned.

Brooke savoured the sweet apple-spiced tobacco, before letting out a measured skein towards the fire. The purge carried his duress away and his shoulders slackened. Though eclipsed in several ways, his stars did align with Gnor and Alghan's counsel.

As the roiling smoke permeated the copse in thin wisps, Gnolin returned and took a deep breath. It finished with a beam. "I love the scent of Quiver's blend."

Quiver grinned up at the pup before sliding it in Brooke's direction. "Have faith, Commander. Your stars will brighten—in our favour."

Brooke removed the cob from his mouth and nudged his chin in the bowman's direction. "How long after Targin arrives can we expect to reach the Hidden Kingdom?"

"He'd have made good time with Thrum—his hawkrike," Alghan replied. "Considering his errand, he'll arrive at Serenthia early on the morrow—if the skies remain clear. As for the pack, without wings, we should reach the Strong Helm inside a fortnight—if the forest remains clear."

Brooke digested the information, finishing the pipe in silence. As he tapped its ash against the side of the log he sat upon, another question surfaced. "Alghan?"

"Yes, Commander?"

"Is Val of the true blood?"

"Yes, he is," said Alghan.

"I see." *Damn you, Targin.*

24: Council
Sonart

Before they left the cottage the next drear, Sonart claimed Seolad's abandoned sword for his own. He fastened the blade to his waist with a makeshift belt and scabbard comprised of leather straps.

With his palm hovering over the hilt, he faced Shayla. "Times have changed. I will need this from now on."

Shayla glanced at the sword. "Indeed."

When the two dwarven started up the ravine, the weather remained calm, skies safely awash in neutral grey. Only a slight wind murmured past their faces, but as drear light intensified and smeared the dull blanket overhead, the wind gathered strength.

The clouds grew heavier and the first drops of rain found their faces. Sonart found the touch of water pleasant enough to quell his nervousness, though not completely.

Water purges all.

Although innocent of the Scourge's wrath, the rain still managed to turn their path into a stream of mud. Sonart's clothes clung to him, sodden and uncomfortable, but he ignored it, as his escort seemed determined to do. He focused instead on the meeting ahead, vacillating between dread and eagerness.

At one point, they came across a Kworn patrol. But the armoured beastmen paid them no mind as they clambered past. Their lantern orbs remained trained forward, lighting the slants of rain like green sparks. But they forced Sonart to recall the cadre that had taken him to the Darkest One.

Mine eyes are your eyes.

A thought took root.

Sonart turned to Shayla after they passed the patrol. "When we near the place of the Gathering, you must do something for me."

Shayla gave him her attention. "Aye?"

"Blindfold and guide me to them."

Her face drew back and bunched into a knot. "Are you mad?"

"Perhaps," Sonart conceded. "Nevertheless, I insist you do. You've not witnessed the storm of my nature—pray you never do."

"I needn't pray. I am warded," she protested.

"But my people are not. If I see their faces, the storm may break again. Any deterrent that might abrogate His influence warrants a measure I must take."

Shayla clicked her tongue and made a dismissive gesture with her hand. Her ambivalence disheartened Sonart and shed darkness over their arrangement.

They walked on in silence.

Drear waned to dimming, but towards the end of their long march, Shayla agreed to his 'bizarre request,' as she had mockingly called it.

At least the rain abated. On its heels, a dry wind came in from the Outereach to sponge the worst of their damp.

Shayla removed a kerchief from her pocket and blindfolded Sonart. For a quarter turn of the dial, she gently led him like a blind man's usher. They slowly trudged down a series of warrens, taking many twists and turns.

Then all at once, Shayla's hand brought him to a stop. A male's harsh whisper penetrated Sonart's dark veil. "Why have you come?"

"The ancient lines have bled," Shayla whispered back.

A moment later, her hand coaxed Sonart forward again. As they moved, a quiet clamour ensued of creaking doors, multiple footsteps, and hurried mumbling.

Three more dwarven had joined them. No, four. One had not bathed: the odour: a mix of ironock dust and sweat. One stank of sour wine.

From the hollow change in acoustics, they had entered an inner sanctum of some large storehouse. Sonart's incarceration in the deep gloom of the Dunge had conditioned him to see—with his ears and nose. Using those skills now, he mapped three potential escape routes.

A short climb up a flight of stairs took them to a second-floor landing where Shayla's guiding fingers bade him stop again. More squeaking wood sounded, followed by one last clank of a deadbolt sliding home behind them.

Locked in, his egress points had been removed—*damn*.

A half-dozen dwarven took shallow breaths all around him.

Sonart dry-swallowed, gooseflesh prickling in anticipation.

After a few anxious moments, Shayla spoke. "We are safe now, Sonart, among allies. Remove the blindfold."

"No," he said, tone unwavering, trying to keep his anger in check. "It remains fastened. Are the Elders present?"

"We stand in an antechamber. They will summon you shortly. Stars, Sonart! You look a fool with the cloth blinding you."

"Better fool than menace," Sonart grated. "It stays."

Footsteps tramped and another woman's voice joined them. It sounded scratchy, frail as if spoken through an old chimney. "All have assembled. You may escort him in. But then you must leave immediately. The Gathering convenes for the Son of Farkshone alone."

"I understand," Shayla said. Then to Sonart, "Come."

Her hand gripped his arm and pulled him forward. Air kissed his cheeks. He brushed what felt like a veil of curtains, its fabric caressing him as he sallied past.

Shayla prompted him to halt a third time.

Despite his induced sightlessness, Sonart could feel many eyes on him.

"Behold the Son of Farkshone," Shayla declared, her voice ringing loudly. "Emissary of the Kusp and vassal of Deathwrought's bane."

Sonart's hands vaulted to his face, digits scrabbling like cast grapnels. Before they could secure the blindfold, it ripped from his face.

As his stricken pupils adjusted, stunned looks assailed him. More than a score of Elders and twice as many armed guards.

He spun on Shayla. "Bitch!"

In a burst of vehemence, Sonart drew his blade. But even as he swung the sword at her, an invisible force deflected the blow. Muscles suddenly taxed, his cognizance followed, diminishing under the same leaden weight.

Shayla shrank away but quickly recovered. A mirthless grin crossed her face—which now glowed emerald.

Even as Sonart's self-control fled, the truth of her betrayal dawned. She had sprung a trap for the Elders. And him, the bait. Shayla was a Proclaimer.

The air around Sonart thickened like fog and his movements slowed further, as though confused by too much drink. In all else, his senses grew sharper than the weapon in his hand.

Through his connection with the Darkest One, Sonart realized Shayla held a similar agency. He could not harm her. Deathwrought's magics armoured her—exactly as the god had done with the Chosen Kworn.

Amidst several cries of dismay, the old woman that first greeted him pleaded. "Peace, Son of Farkshone!"

"Peace, peace," the congregation chorused.

No use.

Deathwrought's will forced itself upon him. Unbridled power infiltrated the dwarven all over again.

"Not now," he croaked from the strictures of his being, forced to fight a desperate war in his mind as he coerced his body to escape. Though disjointed and beleaguered, he marched to the door.

The guards would not let him pass. With so much at stake, they dared not let him flee their most secret meeting.

The guards knew it.

Sonart knew it.

Deathwrought knew it.

Evil manifested, its full tyranny clawing its way into Sonart's mind, but somehow, he held on, seething through clenched teeth, "Let-me-pass."

Unflinching, the guards stood their ground, legs braced, swords brandished, shields poised. The guards glowed emerald too. No, Sonart's whole world shone green. The aura emanated from his own orbs, like that of a Kworn, like that of a Zürshuck!

Mine eyes are your eyes.

His wrath exploded. Sonart roared with Deathwrought's own voice. Sword raised high he surged towards the guards.

The closest dwarven took the point in the heart. He collapsed, bubbling blood.

The blade flashed again. And another fell, hewn at the neck.

A third went down with a ripped throat. The pommel took a fourth on his crown and cracked his skull.

During the murderous spree, Sonart remained aware of his actions, yet powerless to stop them. He had become a sinister tour de force, emulating the berserker Kworn of the Ritual. Identically possessed, bereft of will but not potency.

The guards rushed him from all sides only to fall before the uncanny slash of his blade—tumbleweed in a razor storm. Fed by the limitless energy of a god, his arm delivered death again. Again.

Again!

Rage spurred him.

Bodies of the dead and dying littered the floor of the chamber.

In the deepest recess of Sonart's mind, shouts of anguish sounded, muted as though stuck down a well. Whispers, strangled by evil laughter. His laughter. "Blasphemy and sacrilege!" he sang. "Here is your penance! At one with the Kusp!"

In shrilling ululations, Deathwrought's caterwaul rent Sonart's throat.

He flew at the Elders.

Fuelled by the Darkest One's hate and malice, the blade carved a swathe through the defenceless dwarven, a rabid wolf among a hapless fold of sheep. Before the surviving guards could intervene and distract him, seven Elders lay slain. The floor puddled crimson, the scene, a melange of carnage, terror, fury, and pain.

In the darkest pit of the dwarven's soul, a new voice carried over the cacophony. It banished Deathwrought's seizure so suddenly, Sonart sagged to his knees like a discarded straw doll. Somehow his ferocity receded.

The closest guard seized Sonart's lapse. With a scathing bellow, he threw all his weight behind his sword thrust. The blade bit deep into Sonart's head, splitting his skull. Its dull crack resounded in his ears. Time slowed.

But even as the mortal furrow cleaved his head and lines of blood streamed down his face, Sonart knew he would not die. The wound, which could've easily dropped a Kworn, would *save* him.

Magic closed up his fatal wound. Had the Darkest One's raw power galvanized him? Or some other energy? Blacker than black, the omnipotence persisted, strong and steady. What he'd felt in the presence of the Chosen Kworn, now manifested in his own soul, a hundred-fold. Had he turned the table—now wielding Deathwrought's magic?

As red ichor obscured Sonart's outer vision, his inner sight cleared, thoughts and will swimming frantically away from the Darkest One.

Sonart's possessor had not been entirely banished, but tethered, rendered ineffectual. The dimming's heinous campaign not half-complete.

"Finish it!" Deathwrought struggled to seize Sonart's mind once more.

But could not.

The third unbidden voice within Sonart held the Darkest One in check. That lost voice... from the Cleft Augury sounded once more. '*Flee Vein,*' it urged.

And this time, Sonart listened.

His own fire coursed through his blood once more. With it, he severed Deathwrought's link to him.

The evil power guttered. But before it vanished completely, Sonart stole some to use for his own volition. He regained his wits and by some divinity came back to himself—just as fresh ranks of dwarven assailed him.

A small army's worth attacked, teeth gritted, swords drawn, death shining in their eyes.

Without thinking, Sonart tucked and hurled himself under the closest dwarven, dodging his opponent's raised blade as he did. He spun his foe about and kicked his back, driving him into the combatants converging from the opposite flank. Caught off-guard, peers crashed into one another.

Sonart did not pause. In the same direction from where the first assailant issued, he sped—towards a window, bloodied sword still clutched in his hand.

Pommel first, he dove.

And crashed through the glass, sprawling into brisk open air.

Amidst the raining shards, Sonart fell headlong to the street a storey below. His blind flight into darkness ended with an impact into something soft. As he bounced, an imperious grunt sounded. Then silence as Sonart rolled away.

A portly merchant lay prostrate, out cold beside him. The poor sod—all twenty-five stone of him—had broken Sonart's fall instead of the bags of hogsweed stacked atop his cart.

Bounding to his feet, Sonart wiped the worst of the blood matting his eyelids and cleared his sight at last.

A battle cry went up as dwarven spilled out of doorways lining the alleyway. They raced in his direction.

Sonart grappled his sword from where it lay alongside the unconscious vendor. He braced for the attack, trying to muster strength he no longer possessed.

But then more yowls lifted from the corridor behind him, quelling the mob's blood-song. Guttural cries filled the gloom and the din of a hundred marching boots rose in overture.

The tide of dwarven skidded to a halt.

Sonart spun.

A band of Kworn loped towards him, scattering the dwarven herd.

Sonart recognized them at once; the same bestial company he and Shayla stumbled upon earlier—they must've followed a trail left by that turncape witch.

Instinct took over. Sonart fled into a narrow side alley. It would harry the Kworn's bulk if they gave chase. Down a series of shadow-ridden warrens, he stole from pandemonium's centre, heedless of direction, time, or consequence.

Bitterness his sole companion, Sonart understood at last the truth of the Darkest One's malicious bane. The deepest sleep offered Sonart his only recourse—if not for the redeeming plea of that lost voice.

The answer will find you.

Sin raked his fingers through his silver-blond hair. When they found the pointed top of his right earlobe, he whispered a ghosted curse. Bleary-eyed, he stared out from the massive window of his Killington Vermont mansion. Across the wooden deck and the dale beyond, his attention fixed on the rising sun.

The three-storey room positively glowed, awash in orange light. Sunshine also filtered past a swirling column of steam that escaped the musician's coffee mug. The cup sat politely on the glass table in front of him, its contents still too hot to drink, unless he wanted to burn his tongue.

Burning…

Deathwrought, Darkest One, Octagon, Veins, Siphons, Goodakh, Highprites …Starbond: what did they all mean?

Mine eyes are your eyes.

What did it all fucking mean? Some kind of post-traumatic syndrome after witnessing the death of his parents?

Sin released his long mane, letting the strands fall down his backside. He reached under his shirt for his pendant and studied it. His mom and dad had given it to him the morning of the day they died. A gift for his birthday.

That same sunny afternoon, they set sail aboard their small yacht, *Tide Turner*. Over Pamlico Sound, off North Carolina's eastern seaboard, the vessel cruised towards Cape Hatteras.

Sin loved the ocean.

It had been called the 'Storm of the Century,' but none of the forecast models gave any warning. It just sprang up. Even as his father spun the craft about and gunned the engines racing for shore.

"One in a million you survived the elements, son," one of his coastguard rescuers had said.

"No precedent in recorded history. Neptune's absolute worst scourge," his mate agreed, shaking his head in awe.

But that wasn't the whole story.

Not just a freak storm.

Not just a sorcerer.

Imagined or not, titans had waged a battle in the tempest—with magic. And Sin, their coveted prize. In hindsight, maybe they caused the supernatural storm. Whatever the root, both sides left empty-handed. One power nullified the other. And his parents paid the ultimate price for their attrition.

His entire life, Sin had contemplated the truth of what really happened. Barring the lasting sting of the trauma, growing up had been admittedly easy, fostered in the Seattle home of his selfless uncle, Angus, older brother to his late father, Tristan.

But young Zach never breathed a word about what he saw that night, not to the authorities, not to his uncle or aunt, or any of his four cousins. No one.

Except Promo.

Sin confided in the guitarist, a *Reader's Digest* version of the events. Even that had been the tip of the iceberg, and yet as history demonstrated, a properly placed frozen tip can still sink a ship.

Sin reached down and lifted the mug to his lips, his gaze shifting to the framed platinum records on one brick wall. The abstract painting beside the collection caught his eye and made him ponder.

The thick oil canvas depicted a broad black vertical line running the length of the six-foot-high frame—well almost. The column faded into a machine-grey cloud at its top and a blood-orange swathe at its bottom.

That piece had resonated with him, enough to drop fifty grand for it. The image struck him like a touchstone to his secret world.

After the accident—the brutal attack, Sin's cognizance heightened. And his body began to change, most notably his ears—they elongated and grew pointed at the tops. Now his lobes appeared so deformed, he took great pains to keep them hidden with his hair.

As he always concealed the strange pendant around his neck. It sparked to life from time to time, revealing a dancing blue coruscation within—even in complete darkness. Of late, the pendant flared to life more often, its warmth seeping into the flesh of his chest to cradle his heart.

On that note, it wasn't just his ears and pendant he needed to hide...

In his fifth year, on a Friday afternoon two weeks before Christmas, he received that 'unwanted present,' the one he quickly rewrapped and hid away his whole life.

It had been an unusually warm and rainy day. His father had handed him the 'plug-end' of the outdoor Christmas lights. Young Zach, clad in his yellow raincoat, assured his daddy that he would keep the plug dry, tucked up the sleeve of his oversized vinyl coat.

"Wait till I get down," his father instructed. "I promise, I'll let you light up the whole house when I climb back down, but not before, okay?"

Zach glanced over at the outside outlet beside the garage and nodded up at his daddy. "I pomice—coss my heart and hope to die."

With that, his father scaled the extension ladder, a lasso of lights threaded around one shoulder. He fed the line out as he stepped higher.

Zach watched as his father climbed atop the sloped roof and set to stringing the line. He fastened it to hooks beneath the eaves girdling the two-storey dwelling. When his dad disappeared around the corner, Zach waited.

And waited.

The minutes stretched and Zach began to tap his rubber boots in the puddles. His mind drifted and he pondered over a Christmas carol he'd learned that day in school. He loved to sing, a lot.

And it was a beautiful song, so he started to hum it quietly to himself, "*Si-iiii-ilent Night, Ho-oooo-ly Night. Aw is calm aww is—*"

The string of Christmas lights in his hand suddenly lit up, one at a time, first from where his sleeve swallowed the plug.

Delighted with the discovery, he sang louder as the lights continued to spark up the line and around the house. "*Seep in heav-en-ly—*"

A moment later his father's curse rang in his ears, "Fuck, Zach, are you trying to kill me!"

Zach flinched and stopped singing.

All the lights winked out. His eyes shot up as his father blustered loudly down the ladder. "I thought I told you not to plug it in!" he reprimanded.

Still grasping the plug in his tiny fingers, Zach raised his sleeve and shook his head fervently. "I didn't Daddy, honest. Just came on."

As his father tsked, Zach extended his lower lip but did not pout. His dad quickly forgot his anger. He hoisted his son up, hugged him fiercely, and smothered his cheek with kisses. When he drew back, he smiled. "I'm sorry, Zach. I didn't mean to be so cross. I believe you—must have been phantom power in the line or some such. You scared Daddy. I didn't want you or me to get shocked is all—kay?"

Zach nodded reluctantly, still recovering from his small terror.

"Good," his father laughed. "I'm finished in any case. What do you say, we plug it in now, get out of the rain, and join Mommy inside for some cookies and hot cocoa?"

That day marked the only time his father's warmth diminished from its usual bright nimbus.

Sin had always been surrounded by warmth, even after his harrowing schism—when his uncle took him under his wing.

Despite all the fostering and nurturing as he grew up with his extended family, Sin held a lingering coldness in his soul. That it would prove a 'flawed and fractured shield,' one that would fail altogether, sooner than late.

Who was the dwarf in that secret realm? That 'World in Chaos'?

'No,' the luminous being gently corrected after Sin's latest vision. "On Areth, he is known as a dwarven, as is his race.'

Dwarf? Dwarven? Whatever the name, the little man barely escaped. "But why is he made to suffer, and unwillingly cause suffering—to what end?" Sin whispered back at the humanoid light.

"Why do I keep seeing him like a fly on the wall?" Why did the goddam vision reoccur over and over?

"You are linked to the Four," the being calmly replied. "Like them, you will serve a Blood Scion's calling—as Vein of Fire."

Sin thought he'd been tripping, only to wake and remember he never touched the shit.

It *was* another world, real and not imagined. Granted, no place on Earth resembled it. Magic can't be real, you dumb fuck—it was phantom power.

Then how do you explain the pendant, Sherlock? How do you explain your voice? What it can do? He took another sip of his coffee. It had cooled enough to drink, carefully.

As the caffeine sharpened his mindset, Sin let out a wry chuckle. The hellish microcosm was all bullshit. Areth couldn't be real.

The singer almost convinced himself, for the tenth time this week, that it was only a dream.

He looked over his shoulder at the coffee stand. The pot was empty.

But to have the same vision over and over and fucking over again, began to terrify him. Was he losing his mind?

He needed help—fast.

Stephen Fenech

25: Brapin
Targin

The warm light of the hearth cast dancing shadows against the pub's trellises and arches. It also filtered through the lifting skeins of pipe smoke. The burning tobacco added a sweet resin fragrance to the beer and musk scents of the enclosure.

In an alcove adjoining the main hall, two figures sat facing one another in silence. A small beeswax candle flickered on the oaken table between them, illuminating their faces and the cups of mead before each.

The smaller of the two—a frail white-haired elder dressed in a hooded cloak of hunter-green—broke their stillness with a huff.

He gesticulated with mottled hands. "Are you even listening to me, Targin?" The old one's words came quick and hushed, lost to the boisterous din outside the booth. He craned his neck up and locked gazes with the giant.

"I am listening, Brapin," Targin said. "No need for another reprimand. Merely wanted you to speak with that piehole of yours for a change. My mind tires of communion. We look like a pair of mismatched monks avowed to silence and having a staring contest. Wouldn't be surprised if the other patrons think us statues."

"Statues don't divulge secrets." The Orbical blew out his cheeks. "Fine, speak if you must, provided you listen as well. And verify that you understand."

"Stars align."

"So?"

"So, what?"

"Nightwolf," Brapin grated.

Elbows braced on the table, Targin cradled his head on upturned palms and recited in a dull voice, "Twas a combined effort of the Highprites, brought forth from Limbola. Morgrand stormed Areth with an army of Elementals, demons, and ogres turned to his cause. They descended upon the Kazir. And slew them. The Kalibah Crystal was lost. It instigated the War of the Elementals. Titans clashed—and fucked the Gaia almost as bad as Shirdron. See, my ears did not stray from your ponderous history lesson."

Brapin's eyes narrowed. "What became of the lodestone?"

Targin stifled a yawn. "I don't know. Perhaps it adorns some highborn damsel's décolleté."

"Make mock at your peril, buffoon." The Orbical threw his hands up. "Shirdron found it and—"

"And attempted to use it to curtail the Dragon Wars," Targin interrupted.

"Though not destroyed, the crystal split, its broken pieces scattered. Several fragments, like the one around my neck, resurfaced."

Brapin raised a finger. "But the largest shard passed out of all knowledge. The last account places it somewhere between the Ruin's blight and the flaming chasms surrounding Mount Marwolaeth—in the Land of Fire. And *that* is where you must…"

Targin hunched forward, folded his arms on the counter, and let his chin sag on top of them.

Brapin slammed his fist on the table inches from the Nightwolf's nose. The air cracked and the candle jittered. Their cups rattled, amber geysers flowering up out of each.

Targin bolted upright.

Many heads spun at the commotion.

"Stars *burn* you," the old man flared. "I've waited the full morning and most of the afternoon for you to get your beastly arse off that haystack. The least you can do is pay attention. I do not spew some solipsism. What I impart affects your charge—specifically where you must take them."

Targin raised his hands in defence, and his hackles in anger. "The Kusp of the Testament speaks of Marwolaeth—*Mount Death*, but it's more than a thousand leagues north. And prophetic words can be interpreted—there are the skews from doctrine to consider."

"Vamsah be praised, at last," Brapin exhaled, tilting his head to the rafters. "Welcome back to the land of the living. The Kusp does say something, but not in so many words. Although privy to certain dispensations from the Darkest One, Necatar seeks to capture enough shards to reconstruct the Kalibah Crystal as best he can. Even a fraction of the full gemstone can draw us closer to Obliteration."

Targin ran his teeth over his lower lip. "So sure?"

"Sure as the sun crosses the sky," Brapin answered. "Sure as the mooncycle dictates a woman's blood-let. Barring Shirdron's disaster, it is impossible to surmise what might happen if a reassembled Kalibah is put to evil use. It holds the power to align the planets and stars. Or damn them to oblivion. And if he harnesses its might, the Summoner may trump us all."

"Not bloody likely," Targin scoffed. "Necatar's a pawn—and a blind one at that. He will never get enough of the jewel, not if I can help it."

"Then help—by listening to me," Brapin said. "The crystal was forged at the moment of the Starbirth, its physical form laden with Creation's infinite energy—the wilderen magic of the ancients. But when Shirdron invoked the False Starbond, he threw the Starbalance into chaos. He shattered the gem, casting the fragments in every direction. Even in their present form, the shards can unleash the wildest magic, not enough to invoke the Starbond hysteresis, but more than enough to ensure its failure."

"I've gleaned something of his secret ploy," Targin revealed. "Necatar seeks the pieces to circumvent the Four Siphons, in a misguided attempt to supplant the Darkest One himself. Cele's knave would do Shirdron proud."

Brapin closed his eyes in affirmation. Both parties reached for their mead at the same time and drank.

"Gaegungen believes the shards might also rend a more stringent portal between the physical and spiritual realm," Targin said as he parked his cup back on the table. "The demons of Infern could then come and reap as they please… or something worse."

Over the rim of his cup, Brapin nodded with his eyelids. He lowered the goblet. "Something worse exists. And that is the one 'piece' this Necatar already has in his possession. Beyond the fiery domain of Infern, indeed beyond the Void of Obliteration itself, this primeval abomination resides."

Targin swallowed and looked down at a nimble mouse scurrying for cover along a far wall. "I've seen it." The rodent vanished into a hole. "In my worst nightmares, the monster behind the sniffing nose—I spoke of it last night during Brooke's indoctrination."

The old man dipped his chin. "I have its name, least in the common tongue: *Souleater*."

Targin grunted. "Why am I not surprised, considering what my sprite visions revealed of it? I for one know enough not to take such divination lightly. The nymphs have steered my path away from ruin countless times. Stars, I'm still alive for it."

"Then if you've gleaned the hyperdemon's abilities, you appreciate the threat it now poses to our designs."

"I'll be ready for the necromage, and my Siphon opposite, but with this beastie Necatar dares unleash, I'm lost," Targin confessed. "Still, the sprites have made me aware. It won't set foot on Areth without my knowing." He placed his hand on the hilt of his broadsword, reassured by the sprite-charmed weapon.

Brapin coughed, drawing Targin's regard. "It already has."

Targin started, his grip on the pommel slipping. "What?"

The Orbical raised a hand. "A restrained demonstration, instigated by the necromage to strike his bargain with Deathwrought and prove the hyperdemon's value to the Darkest One."

When Brapin lifted his eyes to meet Targin's, his brows grew weighted. "And prove it he has."

"How—pray? Where—*when?*" Targin probed in escalating measures. Goosebumps prickled the nape of his neck. If something could faze Brapin enough to make the clairvoyant hesitate, it cast the Nightwolf in a doldrum of despair.

"Before your time," Brapin finally said. "And naught but the once." Targin let his broad shoulders slump. Relief flooded through him until rising suspicion dammed it. *Why the Orbical's hesitation?*

Brapin rubbed his chin and observed the candle thoughtfully. "Close to the end of the Second Rennen, it would be." The seer's chin rose. "By— um—Vamsah's holy light, we will stop Necatar before he unleashes the hyperdemon unbridled. If not, the true rapine of Areth will begin—enough to make Shirdron's Folly a mote of dust in the ashes riven of Creation."

The lights of the tavern seemed to dim as Brapin finished. "That is why I fear for you."

"For me?" Targin squeaked.

Brapin pressed his lips into threads and tapped the side of his head with a bony finger. "Deathwrought will not strike the hand or foot of an opposing paragon. But the mind. You would do well to remember that. Countless foes lay dead in your wake, but the threat posed by Souleater... it prowls outside the purview of Creation's strictures, beyond the conflict between Vamsah and the Darkest One. Ungoverned by their dictates. At some point, it will hector your path."

The Nightwolf shifted in his chair, his bulk making it creak loudly.

"Indeed, your eyes tell me it has already begun," Brapin observed.

"Tell me true, Brapin, have I glimpsed my future fate? Does it stalk me?"

The Orbical sighed. "The aberration is real enough. It has already shifted the foretelling writ in the Kusp. Apart from Deathwrought's Four, dark elven also vie for dominion or destruction. Necatar may be Souleater's sniffing tool, but the hyperdemon itself poses a unique threat. Minion to none, of the darkest brood beneath the blackest you can fathom."

"I had hoped the hyperdemon wasn't real," Targin lamented. "A false lure of the Darkest One—but I have felt Souleater's presence in here." He patted his barrel chest with a fist. "Haunts me even whilst awake."

"Likely Necatar's doing," Brapin said absently. He took another drink.

"The necromage must've collected a few Kalibah shards already," said Targin. "Three Sendings from Hell he's pitted against me and mine. He's foiled many a covert mission. Several Nightwolves and countless innocents took the deepest sleep on his account."

Targin gulped as his thoughts veered to Val. He took a deep breath and tipped back more mead. "But my heart mirrors yours, old one. Souleater marks the sorcerer's master card."

Brapin shook his head slightly and the corners of his mouth trembled. "A powerful Orbical am I, but I will neither lie nor soften my import with conjecture. I tell it like it is to toughen you. Souleater represents an immutable piece. I am yet to learn if anything can defeat the entity. Even Deathwrought risks all by allowing it into the Starbond endgame."

"How so?"

"The hyperdemon existed before existence began, before Vamsah and Morgrand."

Targin harrumphed, "How can that be if Vamsah *is* the Creator?"

Brapin lifted his scrawny shoulders. "Creation had a beginning. So too, the Creator."

Fresh beads of sweat trickled down Targin's temple. "Sorgons, Siphons, I can handle, but this horror…" he swallowed past the lump in his throat. "What can you suggest?"

Brapin placed delicate fingers on Targin's forearm and patted it. "Strength, Nightwolf—you wield an abundance of it. Continue your pathless path, but follow your wolven heart. Necatar has not made his grand move with Souleater yet. My heart tells me he cannot. There are stranger forces at work, to which even he must adhere. Souleater's true alignment is to chaos— that much cannot be overstated. Deathwrought must treat with it carefully. And when you face it, so must you. Remember that and you will prevail."

Targin arched an eyebrow. Did the Orbical even realize his riddlesome assurances only added fuel to the pyre?

"A mystery yet to be solved." Brapin clapped his hands and rubbed them together. "But solve it we will." He offered Targin a warm smile and went on in a sprightlier tone. "So, the Kalibah. All who fight for Areth will need as much of that crystal in the Veins' hands as possible. Despite your recklessness and vulgarity, I'm afraid you're the one Vamsah chose to shepherd the Four and serve as Creation's champion. The Starsmith placed this burden on your shoulders because you have the strength to bear it."

Targin clutched the amulet at his chest, felt its weight, and absorbed the power of the Kalibah fragment seated there. The crystal's magic calmed him but not enough. He deflated his lungs.

"Such a *small* charge you lay at my feet," Targin replied, his voice thick with bitterness. "What makes you so sure I'm Areth's only hope? There are Four Veins. Perhaps Gaegungen, or the dwarven sod he seeks to rescue, or the hallowed elven I'm set to guard. Maybe one of them will complete this impossible task."

"True," Brapin allowed. "But it does not fall to one individual. You form symbiont parts to the whole—Four Veins mirroring Four Siphons to One Heart."

Targin nodded emphatically. "The Law of the Octagon—not even the deviations to our so-called prophecy can change that." He let out a hollow laugh. "Does beg the question though: why follow a book of prophecies at all, when it's wrong half the fucking time?"

The Orbical exhaled and took a long pull of mead. "For now, just follow your visions exactly as they've guided you—to Sentinel's Retreat."

Targin frowned. "The Retreat—why?"

"You must go there—to await your three counterparts."

"My warbird can fly me there in a day," Targin said.

Brapin shook his head. "No. Stay on the ground. Approach it along the central stalk of the Relay."

Targin baulked and drew back his chin. "I think you've been at your cups ten drinks too long, old man. A journey into the Relay would take weeks and require many provisions. It's one step removed from the Dead Forest—an unnecessary high-risk folly."

Brapin folded his arms and closed his eyes. "It is necessary. In the sky, you'll risk much and more. You belong on the ground, Nightwolf. And you will have provisions." When his lids fluttered open, his pupils steeled and his jaw set in granite. "This is something I insist you do."

Targin muffled a litany of unintelligible curses, which Brapin dismissed with a brusque wave of his hand. "Now, where was I?" He scratched his earlobe while Targin counted three vexed snorts, each one bringing the candle's flame dangerously close to guttering. "Soon, Gaegungen will collect the dwarven Vein in Grendamaul and hasten him to the Retreat. The elven Vein is an outlander, who resides in Otherworld. His sprite wards know to do the same."

So that's where the prissy's from. Targin made a mental note when a confluent thought glued his eyebrows together. "Why Sentinel's Retreat?"

"The chantry upon its summit houses a wilderen hub, more powerful and secure than a point-to-point translation, but above that, it marks the juncture where the Four Veins will converge." The Orbical steepled his hands together. "Ergo, that is where you must also hurry."

"Why not Galandrium?" Targin asked. "The elven have their own—"

Brapin hoisted his twig of an index finger. "Aberrations will not affect this one event. Even the Darkest One cannot change that. It would hurt his designs more than our own should he deign tamper. Else there can be no Starbond. Trying to malign the Veins ahead of your Merger is his plan."

"This one event seems a fool's errand," Targin said sourly. "Stars, they're all foolish."

"Foolish?" Brapin's eyes blazed anew, making Targin shrink under his glower. "Disregard the words of an alchlemage and he'll call you cavalier. Disobey a king, he'll brand you treasonous and clap you in chains. But dismiss my abilities as Orbical and you pilot the Kusp's divination on a downward spiral that will doom us all. The only real imprudence is to place what you *think* you know above what I *do* know."

"Peace, Brapin," Targin chortled past a bemused smile. "Forgive a barbarian his loose tongue."

Squinting his whole face into a mask of dubiety, Brapin jeered, "Then tell those donkey ears to ward your mouth's bray."

"Stars align," Targin said. He leaned in, sensing another dire revelation on the horizon.

"Deathwrought readies his hammer blow for that precise moment," the seer cautioned. "The Merger will free him of all restraint. To counter this, amass a host in Serenthia—as many as King Johlarin can spare. Tell His Grace to prepare them for war."

Targin splayed his arms as he complained, "Quests, collections, *and* a war? If all three charges knot my convoluted purpose, my stars are truly fucked. How does Johlarin's army play into this wonderful mess?"

"They will serve as your shield," Brapin said. "And Areth's defence, while you guard the other Veins."

Brapin paused, his eyes narrowing into slits. "Be prepared, Nightwolf, for everything and anything. Glamours spring everywhere. Surety is a trick of the light. And not all is as it appears."

"Traps within traps," Targin agreed. "It's why I tread the pathless path."

The Orbical gave him a brief nod and drained the rest of his cup. When the main tavern door opened and a cadre of nightly regulars entered, an evening breeze found its way to their booth and caused the candle to flicker.

Brapin's gaze shifted to the entrance until the door creaked shut and the flame tongue steadied. Then his attention swung back. "If you fail to intercept the Veins, we start the clock to our annihilation—it's as simple as that."

"Simple, if you believe simple words," Targin mumbled.

A fly alighted on the table beside the candle, giving the insect a strangely long and sinister shadow. Quick as a whip, the Orbical's hand slapped the bug, pasting it into the wood.

But when Brapin turned his palm over, the fly docilely clung to the old man's wrinkled skin, wings abuzz. A moment later it flew off to another part of the tavern. "Not all is as it appears," he repeated.

Targin met the old seer's regard. "Frankly, this mule has never trusted the Veins' quest. Indebted to the sprites I remain—but having my life snuffed for a bunch of freeborn folk, such as the citizenry of your precious Riverside and—"

"Orb is my home," Brapin reminded him. "I am strictly passing through."

"—and the dwarven, and we mustn't forget the holier-than-thou elven—those meddling, frolicking, fucking-underhanded elven. Have you forgotten the oaths I swore before the sprites?"

"Move and countermove, Targin," Brapin replied. "And you ought to amend your endearing opinion of elvenkind—the sooner the better. The skews are precisely why you must attain the Kalibah—to maintain parity. Before the Endstorm breaks, you will see how everything connects."

"Endstorm—sounds so final," Targin grumbled in a dejected tone. He drained his glass and stared at the hearth. The fire hissed and popped loudly, bringing him back to the moment. "You know what I wish?"

"Speak."

"I wish I was the simple gods-be-damned brigand the world seems happy to paint me, rich in a free life as I am in wealth, without all the doom and gloom of the Kusp's dirges and verse."

Targin inflated his chest and looked to the bar, a sudden thirst hankering him for a refill. "And if my marriage to Tasmin should fail, well, I'd follow the pathless path into life's eternal brothel, drink deep of the chalice that is woman. Maybe even sire a few pups and live out my days working fertile fields in peace."

"But we both know that's never going to happen, at least until you complete your charge," said Brapin. "Though admittedly, your fantasy sounds nice. I too wish it could be that for you."

"Ah well, if Vamsah ordains the pathless path for me, who am I to question my own maker?"

Brapin straightened in his seat and braced his palms on the table, adopting what struck Targin as a kingly posture. His unblinking eyes twinkled with sagely resolution, ancient wisdom, and a raptor's focus. The sight left the Vein feeling much better about, well, everything.

Stuff what the old man said about the importance of Targin's role. Like the sprites, if Brapin wasn't around to guide his hand, this Scion would have failed long ago.

As the only known, still-living Orbical on the Main, the dogged seer didn't merely interpret the Kusp's prophecy, he could unfold its hidden import before the writer put quill to parchment to log the divination.

"You'll be tried and tested—like that poor dwarven Vein toiling in Grendamaul," the elder said. "But you too will endure. Remember, Nightwolf, Vamsah chose you because of who you are. Heed the disciplines of your sprites and sires and never discount the counsel of Gaegungen. You supply the wind that fills the ship's sails, but let the wizard steer the craft."

Targin glanced over his shoulder as a pair of portly musicians assembled on the corner stage. Another fly swerved into view. He followed its flight to

Brapin's shoulder.

"Remember, Seer, I am only one man. I'll need the Kazir to share this burden, and soon," Targin admitted. "As to my surrogate father and my blood sire, I honour both unto the deepest sleep. Had it not been for the meddlesome elven, Tragmar would still be alive to lead, instead of my enemy's man—this Aviry Brooke. Apparently, you and the wizard, and Dras of the sprites, have better instincts than me."

"You have done right by delegating your pack to the Pathguard commander," Brapin gave back. "All three of us can't be wrong."

"But there are my Wolves to consider—the majority consider Brooke untested, that he will fail or betray them." A shadow passed over Targin's mood, his thoughts straying to Val again.

"Still, I did as you instructed, and they will obey my command. Does that not bespeak how much I heed your counsel?"

"As did Tragmar, your father true," Brapin said.

"Look how he wound up," Targin brooded. Even from the grave, Tragmar's exploits became the stuff of legends. He brought together the fiercest warriors from his race to accomplish what the elven could not. His resolve alone had turned the tide of war.

"Least he's famous. The Second Rennen War took his life and some sod pasted his name on a map to remember him by."

Brapin coughed, curtailing Targin's sour reflections. "Knowing the key role you play, dark elven will conspire against you too. Beware, for they have many indentured servants, many spies."

"Only one thing I hate more than elven," Targin grated, "Stars obliterate the whole cursed lot. That's another reason I follow the pathless path: keep those ugly fish-stinkers guessing."

"One last item," Brapin chimed in. "Except for Gaegungen, the other two Veins remain untried in the wilderen ways. Their power, constitution, and resourcefulness are not lacking, but you may need to help them cultivate their emblems."

"So, am I to be their wetnurse?" Targin mocked. "Shall I sweep their domiciles and clean their privy while I'm at it?"

Brapin clicked his tongue, face hardening with stern ridges. "Put it in their heads to reason on their own, independent of our tinkering or communion. Both must learn self-reliance."

"Of course, I will do what I can," Targin relented.

The Orbical stood and leaned in, his nose coming level with Targin's. "Make sure they know *my* mind in these matters. Word for word, I want you to repeat unto the Veins: 'You would do well to delve deep in Brapin's mind, to hear counsel.'"

Again, the seer tapped the side of his head with a finger. "Thoughts are things, and the thoughts of an Orbical can make things change." He drew back and gave Targin a long look. "Will you remember my words?"

Targin blinked before recalling himself. "Um—yes."

Brapin rose on his tip-toes. "Say—the—words."

"I *am* to serve as the quest's wetnurse," the Nightwolf snickered.

Brapin's nostrils flared. And Targin suddenly felt too tired to laugh. Stifling another yawn, he began in a slow monotone, "You would do well to delve deep into Brapin's mind to hear counsel. For, thoughts are things and the thoughts of an Orbical can make things change."

The Nightwolf raised his hands in surrender. "A truce, Master—please. I've committed every biting syllable and painful inflection of your riddle to memory. But now I am weary and my mind hurts. I've still a fair distance to reach Serenthia ere the dawn. Pray, deem our business here done—I must away immediately."

Brapin smiled. "Words unto deeds."

26: Thrumvedur
Targin

As Brapin and Targin left the booth, the pub's patrons paid them little mind. Immersed in their wine, ale, and conversations, only cursory glances found and left the mismatched pair as they walked towards the barkeep.

While Brapin retrieved his staff, Targin slid five copper pieces across the counter and made his way outside.

Once in the open air, the giant stole across the laneway to await his mentor. He looked out over a sizeable garden plot, facing a line of trees set back a good stone's throw from where he stood.

Through the silhouetted copse, the last sliver of an orange sun waned. He watched the fiery orb dip and spend the last of its fuel.

At length, the sound of fiddle music issued from the pub, then dithered. A moment later, Brapin sidled up beside him.

The Orbical leaned forward, both arms resting on his staff—a sceptre of gnarled wood. "For all your crudeness, you still retain the capacity to dream," he said without pretence.

Targin did not reply. He cocked his head toward the austere stable behind the tavern and beckoned Brapin to follow him. When they reached the entrance, an acrid mix of hay, urine, and manure overtook them.

Brapin bunched up his nose. "Why bring me here—pray?"

The breeze rustled the leaves of four apple trees standing sentry beside the shed. Apart from the odd grunt and clod of the horses within the barn, buzzing insects filled the silence.

Targin chewed the inside of his cheek as he studied the old man. "Just passing through—correct?"

The Orbical nodded.

"It is no longer safe to travel any path by foot or horse—least for the next few days."

"Why?"

"As the sun descended, I caught sight of something moving in the shadows of the forest beyond the glen—spying on me."

Brapin frowned. "Are you certain?"

"It hid when I spotted it." Targin bent an ear. Faint murmurs carried on the wind. "The most brazen of forest animals commune with me. They confirm—it did not come alone."

The wind died and the barn flies fell quiet. Targin tilted his head up. "Listen, all birdsong has vanished. They have fled." His attention returned to Brapin. "Trouble's afoot. Exactly as you warned, I am being hunted."

"Aye, but not this soon."

"Ploys and aberrations, remember? Necatar's a cunning one—perhaps he finally got the jump on you."

"Unlikely," the seer scoffed. "But if dark creatures lurk... Riverside remains charmed."

"I know, but why invite a siege when it can be avoided? Should I linger, I'll only bring harm to the good folk of the haven and its surrounds. Fate has already decreed I'll fulfil my pledge as far as the Merger—but it does not reveal how much collateral I might accrue along the way. I'm afraid that includes you, my wise friend."

"Oh, do not worry yourself on my account," Brapin chortled. "Orbicals have their tricks." His grin straightened. "But remember what I said. Perhaps that is precisely what they want you to do—to get you alone."

"That is *precisely* when I am most effective," Targin answered. "Treading the pathless path. I cannot dally until nightfall, waiting for them to strike. Fate or not, I must be at Johlarin's side if and when he calls the banners. Ensure Serenthia's king is not cajoled into committing his forces to some business he does not relish."

Targin placed a hand lightly on Brapin's shoulder. "Remain here this night and help watch with Klin. More than a tavern owner, he's a stout ally. With their quarry gone from its roost, my antagonists will abandon the pen."

Brapin planted the butt of his staff in the dirt. "You don't know what manner of darkling awaits you beyond the clearing. You haven't a single Nightwolf to assist you if these demons should force your hand, or your thoughts."

"That, they most certainly will not do," Targin assured.

"But how will you escape? By foot? Or do you seek a horse's company as you rush into the deepest sleep?"

"Neither," Targin laughed dryly. "I see my Orbical is not omniscient in all matters, nor has his mockery fled with the passing years. For once, let me enlighten you."

Brapin dismissed the jape with a brusque wave. The pungent barn smells elevated as Targin led him inside the stable, past a row of palfreys, chargers, and a pair of foals. At the rear of the enclosure, an empty pen greeted them.

Targin paused and scanned the gloom for a fifth, non-equestrian eye. Satisfied, he crouched and dug through the hay, scattering loose strands of grass with his thick hand.

In the dim light, the contours of a large trapdoor materialized.

Targin pried it open.

Framed by the hatchway, a ladder sank and disappeared into a shadowed square. Targin lowered himself until the darkness swallowed him.

With deft hands, he struck flint to stone and lit a torch he had left there. A moment later, a warm glow suffused the round walls of a well. From the foot of the ladder, he looked up at Brapin's face peering down at him. The old man's lips quivered as they worked.

Targin signalled him down with his free hand. Brapin's uncertainty was plain in his bunched eyebrows and jowls, both dancing in the torchlight. He glanced over both shoulders, then up at the ceiling before tossing his sceptre below. Targin caught it and waited for the old man to descend.

Down Brapin came, carefully sealing the hatch above him. At the bottom, he accepted his staff, turned, and gaped open-mouthed.

"Only Klin and I know of this tunnel, and where it leads. Now, you will too." Targin gestured with his arm. "This way."

He started down the dank passageway, Brapin on his heels. The further they walked, the less potent the barn smell became. A hundred steps later, it diminished completely as they came upon a wooden door with rusted hinges and crossbars.

"Be silent about this place," Targin cautioned as he pushed the door inward. Firelight filled the sanctum within.

Brapin inhaled, "By the stars. Your steed of flight rests here—and an avatar of the highest heavens at that."

"Hawkrike will suffice," Targin said as he stepped forward. "Though what you say holds true, unlike the elven, I've no need to bestow fancy accolades. Nor does he need to receive them. Isn't that right, Thrumvedur?"

The massive raptor bowed his head, which sat on an extended neck. Not quite a hawk, his rich brown feathers curved around his brawny shoulders and torso, revealing the raptor's great musculature beneath.

Even kneeling with wings folded, Thrumvedur easily dwarfed both men as he regarded them with fierce eyes.

Targin had readied Thrum for departure before he left to meet with Brapin, equipping the warbird with a leather harness, cinched behind his neck and underscoring a pair of immense wings. Stirrups and saddlebags strapped his flanks.

The raptor's feed and water troughs looked near-empty, and he'd picked clean a pair of conies Klin had brought him from his kitchen. By Thrum's bright and alert demeanour, he seemed refreshed and well-rested.

Pleased by this, Targin passed the torch to Brapin and drew up to the avian, stopping just below his curved beak.

"One of a kind," Brapin extolled to his back.

"Bred by sprite lore," Targin added as he raised his hand to preen the warbird's shoulder. "A mongrel true, part hawk, part Ahzarim, taking the best traits of both."

"His name means *thunderclap* in old elven," Brapin noted as he appraised the raptor.

A shadow passed over the Nightwolf's mood. "I know the meaning, but elven?" He turned and studied Brapin. "Are you sure?"

"I am fluent in every tongue spoken in Areth, including the lost ancient ones, so yes, I'm certain."

Targin exhaled. "I thought it a sprite name, considering they conjured him—a breed of one. If not for the love I bear my hawkrike, I'd ask he change his name to something dwarven or Kaziri. I want no part of elven devilry." He stroked the bird's feathers. "Don't worry dauntless one, I already consider you immune."

Targin paused and looked back at the Orbical. "Thrumvedur—*Thunderclap*—is the finest of all air jousters that fly Areth's skies. I'd put him up against any score of elven-bred eagles—and still, he would not be contested."

The Vein scratched the giant bird's crest. "Fine, he is, noble, staunch, fiercest in combat. His constitution, ironock-forged—my stalwart warrior of the skies."

"Seems you do share the elven penchant for avian accolades," Brapin observed.

"Pay him no mind," Targin said as he examined Thrum's sinewy crest. After a brief moment of communion, the hawkrike craned his neck over his shoulder.

"He understands you better than you understand yourself," Brapin noted. "His instincts sharpen—discerns the extent of the danger present."

Targin lifted his gaze to the warbird. "All hawks align with the sprites, old man, and Thrum rises one echelon above them. Of course, he knows what we're up against—that's why the sprites bred the fearless avian to be my bird. But you are both correct. The time has come to leave."

Thrumvedur stood to his full height and fanned his wings. Their tips touched the walls on either side. Folding them again, he waited.

"The creature you spotted—did it bear wings?" Brapin asked over Targin's shoulder.

The Nightwolf moved to a table set against the wall. On it, a selection of armaments lay strewn. "From what I espied, it had none."

Thrum let out a quiet squawk and scraped his talon against the uneven stone floor. "Danger encroaches even as we speak," Targin relayed, "from many fronts." He donned an ironock helm and hoisted up a breastplate. "They move into position to spring a trap for me."

A pair of gauntlets and boots came next, followed by a cape strung over the ensemble. From an angled sheath married to the wall, he retrieved a long telescopic lance that could unfurl twice the length of his body. At present, it extended a third of that span.

Fully armed, Targin climbed onto the hawkrike's back and took the reins. He inserted his feet into the stirrups. Rider and beast became one.

Balancing the polearm between knee and saddle, Targin reached inside one of the panniers and produced a small scroll. He unfolded the document and read its contents, incanting the words in silence.

On the far side of the pen, a thin beam of light stemmed from the bottom of the stone wall to the top. It traced definitive contours, unveiling a portcullis that had not been there moments before. A low grating sound rose as the door pushed outward.

"The real hazard lies beyond that hidden entrance," Targin said to the air. The door splayed open and stopped. "This is where we part, Brapin. Go back the way we came and keep your head low until I am gone. The less you know of my intent, the safer you will be. When my Wolves arrive, give the commander what help you can. He is a seasoned tactician in matters of war, but still green in the way of the Code. Considering what he may represent to my band, I have a feeling he will need much advice."

Brapin flicked his chin. "I will give word and counsel to the Wolves when they pass—especially to their steward. Any message you would have him hear?"

Targin faced forward and hefted the lance once more. "Only to make all speed to the Strong Helm."

"And caution," Brapin added. "On that note, keep your eyes sharp, your mind sharper."

"Have I ever failed?" The question hung in the air. The silence spoke loud enough. "I understand better than most what's at stake. I'll remember your counsel, and the words you bequeath to the other Veins. Farewell Brapin."

The old man's wrinkles softened. "And you, Nightwolf—and to you, Thrumvedur." The raptor gave a curt nod.

Torch in hand, the Orbical moved back the way he had come.

Targin curved his neck around. "Brapin?" he whispered after the elder. The seer turned.

"However riddle-laden and cumbersome your counsel, I always mark your words." Targin did not wait for a response. He impelled his avian mount forward.

Into the shadows, they went.

27: The Ride
Targin

Past the entry, a sloping gully swathed in underbrush awaited. Further veiled by eventide's deepening gloom, Thrum's egress to the surface would be completely masked. Content, Targin coaxed his warbird forward.

The stone door shut behind them.

Thrum slipped through the overlapping curtains of foliage until he emerged onto a dimly lit glade. The renewed zephyr did little to calm Targin's nerves as he scanned the ghost-scape. He impelled the avian into a magnificent vault.

The raptor sprang over a row of woodsmen's logs, and with a crumpling *swish*, landed neatly atop a pile of dead leaves.

Further on, the vale opened. It would allow enough space for the giant warbird to take wing and still clear the closest trees.

In the evening sky, several stars had emerged and the wind whispered a haunting lament, buffeted by the forest's brakes.

Thrumvedur made to extend his wings, paused, and retracted them.

Targin's senses quivered.

Then spiked as a monstrous shadow launched from the canopy, blocking the stars above. It crashed into the Nightwolf, wrenched him out of the saddle, and knocked the polearm from his grasp.

As Targin hit the ground, he absorbed the impact, rolled. And twisted, shifting his foe's direction away from him.

His own momentum fluid, Targin scrambled to his feet in a flash.

His attacker bolted up twice as quick.

The creature's bulk stretched an arm's length over Targin's head. It resembled a wolven kobold—half-man, half-wolf—but one mutated into the largest troll he'd ever seen. Only blood magic could do that: dark elven theurgy.

Claws seized Targin. Hoisted him high above the grizzly canine crown.

Kobold or troll? Before Targin could form an opinion or draw Fang, the awful-smelling creature flung him hard towards the same heap of logs Thrum just cleared.

Pain lanced through Targin as he smacked the strewn timber. But the bone and sinew of his frame stayed intact—one boon to being a Vein.

Targin shook off his stupor and drew his blade. Kobold or troll? He wrestled with the question when the monster lunged again.

With a shriek that filled the glen, Thrumvedur interceded. Wings splayed, claws extended, the hawkrike attacked the creature's flank, forcing it to turn and deal with his talons.

Even as Thrum swept past, tearing at the beast, it spun back and hurled towards Targin in a series of giant bounds.

But the extra moment Targin's mongrel bird bought him proved all the Nightwolf needed—to conclude he did not face a kobold but a troll.

Claws sprawling like siege hooks, the troll pounced. Targin feinted with a swift tuck and roll, swiping Fang in a tight arc as he crumpled.

Still agallop, the bloodied beast swerved but its momentum made it lurch and stumble forward. Feet skidding in the dewy grass, the troll ploughed into the same woodpile Targin had struck.

The Nightwolf bark-laughed, "Your turn."

The troll found its feet and leapt back, howling in fury as it came. Targin gleaned a new tack take shape. He bolted away, racing towards the closest tree—a young spire with an eight-inch trunk.

His feet found air.

Then, the tree.

So swift and powerful was his sprint, he continued to run up the slender stalk.

Clearing four vertical strides, Targin somersaulted back off the stem— vaulting over the head of his foe as it careered headlong beneath.

In a shower of splintering bark and snapping wood, the troll bowled the tree over. Into the underbrush, the beast ploughed, still clasping the trunk in its claws like a drunken pallbearer.

Broadsword thrust forward, hilt firmly gripped in both hands, Targin flew at the troll. Even as his adversary scampered up and wheeled to meet the attack, the blade bit deep into its mottled torso, leaving only three fingers of steel exposed to the guard.

The troll's cry shattered the night air. But it did not fall. It went berserk, doubling its efforts to send Targin into the deepest sleep before death's lull coerced it the same.

Backjointed legs jarred the Nightwolf with a reflexive kick before the monster's burly arms seized and drew him into a crushing embrace.

Targin fenced with the troll's claws but got tangled in his opponent's vice-like squeeze. Ribs bent, lungs pressed flat, air squeezed from the Nightwolf's lungs. He could only wedge his arms against the creature's head to keep it from biting his neck with its gnashing fangs.

Somehow, Targin freed an arm and threaded it into the hollow between the troll's bicep and torso. With a heave, his fingers found the hunting knife the Vein kept tucked in his belt.

He flipped the dirk's tip. Thrust it into his foe's brawny limb. And raked.

Blood spurted out of the widening gorge, splattering both combatants. As they spun and spun in mortal waltz, Targin thought his spine would snap. He could no longer breathe—!

But then, the troll's grip slackened at last. Targin's dirk had severed enough tendons in the beast's arm. Lungs heaving, the Nightwolf greedily sucked air as the troll adjusted its stance.

When the beast shifted its strength to its good arm, Targin saw his chance. Still fending off the maw, he tossed the knife from one hand to the other. In a lightning one-two thrust, he rammed the blade into both of the troll's eye sockets.

Still embedded in the second orb, Targin's stinger blinded the beast and curtailed the worst of its fight.

Shoving off and lolling away, the troll tried to escape but faltered to its knees three steps later. Targin wasn't finished. Legs braced, he made a fist with a gauntleted hand, wound back. And landed a surgical punch to the base of the troll's neck.

An audible crack and the creature pitched over to one side. Dead.

Targin yanked his sword and knife from the troll's carcass and backed away, covered in blood and viscera. "*Cur*! Play at being a kobold, do you? Soiled me, Fang, *and* my stinger, stars burn you."

He cleaned the worst of the troll's entrails from his weapons and person with a quick slide over the grass. "This mess and reek deserve a second death. Come back to life so I can kill you again."

Squaaaawwwkk! Thrumvedur interrupted Targin's grumbling. He looked up. Still atremble, two lessrtrolls lay ripped open from neck to chest. "Guess that'll have to suffice," he said, admiring the raptor's handiwork. "Thank you, my friend."

Although grateful for his warbird's intervention, Targin's roused suspicions peeked. The fury which drove his antagonist was one thing, but to see two more trolls working in collusion quelled any doubt. Typically, trolls roamed as solitary hunters. They'd sooner attack and cannibalize each other than work together. Necromancy orchestrated this ambush, formidable enough to compel trolls. It could mean only one thing.

Dark elven.

And if they had come around, it could mean many things. Many more enemies. Powerful though he may be, Targin was not above fear.

The Nightwolf stood and quickly sheathed his sword and dagger. After retrieving his fallen lance, he joined Thrumvedur. "I believe tonight's festivities have only begun. Time we take our leave."

The hawkrike knelt, allowing Targin to mount easier. Once seated, he secured his weapons for flight and aerial combat.

Thrumvedur rose to his full twelve feet. Abandoning subterfuge and caution to the wind, Targin urged his mount for a take-off run. The bird darted forward, flapping his great wings and building momentum.

Movement erupted all around them as legions of goblins and trolls and freakish things Targin couldn't recognize closed in on all sides. The ground shook with their passage. Elongated faces with grinding fangs filled the glade.

Swift carriages ablur with unnerving speed, Targin's enemies tried to hem their quarry in.

Thrum skidded to a halt.

"Here comes the second act!" Targin yelled as he spun his mount around and around looking for their best possible escape. He found a short knoll in the centre of the enemies' converging lines and spurred the raptor on that course.

Thrumvedur's wings spread wide. Pounded air. Rushing forward, the raptor's legs pumped the ground furiously.

But the gap narrowed. The army behind them pressed to their breaking point by the magic at work. A few moments more and the avian would go down in a tackle.

Targin clenched his teeth and braced for impact. Leaning forward in the saddle, he brought his polearm up so its tip extended in front of the racing bird. He had to deflect any head-on attack—give Thrum a chance to evade the vanguard.

The hawkrike shrieked, ripping the distorting earth with his talons. Adrenaline coursed through Targin's blood. His neck veins bulged. Wind whipped past as his cry joined the raptor's. "Now, Bird, now!"

Thrum bounded in a series of magnificent strides and with an incredible uplift of his mighty parts, launched.

Before the hawkrike could hoist Targin to a safer height, another immense troll leapt high, lifted by magic, desperately trying to gain purchase of the bird's talons. Thrum banked hard in a tight turn and tucked his legs into his plumage.

It was all Targin could do to hang on.

The reins chafed his hands, as they narrowly missed the collision. The massive troll seized air before diving headfirst into the ranks bearing down from the opposite direction. Animate with violent forms, the ground fell away beneath the warbird's wings, now fluttering to a feverish pitch.

Several spears hurled up at the fleeing raptor. Targin caught one with his free hand, spun it on its centre axis and fired it back down to impale the goblin who cast it—and the goblin behind. The pair of skewered fiends pinned the ground for a moment before being trampled in the stampede.

A hundred more spears followed the first volley, each one trying to bring the hawkrike down, but desperation made their trajectories random. Thrum rose safely above their range. The fouled bolts fell back to the earth, dispatching several unlucky goblins rushing to meet them from the opposite front.

Although out of immediate danger, Targin knew he could not simply fly away. He had to conceal Thrum's flight path from whatever dark elven fiend controlled these legions.

Even so, having line of sight, the dark elven might still conjure some other necromantic attack. Being shot down by an elven cursed spear remained a clear peril.

Targin needed to do more than set Deathwrought's minions to rout—he had to disrupt their cohesion. But for the sake of continued subterfuge, he would not use his wilderen magics, potentially drawing one or more Siphons into the melee.

Alas, he never thought to beg a few dragon eggs from his crafty pyromancer, Spifer. But he did possess something that might do as well. Reaching into one of his saddlebags, the Scion produced a rune-covered obsidian stick, given him by the sprites. He made Thrumvedur circle until he found the best target.

Then, with all his might, Targin flung the charmed baton into the roaring press below. It sailed end over end until it touched the ground.

Boom!

The detonation unleashed a shower of fire and earth. At its flashpoint, the blast blew the goblins and trolls apart, eviscerating them en mass. Fiery sparks lanced in thin arcs from out of the fireball to rain down upon the next ranks.

Flames caught their hairy bodies, sending them cavorting in anguished frenzy to quench their relentless burns. The trolls spread the blaze back through the throng as they collided, trampled, and crushed the goblins behind.

The fire quickly feasted from minion to flattened minion, setting patches of dry bracken ablaze. Night became day as the conflagration vanquished the darkness in waves.

Targin nodded in satisfaction when the resulting smoke caused the desired pandemonium. It would disrupt any necromage or dark elven loremaster from completing some evil incantation. As he observed the carnage from a safe elevation, a thin smile touched his lips. Spifer would've loved this show.

When the clearing became, well, not so clear, charged with burning bodies and choking clouds, Targin saw his out. He coaxed Thrumvedur to bank into one last circle to scan for aerial foes.

Spying none, he bade the hawkrike fly due east. Away from the guttering light and chaos below, bird and rider swept over the darkened treetops.

Cool wind billowed past the folds of Targin's cloak. Wearied by combat and lulled by the rhythm of his raptor's easy glide, the Nightwolf grew drowsy.

'*I'd hoped to remain conscious until we arrived at the Strong Helm,*' he communed to his hawkrike. '*But even the sturdiest paragon must rest. Thrum, bring me home.*'

Targin retracted his lance and fastened it to the raptor's saddle with leather straps. Then, tethering himself to the seat with the reins, he made a cloak of his cape, leaned forward, and rested his head on forearms folded over the saddlehorn. His thoughts drifted away with his consciousness.

***

Unbeknownst to Targin or Thrumvedur, during their trials on the ground, a small black wasp had stealthily landed and embedded itself within the thick plumage of the hawkrike's underbelly. There, the insect nested.

All three flew on into the night.

28: Cusp of the Kusp
Sonart

Sonart came to with a start. Fingers scrabbling, he brusquely reached for Seolad's blade—until he remembered where he lay: the cold stone floor of his house. Drear-light filtered through the windows.

Nothing seemed disturbed. But the dimming before, stars burn his shadow, what hadn't he disturbed?

In the aftermath of the catastrophe, Sonart had navigated the dark labyrinth of the village centre. Somehow, he recalled the exact route—as if his mind had been imprinted with a map. He simply followed it, taking a roundabout way to the boulder-ridden ravine that led to his domicile.

His exhaustion clung to him like a ragged cloak as he stumbled past the doorway, locked the door, and collapsed on the floor like a soiled puppet—in true mimicry of himself.

The secluded cottage would serve to wait out one drear while the smoke cleared. Then he would flee for good. Considering how foolhardy the move, it might prove the last place any would search for him.

Sonart touched his forehead. Not even a scar—? Twice now, he received wounds that should've killed him. His nerves froze as the events of the previous dimming struck home: atrocities he perpetrated less than ten turns before.

No coming back from carrying out multiple murders, only forward as a fugitive among his own people—people he'd sworn to help. Whether innocent of the deeds or not, the surviving Elders and guards would only recall what they saw.

Their word would spread quickly.

Sonart held no illusions. Mob rules to be sure—if discovered. Still, the questions gnawed at him. Chief among them: what could he possibly do under such dire circumstances?

He sat up and propped his back against the wall beside the door. Dried blood caked his jerkin and crusted his beard and eyelids. They flaked and fell away as he blinked. Except for the sound of his breathing, the air had quieted.

Ought he give up? Surrender to his brethren? Admit his guilt and throw himself upon their mercy? Should it end on the Hooks, he might find absolution before he took the deepest sleep.

But even as the dark idea surfaced, Sonart chased it away. Not the answer. He possessed more than just a vision of the future. He had a map to it, like the chart that saw him home, free of enemies. He was never evil, only misdirected by it. The Darkest One used him.

Perhaps that in itself harboured the clue he sought. Something lay beyond Deathwrought's reach, some element that compelled the overlord to inflict such torment upon one lowly dwarven.

Sonart clung to the belief that his existence had a greater purpose, as his late father had ordained. Somehow, Farkshone marked the key. He focused on the prophetic words relayed by Rusic, long since committed to memory: *They are all in your keeping now. Only your hands can shape the path of those to follow. You are bound to your doom by a vast conundrum and destiny therein, beyond the lore of any testament. Within the chaos you will find the true path to structure, and deliverance for us all.*

And how could he forget the pleas of the Afflicted Ones? *Save us, Vein. Do not destroy the desecrated. Save us from our corruption. Save us from the land. Save us from ourselves.*

Damn it all, how could he save them from their illness when he'd been cursed with something worse? He was no alchlemage, no healer.

His mind emptied to blankness.

But then, like a cool zephyr freshening stale air, a different thought manifested. Sonart gleaned new insight from Rusic's final words. It filled him with—well, he couldn't quite define the sensation—except that it touched and supported and gladdened him.

Do not seek an answer... the answer will find you. All you must do is survive.

Suddenly, it came back to him. His search about the house had been interrupted when that Proclaimer witch craftily stole him away. Stars, had he come close to uncovering a secret the Darkest One did not want him to find? How could he have forgotten so easily?

Sonart tightened his jaw. He would not do so again.

Ignoring his growling stomach, the dwarven sprang to his feet. His hunger for evidence outweighed his need for food. With new strength and conviction, he vowed to finish the search he'd started.

Sonart opened and closed every cubicle and drawer, shuffled and overturned every bit of furniture, and scanned every scrap of parchment he found. He did not pause for anything until satisfied that it held no hints. His investigation proved long and arduous, but as drear waned to twilight only his refusal to acknowledge failure kept him going.

A thorough scouring of the entire cottage only produced a few ineffectual tools and books. Sonart slumped into a chair.

"Stars burn you, Rusic," he muttered. "Nothing." Could he have overlooked some hidden recess or ceiling slat? No, he'd combed every fucking inch of the abandoned house.

Sonart threw a weary glance at the stack of books he'd amassed during his search. Among them, partially hidden beneath smaller volumes concerned with mining and farming practices, and works of fiction, lay a thick musty tome of his people's lore and history. The Kusp of the Testament.

Judging by its long-neglected leather-bound cover and the sheaves of warped parchment it contained, the book hadn't been opened since he went to live with Auckland and Mila.

Resignedly, Sonart found his feet and sauntered over to the stack. He scattered the smaller books, lifted the large square text in both hands, and blew the dust off its worn covering. The ancient runes, gilded but tarnished, etched its surface:

KUSP OF THE TESTAMENT

Sonart opened it carefully, pausing at each protest the book made. It crackled ruefully, having remained shut for ten and six star-cycles. The decayed parchment smelled its age, not entirely unpleasant.

He sniffed, relaxing somewhat as he set the tome down upon the table, splayed open to its first dogeared page. The title was repeated here but underscoring it, appeared a block of smaller text, which Sonart recognized as the decrees of the first dwarven to swear fealty to the lore within.

Inscribed at the top of the next page the all-too-familiar axiom appeared: *He who suffers most endures all.* Immediately below, writ the common catchphrase which suffixed all psalms therein: *Be at One with the Kusp.*

Well, Sonart stood as *one*, alone—the damned always stood alone. And he held the tome in his hand, so both requisites seemed quite literally filled, just as his dead father had bidden him.

Be at One *with* the Kusp—the exact words Rusic had sworn to bequeath. Sonart inhaled sharply as a jolt of understanding coursed through him.

Seizing the book by its spine, the dwarven regarded it with new eyes. He cleared all else from the table, lit two oil lamps and placed them on either side of the massive volume. Next, he drew up a chair and sat, hunching over the text.

Sonart scrutinized every syllable, stopping only to wolf down a morsel of bread to quell his stomach's protests before returning to the table with a cup of wine.

One turn of the dial passed into his reading session when his lids grew heavy. The light from the oil lamps had diminished; so too, his ability to focus. Four pages later, he read something that made his heartstrings catch. A scribbled footnote inked in haste at the end of a chapter near the bottom of the page:

They are all in your keeping now. Only your hands can shape the path of those to follow. You are bound to your doom by a vast conundrum and destiny therein, beyond the lore of any testament. Within the chaos you will find the true path to structure, and deliverance for us all

Stars, there it was, plain as drear, penned for his eyes. His father's last message to his son, relayed by Rusic, only now in written form—scribed by his father's own hand.

Encouraged, Sonart refuelled the lamps and set about leafing through the Kusp, turning its pages and absorbing the words faster. It only spoke of doom and gloom with penance and obedience being the common thread throughout.

Several pages after the footnote, Sonart noticed a gradual change. The pages appeared equally creased and worn as the first, but the inked words upon them had faded more with every sheaf, until barely discernible from the page they emblazoned. And yet he still understood their meaning.

Saddling his semi-incoherence, Sonart continued to pry the pages open and examine every line of text. When he first opened the book, reading and navigating its chapters came dauntingly slow; the task grew easier the more he read. His exhaustion all but forgotten, it seemed the deeper he delved into the volume, the quieter the book's protests. And the greater his energy.

Sonart grabbed a thick ream of some hundred pages and flipped them together to a random section. His hand drew warmth from the act, more than what the two lamps supplied.

He retraced to an earlier section that he already read, then forward again to a part midway, then past his furthest point to more unread passages. All the while his movements became defter. As though the book itself guided his hand, awaiting some co-signal. Did it recognize his identity? Perhaps through physical contact with—

Sonart swallowed as recognition dawned. Something akin to the power he gleaned in the Cleft Augury. Aye, at last, some positive magic manifested, free of Deathwrought's taint. Subtle to the point of imperceptibility, but it was here, stars align, it was here, imbued in the pages of the Kusp.

Like his experience in the Augury with the Sword, Sonart didn't know what guided his hand, but something deep inside bade him continue—the same instinct assured he would not be interrupted or possessed this eventide.

Sonart followed the sequence of pages back and forth, reading only certain passages aloud, others to himself. With his waking eye, he *saw* the Augury. Each page turn seemed to free a gate-latch, present a new tunnel. And he, the key, or rather the map.

The associations crystallized as natural as breathing. The dwarven's progress grew so rapid that the pages flipped in a constant blur cover to cover. The book evolved into its own animate entity—exactly as the Sword had done.

A flare of light suddenly streamed out from the centre of the Kusp's gutter, casting a hot ethereal glow that lit the entire space, including Sonart's trembling digits. His pupils shrunk to pinheads as he furrowed his brows.

A moment later, the light winked out, but Sonart discerned it presented nothing ill-wrought but a quick signal that did not leave him feeling bereft.

It assured him.

Sonart knew this copy of the Kusp had been charmed and placed here exactly as it had by his father, intended for his son to uncover. And him alone. *Be at One with the Kusp.* He had passed the book's test. As had occurred within the Cleft Augury, Sonart's burden lifted, his weight lessening.

Only this time the magic endured to invigorate him, his uplift lasting and palpable. Without his hand to guide them, more pages turned of their own accord and with greater alacrity. Or responding to his will—*his power*. They slowed, found a mark somewhere in the middle of the thick volume. And stopped.

The nimbus returned, its brisance growing even brighter than before. Flaring tendrils of the book's light spread out from the pages, arcing across the room. They banished any trace of shadow, any doubt.

Somehow, the coruscation made the cottage a haven, rendering it and its lone occupant safe and immune. Immersed in the bizarre conflagration, Sonart stared through a fire with heat but no smoke.

And no pain.

The gush in the dwarven's heart had become as real and true as existence itself.

His anticipation mounted. At long last, Sonart fully understood. The seeking answer had found him.

29: Gauntlet
Targin

Targin awoke to a changed landscape, over which a full moon had arisen. It created an argent glow.

Wings spread and gliding calm, Thrumvedur cast a lunar shadow over the forest canopy far below. Judging by the moon's nearness to the horizon, the hawkrike had flown most of the distance they needed to cover while his master slept.

Targin reached back and patted the great warbird's tailbone. "You do me one good turn after another, my friend," he called over the gusts. "I'll see you re—"

A steady *thrump thrump thrump thrump* cut him short as it escalated over the wind's lament. Targin whipped his head left, right, and back. Nothing below either. Though he couldn't see any winged creatures, his ears did not lie. He untethered himself, coiling the reins tight about one hand.

Next, Targin freed his lance and firmed his grip upon it. "I'm ready. Get us out of here."

The raptor dove to the forested expanse, levelling off some fifty feet above the treetops.

Targin extended the polearm so that its tip pointed over Thrumvedur's shoulder. A sinking feeling assured him he'd need more formidable weapons before this night was done.

Another glance behind confirmed it.

A giant avian silhouette, slightly smaller than his hawkrike, caught the last light of the moon.

No mistaking that hideous bird as it emerged from the shadows of a cloud.

A crowbat.

Bred through dark magic, the raptor bore the beady orbs and beaked head of a crow, but the veined wings, claws, and fangs of a bat. At a daunting speed, it swept in closer.

Targin's eyes lingered. Where one of *those* uglies shows up...

Sure enough, two more crowbats materialized from the same charcoal cloud, forming up behind the lead raptor. Following them, some distance behind, a wall of black avians appeared—more than a hundred crowbats flying in vanguard formation—an entire wingward.

Piercing caws filled the sky.

Brapin's words slipped into the Nightwolf's head. *You belong on the ground.* He cursed and tightened his grip on the reins. "So be it."

A warning screech from Thrumvedur snapped Targin's attention forward again.

Below, another crowbat detached from a narrow cleft in the canopy ahead. Clever—distract him with the main host while this ferret took him out.

Like the murder pursuing him, the lone crowbat bore a hulking snout-faced hobgoblin as a rider. Sweat glistened down his olive-skinned body, wrapped in a sleeveless jerkin of stud-lined leather. Taller than an average man, the corded hobgoblin would tower over the lesser goblins of his wretched ilk. Prove more formidable in combat and as demonstrated, more cunning.

The distance closed. Lance couched under one arm, sword in the other, Targin adopted an aerial battle stance: leaning forward and bringing his knees up in the saddle. Thrum tucked his wings and surged into a lightning plunge.

The crowbat rushed up to meet him, its rider hefting a thick ironock spear. It would be close. Fast. Hard. But Targin had the advantage.

The birds came together in a stunning collision, wings and torsos glancing brutishly against one other. Claws raked the air as their riders' weapons clashed in a flurry of sparks.

Targin deflected the goblin's blow with the lance, but before they separated, the Nightwolf followed through with a back thrust of his blade. The barrel-chested goblin never saw it coming.

But Hob's peers saw it going—as the cretin's head sailed off his shoulders, carrying his gaping mask of shock to the forest below.

With the same momentum, Targin spun the blade on a counter-swing and plunged it hilt deep into the back of the crowbat's neck. The bird shrieked. Lost control of its wings. And plummeted as though trying to return the rider's torso to his fleeing head.

The sound of snapping foliage rose as the forest swallowed the ruined bird.

Targin craned his neck around and gaped. "Fuc—kers."

Crowbats and hobgoblins swarmed the heavens, converging from everywhere. Thrum would be routed or worse, hemmed—

Thwit-thwit-thwit.

Three arrows streaked towards him, shot simultaneously from different points. The hawkrike beat his wings feverishly to avoid them.

Too late.

Targin deflected the first shaft with Fang, but the second pierced his upper arm clear through the other side and the third plunged deep into Thrumvedur's underbelly below the arch of his wing.

The closest hobgoblin let out a guttural cry as his crowbat arced in, "I'll feenish the night-dug!"

And the bold ugly might even succeed. The effect of the poison-dipped arrow impaling Targin's upper limb set in. Burning nettles coursed through his body as he grabbed the shaft by its head and wrenched it free. The toxin dulled his senses, leaving him dizzy with vertigo. He'd better spread his foes' attack thin—and bloody soon.

Targin made to conjure some wilderen magic to blast the fuckers.

None came. *Damnation*, that marked the true grit of the poison they'd stung him with.

The Nightwolf barely managed to get his jousting shaft up as the next goblin collided with him.

Metal screeched and sparks flowered as Targin's lance crashed into his foe's spear. The Vein's weapon ripped from his sluggish grasp, pitchpoling toward the canopy below.

Four wings slapped one another, aflutter in their aerial merger.

Through the entanglement, his opponent produced a hidden scimitar and slashed at Thrumvedur's neck. But the raptor ducked just as the curved blade swung overhead. The hawkrike answered with swift swipes of his beak and talons, keeping both hobgoblin and crowbat at bay.

Frustrated, Hob grew careless, swung wider. And the scimitar sliced into the clod's own mount.

Had Targin not been so enraged, he might've laughed at his enemy's clumsy thrust. But the Vein burned with desperation, fuelling new dexterity and blunting the effect of the poison.

While Thrum dodged the goblin's hacks and jabs, Targin shifted his weight, released the reins, and used his still-functioning arm to bring his sword to bear. He raised his knees level with his shoulders, boots atop the harness.

Braced.

And sprang

The unexpected move caught the frazzled hobgoblin off-guard. Before he could coerce his wounded mount to back off, Targin landed between the crowbat's flapping wings, ploughed into his foe, and jousted him out of the saddle. The cavorting hobgoblin dropped into blackness.

Cries of dismay ignited from the closing ranks of his brethren. They answered Targin's stunt with a ruthless shower of spears and arrows.

But the Nightwolf was ready. He yanked the crowbat's straps, forcing the raptor to veer hard in confusion. Its bulk shielded Targin while Thrum beat his wings ardently to remain sheltered behind the crowbat.

In so doing, Vein and hawkrike dodged the deadly volley, dancing away while the crowbat served as an avian pincushion for the poisoned darts.

The crowbat's eyes bulged. Its beak opened wide in shock, tongue trilling like a rattle made flesh. But no sound emerged.

The surge of venom muted its anguish. Overcome by seizures, the doomed raptor managed a chortled half-croak. Then, it plummeted.

Targin dove off his bucking perch into air.

His flight arced towards the ground just as Thrumvedur shot up beneath him. The Nightwolf landed neatly onto the hawkrike's back. Ignoring the searing pain, he lassoed the reins around his bad wrist in a quick clasp.

"Dive, Bird! Dive!" Targin bellowed, streamlining his torso with the hawkrike's back.

Thrum shot down. His rapid descent shoved Targin's heart up against the roof of his mouth. Through an opening in the foliage, bird and rider dropped, sucked in by brush and gloom.

"Swift, swift!" The hobgoblin urged his crowbat, striking his raptor with a barbed flogger. The hen protested with a piercing caw, but it responded to pain—aye, where there's a whip there's a way—best teacher. The scavenger beat its wings with renewed vigour and dove. "We must, we must, for death we lust," he sang to his companion.

"Eyes sharp, cur," the other goblin warned over his shoulder. "The dug bears fangs." He whipped his own crowbat into a similar fury. "Crush the quarry quick, or Menagerie 'll short-work us."

"Sure as Infern," his cohort agreed. With that, he followed his leader into the only mouth of the otherwise impenetrable canopy.

When they dropped below its green ceiling they found—nothing. Just trees and more trees.

The lead rider wrenched back hard on his mount's reins. Squawking in avian rage, the crowbat billowed its wings and alighted on the closest branch "Where beeg fuckah go?" the hobgoblin yelled, scanning the ground as his winger's crowbat landed beside him.

"Couldn't have gone far," his mate said. "Nor weel-ee. Both our darts flew true, one for the night-dug, one for his pretty pigeon. Poison 'll take hold fore long."

"Surprised they ain't dead already."

"Yessss," a silken voice chimed behind them.

Both hobgoblins wheeled.

Menagerie.

Astride a giant onyx bat, nearly twice the size of their hens, the dark elven king, rose from the ground to meet them. "And why is that?" he hissed as his bat settled on another limb stretching out from the same tree twelve feet away.

Beneath a tuft of albino hair, the dark elven's sneer split his pitch-black face. He regarded the pair with glowing yellow eyes. An invasive smell of rotting fish wafted ahead of the newcomer. It filled the immediate tract with dizzying wrongness. "He might have ss-succumbed to magics, but you did ss-see his ss-steed. Hawks only ss-erve the ss-sprites and the men the ss-sprites pair them with. The Vein's privy to their alliance so it ss-stands that he also benefits from their magics."

Menagerie's bat snarled balefully, revealing a fence of impressive fangs. It leaned forward on its perch and extended its neck towards the two crowbats. They flinched, talons quickly sidestepping as they shied further back along the limb.

"Moreover, that *pigeon* was no common hawk," the dark elven went on, "but a hawkrike ss-sure—ss-suffused with ss-sprite lore. Draws ss-succour it does, wilderen power from the Nightwolf—a Vein of Fire. The raptor's ss-sprite charms buoy the Vein. Ss-so a formidable test lies before you two."

The hobgoblins exchanged glances, still startled by the king's stealth.

"But Masta—?" the first hobgoblin began.

"Ss-silence," Menagerie seethed. "A wolf far from his pack is less the threat and more the target." His serpent orbs flashed bright enough to bathe the surrounding trees in saffron light. The goblins knew better than to question aloud. Not that it mattered. By his icy regard, the dark elven had heard their silent protests nonetheless.

"Hearken unto me! You did not ss-see where he went—my, my, ss-such a tragedy." The dark elven took out an obsidian blade and extended it in a definitive direction. "But I did. He's attempted an expenditure of his wilderen, enough to track him. The trail of magic leads that way—ss-so that is where you go. Remember curs, you must unseat him from his mount to break their connection. If you do not unseat him, you will both die. If you return to me without unseating him, you will both die."

The hobgoblins sniffed the air with recessed snouts. To their relief, Menagerie's magic had heightened their senses to follow a preternatural wake. To them, it smelled like a strong glimmer of the hawkrike's bird scent. They gnashed their teeth impatiently—but knew enough to wait for their master's leave.

"I've diverted the wingward above the treetops to head him off at the next egress," said Menagerie as he sheathed his blade. "I'll remain here to guard the entrance above in case he tries to double back. You two will pursue him beneath the canopy. You have every advantage, including time, for raptor and rider are trapped within my kill box, both compromised by poison and lore. Unlike crowbats, his hawkrike was never bred or trained to fly through a forest at ss-speed."

Menagerie's mount fanned its wings and shrieked. Its master stabbed an ebony finger at them, lantern eyes blazing brighter, fiercer. "Remember, do not ss-stop until you unmount him. His death or yours—that is your only choice. Now fly, vermin!"

Anxious to flee the king's needling scrutiny, the hobgoblins kicked their crowbats' flanks with impunity. Over pained squeals, the black avians sprung their wings and surged off the branch.

Shadow-mired greenery rushed past Targin as Thrumvedur dodged massive trunks and branches. Limbs and leaves and limbs and leaves flashed by in interminable procession.

With the poison coursing through him, the speed-blurred foliage had a hypnotizing effect. Dawn's approach made the maze of shrubbery slightly more visible, but it still proved too dense, too dark—shrouded in the mist permeating the domain.

Targin's hawkrike had been honed to fly beneath such a canopy. Bred for speed and agility in combat, Thrum was, if not for the toxin and spells blunting the warbird's instincts and prowess—and Targin's own for that matter: bereft his faculty of magic. Would that he could command his wilderen emblem now.

Too risky to break cover and emerge above the forest's treetops. Even if he found an opening, Thrum would still have to meet any crowbats on unequal footing. Beyond a doubt, the entire wingward patrolled somewhere above him, waiting for him to make just such an attempt.

Targin's prolonged predicament had devolved from nuisance to mortal danger. He flagged, struggling to stay conscious and alert after the endless trials he'd faced this night.

Thrumvedur did not complain of the venom, strong and battle-hardened, but poison was poison—even the hawkrike could not properly meet the black scavengers head-on. No doubt, the dark uglies had placed a much larger snare, the Hobs pursuing Targin, merely the ruse.

With every moment that ruse gained on him—but only a matching ugly pair—some small grace. The forest creatures communed as much as the raptor streaked past the gauntlet of trees. In such an ailed state, Thrum could not outfly the crowbats in the restrictive space.

Targin had to think of something fast.

When a giant reddenbark tree hove into view, Targin found his solution. He stole a glance over his shoulder before communing his intent to Thrum.

The hawkrike banked towards the twenty-foot-wide trunk, wings fanning to slow his glide before he alighted atop a thick limb on the tree's far side.

Targin dismounted and immediately dislodged the bolt that had pierced Thrum. Next, he removed his cape before reaching into one of the hawkrike's saddlebags. Out came a fist-sized mace.

Its spiked ironock ball hung down from its handle, tethered by a five-foot chain. He set to work propping the saddlebags higher before wrapping them with the cape. *Ever the mummer.*

When their quarry's magical trail led to a reddenbark looming in the distance, the hobgoblins homed in on its musky grass scent. Completely in their element and having the upper hand, the heavy-set goblins slowed their crowbats, erring on the side of caution.

"More stingers," the lead goblin instructed his mate. "Triple volley." He flicked his snout towards the reddenbark. "Dug's behind the tree."

Standing in his stirrups, clamping knees against the saddle, the other goblin readied three poison arrows and nocked them on the same bowstring.

"Ready," he declared, licking his chops.

The pair surged forward, narrowing the gap, fangs clenched, nostrils flaring in anticipation. They spread out to cover both sides and slowed their raptors to a fluttering hover.

"Come out 'n play, Night-dug," the lead goblin taunted as he hoisted his spear shoulder height, elbow locked. The leader's crowbat nudged forward while his cohort's hen held back, wings pounding.

From behind the tree, the hawkrike burst into view, sprinting along the length of the thick branch.

The second hobgoblin pulled his bowstring back until the yew creaked. Sighted.

The lead goblin let fly his spear.

But limbs hidden by foliage fouled its trajectory.

The bolt recoiled, flipped, and went wide. *Curses!*

One bound, two, and the hawkrike took wing, its rider crouched forward in the saddle.

The lead goblin spurred his mount with a savage kick and gave chase, trying to get the hawkrike in the open so his mate would have a clear shot with his quarrels.

As his crowbat shot past, a metal sphere hurled out of the shadows from the far side of the trunk. A spiked mace tethered by a taut chain caught the hobgoblin square in the neck.

His snouted face exploded in a spray of blood. The hobgoblin's head wrenched from his shoulders and sailed in the opposite direction. The headless torso sagged, yanking discordantly on the crowbat's reins. The black bird hesitated, getting conflicting signals until the torso slipped off his back to fall heavily to the forest floor.

Suddenly its own master, the crowbat tried to bolt back the way it came.

But the other hobgoblin, not prepared for three moving objects, let all his arrows fly. Two went wide and the third shaft struck the fleeing crowbat between its shoulders. The crowbat's squawk cut short as the hawkrike rushed in, smothered the bird with his wings, and ripped out its throat with a swift swipe of its talon.

Panicked, the other hobgoblin backed off. The table had turned—upside down. Desperate to flee, he strangled his mount's reins and forced the bird to bank away before plunging into the thickest part of the forest.

***

Thrumvedur sailed beneath Targin, fanning his great wings to remain stationary. The Nightwolf hopped off the branch and onto the hawkrike's back, landing neatly behind his makeshift scarecrow.

Thrum shot down after the fleeing crowbat.

Desperate was Targin's pursuit. This close to his destination he could not afford a legion of hobgoblins hanging on his coattails as he came knocking on Serenthia's front—or in his case, backdoor.

Racing past trees, Thrumvedur must have called forth every sprite charm bestowed upon him, every scintilla of strength and resolve—to catch the frantic crowbat. In the thicker patch, the space constricted, growing more treacherous at every turn. One miscalculation and Targin would smite his raptor into ruin against a trunk.

No doubt, Thrumvedur understood. The hawkrike didn't allow the crowbat to disappear into the brush. He gained on the scavenger, ducked, banked, and darted through the clammy labyrinth.

The hobgoblin demonstrated commendable skills as a flyer, but Targin's tenacity never wavered either. Thrum steadily shortened the distance. When the hawkrike came to within a leap's breadth behind his quarry, the hobgoblin let out a horrific cry.

The gaps between the trees narrowed as the forest closed in. Targin saw this, but Hob didn't realize his jeopardy, too busy stealing panicked glances over his shoulder. His crowbat's wings brushed past webs of branches breaking them off in a shower of twigs and leaves.

For a moment, the horrified crowbat filled with wrath. It snapped and carped at its rider, any chance for survival vanquished. Fuelled by adrenaline, their flight grew erratic and inept, crowbat and hobgoblin reacting with uncertainty.

Another reddenbark materialized out of the shadows, cutting off the hobgoblin's escape. He frenetically tried to slow the crowbat. And tore the raptor's reins off in his terror.

The crowbat spread its wings to stop.

The hobgoblin lost purchase.

Targin leapt.

All four airborne. . .

The crowbat crashed into the foliage, impaling itself on a thick protruding branch. Targin grappled the hobgoblin by the back of the head. Convulsing, the crowbat let fly a stray talon, which tore the hobgoblin's face off and broke its former rider's neck.

Targin heard Hob's death crack even as he slammed into the impaled crowbat. The bird's ribcage snapped as Targin used it to break his own crash.

The Nightwolf springboarded away an instant later, barely avoiding the avian's slashing claws.

Targin fell.

And fell.

...but caught sight of a vine, draped horizontally between two branches. Landing atop the creeper, Targin seized it with his last strength.

The vine squirmed and uncoiled as his body carried the green line past its former perch. Its slack rapidly tightened. Reeled up.

With an abrupt jerk, the vine tautened. But still, Targin dropped. White-knuckled, he held on. Teeth gritted, he held.

And held.

His descent slowed. The Vein's carriage swung out in a wide arc which finally arrested his fall.

While Targin swayed back and forth on the life-saving pendulum, Thrumvedur returned to flutter just below him. The giant let go and settled neatly onto the warbird's back. He grimaced as the ache from the poisonous dart worsened. And what of his hawkrike's pain? They both had to reach haven before midday or neither would live to see the next.

Breaking away from the impenetrable cul in the forest, Thrumvedur found a most welcome—blessedly unpatrolled—cleft in the canopy.

Up and out, he flew to greet a morning sky, clear of hobgoblin swarms and imbued with the orange warmth of a rising sun.

The forest thinned further with every league until it gave way to open steppe. High above, Thrumvedur glided, using the steady breeze to help with his burden and carry him to their destination. The hawkrike showed unprecedented constitution, holding back the effects of the toxin, and the dark magic. But not daring to rest.

Targin did his best to unburden Thrum, casting away all his stores and weapons, save Fang, and bolstering the hawkrike's strength with chants and wards that Gaegungen and Brapin had taught him. Some small measure of wilderen had returned to him to boost the effort, but within an hour of their emergence, bird and rider were flagging.

Targin kept slipping from the saddle when woozy spells of faintness overcame him. Exhausted and compromised, the raptor's flight grew more erratic and it was all the Nightwolf could do to keep himself from falling off or passing out.

When at last, Targin sighted his destination, he intoned heartfelt praise to the Creator. The familiar sinkhole drew closer, scalloping the plains just ahead.

At the base of the hole's clay-mud walls, one hundred and fifty feet deep, sat a mirror of a lake, still shrouded in the morning mists.

To one side of its four-hundred-foot span, a beach skirted the rounded buttress, framed by a swathe of bulrushes with tall fronds. Although the sunken water hole avoided direct sunlight for most of the day, the lake reflected the sky. It gave the water's surface a brilliant sheen to contrast its dark circular frame.

Into the giant pit, Thrumvedur dropped, banked, coasted, lowered, banked, and coasted. Eventually, the hawkrike alighted on the beach, throwing up a cascade of sand under a blur of purchasing talons. He skidded to a halt. With a whisper of a caw, the hawkrike folded shivering wings.

Targin took a moment to wrap his mind around the miracle of their arrival: both drew air to appreciate the familiar surroundings.

To one side of the sandy sliver, the dark mouth of a cave yawned. Within the cavern, a gate of thick ironock bars protruded like teeth. Out of the sand, they rose to join the ceiling and block the entrance.

The dank stench of wet clay and swamp rot smelled pervasive, but Targin breathed deep. His nose told him everything looked as it should. And right now, he needed as much normalcy as he could get. Apart from a few scattered clouds drifting overhead, he and his bird remained alone—a good sign.

"You know as well as I, why we must be quiet and deliberate," Targin said as he slid off Thrum's back.

Agony forked his feverish mind as his boots touched the sand. He staggered three inebriated steps. The poison had spread into his chest and legs. It vacillated from a burning sensation to stinging, became numb, before repeating the cycle.

Thrumvedur snorted wanly in response, a wheezing ghost of an utterance, the hawkrike's sapped strength all too plain. Together they limped up to the gate and waited.

"Stars align, Thrum, we're home. We'll be rid of this damn toxin soon enough. Take a load off my—" Targin stopped midsentence. A disturbance in the lake caught his eye. Obscured by the veil of mist, something moved, causing a sharp ripple to break the surface and fan in all directions. Targin turned and lumbered to the shore where the small wave came to meet him. He watched it break and retreat.

"Odd," Targin whispered to the air. He scanned the lake's entire lay, up and down the cliffs to all points in the sky before returning his gaze to the water. The sentinel only emerges if there's a foe in its midst. "Something vexes the centipus, Thrum." He frowned. "But there's nothing to threaten the Strong—"

The lake erupted in a watery fury as a hundred black tentacles shot towards the sky. Six of them sprang through the corona of spray, coiled about Targin and Thrumvedur. And yanked them off the sand.

Stretched past the limit of endurance, Targin hadn't a shred of strength left to fend off the freshwater kraken.

So, he did not resist as the centipus took him. He had time to hear his hawkrike's stifled squawk before they both plunged hard into the lake's frigid depths.

As Targin sank, the grip of the undulating tentacles grew tenuous. Instinctively he let his body go limp to conserve air—that he might live long enough to find out why the leviathan had made such a grievous error.

When he communed to his raptor to do the same, the centipus immediately loosened its hold. The tentacles hauled rider and bird back to the surface. Through a cascading plume of water, the kraken shoved both on the foreshore.

Targin's vision swam as he wiped the worst of the pond scum from his face. At least the dunk had washed away the bloodstains that his skin and raiment accrued from his recent fights. He looked up.

Thrumvedur had fared only slightly better. The hawkrike plopped in the sand, legs splayed awkwardly in the shallows. Disgruntled but otherwise fine, he ruffled feathers to shake off the muck.

Had the interrogation concluded?

Bright lights emanated from the cave entrance and the gate's bars lifted from the sand with a metallic grating sound. Drunk with fatigue and poison,

Targin staggered to his feet and trudged towards the cave mouth. A figure stood framed and shadowed by the light behind, holding a staff firmly planted on the beach.

When Targin's eyes adjusted to the cave's aura he found an aged woman clad in an ivory robe gilded at the edges, her hair a mix of ghost-white traced with lines of silver. Her skin glowed, pale but smooth and unblemished. The few wrinkles she possessed did not diminish her beauty, they accentuated it. She looked younger than her years.

Atheri.

Set atop high cheekbones, a pair of striking blue orbs shone brightly with compassion and wisdom. The woman smiled faintly as she took in his measure.

"Well met, Targin of Tragmar," Atheri greeted in a gentle voice.

Targin managed a pallid grin, wavering unsteadily on his feet as he drew up, sodden boots squelching in the sand. "Stars align, well met indeed, Atheri—Amah. I still draw breath *to* meet."

She nodded. "My daughter would not think kindly upon her mother if I allowed her betrothed to drown before her wedding day."

"Aye, the kraken—too quick for even a fresh soldier. And Johlarin's beastie did its damnedest. But stars, Tasmin would do worse—is she still angry with me? Did she set your sentinel to this task—to cleanse my person of the troll's blood? *Perhaps it was a kobold after all.* Or to simply teach me another lesson in humility?"

"Targin?"

"I did tell Brooke," he went on, languid gaze drifting to the clouds, then the sand. "The Nightwolves will muster still. There's a problem but food will have to wait. I-ama, *wetnurse*, so very wet" His torso shifted on tottering legs. Water dripped from his soaked person like tears. "Point is—poison comes first. The point—*damn it*, Thrum got bit too—removed that one in the tree. The geezer pointed that much out—lesson one: sub—version of the mind."

Atheri furrowed her brows, her mouth working in silence as she stared up at him, obviously trying to decipher his gibberish. Targin mirrored her frown for a moment until he half-realized what he had said. He checked himself, about to clarify, paused, smiled.

And collapsed in the sand before her.

30: Val
Brooke

Brooke awoke to the thin patter of water droplets against the roof of his tent. Only a faint light traced the details outside. Not quite dawn, he surmised. Beyond the open tent flap, a pair of diminutive legs stood dripping, the only part visible from the commander's prone vantage.

When Brooke rubbed the sleep from his eyes and peered up through the threshold, he found Gnolin, staring down at him, an apology illustrating his face and a small wrapped bundle in his hand.

"Morning, Commander," the boy stammered, colour rising in his cheeks. "I was about to wake you."

Brooke hastily emerged from his tent to find the Wolves already assembled, Wrayns mounted on Warangs talking quietly among themselves. When a few stopped and faced him, his chagrin joined that of Gnolin.

Running a hand through his damp and dishevelled hair, Brooke turned to the pup and pointed to the parcel he carried. "My breakfast?"

Gnolin's orbs widened slightly and they shot down to the package. "Oh, right, yes, Commander. We make haste this morning."

"I see," Brooke said. "In the future, you have my permission to put a boot to this slug who calls himself steward. Please lad, never let me slumber a minute past the first Nightwolf who arises."

"Aye, Sir," Gnolin promised as he handed Brooke the bundle.

"Thank you, and stay 'that' purpose—even if it kills me," Brooke added with a chuckle.

The boy smiled and nodded. Then he ran to join Weet, already striking Brooke's tent.

Of course, the pack allowed the commander the luxury of one extra-long sleep the first morning. But today, they expected him to adapt to their rougher ways.

Brooke quickly dressed and collected his weapons. With his breakfast tucked under his arm, he clambered up onto Maxan's saddle and cleared his throat. "I'll break fast as we break ground. No more words. Let us away."

As they set out, Brooke unravelled the parcel braced against the saddlehorn. He dug into its bounty of scones, dried fruits, and nuts—and began wolfing them down.

Hunger sated, the commander made a point of moving Maxan up and down the line, that he might share space with as many Wrayns and Warangs as he could. He wanted to memorize all the faces in the company.

Brooke easily picked out tireless Gnolin riding side by side with Weet. The commander sensed something peculiar about Gnolin's quiet companion, but he couldn't quite place it. Although Weet birthed of the true blood—from his mother's side—he sure didn't carry himself like one: eyes downcast, his face expressionless.

But of all the faces the steward saw and the names he learned, he'd hoped most to cross paths with Val, who proved as elusive as his reputation.

A few hours past midday, Brooke finally caught up with his quarry, riding in and out of the woods, alone save for his ochre-furred Warang. While the morning drizzle pattered down from the greyness overhead, Brooke stole up beside him.

Val stiffened. With a scowl, he looked away and quickened his wolf's pace.

Unperturbed by the slight, Brooke impelled Maxan on a difficult course to close the distance. Within moments they rode in perfect tandem. If Val had been impressed by the commander's prowess, he didn't show it.

"Val?"

Silence. The Nightwolf kept his eyes averted.

Frustrated by Val's obstinacy, the commander let patience win the moment. Perhaps this wasn't the best time. He slowed Maxan. And Val's Warang doubled her speed. In a blur of ginger, she verged further away from the van until the forest swallowed wolf and rider.

The next time Brooke dealt with Targin, he would confront him about the giant's true designs in selecting him—an untried steward. If that big bastard chose him based on courage, he'd put it to the test, and force the Vein to unriddle everything so it made some kind of sense—because it sure as hell didn't now.

In times of peace, Val's evasiveness would be considered a nuisance, his insubordination, a punishable offence, but in light of what they faced, it could spell the difference between life and death.

The rain continued throughout the day as the company moved stealthily into a darker stretch of the Northern Forest. The smell of musk and decay grew overpowering and the thick air reflected Brooke's foreboding mood. Hours passed and the diffused light faded further, blending into one deep penumbra.

But before the day had waned, breaks in the clouds appeared and the sun peeked through. The commander caught nary a glimpse of Val.

When Gnor's Warang strode past, Brooke kicked Maxan's flanks and caught up with the stout Nightwolf. Before he could ask about the absent Val, Gnor raised a hand to quell any interruption.

Brooke grimaced, caught off-guard by Gnor's actions. Was he playing the same vexing game as Val? But when the veteran turned and met his gaze, the commander knew that was not the case. Gnor's upper lip quivered and his focus shifted left and right.

Brooke gulped. "What is it?"

Gnor didn't answer immediately. He looked off into the mid-distance for several moments before giving Brooke his eyes again. "Trouble."

"What kind of trouble?"

"I tried to commune with the Warangs warding the right flank, but none returned my hails. One pair at least should've joined minds with me."

Alarm bells pealed in Brooke's heart. "Halt the van at once. Make sure we can still commune with our other patrols"

Although the pack had thinned considerably to expedite its passage, Gnor needed only a few moments to bridge minds with the band's vanguard and rearguard. Twenty heartbeats later, he confirmed, "Done."

In the failing light, Brooke inclined his head. "Good, bring them in immediately." He turned Maxan to monitor the converging wolves. "Hearken to me. Regroup and form a phalanx towards our right flank." With an effort he kept his voice calm while urgency prodded him on, dampening his palms into oyster flesh.

When the Nightwolves had reformed the line, Brooke continued, "We'll not be blindsided. We face this head-on. Advance slowly—fifty-yard intervals. Gnor, you and I will take point and lead the van. I want to see what might assail us before it sees us. Now, quietly as you can."

The company started forward, towards the last known location of the unresponsive Warangs.

Brooke's nerves prickled, but his resolve to confront whatever stalked them did not dither a hair's breadth.

He hadn't expected to find battle so soon, but his former career honed his intuition enough to recognize what transpired. His experiences with the razed villages of Pathguard put it beyond a doubt.

After several fifty-yard spurts, the phalanx halted and surveyed again. With no luck. The commander opened his mouth, about to signal them to proceed when Gnor floated an arm. "Wait, something approaches."

Brooke perked his ears and drew his sword. "Curve the front lines, Gnor. Far flanks push forward. Encircle whatever's ahead."

Gnor fell reticent. After a moment, his eyes returned. "The flanks advance and form catching arms."

Branches snapped ahead of them. Who or whatever it was made no attempt at stealth. Soon, the tract filled with the swish of rent foliage and the thud of boots pounding through the underbrush.

A heavyset man emerged from the shadows, sprinting like the wind. Val.

He blazed a surefooted trail, hefting a smaller male's body, splayed like a sack of potatoes over his shoulder.

Brooke stared, too astonished to speak. But he quickly recovered, signalling the wings to close the net. As they converged, Val skidded to a halt and carefully laid his burden on the ground. Pupils downcast, some trauma had turned Val's countenance into a ragged canvas with cracked strokes. The Wrayn made a circling gesture with his arm, beckoning them closer.

Brooke dismounted Maxan and raced up, Gnor and Alghan following closely. Val remained hunched over the prostrate form of an unconscious elder, clad in torn and bloodied clothes. A severe wound, part-gash, part-burn, had opened his torso, but for the moment, his respiration came even. His condition seemed stable.

Brooke drew a sharp breath. "Stars—blacken, what did this?" His focus darted left and right. "Where's your Warang?"

Val stayed silent.

"Answer him!" Alghan demanded. "He asked you a question—and I want to know too. Where's Brax—and the entire right flank for that matter?"

Val's orbs shot daggers at the tall Nightwolf. "Dead. They're all dead."

"How?" Alghan pressed through gritted teeth.

Val hesitated, swallowing twice before he met his interrogator's scrutiny. "Taken by… flames in the shadows."

Alghan put his hands on his hips. "Don't give us flowery speech. Simplify your sordid puzzle—in the common tongue." He glanced around. "Are we in any immediate danger?"

"No," Val snapped. "If that were the case, knave, think I'd be so lax?"

"Understood, Val," said Brooke, lifting his hands in a calming gesture towards both parties. "So, what happened?"

"I branched—as is my custom," Val grated, "to ride out with the furthest flanks. I stumbled across remains, carbonized into the ground. Warangs, by the forms in the residual ash."

Alghan narrowed his eyes. "Why didn't you commune with the main host—as is our custom?"

"I did, stars burn you!" Val seethed. "No reply came. I tried to warn the other patrols—as custom dictates. Something nullified my attempts. I feared our cover had been compromised and raced Brax to return at once. She picked up the scent of other Warangs. I thought strength in numbers—we followed their trail—and found them dead, blasted in the same way."

As the other Nightwolves gathered around, Brooke sheathed his sword and crouched beside Val, followed by Gnor.

"The Warangs weren't randomly slain," Val went on. "Ambushed—my guess—to prevent them from relaying warning. We stole past a third identical scene, and a fourth. Then, along the course of a small stream, Brax and I witnessed the attack unfold."

"Witnessed?" Gnor asked suspiciously. "What exactly?"

"Auras—of light—amorphous but humanoid." Val gulped. "Three of them, swift as flaming arrows, sprang from the base of the trees as the Warangs charged past. They cleaved both wolves and smote them into burning ruin. Giant broadswords of white fire."

Val took a long breath. "They singed the Wolves to ash, branded them into the ground. It happened so fast I don't think the Warangs even sensed their doom. The attackers stood a head if not two above Targin. And their blades, larger than Fang."

Alghan started, then dropped his hands to his sides. "If not for the fire, I'd have guessed ogres." He chewed his lower lip as he pondered. "What you describe sounds like *Colossals*, but in these parts...?" He shook his head. "I have my doubts."

Brooke frowned up at the tall Nightwolf. "What are they?"

"Beings of pure dark magic, the antitheses of the sprites," Alghan explained. "But finding them on the Main alarms me. It would mean—"

"The Four now tread in our midst," Gnor finished for him. "Targin warned us this day would come. The Colossals serve as manifestations of the archdemon Reechabah, indentured to the Siphon they are."

Alghan curved to face Gnor. "I think you're right." He sought Brooke's attention. "From what the Kusp says, Colossals never veer far from their master. The sprites told me tales of them guarding Deathwrought's bastion in Grendamaul—the Darkest One's Highguard." He paused and faced Val again. "Consider yourself fortunate to have survived at all."

"Which brings me to my next question," Gnor complained, pointing a finger at Val. "How did *you* survive?" His eyes dropped to the old man. "And who in seven levels of fucks is that?"

Cheeks flushed, Val met his fire with hotter flames. "I survived, because I spotted them first, Gnor. I came upon them undetected as they sprang their trap. Nothing I could do, except hide and watch from the shadows of the underbrush." His gaze shifted over his shoulder the way he'd come. "Good thing too. Others joined the attackers—rose straight out of the ground."

"More of these—Colossals?" Brooke asked over his empty swallow.

Val shook his head. "Entities the same, cherufes of liquid fire-rock."

Alghan inhaled fiercely. "Lavatrols."

"They moved away," Val added.

Brooke shot to his feet. "In this direction?"

"No, once the Colossals dispatched the two Warangs, the main host sank back into the ground. Their fire ebbed to cold stone and soil. No fire spread as they sank, retreating from our pack, not towards it. But twas no coincidence we crossed paths—I sense intent—bait to lure us in that direction."

"Intentions are piss and wind," Gnor spat. "So, what of Brax, and this scarecrow you acquired?"

Val clenched his jaw, crow's feet quaking. "As-I-said, their main host departed at once. I waited until I could be certain they'd left—before I dared return. When I spun Brax to do just that, this one wheezed loudly, some forty paces away. I dismounted my Warang, bade her hunker down in case I faced a trap and left to investigate."

Val nudged his chin at the old one before him. "He staggered into my strike zone. I sprang and drew him to the ground. Arrested him to silence and immobility. His eyes spoke for him: wild with terror until I assured no harm would come to him. I soon released him."

Just then, one of the Warangs padded up and sniffed the unconscious man's face, once, twice. The giant grey wolf appeared satisfied as he drew back and settled on his haunches, steps away. Ice blue wolfen orbs trained on Brooke.

Val's regard joined them. "Quiet, urgent were his words. A league or so east of where I found him, his village lay—sacked by goblins and razed by 'fire monsters.' He fled with his sister and two brothers, but goblin outriders intercepted them and killed his family. When he took the grievous wound you see, the goblins left him for dead. That's how he managed to crawl away

246

and escape. Nothing more did I learn—he lost consciousness. Over my shoulder, I carried him back to Brax."

Val's face creased and he choked up. "Found her—smote into the earth like the others. Only the Colossals' main host had departed. One must have lingered—perhaps it still lurks in our midst. That is why I came upon you running."

Despite the dubiety in Gnor and Alghan's eyes, Brooke nodded. "A wise choice—they outmatched you. Your death—"

"I don't fear the deepest sleep!" Val flared, springing to his feet. "But if those creatures claimed me, the entire band might be compromised—it still might. I had to bring warning."

"And so, you have," Brooke said, his voice calm and reasonable. "We thank—"

"We're marching into a trap," Val cut him off again. "We must turn back."

In the awkward silence, the giant's demand hung unanswered.

Locking gazes with Val, Brooke kept his voice as neutral as possible. "I agree—about the trap." An overture of headshakes, harrumphs, and murmurs of protest ensued.

Brooke ignored them. "The question is what to do about it? Unseen perils lay ahead. We should not proceed along our present course. Do something unexpected. Perhaps, this village will prove our best option, seeing it has already been decimated. Why destroy the same village twice?"

"Perhaps *not*," Val growled. "The extermination of our right flank says it clear as fucking day. Haven't you been listening? They want us to go to the village." He cocked his head brusquely at the prostrate villager. "Maybe this wretch lies to whet our doubts and entice our course of action. This isn't just another ploy of Pathguard's mad regent to lay the blame for a slaughter at our feet. We are the targets of the slaughter."

"Then, who's to say a retreat does not mark the snare itself?" Alghan pointed out. "The roust true?"

More silence.

"In any case, we cannot linger here," Brooke resolved. "If these creatures truly stalk us, it won't matter which direction we take; we'll only delay the inevitable rout." He lifted his scrutiny to the treetops. "It will be dark soon. There's a lot of bush between here and Serenthia, and we still have a schedule to keep. Considering the village offers us the closest option, we might be better able to assess our plight if we head there first."

Brooke ran his tongue over his lower lip and looked across his shoulder. "Besides that, we may find other survivors in need of our help. Even if not, they could still offer information about these darkling intruders—make us wise to their methods and avoid another ambush."

"Aye," Gnor agreed as he stood. "As good a plan as any, Commander."

Val swore under his breath. "Folly."

"No more than what you propose," Gnor derided.

Brooke expected another rebuke, but Val maintained his silence.

Grateful for the partial truce, the commander blew out his cheeks and faced the other Nightwolves. "I haven't been among you long enough to know my place. But I know my heart, and it points to the village. I agree with Val that our collision with these things is no coincidence, but I press that we move to the village regardless and see exactly what happened there." Then to Val, "Find a mount—and bring your passenger."

Alghan cleared his throat. "Away at all speed."

Once regrouped, Brooke signalled an advance as the sun sank over the horizon. The damp air quickly cooled with the sun's passing. It blew through his cloak and skin and bones. Shivering, he tightened its folds about him. Or was his chill rooted in unease over his less-than-idyllic exchange with Val?

Other dire thoughts kept Brooke's mind occupied until his nose bunched up at a strong sulphuric odour. Moments later, the site where the two Warangs had met their end came into view. Ghosts of smoke still emanated from their burned relief, visible in the last vestiges of daylight.

Soon after, the company crossed the stream Val mentioned and pushed on in the direction he indicated. The way became easier the closer they came to the parish, even as night reigned. Darkness would present both boon and bane here. Maxan trembled but remained serene.

Brooke peered through the gloom, finding it difficult to distinguish the gaps between the tightly packed trees ahead. It left him thankful for the wolves' keen senses in the confusing patch.

But when a distant orange glow became visible beyond the wooden tangle, shifting and shimmering beyond the furthest row of trunks, Brooke could rely on his own sight once more.

It filled him with dread.

The pack approached a series of raging fires, following a tight course towards the nearest conflagration. They emerged from the copse into a cleared glen—cleared and charred. The flames that lit the village's smouldering structures illuminated the entire steading and made shadows dance in multiple directions at once. The din of skirling flames and yelling voices filled the night air. At least, the wind blew the heaviest plumes of smoke in the opposite direction.

At Brooke's command, the Nightwolves halted.

Gnor came alongside. "The village is lost, but I spy many survivors, as you rightly guessed."

Brooke squinted watering eyes past the thinner wafts of smoke. Several frantic people clad in strapped boots, rough-spun jerkins, and rugged leather overalls—woodsmen by the look of them—relayed and chugged buckets of water to douse the flames. Many bodies lay strewn on the ground, some broken, some blackened, all motionless.

The commander turned to Gnor. "It may yet be a trap, but clearly one worth springing."

With a curt nod, the bulldog-faced man impelled his Warang forward at a brisk run. Brooke followed him across the fire-lit plain towards the centre of destruction.

The entire Nightwolf phalanx fell in. Warangs converged behind Gnor and Brooke or flanked them as the host advanced. Forty wolves broke away from the main charge, fanning out towards the treeline. There, they took up different positions to guard the forest's edge.

As the scorched buildings loomed up before him, Brooke was taken back to an almost identical scene in his recent past: Pathguard on fire, less than a fortnight prior, yet now a lifetime away. Rekindling the irony of his fate, he gauged the dismal situation with the same grave temperament.

The van kept a safe distance from the closest ruins, filtering past the corpses strewn in heaps across the clearing. Amid the catastrophe, the survivors' desperate shouts added to the roar of the blaze.

Until the villagers saw the approaching Nightwolves. Then, they dropped their buckets and picked up their axes and swords.

"Come no closer, dogs," one of them bellowed, a burly bearded man.

Brooke brought Maxan to a stop and lifted an arm. The rest of the pack halted. "We mean you no harm." He pointed to the old man laid out across the back of Val's Warang. "We found this aged one in the woods, not two leagues west of here. He's one of yours. We've also been attacked by the same creatures. And sustained losses."

"Not as great as ours," the man shouted back. "We're a little busy now, so leave the geezer, turn around, and be on your way."

"Stars chase your shadows, man. Let us help you," Brooke entreated.

"More hands will achieve your goal quicker. We only seek information about that which wrought this. It will be safer for both parties."

The bearded man brandished his sword higher. Brooke disregarded the trenchant display and dismounted Maxan. Slowly, he approached the woodsman.

"I said *no* closer," the villager sneered. "Or you'll taste ironock, Nightwolf." The man cleaved the air for emphasis.

Brooke raised an eyebrow. "So, you're familiar with our band. And yet your weapon still trembles before us?"

"Aye, you may not share their dress, but I recognize the black-clad savages behind you. Villains who sack kingdoms and villages for plunder, I name them. We've nothing left, knave, save fire—plenty of that—or do the rumours hold the truth? You've come to eat our dead?"

"As it so happens, we are not hungry," Brooke said, calm fretting his ire, "As to the rapine of your village, seems someone beat us to the task."

"Then leave us in peace to lick our wounds without your outlaws pilfering the dead's pockets for coin and spoils."

Brooke unsheathed his sword and threw it to the ground at the villagers' feet. He moved closer until he stood directly before the startled man's quivering blade. Without taking his eyes off him, the commander stooped and picked up one of the wooden water buckets. He walked to the fire, hefted the pail shoulder-high, and cast its contents against the closest dwelling. A section of the blaze petered out with a sharp hiss and a rising column of steam.

Brooke turned to the villagers and shouted angrily, "It still burns! The Nightwolves shall leave you in peace, as soon as I'm convinced you will not be left in pieces."

The leader's jaw dropped in stunned silence. So did his blade.

"Now," the commander snapped as he strode back and reached for a second bucket, "promise not to perforate us with arrows or give us haircuts one neck too low—and I'll spare two hundred backs just as capable—to save what we can."

The villagers lowered their weapons.

31: A Glimmer of...
Sonart

Sonart's eyes cringed into slits at the overwhelming brightness. Yet he could still read the characters on the page. They appeared like silhouettes standing before an intense flame. The text spoke only of the Kusp's apocryphal dogma, centring on a typical parable concerned with sacrifice for the greater good. Despite his disappointment, Sonart read on, feeling more abject with every sentence.

But before he finished the third stanza, the words shimmered and vanished. Through the luminous veil, he discerned new words forming, inscribed by the light itself.

Sonart took a deep breath, rubbed his sore eyes, and read:

As Greatest Powers clash
Blood will burn and orbits churn
Veins of Fire Four
Siphons add Four more
To the bidding of the Octagon
To the Bonding of the Stars
Eight sides face the draw
All fates face the Starbond
All souls mirror the Stellar Dance
Of the First, or of the Second
Time or Void
Those who end the last
Will outlast the End

Spellbound, Sonart held the tome's edges in a white-knuckled grip. And stared. Foreign to the original text suppressed beneath, these words—were clearly forbidden words.

His pupils drifted back to the top of the page. He reread the entire passage many times until he'd committed it to memory, logging it beside Rusic's epitaph.

But when Sonart looked up, befuddlement left him in a fog.

...Or had it? He recalled one word he did understand—was meant to understand: *Vein.* He finally comprehended what it meant for him *to be* a Vein. A title, an accolade, a rite of passage to limitless magic. And that fount of infinite energy—that sigil—belonged to him—and three others like him.

They shared his charge. Relief blew the fog away. No longer did he have to walk his path alone.

Sonart cleared his throat. "I am—a Vein—of Fire. *One of the Four.*" Though he did not grasp his full export, by declaring his agency aloud, he affirmed the title not only to himself but beyond the Cradle and Void, to the Universe at large—reciting a litany before his indoctrination.

An image ingrained Sonart's mind and immersed his senses within. He saw an abandoned building on a neglected warren in a town much larger than Farkshone Village. He looked around. By the size and greyness of its urban sprawl and the considerable height of many of its buildings, he glimpsed the inner streets of Bulkforge.

Something stirred in Sonart's gut. The edifice only appeared derelict... Could his answer lie within? Salvation perhaps? He branded every detail of the picture in his mind's vault.

The nimbus emanating from the book tapered, calmed, and faded completely. It left the page lit as before, by the orange flicker of the twin lamps. But the ghost of the strange prophetic text lingered.

A new sense of purpose infused Sonart. He must seek this place out, for it might offer an accord between his fate and that of his people. Then he could begin to undo the damage—if he could keep the Darkest One from undoing him first.

A shadow passed over his certitude. Until he fixed everything, he could never again face Auckland or Mila. When news of his crimes reached their ears, they too would be forced to shun him as an agent of evil. And rightly so.

Apart from that demoness, Shayla, Sonart was the only dwarven who knew the truth of matters. He'd been an unwilling partisan, possessed by the Darkest One. But to the masses, none of that would matter. Until he joined the other three Veins, he must walk his attainted path alone and under a constant cloak of subterfuge.

Rumour may serve him yet as an ally in that regard. Dwarven would ostracise him to be sure, but they would also avoid even a chance encounter. His disorder—more abhorrent than any Afflicted's malady, his spite—sharper than that of the most ruthless Proclaimer.

As such, he wouldn't inflict any more malice in Deathwrought's name—the atrocity would monger such fear. But for certain, he had to leave for Bulkforge at once.

"Coming from Farkshone?" the geezer asked.

"Aye," said Sonart, guarding his tone.

The old dwarven unslung the pack from his hunched back and regarded Sonart carefully beneath the rim of his hat. "Where you heading?"

"Bulkforge."

"Can't say I blame you—with the mayhem happening in those parts. Stars, I'm steering clear of that village, if I can help it."

Sonart swallowed. "What have you heard?"

"What I hear lad, naught but convolution. Most travellers who passed before you say the carnage be the work of Kworn. Sighted all over the streets of Farkshone, they were. And their footprints carry the stain of the slain. If Bulkforge be your destination, I suggest you make all haste."

The old one removed his hat and wiped his forehead with a mottled hand. "Been tell of Kworn raiding parties in these parts too, and not much in the way of shelter between here and that town, should the Scourge send a razor storm your way."

Sonart nodded. "Thank you. I will."

The geezer shot him a sideways look. "Why you heading there at all, Red? Seem able enough. Shouldn't you be in the mines?"

Sonart placed his hand on the hilt of his sword and drew the blade a finger's breadth from the scabbard. "I have business in Bulkforge, needs attending. I—proclaim, that speaks for itself, and all you need know." He sheathed the blade to punctuate his ire.

"Point taken," the old traveller relented as he reseated his hat. "I'll be along now. Forgive an old man his tongue wagging. Be at One with the Kusp."

"Words unto Deeds," Sonart growled.

With that, the old man lifted his pack and scuttled away. Sonart watched him go, smiling to himself. A powerful ally indeed.

The drear had waned by the time Sonart reached the outskirts of Bulkforge, the largest urban centre in the Cradle. Set precariously close to and above the inner edge of the Lobe, the town perched on the Steppe like a series of grey juggernauts.

Industries loomed in the distance, rising above the intermediate buildings. Smokestacks, six storeys high, puffed great gouts of smoke. A charred sooty smell permeated the air and dried his nostrils.

Small wonder: Bulkforge served as the manufacturing centre of the Cradle, where blasted ironock was carted on tracks from all the mines across the land. Here, dwarven forged raw ore in the fire pools fed by the River

253

Seething and tooled it into myriad materials, tools, and weapons.

The city's size and the tight lay of its warrens and structures protected it from the brunt of a razor storm. As such, it provided a haven for the 'bulk' of the dwarven people.

With so many strangers coming and going, Sonart would be able to search for the mysterious edifice unnoticed.

"Sir?"

Or so he thought.

Sonart spun.

Beneath the rock-hewn awning of an austere cottage, a young woman with flaxen tresses stood staring at him.

"Sir?" she called again. Beside her, a frail dwarven man sat hunched in a rocking chair. His weathered countenance seemed archaic, even by an Elder's standard. By his wheeze, sputter, and the loll of his prunish head, he did not look well.

Sonart wanted to ignore the pair and keep walking, but something in the woman's pale grey eyes kept him rooted to the dirt track.

Holding the folds of her skirt, the maiden left the old one's side and hurried up.

"Good sir, though no longer contagious, a derivative of the plague has taken part of my father, the mines and age, the other parts. His wits have grown addled."

Sonart contemplated trying the same Proclaimer-on-errand mummer's ploy that he used with the traveller on the road. But he detected a strange familiarity with this woman, something he could neither peg nor abandon. And her batting eyelashes made his ears twitch and warm.

"You speak as though Zürshuck have made sport of him," Sonart said, his regard flitting over her shoulder at the gaunt man.

"The fates more like." She curved around, giving Sonart her profile as she looked back.

"He was smitten with the earliest stages of the Afflicted's illness, before I arrested his ailment" the maiden confessed, ambivalence fretting her tone. "But the damage was done. He raves, more than his usual. And I know not the nature of his rant this day. Only that he would speak with you, if it pleases."

It did not. But Sonart could not refuse her. He exhaled and before realizing it, he followed her back to the cottage porch and her emaciated father. The pungency of the old man's sickness quickly became apparent as they drew up: rotten vegetables and a neglected privy.

Through a single glazed orb—the other swollen shut—he looked up at Sonart and harrumphed. "Ah child, fetched him you have," he cackled without looking at the woman. "Your livery might be shit but not so your brains—aye, that you take from your mother and me, something lost on your sister."

His face rolled towards his daughter. "Now, fly girl. I will have words with this one alone, and if this cursed illness doesn't claim me first, warrant I'll be facing the Hooks ere long—once he hears me out. Losing one seed to them jackanapes has given me misery enough. Already dead, she is. I do not wish you to join her or me this drear."

His daughter blinked and stared down at him.

"Go!" he barked. "Now!"

She retreated a few steps but did not leave, which made the old man fulminate and stammer incoherent expletives about fornicating Zürshuck.

The maiden flushed and splayed her arms. She turned to Sonart, a note of pleading in her visage as she ran a shaky hand through her hair.

Startled as much by the oldster's bane as he was by the abusive tone the prune took with his daughter, Sonart held both in check. Beneath her father's harsh demeanour, Sonart sensed long-cured mettle that reminded him of Seolad's contempt and firmness. And the blackbeard's ruthless courage.

The prune's good eye searched and squinted until it found Sonart. Then it bored holes into him. "Hooks and Dunge, it is you, Son of Farkshone. Left quite a mess back in your father's village, you did—the tall one told me, but I reconnoitred ahead of the scourge. Your fatal journey has only begun, Saviour."

The old man paused and let out a horrible guffaw, which sounded more like a snarling wet cough. "Stars, the only thing you'll save me from is this horrible existence. Seeing I won't get another chance, let me thank you for speeding me into the deepest sleep—something I've craved of late. Bedtime comes a little sooner than late I expect—much the better in my broken condition."

Sonart gulped, eyebrows unhinging as he exchanged an incredulous look with the man's daughter. She spun on the decrepit man. "Father, please. He is but a stranger, trying to assist you."

Turning varying shades of purple and red, Fossil-face griped, "Thought I told you to disappear—fuck a Siphon!" he griped. He rocked his chair forward and back, forward and—paused, gaze swerving up to Sonart. "Listen to me, Farkshone son. The answer which seeks you *hides* here. Haven and help. Look to Bessel of the Golan Hob. Share a pint. Your fire will burn all the brighter for it. Let the fire of ale light your path the rest of the way. Stars burn me, you'll need lots of it."

He slapped his frail hands on his bony knees. "But if it's any consolation, even a sword intended for evil can cut both ways. Cut through the lie to get to the heart of the truth. Either way the blade will cut, you must decide which way. And how deep. The tall one spoke sure, but I have my doubts as to your business here. Except for one certainty."

Sonart's curiosity was piqued. "What is that, pray tell?"

"You will kill me—and both my daughters."

The woman gasped, eyes widening until Sonart believed they might pop from their sockets. They veered back and forth between her father and Sonart, but she braced her legs, folded her arms, and stood her ground.

"Sire, I beseech you," she interceded. "Do not lay false accusations at the feet of a stranger. Malicious ears are never far. They listen."

"Aye, Father," Sonart grated. "Heed your daughter's wisdom. A foul tongue dipped in such rancour earns an audience with the Proclaimers. Your mind's obviously Dunge-bound, but do not endanger your own kin with such wanton raving and disregard."

"Balls of a Kworn to that," the old man hooted. He flicked his wrist dismissively while a litany of curses meshed into a series of offensive sounds.

Sudden vertigo jolted Sonart and seized the back of his mind. The static manifested, suppressing his thoughts as they merged with those of the Darkest One.

His pupils lifted to the overcast sky, trying to make sense of the old man's words, but the roiling clouds offered no surcease. Sonart remained bound, trapped by the internal maelstrom. He struggled to maintain control, but his grasp slipped like the ebb of a sandy dune in the throes of a razor storm. He could use one of those right now.

Sonart grimaced, forcing himself to look down at the old man's face. "Who *are* you?" he jumbled.

"Me?" the old one snivelled. "Nobody. Just a messenger."

"His name is Xoral," the woman meekly offered, drawing Sonart's focus. "And I am his daughter, Iomi."

Could he be...? Sonart turned back to face the elder. And shuddered. Xoral's body flickered with the telltale iridescent glow. The same green that had imbibed Shayla, the same aura within the State. The old man screamed into Sonart's face. Cut through his blindness and reawakened deaf ears.

Sonart howled back, mirroring Xoral's pyrexia. An infuriated voice inside his head drilled the redbeard. '*What did he say? What did he say? What-did-he SAY?*'

Despite his mental tempest, Sonart gleaned something profound. Although he understood what this Xoral had said, Deathwrought could not comprehend the elder's words. Only that he had spoken them.

A mortified Iomi shrank back and gaped, her hand shooting to her mouth. Sonart flexed and reflexed, his fingers found purchase on his sword hilt.

Out the weapon came, ironock singing as it skinned his belt buckle.

Three children turned the corner around the cottage, no doubt to see what had caused the disturbance. When Sonart's eyes found them, they jumped an inch off the ground, screamed, and fled in terror.

But then something cracked Sonart's delirium, silenced the Darkest One's wail, and impelled Sonart to run himself. He bolted, sheathing his sword as he sprinted away, tearing the ground beneath his boots. His seizure lapsed, its puissance diminishing the further he raced into the heart of the town. Stars align, he had stilled the seed of evil once more.

Several snaking turns down alleys and cross-warrens later, Sonart's fire expended itself. It left a vast emptiness in its stead. He stopped, heart threatening to burst from his chest, and waited to make sure no one had followed him. As his vitals steadied, he donned a cowl and made his way into the centre of Bulkforge.

Either way the blade will cut, you must decide which way and how deep... Mine eyes are your eyes. But if his success with Xoral meant anything, perhaps not for much longer. A simple fluke of circumstance? No, the Darkest One's rage had not been feigned. Sonart held a secret from his nemesis. *Look to Bessel of the Golan Hob.*

He had won a tiny victory, but how would Deathwrought retaliate? Surely obliteration in the Afterworld could not surpass such inescapable condemnation. What other choice did he have, forced to continuously fight against the will of a god?

Just then, a gap opened between two buildings and Sonart stopped. The Lobe of the Cradle loomed beyond: a seemingly interminable plane of barren desert. Twas vast but not vast enough: as a single strand of hair appears scarcely visible atop the crown, Sonart spotted the spires of the Outereach. They shielded the Cradle from the Void of Obliteration—the abyss of nothingness on the far side of that mountainous cordon.

Sonart found the prospect of hiding out there alluring, but he knew that promised certain death. If the Zürshuck did not make waste of him from on high, the elements would. As his father once told him, fouler terrors still dwelt within the Lobe's sand itself.

He stole a glance in the opposite direction. The Innereach loomed much closer. The Four Peaks circled the core where Deathwrought pervaded. Where He surely watched Sonart now. Or ...could He?

A vanguard of lightning strikes behind Sonart shook him out of his contemplations. Thunder cracked and echoed an instant later. He wheeled around as searing forks lanced down over the vast plateau. A heavier-than-usual air mass settled into a dead calm. He needed no great seasoning to parse what approached.

Sprung into action, Sonart bolted down the street in search of an abandoned shelter where he might wait out the encroaching razor storm. Within seconds he heard and felt the rumbling all around him.

The spiralling clouds overhead turned black while the wind whipped into fury. Electrical strikes split the sky like crooked legs of light feeling their way across the terrain, stalking him. Nearer. Patches of bulrushes on the edge of the Lobe caught fire with each strike, their cinders still burning as the gale ripped them away and sent them flying.

The gusts steadily gained strength, propelling Sonart forward. The interval between flash and crack lessened dramatically.

But the sand carried on the Scourge's relentless gyre posed the greatest threat. If that caught up with him before he retreated indoors, Deathwrought and prophecy would be the least of his worries. His flesh would be grated clean off his bones; his skeleton erased from existence.

By some divine intervention, Sonart happened upon a stable, set on a rutted slope mere feet from the escarpment.

The gathering storm rendered the entire district deserted and dust-blinded. Seconds later, visibility diminished to a few feet.

So, when Sonart broke the lock to the shed's door with the pommel of Seolad's sword, no one saw to cry umbrage. Nor heard the hammering in the tempest's caterwaul.

Small shards of rock unhinged from the ground and pummelled Sonart's cloak as he passed through the portcullis. He shut the heavy door moments before the storm turned deadly.

Sonart chose a random stall, inset and as far away from the metal-lined door as possible. He lowered his pack to the floor. As Auckland had revealed, no livestock filled any of the pens, only the grainy smell of harvested hogsweed, stacked neatly in two-foot square bales halfway to the sloped ceiling. With no creatures to contend with, he had the stable all to himself.

In the failing light, Sonart pulled out three of the bales and arranged them into a makeshift bed. He didn't bother with his bedroll, collapsing on the welcoming mounds. Despite the rattle and squeal of the tempest outside, sleep overtook him as soon as his head sank into the cushioning weed.

Look to Bessel of the Golan Hob.

32: Fire and Fang
Brooke

Two hundred Wrayns dismounted and set to work assisting the impoverished villagers. They doused the worst of the flames and salvaged what structures and chattel they could. Several Warangs helped too, shuttling refilled buckets from nearby streams and wells, saving them time and effort.

When the last of the fires had been extinguished, the dead were set atop a pyre, extruded from the unsalvageable bits of charred wood. Shindu, the leader of the woodsmen, set it ablaze.

Though the red-eyed villagers had worked in conjunction with the Nightwolves, they did so in silence and with blatant distrust. Some flinched if a Wrayn came too close—doubly so with the Warangs.

Brooke understood their hesitation: not all of it stemmed from lingering suspicion. Loss and trauma had left many rife with grief, only to be shocked anew by the band's offer to help.

Like himself, their ingrained beliefs about the Wolves conflicted with what they had witnessed firsthand. For their part, the soot-stained Wrayns did not engage the villagers, focused instead on the immediate task.

When Brooke informed the woodsmen that the pack would camp the night on the edge of the clearing, they stared at the ground.

Shindu stepped forward and bowed. "Then you have my leave and my thanks, Nightwolf." When he lifted his eyes, he swallowed and coughed. "Also, my apologies."

With the tents unpacked and set, embers from cookfires soon crackled and popped, lighting the glen in another orange glow. But before any beds of coal could be used for their meals, the Warangs guarding the forest's eaves raised their canine heads to the sky and bayed in unified alarm.

Gnor rushed up and seized the commander's arm. "Trap's sprung. We are beset!"

Brooke dropped the cup he held and bolted to his feet. "What?"

"Lavatrols," Gnor cursed.

Fear ratcheted up every knuckle of Brooke's spine as he digested the news. But he didn't hesitate.

He raced to Maxan, leapt into the saddle, and wheeled the destrier about.

At the edge of the forest, abominations emerged out of the ground. One and a half times the height of a man and twice the width, they trudged forward.

The lavatrols towered over the closest men and wolves. Formed of molten rock and pyroclastic mud, covered in a layer of smouldering ash, they smoked and sputtered flame. It trailed them, causing small conflagrations in their slow tracks.

Magma infused the lavatrols' bodies, in a kind of semi-liquid, semi-solid flux. Red light shone through myriad cracks in their grey shells, arranged like fragmented tiles of igneous rock.

Without warning, the fiery creatures erupted beneath a pair of Warangs, catching them unaware and incinerating them.

Villagers cast buckets of water at the advancing fire-gorgons. But what didn't splash off their molten crust evaporated on contact, sending screaming columns of steam spiralling up into the night air.

To Brooke's horror, arrows and spears had no effect either. Any creature stuck with one merely melted the projectile as soon as it pierced its shell. Swords would be equally useless. Implacable, like the Sorgon had been— but even the demon had a chink in its armour.

"Stars burn me—if the monsters don't!" Brooke yelled. "Swords and arrows are useless here. Use your shields to deflect anything thrown!"

At what was surely their most vicious, Warangs gambolled along the inner flank, hectoring the cherufes. The canines bought the Wrayns time as they goaded the flaming creatures away from the main host.

Slow and ponderous, the lavatrols responded exclusively to their closest target, not thinking beyond, if they thought at all. For the moment, thank the stars, the Warangs' tactics kept the monsters at bay. But, confused as they were, the cherufes remained impervious to attack.

Brooke spurred Maxan at full gallop towards the frontline. "Follow me! Form a phalanx!" he cried over his shoulder.

Within seconds several Wolves formed up behind his horse. An eyeblink later, Gnor came alongside, astride his smoky-brown Warang, Fram. She kept pace, matching stride with the commander's horse.

Brooke's heart raced ahead of Maxan's thundering hooves. Halfway into the cataclysm, the horse faltered.

Knee-jerked, the commander corrected his mount's misstep, edging him on a different tack.

Even Brooke's long experience could not have prepared him for such a battle. Would this be his rite of passage with the Nightwolves—a branding rite of fire at that? Or the deepest sleep? Doubt plagued him. But courage vaulted over all.

As Brooke led the charge, revelation dawned and he gave it voice. "Gnor, commune with the band to keep swords sheathed, bows unstrung. Tell them to use only the natural elements they see. No forged ironock. Horde and launch sticks and stones. Let's see if that impedes them."

With a curt nod, Gnor confirmed that the flanking Wrayns understood.

Brooke gave the command. "Attack!"

Despite their immensity and apparent immutability, the closest lavatrols hesitated at the sheer ferocity of the counterattack. The Nightwolves' onslaught caught them unprepared.

Had they ever been attacked before?

As the Wrayns swept in, launching fusillades of rocks and debris, many of the fiery monsters slowed, jerked away, and bowled over like felled trees.

Bits of fiery lava sparked off their shells to scorch the commander as he drove past. He ignored the forks of pain from the red-hot bits that rained past his shield. As did Maxan. Luckily the barrier absorbed the brunt of them.

The company shot away from the lavatrols before rallying in a wide circle for another pass. Again, the Wolves ploughed the fire-gorgons over.

Brooke set his jaw, encouraged by the standstill, until his eyes caught sight of the treeline at the opposite side of the glade.

More lavatrols appeared.

"Quick—divide into two groups!" Brooke ordered. "We're surrounded. Gnor, take the second vanguard and push those bastards back to hell. Shields! Shields!"

As Gnor tore away, leading a contingent of Warangs, a scratchy voice grated beside Brooke's ear. "Begs yer pardon, Commander?"

He whipped around and flinched as Spifer's canine face came within inches from his own, a crooked smile playing on his lips—and some bit of news he was plainly anxious to impart.

"What?" Brooke shouted impatiently over the din.

"True Blood or no, learned as a *combart* veteran to fight fire with fire— *my* fire."

From one of his side-sashes, Spifer produced an ebony sphere, twice the size of a chicken's egg and held it up. "The fucks' seem handy with fire— see how they like it when fire fucks 'em right back."

Fast as lightning, Spifer wound back his arm, aimed, and shot the sphere at the closest lavatrol. The creature exploded into a hundred fragments, which blew apart three more trolls in its immediate vicinity and dismembered the arm and half a torso from a fourth.

Spifer let out a demented bray. "Dragon eggs—nothing like natural explosives—furder charmed to brighten yer day. Or yer night."

When Brooke's eyebrows reseated their hedge, he felt a grin cramp his cheeks, competing with the firemonger's violent smirk.

Brooke regarded Spifer with a new appreciation. Stars, the pyromancer *was* a gods-be-damned dragon.

Astride his Warang, Alghan sidled up, charred face shining at Spifer's demonstration. "I never knew you had any left after Pathguard, man."

261

"Alghan, fast, race some of Spifer's eggs to Gnor's party," Brooke instructed.

Spifer gave the tall Nightwolf a satchel filled with his explosive hoard. "Just don't drop 'em," he warned before handing Brooke a comparable sack. "Let's wager on the best marksman."

With a brusque nod, Alghan impelled his Warang forward, careening away to aid the Bulldog's contingent. Spifer's mount surged in the opposite direction.

"Where are you going?" Brooke called after him.

"Off to bag me one o' dem Colossals Val boasted about. Otherwise, this party'll never finish." The pyro yelled a string of obscenities but they were lost on Brooke.

The lavatrols forged closer.

Brooke swivelled Maxan around and swept past his share of the battlefront, bombarding the closest lavatrols with the oblong projectiles.

The dragon eggs worked fabulously. Cherufes detonated, causing an explosive chain reaction down their ranks and back through the press. The commander shattered the lavatrols' momentum while Nightwolves under his command threw the surviving monsters into disarray with volleys of debris.

Brooke chanced a look at the battle on the far side of the dell. Multiple plumes of lavatrol fireworks lit up the night sky. Their explosive strikes met with equal success. The tide of battle turned as the Nightwolves nearly halved the lavatrols' numbers.

But then another cry went up, from the ruins of the village. To Brooke's dismay, a new wave of cherufes emerged from the ground and stalked the villagers themselves. They'd soon be overrun and incinerated.

And still more of the fire-gorgons rose from the blackened earth behind the remnants of the initial two flanks. Brooke kicked Maxan's stirrups. The destrier's hooves pounded the ground as he ran to the front of the third wave.

The commander had to drive a wedge to get the villagers out before the lavatrols completely engulfed them. Random wolves fell in behind Maxan as he shot past. But at full flight, the warhorse pushed well ahead of the Warang pack by the time he reached the first buildings and the front row of cherufes surrounding the villagers.

With one hand, Brooke fished out two spheres from his stash. Coiled his arm. Aimed.

The ground in front of him buckled and swelled, throwing Maxan off-balance. The charred crust flared in patches, cracking the glass-fused earth into triangular shards as it rose. Brooke's mount skidded to an awkward halt. In every direction, lavatrols rose from the fibrillating ground. The monsters had cordoned him, forming a wall with their flaming bodies. They all but ignored the inhabitants.

The cherufes converged—on him!

Stars be merciful, *he* was their target.

As the fire-gorgons lifted to their full height, they cut him off from his band and the villagers. Alone, Brooke would pay for his haste with his life.

The lavatrols' acrid smoke choked the air, stung his eyes, and obscured the monsters that created it. But Brooke forced them to stay open.

Through the maelstrom of confusion, a bolt arced towards him. It overshot the advancing creatures, a trail of fluttering blue fire marking its perfect trajectory. Another bolt followed it. And another, and another. Each shaft struck the ground beside the one before it, embedding the tract, forming a series of burning fence posts between Brooke and the lavatrol van.

When the encircling monsters tried to cross the flaming barricade, they detonated en mass, causing an eruptive train of events left and right. Whoever had loosed the impossible fusillade was charmed—the hands-down winner of Spifer's marksman wager.

Brooke would not squander the let. He flung his last spheres wildly as Maxan tore through the burning gap. A shower of lavatrol body parts confirmed his success. Horse and rider sailed past the monsters' fractured third flank.

And into a fourth. *Stars!*

Brooke spun his now-terrified mount hard, desperately searching for another escape within the miasma of line and breach. None did he see. The smoke cleared, revealing a thicker swathe of converging forms.

Maxan whinnied in terror as he reared up on his hindquarters, ready to make a last desperate run.

Chaos reigned as the horse came down on all fours.

Maxan surged towards the cherufes, hooves pounding the earth.

Over his head, Brooke windmilled the full satchel of explosive spheres as the wall of lavatrols rushed up to meet him. Ordinance ablur, he would carve his own bloody breach.

The ground convulsed beneath Maxan's hindquarters, vaulting him savagely forward. The horse lurched, stumbled, and trumpeted as he went down.

Bones snapped.

The impact threw Brooke clear. He got to his feet just as two ragged claws shot up through the ground and clamped the horse's torso. The destrier didn't have time to cry out as he ignited, consumed instantly by a lavatrol's embrace.

As the monster gouged the horse's flaming underbelly, Brooke dove out of the way, a moment before another explosion rocked the earth beneath him.

He landed hard on his back and skidded over the baked ground. The dragon eggs—wasted.

His world reeled. Ears ringing.

The creatures loomed closer once more.

This time, Brooke had no spheres.

He had no horse.

He had no chance.

A hand suddenly seized him by the scruff of his neck, hauled him off his feet, and impelled him forward.

Brooke collided with fur. Heard a snarl and turned to see a Warang, eyes trained forward, moving like the wind. A field of its grizzled coat whipped the commander across the face.

What wind his earlier impact left in his lungs fled as he bounced unceremoniously on the back of the Warang. Until the giant wolf left the ground altogether. Time stretched as the canine arced high—an impossible leap—over the heads of the lavatrols.

To land hard but true beyond their barricade. The wolf's snarls turned to pants as he raced away. But he still breathed. Still ran.

When the Warang skidded to a halt. Brooke raised his head, pupils sweeping the clearing between the three-fold attack. He lifted his gaze higher—and stared.

Val's unreadable face stared back.

Remembering himself, Brooke sputter-croaked, "The others?" Smoke had turned his throat into a chimney.

"Gone," Val answered gravely. "Cut off. Without more dragon eggs, they'll die. We'll follow shortly—the cherufes have encircled the entire village."

"Never!" Brooke galvanized his resolve and took it in another direction.

"Commune with a Warang," he demanded while righting himself in the wolf's saddle. "I need to save them, Val—I can—I've seen it. The lavatrols seem intent on slaying me. I'll lure them away. Get the wolves to disperse—no time to lose!"

Val slid off his mount. "Take mine."

Before Brooke could protest, Val ran back into the choking cloud, lost in seconds.

Panting, Brooke shifted in the saddle and took the Warang's reins. The wolf tilted forward into the fray, paws reigniting with unbelievable speed.

A quick circle showed the Nightwolves still kept the lavatrols in check, but they'd lost too much ground, effectively penned in without dragon eggs to break the monsters' lines—now too deep for a Warang's leap. The trapped wolves could do nothing except wait for incineration to ferry them into the deepest sleep.

Brooke hefted his sword high and hearkened the Wrayns outside the cordon. "To me, to me!" he cried.

The Warangs and their riders converged, breaking off their deadlocked engagements to join him. They formed a tight wedge, some distance away from the closest lavatrols.

Brooke expected to see defeat on the Wrayns' faces as they made their final stand. He couldn't have been more wrong.

They all grinned—the fuck—some of the more brazen laughed.

"A merry pickle, eh Jaak?" Gauley bellowed.

"The merriest!" Jaak yelled back as he flung a large rock. "I'd hoped to run wagers on the highest count of goblin heads."

"Long gone—those runts," Gauley said.

Jaak nodded. "I should thank them." He flung a stone so swift it took out half a lavatrol's head before it fell back. "Haven't had such a good workout since I bedded my wife the night before we left Serenthia."

"Workout?" Shora, one of the female Wrayns harrumphed. "Way my sister described it, you proved 'worn-out!'"

A chorus of laughter rippled up and down their line, fracturing Brooke's desperation like a smith's hammer. Their acceptance—or madness—rallied his resolve! Of such a dauntless well of fortitude, he too must drink deep.

Gnor stole up just then, feverish eyes penetrating Brooke's, "We still have air and strength, and sure as Infern we have hope."

That clinched it. All the remaining Nightwolves formed a circular phalanx and awaited the lavatrols with an air Brooke best-likened to fierce serenity.

Through the smoke and fire, the wall of lavatrols closed in.

"To the Purpose!" Brooke cried as he raised his sword above his head.

"To the Purpose!" the Wrayns roared back as they lifted theirs.

"To the Purpose!" the commander bellowed louder.

"To the—" Their voices faltered.

Amidst the ruinous smoke and fire, the prevailing gyre of ash and soot, and the overture of cracks, hisses, and howls, a new sound entered the battlefield.

Deep guttural base notes droned so low it made Brooke's heart flutter. His bones trembled as the ground beneath his feet quaked. Puddles of water in a few ruts shivered. The fire-gorgons paused and dithered.

In the next instant, smoke clouds jarred as if suddenly sucked in and exhaled from a god's own bellows. Somewhere beyond the trees, the air clapped, imploded, and concussed. Then, the sharp clangour of battle chorused in cantankerous refrain.

Fierce fighting had begun somewhere outside of the lavatrols' cordon. The trolls made an about-face and moved *away* from the trapped Nightwolves and Brooke's contingent.

Like a drawbridge slowly opening, Brooke's lower jaw lost purchase from his upper.

The lavatrols reformed their lines and shifted to their flanks as though unravelling a burning slipknot. Somehow, something—or things—more formidable than the Nightwolves harried the cherufes from behind.

The commander's instincts took over. "Hold your ground, Wolves. Do not engage or harass our enemies. Let them leave."

His reason soon became apparent when a plume of lavatrol body parts rose fifty feet into the air. Molten appendages rained everywhere. Heads sailed in random volleys like blazing potshots, arms and legs pitchpoled the same, out from the lavatrols' rearguard.

The monsters' frontline heaved away with greater, more strident effort. It pushed outward, widening the gap even further between wolf and lavatrol.

As the troll ranks thinned, so did their obstructive smoke. Above their heads, a moving forest of massive axes, cudgels and clubs swung, arced and felled. Each weapon, the size of a tree trunk wielded by a gargantuan hairy arm, thicker than a tree trunk.

Brooke could only gawp. The new combatants stood more than three heads above the trolls, twice the height of a man.

Seemingly unaffected by the lavatrols' flaming bodies, the new army advanced like a line of giant farmers thrashing a field of burning hay. The bigger monsters purged forward as they decapitated, disembowelled, and pulverized every lavatrol with impunity.

Some of the cherufes turned tail and tried to escape by penetrating back into the ground, but they could not move quick enough: their opponents wrenched them back up as easily as uprooting weeds. In the end, every single lavatrol succumbed. Vanquished utterly.

And Brooke found himself facing an even larger, more formidable set of potential foes. He swallowed past what felt like a scorching nugget of coal lodged in his throat. Despite the residual heat, icy shivers coursed through his body as the indomitable army of grizzly beastmen closed the gap between them.

33: Verdict
Sonart

Sonart breaks away from her naked embrace. He avoids her eyes, not wanting her to see the anguish that fills his face—after the tender moments they shared. But she had betrayed him.

She is dangerous.

He is dangerous.

Sonart must leave her—before he kills her. Such obstruction marks his path: the damned walk alone, always.

Yet here he lies, safe for the moment, but surrounded by his plight.

Her plight.

Reality and dream fuse into one existence. One nightmare, the truth of being in the Cradle—that will never change.

He pulls her to him. Kisses her mouth tenderly, the stir of desire for her drives him mad. An enchantress, Shayla poses a lie, a wound too deep. But also, a salve. Another seduction to tempt him down evil's path? Or star-crossed love cleansed of Deathwrought's ataintment?

Despite his fear and guilt, impeded by a darker melange of conflicting emotions, her warmth penetrates his tormented soul.

His suffering eases. The weight lessens.

Her respiration becomes heavy. "I hunger for your kisses."

He obliges her. Shayla pulls him down to the floor. Tries to haul his body on top of hers, but he breaks away.

She frowns, confused. "What's wrong?"

Sonart swallows in contemplation and buries his head in the hollow between her breasts. Through a clenched throat, he whispers hoarsely, "I cannot. He dismantled me. My—"

Shayla sits up and coaxes his head into her lap. The soft skin of her thigh gives comfort. She gingerly strokes away loose auburn strands of his dishevelled hair and the tears from his face. She leans in and kisses his temple, enfolding him in her arms. As if in absolution.

"Sonart?" she whispers.

"Yes?"

"I know you hate me for what I have become—I do not blame you. But I too am blameless."

His pupils tilt up to meet her regard. "What do you mean?"

Her eyes ignite with scarlet light and in a voice not her own, she declares, "Had I not foreseen to possess and taint her, she would've been your greatest ally. Now, wed her doom to the toll of your folly."

Sonart awoke panting in the darkened stable. A cold sweat suffused his back, dampening the hogsweed hay stacks beneath him. Bile caked his throat as he brought his breathing under control. He had outlasted the gloom.

The razor storm had spent its fury during the dimming—the wind free of its telltale grating sound—but its rapacious lament still whistled and shook the chattel outside.

His dream had been a lie, but he still winced at the memory of it—his inadequacy brought on by the pain he endured in the Hive. His mangled innards seemed nothing compared to the mental duress, denied even the feigned pleasure of a dreamt fantasy.

BONGGG-G—G---G!

Sonart's ears perked. The solstice drum which signalled the halfway point between mid-death and mid-drear sounded. Morning. He brushed loose hay from his face and beard. Stood, stretched, and hoisted his pack.

When he unlatched the door and peered outside, the usual sullen grey sky greeted him. He quickly gathered his things and slipped out. Several steps from the refuge, he slid his blade into its makeshift scabbard.

Bulkforge would mark his final attempt to master his situation and solve the mystery of his purpose. If the town offered him nothing new, he would put matters to rest—with one final march.

His conviction gave him courage, galvanized by pain and anger. But then his stars eclipsed. Shayla still haunted his dreams—still stalked him. And as much as he wanted to put the Proclaimer's lights out, he had to avoid her at all costs. *Damn her.*

In the remnants of the storm's wind, the front doors to the row of cottages flapped and creaked on their hinges. Something wasn't right. Sonart had not seen or heard a single dwarven since he had left the barn. He randomly picked a dwelling and called out to any occupants. His hails went unanswered. He tried the adjacent building. No one. Twas as though the whole of Bulkforge had been abandoned or emptied.

Near a cluster of houses towards the main square, Sonart came across a shamble of dwarven bones picked clean by the Scourge's recent vehemence. As he crouched to examine the unlucky party, a din of voices rose above the wind's skirl.

Of course. A gathering in the main square had convened. But the last time there'd been such an assembly… Shoulders tense, Sonart sprang to his feet and shambled at a run, pulling his cowl over his head as he raced on.

In no time, he reached the vast opening between the central buildings of the town. Here stood the stockade tower—a massive ironock pillar, eighty feet high, impaling the middle of the square. The tower soared over the masses like a thick spear—a diminutive version of the Hive itself.

Zürshuck either flew overhead or alighted on the roofs and terraces surrounding the square while Kworn policed the dwarven and cordoned off the area.

So close, the mere sight of the Winged Ones sent icy nettles down Sonart's spine. He kept his gaze level.

The dwarven congregation milled about, packed shoulder to shoulder in the enclosure. They formed a field of grizzled beards: brown and black, some grey and white, earthen-coloured hoods, hats, and jerkins.

All the adults tilted their heads up, towards the top of the tower, while their children ran underfoot. Mothers stood with babes in arms. Their conversations held an infectious air of expectancy, uncertainty, and dread.

Sonart had witnessed this kind of function before, in the dark times prefacing his arrest.

The top of the ironock monolith shone onyx with a cold sheen against the dull grey sky overhead. The prongs of that lofty crown erupted in spiralling flames, channelled up through the same conduits that left the Hive's moat and found their way into the town's smelting forges along the River Seething.

Distant doom-drums thudded a funereal cadence from one, then two, then three different locations. The drums had come back to stay it seemed. Sonart discerned their numbers by the strength of their impedance against his chest. Some sixty of the giant tocsins did the bestial Kworn hammer. As to the purpose of such a massive overture, their sound amplified the throng's unease. It spread like a contagion over the hushed crowd.

The percussion formed its own storm. It oppressed the throng, made the children cry out and the elderlings seem frailer—a few hunched over and clutched at their hearts.

Everyone in the citadel appeared loath to attend, but they remained transfixed, rooted to the cobblestone—the Kworn and Zürshuck saw to that. And with Proclaimers filtering through the press, no one dared exit or voice their dread. Or worse: gainsay the proceedings.

Sonart had learned from childhood that a gathering meant a Trial of the Kusp. Not attending was considered tantamount to treason and carried punishment in the Dunge or the Hooks. The latter marked the verdict of this assembly.

Near the top of the pillar, a long hatch sprang open with a cantankerous thud. It formed a narrow ten-foot-long platform when fully splayed, fastened to the tower by a pair of thick ironock chains.

The ratchet of a windlass uncoiling sounded within the spire. Through the vacant maw, a huge beam of wood thrust outward. On the tongue of the rafter, a black sack, four feet high, jostled erratically on a short tether, swaying like a drunken pendulum.

Another pair of chains hung from the sack with handles attached to the ends. The grips danced and clanked sporadically. The beam extended and came to a stop a further five feet beyond the lip of the platform, a full thirty feet from the opening. The ebony bag suspended from its tip, jangled in mid-air.

Stifled whispers fell over the crowd like a pall.

Moments passed.

Everyone froze.

A lone Zürshuck flew across the square, wings beating fervently as it drew up to the sack. The demon grappled its tethers and with a quick jerk, yanked them free.

The sack fell away, followed by a drizzle of blood, which cascaded over the crowd below like red rain. Sonart did not follow the bag's plummet even as it landed close to where he stood. His regard fixed on the dwarven elderling that hung up there, barbs piercing his body in several spots.

That was the way of the Hooks.

Above the gut-wrenching scene, another rain began to fall. A blast of thunder followed—but no dead calm preceded it—so everyone stood their ground, assured that no razor storm would break.

As the sack settled on the ground, a cry of dismay chorused through the square. Sonart followed their gasps and forced his scrutiny down. A note marked the outside of the coarse-spun bag. It read:

PROCLAIMED BY SONART OF FARKSHONE

Sonart blanched under the shadow of his hood but he squinted upward. And was crushed.

High above him, the face of the condemned belonged to the crazed old one, Xoral. Sonart's heart forgot how to beat, escalating his torment. He could think of only one recourse.

Run.

Sonart bolted, shoving past the ranks. He got as far as the square's perimeter when something jarred the side of his head and dropped him senseless. He lay on the cobblestone, ears ringing from the blow someone dealt him. His body shook, eyes shut, head reeling in a vertiginous daze.

The Proclaimers had found him.

Sonart would join Xoral atop the spire.

The moment of his doom was at hand. And that hand belonged to Shayla.

But a wroth male's voice quelled his panic. "He's lost it: fucker's mind is Dunge-bound," he shouted over Sonart's prone body.

"Hooks and Dunge, man, he's grief-stricken, nothing more," an older voice gave back. "The sentenced sod—his uncle. And I knew both. Begone from my sight and spend your malice with a hammer in the mines. Tis a family affair."

A tempest of ire stormed the first speaker's yell, "Then leash your knave, for grieved or not, next time he tries to plough through me, I'll gut him—string his fucking beard from one Reach to the other."

"I heard you, stars align. Now pray, away with your foolishness, before you draw a Proclaimer's attention—and they gut us all."

"Words unto deeds, Wetnurse," the first speaker grated.

Rain began to fall steadily on the departing crowd.

Strong arms heaved Sonart gently to his feet. Face downcast, still veiled by the cowl, he leaned heavily on the arm of his rescuer and allowed the dwarven to lead him out from the main square into a deserted alleyway.

The noise of the crowd diminished, blending with the soft sound of the falling rain. Calloused hands propped Sonart against a weeping wall. A rough finger pad touched his forehead.

"Not too bad—just bled a lot."

Sonart's vision swam, but he recognized the voice. "Auckland?"

"Aye, it's me."

Sonart's carriage sagged. His guardian, here? He forced himself to meet his uncle's stare.

"What is happening to you?" Auckland pressed, his pained tone rent ragged. "Saw the decree. Heard tell of the massacre. The Elders? Why?"

Water streamed down both their faces. After the Kworn lockdown in Farkshone, there could be only one way Auckland found out so quickly.

"What did Shayla tell you?" Sonart croaked.

Auckland hesitated. "Enough. I rode an ore wagon to intercept you.

Stars chase the shadows, does she speak sooth?"

Myriad questions rooted Sonart's mind, but before he could voice one, Auckland went on. "Mila—she knows nothing of this."

Grateful for the small mercy, Sonart found the will to speak. "Stars burn me, I've been damned from the drear they cast me into the Dunge—no, when my father disappeared. Everything I see is being watched—not by Proclaimers but *directly* by Him, the Darkest One."

The fear writ in Auckland's widening eyes and the quivering of his jowls completed Sonart's defeat.

Despite the danger of discussing such matters, Sonart forced himself to say more. "He impels me to spy, and roust any dissidents, to enact his evil. Not by choice—stars, believe me, not-by-choice."

Auckland gulped. "The dwarven back there—upon the tower?"

"He dies because of me—aye." Sonart's eyes filled with tears. They blurred his vision as they dripped to join the rain.

Auckland shook his head vehemently. "Sonart, you rave. You would never. You are blood—son of my noble brother."

Sonart grappled his uncle's tunic and wrenched him forward until their beards touched. "Listen, damn you! That is precisely why he made me a pariah—*because* of my sire. My father intended for me to lead our people, but who would follow such a murderous outcast? Such a malefactor? Such a Proclaimer? You sensed it yourself in my father's words." *You who wisely refused to attend the Ritual that cursed my line forever and anon.*

Tears welled up in the elder dwarven's orbs. "Stars eclipse, for what cause?"

"I don't know!" Sonart cried. "Fucking hell, would that I could fix what I've wrought and glean the truth. Think you that I act so of my own volition? Hooks and Dunge, I've been smitten—a pawn of both good *and* evil. One way or another, light or dark, my soul is doomed, hauled towards one, then the other, like a bloody plumb."

Sonart pushed his uncle away. "But the curse I bear—I'll not suffer you to share its burden. The hex will consume you as it does me. Mila too is not safe. You must go, Auckland, and never seek me out again."

Sonart's gaze dropped to Auckland's sword. *That's it.* "Do me a kindness and all dwarven a justice—strike me down, here and now." *You may have better luck than the last two—for I seek it.*

Sonart sank to the ground of the corridor and gripped his mentor's boots, islands in the running stream that formed from the downpour.

Auckland drew his weapon.

Hearing the metal's song, Sonart closed his eyes and held his breath. Absolution...

The sword clanged and splashed a few feet away. "I will not end you," Auckland spat in disgust. "It is too late for that—the damage, done. Sonart, get up," he commanded. "Look at me."

Sonart rose and faced him, anger flaring, fists balled. "I cannot *control* what I've become. His power over me strikes at random. If you do not take this one chance now, you'll regret it. I will haunt you. Hunt you. I may even kill you. With His might fuelling my hands... I have committed *murder*. Kill me, before I destroy all you hold dear!"

Hurt etched Auckland's troubled face like the aftermath of a storm. "I've regretted much in my existence." His wrinkles warred like opposing battle lines, expanding and contracting.

Auckland dallied, and finally forced his glare away. To the rain, he moaned, "Stars, Farkshone, an answer, I implore. The chance I take now decides the fate of our people. Was *this* part of your bane? Pray tell, your hidden design for deliverance? Upon the Kusp, I beseech it sooth."

Every step heavier than the last, Auckland lumbered towards his castaway sword. It lay strewn, half-submerged in a shallow torrent. He picked it up and pointed the blade at Sonart. "I am sorry. I've no place to judge you, for good or ill—I remain incapable of either."

He took a deep breath and another. "But I must hold to an oath I made to my blood—to my line—long before your birth. You stake part of that line. In that much, by the stars, we bond the same."

With a sharp clank, Auckland slid the blade into its scabbard before returning to Sonart's side. He opened the younger dwarven's palm and placed a small coin purse there. "Prove me right. May the stars light your way and reveal a path from your darkness."

Sonart swallowed and steeled himself. "Farewell, Uncle."

Thunder rumbled in the distance.

Auckland gave him a brief but reassuring nod. Without another word, he turned and walked away, pushing through the curtain of rain into the main thoroughfare where the wind wailed in lament.

Stephen Fenech

34: Helmdak
Brooke

Brooke held his breath as he focused on the towering beastmen looming closer.

Closer.

Although unsure of their intentions, Brooke sensed no immediate threat or hostility. He remained put. But stars, what *were* they? For certain, an ilk unknown to the masses, if not the Kusp itself, returned from some long-forgotten arcane past.

Wiry black and grey fur covered their sinewy bodies, flaunting an unbelievable musculature beneath. Under longish manes, cavernous eye sockets berthed pupils that shone like onyx glass. Upturned snouts fell to maws arrayed with small fangs, protruding over cracked lips.

The ferocious faces displayed during their engagement with the lavatrols had turned strangely impassive. As they drew near, they regarded the Wrayns as if observing shocked squirrels frozen to stillness.

When Brooke finally exhaled and drew breath again, a musky smell of oxen filled his nose. The scent quickly permeated the night air, overpowering the sulphuric stench of the lavatrols. Not an entirely unpleasant smell, the commander decided, but one that would surely bar him from entering his wife's bedchamber.

Apart from leather girdles and pairs of rawhide bands that formed an X across their barrel chests, they wore no clothes.

Rows of corroded ironock spikes lifted three inches from their leather raiment. The metallic thorns enhanced the monsters' ferocity—not that they needed it—the lingering bits of lavatrol viscera covering their bodies proved ample. The bits still burned and smoked, but the giant combatants seemed oblivious, or impervious to it.

Brooke could only gape and marvel and tremble.

At these close quarters, the beastmen didn't need their mighty cudgels and axes. They could easily stomp the life out of every Warang and Wrayn with their massive legs.

The brutes did neither. They halted and lowered their weapons, resting axe blades and hammer barrels on the ground. Thick arms settled hand over hand atop their pommels.

The mammoths relaxed. Corded muscles slackened and they fell still as behemoth statues, heads tilted down as if in silent prayer.

But their eyes—every last set—fixed on Brooke.

He swallowed, teeth chattering.

"Say and do nothing, Commander," Gnor said from the corner of his mouth. "We are being judged. If myth holds true, we've just been saved by the ancient ogres."

Brooke couldn't take his eyes off the grizzly giants rising over him, but the name Gnor whispered...?

The commander suddenly wished he'd paid closer attention to his childhood lessons: specifically, the primeval histories of the Kusp. He slowly swivelled his regard to the bald Nightwolf.

"Unless I miss my guess, we'll not have to wait long," Gnor assured.

The Bulldog had surmised correctly, for moments later, the redoubt of ogre carriages parted down its centre to form an aisle. Through it, another ogre approached at a sturdy unhurried pace.

The newcomer looked the same size as the others, but his confident strides and air made him seem larger. His fur, a lighter grey than the rest.

And in the centre of his chest, affixed at the crosspoint of his X-shaped jerkin, rested a striking red crystal set in a black metal amulet. In place of a weapon, he carried a staff of gnarled oak clasped tightly in one fist. If one's countenance could be called 'god-like,' stars, this hulk embodied it.

Yet tempering this intimidating impression, Brooke identified a weathered face that bore a wizened look of forbearance and experience, and beneath that, an unmistakable sadness reflected in his ebony pupils.

Clearly their chieftain, the ogre comported himself with poise, his gait and the thrust of his chest, determined.

He emerged from his company's front ranks and halted, soaring over Brooke's craned neck.

The chief planted the butt of his staff on the charred ground. "Prove true, and your army and the villagers under their protection need not fear."

He *spoke*. The juggernaut's voice gurgled like pebbles meshing in the surf while thunder rumbled in the distance. "I have sent several of my warriors to their homes, industries, and forest environs to curtail the destruction. All residual fires will be quelled shortly."

Every Wrayn gaped. All the Warangs folded back their ears and set their tails between their legs. Brooke couldn't blame them. If he had a canine tail, that's precisely where it would have retreated.

The villagers had wisely distanced themselves from the two hosts, peeking out from behind wagons or any viable structure.

"As you've undoubtedly deduced," the chieftain went on, "my kind bear natural armour against all forms of fire, including that of the lavatrols and the cremating flames of the archdemon's Colossals."

Brooke meekly pointed to a smoking nugget of lava that clung to the giant's chest fur. The ogre's eyes followed the commander's digit down and flicked the magma-coal away with a thick finger.

Then he looked back over his immense shoulder. "As for the trolls, and the Colossals that impelled them, they will trouble you no further. We smote the lot, their ghosts forever riven back into the Siphon's hell, which spawned them."

Brooke had to work moisture into his mouth to speak. "There were goblins too—in the initial assault on the woodsmen's village—what of them?"

The ogre shrugged. "Bugs crawling underfoot—a mere nuisance we flattened into the earth. I lament the ground, having to endure their taint until the rains can rinse its soils clean."

A gruff horselaugh to Brooke's left drew his notice.

Spifer—! Fresh scalds, cuts, bruises, and carbon scores painted his carriage head to toe, but the smirking firemonger was alive and well—a miracle in itself.

The chieftain also turned his attention to Spifer. "Greetings, Egg-hatcher." He nudged the headpiece of his staff in the Wrayn's direction. "This brass one saved me the bother of disposing of two Colossals—a risky venture for one man. I thank you for conveniencing me, a service not hardily rendered, or easily accomplished."

"Words unto—detonation," Spifer snickered. When he gave the ogre an unsteady bow, a great burden alighted off Brooke's shoulders. He relaxed enough to chuckle at the madman's awkward gesture. Several Wrayns joined the commander in his mirth.

The ogre acknowledged the pyromancer with a terrible fang-lined grin, guaranteed to give younglings nightmares for weeks on end, and yet a smile nonetheless.

However, the smirk did not reach the monster's orbs when they found Brooke again. "You and I will have words, but I cannot look down upon you if we are to treat as equals."

Leaning on his staff, the ogre lowered himself and rested his rump on the backs of his calves. Even in such a squatted position, the chieftain stood taller than Brooke at his full height. "Better you not feel intimidated when you tell me your true purpose here."

Brooke searched the trees, uncertain how to reply. "I, thank you for your consideration, but we owe greater gratitude to you, for your tribe's intervention."

"Dwell not too strongly on our assistance, little one. We would have joined battle with the lavatrols regardless. As to your affair, we bore a common enemy—I seek to know if it reveals a common purpose."

"All races intertwine in this business. All fates face the Starbond. All souls mirror the Stellar Dance," Brooke answered, surprised that he could recall the psalm from scripture. "If it be for the greater good and the preservation of life on Areth and beyond, then our stars indeed align."

"True words of the Kusp," the ogre allowed noncommittally. "But since the Testament was first penned, history and prophecy have tangled. Aberrations must be unknotted to glean the true path. There are traps within traps—especially for my kind. Of all creatures, we ogres must tread our route most carefully. And place our trust not so hastily as you."

The beastman leaned in and narrowed his eyes. "Things are not always what they seem." He tightened his grip on his staff until the wood creaked. "Defend your purpose—or defend your life."

Brooke started at the threat. Until he saw the ogre's point. "When you say *we*, do you speak on behalf of the entire host gathered behind you?"

"I do, for though an ogre can tread any land without fear of where his foot falls, history has shown we must be extra-vigilant to usurpers of the mind—that has proven *our* weakness. I am chieftain, my brethren's chosen emissary. Because of my station, I am the only one gifted with speech and the right of embassy and judgement."

The ogre paused and examined the gnarled bulges on the head of his sceptre. The storm behind his tone sharpened. "So, I ask you again."

"My name is Aviry Brooke," the commander blurted. "Until recently, I served as one of Pathguard's officers, sworn to King Cele, but fate and truth have displaced me a great distance from—and at odds with—my former station."

Brooke stopped, his regard drifting to the Wrayns and Warangs along his flanks. "I've been chosen to steward this band by one named Targin. He is a renegade marauder to most, a hero and liberator to some, but radical to all. We are known as the Nightwolves, and we await the Night without Dawn—the Starbond. In that, our truest purpose—is to hold back the Darkest One from tipping the stellar balance into endless dark. We strike back as we may, to maintain that balance."

So far so good. Ogres, Nightwolves, and villagers alike remained silent and serene. Other than the sound of crickets and the odd pop of the fire, Brooke still had their ear. "The Noirlunen—ancestors to many who stand before you, suffered great betrayal at the hands of the Darkest One, their lands blighted and eternally damned, their people slain—because they would not follow him into war."

Brooke caught Alghan nodding at his explanation. Encouraged, he went on, "Their defiance cost them dearly, but it also forged who they became. An inherent debt is owed them, passed down their ancient lines of blood. Although my line differs from their origins, we share the same purpose. At the behest of the sprites, we follow what we call the pathless path."

The ogre's coarse brow arched but he remained stoic and attentive. Brooke spoke as one voice in the night. He stepped forward until he stood within striking distance of the giant.

There, the commander raised his arms palms outward. "In earnest, my stars eclipse as to my full role within this resolve. I can defend only what I know—that I've been handed my part, as all life hastens towards a converging and final twilight."

The ogre let out a gust of air that sounded like it passed through a narrow mountain pass. "You've stated the point of your purpose," the ogre said, his guttural voice losing its menace. "But why are you here? To where are you bound?"

"We make for the Hidden Kingdom—Serenthia," Brooke said. "An unprovoked attack on our flanks left many Wolves slain and led us to this village, only to be ambushed again—even as we quelled the harm done by the same villains you slew."

Brooke gulped and met the ogre's enquiry. "Though I wish no enmity between us, judge me as you see fit, Emissary. Regardless of your decision, I stand grateful—if not for your intercession, more than half our numbers would have perished." The commander bobbed his head and said no more.

The beastman nodded slowly. "You speak plain—it does you credit. More than defend your purpose, you have aligned my stars to it. Henceforth, I shall name you, *Stunted Tree*. Small though you may be, you yearn towards the same sun as all creatures of the light. As for me, I have no true name to give you in return, nothing in any tongue of men, dwarven, or elven, but you may call me Helmdak. Tis a name the sprites dubbed me when I swore fealty. It means *One Who Leads through Hell*."

Brooke wavered between reprieve and doubt. "Forgive my question, but why come to our aid when you must judge us, true or false with mere words, *after* the fact? Why intervene at all?"

Brooke expected umbrage from Helmdak, but the ogre chieftain only cracked his black lips to reveal another smirk, no less hideous than his first, yet somehow warmer and more endearing.

The emissary cleared his throat. "I will sate your curiosity, Stunted Tree. We still have several hours ere the dawn, with time for you and your pack to rest in between. Even the tightest of schedules can afford us the chance to reach coven, before we go our separate ways."

Brooke's shoulders sagged in relief.

Helmdak looked off into the middle distance and let out another sonorous squall of breath. "The ogres' tale is a dire one, but trading stories lessens the weight of their full burden. Even a heart strong enough to suffer alone always strengthens when joined."

"As when stars align," Brooke said without pretence.

The ogre lifted a finger and pointed it to the red stone fastened to the centre of his chest. "The answer to your questions lies here. This stone determines how I learn and act, since our emancipation. A token of the sprites, a sigil given to seal a pact long-standing between sprite and ogre."

Sprite and ogre. Brooke creased his forehead, casting his doubt over his shoulder. "Alghan?"

The tall Nightwolf coughed. "I am well-versed in the lore and histories of the Kusp. In truth, Commander, this is news to me."

"It would be," Helmdak growl-chuckled. "Twas a secret pact." The ogre's eyes found Brooke again. "In the ancient days, not long after the Starbirth, the War of the Elementals threw Areth into another great calamity. The Highprites fought fierce battles between those aligned to light and life against Elementals who flocked to the banner of the Darkest One. Vamsah's loyal Highprites made the Kazir, a race of wizards, invested with magic."

Helmdak's face tightened. "As the titans' war raged, the Kazir used their formidable power to repair the damage done to Areth. Vanquishing most of Deathwrought's minions, the Kazir's victory seemed all but certain. The darkness retreated."

The ogre lifted his staff a foot off the ground and brought it down with a jarring thud. "But then, the Darkest One resorted to heinous means to force the pendulum back to centre. Like the Kazir, ogres never birthed in this realm. Our world lies beyond the Hinge: the most savage of all places, one step removed from Infern, lacking only its fire. Life proved a curse from birth, eking out an existence in a hostile and unforgiving land. Only the most ferocious among us survived. Resorting to violence and cannibalism, we'd have destroyed ourselves if left to our own devices."

"What is your world called?" Brooke asked.

"Our globe had no name. It just—existed." Helmdak faced the heavens. "Where your sky colours blue and cheery by day, the sky of my realm appeared crimson like dying embers, the land, an arid blight with more shadow than light, even at midday when our small red sun reached zenith.

"Though we did not know it at the time, Deathwrought had created and conditioned us to subsist—indentured servants, relegated apart from the inhabitants of Areth. Until called upon.

"Our purpose revealed itself only when the Darkest One appeared for the first time to unleash us against the Kazir. He translated us from our world here to Areth—at the time, a realm consumed by the throes of war but still unprepared for our singular purpose. Without any governance of our own, we bent to Deathwrought's will from our inception."

Brooke frowned and took a step closer. "How so?"

"The sprites believe he extracted our soulless essence from the demons of Infern—that makes us impervious to any fire, be it lavatrol, Colossal, or dragon."

Brooke stared at his feet, lamenting the ambushed Warangs and Maxan, his faithful horse. They could not claim the same. He hadn't yet learned the full count of fallen Wrayns and Warangs, but judging by the numbers of wolves and troops gathered here, he calculated their casualties light, all things considered.

Helmdak cut into the commander's reflections. "Shantisan—he goes by other names: Stardimmer, Nitevesel, Deathwrought—brought us into what is now the Dead City. We helped make it so, already a hardened race, bred for war, carnage, plunder, and destruction. It was all we had ever known. As such, we visited great wrongs upon Areth, beginning with the defilement of that city."

Three Warangs padded into the narrow space between the two armies, sat back on their haunches and began to lick their burns and wounds. With a tilt of his massive head, Helmdak paused his tale to study them.

"We scoured the countryside," the chieftain went on in a subdued tone. "Slaying the First Children with impunity, as a rite of passage in the new realm and the promise of salvation in our own. Ogres of that age became a mindless scourge upon the land, mirroring the evil that wrought us."

"What happened?" Brooke pressed, drawing the ogre's regard once again.

"The Kazir rallied—and prevailed. With the help of the Highprites, returned from their place in the heavens, they decimated our numbers, as they sought to manacle the Darkest One and his Four. The Siphons and their Master escaped their bastion in the Land of Fire. Leaderless, the survivors of my fold scattered and went to ground—but by no means won free."

The rigidity in Helmdak's black orbs sapped and his thick shoulders slackened like weighted tree boughs. "Shantisan fled and troubled Areth no more. It became an age of rebuilding, though also estrangement—of lost racial ties and newly forged ones. But the one thing the races shared after the Great War was a loathing of my kind. They vowed to hunt us down to extinction. We had to disappear."

"You did," Alghan said from behind the commander. "The Kusp says as much but leaves no record of how."

"The sprites," Helmdak answered. "Despite the countless ills we had wrought, they sheltered and offered us amnesty. The nymphs saw that we never had a choice in what we'd become and only followed the edicts of our nature. They nurtured the belief that we could do more—if we sought to protect the light instead of trying to extinguish it. Ogres found the power to change, to make reparation. But only if we could be fostered away from Deathwrought's evil."

Alghan and Gnor sidled up beside Brooke. When the three stood abreast, the commander faced them in turn. Alghan's bright eyes bespoke fascination. Under Gnor's heavy brows, a shadow of dubiety.

"What did the sprites do exactly?" the Bulldog asked.

"They released us from the Darkest One's coercion—though not his full taint. All they could do on that count was to shroud us through their lore. We lapsed into a dreamless slumber within the earth itself—not unlike what lavatrols do. The earthen sleep protected us from the vengeance of the races while keeping us safe from the pry of Shantisan."

Helmdak inhaled fiercely. "Wise beyond all measure, the sprites understood the War's uneasy victory would prove ephemeral. And the will of the Darkest One would fester again, in some other form. He would return to finish what he failed to do with us."

"He failed with my people too," Alghan said in a voice thick with emotion. "And similarly, the sprites intervened to save us."

Like an apparition, a great wolf appeared by the three closest canines. By far the largest Warang—a snow-white beast with ghostly blue orbs. It was the first time Brooke laid eyes on the spectral wolf and by his size, colour, and the strength of his stance, it must be their chief, Yerik.

Yerik sat back, flicked his snout to the sky and howled. When he lowered his head, his attention sought the ogre chieftain. They exchanged nods.

"Appointed in deeds—you are, noble one," Helmdak said to the pale wolf. His focus swung back to Brooke. "Like your own, Stunted Tree, the role of ogres in the Endstorm has yet to be fully revealed."

More Warangs and a few villagers came and settled in their midst. Helmdak paused to study them. When the beastman's scrutiny returned to the three men, they glistened with what looked like mourning. "I had hoped that during our sleep the sprites could cleanse us of the evil stain that created and suffused us. But the roots of the Darkest One ran too deep in our blood. Every ogre now carries a guilt and grief, knowing that we can never be wholly saved. We can only seek to atone by serving the sprites—and accepting our doom."

Gnor scratched his head. "For millennia, not a single ogre has trodden the lands of Areth. Why now?"

"We too await the Night," Helmdak said. "Our fate is tied to the Darkest One's resurgence. With the fast-encroaching Starbond, forces reawaken. The ground trembles as wilderen magics stir again and mingle. The Kalibah calls.

Even in its splintered state, the Starbirth crystal flares anew. Everything that transpires on Areth fosters the question of balance. Colossals and lavatrols have come from the north to spread devastation. Like you, we have risen to meet them—that underscores our purpose. One we deem honourable."

Brooke surrendered a mild laugh. "Considering we still draw air because of your purpose, I don't think anyone here would find fault or murmur a breath of gainsay to that."

"Sooth," Helmdak agreed with a dip of his chin. "But the sprites did not revive my tribe only to leave it powerless in other matters. They bestowed gifts to armour us against the approaching storm—one of which I used to judge you. And though we fight different iterations of darkness, our foes fount from the same source. Twas not your words that spoke for you, Stunted Tree, but your heart. Aside from giving me the ability to speak, my stone hears the truth in voices."

The ogre's visage warmed, the corners of his fang-lined maw curving up. "I envy the truth in your heart—it is most rare. Owing to the strength of its fire, you've been well chosen."

"So Targin and this lot keep assuring me," Brooke said. "Truthfully, I have my doubts."

"We may not know each other, but the goal of our purpose is one," the chieftain said. "The Darkest One will not adhere to any rules. He's manipulated divination unto meanders, which the sprites strive to rectify ere the Starbond. Shirdron's Folly and now the emergence of your band evinces two such aberrations that I have discovered since my resurrection."

"There's the prophecy of the Four to consider," Alghan added. "The Law of the Octagon must need stay intact—that sets the true crux."

"But the foundations of that construct were built on fractured ground," Helmdak countered. "Shantisan has returned to draw his deepest lungful, spit his most nefarious venom. He walks the ground of Areth disguised in corporeal form—hence my demand for you to defend your purpose."

Helmdak's attention dropped to his free hand. He closed and opened his palm. "The Darkest One resides among us to make certain his final vengeance is had."

"Among us?" Brooke looked around and grimaced. "How can you be certain?"

Helmdak held the commander's gaze. "I can feel him in my veins still. That... asserts the bane of our existence. We form part of his paradox. Deathwrought created us. Our races never would have met otherwise. Now, we act as simple vessels, extensions of his power. Like any creature of flesh and blood, we can be killed, but our souls remain bound to his. As long as he endures, we exist."

Brooke chewed the inside of his cheek as a shadowy thought occurred to him. "But—if the Darkest One is destroyed—" he stopped midsentence.

"Yes—precisely," Helmdak finished for him. "In that, the sprites failed, though through no fault of their own. Same as us, the little ones are limited by the strictures of their nature."

Helmdak deflated his chest and straightened his back. "But let us not dwell on the inevitable. No point worrying over things you have no control over. All one can do is make the most of the time and purpose granted you—keep the truth as the foremost beacon in your heart."

"Wise words," Brooke acknowledged. "True words."

With some effort, the ogre cracked his fourth grin. "Another dawn fast approaches and our parlay draws to a close, but I would like to learn more of your story, apart from all our cryptic diatribes. No talk of Blood Scions or doom. Something simple to bestir the flames of hope."

Helmdak extended his hand and lightly traced the length of Brooke's arm. "I sense love and yearning in your heart. Tell me, Stunted Tree, have you seeded any saplings? Or taken a wife to wed and garden with the promise of seedlings?"

Despite everything that had happened, Brooke's insides glowed at the unexpected question. He gave the ogre a tired smile, but one that came easy. "Now that, Helmdak, is an effortless regale for it shines as my beacon, guiding my heart hither and anon. The purpose I defend—the purpose of my purpose, the motive for my defection. And the reason for my life."

Brooke went on to describe the more pleasant highlights of his former life while the ogre listened without interruption. When the commander finished, the treetops underlined the first blush of dawn.

Helmdak stood and leaned on his staff. "Half my tribe will accompany your Nightwolves to the next village. Half will remain here to ward the woodsmen and help them rebuild what they can."

Brooke opened his mouth to protest, but Helmdak raised an enormous palm, his stance adamant. "Reprisals may seem unlikely, but if the lavatrols ambushed you twice at a Colossal's behest, they may try so again."

The ogre tilted his head to one side and nudged his chin at Brooke. "Besides my caution, as the first man in history to treat with an ogre—without ironock, I consider you a friend, even should you choose to revile my kind forthwith. I have a strong conviction that will not be the case. If we tramp in lockstep for a spell, we just might forge new stars to align and burn that much brighter."

"I'm honoured by your pledge, but..." Brooke looked to Gnor for some refute, but the Bulldog only splayed his hands and shrugged. When Alghan nodded assent to the arrangement, there was nothing for it.

Resignedly, Brooke turned back to Helmdak and placed a hand on the ogre's massive arm. "You also have shown yourself true of heart, my friend. I will hold to that; join it to my own coven unto the deepest sleep."

Although Helmdak dwarfed Brooke, the ogre's brutishness seemed to soften. "That gladdens me greatly, and I thank you, Stunted Tree."

Brooke smirked up at the giant and chuckled, "Now what?"

"Tell your band to take what scant hours they have left ere the dawn, to rest with ease. They need not fear. We will ward Nightwolves and villagers alike. Barring our sprite-wrought hibernation, ogres do not sleep."

"Then I will leave you to your thoughts," Brooke said gently. With a mind full of mixed emotions, he took his leave of the gathering and retired.

When Brooke reached the tent prepared for him by Gnolin and Weet while the two hosts conversed, the commander glanced over his shoulder.

Staff in hand, Helmdak's hulking silhouette stood out against the backdrop of fleeting stars. Brooke may have imagined it, but the ogre chieftain appeared to tremble, or weep.

Pained by the sight, Brooke turned back to his tent, crouched, and unfastened the front flap. Was this strange truce a glint of the real reason that the sprites' chose him?

Brooke did not have long to contemplate the question. Upon entering the tent, he lay down atop his bedroll and fell fast asleep.

Stephen Fenech

35: Serenthia
Atheri

Queen Atheri crouched beside Targin's unconscious form. When she placed a hand on his forehead, it burned. A putrid odour made her bunch up her nose. Only then did she notice the dark wet spot on his cape where it draped over his arm. She pulled it off and gasped. The angry wound perforating both sides of the appendage had festered into a blue and purple tumour fretted with pus-filled lesions. They throbbed. They hissed.

Atheri leaned in closer. A thin wisp of black vapour escaped the lesions. Stars be merciful—twas shadowed magic at work—the taint of dark elven.

Without taking her hand away, the old woman threw a glance over her shoulder, then closed her eyes in concentration.

A minute later, five guards rushed out of the cave's inner recess, carrying a simple palanquin between them. One tried to take Thrumvedur's reins, but the warbird resisted and made to attack with his curved beak.

Only when Atheri extended her palm and made a hushed cooing sound did the raptor relent. With a lurch, he allowed the guard to guide him, moving forward on unsteady legs. Into the cave, they went, drops of the raptor's blood trailing in the sand. Targin had revealed as much before he lost all coherence—Thrum had been struck by a poisoned shaft as well.

Atheri stood and moved back a few steps to give the remaining four some room. They laid the gurney down on the sand beside Targin and rolled him carefully onto it.

With some effort, they lifted the palanquin and carried the unconscious Nightwolf behind the hawkrike. Atheri stayed back. Both hands on her staff, she cast her severe gaze over the lake.

Placid. The centipus seemed satisfied—which somehow troubled Atheri more. Uncertainty knotted her mouth and knitted her brows. But after several moments probing the sinkhole, she could discern nothing amiss and followed the urgent procession inside.

***

On a jutting rock halfway up the cliff face, not a hundred feet from the slowly closing cavern entrance, a tiny wasp perched. It conveyed all that it had seen to its necromage master.

A second later, the insect took wing. Timing its flight perfectly, the wasp managed to slip inside behind Atheri's procession a moment before the entrance sealed shut with a loud thud.

Inside the gate, four Highguard sentries intercepted the train. All armoured in ironock helms with nasal bars, breastplates, gorgets, and hauberks draped in crimson cloaks, they fell into step beside Atheri.

"Clear the passage for us," she commanded two of them. "We must bring him straight to the nurses in the Chamber of Healing. Targin and his mount have been poisoned by dark elven."

The sentries charged ahead, capes billowing in their wake. "Hear, hear!" they shouted in tandem. "Make way for Her Grace! Yield the corridor!"

Atheri turned to the other pair. "Summon the King's alchlemage. Have him meet us in the Chamber." *I cannot reach him through communion. Tis too early for Thorian to have risen from sleep.* "And get the most capable physician available to tend the hawkrike in the stables, till Thorian can see to him. Make all haste."

"As you command, My Queen." With firm bows, the pair sprinted ahead of the procession.

Into the sanctum of the underground Kingdom of Serenthia, Atheri's van strode. They passed several more sentries, some of whom were given further instruction from the members of their order in the know.

Fore long, many more soldiers, knights, and squires hastened in different directions carrying out related errands. Atheri and her escorts swept past them, disappearing around a bend in a forking tunnel a moment later.

At this juncture, Thrumvedur's wards led the mirky-eyed raptor down a different causeway. Guttural puffs escaped his beak, his pink avian tongue slack, dangling down one side like the corpse of a skinned rodent.

Stars, two lives hang in the balance of my timeliness, with naught an hour separating them from the deepest sleep. Mercy, Vamsah, sanctify our efforts. Atheri prayed and inhaled and prayed.

Further in, the corridor grew more linear, with hard angles replacing the unevenness just prior. Set in the smooth walls, crystal-lit sconces cast glowing swathes that mimicked daylight and illuminated the way. Intersecting warrens appeared with greater frequency, all blocked by guards holding back common folk dressed in earthen garb of grey, green, and brown.

When the train came to an abrupt halt before an arched portcullis framing a double set of glass doors, the queen jabbed her staff towards the sentry posted beside it.

His eyebrows sprang to attention, barely managing a fumbled salute before hastening to splay the doors open. The procession swept in.

A bevy of young and middle-aged women in blue-grey smocks and kerchiefs sat by a row of empty beds interspersed with small tables. Stands and shelves filled the space, laden with poultices, bottles, vials, and flasks topped with white, blue, green, and ochre creams and gels. A neat array of surgical implements, there was also. A short-bristle eggshell carpet lined the floor of the vestibule, contrasting the naked stone of its organic walls. The room's fresh lemony scent attested to its cleanliness and upkeep.

By the nurses' casual demeanour, it had been a quiet day. And a quieter week.

That all changed when Atheri stormed in. The nurses froze for an instant before snapping to action under the sharp commands of Bruna, the head nurse. Her jaw set, the robust elderly woman looked the embodiment of authority. Stern of comportment, she delegated specific duties and tasks, loudest of all: getting the passage cleared.

Amidst the sudden chaos, Bruna ushered the guards into an adjoining chamber set apart for special cases. The guards positioned the pallet next to the only bed in the room while the nurses fastidiously removed the Nightwolf's armour and clothes. When all but his small clothes had been stripped, the guards transferred Targin's pallid form onto the waiting bed. Under Bruna's supervision, her underlings came and went, carrying an assortment of supplies and setting to their assigned tasks.

Once they had done all they could, the head nurse beckoned the guards and nurses to leave. Her eyes found Atheri, who had silently watched them work, back pressed against the wall to stay out of their way.

"Thank you, Bruna," Atheri said.

"My Queen." The nurse dipped her chin and left the room, closing the door behind her.

Atheri's gaze fell upon Targin. The gentle rise and fall of his chest encouraged her as she maintained her lone vigil. But not for long. A gentle rap at the door drew her regard. "Come," she said.

The door opened revealing a breathless soldier and an equally winded alchlemage in tow, a small wooden case tightly couched under one arm. Flowing greyish-brown robes half-hid what had become a frail body. By his dishevelled hair and loosely fastened attire, Thorian had been jerked from sleep and hit the ground on the run—the poor sod. What once had been a carriage of sturdy bones had surrendered unwillingly to the passage of time and a life of combat.

Beneath his cowl, the mage's face had a look of worn leather. Although dark circles underscored his sunken eyes, he still maintained a hard strength tempered with patient resolve. Wearied with the years, he still bestowed kindness and competence with every glance and gesture.

"Your Grace," the mage greeted with a solemn bow. He turned his attention to Targin.

"Lord Thorian," the Queen returned. "Our champion took quite a wallop this time," she explained over his shoulder. "It's a bad one."

"Always is for me." He set to work, splaying the case open on a small stand beside the bed. "Otherwise, you wouldn't have summoned me."

"Of course." She smiled in spite of herself. "Can I assist you?"

"Assist?" He examined Targin's infection, ran a hand across the giant's temple. The alchlemage bit his lower lip for a moment before returning his focus to the open case. "Nay, My Lady, the nurses will be adequate in that regard. Not the first cursed wound I've had to treat. He'll be fine."

Atheri released a sigh of relief as Thorian selected three vials containing powders from his trove. "But the pleasure of your company will help motivate this old heart."

"Then you shall have it," Atheri laughed. "Until you sicken of me."

Thorian looked up for a moment from his mixing, a frown drawing his eyebrows together. "Your Grace, you name a sickness I shan't ever seek to remedy." He dropped his eyes to Targin. "But as to the malady assailing your daughter's betrothed, I must now press all my resources. Time is of the essence. I took the liberty of sending my apprentice to see to his hawkrike. She'll ensure the dark elven's hex is removed and the poison arrested in time." He took a breath. "But as to the healing of the raptor's avian parts, I'm afraid that remains beyond Jana's abilities. You'll need a proper bird-master for that."

"When Jana sends word, I'll appoint the master of all masters," Atheri promised.

"Thought as much," said Thorian, a benevolent smile warming his countenance, further brightened by rosy cheeks.

The alchlemage uncoiled another bundle of medicines and busied himself with his mission, adding water to the powders to make a thick paste, while Atheri looked on.

Sin watched with tired eyes as the trail of smoke rose from his cigarette heater. In a thin undulating column, it wafted up past the resigned faces of his bandmates. Their expressions mirrored his own sentiment.

Inclement weather had delayed their flight to Gothenburg, forcing the band to wait it out in the First-Class lounge of Stockholm's Arlanda Airport. Bobby would've made the attempt, but the band's jet had also been grounded, in need of a vital avionics part.

Bobby was a first-rate pilot, having cut his teeth flying daring missions in warzones before retiring from service. That's when Sinathor hired him. A well-honed trooper, through and through, Bobby could handle just about anything Mother Nature whipped up, with easy calm. So, when he said *Song's Swan* should stay nested, no one contested him.

Sin took a drag from his cigarette, blew out the smoke and took a sip of his Americano. Bobby was a character to be sure, but stalwart, resourceful, and as unflappable as they came.

More and more characters entered Sin's life. Some like his pilot in the 'real' world, some from Areth, a world that steadily edged towards reality. In that regard, Sin finally accepted it as real—entwined with his life, his fate an existential part of it.

All fates face the Starbond.

First, the dwarven and all the shit he'd been forced to endure. Now this barbarian. Sin dreamt of the new player for the first time three nights ago. The giant just finished relegating his small band to an enemy soldier. No, a higher-up—a commander.

Then last night came another vision as the barbarian flew a bizarre-looking bird, chased by a gangly crew of hobgoblins astride giant crows with veined wings like bats. The goblins stuck him with a poisoned arrow.

An insane flight ensued, through a darkened forest of trees that would've dwarfed the coastal redwoods. The giant made it home, but would he pull through? Sin put his money on yes. Like the dwarven, this barbarian struck him as a survivor.

Strange, although Sin could see the events play out as they had with Little Guy, he never could make out their faces—they always appeared blurred out, defocused.

And again, the luminous beings assured Sin with their ghostly voices that he would learn the truth in time ...when he needed it.

For now, they maintained, he had to concentrate on his singing. If that wasn't fucked-up advice from beyond, he didn't know what was.

Sin played with possible lyrics: 'Beyond fucked-up', 'Fucked from beyond'... 'Be-fucking-yond.' More like yawn, he concluded as one escaped his mouth.

Turning inertia drew the singer back to the present. Sin reached for the pendant beneath his shirt. It grew warm, unnaturally hotter than from touch alone. Still, that might just be his imagination. Add fucked-up imagination to the pile. But who was kidding whom? A storm was coming; he heard the first rumble of thunder. It loomed just over the horizon.

An announcement interrupted his cryptic thoughts and a thick Swedish accent came on the terminal's intercom. "We're sorry, but Flight 257 to Gothenburg has been cancelled."

Seven days later, outside Targin's room, Bruna strictly reprimanded a soldier. Atheri recognized the man's voice. The ranger, Lorin.

"Listen, Pup," Bruna seethed. "No one—and that includes the likes of you too, Lorin—shall enter the hospice until Thorian has finished, and even then, only with Queen Atheri's blessing. Is that understood? Or do I need to bonk you on your ferret head to give you incentive? Now, out from my ward."

"Stars burn you, woman, and whatever plague of the First you've contracted," the scout grated. "That Targin be placed under your care, while his troops—while I—toil in ignorance through a storm of your sarcasm."

"Only the plague caused by your wagging tongue. Now shut the hole from which it escaped and begone with the rest of you before I have you thrown to the centipus for disturbing the alchlemage!"

Inside the room, Atheri exchanged a resigned look with Thorian. "Appears I can be of service after all." With that, the queen slipped out of the room and quietly closed the door behind her.

An exasperated Lorin greeted her. Tousled brown hair matted the handsome ranger's tanned face. Flushed and weathered when the queen appeared, it went crimson and he stared at his feet. "So sorry for the disturbance, Your Grace."

"No offence incurred, Lorin," Atheri said. "What vexes you?"

"Her." He stabbed a finger at Bruna. "I'd fare better reasoning with a rabid boar!"

"Stars align, the incorrigible pest and I have come to an understanding at last," Bruna gave back, no less trenchant.

Lorin threw up his arms, spun, and stormed out of the chamber.

Bruna shook her head slowly, watching him go. "He can be such an ass, but I like him."

Atheri shared a brief chuckle with the head nurse before reaching out to the ranger, through communion. '*Lorin?*'

'*Yes, I hear you,*' his voice answered sourly.

'*Do not discount your captain's resilience,*' she comforted. '*Any other man and I wouldn't dispense such assurances. But for seven days his condition has not worsened. He is a Vein of Fire. I assure you, Targin will heal himself, and quickly now that he lies in Thorian's care—an alchlemage of the highest order. Also, my daughter's arrival will guide Targin away from the deepest sleep. Cocky and overbearing he may be, but your captain is one tough bastard.*'

The Queen paused before adding, '*The poison took a much firmer grasp on his raptor. Thorian's student has kept Thrumvedur from the deepest sleep. But with your exceptional knowledge of the wilderness and its denizens, perhaps your time would be best spent tending to the hawkrike. Possibly conjure a cure from your vast trove of plant lore.*'

Atheri sensed Lorin stopping midstride, his earlier ire evaporating. She felt the smile crossing the scout's face. His heart softened and he spoke to the air in front of him. "Stars align and with sincere thanks, My Queen. Ever you champion the truth of diplomat and confessor, your counsel just and astute. On my oath, Thrumvedur will soar again." With that, the ranger quickened his pace towards the wingwards' aviary pens.

An hour later, Atheri's appraisal of Targin proved true. She left the hospice and addressed a gathered company of soldiers in the corridor beyond. "The king's alchlemage assures me Targin will make a full recovery. The worst is behind him, thanks to Thorian. I am grateful to all of you for your concern, but you need not tarry further."

Shoulders sagged and many exhalations and nods followed, but Atheri discerned lingering doubt in the troops' faces and minds—all too palpable, all too justified. Their mighty leader had never before fallen, so they held a common belief that Targin was unstoppable. Indomitable.

Set jaws and hard gazes masked the air of uncertainty as the congregation disbanded. The soldiers took their misgivings with them to the other districts of the Strong Helm.

An impenetrable blackness seeped into the confines of the circular tower room, further darkening its near-unsolvable shadows. The penumbra coalesced into an opaque cloud, blotting out the night sky outside the windows.

Inside the spire, a small sconce strapped the peeling mortar walls, its flame cowering before the entity's advance. All light guttered and died.

Necatar bathed in the being's presence like one deranged in the ecstasy of a gratifying vice. But the necromage braced, careful not to forget his place in the greater daemon's essence. He opened his mind and welcomed the possession, as he knew he must.

Twas the only way to safely communicate with the dark messenger. Maleficent thoughts chiselled into his brain, as though his own. This mark—this arrangement—would not be detected by any mole of the sprites, or the elven, any Vein or Siphon component to the Octagon.

Nor the Darkest One himself.

The wheel of prophecy had sped up. Its import ramped higher with every passing day, but its spokes were bending to his direct influence, aligning to this new arrangement—to the deviation Necatar had forced.

Let the Four Veins plunge on, move towards Merger and conjunction, ignorant of their ultimate fate. When they realized the truth of matters including their dark destiny, it would be too late.

Brooke may have escaped his snare, but that jackanapes would meet his end soon enough. With the jaws of war firmly opened now, the armies would be unleashed exactly as Necatar had intended. Only now, with the help of Menagerie and his dark elven, a greater secret had been revealed.

The armies would make a slight diversion. And the Nightwolf would pay for his folly when he sees the final tally. That will evidence the most glorious of Creation's moments—for it will mark its last.

Necatar would see to it. He would see to a great many other things as well. The first of which flew on the wings of his special envoy—a tiny wasp bearing the loudest message of all.

36: Tasmin
Targin

Targin awoke to a row of lovely young nurses hovering by his bedside and staring at him. A bear's yawn escaped his lips before finishing in a full-blown grin. He stretched and corded his arms until the veins rippled across his skin.

Brawny shoulders sagging, he blew out a great breath. Then tilting his head to one side, he probed the nurses' expectant faces. "How's my bird?"

"Your hawkrike's on the mend, and fine," the nurse to the far-right blurted. "Lorin said that would be your first question upon waking—made sure we would tell you."

"Smart lad," Targin said. "Stars align, good news, that is." He let out a gust of a sigh and slapped his belly with both hands. "Now that that's settled, my stomach needs settlement as well. I've the hunger of a ravenous ogre. Pray, bring me food before I wilt away to nothing."

They laughed at the absurdity of his quip, but when the moment passed, two of the nurses who Targin recognized—Anora and Alitha—scurried away.

They returned a few minutes later, Anora cradling a tray piled with steaming venison and roasted vegetables. Alitha held a basket of bread and a half-flagon of wine.

Targin ate boorishly, engaging the bevy between bites with endless japes and a few tales of the Nightwolves' exploits. "If Barget," *chomp, chomp,* "had sequestered as many maidenheads," *chomp,* "as he boasts, would not Serenthia's population be double?" He lifted his knife and waggled it before his arching eyebrows. "Unless, of course, he speaks sooth but knows not where to point it."

The giant cleaned the tray amidst an overture of giggles and scandalous scoffs. He sopped up the lingering meat juice with the bread and washed it down with the last swallow of wine.

"*Mmm,* that was well done and better received," he exalted as he wiped his chin with a napkin. "And I thank you, my ladies. But now, I must put my replenished energy to good use—and see to more pressing matters. If you'd be so kind as to pass me a robe."

"Milord," Anora replied meekly. "Thorian stressed you must remain in bed until he gives leave."

Targin scowled, throwing her a look of umbrage, not entirely feigned.

"Also, by command of the head nurse," Anora added hurriedly, clearly hoping the mention of Bruna would carry more weight.

It did not.

"Nonsense, woman! I'll not be imprisoned in an infirmary when I feel well enough to argue with you. I must consult with the King—once I see to my hawkrike." Targin let out a sonorous squall and locked gazes with the nurse. "Anora, I officially exonerate you and your peers from any dereliction and release you all from your charge. Now, pass me my robe, or naked I shall—"

"Hold!" a woman's sharp voice silenced his protest.

The nurses' heads whipped around.

"You will do nothing of the sort for this barbarian."

Targin recognized the voice—and the manner. A minute burp escaped his mouth as he braced his ears for the forthcoming tongue lashing.

The nurses shied away as a tall woman, cloaked and hooded in a hunter green robe, swept lithely to the Nightwolf's bedside. The cowl concealed the face within, but the unbridled strength and poise of a wildcat underlined her carriage.

The woman drew to a stop before Targin, who sat a head below her. Crisp pale hands moved to her hood and drew it back, revealing a piercing set of ice-blue eyes. They locked with his—and froze him.

The room dimmed before her like a storm cloud suddenly penetrated by a sabre of intense sunlight. Such, the radiance this woman bestowed, such the thunder of her countenance. If beauty could be called fierce, this woman imbued it. The finely chiselled face adorned by a straight nose, high cheekbones, and full lips, depicted a trove of tenderness carefully stowed. Now her jaw had firmly set, sculpted by determination and scorn.

Straight locks of silver-blonde hair glistened in the torchlight. Her hard stare never left Targin as she reached back and lifted the full wealth of her mane, letting it cascade down her back.

As though held in trance, all eyes were drawn to her as she loosened the folds of her robe. It revealed a ranger's boiled leather gorget, vambraces, knee guards, and riding boots.

Targin swallowed hard and gaped. The woman before him was a layered paradox, beyond mystery. All present waited on her next word, none more than him.

She slapped Targin across the face, so hard the clap echoed across the walls. Her next word—spoken.

Jaw tightening, the Nightwolf glowered at his own reflection in the bedside mirror, as the red imprint of her hand appeared on his cheek. The nurses gasped, their faces coloured equally red. Hands covered mouths as they looked away in shock and chagrin.

"Leave us," the woman commanded over her shoulder. In a bustle, the nurses hastened out of the room, apparently relieved to be dismissed. How

Targin longed to join them.

When the door shushed closed behind the last orderly, the room felt suddenly cramped. An awkward silence filled it.

"So, it is true."

"Targin furrowed his brows. "So, is what true?"

"You bear greater love for a bird than the one you swore to honour forever."

"Tasmin!" the Nightwolf half-blurted half-laughed. "Do not yammer so." He reached to draw her in, but she shrank back and batted his hand away.

"Oaf! I rode hard for the better part of a week to egress the forest and rendezvous with a hawk—to spirit me to your side. Lain awake, keeping vigil each night for another fortnight, watching as Thorian dragged your miserable carcass back from the deepest sleep. I've helped the alchlemage nurture you to the land of the living. Three weeks in total. And your first conscious thought, ahead of His Grace and your betrothed veers towards a beast you keep in an aviary?"

"Stars burn you, woman," Targin growled, "Thrumvedur took a far more grievous wound than I, swollen with the same poison. But he does not possess the same wilderen store to help heal himself."

The Nightwolf let out a rush of air. "Of course, I'd have greater concern for his wellbeing. Matters of court, including your trials of the heart, can wait a few hours while I ascertain Thrum's condition."

"Matters of court? Trials of the—!" Tasmin fired back. "Is that what you think my lot in Serenthia? Think I scamper beneath the war board, ignorant of what transpires above?"

Targin looked away but she punched his arm, snapping his attention back. "That I sit idle and immerse myself in frivolous affairs of the kingdom, doing needlepoint with highborn maidens? Do I wait, hand on breast, while you play jester every time you set foot out the fucking door? While you turn another notch in the gears of war or prance about the woods with that bunch of filthy dogs?"

"Do not mock my Nightwolves, for without them the gears of *everything* would have already come to a screeching halt. And no, I understand you tirelessly perform a senate's worth of political, diplomatic, and extra-curricular duties to address the needs of your father's kingdom."

Tasmin folded her arms. "So, *that's* what I do for the Strong Helm while you forage on your savage meanderings?"

"Why should I think any different?" he thundered.

"Yes, why—and that's exactly what you should contemplate tonight when you bunk down in a pile of hay with your steed in a stable pen instead of a warm bed with me. I will not stand between you and that overgrown fowl you prefer to wed!"

"At least Thrum will not crucify me for an innocent slight. And allow me parlay with a reasonable mind—not one that is always filled with such wrath!"

A tight-lipped smile crossed Tasmin's cold face. The princess spun with a practised flourish, letting her cape flare and reveal the exquisite figure beneath. She *knew* the effect it would have on him. His mouth went dry as his eyes translated what his loins suddenly craved—and would be denied.

As she reached the doorway he said to her back, "Farewell, vixen of unfairness."

Tasmin did not answer him as she opened the door and left. She had bested him, again. Curse her.

Targin did not seek to call her back. He would be equally unwavering, and in a small way glad to be parted from her vehemence.

When his anger abated, the giant marvelled at how she affected him. In the briefest of exchanges, Tasmin could anger him more with mere words than a thousand demons prodding him with forks. Suppress him with a more efficacious poison than any ten goblin bolts. And injure him with the most direct weapon of all.

37: Allied Forces
Brooke

Stuck on the losing side of a calamitous battle, Brooke struggles not to despair. The men he commands are on the verge of mutiny, blaming him for their predicament—he deserves every syllable.

There stands a magnificent crystalline statue of a female deity, a hundred feet high, carved from a sapphire pinnacle overlooking a vast canyon. She holds a long golden horn to her mouth with one hand, a time-dial couched in the crook of her other elbow. Above the statue on an adjacent perch stands a domed chapel.

A flash swallows the scene and deposits him in an immense cavernous domain. It rises high above him, a husk of what had once been clean lines joining enormous balustrades and balconies. But to some unholy scourge, the natural cathedral has succumbed. Dank and dark, it has devolved into a tomb, defiled by horrors, littered with mounds of half-rent and burned corpses.

Thousands of giant bats crawl up and down the walls and floor of the enclosure like an angry insect horde. Penned in, they walk on their wings to clear a passage through tunnels, crushing the bones of corpses as they press forward.

Blood has splattered the broken monuments and structures. Across the vast tiled floor, the crimson fluid trickles and pools and seeps into hidden crevices. Into the maws of the bats.

They turn, sniff, and catch Brooke's scent. He wants to bolt but cannot. His feet are shackled to the stone rampart. The bats bear down on him, shrieking in umbrage for disrupting their den. Of that too, he is to blame.

Reality blots out as the black droves pounce.

Darkness...

Brooke awoke in a cold sweat, his body trembling in capricious waves. This was no dream: this had been a vision. He recognized its texture—identical to the one Targin forced him to watch. He lay awake in silent contemplation until morning came in earnest, bringing light and a crisp breeze.

Despite his stricken mind, stiff muscles, wounds, burns, and bruises, Brooke felt strangely purged as the first rays of sunlight streamed into his tent.

When he dressed and crawled outside, shock assailed him. The entire contingent of ogres bustled with a handful of villagers and Nightwolves, all hard at work rebuilding the village. They felled trees, held, braced, or nailed walls, drove stakes into the ground, hauled logs or sawed them, even supported entire roofs. The enormity and strength of the ogres had sped up the workload and an astonishing amount of progress had already been made. At this rate, seemed they would complete the restoration by day's end.

Brooke caught sight of Helmdak, hoisting a log up to a pair of ogres straddling the apex of a roof. The chieftain turned and smiled his horrible smile.

"A-hum!" Helmdak called in a booming voice. "As I said, even the Stunted Tree will rise to meet the Sun. Greetings. Have you broken fast?"

"Nay, Helmdak. I would you—" Brooke stretched his arms wide and let out a canyon-wide yawn. "—sate my curiosity first."

"Nothing really. We simply set to work after you fell asleep, waiting only long enough to ensure we would not disturb you. But in truth, this ogre has had enough for now." Helmdak made a silent gesture to his brethren, who answered with gruff nods. He faced the commander again. "The ogres will continue the reconstruction after we leave. I would have us depart as soon as you are ready."

"As would I," Brooke said. "Let us leave then. I've no appetite that can't be quelled by a saddle's dry stores."

Even as he said it, Brooke winced, remembering his lost mount. The bereavement of Maxan proved all the more biting now. He looked to the sky and intoned a silent prayer for his valiant steed.

After a few moments, he turned his attention to the task at hand. Easier said than done, unsure about riding a Warang for any great length—provided one would suffer him to try. A Warang was not a horse.

By the grimace on Helmdak's face, he'd detected Brooke's sorrow as he stole up. "I'm told you lost your mount. Would you honour me, by sitting atop my shoulders and allowing me to carry you this day?"

Disarmed by the offer, the commander's jaw fell open, but before he could think of a response, Alghan, astride a swift Warang rode into view. Another wolf trailed close behind. The second canine looked beautiful with a melange of grey and white fur and a striking set of mismatched eyes, one blue, one brown.

"Good morning," Alghan announced as his wolf drew to a stop before the pair. "The Warang behind me is Ralaus, Commander. His rider, Wals fell last night. The wolf has agreed to bear you today. As for tomorrow, he will commit pending the outcome of your ride this day. The first trial decides the Warang." Definitely not a horse.

Blood rushed to Brooke's ears, unsure which offer to accept. He looked up to Helmdak, but the giant only rumbled with laughter. "You do not require my leave or sanction for such things. If before the morrow the Warang resolves you unworthy to bear further, my offer still stands."

Brooke smiled. "Thank you—all of you." The commander bent a knee before the Warang and placed a hand under the wolf's giant muzzle. "I am humbled and honoured that you deign to carry me, Ralaus—even if it be for one day."

The Warang nuzzled Brooke's open palm before pawing the earth lightly. Then he lowered his stolid frame until his body rested prone.

Brooke got to his feet, moved alongside the Warang, and swung his leg over the worn leather saddle strapped to the wolf's back. When the commander's hands adjusted and secured the reins, Ralaus slowly rose and waited as Helmdak, Alghan, and Gnor came abreast.

"Commander?"

He glanced behind. And spotted Weet and Gnolin beside his tent, pointing to it.

Brooke inclined his chin. "Aye, lads, strike away."

The pups set to it at once.

Brooke trained his eyes ahead and cleared his throat. "We move."

Ralaus started forward.

The two armies filtered past the woodsmen, who stopped their work to see the procession pass. Brooke espied Shindu, the same bearded leader he had exchanged harsh words with when they first met. Shindu dry-swallowed as their gazes locked. He pulled at his collar.

If his weighted brows and the slight press of his chafed lips gave any indication, all malice had drained from the woodsman's face, replaced with a mix of gratitude and guilt.

Brooke offered him a thin smile. The two men raised hands and waved to one another in silence.

As the company crossed the clearing to the far side of the village, they passed under the shadow of the remaining contingent of ogres. Without pause, the beastmen continued their tireless work under the supervision of the villagers.

Brooke trained his eyes ahead. The narrow forest road they followed forced the two hosts to thin their lines. Within an hour, the van had elongated such that only two Warangs could pad side by side. The commander rode abreast of Gnor, seated atop Fram.

With the bridge Brooke had forged with Shindu fresh in his mind, his thoughts turned to Val. And no sooner did Gnor glean his inadvertent communion.

Speaking only so that Brooke could hear, the Bulldog broached the subject. "Traps within traps—is that not how our ogre friend phrased it? I suspect such a root runs deep in Val's purpose."

Brooke started. Targin had warned him to be mindful of his thoughts.

Something else he'd have to work at—on top of his growing list.

"If not for Val's diligence, gall, and self-sacrifice, I would have perished last night," Brooke reminded him.

"Aye, but many Nightwolves sacrificed themselves in the wake of that rescue," Gnor countered. A scowl formed on his face. "Look to the plaintiff's words of yester. Val did not commune with our main host when he should have. I piss on his claim that he heard no return hail anywhere. Regardless of custom—whatever foe might've gleaned his news—his first duty is to the pack. Not some old crow."

Gnor blew out his cheeks and his features softened. "In the kind of business we're in, Commander, callous though it may sound, the old villager was expendable. How many of your people were similarly killed in our campaign against Pathguard? Val should have made straight for our host with warning, not investigate the flank's silence alone. And then, how convenient that the cherufes consumed his Warang? I sense his actions plot and parcel to the ambush."

Brooke tightened, his ire rising. "Stars, Gnor, he beseeched us *not* to enter the village—that was my decision."

"Convenience again, and cunning. He counted on your animosity to do the opposite of his request—traps within traps."

Around the reins, the commander made fists as his anger grew, but he kept his voice in check. Cele's council sessions had taught him something of that. Still, a phantom of doubt stole over him, but of whom should he be suspicious? Had someone sought to manipulate him into shunning the introvert? If so, why?

"I harbour no such animosity towards the man." Brooke met Gnor's penetrating stare. "Only incomprehension. As steward, I will not hold Val suspect in this matter until I have solid evidence of his collusion. Perhaps my findings will attest to the truth of the trap, and show you, the ensnared."

Gnor raised an eyebrow and studied the commander. "You may wharf no suspicions, but he's riven with them towards you. Val has always been a quivering bolt, held taut in anxious hands. He makes his way on the outermost fringe of the pathless path for a reason."

"Such a course is needed," Brooke defended, "in our business as you say."

"True, but he sheds a darkness any among us would be quick to point out," Gnor pressed. "It's what segregates him, keeps him so damnably alone, and barren of cheer. His actions have always been suspect—now even more so. If any of us would fall sway to the Darkest One's treason, it would be him."

"Your opinion is noted," Brooke said, his tone wooden. "As is your enmity."

"Then note this, Commander. The other Wolves will shun him—after the events of last night. More than ever, they will be loath to trust your decisions, especially about him. And they will never again let Val watch their backs."

"That sounds like a veiled threat," Brooke said, sharper than he intended.

Gnor let go of his reins and splayed his hands, jowls flapping. "Not at all. I only give voice to the sentiment of the entire band, for your benefit. Near two hundred Wrayns and their same number in Warangs. Just remember, you serve as steward to all, not just the one."

Brooke locked eyes with the bald Nightwolf. "Aye, but tis the one who seems most in need of a steward, if not a friend."

"Need and want are different beasts."

The Nightwolf's words sickened Brooke, enough to sour his stomach. He wanted to bridge the gulf with Val, not ostracize the man—such a capable warrior—as demonstrated.

Brooke faced forward and said to the air, "I think you're wrong, Gnor. Val's burdens differ from our own, and though I'd be the first to agree Targin's Second is a secretive and troubled recluse, perhaps you misunderstand what he faces."

Gnor snorted back and spat on the ground, showing quite plainly what he thought of that notion.

Just then, Alghan pulled up beside the pair, giving them curt bows in turn. Suddenly grateful for the tall Nightwolf's presence, Brooke beckoned Alghan closer. "I'd like you to weigh in on something."

"Commander."

"Pray tell, where falls your opinion of last night's business with Val?"

Alghan surveyed the area behind him and to either side before replying. "Of last night, and the rogue's part in it, frankly Commander, I don't know what to think. But I do know Val. He may not be a pub of mirth and camaraderie, but you can trust him—he'd chop off his own arm if it meant following the Code. Like Quiver, he's the *first into the worst*—which is to say, he's always the first Targin sends on any mission with the greatest personal risk—oft as not on Val's insistence."

Alghan adjusted his grip on the Warang's reins, loosening his hold as he rolled his shoulders. "As much the conundrum, Val remains a valuable asset to have on your side when you duck past the breach, or storm it." His eyes drifted to Gnor. "Unfortunately, my peers do not share my opinion."

The Bulldog scoffed.

Brooke gave Alghan a firm smile, grateful for his appraisal, even if it was only slightly more positive than that of Gnor. In any case, a lot less hostile.

Alghan sighed and looked away. "That said, I maintain you should keep your distance and be wary of him. Like a sword, Val bears a double edge."

Brooke nodded. The Nightwolf's counsel confirmed what he should have done at the outset.

When the three riders drifted apart, Brooke leaned forward and whispered into Ralaus' ear, "Bring me to Val. But please, do not commune my intent."

Ralaus wheeled right and lurched into motion, leaving the road in two heartbeats. Tearing through the underbrush, the Warang careered ahead of the pack, surefooted and spectre-like. He threaded a rapid course, branching out from the host's right flank and into the deeper folds of the forest.

It didn't take Ralaus long to pick up Val's scent. The giant wolf stopped, raised his head, sniffed the air, and broke into another sprint, adjusting his course to the left. Within minutes the gap between the two men joined. Brooke slowed his Warang to match pace with Val's canine.

As expected, Val glowered and turned away. He kept his eyes averted as the commander drew up, but he didn't baulk or shoot away. He allowed Ralaus to come alongside his charcoal wolf.

Encouraged, Brooke began, "Val, I will have words with you."

Only the sounds of the Warangs' snorts answered him.

"It was never my wish to supplant or rob you of your agency," the commander went on. "Your chief thrust the charge upon me for reasons I still cannot grasp. But give me a few moments; lend me your ears and voice—for the sake of understanding. Then you'll have my leave to go on hating me, in solitude."

Head down, Val gave no indication that he'd heard the commander's words, but his Warang did not break stride with Ralaus—response enough. "I will not waste your time, mincing some shoddy truce. Your peers tell me not to trust you—which only makes me adamant that I should."

Val tightened his lip and his grasp on the Warang's reins but kept his grimace fixed onward.

"In turn, as your steward, I must ask. Why do you mistrust me?" Brooke pressed, his eyes searching the other's stone visage. "Please know, if there's anything you wish to share, to lessen the weight, you'll find impartial ears. I bear you no ill will. Stars, I have seen your worth firsthand—that I still breathe is proof enough. You have more than earned my trust, and with it my—"

Val spun on him. "Do not fan the flames of my ire, lest-you-get-burned," he sneered through clenched teeth, "I don't need your trust! Or your thanks!

You'll only cross more stars with me. Just go back—to being the singular puppet." He brandished a quivering finger at the commander. "Nightwolves are dead who would be alive today had you listened to me."

"You know that's something I cannot—"

Val lunged at Brooke, knocking him out of the saddle. The pair went down in a tangle of limbs, striking the ground with a crunch before ploughing through the underbrush.

The impact left the commander in a daze, but he discerned the two Warangs howling as he scrambled to his feet—just in time to meet Val's second attack. Even so, the Nightwolf proved too quick. Before the commander could get his fists up, Val landed a brutal blow to his gut.

Brooke rolled with the punch, tucking his stomach in, and tensing to dampen its power. The momentum impelled the commander backwards but he kept his legs under him, crouched, and sprang back, striking Val square in the face with his own balled fist.

Val absorbed the blow and used it to get inside Brooke's reach, smothering him into a bear hug. He lifted the commander and bore him down to the ground. Before Brooke could rally, Val held a dagger's tip, poised under his chin.

"Shall I prick you to drive my point home, knave?" Val spoke softly but his voice implied a shout. "I'm wise to your folly so let me make this clear. Stay the-fuck away from me, or so—"

Val's bulk suddenly wrenched off Brooke.

In the next instant: Ralaus loomed over the commander, growling balefully at Val, a mouthful of the Nightwolf's black jerkin clamped in his snarling fangs.

Brooke clambered to his feet just as Helmdak and Gnor raced up.

Eyes wild, Gnor demanded, "Stars burn me, what's going on here?"

It didn't take a soothsayer to see the Bulldog knew perfectly well. But Brooke played along between pants. "Away with your dread. It is nothing, a quickstart of control—my fault really. Isn't that so, Val?" He faced the Nightwolf, busy massaging the torn patch on his back Ralaus that had caused.

After some hesitation, Val gave a terse nod and the commander continued, "Still green I'm afraid when it comes to riding a Warang. Val and I collided and stumbled is all, but enough to drive the point home. I'll know next time how to better handle my wolf—how unpredictable they can be."

"Are you all right, Stunted Tree?" Helmdak asked, brows arched, concern fretting his rumbling voice. "Any broken branches?"

"Apart from some embarrassment, no worse for wear, my giant friend," Brooke assured. He feigned a chuckle.

Gnor was no fool. He held his tongue, but his eyes shot daggers at Val, chasing the other's glare away. Val turned and made for his Warang.

"Then, follow me, Commander," Gnor said in a cautious tone. "We are still hours away from Riverside and, tried or not, our leader is not an outrider. You should never stray to the flanks, where enemies may still lay in wait."

With that, they split up. Brooke, astride Ralaus, fell into step with Gnor mounted atop Fram. Helmdak marched stoically behind.

Val spurred his Warang away from the main host. The wolf careened through the trees, swallowed by the thicket in three seconds.

38: Golan Hob
Sonart

Only after Auckland had gone did Sonart look down. By the weight of the purse his uncle had given him, he had enough coin to keep him in good stead for a fortnight. No small sacrifice, and considering he had money of his own, why had the elder dwarven bothered?

Perhaps the damnable fool deemed it restitution for what he refused to do—what he had allowed to be unleashed. Or perhaps Auckland had done it as an act of stolid faith.

The rain showed no sign of respite as Sonart staggered through the streets of Bulkforge, gripping his drenched tunic with both hands. The hollows left in the mud by his footfalls caved in as soon as he made them.

He would lodge in Bulkforge, if he didn't collapse or get struck down by lightning first. But even as the notion rooted, it vanished twice as quick. As a minion of the Darkest One, neither would be allowed to happen.

Sonart pressed on.

The wooden plaque swayed beneath the ironock finial beside the entrance. Emblazoned on its painted green surface the name read:

GOLAN HOB

Sonart wasn't surprised when he stepped inside the cosy establishment and found the proprietor waiting nearby, a warm and ready smile on his blocky, pockmarked face. Ruddy cheeks and a shock of white hair flanked his bulbous nose. A thatched beard hung from his chin in web-like strands. Stars, he looked older than the Cradle itself.

"Name's Bessel," the innkeep greeted. *Exactly as Xoral revealed.* "What can I do you for? Sorry, bad joke."

Sonart cleared his throat. "A room—if you have one to let—possibly long term."

Bessel's grin widened full-blown. He leaned on a wooden cane as he reached into an apron pocket and fished out a large bronze key. Without hesitation, he handed it to Sonart. "Fourth door on the left."

When Sonart blinked, Bessel lifted his walking stick and pointed it towards a staircase leading up to the pub's second landing.

"But we haven't discussed terms or price," Sonart protested.

"Stars align, heard the jingle of your purse when you strode in. So long as you're tidy, and not too rowdy when in your cups, that's good enough

307

terms for the Missus and me. And don't worry about the price. Pay what you can afford."

Disarmed, Sonart could not believe his good fortune. "Um, thank you, Bessel."

As the old dwarven led Sonart up the stairs, he bore himself with a more able carriage than first seemed possible. Perhaps the cane served merely for show when the innkeep first met a stranger. Twirling and spearing his cane here and there, Bessel deftly handled it more like a weapon.

Sonart instantly liked him—and the room he offered. Atop its rustic wooden floor, a quilt-covered bed splayed before a rug of rough shag. A small table and chair butted one wall; a wood stove and washbasin adorned the other. Set into a third dedicated alcove, was a small, curtained cubicle containing a privy. A large window above the bed overlooked the back alley behind the inn.

"You're my first tenant in more than a star-cycle," Bessel confessed. "Wres, my wife, insisted we keep the rooms clean and respectable."

"In that, she has earned my respect. And you, Bessel, have earned my trust." Sonart handed him Auckland's full purse. "Keep this and take what is owed for my room and board."

Bessel nodded. "I'll mark a ledger every drear. You can square up whenever you decide to leave." His voice trailed off into silence.

Sonart held his breath when the innkeep began inspecting him closer, wizened orbs drifting from his auburn crown to his waterlogged boots.

After an anxious moment, Bessel said, "Beg pardon, but I think you'll need some dry clothes. Set yours by the stove. I can lend you some of mine for this dimming."

Sonart released his detained air. "That sounds good."

"Right then. I'll go fetch them. Once you clean up and get settled, come downstairs for some supper."

"That sounds better," Sonart said, and meant every syllable. Only after Bessel left did he realize that the innkeep had not even asked him his name.

When Sonart had bathed and rested, his sodden clothes drying on the chair, placed near the wood stove, he donned the livery and shoes Bessel had loaned him and refastened Seolad's sword to his side. Then he locked the door and marched downstairs, taking a seat at a corner table by the hearth.

Through the haze of pipe smoke, he counted thirty or so patrons huddled in quiet conversation. Each with a plate of food, a large stein of beer, or a flagon of wine in front of him or her. A circle of four engaged in a quiet game of dice. And one solemn lass played a pleasant tune on a hollow-sounding wind instrument.

Sonart bent an ear to her song. It struck a chord with him: even in the face of such depravity with naught a glimmer of betterment, that one could find the strength to create something so beautiful. A wonder—perhaps, that was the key to survival, for them all.

The welcome smell of baked bread and spiced fare wafted in from the kitchen. It mingled with the musky scent of pipe tobacco, yeasty beer, and the heady fragrance of wine. All the smells and sounds put Sonart at ease, but not too much.

With only a hearth and a few table lanterns to light the tavern, it appeared dark enough for strangers to remain strangers. Which was well and good. Sonart turned his back to the crowd and faced the flames. A jumble of three logs burned and crackled softly.

The sound of rolling dice behind him put a thought in Sonart's head. His arrival here was a gamble. Would his dice roll on the side of good or the side of evil? If the dying (or dead) Xoral proved as right as he'd been about Bessel and his inn, then Sonart's arrival should illicit results.

The answer will find you.

Just then, a steaming bowl of Mulweed—vegetables covered in a creamy orange sauce layered with black pepper—landed gently on the table before him. Half a loaf of bread and a pint of beer joined the bowl.

He looked up at Bessel's happy face, wrinkles lax in the firelight. "Best in Bulkforge, or so the wife insists."

Sonart's mouth watered at the arboreal aroma of the dish. His smile joined Bessel's, before a woman's holler from the kitchen interrupted them. The innkeep limped away.

While he ate, Sonart's thoughts turned to the mysterious building he had seen in his vision. He would begin a search for it on the morrow.

He washed down the last of the bread with a long swig of the bitter ale before ordering another pint. Meanwhile, the Golan Hob's patrons trickled out in ones and twos until only a handful lingered. The dimming had lengthened, and most would be bound for the forges or the mines the following drear.

When Bessel brought him the drink, his eyes lingered, his cane gone, and two full glasses sat on his tray.

"Something on your mind, Bessel?" Sonart asked in a guarded tone.

The innkeep's attention shifted between Sonart and the drinks, his consternation plain. "About to ask you the same thing. Forgive the intrusion. May I sit with you awhile?"

Sonart wanted to say no, but after studying the man for a moment he gestured to the chair. "If it pleases."

Bessel set the tray in the middle of the table, sat down, and let out a long sigh. "By the stars, achin' feet and hinges rejoice." He took a long draught from his glass, wiped his lips with the back of his sleeve, and levelled his gaze at Sonart. "Before I say anything else, allay your fears. Long has the Hob been charmed. You're free of Deathwrought's probes and minions here—know that beyond a doubt."

Sonart started, but Bessel raised his hands in a calming gesture. "I know who and what you are, Sonart. Intimate with your line. Close to your kin, Farkshone and Auckland. And I know why you've come."

Sonart shifted in his chair. His eyes instinctively shot to the others in the room before fixing on the main entrance.

Bessel coughed. "I'll say it again: the Hob's charmed—and so are you—a Vein of Fire. Had I made such an admission, steps outside my establishment, you'd have wound up in a craze and made short work of me with the blade at your side."

To Sonart's shock, Bessel spoke true. No wave of evil overcame him. If anything, his weight lessened in this place, more so in its owner's company.

"Xoral—the alchlemage—secured your escape, paying for it with what sad existence he has left him," Bessel revealed. "He functioned as an intermediary—a messenger if you will, who spoke to you in the ancient tongue of the sprites, a language the Darkest One could never comprehend. You heard Xoral's message in the common tongue, correct?" When Sonart bobbed his beard, Bessel explained, "Only a Blood Scion, a Vein of Fire, or someone fluent in sprite lore would have understood."

Sonart swallowed. "His daughter, Iomi seemed to understand well enough."

Bessel allowed himself a brief chuckle. "She is his daughter. Blood of blood, traits and gifts of the ancients pass down the line—as they did with you—in your case, from the most primeval of our kind."

The elder dwarven took another drink and this time Sonart joined him. The bitter ale helped steady his nerves.

"So, the weirding of Xoral's words did more than confound Deathwrought," Bessel went on. "It cracked His hold on you, long enough to bring you in safely."

"Bring me in?" Sonart narrowed his eyes. "Into what?"

Bessel leaned forward. "The dwarven underground."

Sonart drew his head back.

The innkeep exhaled. "Sadly, if he hasn't already, when Xoral takes the deepest sleep, the magics he set to ward you will dissipate. But within the Hob, you'll evade detection and stay safe. Deathwrought, his Four, and their minions—will remain blind to you as they've ever been to me in here. The Hob serves as a haven, Sonart. You must've sensed it already."

"Aye," Sonart admitted. "I have."

Bessel cocked his head towards the entrance. "But outside that door—which you just considered escaping from—you're as vulnerable as me." He surrendered a brief half-smile. "Xoral's grasp of the wilderen magic was strong."

Sonart angled his eyebrows down. "Wilderen? I am unfamiliar with the term."

"An arcane word, loosely translated in the common tongue means *wildest.* And for good reason. It describes the most chaotic of all the seven disciplines of magic—at the top of magic's food chain if you will. Even besot with the Afflicted's curse, Xoral will not go to the deepest sleep lightly. He will continue to ward you with his dying breath. But make no mistake, it will come."

"Then, underground or not, I cannot linger here forever," Sonart pointed out. "Stick my head in the ground like one of the Cradle's trees and wait until the Void claims me. I've had visions that indirectly led me here. But what I truly seek, Bessel, is *not* here."

"Stars no," the innkeep quickly agreed. "I may be blind to exactly what you hunt. But tell me what you've gleaned so far and I will offer what I can to ensure you find it."

Sonart looked towards the fire as he framed a response. Unlike with Shayla, something in his soul urged him not to spin a yarn to this aged dwarven—that by doing so, he would only prolong his own ignorance and suffering. And that of every dwarven in the Cradle. Still, he resisted.

Bessel slanted closer and pressed, "Sonart, I am part of this underground movement—even led it for a time—a crusade instigated by Rusic and championed by your father. On the surface, nothing happens, but trust me that the underground plots and will hearken to you when the time ripens. Why do you think the Proclaimers formed? My associates and I need and covet the opposite—for you to succeed."

Sonart glowered, but something in the other's eyes quelled his anger and distrust.

He told the innkeep everything.

When Sonart had finished, Bessel only nodded. "That sounds like a place I might know, and it's not far from here. I can point you in the right direction but I must remain hither. As I said, this cover provides my only sanctuary from Deathwrought. I know of your 'decree,' and it would be wise for you to hide yourself whenever you leave the Hob. Proclaimers are afoot and they will seek to subvert you, especially now since their master has been blinded to your whereabouts. He will try to recapture you and punish any who aided and abetted you—as He did with Xoral."

Sonart gulped, feeling the bite of the recollection and the hard truth it bespoke. He sized up his companion with new eyes. "What do you suggest?"

"Protect yourself—and if you can, defend my wife and me. But above all else, shield the movement. Seems a good omen that we should meet here in safety." Bessel reached across the table and gave Sonart's arm a firm squeeze. "Consider me an ally."

Sonart took another sip of beer, squared his shoulders, and matched the elder's stance. "So, you knew my father."

"Knew him?" Bessel harrumphed and stared at Sonart as if he'd grown another arm. "How could I forget him? Farkshone—a hero of the people and the noblest dwarven I ever met. Do you not recall the Neglect?"

Sonart mouthed the word in silence and frowned.

Bessel looked up at the rafters as he pondered. "No, you wouldn't have—you'd have been a babe then. Twas Farkshone who delivered us, stars guide him. That time claimed many souls, finishing half this street alone."

Bessel shook his head in slow marvel. "When his anger outweighed any fear, your father stood against Zürshuck. Imagine the audacity—a dwarven rising up against Winged Ones—and besting them."

"What?" Sonart let down his mug with a thud. "I've never heard tell of this before."

Bessel flicked his chin up and down, making his beard strands jig. He flashed Sonart a knowing smile. "Farkshone rallied three dozen dwarven, right here at the Hob, he did. Ingenious, I tell you, stealing away in the shadows of a dimming with his small company, right under the demons' very snouts. The fiends had the Kworn stockpile our livestock and hogsweed grain way out on the plateau before poisoning the soil."

Bessel paused and took a long haul of beer. The glass shimmered while firelight danced against the senior's face. He put the vessel down and sucked some air. "Your sire's band advanced covertly on the Zürshuck. Moving as wraiths, they fell upon the winged guards, dispatched the whole unsuspecting lot, and burglared back *all* the neglected stores."

"In a single dimming?" Sonart asked, unable to hide his incredulity.

Bessel inclined his head. "They attached food sacks to the backs of the stolen livestock—while such creatures still roamed the land—and had them carry everything from hogsweed seed to wild medicinal plants, to cure the soil's taint and such. Then, they drove the massive herd for leagues straight into our hungry hands. A larger company stood ready to distribute everything to the people across the breadth of the Steppe."

Drawn in by the tale, Sonart shifted closer and whispered. "What did Deathwrought do?"

"We feared retaliation and maleficence—aye, but the Darkest One sought penance from the Kworn and Zürshuck responsible instead. With us dwarven, He stayed His hand—could not fathom the reasons, nor did I care. By the stars, my full belly remained un-gutted."

Bessel stared off into the mid-distance before returning his attention to Sonart. "But I am sure Deathwrought had His reasons. For a while at least, the hard times ended." His voice petered into silence.

Sonart downed the rest of his ale and stirred at the first flicker of purpose and friendship with Bessel. More of Xoral's words came back to him in that instant: *Let the fire of ale light your path the rest of the way.*

Hearing the warming story of a father he never really knew put Sonart even more at ease. He settled back into the comfortable chair and suddenly felt better about everything. "Bessel, you embroider a tale with threads unknown to me, but I'll not deny the comfort I find wrapped in its folds."

Bessel gave him an appraising look. "From what I can see with my unwise peepers, the darkest times will soon reconvene. The weight will return. But knowing that the son of our saviour walks among us once again: the dwarven emissary of the ancient line—stars, truly makes me feel young—a proud warrior again."

Sonart straightened. "Bessel, as a former leader, you must retain some pull with this underground of yours."

"I did. Nowadays, nobody would listen to an old fool like me." The innkeep pointed to his cane propped up against the bar. "Least, that's what the wife keeps assuring me," he added with a smirk.

Sonart's grin matched it briefly before uncurling. "Regardless, even from them, I trust you to keep my business here quiet."

"A given. The less who know, the better." Bessel lifted his shoulders. "Still, you needn't worry on that score. Soon, you shall meet your true redeemer—an outlier of kindred might."

Sonart frowned.

"Fret not," said Bessel, "We're on the same side. For now, under Bessel's roof, you'll find no unfriendly ears. As I said, my place is blessed— a haven in hell."

The oldster took another long pull of his beer. The fire popped loudly. "Though they still might, in all my drears as proprietor of the Hob, I'd not seen a single Proclaimer enter her doors. Don't ask me how or why but there are other forces at work besides the will of the Darkest One."

Sonart gently gripped the elder dwarven's arm. "You have lifted the weight—substantially." *Haven and help: how could the dying geezer have known?*

"Stars align between us, Sonart. I may be old, and certainly odd, but I sense great purpose in you, perhaps greater than you know yourself."

This heartened Sonart so much that for the rest of the dimming he all but forgot his burdens.

39: Orbical
Brooke

The day drew to a close as the Nightwolves and ogres reached the clearing that marked the outskirts of Riverside. As they emerged from the treeline, an amber sun cast a warm glow on their faces. The full company formed up, awaiting the commander, who rode alongside Gnor and Helmdak. The beastman's towering contingent drew in behind.

With both hosts assembled, Helmdak dropped to one knee. He met Brooke face to face, even as the commander sat astride Ralaus.

The ogre spoke in a quiet voice that sounded like distant surf, "We must part here, Stunted Tree."

"Will you not accompany us into the village proper?" Brooke asked. "Gnor tells me Riverside is a haven for our band. They would be more open to having you rest here the night, provided the Nightwolves went ahead to vouch for you."

A half-smile traced the ogre's cracked lips. "I would be more than honoured to extend the time of our liaison. Alas, I cannot. The fewer eyes that fall upon the ogres, the better. Ere the Starbond, my brethren's purpose marries to that of the Colossals and their lavatrol legions."

"My kind of wedding," Spifer chuckled from somewhere within the ranks.

"Wherever they should rise, we must intercept them to mitigate their scourge," Helmdak went on, his ebony orbs never leaving Brooke. "So, we return at once to rejoin our brethren. United, we present a force to be reckoned with, treading a course akin to your pathless path—until our true purpose is revealed."

Brooke nodded in silence. Ralaus whimpered and wagged his tail.

"Though I dismissed it out of hand when first our hosts met," said Helmdak, "my heart tells me that our meeting was no coincidence. That our stars orbit and somehow entwine. In earnest, Stunted Tree, I would bestow one further title upon you—and with it a pact—if you will have it."

"Stars align," Brooke answered. "By all means."

"Then, I name you, True Heart," Helmdak proclaimed. "And vow that should trouble find you—the likes of which you cannot contain, say my name. And if the sprites deem it dire enough to outweigh the charge they've already given us, this amulet will toll against my chest."

Helmdak paused and looked down at his ruby pendant. He drew it forward with thick fingers and presented it to Brooke. "Place your hand on the stone."

Brooke did. Its heat instantly permeated the flesh of his fingers and into his bones.

"I will hear your voice through my amulet," Helmdak explained. The scarlet light of the magnificent gem danced like fire in the chieftain's pupils. "Forthwith, you and I share a bond and a brotherhood. At *any* turn of the dial, my tribe will hasten to your plight, for as I said, ogres do not sleep. But only if the sprites in their infinite wisdom deem it your most dire need."

"I can only hope I never find myself in such straits," Brooke replied as he removed his hand from the ruby crystal. "But I accept your pledge and allegiance, and sincerely thank you for both, Brother." His eyes dropped again to the ogre's amulet. "Your stone is a great gift for a worthy keeper—with as many purposes as it has facets."

"Many purposes," Helmdak agreed, a strange timbre entering his gruff voice.

In the awkward silence, leaves rustled in the trees immediately behind the chieftain. Helmdak recovered a moment later, face brightening. "We are well met, True Heart, Stunted Tree. Pity we did not encounter each other in happier, less-hurried times. If by chance our quests align again, it will be a glad occasion of fellowship and jubilation. If we should not meet again, know that in sooth, you have earned my gratitude for the same clemency the sprites showed my ancestors. It is something I have never known before. I will always consider you an ally. And a friend."

The weight of Helmdak's words burdened Brooke. He reached up and clasped the ogre's giant arm above the elbow. "And I, you, Giant Tree," he said. "For we share the honour of this second name you've bestowed upon me."

Helmdak stood, gave Brooke a deep bow, and the two armies parted ways.

The Nightwolves moved in double-file towards Riverside while the ogres turned their backs to it, marching into the shadows under the forest canopy, the way they had come.

Brooke marvelled at how quickly he'd grown to empathize with the ancient ogres' cause. He also gave thought to Helmdak's parting words as Alghan and Gnor's Warangs fell into step with Ralaus. Three abreast, they led the Nightwolves into the heart of Riverside.

The village looked strikingly different from the previous one. Its houses, hewn of ancient wood and stone, stood back from the main artery, but visible to all passers-by. Hanging plants with blue and gold flowers adorned their facades. Shrubbery and gardens lined the cobblestone footpaths that led up to the buildings.

Separate stables occupied parcels of land in each steading where livestock grazed. Even in the warrens between, small wild animals and birds moved casually without fear. A swift river ran through the middle of the village, traversed by a wide bridge of carefully laid stone and oak.

Balustrades lined the construct to each side while stone columns supported the bulwark in three stages across the narrows. The smell of birch and baked apples wafted past.

Over the bridge, the Nightwolf procession made its way to the main square on the opposite bank. Here, locals milled about market stalls, filled with a colourful bounty of produce, sacks of grain and animal feed, wares, clothing items, and sundries. A prevalent air of laughter permeated throughout the press as people engaged in commerce, ran errands, or shepherded small flocks of goats and sheep.

When Brooke and his band filtered past, the villagers stopped their work—but only to wave or exchange friendly greetings. Their mirth never ebbed. Strikingly different indeed.

The locals' openness disarmed Brooke—he wanted to keep his eyes downcast but found himself floating an arm and smiling at their endless hails. Had this been a village in Pathguard's prefecture, every Nightwolf would be escorted to the gallows, a welcoming noose fitted snugly around his or her neck.

On the far side of the central square, the road curved to the right. Past the last edifice, they came to a pair of open parks on either side of the path. Rows of large willow trees filled the two tracts, interspersed with gardens containing long-stemmed violet and orange flowers.

Gnor took point and led the van into the park on the left. The Wrayns dismounted their wolves and gathered in groups along a small canal, three hundred feet in from where the park met the road. A skein of more willows swayed lazily in the fresh breeze and offered a shady respite.

Set to one side of the channel, a wooden watermill perched, its thirty-foot-high wheel turning slowly. More than in harmony with nature, the peaceful settlement seemed an extension of it.

"Make camp," Gnor called out before facing Brooke. "We'll have sanctuary here in Riverside, Commander. The pups will visit the market and buy what supplies we need with gold from Serenthia's coffers. Let the Wolves settle themselves—we'll join them later. For now, there's someone I want you to meet."

Brooke dismounted Ralaus and scratched a tuft of fur behind the Warang's ear. He bent close to the giant wolf and whispered, "My thanks again for the lift—and your earlier intervention."

Ralaus licked the front of Brooke's hand, which made the commander smile as the canine's hot breath misted over his palm. He gave the wolf one last pat on the flank before straightening.

Then he turned and joined Gnor, patiently awaiting him. The stout Wrayn led him back to the road and past the main square. Brooke counted two crossroads before Gnor turned down a third.

"Where are we going, Gnor?" asked Brooke.

The bulldog-faced man grinned. "To the pub."

Brooke's stare made Gnor laugh out loud. "Don't worry. We're not going there to lose our wits—quite the opposite in fact."

The pub resembled a stable, but one dolled up in a mix of deep and bright-green filigree. Garland adorned the windows, doors, and the lattice that traced the entire frame: rough and charming at the same time.

Set back against the edge of the Northern Forest, the tavern stood at the bottom of a lazy dip and bend in the narrow road. Past the tavern, the lane sloped up another rise.

The corners of Brooke's mouth curved high when he and Gnor drew up to the pub's carved wooden sign. Suspended from a black metal finial by a pair of thin chains, the rod and sign extended out over the laneway from the tavern's front façade.

In gilded letters, the plaque read:

KING'S THRONE

Beneath the ornate title routed into its lacquered surface, a painted caricature of a king sat atop a jewel-studded privy, a lopsided crown on his head and his britches down to his ankles. One hand clutched a pile of leaves.

"Any resemblance to Cele?" Gnor asked with a snicker.

Brooke guffawed at the remark. "If this indeed depicts my former Liege, Cele's Haft would replace the shrubberies. Though, like as not, King and Haft's roles would be reversed."

"Stars align," Gnor said, his smiling eyes fixed on the sign.

Frequent patrons entered and exited the pub's doors, true testament to the Throne's popularity. Not that it needed it: the music and laughter spilling out into the laneway stated it well enough. It sounded like a raucous party inside.

Gnor lowered his gaze to Brooke. "Shall we?"

They followed a middle-aged couple into the pub.

Warm smoky air filled the interior, carrying the scent of old wood, tobacco, roasted meats, and stale beer. The main room had a high-vaulted ceiling supported by beams of wood. Traditional farming implements such as hoes, saws, axes, and pitchforks decorated the walls and rafters. Scarecrows clad in farmers and loggers' raiment hung on display between faded tapestries and banners.

A stack of kegs rose in a triangular pile to one side of the room and tables topped with beer glasses lay scattered in disarray.

Clutching pipes and mugs of ale, common folk crowded the enclosure. They sat on benches or the tables themselves. Many stood in circles of three and four. The tavern bustled and buzzed with loud convivial excitement.

A cheer went up as a fat old man and a larger old woman sat themselves on stools in the middle of the congregation.

Brooke paused as they began playing a merry jig on a pair of string instruments, keeping time with the jovial crowd's handclaps and foot stomps. Through the press, a few sots danced arm in arm.

Facing one another, the musicians sang in mock scorn, each taking a verse.

> *Seasons come and seasons go*
> *Though m' wife may tell me so.*
> *Sh' works too hard with seeds to sow*
> *I'll grow m'crops to feed me cow.*
> *Plump my Hen but fair as sprites*
> *I never want to let her go*

> *Tra la la la la lalaaaaaaah*
> *Hoo! Hoo!*

> *Seasons go and seasons come*
> *Though m' husband meets my sum*
> *Yanks the weeds, green pastures fair*
> *So m' table's never bare*
> *He works too little lest prompted so*
> *Hadn't the heart to let him go*

> *Tra la la la la lalaaaaaaah*
> *Hoo! Hoo!*

"*Hoo! Hoo!*" the throng chorused back before the old man took the next verse. Patrons revelled, cheered, and clinked glasses so hard that beer and mead sloshed, sputtered in plumes, and fell like rain. The rollicking banter at the old couple's spirited music offered its own harmony.

The scene warmed Brooke's soul, seeing such earnest and enduring love proudly expressed between husband and wife. Bittersweet thoughts drifted longingly to Dayanthi.

A tap on his shoulder brought Brooke back to Gnor's apologetic smile. With a tilt of his head, the Nightwolf led him past the long bar, where every stool was taken by an applauding or foot-thumping customer.

Inset the tavern's back wall, a series of booths awaited. Each housed a heavy wooden table and a pair of benches. In the corner of the furthest booth, a cloaked and hooded figure sat, his face hidden in the shadow of his cowl, save a white beard. It appeared carroty in the combined light of a beeswax lantern, stuck in a sconce above the enclosure, and a lone candle planted in the centre of the table.

Although Brooke could not see the mysterious figure's eyes, he felt their scrutiny from across the room.

"That's him," Gnor confirmed as he strode up to the stall.

A frail hand emerged from the folds of the old man's earthen-grey robe. Clutched in it, the barrel of a wooden pipe. He used it to point to the bench opposite him.

Gnor slid across the seat to make room for Brooke. "Did you lose your tongue, Brapin?" he asked in a bewildered tone. "Or do you insist on communion to befuddle my companion—as it always does our chief?"

A puff of smoke, a quick cough, and quicker cackle answered the Nightwolf. "Neither." With his free hand, Brapin pulled back his cowl. "I preferred to study this misplaced—and all-too-well placed—steward of yours in peace."

Gnor threw a glance over his shoulder at the obese musicians. "Think you've come to the wrong place for that."

More laughter. "The peace in an Orbical's mind, Master Gnor, can only be distracted by the sounds of his own thoughts." His smile dimmed as his studious orbs settled on Brooke. "The talking ogre named him, True Heart. I wished to see if he deserved the accolade."

When Brooke flinched, Brapin hooted and extended a bony finger.

Gnor waved him off with a chortle. "Don't let him caper you along, Commander. Brapin may be an Orbical, but he's equally apt a listener—in a place where many voices can be overheard."

Gnor swivelled to Brooke. With a good-natured snort, he hiked his thumb in Brapin's direction. "A pair of jackrabbit ears, this one has—to flank his sharp tongue and sharper wit, so pointed it sometimes stings. Targin would attest to that in a heartbeat. Isn't that right, old man?"

"Oh, do relent, Nightwolf." Brapin put the briar to his lips and drew in more smoke. "I hear many things, but tis the source, not the echo that reached my rabbit ears. And my tongue verses in many languages, for many reasons."

"And vexes in all of them," Gnor sniggered.

Brapin shrugged. "I've had to hone its sharpness to great fluency, to drive my points home—and points, are something the commander has had some experience with of late."

Brooke swallowed. He wanted to say something, but genuine curiosity of Targin's mentor compelled him to remain silent.

The odd seer blew out the smoke he held in his mouth. "Tell me, Gnor, how fares your blood? The pup continues to sprout, in body, stature, and wits. He is destined for greatness."

"Stars align, ever the eager weed, the lad," Gnor vaunted, his eyes bright. "Gnolin is my son's boy, a match in every sense when Gnail was of that age. Soon, the pup will hunt as a full-fledged Wrayn."

"And find, no doubt." Brapin gave Gnor a sad smile. "Gnolin's a joy to tired hearts, yours and mine. I wish to hear more of him in time." His gaze shifted back to Brooke. "For now, to this one I grant an audience, and a mirror. Much to discuss."

Without taking his eyes off the commander, the Orbical said, "Gnor, do be so kind and bring us some grog—to loosen the knot in Brooke's tongue and blunt the sharpness of mine. We'll all need our thirst slaked ere long."

"To the Purpose, Storm Cloud," Gnor quipped. "I promised the Commander that his wits would not be addled by drink. But a pint or two will do him no harm either." Brooke slid out of the booth and stood to let Gnor exit. As the stout man abandoned the table and strode away, Brooke reseated himself.

Brapin watched Gnor join the back of a short cue by the bar. Then turning to Brooke, the eccentric man set his cob down beside the candle and leaned forward. "Show me your hands, young ranger. Don't be afraid. I shan't sting you—much," he added with a smirk.

Brooke frowned, but after some hesitation, he held out his hands, palms open.

The Orbical took the commander's hands and brought them within inches of his face. He pored over each in turn with the meticulous care of a surgeon checking a mysterious abscess. "You've come here by a long, arduous route, Aviry Brooke—Stunted Tree. I'm afraid it shall pale beside the one that lies ahead."

A shiver coursed down the centre of Brooke's spine.

"That said," Brapin went on as he released the commander's hands, "I assure you that your chosen course of action will prove your best course of action. As to your role along that path, only you will decide how far it will take you, beyond the Merger."

Despite the cheery atmosphere of the pub, Brapin's cryptic divination made it dim.

"But Gnor did not ask you to see me for this," Brapin said a moment later. "Orbical or not, I would only vex you further to say more than I already have at this juncture. Trust that it's too soon for you to hear more. Val's timeliness also proved amiss in seeking my counsel—but let's not dwell on your other challenge either."

Brooke coughed. "Val has come to see you?"

"Aye, earlier today," Brapin confessed. "But our discussion has no place in your ears. Know only that we had one."

"I understand, but there may be greater repercussions if left to fester unaddressed." Brooke rubbed the back of his neck. "Brapin, is there nothing I can do to bridge my widening gulf with him?"

"Bridges may be built in more than one way, Commander. The key is learning what materials to use for your construct, which gulf to cross, and most importantly *when* you must cross."

Brooke gave the Orbical a thin chuckle. "Gnor spoke truly of your riddles, but that's one conundrum I vow to unravel. It means a great deal to me."

"You'll succeed where others have failed, True Heart," Brapin added with a wink. "Yet, there is much and more for you to learn, apart from the stunts of a Stunted Tree. Have faith in the reason why Targin and the sprites chose you and not Val to lead his band into the Night."

Brooke narrowed his eyes. "Gnor said you chose me as well. What prompted your reason?"

"I have several prompts. And several reasons."

Brooke tried to keep his voice under control. His throat suddenly went dry. "Then for pity's sake, tell me."

"I know the reasons," the Orbical repeated as he picked up his briar again and lit it. "But it is precisely because of pity that I'll not reveal them to you. They may jade your conclusions—and your course of action. The Kusp is replete with aberrations. I will not conjure another. Think of it as another bridge to be crossed—one you can only realize when you draw near to the ford."

Defeat pressed Brooke's chest as he leaned against the seat's backrest.

The Orbical let out a puff of smoke which made the candle flicker. The small tobacco cloud carried a scent of bergamot and cedar. "Have faith. In the Nightwolves' purpose and your own. You need only to stay the course."

Brooke's conflicted thoughts waged a silent war in his mind, but slowly, by focusing on the pleasant smell of the old man's tobacco, he impelled them to retrench and lay down arms. "As you say."

Brapin's wrinkles softened. "Let us talk of Val now. I will not reveal exactly what I said to him, but I can say this. Pathless though your roads may be, his lies upon a separate course than yours. Val represents a piece destined for a different role in the endgame."

"Endgame? You mean the Starbond," Brooke guessed.

The Orbical's forehead tilted forward. "Make no mistake, the Starbond is a board of ending—a tableau upon which we must now all cast dice and move pieces. Val cast his lot, same as you, and Targin, and me. Val's purpose, for good or ill, will reveal itself. Where he must go and what he must do leads not where the Nightwolves may follow, not yet."

A small black kitten darted from under the adjacent table, drawing Brooke's attention. It paused and looked up at him with green eyes. Until a slightly larger tabby veered into the corridor and chased it away. Both felions disappeared.

"But I can tell you this," said Brapin as Brooke attended him again, "he will have his part to play. Watch him. Watch your back. The world fills to the tipping point with corruption. And it seeps into the most trusting circles. The Wolves are strong but by no means infallible. And Deathwrought's digits have grown long. Ever they reach and probe like that of a spider, casting webs of entrapment in the gathering gloom."

Brooke swallowed. "What should I do?"

Brapin arched an eyebrow. "Why, follow your heart of course— Helmdak named you True Heart after all. It has been the compass that steered you clear of harm's way before. It served you well enough on your liberation from the malignancy that engulfs Pathguard. It will continue to point true— if you heed its needle."

"In sooth," Brooke lamented. "I would it point me elsewhere."

The old man smiled. "Fear not for them, Commander, just stay your purpose and the compass needle will eventually take you there as well."

Brooke might've shed a tear, if not so disarmed by the Orbical's perceptiveness. "Riddles or not, where my family is concerned, your words are thick, a poultice to the wound in my heart."

"Your wound only shows your love for them is real—and love *is* the needle that will point you there."

The creases in the seer's temple diminished and he fell reticent as he observed Brooke, cushioned in understanding and catharsis.

A clink of glasses jerked Brooke out of his sentiment. Gnor returned, three mugs balanced in his axe-hewn hands.

"At last," Brapin announced in a breezy voice. "So long as we arrive in one piece, the mode of our journey matters not. We'll talk more ere I see you off, Commander."

Gnor placed the mugs on the table and took a seat.

While the Nightwolves blew the froth off their brews, Brapin placed his cob between his lips. His cheeks formed small bellows as he inhaled and exhaled smoke in slow puffs.

Wavering vapour accompanied the Orbical's next words. "As you know, Targin passed through here a few days ago. His message to you was simple— make all haste to the Strong Helm."

"We will away on the morrow," Brooke acknowledged as he raised his cup.

"Good and well," the Orbical agreed, pipe smoke jittering in the air as he nodded. "What route will you take from Riverside?"

Brooke looked to Gnor for answer as he tipped back the beer. The bulldog-faced man lifted his shoulders. "I intended the pack to follow the river as far as the Plunge. From there we'll scale the Ridge and follow the Southern Arm until we pass the old caravan roads cutting through the lowland forest. After that, it's not far across the plains to our journey's end."

"I see," Brapin pondered as he stroked his beard and studied the Wrayn. "Might I propose an alternate route?"

Gnor raised an eyebrow. "Pray tell?"

"Ply the Northern Arm towards the Spires' Crest instead. Take your company into the Highlands, in the direction of Sentinel's Retreat."

Gnor tightened his grip on his mug. "If we are to make all haste, the Northern Arm of the Ridge would take us too far afield, with little in the way of food or cover. It would add considerable time—more than a week to reach the Hidden Kingdom. We'd miss Targin before he embarks."

"True," Brapin conceded. "It would add time and distance to your journey, but better to arrive late and alive than dead on time."

Gnor's mug had since found its way to his lips. Over its rim, his eyes became slits as he levelled them at Brapin, their doubt plain.

"My rabbit ears do hear, as you pointed out," Brapin went on. "Some distance where dangers may loom—snares of which the forest creatures may be unaware—or prevented from communing to the pack."

Gnor's mug dropped with a dull thud. "So?"

"So, if you value their safeguard heed what an Orbical's pointed lobes relay to his sharp tongue," Brapin replied a little testily. "The Southern Arm's beset by more than just goblins and trolls. Dark elven have been sighted, setting their will and other beastly things upon any who trespass, including Wolves. Forest hordes threaten those tracts, and these parts—evidently right to Riverside's doorstep."

Brapin pulled the briar out of his mouth and prodded it up over his shoulder like a schoolmaster with his chalk. "Tramping that southern route would add substantially more than a week to your intended journey if you're forced to spring ambush after ambush."

Fresh lines of dismay creased Gnor's face. He shook his head slowly, his hesitation and ire plain. "How secure are your sources, Old Crow? Even rabbit ears may hear false."

Brapin scowled. "Secure, their import sooth—ask your chief when next you see him." He shoved the cob back in his mouth and tapped his index finger on the table, making the candle flicker. "Right here—immediately outside the enchanted wards that guard this centre. Such a host beset Targin before he escaped. Though they consume their own dead, the following morn, I detected evidence of their full number. It was vast. As was their strength, indicated by the magical residue of dark elven enchantments. Not to mention the burned tract he left in his wake. Your chief's melee on the ground must've been savage. He and his hawkrike got away—but part of the horde followed."

Gnor bolted upright, jarring the table. Beer spilled from the three mugs and the candle's flame guttered. "We must leave at once."

Brapin raised a hand to quell the Nightwolf's fire. "Peace, Gnor. And faith."

Still startled, Brooke sought the Orbical's attention. "What of Targin? Tell us everything."

The seer gave a few details of his meeting with the Nightwolf chief. "At parting, he bade me ward the village and raise the alarm if something threatened. I spent the rest of the night on vigil. Nothing untoward happened. As Gnor can attest, Riverside remains a protected refuge, since the ancient days. In fact, they worked to douse the encroaching flames before they could spread to cause any harm to the surrounding forest. Even so, the dark elven lurk closer all the time, testing the town's boundaries in the witching hours."

Brapin reached for his cup, took a long pull and wiped the bulbs of foam from his beard with the cuff of his sleeve. "As I said, come dawn, I descried the proof: amidst the large swathes of blackened grass, ran troll and goblin tracks. Felled trees, ripped underbrush, and ghost traces of dark magic scorching the ground, there were also. Our comedian Vein faced a sore and unruly audience that night."

Brooke blinked. "Do you think he survived the flight?"

"Depends on your definition of survival—physically, for a certainty. As a Vein, he's destined to attain the Merger. But where the body forges rock, the mind remains fluid, a vast ocean susceptible to storms of evil metamorphisms."

Gnor scrunched up his face, angling his scowl towards Brooke. Seemed the commander wasn't the only one completely perplexed.

"I believe Targin survived even this," Brapin concluded, drawing their focus again. "Reckless, incorrigible, but also one tough son of a witch."

The old man locked gazes with Brooke. "And he's no fool—Targin anticipated the attack even before he left my side. He would've taken steps to avoid the worst snares. Aye, your chief has reached Serenthia in one piece."

Gnor eased back into his seat, eyes dropping to his beer. "If an Orbical says it so, Commander, then it must be."

Brapin acknowledged him with a curt nod. "Then if your faith in my counsel has been restored, heed an Orbical's advice. Take the Northern Arm."

"We understand." Brooke raised his mug.

Brapin's face darkened. "Not yet."

The cup of beer stalled and quivered halfway to Brooke's lips.

"You, must go to Serenthia," Brapin maintained, his tone strident.

Brooke's frown began to hurt his face. He looked to Gnor who gave both companions a blank stare. The commander took a breath before shifting his full regard to the Orbical. "That is our intent."

"No, you do not understand yet. Upon Targin's Merger, you too will be tested. You may not be a Blood Scion but your stature rises in importance—cynosure towards the same juncture. If a choice falls at your feet, *you*, Aviry Brooke, must elect to go to the Strong Helm. Take as many Nightwolves as suits your purpose, but it must be you who leads them and no other."

"Stars, Brapin, no need for such obscure counsel. I assure you, that is precisely what Targin charged me to do. On my life, I vow to take that course."

The old man narrowed his eyes as if weighing Brooke's resolve. After several moments he relented. "Good." With his pipe, he poked the air in front of the commander. "But if anyone—be he Wolf, wizard, king, Vein, or Vamsah himself, tries to dissuade you from this purpose, you must stand your ground—adroit, adamant, firm as gutrock."

Brapin slipped the cob back into his mouth and scratched his cheek absently. "While on the topic of charges, following your venture to Serenthia, if you should find yourself in the shadow of Sentinel's Retreat—the same edifice described to you in your recent visions—guard it with your life. Tis the crux of all that we seek to achieve." He shot the commander a look from the corner of his eye. "Tell me, have you had any more visions of late?"

Breath left the commander and his palms went clammy. Gnor stole a glance at him and pulled his chest back from the table, biting his lower lip.

A quick hacking sound from the Orbical broke the awkward moment. "When that time comes, and it will, remember..." His voice trailed off like a departing wraith, its verdict lingering in the air, suddenly gone cold.

Gnor shifted in his seat and cleared his throat. "Will you accompany us on our journey?"

"Nay," Brapin said with more familiar rue. "I must needs attend many other matters. There's always something that requires looking after—story of my life, that is," he laughed.

By the wry dance of his orbs, the seer reflected on some humorous irony, of which he alone was privy.

Gnor sighed with a touch of finality and relief. "Then, let's finish our ales and tales. We need to hold audience with the Wolves—and settle the inevitable deliberations over this change of plans."

Brapin pulled the cuffs of each sleeve and offered the stout Wrayn a knowing grin. "Words unto—debate."

40: Crossroads
Brooke

Under a darkening sky, Brooke sat atop a tree stump twenty feet from the main campfire and explained the dilemma to the gathered Nightwolves. Some of the Wrayns settled on logs while the rest stood, forming a wide circle around the commander.

When Brooke finished, he took in their reactions. Most shook their heads and opted to continue as planned, citing Targin's choice.

The commander's scrutiny tallied up and down the line of faces searching for Alghan but could not spot the tall Nightwolf. "Where's Alghan?"

A burly Wrayn named Sejan spoke up. "Our scholar sensed the dark elven's taint, Commander. Took his Warang to scout the immediate lay. He left message that he'd return fore the night's done."

Brooke nodded, taking in the news with quiet poise. "We might as well finish our discussion now. Alghan can weigh in when he returns. I'll consider his advice if he can offer me something new. What say you? Anyone?"

Several murmurs of debate ensued, but it seemed no one wanted to discuss it in open forum. As the fire wheezed and cracked, Brooke considered the matter closed and made to retire, when much to his surprise Val stepped forward.

"Heed the Orbical's words," the Nightwolf declared. "Brapin alone was aware of whatever calamity transpired here. He has counselled Targin several times before—changed the chief's mind—and in so doing, helped us avoid snares, capture, and death." With a gloved hand, Val gripped the vambrace of his opposite arm, looked around, and locked gazes with Brooke. "Besides that, when he first directed us there, Targin knew nothing of this potential danger along the southern reaches beyond the Ridge."

A hulking tower of a man brushed past Brooke, strode up to Val, and spat on the ground before him. "Of course, the loner rushes headlong to agree with the Storm Cloud."

The mountainous back turned. As the firelight caught the newcomer's terse features, Brooke recognized the speaker. Lonus, the Wrayn who nearly fell in their struggles with the lavatrols—the true blood Gnolin had warned him about.

Brooke shifted his weight six inches across the stump beneath him. An uncomfortable knoll had dinted his ham.

Val's rebuttal proved no less trenchant. "Maybe, the trolls have scourged your resolve, Lonus, rendered your wits to ash with it. Least I know sound counsel when I hear it."

"Ballsuva-fucked-up-hellspawn, I name you," a tempestuous Lonus cursed. "Perhaps, you'll hearken to the counsel of my fist, as it cracks your turncape face. Forsooth, it'll be the last sound you hear before I whisk you to the deepest sleep."

"Cross stars with me and we'll cross swords," Val gave back. He gripped the hilt of his blade for emphasis. Lonus mirrored the gesture with his own weapon.

Brooke shot to his feet. "Enough." He spoke quietly, but his tone basted in fire. "Val's no traitor. Remember the Purpose—that includes refraining from insults, labels, and threats."

"I only label those who merit such," Lonus returned acerbically. "A senile old crow and his rotten egg—a defector adept." The tower stabbed his finger inches from Val's glare. "And my threat still stands."

Val knocked Lonus' hand away. "Want to put that to the test, knave, here and now? A trial of combat?"

"I said enough!" Brooke rushed in between the two combatants and brusquely pushed them back from one another. "I'll not suffer such dissension, do you hear?" The air tightened around the three men in terse silence. Only the crackling fire counted the anxious seconds.

Stars align, Lonus retreated a step. But he still glowered at Val, grumbling some litany in his Noirlunen tongue under his breath.

Brooke couldn't make sense of what he said.

But Val clearly did. He balled his fists, spun on his heels, and stormed out of the inner circle's firelight.

Unable to mask his anger or his disappointment, Brooke could only shake his head as he watched Val go. Though Brapin stood not a stone's throw away, he faced away from the scene, whispering into Gnor's ear. The bald Wrayn did look towards the fire, dipping his chin slowly to whatever the Orbical was telling him.

Heart thudding in his chest, Brooke strode to reprimand them but as he drew near, Gnor cleared his throat. Brapin's whispers petered to silence. He turned and met the commander's eyes. Brooke read neither apology nor awareness in the old one's innocent expression.

Damn it all, he could've used their support in quelling the heated debate. It bloody near sparked a fistfight, or worse—over a decision these two helped forge! But even as his chest tightened and his lips quivered, realization dawned to quell his irritation. *I need no sanction.*

Brooke skidded to a halt, wheeled about, and directed his voice at the Wrayns. "Targin put me in charge to make such decisions on his behalf. While I'd follow his course unwaveringly, your chief heeds Brapin's guidance ahead of his own. Fretted with riddles or not, in light of his troubling news, I must weigh alternatives—and if need be, twist the path—even a pathless one."

The commander paused and looked over his shoulder at Brapin. He wasn't entirely sure but he thought a ghost of a smile played at the corners of the Orbical's mouth. Gnor looked ghostly, his face impassive and devoid of mien.

Brooke curved towards the pack again and squared his jaw. "If a trap awaits us on the Southern Arm, why spring it, when a way around exists? Avoid it altogether. I elect to heed Brapin's direction."

No rebuttal did any Wrayn voice, not so much as a whimper from the Warangs either. Brooke straightened the bottom of his tunic and meshed his fingers together. "Much can still happen before we reach the Plunge, which marks the point where the two arms diverge. You have until then to dissuade me. Agreed?"

A chorus of, "Aye, stars align, agreed," and "to the Purpose," filled the copse, seconded by a few Warang yelps and yammers.

Gnor stepped lightly beside Brooke. "Well said, Commander. Seems settled."

With a brisk nod in Gnor's direction, Brooke muttered, "For now."

Brooke's thoughts kept him awake for some time, but he eventually fell into a tranquil, dreamless sleep for a change. And come next morning, he awoke pleasantly surprised to find he'd risen first of all the Wrayns. He emerged from his tent to find the pups, busy lighting the morning cookfires.

He quickly spotted Weet, Gnolin's quiet friend, crouched beside the closest pyre.

The boy struck a flint, making orange sparks dance in the pale light. Soon he had ignited the skeletal cone, comprised of kindling and strips of bark. He looked up, trembled, and gave the commander an uncertain bow. Thank the stars, some progress.

As the camp stirred, Weet moved off.

Brooke donned his outer vestments and boots, strapped on his sword belt, and walked over to the fire the boy had made. Already an intense blaze, the fire helped the commander work out the damp and stiffness from his arms and legs.

Two tents down, Gnolin appeared carrying a kettle. The pup beamed as he drew up. "Kofei will be ready soon, Commander."

"That is good," Brooke said. "But my head needs a jolt of insight first—I have a question." The lad blinked and straightened as he gave the commander his full attention.

Brooke cleared his throat. "No doubt, you heard our discussions last night."

Gnolin offered a faint grin.

"Given the circumstances, Gnolin, what advice would you dispense concerning my decision? Be truthful—I'll not hold it against you."

The pup bit his lower lip. "Well, Targin's our leader and all. The pack follows his command to the letter. But Brapin, see—well, he's kind of like the quill that inks those letters. Gramps says, the Orbical only imparts what truly needs hearing and not a syllable more."

Brooke smiled, his admiration for the lad growing by the moment. Unlike a typical boy of his age, full of mischief and wilfulness, Gnolin spoke and acted like a proper lordling with wisdom that belied his years: someone three times his age. "Thank you, Gnolin. I admire plain talk—it reflects your honesty." He clapped his hands and rubbed his palms together. "Now, how about that kofei?"

"Coming up," Gnolin replied with enthusiasm. As the boy darted off, Brooke's thoughts shifted to Cele. That dotard could learn a thing or ten about nobility from that pup.

Inside an hour, the company had eaten, their fires extinguished and all but their final decamping duties completed. Ralaus padded up to the commander and lowered himself to the ground.

Without Brooke's asking, the Warang had agreed to a second ride. More progress. First Weet, now Ralaus. Perhaps there was some hope for this steward after all.

Brooke mounted the wolf's saddle. "When you are ready, Ralaus, to the Plunge we go."

The giant wolf started forward. Gnor, astride Fram, came alongside to match pace. And the rest of the Wolves fell into step.

As Riverside disappeared around a bend in the forest road, Brooke's mind drifted to Brapin's promise in the King's Throne. The commander needed to believe that he would hold Dayanthi again and watch his sons, Ferin and Hue, grow into men.

Brooke pressed his lips together. Hope and love would steel his resolve—and make it just so. But first, he had to endure what the Orbical referred to as the Merger. He let out a long breath and trained his eyes forward. *One test at a time, Commander.*

As for the test of tests beyond, he'd just have to wait. See.

…and pray.

41: Reunions
Sonart

Thud, thud, thud!

Heart and mind racing, Sonart woke to a fervent knock at his door. His shock subsided when he realized he still lay abed in his darkened room at the Golan Hob, the turn of the dial, late.

He held his breath, ears perking.

Bessel's voice whispered urgently in the gloom, "Sonart, you in there?"

Sonart dragged his body out of bed and lumbered to the entrance. He fiddled with the latch and opened the door.

The innkeep's troubled face greeted him, flickering orange in the light of the candlestick he fisted. "Several dwarven roam the streets searching blindly but meticulously. Proclaimers—I can smell it. They're looking for you. A woman leads them—pretty thing, but damn persistent."

Sonart cursed. "Shayla."

"She made some inquiries earlier, but I sensed a threat hidden behind her words." Bessel paused and checked himself. "The evil magics cannot detect you in here—that remains. But the Proclaimers may still enter and sweep the inn. Judging by her tone, her suspicions seem roused but not confirmed. They'll have eyes on the Hob. You mustn't leave—least not through the front entrance."

"So, we're beleaguered," Sonart mused darkly. "Precisely why I must leave, Bessel. Their net will only tighten with each turn of the dial."

After some hesitation, Bessel nodded. "Then get dressed and don your weapon. My wife guards the door, but if they choose to come in, she must let them. I'll have to smuggle you out."

As Sonart dressed and gathered his things, Bessel grimaced, his face flushed. "Stars, I know how much you needed a bastion, but I think my haven's run of blessed drears has expired. My assurances be buggered, I fear you're no longer safe here. I've failed you in my service."

Sonart retrieved all that he dared. "I'm not safe anywhere, my friend. And no longer can I skulk in the shadows. I must confront this foul business." He put a hand on the innkeep's shoulder. "The last four drears have given me the reprieve I sorely needed—and your companionship much more than that. Your inn's very shield may have been what drew them to these warrens. But I've no doubt its sanctity endures. If not so, the reprobates would've stormed it already. As to your service, it already holds a debt I can never repay."

Bessel gave him a brave smile. "You might be surprised about that. We're all in grievous stead, but your advent has lifted the weight. Although my body has addled with the star-cycles, my heart sees clear enough." He lifted his chin and clasped Sonart's forearm where it bridged the innkeep's shoulder. "I foresee you will rise. And become our saviour."

Sonart clenched at Bessel's support. He dipped his beard and forced a grin as he disengaged the old one.

Bessel's eyes hardened in the candlelight and he looked around. "Now, I'll set you well away from the hazards roosting in my hood. With any luck, Xoral's ward still holds and—"

Shouting outside the Hob interrupted the innkeep. Both dwarven paused to listen. Down on the first floor, hammering knocks sounded against the tavern's entry door. It swung open brusquely. The commotion of voices intensified.

Or not.

"Stars burn that fool head of yours, are you deaf or just dim? The plaintiff's voice belonged to Wres, Bessel's wife. "I tell you we *have* no guests!"

A scuffle and loud footsteps followed and a burly voice commanded, "Stand aside, Scarecrow, or my axe will be your guest—as it cleaves that rotting skull of yours."

"Quick," Bessel urged. "Out the window. There's nothing for it."

Abandoning his pack, Sonart ran to the window, heaved the pane open, and climbed up into the frame.

Over his shoulder, he whispered, "I'll never forget you."

Then he jumped.

Sonart landed hard on his feet, stifling a grunt as he crumpled to absorb the impact. He scrambled to his legs and raced down the alleyway to the closest side street. Picking an arbitrary direction to his left, he followed it to the first crossroad.

But before he emerged, a cry erupted behind him. "There he is! Seize him!"

Sonart glanced back. At least a dozen dwarven sprinted toward him.

As though borne on the Scourge's wind, Sonart tore away, down the conjoining alley. He made a series of sporadic turns at each intersection, trying to throw off his pursuers.

A gloom-ridden warren hove into view.

Panting, Sonart careened into it. Once in the darkened artery, he hid in the thicker shadows behind a massive pile of refuse. A moment later, a pair of Proclaimers raced past, oblivious to him.

The knaves would soon find him if he lingered. Sonart quickly saw the folly of running in the opposite direction. Having lost his hunters this close to the alley's mouth, his wisest course lay deeper within the maze. And he did not know the extent of Deathwrought's blindness.

Into the alley, he stole. Fifty heartbeats later, the urban fissure narrowed until a mere four feet separated the walls.

Sonart slowed and gathered his thoughts. He had to go to ground and somehow get to the place Bessel suggested.

Poor Bessel—if discovered, he'd pay for abetting the Darkest One's prize. But perhaps not: the stalwart innkeep proved a crafty one, having survived this long, leading an underground movement no less.

Sonart turned into a more confined cleft. It required him to shimmy sideways to pass the last five feet of space between the damp walls.

Out from the tight gap, Sonart spilled into a wider rhombic space. A good sixty feet separated its asymmetrical walls. He trudged into the centre of the enclosure—and found a dead end.

Heartsick, Sonart peered up at the black sky for a long moment. Stars burn him, other than turning back, the only way out was up.

Something clicked behind him.

Sonart wheeled—barely avoiding a dagger as it whizzed past his head. He dropped to a crouch. Drew his sword as a Proclaimer rushed him, hefting a morning star in his gauntleted fist.

Sonart feinted as the spiked ball came down. Quicker, defter, he danced away from the blow. But not far enough to answer with his own swing.

Metal rang as his foe's head collided with the flat of Sonart's blade. His foe surged past, doubled over, and sprawled senseless to the ground.

Sonart leapt on his opponent, grabbed his tunic, and pummelled his lights out with a fist that cracked the bridge of his nose.

The Proclaimer did not rise again. Sonart put his ear to the dwarven's chest. He still breathed.

"You're trapped, Son of Farkshone!"

Sonart spun as more Proclaimers filed into the cul de sac. When the last of them had entered, he counted eight of the turncapes.

"Turn around and leave," Sonart hailed as he retrieved his sword and rose. "Else this place will be a dead end in more than one way."

"She said you'd sputter something like that," their leader scoffed as he brandished his sword.

Sonart lifted his own weapon and spoke with an eerie calm, "All you will do here is serve as fodder to elicit a response. All of you will die."

This time, his words did not fall on deaf ears. The Proclaimers' faces blanched. Lips atremble, three among them exchanged uncertain looks.

Even as they absorbed his threat, the first wave of dark power welled within him.

This time, he welcomed it.

One of the spooked dwarven gasped and pointed a shaky finger. "The bloodbeard's eyes glow green!"

"Burn her," their leader grated. "She assured me the red bastard wouldn't change."

Noise flooded Sonart's mind. Tears swamped his orbs. His vision swam in emerald waters. He clung on like one trying to harness open flame with bare hands. His volition burned away.

But his sight held. His Eyes. Mine Eyes. *Mine Eyes are Your Eyes*. Like the Chosen Kworn, he had become a vassal of the Darkest One.

The Proclaimers fanned out, trying to surround and grapple him. But his black power swelled past a tipping point and they shrank back.

Reality split into a double image, one ghosting over the other. In one iteration he dealt death, cleaving blade ablur, lopping heads from shoulders. In the other, the Hive, the Augury, swirling veridian mist, candles, crystals, and clouds—just as before.

No, not as before. This time, an unbidden thought took root—and held the Darkest One's possession in check. *Either way, the blade will cut, you must decide which way, and how deep.*

To his utter shock, Sonart cast the invasive spirit from his body. Reverted to his dwarven self. But Deathwrought's presence still came. The cloud before him solidified into His face—no, not just the face, but his entire sodding body. Thin ebony fumes shot into the nebulous form like arrow shafts.

The figure's skin became grey, sizzled, and fractured. Pus-swamped entrails burst out of multiple fissures before burning up in the acrid vapours.

Metamorphosis complete, the smoke dissipated into wisps. The form, three times Sonart's height, a full ten feet, stepped towards him. The sound of ripping scabs tainted his ears as the Darkest One loomed over him.

Sword raised above his head like a dagger on the plunge, Sonart whirled—to face him head-on.

And sprang.

Like a lightning bolt, the blade passed through his nemesis—into shadow—buried to the hilt.

A primal scream sounded.

And the veil lifted. The nefarious lord winked out, replaced with that of the Proclaimers' leader, impaled, eyes frozen in shock. Crimson syrup bubbled from his breast as he sagged to the ground and lay still. Deathwrought had used his presence to goad Sonart into employing his *wilderen* power.

On wooden legs, Sonart slouched against the far wall, panting heavy breaths in the shrouded alley. His lungs hushed into a soundless vacuum.

Something caked his face and arms. He looked down and gawked.

Strewn before him in heaps, connected by a widening red marsh lay all the Proclaimers who assailed him.

Save one.

A snicker made him spin towards the narrow entrance.

Shayla stepped from its shadows.

"You do not disappoint, Scion," she rasped, her voice a mix of honey and acid, her face a cold mask of vindication. "Vein bled, Sword broken, Seed thwarted, I *proclaim* my work done. The exalted sisterhood within the Darkest One's coven awaits, elevated above the Cradle's sorry existence. My foster father, *Wroughn*—Deathwrought will have your blade now, as He claims you—and I'll be the one who brings Him both."

Betrayed *utterly*.

As Shayla advanced, a Zürshuck alighted on the ground behind her. The Winged One blocked the entrance as the dead Proclaimers had done.

To Sonart's shock, the alley floor beneath him began to smoulder. The smell of brimstone choked the air.

Sonart coughed as it assailed his lungs. He gaped while markings etched themselves into the ground directly under him. Claws of onyx light traced canals. They formed symmetrical patterns he recognized: a double-crucifix inlaid within an octagon. Lines crossed, chiselling deeper hollows within the cobblestone.

He scurried away and backed into a corner as a caesura opened, revealing a translation window directly back to the chapel atop the Hive. The same altar materialized. The harsh reek of deathbreath overpowered his nostrils. Sonart pressed his back against the smeared crook behind him, as though he could will the trap away and avoid recapture.

The Zürshuck extended its wings, forming an inverted V, its claws protracted forward like grapnels. No more escape.

Svishh.

Shayla wheeled at the tearing sound. Sonart gaped. A poniard's worth of ironock sprouted from the demon's chest. Drove up and twisted. The Winged One's surety blinked into stunned surprise. A mortal screech escaped its maw, reverberating off the walls of the enclosure. The demon gagged on its own fluids as the cavity erupted in a sluffed flower of viscera.

The Zürshuck's razor wings fanned wildly, whipping the air into furious gusts. Black blood sprayed Shayla as she scrambled to get clear.

To Sonart's shock, the Winged One pitched forward and crumpled to the ground. Its membraned appendages beat fury, shoulders clubbing the cobblestone in its death throes. Then all at once, they folded and grew still. The transcendental portal winked out.

Behind the fallen Zürshuck, the shadowy outline of a dwarven male emerged, blade held firmly in two dripping arms.

"Get out," he roared at Sonart like a hammer pean striking another. "I'll settle your score with this bitch."

Sonart knew the voice, and the manner. Seolad, Rusic's son.

Without another word, the blackbeard rushed Shayla.

But before Seolad cleared four bounds, another winged shadow fell from the heights. And a second. And a third. *Damnation.*

The three demons landed and barred the dwarven's path.

Seolad dropped on all fours.

Behind him, a horrendous burst of lightning ignited. It erased everything in a white flash. The Zürshuck wall detonated in a blossom of flaming parts. It concussed Sonart's head against the wall behind him but he remained standing.

Seolad jumped up, sword arcing high. And fell upon Shayla as she staggered towards Sonart, managing two steps before Seolad parked his blade hilt-deep between her shoulder blades. A muffled cry escaped her lips as she toppled and stilled.

A fifth Zürshuck pounced on Seolad from above, claws and wingtips extended.

But the dwarven proved too swift and agile. He fell back and rolled in a spectacular move, catching the demon off-guard. Seolad flung his blade.

And the Zürshuck alighted—with the blackbeard's sword skewering its throat. Wings splayed, the demon collapsed backwards, double-jointed legs spasming.

Seolad regained purchase on his steel. Hands fastened to the hilt, the insane dwarven rode it up and over his foe even as the Winged One stumbled onto its back.

The Zürshuck clawed at the air in a manic effort to rid itself of the mortal weapon—blade and executioner. But its jerky movements quickly slowed to rigidity.

Using his boot for leverage, Seolad yanked the sword free. "Here, let me help you with that!" In a wide arc, he swung the blade like an ironock wraith and lopped off the Zürshuck's head.

The sound of pounding wings filled the space as more Zürshuck descended from high above. Seolad's scowl lifted to them, reddened, and tightened like stifled combustion. "Apparently, the idiot didn't hear me the first time!" Body and face twisting fresh cracks at Sonart, the dwarven hellion bellowed, "Get the fuck out!"

Sonart's head reeled. But his legs responded to the blunt sharpness of Seolad's ire. He slammed his blade into its scabbard and rushed past the dead Zürshuck and Proclaimers, past the corpse of Shayla and the volatile face of his enraged redeemer.

Into the deeper darkness of the slim egress, Sonart dashed as fast as he could sidestep. Just as he achieved the wider alley beyond, a pair of hands seized him, clamped his mouth shut, and stopped him dead in his tracks.

Stephen Fenech

42: Rite of Passage
Sonart

Before Sonart could panic, the towering silhouette spoke, his urgency plain. "The place Bessel told you about—go there now. Seolad and I will cover your escape. Now flee."

When the giant released him, Sonart raced away into the unknown weave of alleys and warrens.

Damn it all: every effort to put the trauma of his heritage behind him and reach the end of his pursuit only incited more vigorous assaults.

And that stranger—only slightly shorter than a Winged One. The same size as... as the corpse he and Malrik discovered in their Dunge cell.

Implications turned into a carousel of ignorance and torment. Spun his mind about in a confused delirium of roles, emotions, and allegiances. They meshed until everything became nothing, and his pounding heart spurred him on, following a map—writ inside his head.

Hand welded to his sword, Sonart pushed through the doorway and descended the six half-steps to the bottom landing. This building matched the image that had lifted from the Kusp's glowing sheaves in his home.

Somehow, after the tall shadowy interceptor released him, Sonart homed in on this place as naturally as rain falling to the ground.

Haven at last?

But as Sonart's boot touched the sunken floor, a wail pierced the air behind him, chilling his marrow to ice. He spun as a Zürshuck alighted on the passageway outside.

Backlit by a street lamp, the Winged One's shadow spilled through the open doorway and down the stairwell. The demon tucked its spread wings as it entered.

Sonart wheeled. The demon's shriek chased after him as he darted for the door at the opposite end of the cellar. Found it locked. Twisted back. Curses, he'd been led into another trap.

Fangs bared, claws extended, the Zürshuck came at him.

Sonart brandished his sword, fear resurrecting his primal fury.

He focused it through the weapon.

But before he could fully get the tip up, the Zürshuck batted the blade from his hand. Sent it sailing.

339

As the sword clanged to the floor, the demon's other claw raked Sonart's cloak, rending the fabric to shreds in a single swipe. At least the confined space denied the demon the guillotine use of its wings.

The Zürshuck wrenched Sonart off his feet and hurled him against the wall. Twirling as he flew, Sonart just managed to get his feet under him as he struck. The impact still rattled his spine and jarred his joints but no bones snapped as he bent his knees and rebounded.

The stunt left him shocked at discovering himself capable of such a feat. Equally fortuitous, he landed upright and found Seolad's sword within arm's reach.

And quickly snatched it up.

Though not quick enough. In three bounds, the Zürshuck pounced again. Long sinewy arms clasped Sonart about the waist and hauled him into the air a second time. The demon's maw gaped for a killing bite.

Sonart blocked the assault with his blade.

The Zürshuck's jaws clamped metal.

Glowing metal—!

Sonart kicked the Zürshuck in the ribs. The metal plate in his boot toe cracked several bones in a sharp cascade. The demon dropped him as it buckled and doubled over, hissing fetid air. It gnashed against the blade, wedged into the bone of its inner jaw. One claw grasped at its dinted chest while the other sought to remove the lodged blade.

Recalling Seolad's brazen move, Sonart jumped aside and yanked the blade free from the demon's jaw. Blood traced an arc in the air—lit by a ghosting curve of azure light.

Howling in pain and frustration, the Winged One swung its tail and bowled the dwarven's legs from under him.

Sonart flew back. He hit the floor with a grunt and skidded to the far wall in a heap.

Vision swimming, he tilted his head down the length of his arm *and* blade. Stars, he still grappled it.

The tormented Zürshuck lunged at him along the ceiling—no the floor.

Hooks and Dunge, he was upside down! With all the strength left him, Sonart kicked his boots at the wall and catapulted into an upright battle stance. But cornered he remained, the wall at his back, any escape blocked by the demon's wings as it drew up.

Sonart cried out, an unintelligible curse.

The Zürshuck's claw lanced towards his face.

Impossible to parry.

The sword suddenly raised *itself,* bringing Sonart's arm up with it to repel the demon's attack.

Of its own volition, the blade acted, galvanizing its wielder.

The sword matched the Zürshuck's thrust.

When the demon overextended an arm, the sword's backstroke severed it below the shoulder.

The Winged One's triumphant roar died. Its snouted face screwed into a mask of umbrage and horror as blood spurted from the stump.

On unsteady talons, the Zürshuck darted back—far enough for Sonart to press his attack. He spun the blade over his head, around and around into a whirlwind, a cobalt radiance trailing the sword's wake.

As the Zürshuck cringed like a trapped animal, dwarven and demon shared a truth: their roles had reversed. Predator had become prey.

Sonart roared in a voice that stole and detonated his senses. "I shall not—DIE."

He let the sword fly. It streaked across the short distance, an arc of caerulean light connecting Sonart to his foe like a lightning fork.

The blade buried itself in the Zürshuck's torso, driving it back with such force the demon hammered the wall behind it with a crack and poof of stone powder.

The sword pinned the Zürshuck to the mortar, where it remained. The demon's convulsions proved brief. Within moments, it sagged, head lolling to one side, luminous eyes guttering as it stilled.

Then, the sword pommel, still infused with an intense sapphire nimbus, vanished.

The Winged One slid to the floor.

Sonart gawped in disbelief. Until he remembered what a possessed minion could do—as the doomed Chosen had done during that last Kworn ritual. *All you must do is survive.*

"Stars be—merciful." Sonart limped over to the demon, his antagonist, his victim. Standing over the dismembered corpse, the dwarven confirmed the impossible: the hole in the wall left by the weapon remained, the cauterized wound in the Zürshuck's chest still gaped, but Seolad's sword had disappeared.

A shadow crept over Sonart's relief. Had the source of the weapon's power gone as well? Had Deathwrought found out about this sanctuary? If so, what would the Darkest One do now? *Mine eyes are your eyes.*

"Fear not, young dwarven," a voice said behind him.

Sonart jumped, hand diving for his empty scabbard as he veered about

341

to meet another attack.

He stuttered and froze. Twas the impossibly tall stranger who intercepted him in the cul de sac, where Shayla and her thugs—and most likely Seolad too—met their end.

"Time and time alone will show you this truth," the cloaked figure went on. He wore a cowl that hid his face in a veil of shadows. His stance exuded an air of confidence bordering on defiance. The spectre had arms and legs in all the right places but he stood taller than any dwarven or Kworn had a right to be. One hand braced a staff of gnarled wood.

Despite Sonart's trepidation, he sensed something familiar about the towering stranger. His presence stirred warmth in the dwarven's soul like a shift of coals in a pyre to coax new flames.

But Sonart would take no chances. Holding caution as tightly as his resolve, he raised a weary arm and pointed an accusing finger. "Did you bring this terror? Are you—Deathwrought?"

The figure chuckled with a mirth Sonart had never known. It instantly disarmed him, rendering the dwarven ambivalent as he shifted from one foot to the other.

"Heavens forbid," the enigmatic figure said at last. "Now, away with your wrath and fear. You needn't bear either in my company. As you've just learned and verified, you serve as your own weapon. But stars, please, don't point it at me."

Sonart folded his arms. "I'll be the judge of that."

"As you should," the stranger mused. "I ask only that you hear me out before you pass judgement. I guarantee that by the time I am finished, our stars will align like no two stars have ever done so before. The Kusp of the Testament has long-divined this—the true Kusp, that is."

Sonart grunted and gave him a long look but did not attempt a rejoinder.

The tall one's cowl drifted to his staff and he slowly rotated its length. "That said, you will need your weapon eventually, but for the moment, I assure you that you are quite safe."

"Safe?" Sonart's eyebrows sprung off their perch, causing the caked blood gripping their strands to crumble. "I haven't been safe my entire sordid existence." He stabbed his index finger towards the floor, then at the stranger.

The digit hung in the air quivering like an arrow stuck in a target. "Tis a dark mockery, knave. From whichever Dunge pit you've emerged, you bear the mark of a spider, trapping me down here with this devil."

"No, Sonart of Farkshone, I had no part in the Zürshuck's presence here. It followed you out of the alley from on high, much faster than I could hunt it down." He let out a weary sigh. "I feared I would arrive too late. But to my relief, you proved me wrong. Faced with mortal combat as you were, you've earned your claim as emblem bearer. You are a Blood Scion. A Vein of Fire."

"I know all that," Sonart replied tersely. He hesitated, curiosity piqued. "What bloody emblem?"

"Why, the Sword you just used to slay that foul beast." The stretched figure gestured to the crumpled demon. "And the map you offer our... 'fellowship-to-be.'" He slowly moved his cowled head from side to side. "Make no mistake, Sonart, by dispatching the Winged One, you most certainly *un-trapped* yourself."

Sonart saw the truth in the tower's words. He had carried out the act through possession—though now that he thought about it, he had been the possessor. And only grew stronger for it. More—more? Stars eclipse him, he found no word to describe the new emotion.

Stretchy noticed his shift for he began to nod. His manner seemed accepting, without pretence, filled with good nature. Sonart made every effort to hold onto his anger and distrust of the tall one.

And failed.

Still, he made himself ask, "What do you mean?"

"You were told that the answer would find you—were you not?" The spectre laughed. "Well, my little fire-bearded friend, I am that answer. For I also bear an emblem." He gestured to his staff. "I too hold the rank of Blood Scion. Like you, I am—a Vein of Fire."

Sonart's mouth gaped. "By—the—"

"Stars, indeed," the stranger chortled. "For *by them*, I found such guidance to you. Tis time for new beginnings, Sonart of Farkshone, the moment for you to learn of our shared agency. And the whole truth of everything, and everything within the truth."

The dwarven's ire returned and he glared, blood rushing to his cheeks. "Ever you speak in riddles. Can you not speak plainly, stars burn you?"

The stranger spread his hands in surrender. "Forsooth, I wouldn't have it any other way."

Sonart gritted his teeth. "If you seek to ensnare my heart, stow your cursed spell, conjurer. Hooks and Dunge, I've wizened up to turncapes of late and can give as good as I get. But—if you do not serve as that she-demon's ilk, why are you so deformed?"

That drew a belly laugh from the stranger but he didn't answer the question.

Eyes narrowing, Sonart scrutinized the lofty riddler up and down. "What are you? And what in hellish blazes do you want from me?"

The cloaked one's gregariousness ebbed and he straightened, his voice becoming earnest as he splayed one hand across his chest. "My name is Gjengaegungen—a rather long ponderous title I'm afraid. So, for the sake of brevity please call me Gjen. I am a descendant of the ancient Kazir. But of all who dwell upon the Main of Areth, I am most closely identified with the race of men. If by *what*, you mean my profession, I do perform 'conjuring,' of a sort, in the same field as an alchlemage. But what I truly am—is a wizard—of magic—wilderen magic."

The spectre drew a deep breath, taking Sonart's away as he did.

"As to my purpose in coming to *Grendamaul*—your Cradle, well my feisty firebrand, I have come to rescue you."

43: The Plunge
Brooke

The first murmur of the Plunge sounded in Brooke's ears a half-league before its fine mist sifted through the trees. As the Nightwolves tramped the damp forest road, leading up through the foothills of the Spires' Crest, the vapour thickened. The cataract's ambient noise also continued to rise above the sounds of the woodland—until quite suddenly the natural wonder appeared.

Now that he beheld the full extent of its grandeur, all the commander could do was gape. Teal trees and sage-coloured moss accentuated the majesty of the horseshoe waterfall, which stretched three hundred feet across. Its turbulent waters gushed over jagged boulders near the edge and dropped more than a thousand feet into a mist-shrouded chasm. Clouds of vapour detonated far below, obscuring the deep pool somewhere at the chute's scalloped basin.

As Brooke peered over an adjoining cliff face, wind-charged spray fanned and matted his hair. With such raw power, the cataract made it rain upward.

"Impressive, isn't it?" Gnor shouted over the din.

"Aye," Brooke acknowledged as loud as his voice would carry. "Eponymous, its name!" He shifted his gaze away from the vista to see the stout Wrayn's smiling face. Beads of water dripped from his bald head to the white stubble on his chin. "The survival of such magical places underlines the reason we ride so hard. Our Creator has wrought perfection here."

Gnor gave Brooke a firm nod. "That He has." The Bulldog faced the waterfall again. "Yet despite the magnificence of the Plunge, Targin speaks of another cataract far to the north. Etern's Drop."

"Where the sprites' bastion stands—no?" Brooke yelled. "Their first domain?"

Gnor sopped the droplets from his face and inclined his head. "The Chief has ventured there on occasion and spoke often of it. 'The Plunge rains but a faucet's trickle compared to the Drop,' Targin swore."

Brooke tried to imagine something grander than this immense natural cathedral—and failed.

"For a thousand eons this chasm has stood," Gnor extolled, "unmolested by Shirdron's Folly. And still, the Plunge flows ever strong and stalwart, holding audience with the grey pines and evergreens." He swept his arm across the gulf to where the trees formed ranks to the very edge of the falls. A swathe of yellow and orange marigolds draped their trunks and the surrounding underbrush. "The White River's glacial waters provide the greatest tributary to the almighty Run."

Charged clean and wet with vigorous spray, the air smelled of fermented bark, blue spruce and honey-scented mountain shrubs—sweet decay mingled with new life.

Brooke breathed deep, an unexpected but welcome catharsis washing over him as his lungs filled. "Perhaps one day, Gnor, our paths will take us to the Drop, and we can decide for ourselves."

"The pathless path ranges far and wide, Commander, so yea, one day let's." Gnor leaned forward and looked straight down. A blast of water rivulets showered his crown anew, and he chuckled heartedly. "Stars align, that would surely be a day to remember."

A shadow crept over Brooke's mood at Gnor's comment. It brought him back to the crux of their arrival here—the moment he'd been dreading since the company had left Riverside.

The road they followed stopped just short of the Plunge. From where they gathered now, the route split: one path branching north to form the Northern Arm. The other followed the river a mile upstream to its narrows.

At this bottleneck, a dwarven-hewn rope bridge traversed the torrent. On its opposite bank, the Southern Arm began. The carrefour allowed Brooke no more time or room for any great deliberation.

Either way presented a challenge, slowly ascending along separate ridges even higher than where they stood now. Eventually, the paths would level off to follow their respective highland roads. Both arms would ultimately curve east to run a relatively parallel course towards Serenthia.

Brooke's options looked equally precipitous, not so much for the path he picked as the band's reaction to his choice. His eyes swept the press of Warangs lying prone or sitting back on their haunches amidst the trees. Some licked their fur, others scratched their flanks with their back paws, and a pair watched a blue butterfly with pink dots flutter past.

The Wrayns sat or stood in circles scattered among the canines. All of them awaited their steward's decision.

Brooke hardened his jaw and cleared his throat. "Nightwolves, I've weighed options and considered the counsel of many regarding our route forthwith. We shall take the Northern Arm as Brapin suggested."

Most of the Wrayns inclined their chins or jutted them. Val stared down over the Plunge, giving everyone his back.

Expecting as much, Brooke sighed. "If any should gainsay, I would hear it now."

When Alghan stepped forward, Brooke lifted his eyebrows in dismay.

"Commander, I must." As gently as the Plunge's overture allowed, the tall Nightwolf explained, "As you know, I've scouted a good length of the arms ahead—north and south. The Warangs that accompanied me found

346

scent trails. They indicate the minions of the Darkest One have indeed passed to the south, but their trail appears long-cold. To the north, the wolves found more recent evidence of… well worse things. Forest creatures confirm this."

A few Wrayns nearby nodded and a pair of Warangs chuffed and tossed their snouts.

Brooke cocked his chin at them before facing Alghan again. "More lavatrols? Colossals?"

Alghan shook his head. "Nay, something different, more elusive."

Brooke's frown deepened. *More* elusive? "Do you suggest I reconsider? Have us take the Southern Arm?"

"I'm only saying that trouble exists in either direction. I wanted to present you with all the facts—to weigh them accordingly." Alghan paused and looked past Val, into the abyss. After a moment, he regarded Brooke again. "But there is also the question of time. The scent the Warangs picked up to the south suggested the enemy was heading towards Serenthia. They are legion."

"Ah, that word—*but*." Brooke inhaled through his nose. "The crux of our dilemma, like the narrow waist of the hourglass that sifts the preamble above into the truth below."

"But," Quiver laughed. "Sometimes the horseshit you start with before the waist only leaves you with a larger heap at the bottom. Wait long enough, mayhap some broken glass too."

Divining Quiver's meaning, Brooke handed the bowman a thin smile. He tilted his head to the ground and kicked a small stone with the side of his boot.

When Brooke faced the pack again, he drew a deep breath and clapped his hands together. "Thank you for your report, Alghan, and your counsel. Nevertheless, I maintain we take our chances along the Northern Arm. Luck may favour us there. But if a formidable host ranges the Southern Arm between us and our goal, best to avoid it—give Serenthia fair warning, by staying alive to deliver it."

"Tis the Hidden Kingdom after all," Quiver put in. "Protected by no lack of sprite wards, glamours, and monstrous sentinels. Even if Deathwrought unleashed the whole of his army, they'd never find it."

Brooke dipped his chin before shifting his attention to Alghan. "Best to meet them safely entrenched, surrounded by allies within an impregnable keep than dealing with them on our own in the wild."

"As you wish, Commander," Alghan said with a respectful bow.

Brooke strode over to Ralaus, his steps deliberate. Lifting his boot into the stirrup, he clasped the pommel and swung his other leg over the saddle. "Up the Northern Arm, Ralaus, if you will."

The Warang rose and moved away at a brusque pace. The riderless Warangs fell into step while the rest awaited their Wrayns to saddle up. In ones and twos, the giant wolves filed up the ascending trail, between rows of cedars and pines.

With every step Ralaus climbed, the more exposed the way became. He trudged over the rutted, pebble-strewn ground, sallying past a series of throne-sized boulders.

The wind freshened the air and smelled clean of morning dew, scruff berries, and tall mint. Trees still flanked the trail but grew sparser the higher the pack climbed. The gaps allowed slats of sunlight to bask large patches of earth beneath the thinning canopy.

Daylight petered and deepened the colours of stone and tree alike as the van rounded a sharp bend in the trail. It marked the start of the Northern Arm. The ochre sun began a slow descent, shadows lengthening before it. With Ralaus padding away from the sinking orb, Brooke could feel its fiery intensity on his back as the day waned to dusk.

When the sun had all but abandoned them, the air grew colder, carried on more insistent gusts, but the company pushed on at Gnor's behest. "I know a campsite, not half a league distant which will cater nicely. It lies within a hollowed cove to shield us and our fires from the full brunt of the squalls."

Before they covered half that distance, they came across fresh tracks: some clearly made by human boots, but others dug wider trenches. They belonged to something large, bestial. Pounded into the dirt, the paw prints were not made by any wolf or bear. In places, crimson spots marred the earth.

When Brooke gestured towards the troubling sign, Gnor moved his head from side to side. "Blood—aye. The Warang scouts commune; they say we still tread safely. The lead wolves have passed the haven I mentioned and now spread their patrol out in all directions beyond. Nothing threatens. If the Warangs sense any danger, they will alert us."

Brooke could not shirk his doubt; their recent ordeal with the lavatrols fresh in his mind—the monsters had *targeted* him. He looked away from Gnor and swallowed, deciding to keep faith and let it pass. What option did he have? Having taken this charge, he had to justify the sprites' choice in him, even when it became difficult, even if it killed him.

And stars, it almost did.

By increments, the forested path levelled off. Minutes later, Ralaus snorted as they came upon Gnor's intended campsite. And a wonderful spot at that: set in a naturally formed half-bowl filled with evenly placed evergreens. Beyond the basin's upper lip, the trees cloistered closer together, their needles thicker.

But their trunks rose taller, and with little in the way of underbrush, the ground looked easily accessible, with only a carpet of brown nettles to cover the forest floor. Pine scented every breath.

Near the middle of the depression, twin creeks gurgled past. Four feet wide and some sixty apart, they flowed towards an open edge two hundred feet out from the trail. This empty side of the bowl resembled an upturned horseshoe made of evergreens that framed a cloud-scattered sky beyond.

Ralaus stopped.

Despite the prevailing melancholy of the band, it could not detract Brooke's appreciation of the site's natural beauty. While the Wrayn pups dismounted their Warangs, he guided Ralaus to follow the creeks to the last skein of trees warding the precipice. Shade reined the dramatic drop below, but at eye level and above, the afternoon sun painted the sprawling vista bright orange, including the upper clouds, the distant snow-capped peaks of the Swordswathe far to the south, and the Spires' Crest to the north.

Though hardly a dribble combined, compared to the violence of the Plunge, the creeks' drop gave a higher vantage of the valley below. But their waters cascaded down the sheer plummet no more than fifty feet before the high gusts swept their fill into a swathe of vapour that made the cliff face weep. Their waters rained down upon the rocky banks of the White River, the same upper torrent that fed the Plunge.

Even from this height, Brooke discerned the hum of the potent artery raging below, lifted by echoes on the wind.

He alighted Ralaus and bade the Warang take his leave. When the canine sauntered away, Brooke just stood there and absorbed the panorama. As always, his thoughts drifted to Dayanthi and the children.

Brooke closed his eyes. *Imagine them and it will be so... 'love is the needle that will point you there.'* After a moment, he exhaled and turned to join the others. The pups had started erecting the tents and gathering wood. Seems once the commander had made up his mind, the band just fell in, prepared to follow him to whatever end—as Targin proclaimed they would.

But Brooke had Val to consider. Did the troubled Nightwolf renege on that particular oath? If not for Brapin's riddlesome insinuations to the contrary. Time would tell.

Instinct and experience assured Brooke he must travel in deepest stygian darkness before seeing the light. He held no illusions about that. But then he remembered Helmdak's pledge of fealty. How would he know the Nightwolves' direst need? A prophecy foretold in the Kusp, or an aberration diverging from it? Did it preordain his own life's purpose in that scripture? Or did he only serve as a scapegoat for the manipulations of the renegade, Targin and his Orbical-mentor?

Only courage would win the truth of matters—or die trying to wrest it free from the future. Contemplating so many questions left Brooke feeling small and too wearied to care. He'd rest early tonight, give himself more time to sort the quandaries. For now, he needed some company.

By the stars, he spied tireless Gnolin keeping an animated conversation with his impassive cohort, Weet. He approached them. Gnolin's quiet companion made quick spidery gestures in the air with his thin digits, but not once did he speak aloud. Then it struck the commander. Weet had *never* spoken—the boy was a mute. And, by Gnolin's quick responses, he understood every silent gesticulation Weet made.

Brooke stopped in his tracks, deciding not to interrupt the boys' happy exchange for his own paltry need. He watched them from a distance, heartened at how easily their camaraderie came—a model for the older Wrayns for certain.

After the better part of a minute, Brooke moved on. He found Gnor bent on one knee, nuzzling Fram, his calloused hands scratching the tufts behind the smiling Warang's ears.

Gnor turned his head slightly at the sound of Brooke's approach. "Commander."

"Your senses are sharp," Brooke extolled.

"I'm an old dog," Gnor said with a gruff laugh. "With much time to learn a few tricks."

Brooke smiled. "Apparently, a few good ones."

Gnor gave his great wolf one final pat before standing to join the commander. "The forest sleeps." He pointed toward four different spots in the woodland. "Double Warang patrols guard beyond the perimeter. They'll keep vigil and maintain constant communion with the main host."

Brooke nodded gravely but averted his eyes. "That is good."

Within the hour the band had settled. The commander sat before one of the modest fires, joined by a wide circle of men and women, all busy gnawing strips of venison and drinking cups of mead.

Brooke too settled—in body.

Not so in mind. Despite Gnor's assurances about the added watches, he remained uneasy, recalling the blood trail they found a scant distance away.

"We'll start earlier on the morrow," Brooke said to the fire. "If Brapin tells us true, our way is safer, albeit longer than the Southern Arm. So, we shorten it through greater haste and distance each day, enough to make up the difference between the two routes."

"Haste will not harry our journey overly much," Alghan said from his seat to Brooke's right. "The Warangs are all fed and can draw deeper strength to quicken our passage. We will be spread thinner, but the flanking scouts will alert us if anything untoward approaches."

Brooke dipped his chin in appreciation. "I would hear more about the lay of the land ahead, specifically alternate routes in the event of—well something *untoward*."

"I can do that, Commander," Gnor said. "I know this country like the back of my hand. The environs stay thinly forested for another league or so. Then the sparse grove will thicken for a while as we travel east. Eventually, the terrain will slope downward on our left flank while our right flank continues parallel with the sheer drop to the river below."

Gnor tipped his cup back and burped. "As the road merges with the Relay's defiled course, the lay will switch, with our right flank to the south filling as the river comes up to meet it. The left slope will then become more pronounced until it forms the sheer drop. Technically, the heights of that juncture mark the start of one of the side channels into the Relay."

"One of many such fissures, component to the central stalk of Shirdron's abyss," Alghan added, drawing Brooke's attention. "The blighted confusion of the labyrinth owes its existence to the tragic Lord. The cataclysm he incurred when invoking the False Starbond gouged the original canyon to a depth of five miles in places, or so I've read—never actually penetrated more than a mile down."

"Not the safest place to camp," Gnor snuffled as he ran a hand over his bald head.

Alghan offered the stout Wrayn an amicable grin before continuing, "In the millennium since, the usurped river system forming the original canyon was diverted to Vamsah knows where—its web of torrents furthering the derangement of the Relay's countless formations. The rivers dictate any path through that maze now."

Gnor drew his arm back and gestured over his shoulder towards the road they took up from the Plunge. "Dwarven blazed the Northern Arm to efficiently navigate the Relay's myriad switches while staying clear of its deeper reaches. It offers the shortest route, but one seldom travelled."

"Why is that?" Brooke asked.

Gnor lifted his shoulders. "No steadings or villages for one. Grows barren and cold for another. Here, we truly slog an unforgiving wild, Commander—alone as any can be."

"But—we're not alone," Brooke mused darkly. "Someone or something as deadly as the lavatrols ranges these tracts, evinced by the grizzly scene we stumbled upon." *And now we camp upon its very fringe.* He tried to suppress his anxieties but they refused to release their grappling hooks on his mind's holdfast.

A none-too-gentle tap on his shoulder brought him out of his brooding.

He looked up. The mountainous form of Bhom grinned down at him, a flagon full of spritewater shoved out in offering.

Brooke lowered his cup of mead to the ground and accepted the flask. When he tipped back a swallow of the draught, he tasted fire. And doubled over, half-coughing half-sputtering the potent contents.

But when Bhom sniggered, his mischievous eyes darting to his peers, Brooke drew some air and took another swig with greater success. Wiping his lips with the back of his arm, he handed the flagon back to the heavy Wrayn. "Stars, did you bottle that in Infern?"

"Someplace hotter!" Bhom snorted laughter and rumbled an approval.

Smiling, Brooke turned to Gnor, who only shrugged.

A commotion behind the stout man caught Brooke's notice and the grin died on his lips. Gnolin raced towards him. Wide-eyed alarm registered on the boy's face, unmistakable. Contagious.

"What happened?" Alghan asked. The others spun to face the pup.

Between pants, Gnolin managed one word. "Weet!"

Brooke shot to his feet, knocking over his cup and spilling the mead on the ground. "What of him?"

More panting.

"Speak, lad," Gnor pressed. His strident tone shook the pup out of his delirium.

"Weet has... 'the Fear' upon him... collapsed on the ground ...huffing, fingers stuck together—like this." Gnolin shakily made two claws of his hands with the index fingers extended, placed in tandem like an arrowhead.

"The *fear*?" Brooke mouthed, his chest tightening. He and Gnor exchanged frowns before meeting the boy's bulging stare.

Gnolin got his breathing under control. "I tried to comfort him—bring him to the fire, but his position's all skewed, off-kilter. I didn't want to risk further harm so I left him there on the ground."

Brooke placed a firm hand on the pup's shoulder and sought his regard. "Gnolin, take us to him."

They found Weet splayed on the ground, legs extended awkwardly, hands clasped together as Gnolin had described. Under the light of handheld torches, the pup's glazed eyes stared up, mouth frozen in a gaping O.

Dead?

Brooke stooped beside the boy's ashen face and brought an ear close to Weet's mouth. He detected a hint of respiration and the faintest rise and fall to his small skeletal frame. The commander had seen this condition before, in the aftermath of battle when a soldier became mentally overwhelmed by carnage, fear, or both. Weet appeared stricken by the same malady: shock, paralyzed by a witnessed trauma but otherwise physically unharmed.

"Before his seizure," Gnolin said, "he kept signing some gibberish about, 'staying the same course.'"

Weet's hands meshed, his index fingers joined together as if bonded, stabbing the air, pointing at... Brooke stole a glance over his shoulder, and wrinkled his nose. Trees?

The commander clasped Weet's outstretched arms. The boy's skin felt cold and clammy, his muscles, rigid and unyielding as if they had atrophied, or flexed under impossible strain.

His legs proved the opposite: all-too-pliable, as though the bones had been removed altogether. The pup had also wet himself.

"Bring a blanket," Brooke instructed behind him. "And make a litter. We'll move Weet exactly as he is to the tent closest to my own."

When the makeshift palanquin of thatched sticks and a blanket had been set beside the afflicted mute, Gnor and Alghan gently placed him on it and lifted the gurney. The party set out for the centre of camp when something stopped them short. And made Brooke bite his lip.

In the orange flicker of the closest firelight, Weet's arms rotated like a compass needle as the two Nightwolves moved away from the site. His hands fixed on the same point in the woods.

"Back up," Brooke instructed. The pair did so.

Sure enough, Weet's arms returned to their initial position.

Gnolin shivered, his face blanching as he looked on.

"The pup's trying to tell us something," Brooke observed. *But what?* Years of experience taught Brooke not to disregard anything unusual, especially when in unfamiliar or hostile territory. "Summon Onis. Alghan, when you've secured the boy, I want a detail in this area to re-examine the direction Weet pointed at. And triple the watch everywhere else."

"Words unto deeds," Alghan replied with a curt nod.

After Weet had been bedded down properly, Alghan assisted Onis as he worked a salve into the boy's stricken appendages. By slow increments, the mute's arms surrendered their terseness and slackened. His eyes and mouth closed and his breathing evened.

"Never seen him like this," Gnolin croaked over their shoulder. "Not even the first time I met him—when Gramps brought him back."

Brooke lifted a brow. "Back? From where?"

Gnolin cleared his throat. "A steading, on the outskirts of a village where his family lived. They were attacked."

"What happened?"

"Weet was only five. Both his parents were butchered by a band of trolls, led by dark elven. He told me he dreamt about it that same night—

hours before it came to pass."

The hairs at the nape of Brooke's neck stood on end. "Go on."

"When he woke, he found his parents unharmed and dismissed the nightmare. All clammy from tossing in his sleep, Weet needed air and water. Rather than waking them, he tiptoed out of the cottage and down to a nearby stream. He planned to tell them about it in the morning."

Gnolin's chin quivered and his eyes glistened. "When he returned, the trolls had come for real. They strung up his parents while the dark elven put them to question. The elven grew angry about something and in a fit of rage cut his mother's throat to get Weet's father to talk."

Gnolin gulped and stared at his feet. "But he kept silent, even as the trolls feasted on her body right beside him. Then, they did the same thing to Weet's father. He never told them what they wanted. They slaughtered everyone in the village. Weet saw it all," Gnolin finished, his mouth trembling as he met Brooke's solemn gaze.

The air inside the tent cooled.

Brooke swallowed past the lump in his throat. He couldn't imagine witnessing the horror at such a young age. Stars, Gnolin's recount sounded harrowing enough. Guilt clenched the commander's heart at pressing the lad so. He placed a hand on Gnolin's shoulder. "Would you stay with your friend and assist Onis?"

Gnolin snorted and bobbed his head. "I'll not sleep until he wakes."

The boy's loyalty—his nobility—disarmed Brooke. The lump in his throat doubled in size. He had to work moisture into his mouth to speak. "Then, Weet will receive the best care. That said, pray get some sleep as well, Gnolin. I won't command you. But ask it out of concern."

Brooke left the tent, Alghan following behind.

"Stars," the commander grated, "if not for the pup's state, I'd have us strike the tents and leave this cursed tract at once." He tilted his head up to those same celestial light points, peeking out above the pines. "Alas, dawn will herald better prospects."

"Aye, Commander," Alghan agreed. "A wise course under the circumstances."

After some small talk of direction and deployment, Brooke retired. As he lay his head down, it occurred to him that he forgot to ask Gnolin about Weet's 'fear' business. Too late to question the pup now. He resolved to inquire come morning after Gnolin got some rest—and only then if the lad felt up to it.

Brooke's sleep troubled him with dreams of falling, pits of fire.

And traps within traps.

44: Quest—ion
Sonart

"*Rescue me?*" Sonart flared. "Cocks of a dozen Kworn to that." Balling his fists, he advanced on the tall figure. "And what in buggered hell is a wizard? Sounds like a molester of children. I heard en..." He skidded to a halt, his retort petering to silence as Gjen removed his hood.

This was no demon, but a stretched-out, near-beardless dwarven—a handsome one. His dark face bore a weathered sternness. Streaked with white strands, Gjen's brownish-grey mane hung shoulder-length, framing a straight nose and blue-green eyes.

As they fixed on Sonart, they exuded hardness, calm, and rectitude. A scar presented the only mar on the wizard's face. It cleft his chin past his right cheek up to his forehead.

Gjen floated his arm and pointed towards the corner of the room. Sonart followed the finger's direction—and gasped.

Seolad's sword lay on the floor there.

The wizard harrumphed. "Think you stuck the Zürshuck with that?"

It couldn't be.

"Aye," Gjen growled, though in good humour. "*That* sword did indeed belong to the son of Rusic. The blade you brought from your childhood home after your skirmish with my dwarven ally, the same weapon this foul creature knocked from your hand."

Gjen approached Sonart. Leaning on his staff, he dropped to one knee until their heads matched heights. "You did not recover it as you first thought. You retrieved something else—something much more valuable."

A pit formed in Sonart's stomach as realization dawned. "The Sword from the Cleft Augury!"

Crow's feet softening, Gjen smiled with his eyes. "One and the same. It has come to you before—several times in fact, only along magical tangents beyond your fluency. I seek to remedy that. Alas, in this instance, it only came to you out of primal need. Your survival instincts took over."

The dwarven shifted his attention from Seolad's weapon to the dead Zürshuck, and back to Gjen.

"As to the *correct* definition of a wizard," Gjen went on in a kindly voice, "let's say I know my way around the lore of my staff, and have some experience with the craft of magic—you do know what that is, I trust?" He arched an eyebrow.

Chagrin made Sonart's ears go hot, but he forced himself to nod.

"Good," Gjen laughed. "Then I won't have to begin your training with basic grammar. On that magical note, the dark powers have been busy of late, trying to thwart me and claim you. All the torment you've endured since your wilderen inception: becoming a pariah on errand, ousted by your own kind, has been done to limit your options when you claimed the talisman."

Gjen scratched the stubble on his chin. "This new order of Proclaimers, under the guise of policing your brethren and disrupting the efforts of the resistance, is merely a front. Their true purpose was to help find and undermine you."

Sonart cringed, remembering Shayla and her death at the hands of Seolad.

"The Kworn were partly component to that same effort," Gjen went on. "The Neglect Bessel spoke to you about happened shortly after your birth. Deathwrought put such a strain on your people to help flush you out. For your power would manifest when physically taxed so. He knew a Vein had come into his midst but even as a babe your wards included defences against detection. When his ploy reaped no prize, he changed tack and waited, letting your people regain their former health—and resume their work in the mines."

As Gjen spoke, Sonart sniffed at the dead Zürshuck strewn across the floor. The scorched odour began to tell. From the cauterized hole in the demon's chest, wisps of white vapour still trickled.

He had done that. But behind Sonart's amazement chased apprehension. *Mine eyes are your eyes.*

Gjen let out a wry chuckle, breaking the dwarven's doubt. "Your eyes will remain your eyes, if we keep true to each other, heed the prophecy—and honour the Scions' coven."

Sonart felt his cheeks colour. "Stars burn you, must you invade my mind as well?"

"No, Sonart," the wizard said firmly, "I only listen without incursion. You cast your thoughts like a wayward beacon. That can be a curse, but also a gift, known the length and breadth of Areth as *communion*. I seek only to enlighten you with your true purpose. In all solemnity, you have dwelt too long in the darkness. The time has come for your illumination."

Gjen stood to his full height. He waved his palm in a circular motion over the headpiece of his staff. The crown ignited with a brilliant light— exactly as the Kusp had done in Sonart's home.

When the glow ebbed, Gjen lowered his hand and with fingers splayed extended it towards the dwarven.

Sonart's breath caught as the warmth and ease and familiarity he first sensed in the wizard's presence increased into something wonderful. It nurtured his soul and erased all the soreness from his deadly fight with the

Zürshuck. A wispy sound filled his ears while his chest and midriff tautened.

Sonart looked down and gaped. The torn fabric the demon had rent from his tunic had sutured and all the grime and blood stains had been cleansed from his livery and person—not even a fleck of crust embedded his beard.

"Xoral is not long for this earth," said Gjen, drawing Sonart's regard. "But he hangs on yet—to shield you until I could take up his mantle. I have. Even now, I feel him slip away into the deepest sleep. But you will continue to elude the Darkest One's surveillance."

Gjen paused and gestured to the cellar's main door, still open from when Sonart first entered. "Ahead of your arrival, I conjured a ring of enchantment over this safehouse, like the one that protects the Golan Hob. But I've added something to the spell just now. It will shelter you wherever you tread henceforth."

Sonart blinked. "But the Zürshuck?"

"Was the last and it saw you flee from on high. Its master, on the other hand, cannot see you, or that which you see yourself. While you walk in my shadow, he can possess you no longer. But I'll not lie to you, Sonart. You will have to face his treachery again. When you do, I feel confident I can intervene on your behalf. And if we must separate, the better prepared you will be. Trust me: you'll *never* do evil in his name again."

"Trust? You know nothing," Sonart fired back, raising his walls anew. He could not put any faith in this one's words or parlour tricks. "I'm watched at every step. And any place that invokes an absence of sight only leads the Black Eye directly to it—as did the Hob."

"The Hob remains safe," Gjen maintained. "So too with Bessel and Wres."

"But not me," Sonart returned. "You do not know the price of serving as thrall to Him. You talk of facing the Darkest One like some thumb wrestle in a tavern."

Gjen's face tightened, his orbs growing stormy. "Do you think I speak lightly when I say it can be done?"

Sonart's throat clenched and he buried his head in his hands. "How can you illuminate that which is damned and doomed to die in darkness?"

"Nay, my friend," the wizard soothed. "Not if I can help it." With two fingers he lifted Sonart's chin until their eyes met. "And I can help a great deal."

Gjen pressed his lips together as he appraised Sonart. "Together, we shall embark on a great quest."

"Quest?" Sonart soured again. "What quest?"

"I have great need of your talents—and your emblem—to stem the tide of darkness. Forsooth, it sweeps far beyond the fortressed borders of the

Cradle, and the Whole of Areth, across all the realms of Creation under the stars. I speak of an apocalyptic event the Kusp foretells. The Starbond, it is named. Together, we will save Creation."

Sonart swallowed his bitterness. Like Mila, he had an inkling of the Starbond prophecy: the storm of storms. The Darkest One had mentioned it too—more than once. *... the nexus of the Starbond draws near. Can you not hear the storm winds build? ...when they reach gale strength, left unchecked, existence shall cease.*

Outwardly Sonart could only stare at Gjen. He seemed coherent enough but his proposal—the convoluted ravings of an Afflicted.

The dwarven's hackles rose, enough to make the bile he recently forced down his throat to come back up. "And just like that, I'm supposed to drop everything here and throw in with you?"

The wizard said nothing, his face a blank slate.

"You know what I think?" Sonart derided, his croak sharpening. "I think you're false—another crony full of mischief. You seek to subvert under the guise of making mock—so Deathwrought can reclaim me. The Cradle brims with shite. I don't need to add yours to my growing pile."

Sonart strode over to Seolad's blade, hoisted it up. And slammed it home in its scabbard. "Fuck your quest."

Lips aquiver, arms folded like a barricade, Sonart stomped past the self-proclaimed wizard, his scowl daring the bizarre doomsayer to stop him.

Gjen only stepped back and let him pass. Sonart reached the top of the stairs without incident. Once through the doorway, he dashed out into the night.

On the darkened street, Sonart's thoughts raced ahead of his legs. He half-expected the stranger to assail him as he fled, but he didn't. So much for Gjen being Rusic's answer.

Three blocks later, Sonart slowed his pace. The dimming's witching hour harboured many stalkers, of which he must needs be wary: Afflicted, Proclaimers, Kworn, Zürshuck.

But the streets remained empty. He continued alone.

And the damned always walked alone. Always.

So adamant about salvaging his sorry existence, Sonart had blinded himself to the one true course that could erase his pain for good. The solution was simple. He hadn't fully considered crossing that line but this latest encounter tore him past his breaking point. Sonart of Farkshone would let it all go. Fight no more. He would set *out*, immediately.

With the Innereach mountains looming above the tops of the city's buildings, it proved easy to get his bearing. He only had to keep moving away from the granite sentinels.

Within a half-turn of the dial, Sonart passed the outskirts of Bulkforge, the undesired parts of the city, less cramped, more exposed. Shelters that might've served as a refuge from a razor storm grew infrequent. Soon, only dilapidated stables lingered—a heap of discarded structures, one storm away from being flattened.

For the taking, the buildings were, but he'd fare just as well in the open—if he'd been of a mind to survive. Sonart trudged past, not breaking stride until he arrived at the lip of the escarpment. There, he paused, absorbing the endless expanse of sand beyond the plateau. Let the horrors of the Lobe take him, and not soon enough it would be. All would be resolved.

Sonart started down the bluff, his footfalls heavy and jarring as he slogged its craggy defiles. The trenches deepened as they bled away from the Steppe's flat top, towards the vast grave of the Lobe's shifting dunes.

Shadows clung to the fissures, shielding Sonart from the crimson glow of the River Seething's many forks. Their molten flow generated an aura across the plateau that reflected off the clouds. The afterglow chased darkness over the dips of the Innereach and kept full gloom away every dimming. If he let his guard down, the light would find him, and like as not, the scrutiny of the Four and their master.

One adversary at a time. Eyes down, Sonart concentrated on his feet as he neared the uneven ground at the bottom—lest he trip and sprain something. No half-measures. It must end utterly.

When his boot imprinted its first swathe of sand, Sonart looked up—and collided with a tall figure silhouetted against the scarlet dunes.

Gjen—!

Long arms encircled Sonart, gripping his shoulders like manacles. It was all he could do not to scream. How the spectre had gotten ahead of him, he could not fathom. Then again, he'd been clever enough to evade Deathwrought for an impressive stretch.

"So, you want no part of my quest," Gjen said, his calm tone full of irony. "Yet you found the gumption to embark on it anyway. Or have you conjured one on your own? Pray tell, what might it be—a form of escape perhaps?"

Sonart gritted his teeth. "I only wish to escape you, and my pain, which presently takes the form of you. Impetuous Zürshuck with plucked wings, I name you."

Gjen clicked his tongue. "The deepest sleep is no answer."

"Yes, it is," Sonart shot back. "So, unless you want to expedite my quest, Wizard, get out of my bloody way."

"That is the last thing I want," his captor replied earnestly. "In fact, I shall release you."

When the towering demon did, Sonart promptly started walking.

"But," Gjen said, falling into lockstep beside him, "as it so happens, we share the same route. And I could sorely use some company. So, might as well join your merry jaunt."

Sonart skidded to a halt and stomped his boot in the sand. The move cupped grains into his shoe's collar and pushed hot blood to his temples. "Hooks and Dunge, this is my path, old man. Find your own, lest you draw the Darkest One's doom. I advise you, Gjen, and whatever the rest of your irksome name, I cannot control what I've become. Haranguing me will only hasten His rout of you. This is my choice, my quest—and your last warning. Or do you wish to end yourself as well?"

"Again, my troubled friend, on my ladder of goals this night, I'd place that notion one step below my bottom rung."

Sonart groaned and plodded on. For several moments, only the *shuh-shuh, shuh-shuh, shuh-shuh* of his footfalls in the sand made any sound.

"As you probably know," Gjen said behind him, "there's no turning back now. You can only move forward until the traps of the Lobe or the denizens of the Outereach consume you. Or—you can take your chances with me. I'll not steer you away from your course, seeing you've no desire to turn from it."

"Finally," Sonart grumbled, seizing two handfuls of his auburn beard. "An accord."

"The first of many," the wizard quietly vaunted. "I promise that the stars will align between you and me, like no two celestial orbs ever have. I can see you through and beyond—far beyond."

Sonart threw his hands up. "Riddles!"

"No riddles!" Gjen flashed. "Truth, Son of Farkshone." He took a deep breath and slowly deflated his chest. "Whether you like it or not, your role remains: You are a Vein—nothing can change that. The sooner you embrace it, the better. I can help you understand everything—if you let me."

Gjen lifted his staff—his *staff*? Sonart flinched as the wizard inspected it, hood shifting in line with its headpiece. The sceptre was not in his possession when he intercepted Sonart at the bottom of the bluff.

"But, if you opt not to acknowledge it," Gjen pressed, "Deathwrought will surely help himself to you. Either way, you live and die a Vein of Fire. Either way the blade will cut, but as a Blood Scion, you must decide which way, and how deep."

Sonart's frown cracked his defensive walls some. Hearing Xoral's words repeated by Gjen disarmed him. He tapped his fist against his lips, resolve wavering. But distrust and anger kept him steadfast, and he hastened his march.

Gjen matched it. "Ask yourself, how I could've known about the Sword, or the Kusp's secret message that led you to Bulkforge and the haven of Bessel's Golan Hob, about Xoral's sacrifice, and his words? Did he not refer to me as the tall one? And what of Bessel? Did he not say that you'd soon meet your true redeemer—an outlier of kindred might?"

Sonart gulped. He had no riposte.

"I know, Sonart because with the likes of Seolad, Xoral, and Bessel, we carefully mapped out your rescue long before this night. You have nothing to lose by hearing me out, except the prison of your self-imposed ignorance."

That stopped Sonart. Tears welled up in his eyes. "The weight crushes me, Gjen," he sobbed. "If I become nothing, I'll have nothing left to lose, and I will not care."

"I understand," Gjen relented, inclining his head. "But the truth is, you do care. Overwhelmed by obstacles that would've crumpled the strongest champion, you feel helpless—enough to seek death as your escape."

Gjen raised his hands in a placating gesture. "But what if I offered you another way to escape him? To right the many wrongs he must answer for?"

Sonart sniffed back through his nasal passages and rubbed his arms. "I would call you a liar."

"If you persist and won't hear reason, you would force me to lie—about giving up on you—something I would never do."

Silence.

"So, here we are," Gjen said. "I will accompany you, and see what happens. In sooth, I hadn't planned to leave Grendamaul so hastily and ill-prepared. But in truth, I *was* heading in this direction—I swear that on your father's good name."

The wind briefly gusted, filling the awkward moment with a passing curtain of sand. When the particle-speckled breeze abated, Sonart wiped his face and continued more calmly. "No more hectoring, traps, or surprises. You will not stop me."

Much to his vexation, Gjen laughed. "On the contrary, I shall impel you to go. I would push, even drag you kicking and screaming. I only ask that we take a few provisions, and a few precautions, to facilitate your quest. Please, come back with me. We will be off soon enough—a matter of a day—um, drear, two at most. I promise."

The dwarven wandered three steps to his left, swept his gaze over the sandy expanse, and rejoined his companion. "I'm listening."

Gjen nodded. "Good. We can face our doom as the Kusp divines we should—together. We won't tarry, searching blindly throughout the villages and towns of the Cradle, or a chance death in the Lobe. Stars, might as well do it right the first time with 'no half-measures,' in the Void of Obliteration."

"Uh——*what?*" Sonart froze and narrowed his eyes, sensing a smile hidden in the shadows of the tall one's hood. Clearly, this Gjen was an eccentric provocateur, who spoke in frustrating semi-truths. But for him to offer a better plan for ending Sonart's despair... the dwarven began to suspect this *wizard* was madder than himself.

When Gjen placed his hand on Sonart's shoulder, the dwarven felt the same magnetic buoying sensation lift his soul and crisp his clairvoyance as when they first met—only much stronger. All at once, his walls came down and he surrendered a chuckle. Either plan carried a surety that the crazed conjurer would never leave his side.

They turned back.

45: Lorin
Targin

Targin lumbered out of bed and wrapped himself in a finespun silken robe that dropped below his knees. Next, he donned a pair of slippers that had been laid out for him.

For a moment, he regretted asking Tasmin's hand in marriage. But then remembered why and his mood softened towards her. His mental turmoil over that inexorable woman expunged, he returned to his jovial self. And indeed, his thoughts immediately shifted toward Thrumvedur.

Still somewhat lightheaded, the Nightwolf made his way to the door, into the foyer, and past the protesting nurses. He timed it perfectly—so the kraken, Bruna would not be there to add her substantial weight to the press.

By the time he started his march down the well-lit corridors, his mind had cleared of its fog and his stride quickened.

The soldiers and sentries he passed en route to the stables acknowledged him with brightening looks, bows, and salutes. He responded in kind with nods, smiles, brisk courtesies, and the odd quip over his bedroom attire being Serenthia's new formal dress. Such displays of recovery would go a long way.

Crowds of civilians, merchants, and tradesmen proved too busy handling or exchanging their wares to pay him any notice. That they went about their business also boded well with Targin. It meant everything remained normal.

His path led him into a central vestibule supported by monstrous columns. The vast enclosure had been partly hewn from a magnificent crystalline cavern. Gem-veined rocks basked the space in azure light.

Engineered from days long past, the translucent formations channelled sunlight through fissures far up at the surface. Fires burned in six-foot-wide hearths, set at regular intervals along the various warrens and squares. Their warm glow tempered the crystals' cool nimbus. Combined, the two auras balanced one another and filled the chasm with daylight.

Trees and flowers such as jasmine, gardenia, and alyssum proliferated, adapted to the underground sanctuary. They flourished in every alcove and garden, filling the space with colour and fresh scents.

In the centre of the esplanade, an enormous fountain, five storeys high, shot jets of water twice its height into the air. The stone construct flaunted four glorious statues of warrior Highprites. The figures faced outward from the central column to match the four main points of a compass rose. Each warrior bore a different stone weapon and shield, indicative of the Lines of

Blood and the Four Veins of Fire.

Their sculpted granite capes appeared to flow with the movement of the water as it cascaded down their length. Into a circular basin, the water pooled around the Highprites' sandaled feet.

Several smaller statues of men, horses, wolves and warbirds filled the gaps between the titanic colossi.

The rushing water sounded like a symphony to Targin's ears. He paused to admire Serenthia's masterwork, heart gladdening as his eyes drank in the dwarven-wrought grandeur. Worthy of the heraldry and proud history of the kingdom that never fell.

His latest tryst with his betrothed all but forgotten, Targin reined in his devotion and continued his march. He left the main concourse and turned down a straight thoroughfare. It tunnelled another four hundred feet before widening into a higher cavern than the first. This enclosure served as a hub.

It encircled a dais, adjoining several alcoves scalloped into the high walls. They all marked the mouths of branching tunnels.

Targin took the second tunnel on the right. Thirty feet in, he came to a spiral staircase. Several winding flights brought him down to the garrison landing.

The Nightwolf strode along another long corridor, past several cavalrymen, ostlers, and wingward flyers. His slippers made a shushing clamour against the uneven stone that drew the soldiers' attention. Anxious to be reunited with his avian steed, Targin kept his eyes downcast.

His anticipation mounted as he drew up to an arcade with a high-vaulted ceiling. The space was larger and darker than the other precincts, but he didn't need much light. Targin simply followed his ears and nose past the musky smell of the horse stables and pup kennels, to the aviary.

The familiar odour of bird guano and grain assailed Targin's nostrils as he pushed through the set of massive swinging doors. The air thickened with humidity from all the rooks and raptors. Hundreds of stalls lined the walls of the vast passage, most occupied by giant hawks.

Their squawks and occasional shrieks created a constant din as they conversed with one another in their avian speech.

Giant bails of grass stacked against every inch of available wall space, while troughs filled with carrion and feed occupied their own section at the far end of the enclosure.

A dozen stable boys milled about. They cleaned the pens with corn brooms, pushed wheelbarrows filled with provender, spread fresh hay with pitchforks, or groomed and tended the hawks.

Here, every face looked familiar. Many of the lads stopped their chores to give Targin an enthusiastic wave or call out to him. None of the stable boys commented on his strange attire, nor would they.

In this den, Targin truly belonged.

Two-thirds of the way down the corridor, the Nightwolf found Thrumvedur, occupying the aviary's largest pen. The raptor's tail was to him, but as his master rounded the stall's open gate, the hawkrike surged to his taloned feet, spun, and squawked a loud greeting.

Judging by the brightness of the raptor's preened feathers and the alertness in his sharp pupils, he'd been well cared for.

Targin's pent-up tension evaporated as he came alongside, reached up, and fanned a palm over the warbird's plumage. Together, they shared a lucid moment.

A shadow fell across the coop behind them, interrupting their communion. Targin looked back. The flare of a sconce's crystal light behind the figure cast his lithe form in silhouette. But Targin recognized his medium-set carriage and easy stance.

"Hello Lorin," Targin hailed in a tired but not unkind voice.

"As Queen Atheri promised, you do recover quickly, stars align." The ranger strode in and clasped Targin about the shoulders. "It is good to see you on your feet." His gaze dropped. "Nice robe."

"You noticed."

"It doesn't take a veteran scout long to notice such oddities. If it did, he wouldn't be a scout for very long."

"Good to see you too," Targin said with a chuckle. "But I wouldn't call three weeks unconscious a quick recovery."

"I had cause for concern," Lorin confessed. "First time in the long years we've served together that you fell."

Targin blew out his cheeks. "If you only knew."

"Sent a spike of dismay throughout the Hidden Kingdom."

The Nightwolf laughed. "Sorry, I'll try to be more considerate next time."

"I suppose even a Vein of Fire can be tested," Lorin said. "As for my own trial, if not for Her Grace, I think it would've come to blows with that impetuous hen of a head nurse."

"Bruna?"

Lorin nodded. "The ruthless harridan chased me away from your side. Queen Atheri offered kind assurances to mollify me, but after tending to Thrum here, I returned in the dead hour. Twas Tasmin I found kneeling by your bedside. She promised she'd keep vigil and never allow the deepest sleep to claim you. Only then, could I return to peace."

Targin turned away to hide his grimace. Guilt coursed through him over his harsh words with the princess.

Lorin seemed to sense it all the same. He touched Targin's arm, drawing his attention. "Tasmin's been securing the forest roads, allowing food trains to reach the frontier villages along our southern borders. In your absence, they've been repeatedly hammered. Not just the usual minions, mind you. Evidence and testimonies confirm: lavatrols have beset our lands.

Targin jerked his head back. "Lavatrols? They're relegated to the blight of Marwolaeth. They've never been south of the Land of Fire, let alone the Ice Wastes which entomb it. Not even during the Ages of Ice, not *ever*, Lorin."

The ranger inclined his head. "Who knows what anomalies to prophecy usurp the natural laws ahead of the Starbond? The Endstorm draws nigh, Targin. The skies will open soon."

The Nightwolf exhaled. "Ever true you speak, my friend. And always the hard truth—for which I both hate and respect you beyond measure. Tell me all of it, please."

Lorin took a position on Thrumvedur's opposite flank and stroked the hawkrike's feathers beneath his wing. "I'd been on a routine ranging patrol when I came upon the devastation of the latest attack. It was bad. Corpses turned to ash. Villages razed, consumed... stars, the very earth turned to molten glass. I communed with my rooks to make all haste and bring word to King Johlarin. Tasmin came at once in force, with a contingent of her father's troops—three heelwards supported by an entire wingward."

Lorin drifted to Thrum's crest and preened it gently. He tilted his head up at the hawkrike's orbs. The warbird regarded him docilely. "Tasmin believed the villages' destruction, a ruse with the enemy still close at hand, waiting for her men to secure the villages. That they'd launch another covert attack while her troops' backs were turned. Rather than concentrate on securing the refugees in the village ruins, she conscripted the survivors and took the fight to the attackers before they could regroup."

Thrum's neck craned right. He gently plucked at a few errant feathers along his shoulder ridge.

"So, was she right?" Targin asked.

Lorin dipped his chin. "While the hawks flew sorties, communing with the ground troops, Tasmin blanketed the area with traps and sentries armed with dragon eggs—you'll recall how volatile those can be."

"Too well. Spifer reminds me every chance he gets."

"Ah then, the pyromancer would have loved this," Lorin chortled before the earnestness returned to his face. "Tasmin set the rules of engagement and used them to their greatest efficacy."

Lorin bestowed his admiration for the woman without reservation. "We routed and slew the attackers to the last foe, but before we put the final goblin to the sword, he confirmed what Tasmin suspected, and more."

Targin slanted forward, his throat going dry.

Lorin met his stare. "The assaults on the villages and caravan routes had been part of a greater campaign against Serenthia—their true objective."

Targin swallowed. "What did the cretin reveal?"

"He declared Johlarin's kingdom was already lost, that no matter what we did, it would fall next. The Princess concluded the attack had not been thwarted—and is only just begun."

"All fates face the Starbond," Targin said absently. His regard lifted to the hawkrike's fierce countenance.

"The situation remains grave," Lorin said beside him. "But Tasmin sought to address the villagers' more immediate needs first. The common folk feared reprisals, so she had them relocated to other centres and saw the defences of those villages bolstered. Left garrisons at each accompanied by rooks to relay warning and maintain surveillance over the entire tract."

"Johlarin's daughter is a shrewd one," Targin allowed past the catch in his throat. "Wise moves, the lot."

"Her arrangements satisfied the villagers and men-at-arms," Lorin said. "But not Tasmin. Worry over our borderlands haunts her still. She lingered to survey the network of roads on horseback, while I ranged the surrounding forest on foot. Tasmin planned for us to stay at it for another month or so."

When Lorin paused, the Nightwolf returned his gaze to the scout.

"But then, message of your dire return came. Tasmin and I met and thundered away, sharing her mount, several days' beeline to clear the skirts of the forest. She summoned a hawk and flew back at once. I took her horse and, after communing what delegations I might, made all haste in her wake. For the time being, I'm confident she's left the borderlands in relative safety. Truly Targin, you found your match in your betrothed."

Targin ran a hand through his hair and gave Lorin a slight bow of admission. More percolated beneath the scout's words than he let on, but if Lorin deemed something safe, then it was beyond any doubt.

"Ever distrustful, you're not one to delegate swiftly," Targin said. "And I know how you loathe burdening any animal to carry you unless absolutely necessary."

Lorin idly kicked at a clump of hay that had covered his boot. "I scout swiftly, think swiftly, but I'll not delegate so—if at all."

Targin raised an eyebrow. "You must trust in others and divest some responsibility in order to lead."

The scout lifted his shoulders. "I do not wish to lead any man, but myself."

"Why is that?"

Lorin narrowed his eyes. "Life's taught me to place my trust in the only person I know will never let me down. Me."

"A lonely existence, no?"

The ranger shook his head. "Nay and never my friend. I have the best companions—the creatures of the forest." He started, then swallowed, as though remembering something he'd neglected.

"And—one old hermit," Lorin added astride a slow exhalation. "Quite dear to me, this wise elderling—he's become somewhat of a mentor."

"Indeed? Pray tell."

"He lives in a humble log cabin north of our gates. Shares my love of nature and animals and vaunts their truth and authenticity. Such traits compel him and me to live the way we do amongst them. Animals seem immune to the duplicity that attaints so many freeborn. My furry friends act as they always have—with sincerity, purity, and gut instinct."

"Animals, I understand and trust. And your reclusive friend sounds a lot like my own mentor." Targin cocked his head and laughed. "So, now I know the true reason why you've evaded my repeated requests to join the Nightwolves! All this time, I had thought it was because you don't trust me!"

"That stands. Stars, I trust you least of all." Lorin grinned. "As much as I respect Brapin's counsel and all that your band does, I'd never fit into that hierarchy."

Targin admired the ranger's independent mind. Conversations with Lorin always proved a boon—for the man's refreshing point of view if nothing else. Perhaps that was why, of all Targin's many associates, Lorin was the only one whom Tasmin openly approved.

Targin placed his hand on the ranger's shoulder. "I appreciate your reasons, Brother. But if you ever change your mind…"

Lorin met his gaze. "Aye?"

"I'd exempt you from any initiation," Targin said. "You've already earned twice the highest echelon among the pack."

"Thank you, but again no," Lorin replied.

"Then by the stars," Targin said. "Tend your sibling creatures. Range the forested domain—continue to keep it safe for us. May your special path be swift and free of burden."

Lorin gave a courteous bow. "I do yearn to return to the forest—my rightful domain. Ere long, I'll tend to its denizens." He let out a heavy sigh. "And now that you've jogged my memory, I must pay my wise friend an overdue visit."

The ranger gave Targin a long look from the corner of his eye. "But if I may say so, Targin, I believe your path must also be swift, towards your chamber. Go, tend to her."

When the Nightwolf crossed his brawny arms, Lorin quickly put in, "Thrum's a mighty steed. I took the hawkrike under my wing during your recovery. It will be no great task to watch over him a little while longer—ensure his full recuperation to my own lofty satisfaction."

"You've clearly shown Thrum the same love and care as I, and for that, you have my thanks." Targin deflated his chest. "But Tasmin's the one in need of repair. I cannot even emerge from the hospice before I'm made small in front of my own subjects by her scathing diatribes. She's beyond mending, I fear. Or at least in need of more sutures than I can stitch. Damn it all, how can I care for the daemon that dwells in her mind? Forever a mystery to someone practical like me."

"More the reason why you must go, Targin. To be more *impractical*. You may live to reevaluate your regard for her." Lorin spoke plainly with no lilt of accusation, but it caught the Nightwolf off-guard all the same.

"That is bold," Targin growled as he leaned in. "Even for you."

Lorin shrugged, "I only say what you need to hear. Practical words for a practical man. Want my advice, swallow your stubborn pride and begin the healing forthwith. It grieves me to see you at odds with one another. Such a state of upheaval between two of my closest."

"You needn't worry for me."

"Aye, but there's Tasmin to consider."

Targin flushed with anger and forced himself to look away. After a moment, he let it pass. "Your words administer bitter medicine to my ears, but stars burn you, Lorin, I'll heed your counsel. Take care of my bird."

When Lorin ran his hand up Thrum's neck, the hawkrike's beak lowered to meet it. The scout scratched the small tuft of down just below, drawing a rare avian smile from the raptor and a purr. "Your steed will be treated equal to the eagles we house."

Targin blinked. "Eagles?"

He spun his head left and right. "Here?" His ire resurfaced, before vaulting off the ground. "Why?"

"Greater machinations come into play in light of recent events—some of which even you and I remain unaware."

"Unaware, or not privy, cause Lorin, I'm mindful of much. Why wasn't I informed sooner? Such notice could have easily been communed to me. If we stable eagles here, then stars burn my scrotum black, their fucking girly riders can't be far behind."

"They're here."

Targin finally snapped. "What in seven fucks for?"

"Council—I believe you were alerted of that much. The elven arrived yesterday and His Grace hearkens to hear their tidings."

"King Johlarin summoned me to the council, aye. Whom to counsel, no." The Nightwolf gritted his teeth and balled his fist so tightly his knuckles cracked. "When is this farce?"

"Tomorrow," Lorin answered. "Will you attend?"

"Aye," Targin grated. "I'll bloody well be there. Someone in touch with reality has to filter their pompous honey-taint. Besides, Johlarin would not think kindly of me if I skipped the party just to spite them."

"Perhaps you could... return to Bruna," Lorin quipped. "Feign a relapse of your malady."

"Or bed in the lake depths with the centipus," Targin seethed. He let out a sonorous breath, shoulders sagging. "Pray, tell me you have no more pleasant surprises to further darken my mood this eventide?"

"Only if you don't attend your lady," Lorin laughed.

Targin sniggered and clapped the scout on the back. "I don't know what's worse—mincing words with flowery elven twats or dealing with the she-wolf's verbal claws."

"I think you know the answer to that question," the ranger said.

"Indeed. Well then, I'd better face the princess tonight and find out what I'm up against. The sooner for it to be over."

"May I offer you a small suggestion?" the scout asked.

Targin waited.

"Flowers—wild trinsic—they're her favourite. A few shops along the main arcade still carry them this time of year."

Targin chortled. "They're her favourite because I always pick them for her when I'm afield in the hinterland."

"Yes," Lorin agreed. "I know."

The Nightwolf raised his hands in mock defence. "All right, all right you rascal, now I beg you no more cunning words. Take care, my friend. I'll see you on the morrow."

Lorin smiled and Targin turned his attention back to Thrum. He slid a hand under the hawkrike's folded wing. The raptor softly trilled his tongue. "With Lorin at your service, your return to the skies will be swifter than the wounds to my pride. Farewell"

He took Lorin in with his eyes. "Both of you."

46: Enlightenment
Sonart

With dawn less than a dial-turn from breaking, Sonart and Gjen entered the safehouse. The wizard had disposed of the Zürshuck's body before he tracked Sonart down, and apart from a hole in the wall, nary a trace of the demon's presence remained. Not even a whiff of the burning odour.

Confusion chained Sonart, but Gjen's words had made sense, and his assurances that their return to the refuge would go unnoticed proved true.

Upon entering this time, Gjen locked the door behind them and added a thick metal crossbar. "For good measure," he said.

Gjen showed Sonart to a room where a simple cot awaited. Covered in earthen tone blankets atop a grey linen sheet and straw pillow—nothing ever looked so inviting.

In tired silence, Sonart removed his boots and the scabbard that still held Seolad's blade. Not bothering to undress further, he lay his head down on the pillow and fell fast asleep.

For the first time in his existence, he slept without dreams.

Sonart awoke to a drear's pale light. After donning his boots and sword belt, he lumbered into the main hall to find Gjen slouched over a small wooden table, arms folded atop. His face appeared haggard, pronounced circles underscoring his eyes. Had the wizard slept at all?

Gjen's gaze lifted as the dwarven approached. "I have good news, Sonart. It is done. While you slept, I severed the link and collapsed the tunnel through which the Darkest One bore down on you. His taint has been completely exorcised from your essence."

Sonart frowned and tilted his head to one side. "Exorcised?"

Gjen gripped his chin and nodded. "Expunged—removed and blocked from re-entering your mind."

Sonart blinked, not daring to believe it. At length, his cynicism croaked on his behalf, "For the moment." He looked around. Gjen had removed the crossbar from the door, but it remained closed. "What is the turn?"

"Three hours—sorry, turns of the dial, past midday, your mid-drear."

"Considering all that happened yester-drear, I didn't get much rest. Strangely, I do not feel tired."

"A very good sign," said Gjen. "A hardening constitution under duress heralds a Vein's rising strength. Twas the same for me. Mind you, the seed of that power took root with your birth. When you feel the draw of the Starbond more acutely, your emblem's presence will flourish."

Sonart sat down to a meal of nut-encrusted bread and... orange cheese? His mouth formed a circle and when his eyes sought the wizard, Gjen chuckled. "No, I did not bring a cow or goat with me. Tis an elven trick conjured from a charmed powder they concoct. Sadly, I used the last of my store for that brick. Consider it your first taste of freedom."

Sonart cut a wedge, took a nibble, and smiled as he savoured the tangy morsel. "I've not had such fare since my imprisonment."

"Yes, I know," Gjen said.

After he had supped, Sonart cradled a mug of hot herbal tea Gjen had prepared for him. Its woody scent filled the room with a soothing aroma.

While Sonart sipped the mossy concoction of bitters, the wizard piled kindling onto a small hearth. With a subtle wave of his hand, blue fire sprang from his digits to the fuel. And the pyre ignited into a crackling blaze.

Sonart formed a second O with his lips, though only to blow lightly over the tea to help it cool. "So, my power grows?"

"Aye."

"Is that why you said I would not need this one ever again?" Sonart gestured to Seolad's blade.

"Yes and no," Gjen replied as he rejoined Sonart by the table. "Your power is surely a factor, but it is the Sword you've yet to master with that might—that marks the real reason. The weapon hidden inside you serves as your emblem to focus your wilderen magic. The limitless power of the First Father and Creator. Vamsah."

Vamsah? Sonart started. "What is—"

Gjen raised a hand. "Perhaps we should not get ahead of ourselves. Let's begin with your experiences in the Cleft Augury."

"I'm not so sure the Augury is real," Sonart confessed as he sipped his tea. "Every time, I'd been in the State—a ghost travelling outside my corporeal form. Deathwrought interrogated me about it, tortured me, slaughtered any prisoners in the Dunge who shared a glimpse of it. In truth, I do not understand its purpose."

Gjen placed his palms together as though in prayer. "The Cleft Augury represents Deathwrought's greatest threat, housing the one weapon that can instigate his undoing. It therefore garners his greatest malevolence. The Augury is precisely that: a place of Creation—both forum and fount of all the wilderen energy inherent in every Verse."

Sonart wrinkled his nose and gulped his tea, more confused than before the wizard began his bizarre explanation.

"The Cleft also serves as an omnidirectional portcullis," Gjen elaborated, "to all the stars across the cosmos and the nether regions beyond—the planes of the gods."

"Gods?" Sonart harrumphed latching onto the one word he actually understood, and sputtering a few hot drops for his effort. They formed beads on the table. "To speak thus of the Darkest One and the stars is heresy of the highest order, Gjen. A sacrilege against the Kusp carries a penalty of death. The tome plainly states, 'Deathwrought is the one and only true god.'"

Gjen bit his lip and gave Sonart a long look. "What know you of the stars, pray tell?"

Sonart lifted his shoulders, recalling that he knew something of those too. "Fabled constructs lost in the eternal clouds far above the Cradle—I've never laid eyes upon them. No dwarven has. Though the Kusp does speak of them."

"And what exactly does the Kusp say?" Gjen asked, pinching the bridge of his nose.

"Long ago, Reechabah's Colossals sacrificed part of their essence to assemble bastions with their darkling light. Stars, they were named, warding the Cradle against menaces that lurk within the Void of Obliteration. The Outereach offers us this same protection. Ever these terrors seek to destroy us from beyond. The written psalms refer to one called 'the Second' as the most nefarious."

The fire in the hearth popped loudly, snapping Sonart's attention as a cinder launched towards the ceiling. When the pyre resumed its crinkling din, the dwarven went on. "Stars align when we become 'One with the Kusp.' We pay homage to the stars in all matters. Our existence would not be possible without them." He shifted his regard back to the wizard. "We must fear and obey them."

"Fear and—?" Gjen made a gruff sound before shaking his head. "Seems your imprisonment has not been limited to the pits of the Dunge. The entire Cradle is a Dunge—of the mind. The dwarven race has been suppressed by an epoch of lies and half-truths. It will make it difficult to redeem them before the Starbond. But redeem them we must."

Gjen let out a deep breath and rubbed the back of his neck. "Trust that what I'm about to tell you offers the Kusp-truth. It most certainly will sound heretical, outlandish, even painful to hear. But I swear it will only be the truth I impart this eventide. Will you hear it?"

Sonart shifted in his chair, feeling a tingling sensation at the base of his spine. He hesitated before meeting the wizard's scrutiny. "Aye, Gjen, you have my ears."

"Now listen carefully: stars are in no way evil. And no indentured servant of the Four created them. The powers that work in the cosmos far exceed what you or I could fathom. Countless worlds beyond our own. Areth forms one such world, of which Grendamaul—the Cradle—occupies but one isolated landmass. Our world is a sphere, and the Cradle rests upon its underbelly. Stars—are immense celestial globes floating on an astral plane."

Sonart finished his tea and brought the mug down on the table harder than he intended. "But the Void of Obliteration maintains a constant peril. It encroaches on the Cradle, and if not for the Outereach, we'd all be consumed by nothingness."

Gjen exhaled. "If that were true, then I too am nothing, for I crossed your Void to collect you."

Sonart's jaw drifted down, his beard mopping some of the liquid he spilled on the table.

The wizard pursed his lips and leaned back in his chair until it creaked. With a sigh, he tilted his head up and studied the darkening ceiling. "It has evidenced a void of sorts, as far as Grendamaul's dwarven are concerned—an abyss of ignorance." His eyes found Sonart again. "But no longer. You shall be the first drop of water that reawakens the ocean."

"Why?"

Gjen fished out a pipe from the folds of his robe. "As I said before, there are unfathomable powers at work. What I know describes but the tip of the iceberg."

Sonart threw up his hands. "Ocean! Iceberg! Why do you conjure terms I cannot possibly comprehend?"

"I warned you," Gjen laughed as he began stuffing his briar with weed from a small leather pouch. "When we arrive in safer lands you will learn much and more of these things, but time is of the essence. Your beliefs have been ingrained to aid Deathwrought's purpose, and to feed your naivety. As to your importance, it remains beyond paramount. The First Father chose you, me, and two others like us. I warrant you know nothing about him either—nothing correct in any case."

Sonart began to shake his head and stopped in sudden realization. "Atop the Hive, the Darkest One mentioned the First Father… called him Vamsah. Said I would be 'instrumental in his dark plan,' that he planted a seed in me to spread poison fruit. Left unchecked, existence shall cease."

"The Darkest One described himself," Gjen spat, emphasizing the point with a flick of his unlit pipe. "To confound you of his designs. As writ in the uncorrupted Kusp of the Testament, Vamsah is all-benevolent, the Creator who fathered the children of Areth, and her Sister. Alas, the actual theological doctrine has been perverted here in the Cradle—its truths twisted. Vamsah has existed since the beginning of time and set the laws of the Universe into motion."

"You need not add *Universe* to your list of befuddlements," Sonart put in. "That term's in the Kusp. Then again, as you say…"

Gjen grinned. "The Universe, which they falsely led you to believe was a Void, is in fact an infinite realm filled with uncountable fiery orbs called *stars*, worlds that encircle them, energies, and magics that hold it all together."

Sonart found himself nodding at the wizard's explanation. What Gjen said resonated—insofar as the Kusp's falsehoods. Lies, Sonart had swallowed his whole existence.

"But within that scope, you cannot generate light, without also creating shadow," Gjen pointed out. He stood and walked to the hearth. "Linked and counterpoint to Vamsah's birth, an antithesis of purest evil manifested—initially in another sentience of the most ancient sort, then passed onto, or rather meshed into the Darkest One. Likewise, with Vamsah's Creation: its conception brought into existence a polar opposite."

"The Void?" Sonart ventured.

"Precisely," Gjen sounded impressed as he inserted a twig into the fire and held it there. "Now, presiding over all reality, a duality exists: good versus evil, light to dark."

When the twig caught a tongue of flame, Gjen used it to light his pipe. After two long puffs, he continued. "By the nature of his inception, Deathwrought is innately riven with hate towards the First Father and that which he created. Ever and anon his malice takes myriad forms, eternally bent on destroying Vamsah and usurping the Balance of Creation to the ever-dark."

"When you said outlandish, I didn't think to take you at your literal word," Sonart chortled. He inhaled deep as the arboreal scent of the wizard's tobacco found his nose. "But better antithetical, uncanny, and true than an accepted mendacity."

Gjen offered a warm smile but it faded as he returned to the table and sat down. "The Cleft is a place in the centre of the Universe which binds the forces that keep us in this—" Between his thumb and forefinger, the wizard gently pinched Sonart's forearm, "—solid form. Think of it as the heart in the body of Creation."

Gjen's gaze held Sonart. "That Heart is dying. And as the veins of your body carry blood back into the heart—"

"I am that Vein," Sonart finished for him. He took a deep breath. "One among four, sharing a common purpose."

"Aye, we do," Gjen agreed as he took a long draw from his pipe and let the cloud escape. "Together we grow stronger than the sum of our parts."

Sonart chewed his lip as he pondered. "Is that why I feel an upwell of strength and clarity in your presence?"

"Forsooth, my good dwarven, as I feel in yours," Gjen said.

"The Darkest One said that as a Vein I'd bleed fire for Him. Shayla knew that name, as did Bessel. The Afflicted Ones in my dreams called me Vein, begging me to save them. The hidden message I read in the Kusp, in my childhood home, confirmed the title as well."

The wizard removed the briar from his lips and used it to gesture at Sonart's heart. "Even as you speak the words, your stars realign to their true orbits. You begin to see the truth behind your role. With the Kusp's revelations as our compass, we Four Veins must replenish the Heart of Creation with the blood it needs to go on. The Four Siphons attempt to drain it."

Gjen turned his pipe upside down and tapped the spent ash into a small plate sitting on the table. "The blood that the Heart needs—is Fire, the limitless power of wilderen magic—the magic of Creation. To that effect, you, Sonart of Farkshone will supply the conduit for Creation's infinite energy. Your emblem's been handed down to you through the ancient Highprites, along one of the four stringent lines of blood to bring that power back into the Cleft Augury, when the Starbond comes to pass."

Sonart scratched the side of his head, his puzzlement unrequited. "You've now told me in plain words, and some not-so-plain, yet still I do not grasp the nature of the Augury."

Gjen busied himself stuffing the cob with fresh tobacco—no doubt realizing the dwarven's thickness would require more tutelage than first expected.

If he'd gleaned Sonart's wry reflections, Gjen's patient reply did not indicate it. "The Augury forms the First Circle, from which Creation sprang, the central locus that forged an undying crystal called the *Kalibah*. It *augers* a paradoxical crux where the spiral dance of the heavens ensued. When the time ripens, you and I will go there. That is why you are so important. As Blood Scion, you bear the mark of the ancient line—One of the Four."

Sonart winced. "One of the Four? That is the distinction bestowed upon the archdemons who guard the Inner—stars burn my addled wits. With my own voice, I recently asserted that title for myself, after reading the glowing missive left for me in my home."

Gjen nodded briskly. "Against the Four Siphons, you, me, and our two counterparts form a wilderen quorum, each of us directly matched to our respective antithesis, paragon to malefactor. You, Sonart, stand in direct opposition to *Maudlin*—the Scourge as the archdemon is called in the common tongue."

Sonart quaked and nearly fell off his chair. "Hooks and Dunge, the devil responsible for the razor storms?"

"Aye." Gjen relit the pipe, though this time with a simple snap of his fingers. Then why the twig earlier—? Forget his baffling words, this confounded wizard was a question mark made flesh.

Gjen puffed out his cheeks like smelters' bellows and soon let out twin plumes of white smoke from the corners of his mouth.

The herb crisped Sonart's mind, allowing him to see matters with greater precision. "Why didn't the First Father heal this Heart himself? If he made Creation possible, would he not be omnipotent? Could he not destroy the Darkest One and reclaim his work?"

"An age-old question asked for all time." Gjen placed his palms on the table and drummed his fingers twice. Around the pipe's stem, his mouth worked. "Sonart, in this vast arena, mysteries tier upon mysteries, cloaked in an even deeper conundrum. But it all comes back to the question of balance, as ordained by the ancient Highprites—Vamsah's First Children, passed down through the ages as prophecy and writ into the Law of the Octagon."

When the wizard paused, a buzzing sound filled the silence. Sonart spotted its source: a pair of flies meandering in the air between him and the brazier. They both landed near the far edge of the table, casting elongated shadows toward Sonart.

"My feeble understanding is scant at best," Gjen resumed. He too observed the insects until they launched and flew off. "Only, that to ensure Creation's survival, Vamsah was forced to become dissolute. Removed from the microcosm, so that his bane, Deathwrought, would remain sealed within, trapped in deadlock. As Veins of Fire, we can break that impasse, chosen to carry out this task of tasks started by the Highprites."

Dissolute—deadlock—chosen? A fresh wave of scepticism crashed into Sonart. "But I am just one lowly dwarven. I bear nothing but a power and a vision I do not even understand. And others, outside the Dunge, have had visions too," he protested.

"To shield your acquisition of the wilderen emblem, bewilder sniffing noses, ultimately to safeguard you."

"Safeguard!" Blood rushed to Sonart's cheeks as his anger welled up. "And who's safeguarding them? Sacrificial decoys!" He pounded his fist on the table. "I abandoned Malrik to a horrific death. I've slain my own people in the name of this safeguard."

Gjen gagged slightly on his smoke, spooking the cloud into twin wraiths. "Such sacrifice—*cough*—is a small price to pay—*cough, cough*— considering what's at stake."

"Says you," Sonart returned acerbically. Movements brusque, he pushed away from the table, making his chair's legs grate against the floor. "Easy to voice. Not to behold. Do you consider it a good omen to kill your peers and then toast to your continued safety on the same drear?"

Gjen said nothing while Sonart vented. But his brows grew so heavy they appeared to press his glistening pupils like vices. The edges of his mouth curved down, giving the wizard an expression so grieved, Sonart's reproach and vehemence guttered.

"Malrik was my friend," Sonart croaked in a calmer tone. "Since childhood, he trusted and supported me, even when faced with the horrors of the Dunge. He helped me interpret what I saw in the State. His existence snuffed—to protect a killer?"

Between sputters of smoke, Gjen said in a small voice, "I mourn your loss and feel your pain, as you do mine through our wilderen connection."

Gjen faced the hearth, its firelight dancing amber in his eyes. When he spoke again, his words sounded fretted with anguish held in check. "I too have known bereavement in this campaign—mine own lifelong companion."

He slipped the pipe from his mouth and hung his head. "Laethan was an acolyte, but also my peer. He took a fateful misstep when we attempted to translate you from your cell in the Dunge."

Sonart gasped, eyes widening as realization dawned.

"Twas my wish to extract you long before the first brunt of your torment, but due to our proximity to the Hive, we had to play the most subtle hand. For the translation to work undetected, one of us had to stay behind to hold the portal open. I wanted to take you away myself, but for the quest's sake, and my role in it, Laethan insisted that he be the one who retrieved you."

Gjen took a protracted draw from his pipe and studied Sonart. "We'd come too late. Some immutable ward discovered Laethan before the translation could be completed. A ghastly demon set upon him, which in all my long experience," his fingers floated up to his considerable facial scar, "makes me shudder to recollect."

All at once, Sonart remembered the soothing voice that had cautioned him in the Augury. And the horrific presence that intervened, filling the sanctum with its unearthly scream, its attack, and the dwarven's purge from the Augury."

"I sense your thoughts. Aye, you heard Laethan's last counsel. And caught a glimpse of this... *hyperdemon*," Gjen noted.

Sonart leaned in. "Stars blacken, what was that thing?"

"In truth, I do not know. The entity did not birth in our realm, or any known plane. The sprites call it Souleater. An intruder even Deathwrought must respect—my heart tells me. Tis an anomaly not of his making."

378

Sonart narrowed his eyes as Gjen closed his. "Unprepared for such a black sentry, I had to choose quickly—and that choice meant the death of my apostate and most beloved ally."

"Was it your friend that Malrik and I found slain in our cell?"

Gjen's eyelids opened and he inclined his head. "Yes. Laethan's essence—his soul—permanently severed the connection to his body to confront this Souleater, distract it long enough to help you win free—and to defend me. Tragically, he can never rejoin his corporeal form because the hyperdemon destroyed it. I can only hope he escaped the entity and found his way to the Great Beyond."

The wizard exhaled and downcast his regard to the table. "But he is dead and gone in our physical world. Bereft of his companionship ever since, I've been forced to walk my path alone, hidden from all but three of your people. So, you see, we both share a part of the same guilt."

Remorse and shame weighted Sonart's shoulders and pushed in his chest. "Forgive me."

Gjen placed a palm on Sonart's shoulder. "Nothing to forgive. The burden of pain and loss, we also share."

Sonart nodded. "You stated that Vamsah no longer abides in the heavens. Does that mean he has died as well?"

The wizard moved his head from side to side. "Locked out of the realm he created, which doubly functions as a prison for the Darkest One—his Dunge. Now do you see the paradox manifested by the nature of the construct? Immortal though he may be, the Creator's power and that of Deathwrought balance in equal opposition and entanglement."

"So, Vamsah can't get in, and Deathwrought can't get out," Sonart ventured. "The paradox,"

"Just so," Gjen affirmed.

"Stars, you did not exaggerate about your truths being sacrilegious as well," Sonart said astride a chuckle. "I think we went and blasphemed every sodding syllable in the Kusp."

Gjen tossed his head back and let out a heartfelt laugh. And Sonart joined him, surprised that he too could make light of such overwhelming concepts.

When the moment passed, Sonart met Gjen's eyes. "I just wish I could shirk my ignorance. This magic I wield seems to come and go on its own whim. I cannot control or command it forth at will." The dwarven blew out his cheeks. "I wish I didn't feel so small."

"Sonart, you cannot measure the potency of power through size. Smallness does not mean insignificance." Gjen lightly pressed his finger on Sonart's forehead. "The wilderen seed lies planted within your mind."

"But," Sonart lamented, "the Darkest One swore that I'd be destroyed before I could flourish."

"Nonsense." Gjen's face tightened. "Vamsah as my witness, you will flourish and make the Darkest One eat his words. As for my own—mark them: He will rue the moment he sought to subvert a Vein of Fire."

Sonart gulped, doubt nagging him. "You sound so sure. Would that I could take such conviction and call it my own."

"You will," Gjen promised. "You'll come to see that Areth is a place of miraculous wonders, not only the horrors that have sadly governed your entire existence. And smallness being the theme, though stout in stature, the dwarven too will soon rise—their might surpassing that of all the freeborn races that inhabit this good earth."

"Enough questions," a voice grated behind him. "Enough answers."

Sonart bounced an inch off his chair, wheeled about, and froze in shock. Framed in the open doorway, a small brown rucksack slung over his shoulder, stood Seolad.

The black-bearded firebrand Sonart had almost killed, who intervened before he could be translated back to the Hive, who ended Shayla and single-handedly slew Zürshuck, saving Sonart in the process. But how-in-ten-plus-two-hells?

Sonart had left Rusic's son for dead, yet here he was, legs braced, face creased into his usual scowl, hard eyes regarding Sonart with a mix of impatience and apathy.

"The wizard speaks sooth concerning our brethren," Seolad growled, "but like all Kazir, tends to ramble on. Gaegungen, save your explanations for when we can afford to hear them. Are we ready for this suicide mission of yours?"

Although Seolad mentioned the word *suicide* in dry jest, the notion Sonart had been determined to carry out lost much of its former appeal. But had Gjen spoken truly about attempting the Void? Only time would tell. For the moment, Sonart's amazement and delight at seeing the gruff dwarven held sway.

"You—survived!" Sonart exclaimed.

"Astute as ever," Seolad said. He surrendered a fierce slash of a grin, but his glower never wavered. "Except that would be twice I endured, where you're concerned, Red."

A long sigh made the blackbeard's chest cave. His countenance softened—somewhat. "I'm quite stubborn when it comes to taking the deepest sleep. And I don't like pain—it hurts me."

Seolad closed the door, descended the steps, and dropped his rucksack to the floor. As he drew up to the table, his scrutiny fell upon the blade still fastened to Sonart's side. "Still have my sword I see."

Knee-jerked, Sonart immediately made to remove the scabbard from his belt, but Seolad stopped him with a dismissive wave of his hand. "Nay, keep it. Found one better since our first reunion. When I tried to relay the wizard's message, and you tried to snuff my existence."

Sonart spun on Gjen. "How—?"

"Rusic," Gjen said.

"Heard tell of the Kazir from my father—aye," the blackbeard cut in. "Unlike you, I listened to my sire while I could, before he went and got himself slain—Vamsah protect him."

Sonart searched Gjen's orbs as understanding took root. "You've …been to the Cradle before."

Gjen dipped his chin.

"A wonderment, to be sure," Seolad said with blatant asperity. "Yet another tale for another time. As we're so damnably short of it—thanks to your procrastination, let's get moving already."

Sonart turned to the brazen dwarven. "How did you manage to get away from the Winged Ones, completely intact?"

"What is this—a thousand fucking questions?" Seolad grumbled, raising his hands in exasperation.

Sonart and Gjen stared.

Hands still aloft, Seolad walked to the hearth and warmed his fingers over the coals. "You recall my first customer feel my sting," he said over his shoulder. "Gaegungen used his tricks to incinerate the next rabble. After I put that witch in her rightful place—and offered my second winged mark equal hospitality—the sky grew lousy with a swarm of the fuckers. Most kept going in your direction, so the Kazir chased after your sorry hide."

Seolad took a deep breath and turned around. "I dealt with the ugly batch that didn't. But couldn't push my luck. Slipped into that tight warren moments after you. Zürshuck couldn't follow—them pretty wings won't allow it. Still had a bit of knife-work to do with a few stray rodents—of the Proclaimer sort. But stars burn the lot, the turncape mummers proved easy by comparison. Went to ground after that. And now here we stand, as allies and outlaws. Illuminate that riddle to the stars."

A smile spread across Seolad's feral visage as it locked on Gjen. "So, wizard, when do we depart?"

"Morrow's eve," Gjen said. "We'll embark under cover of darkness, after the drums signal the turn to mid-death. We need many provisions—one in particular—before we challenge the Lobe."

Seolad's grin vanished, a ghost of his former scowl etching his crow's feet anew.

"Both of you are fugitives now, so you must remain here," Gjen said as his regard found Sonart. "Magical lenses are blinded to you but I cannot risk someone recognizing you on sight. The Proclaimers will be out scouring the Steppe in search. I must get what we need alone."

Gjen looked to the door, then back. He lifted a finger and wagged it at Sonart. "And no more foolish talk of the deepest sleep from you. Once we're away, I'll retrain your mind. For now, we start by correcting two words erased from your vocabulary. I want you to repeat them and understand their import, for they underscore the purpose of all Creation." Gjen's voice dropped low and particular. "One of the words is *hope*, the other… *life*."

Gjen tapped his second batch of ash remnants into the same small dish and deposited the briar back in his pocket. "Since you'll be keeping each other company in the interim, Seolad can tutor you further."

"Splendid," Seolad snorted, clearly less enthused by the wizard's charge than the delay. Rigid eyes searched the enclosure. "Got any wine?"

"As Seolad so adamantly pointed out," said Gjen as he stood to leave. "We mustn't linger a moment longer than necessary."

"Where will we go?" Sonart asked, his heart aflutter.

"What I said last night on the fringe of the desert was no jest for the sake of mock. When we are ready to do so, my good dwarven, we shall cross that great expanse you call the Lobe. And escape the Cradle."

47: Trap Tripped
Brooke

A high-pitched scream shattered the silent gloom, jarring Brooke awake. Heart racing, he checked himself, unsure if he imagined it or remained stuck in his harrowing nightmare. No, he lay in relative darkness, staring up at the roof of his tent.

His ears perked. The sound of chortled gagging lingered.

Brooke cast his gaze down the length of his prone body to the canvas flaps at the entrance. They danced with ochre light from the campfire beyond.

A sudden tumult of shouts erupted everywhere.

Clad in naught but his small clothes, the commander threw off his bedding, donned his sword belt, and bounded outside.

Into anarchy.

Through the steady stream of running wolves and warriors, Brooke had just enough time to see Val wrench a sword from an impaled Wrayn. The commander could only gape as the writhing man gasped his last and crumpled to the ground before Val.

Behind them, more cries went up.

"Our defences have been breached!" a voice shouted. "Hearken to the Commander!"

"Nightwolves all," another Wrayn bellowed from further off. "Close the gap!"

The shrill notes of baying Warangs ensued and multiplied, joined by more canines in the distance. Their collective howls escalated as they swept in.

Though the commotion staggered Brooke as it rumbled the soles of his bare feet, he focused on Val. Targin's Second took up a defensive stance, eyes darting left and right. But he stood his ground, making no attempt to flee or attack.

The turmoil abated as the Nightwolves converged. The Warangs settled shoulder to shoulder and any gap quickly filled with standing or crouching men and women. They formed a tightly-closed semicircle of bodies, fifty-feet wide. It effectively cornered Val against the cliff's edge a few paces behind him.

"I told you he'd prove the one!" Lonus seethed as he strode forward. "The villain in the shadows. But no more." He stabbed a finger at Val's hands, covered in blood rendered black in the firelight. "Now, the snake has been caught red-handed."

Brooke defied the Warangs' riled barks, ignored the Wrayns' warning shouts—and stormed in, centring himself between Val and Lonus. His scrutiny shifted back and forth between the two giants. He could not believe his eyes, trying to glean a motive, finding only mist and mirrors.

Fists balled, face clenched, Lonus was all fire.

Val was all stone. Expressionless. Calm.

Of the two, Val looked the more dangerous.

Low and catlike, Val poised in a battle stance over the body of the fallen Wrayn, his bloodied foil clenched in an iron grasp, eyes fierce, emotionless.

Lonus drew a spear and slowly advanced, matching Val's *combart* form in every detail.

"If that be the way of it," Lonus scathed. "I'll be the one to dance with the knave. And when he flees, I'll carve a fabulous cunt of his back."

"Hold, Lonus!" Brooke bawled. He raised his arms to bar the Nightwolf's path. "Hold I say! We meet the truth on fair ground."

Lonus lowered his spear and threw him a fulsome laugh. "None fairer, Commander. I found dead Nightwolves by the trees near the road—impaled by a blade the same. With our *own* eyes, we bore witness to the villainy of this turncape. The ground will be laid fair, when it mingles with his blood." He raised his weapon again and shoved Brooke aside.

A white blur leapt over the heads of the closest Wrayns. Before anyone could react, Yerik, the Warang Chief, sailed into view landing neatly in a crouch, between Lonus and Val. Wheeling to face Lonus, the massive wolf bared his fangs, spittle frothing between them as he snarled.

Yerik intimidated Lonus—enough to make the Wrayn retreat a step.

But only one.

Lonus hefted his spear. Fired it at Val. The javelin flew true, but as it shot over Yerik, the Warang sprang. He caught the projectile midway in his mouth. Clamped down hard. And snapped it in two, just as several other Warangs entered the fray to support their chief.

Lonus pounded a fist against his chest and howled in rage.

Yerik howled louder.

"What is this?" Lonus cried. "Are you all in league with this demon? Stand aside, Warangs—do not cross stars with me. I have no quarrel with you—yet."

Yerik yelped over his shoulder. Then dropped his head low and stared Lonus down. The other Warangs twisted about and faced the press of Wrayns, growling vitriol.

Stars burn them all, it was a standoff. Or a mutiny.

Before Brooke could find his voice, another spear shot at Val from somewhere in the shadows, followed by a volley of arrows in quick succession. With an assassin's grace, Val evaded them all, dancing lightning-fast feather steps while shifting arms, head and torso.

Others of the same opinion as Lonus had also decided to take matters into their own hands.

Lonus jeered.

Brooke cursed.

Val braced.

The trapped Wrayn did nothing but stand his ground—all he could do, unable to escape the barrier of bodies corralling him.

Thwitt-thwitt-thwitt. More shafts flew. This time, the Warangs were ready. As the bolts arced over their heads the wolves leapt up and snatched them out of the air. But not all.

Some shafts went wide, striking the ground. A pair collided with each other and thwarted themselves. But two quarrels sallied past the wolves' defences and found their mark.

The first bolt impaled Val's thigh. The second darted towards his heart when a *third* arrow loosed from the canopy rammed the shaft away, sending both pitchpoling over the drop. Along the same trajectory, a fourth, *headless* quarrel struck Val below the shoulder, lodging in his leather gorget. The blunt impact did not penetrate past his armour but it forced him off his feet, dropping him to the ground as though punched by an ogre.

"No!" Brooke cried. He drew his blade and surged forward. "Damn you all. Lower your weapons. Stand down!" He wheeled on the inner circle of Warangs. They barred him from approaching Val, gnashing teeth and snarling thunder.

"I only seek to give aid!" Brooke raged, feral eyes shifting between Yerik and the other Warangs. But the canines wouldn't relent. Their ferocity escalated.

The commander threw his hands up in frustration. "What happened to your precious Code?" he scathed. "Does my command mean so little? You all do Shirdron proud to divide so readily. Stars *burn* the lot of you and your sordid Purpose."

Brooke's red gaze swept behind him, muscles corded, blood blazing until he spotted Gnor. The Bulldog stared back from a distance, his face grave and unyielding.

"For fuck's sake, man, commune with the Warangs to let me pass!"

No one moved. Brooke wanted to explode. How could their order fall apart so quickly and completely? He spun and moved forward again.

Yerik strode up to meet him, foaming suds of spittle, snapping viciously. He crouched, tendons winding, about to launch.

The commander's apathy surpassed any fear. He raised his sword and made to break the line, even if he had to attack the Chief of the Warangs to do so. But a glimpse of movement stopped him in his tracks. Over the heads of the wolves, Val regained his feet.

His hands reached for the shaft lodged in his gorget and wrenched it free. Then he snapped the stem of the second arrow just below the fletching. The rest of the bolt still protruded from his thigh muscle, but with an effort that made him grimace, the Nightwolf drew it out from the other side.

Val straightened and squared his stance. He did not grovel, voice objection, or plead innocence. He sought Brooke's eyes. And held them. Was he trying to tell him something?

Before the commander could guess, Val twirled around, offering his back to the throng.

And bolted towards the cliff.

Reaching it in six giant strides.

Brooke's voice caught as Val leapt off the precipice.

The black abyss swallowed him.

48: Ice on Fire
Targin

When Targin emerged from the stables, his emotional unrest over Tasmin filled his thoughts like overcast skies, rumbling in places, flashing in others. Would she hear him out or would she spur him on sight? As he deliberated, his heartrate quickened and his breath came in short hurried spurts.

He took a different path, down a narrow stairwell that opened into a wide and busy concourse. Exactly as Lorin had indicated, he found a flower shop that carried his aromatic prize: a magnificently arranged bouquet of three-toned green flowers.

With no coin on his person, Targin offered to sign the shopkeeper's ledger and have him charge the purchase to his royal account. The flower merchant graciously agreed. Bouquet carefully tucked under one arm, the Nightwolf considered himself better-equipped as he hastened to his next sparring session.

Targin turned down a ramp that branched into a recessed but wider esplanade, then up a series of carved switchback staircases. They led to a motif-and-statue-laden causeway that ended at an arched portcullis.

The entrance to the king's palace.

Two rows of twenty stern-faced sentries flanked the bridge. All wore silver armour draped in hunter green capes and bore shields emblazoned with Serenthia's teal kraken sigil. The guards also hefted eight-foot pikes, positioned exactly so that each blade point touched the pike of the guard on the opposite side of the causeway.

Targin offered them the briefest of glances as he strode beneath their triangular pike fence. The guards did not react to his passage or his dashing attire, least not outwardly—only Lorin would do that.

They should all know his face, and even if they didn't, the magical sprite wards vouched Targin's identity and purpose safe.

A few strides later, the Nightwolf emerged into a splendid hall of the inner palace. Carpet runners of red and grey ran the length of the floors, expertly woven into an artistic pattern. Striations of blue crystalline veins threaded the deep-grey and black marble walls, which supported a high-vaulted ceiling adorned in silver filigree.

Targin moved past a procession of ebony sconces, set in alcoves lining the walls and rounded columns, four rows across and twelve deep. Foot-high columns of flame danced in all the braziers. As in other parts of the Hidden Kingdom, their warm aura combined with the blue shimmer of the crystal veins to produce as close a semblance to natural daylight as possible.

Aglow in more than one way, Targin slowed his pace, apprehension burning as he closed the distance to Tasmin's private chamber. Still fresh and volatile, their previous conflict had been bottled. When—if—that door opened, the bottle would either open gently with it, remain corked, or shatter and explode.

Before the sealed entry, he paused to compose himself. The fragrant smell of the wild trinsic helped suppress his anxiety but he still harboured a nagging doubt. He took a deep breath, made a fist, and gave the heavy oaken door a firm rap.

Nothing.

He knocked again and waited. Knocked again, waited longer...

His throat went dry as his patience waned.

"Stars cross you, Tasmin," he huffed. "Allay your wrath and unlock this cursed door!"

Silence answered him. He frowned. Could she have left the palace? He waited with simmering tolerance a few moments longer before turning to go. A murmur sounded within. Or did he imagine it?

He put his ear to the door, hoping, and when that faded, he dismissed it as the product of his overwrought mind.

Targin raised his voice again, most likely to an empty room. "I heard of your valorous deeds in the borderlands. And regret how boorish I proved as your reward." He kept his tone measured. "Lorin tells me you are my equal in many noble ways—perhaps you can make a show of clemency one of them. My priggishness blinded me, but I would like to explore equality with you."

He filled his lungs again and exhaled. "I offer a truce—if you would but hear me out, face to face. I'll make proper amends for my oversight—to *your* satisfaction."

The lock clunked loudly, the door swung inward, and Tasmin stood there framed in the threshold like a living work of art. Dressed not in armour but gossamer, her thin white gown hugged her firm carriage. Its translucent fabric flowed over and flaunted every curve. Her lavender perfume spilled out of the chamber and diminished the minty cinnamon scent of the flower petals under the giant's nose.

Targin's body tensed and his mouth went dry. It now harboured a desert as his betrothed studied him with big expressionless eyes. Eyes that dropped from his hungry scrutiny to his bizarre robe—one brow lifted at that—before settling on the brilliant bouquet clasped tightly in his sweaty palm.

Twas as though she didn't even see the flowers. But her dark orbs spoke volumes when they slowly lifted and fixed him with an expectant look. The faintest trace of a smile curved the corners of her lips.

Much to Targin's chagrin, he had put himself at her mercy until she declared otherwise.

"Your eyes tell me I am worthier than you dare demonstrate when among your peers. But if you acknowledge me as your peer, I *may* be inclined to grant those ravenous peepers an audience. And you may do more than just gawk."

"I did say it!" Targin remonstrated.

"No, you simply quoted Lorin," she shot back haughtily.

"Why do you believe it his idea?"

"Targin, my love, Lorin's the only one of your brood intelligent enough to know worth and wisdom in this gift." She made a show of presenting herself, floating her arms, palms upward. "So, naturally it was him. Besides, he's the only one wise enough not to join your dog team."

"How many times do I have to tell you not to mock my brethren Nightwolves?" Targin grated. "Their campaigns have kept your father's realm intact. It would be wise to remember that, taken away, the hand that protects that pretty face of yours will make such weapons less effective."

Tasmin laughed, her voice innocent and musical. "You mean *paw,* for they are dogs—sorry wolves—who do your bidding. Until I am convinced otherwise, I deem their protection a gesture of bravado. They simply follow their master's commands. Heel! Sit! Play dead."

Targin growled at her taunts, as was her lewd wont, so he stopped, smiled, and drew closer to her until they stood inches apart. This close, her fragrance not only overpowered the flowers he now crushed, but the last remnants of his resolve as well.

Her smirk joined his as she shoved him back. "Say it, from *your* lips." Her gaze drifted down. "If you want to unlock mine."

"What?" he fumed, sweat bathing his back into a slather.

She ran her tongue across her bottom lip. "Say it."

With some effort, Targin obliged, "You are, my equal in valour, *and* my superior at torture—stars burn you!"

"And that is why you love me." She drew up, engaged his trembling bulk against her lithe form. And kissed him on the mouth. Though his shock made his return awkward.

Tasmin broke away. "What's this?" She indicated the flowers with a nudge of her chin.

Targin thrust the bouquet at her but said nothing.

"Your idea, I hope."

The Nightwolf cleared his throat, evading her gaze.

Tasmin's laugh sounded like the finest wine wrapped in silk. "It matters not. I accept your apology. Now, you may come to me."

He tried to resist as she reached for his phallus, but her charms won him over from the inside out. He stiffened. With her free hand, she took the flowers from his grasp and cast them uncaring to the floor. He returned her second, more voracious kiss, with desperation, enjoying the strange euphoric moment of calm it instilled—perhaps because he'd paid for it with a thousand more of frustration.

But it seemed paid in full—and worth the price. Such was their relationship. Such was their love.

Tasmin drew away from his kiss and, closing the door, whispered moistly in his ear, "Now you have earned my audience. Attend me, Nightwolf."

Her words and their delivery intoxicated him like a triple-measure of spritewater. For all the trouble, having to swallow his pride, this feeling verified its worth as they enveloped each other a third time. Targin stood only a head above her. Aye, they were well matched.

Giving a silent note of thanks to Lorin, Targin lifted her body in his thick arms. She wrapped her legs around his waist as he carried her into the inner bedchamber. Not the largest or most finely decorated of the palace's appointments, but its beauty lay in its simplicity.

Smaller warmer versions of the light-emitting crystals in the main foyer lit this sanctum. Two hearths burned and crackled softly, their flames making dancing red and orange patterns against the rough stone walls and wooden furniture, inlaid with deep brown cushions.

Myrrh-scented incense sticks splayed like thin fingers from out of a clay holder that sat on a granite table to one side of the room. Their glowing tips sent thin, unhurried columns of smoke into the air. The wisps jittered as the two entwined bodies entered.

In the centre of the magnificent space, a cushion-littered silk bed awaited them. Above its headboard, an intricate tapestry mapped all the kingdoms of the Main. At the bed's foot, a thick bear rug.

To that bed, they moved as one.

When Targin let Tasmin back down onto her feet, she slipped off her garments and his robe. For a moment they stood, toes cuddling the rug's thick fur. They breathed and swallowed and faced each other's naked form. Targin grasped her buttocks in his hands and hoisted her into the air a second time, allowing her to straddle him. Then he entered her.

She attacked his mouth with savage kisses, biting his lip. In such a wondrous tangle, they sat on the bed and formed a single being like a swaying tree yearning towards the sun.

After an unhurried and blissful sharing and release, Targin alighted and rested his weary head against Tasmin's breast. They lay together and let the tribulations of their love and war merge into a single entity.

A strange emotional aura basked them equally before it slipped away, taking Targin's silent contemplations and his consciousness into a haven of serenity.

Targin awoke alone. After his initial disappointment, he resolved that this morning it was preferable. He did not want to involve Tasmin with early brooding over the day's forthcoming trials. It may only be a political arena, less dangerous than his recent test, but much more vexing. He couldn't rely on wild trinsic, or Fang, to resolve his inevitable differences with the elven. No, Targin stood in Johlarin's house now, so the King's Rules and the King's Peace and the King's Justice would prevail.

Targin would have to keep his sword sheathed, which meant a lot of tongue-biting. All the same, he prepared for blood.

Still, part of him felt a measure of relief to face his fate head-on, to act under one banner, even if it meant painful dalliance with the holier-than-thou elven. Prophecies and their myriad aberrations, visions, premonitions, machinations, plots, and subterfuge—would that he could cast them all aside and simply fight. The storm of war gathered strength. As a Blood Scion, the pull of the Starbond reached out to him. Ready or not, the real action would soon begin.

A firm knock interrupted Targin's thoughts. He slipped on his robe, walked over to the entry, and unlatched the bolt.

When the door opened, Lorin stood framed in the doorway a knowing grin on his visage. "Targin, you son-of-a-witch."

Targin threw a mock glance over both shoulders before returning the ranger's smile. "You mean *which*."

"Stars align," Lorin chuckled. "By your face, amends were made."

"And had," Targin said.

"Well, you definitely look mended," the scout chided. "You can thank me later."

Targin's smile joined Lorin's. "Who's to say what may happen the day I prove too weary to live up to her expectations."

"When that day comes, will you ask yourself if she is worth it?"

The question hung in the air unanswered. With his arm, Targin gestured for Lorin to enter. "What time is it?"

"An hour before midday," the scout said as he entered the foyer. "The council will commence in two hours, giving us just enough time to properly break fast—and facts."

Targin closed the door. "Good. Both will help me stomach our elven *betters*."

"Then might I suggest a change of wardrobe or do you seek to match their finery as well as their words?"

"Well said," Targin laughed. "And no, I will be but a few moments."

Lorin waited patiently for Targin to bathe and dress into more stately attire: a long buttoned grey doublet bearing the freshwater kraken insignia of Serenthia, black britches and boots polished to a mirror finish. When the Nightwolf declared himself ready, Lorin made for the door.

To his back, Targin said, "Right then, let's get this over with."

Closing the door behind them, they made their way into the central palace. A wider corridor presented itself almost immediately, with a high ceiling and spires recessed along its flanks. Targin led Lorin into one of the recesses.

The scout raised an eyebrow in obvious surprise. "Will you not break bread with the highborn?"

"Nay, I'll see Johlarin's royal flock in due course. For now, I'd rather seek audience with the officers and soldiers who actually tread the shite around His Grace's realm—maybe glean a few extra morsels of information before the council session. I suspect an ache in my belly regardless, but anything to better arm Serenthia's position against the elven will be a benison."

"You make it sound like they are the enemy and not our sworn allies," Lorin chortled. "But I understand. They have all the answers, and we get the sore necks from nodding obediently."

Targin stopped and faced his companion with appreciation. "Insightful to a fault, you are." The giant sighed and straightened his tunic. "I hate this fucking thing. I'd sooner dress in motley and juggle."

"To me, that is motley. And you will be juggling soon enough—debate with the elven."

That drew a thin smile from the Nightwolf. They resumed walking. "In any case," said Targin, "by immersing my voice and ears among the troops, I keep morale high. It also keeps me abreast of many things that might present a death sentence."

"Good policy," Lorin agreed as they entered the great dining hall.

Filled with long tables and three hundred boisterous soldiers of various ranks, the din of voices and clanging cutlery on porcelain echoed throughout the vast room. Targin and Lorin lost themselves among the soldiers. For the first time since he arrived at the Strong Helm, Targin truly felt at home.

49: Provisions
Sonart

Sonart raised troubled eyes above the cellar window's bottom ledge. It had grown dark outside, and Gjen was several turns—*hours*—overdue.

"Don't trouble yourself over the wizard," Seolad said to Sonart's back. "Gaegungen crossed the perils of the Lobe to come here unscathed—twice. He concealed himself for months, unnoticed in Deathwrought's very midst. Do you think he would slip up now procuring a few supplies?"

Sonart glanced over his shoulder at his companion, seated at the table, busy sharpening his sword with a whetstone. Its grating sound filled the silence that followed the blackbeard's question.

Firelight danced against the walls and played havoc with Seolad's features, deepening his frown lines, but his jaw remained set in granite.

"Aye, but that was different," Sonart pressed. "After what happened the dimming—*night*—before last, I wouldn't be surprised if the whole of Bulkforge is under lockdown. Besides that, Gjen said he'd be back by now."

"Plans change. He will show ere long. And we will wait," Seolad said in a wooden voice, clearly bored with the matter.

"Coming from one who lectures about procrastination," Sonart rebuked. "Recall the wizard's words? Hope and life? Here's another: *trust*."

Sonart turned and approached the table. "Maybe we should search."

Seolad tightened. "Hooks and Dunge, enough already, tis you they want. Gaegungen has his tricks."

"But it's Gjen's life. How can you sit idle?"

Crow's feet quivering, Seolad lowered his whetstone and fixed Sonart with a corrosive glare. Sonart regretted his words immediately. The last thing he wanted to do was push Rusic's temperamental son away—something easily done. But he acted so sluggish.

If Gjen had been captured or slain, it would be up to the two of them to somehow rally their people.

Their people—Sonart's thoughts plagued all the more. Why abandon the Cradle when it faced its direst hazard? And how *does* one enter the Void—the same abyss the Darkest One had warned threatened all life in the Cradle? How could they possibly cross the Lobe for that matter with the added burden of supplies?

After a vacuous pause, Seolad spoke, his words rumbling like distant thunder. "We will sit, and we will wait, exactly as the wizard instructed. Your name means agony in the hearts of all dwarven now, not only the Proclaimers. You allowed Deathwrought to lop off the head of our resistance. After your merry jig with the Elders, the Kworn took out the rest. In one night, you didn't just kill the organizers, you destroyed the whole fucking movement. All hope of rebellion is now quashed."

The images of Auckland and Bessel appeared in Sonart's mind. He met Seolad's acrid gaze. "Not all."

An uncomfortable quiet fell between the two dwarven. Seolad muttered something and returned his attention to honing his sword. It grated even louder.

Sonart let out a vexed breath, sat down opposite his cohort, and stared at the fire. Perhaps Seolad was right. Gjen had magic as his ally. He dispatched three Zürshuck with one blast from his staff. He could take care of himself.

Scratchy creaking interrupted Sonart's meanderings. He spun as the heavy door at the top of the landing slowly opened.

Seolad dropped the stone to the table with a clunk. He bolted to his feet and hefted his weapon.

Before the door splayed fully ajar, Gjen's voice filled the room, and Sonart's heart, with relief. "Only me." He stepped out of the shadows into the firelight.

Gjen carried a large pack across his back and another smaller one hung from his shoulder. "I've brought the provisions I mentioned—including the crucial item."

Sonart and Seolad inhaled together and exchanged nervous looks as a cloaked dwarven sidled up beside the wizard. When the conscript removed his cowl, Sonart did a doubletake. He—was a she—and not just any she. Bordered by the doorway, stood none other than Xoral's daughter, Iomi.

Seolad sat back down and lowered his blade but not his scrutiny. Sonart shifted uncomfortably in his chair as Gjen turned to close the door and Iomi descended the steps.

The maiden's grey orbs never left Sonart as she approached. Cold, impassive, they remained until she stood before him.

Then she lunged at his head, dagger in hand.

Caught off-guard, Sonart barely avoided its ironock bite. He seized her arm below the wrist before the dirk sailed home between his eyes.

But her momentum toppled him off his chair. Together they went down.

A moment after their impact, he managed to spin her about and hold her fast.

"Stow this madness!" Gjen cried, fire igniting his words as he pried open her fingers and removed the knife from her hand. "Sonart, release her."

"I will unhand you," Sonart began tentatively, "but raise your weapon at me again and so help me, I'll silence you with your own toy."

When she nodded, he let her go. Both stood.

Iomi inclined her chin at Gjen and brushed the dust off her cloak. Then she turned back to Sonart.

And promptly spat in his face.

He growled as he wiped the glob of spittle worming down his cheek. But swallowed her vitriol—and the urge to strike her.

"Bastard," she seethed, "You owe a blood price for my father's death, the tally doubled for his suffrage on the Hooks."

Iomi stiffened when Gjen gripped her shoulder. But he managed to coax her to turn towards him. "The blood of Xoral is solely upon my hands."

All three dwarven stared up at the wizard.

"When my first attempt to rescue Sonart failed, direct extraction was no longer an option. The Darkest One had been alerted to my magics and heightened his surveillance for them." Gjen exhaled as he released her. "After Seolad had been discovered, I needed someone to convey my message to Sonart—a vital message. With so many eyes upon him, Sonart's liberation could only be accomplished through sleight of hand."

Fatigue overcame Gjen's face and the corners of his mouth dipped. "Trust me, I know."

The maiden folded her arms and pressed her mouth so tight, the colour left them.

"Your sire was my friend, Iomi," Gjen said as he studied the storm in her countenance. He gestured to Sonart and Seolad. "Allied to both their fathers. Besotted with the Afflicted Ones' illness, Xoral insisted he be the one to impart the vital message, giving him a worthy death—one, he said, would 'emblazon the resolve of his once-proud people.' Rather than submit to the affliction corrupting his body, he would go to his doom content and vindicated that he struck back at the Darkest One."

"You lie!" Iomi flared, throwing her hands down as she glowered balefully at Gjen. "False words to placate me!"

"Did you ever ask yourself why Xoral implored you to solicit Sonart's help and that of no other?"

Eyes ablaze, she stuttered a rebuke, but it petered.

"Xoral was an alchlemage true, aye, but also an agent," Gjen consoled, his words nursing and calm. "A hero for the Creator. Make no mistake, he dug in his heels, more than willing to suffer the Hooks, to save Sonart and me, and the cause—ultimately to save you. By the stars, I swear it sooth."

The maiden's eyes glistened, tears threatening to wet her cheek but she brushed them away and gritted her teeth. "I'll aid your quest, Wizard. I'll do what I can with the skills my father taught me. But—"

Iomi made a dagger of her index finger and stuck it in Sonart's direction. "Mark my words, fiend: my business with you is far from over." Her hard gaze lifted to Gjen. "Or must I suffer the same fate as my father to save *him*?"

Shivers rattled Sonart's bones in sudden recall of Xoral's bane. *You will kill me and both my daughters.*

Gjen let out a slow breath. "The quest and your business entwine. We will rid the Cradle of the Darkest One's malfeasance and the endless harm his Four have caused. With your abilities as a healer, you can avenge your father. Take up his mantle, Iomi, and let us usurp Deathwrought and his disciples together."

She buried her head in her hands, locks falling forward like a veil. "You must truly be desperate to recruit me," she retorted through a clenched throat. "I only arrested the contagion of my father's malady but failed to heal him of the affliction. Seeing him up there on the stockade, rendered me utterly helpless."

When she raised her head again, her eyes shot quarrels at Sonart. "But I swore on his good name, I'd exact rightful vengeance upon this one." She turned towards the hearth and sobbed at its guttering flames. "And now, I have failed in that as well. Forgive me, father."

"That is not your failure," Gjen soothed quietly. "It belongs to Deathwrought."

Cheeks burning, Sonart's guilt masticated his soul, but he had to offer her something. "Gjen speaks truly," he croaked. "Xoral's death can be laid at Deathwrought's feet alone. I wept dearly for the old one as well, but I swear to you on the memory of my own lost sire, my sole part in his tragic end compares to that of the rock thrown to kill. A blameless tool. Ever the slave to the Darkest One I have suffered but," he paused and swallowed, "no longer. Tragically, your father paid for my emancipation with his life."

Iomi opened her mouth to baulk but a look from Gjen quelled her to silence. Her hatred and enmity appeared to dim, her resolve wavering. It made her face soften and look lovely in the firelight. A face so much like...

Sonart flinched, deducing something from his dream about the Proclaimer. The Darkest One's last revelation: *she would have been the greatest ally to you. Now wed her doom to the toll of your folly.*

Seolad broke the confused moment with a verbal hammer. "For fuck's sake, Gaegungen! Is your mind Dunge-bound?" The turbulent dwarven's face flushed red, beard shaking in rage. "To bring a stranger into our midst. We need a warrior or a ranger, not a fucking healer. I don't trust her."

"So, you trust Gjen, but not his decisions," Sonart seethed, his voice raw and hoarse. "He had a reason for adding Iomi to our party. That is good enough for me."

"At last, the idiot takes a stand. What know you of good enough? Good enough for you to squander, or kill perhaps?" Seolad's tone dropped low and controlled but held back a razor storm of violence. "Do not cross stars with me, Son of Farkshone—or we'll cross swords. Unlike you, I know when and how to act in my father's stead."

"And how is that, hellion?" Sonart scathed.

"With honour and courage. And I understand the sword cuts both ways, so quell your foolish furnace, before I piss all over it."

Sonart ignored the threat, but Gjen interceded, "Please, both of you, such cruel banter will avail you nothing but more cruel banter."

The circles under the wizard's eyes deepened and he rubbed a hand through his longish mane. Consternation fretted his plea. "We are allies here. You must all put aside your differences and trust that every one of you remains component to a successful traverse of the Lobe. Seolad, you know I would never risk anything that might jeopardize our quest. Vamsah's light illuminate your stubbornness, everything will unfold as it—"

Seolad threw his hands up. "Choke me with my own beard, Kazir, we have you for that. How can we hope to be rid of this cursed place with her to burden us?"

He hiked a thumb like a pick-axe at Sonart. "The idiot is enough. We're not heading to the bakery for scones, Gaegungen. Stars burn my eyes out and take my manhood along for the ride, we're planning to cross the most hazardous blight. Something only you have any experience with. More bodies mean more risks."

"She may surprise you, Rusic son," Gjen said, raising both hands in a calming gesture.

"Balls of a Kworn—she's a woman—and I-don't-*trust* her!"

"But you trust me still, I hope," Gjen chuckled. "And Iomi is my decision."

"You may rue that decision, Wizard," Seolad griped.

"Fine," Sonart chimed in, stomping his boot on the floor. "I guess that makes you a hypocrite, considering how you carried on about faith before they arrived. Surprise, I don't *trust* you, yet here we stand together, as our fathers did years ago, brethren and forsworn allies. They trusted each other implicitly. Perhaps you can heed your own declaration and *act* in your father's stead, as you claim, or was that simply more angry piss and foul wind?"

That silenced Seolad. To Sonart's shock, the blackbeard regarded him with what looked like new appreciation. He even allowed a thin crooked smile to crease his crenulated features. Perhaps, because Sonart handed him back his own tempestuous quip.

"Words unto deeds," Seolad said.

50: The Lobe
Sonart

The night sky's crimson aura suffused the vast desert that made up the Lobe. Its light stemmed from the molten rivers and lakes on either side of the Innereach and reflected off the blanket of clouds throughout the Steppe, now at Sonart's back.

The sandy expanse spread out before him as he trailed his small company. And for the first league or so, it stayed lit. But after that, the glow and the desert faded into dark nothingness.

Since they had left the safehouse earlier that eve, Sonart had not let his guard down. Neck muscles taut, eyes darting left and right from beneath his cowl, he had followed Iomi and Seolad. Gjen was not among them on that first anxious leg.

As the three dwarven stole past streets milling with people, Sonart remained doubtful of the special grey cloaks Gjen had given them. Every passer-by could be a Proclaimer, alert to their movements.

The wizard promised the raiment would conceal them from the unfriendly noses of the Cradle's more scrutinizing malefactors. But after what the Darkest One managed to do with him, Sonart had convinced himself clothing alone would not so easily fool a Colossal or Zürshuck, let alone One of the Four.

But so far, despite his dubiety, Gjen had proven him wrong. The three passed unchallenged.

From the top of the bluff, Sonart and his two companions had kept to the shadows of the slope's deeper ruts. It made their descent difficult, occasionally stumbling on loose rocks, but their route also kept them completely hidden from the glow above.

When Gjen stepped out from behind a large boulder at the escarpment's base, rune-etched sceptre in hand, Sonart let his shoulders sag. Coincidently, they reunited on the same tract where the wizard intercepted him, not three nights before—the furthest point out Sonart had gone in his *life*.

Gjen had warned them before they set out to remain silent on the march. So, he did not greet them with any verbal salutation. He merely raised his free hand and bade them stop. He looked out over the Lobe as though listening for some sound while the three dwarven waited. Sonart enjoyed the respite to work out some of the nervous kinks from his joints.

After several moments of breathing and being, Gjen lifted his staff and gestured with it for them to continue. He led the silent procession out of the scarp's gloom. But then, just before the red afterglow cast four vague shadows on the sand, the wizard began humming a soft incantation, no louder than a ghost's murmur.

Gjen's other hand joined the first where it clasped the middle of his staff, its gnarled wooden crown of branches braided around a large blue cabochon pointing forward. The wizard's eyes remained closed in apparent concentration. He resembled a blind man, feeling his way with a walking stick, along a route he'd committed to memory.

For what they set out to do, the gear they carried in their packs struck Sonart as strange: an odd assortment of hooks and contraptions, hides and boots with small serrated blades affixed to their soles.

Questions for another time.

Sonart dropped his eyes to his new attire and arched an eyebrow. The colours of his raiment blended with the dunes. To a passing Zürshuck or dragon, the party would appear as errant rocks in the sifting sand—provided they all kept still.

Some four turns of the dial had passed—*hours* as Seolad often corrected him, after mid-death—*midnight*, when Gjen brought them to a halt inside a shallow fissure. The shadows appeared much deeper within the narrow cleft until the wizard sparked an azure light from his staff's headpiece. It cast a soft cool glow against the walls of the defile and all their faces.

Gjen rested the sceptre against one of the cleft's walls and turned to them. "This wilderen light is visible only to our eyes." He tilted his head up to the foot-wide crack in the fissure's ceiling. "And were that not the case, our enemies would have to be directly above us to see it. So, you needn't worry on that score."

Gjen dropped his gaze to his three companions. "But all the same, I should impart a few words of caution at this juncture. Undertaking such a journey, my friends, you must take great care of your bodies as you do the equipment we carry."

"How long will the journey take?" asked Sonart.

"If all goes well, within a fortnight we should bear sight of our destination."

Iomi started. "We do not have enough rations or water to complete such a trip. We would perish in half that time."

"Look above you," Gjen said. "The clouds which blanket this land are comprised of water. I carry a device in my pack called a trapper draw. It collects water from those clouds, even if it does not rain—enough to slake our thirst and bathe for that matter. As for food, trust me, Iomi, neither starvation nor exposure shall claim us."

"But the minions of Deathwrought might," Seolad reminded him.

Gjen faced Seolad. "Not if we travel according to my clandestine plan. That will require a measure of foresight and subterfuge on your part. I will not lie to you. Our task is daunting, but if anything shall seriously thwart us, it'll come from our own minds. Take heart that with every step we move away from the fount of Deathwrought's power, the greater our chances of escape. Even as we speak, I sense the Darkest One straining harder to seek us. He drives His Four relentlessly atop their peaks. But to no avail."

"Does His power weaken as we draw away?" Sonart asked hopefully.

"In this realm, after a fashion, aye. But more so for the fact that he searches elsewhere, based on a certain premise born of his interpretations of how events will unfold. Still, do not misplace hope in such revelations. As you all know, even the true Kusp had been corrupted."

The light in Sonart's heart dimmed. "Another riddle for certain, but I do trust you."

"My magic will continue to aid us, but if I sense a hazard approach, you must buckle down to task. Our stealth must be unilateral and unwavering, not just in body, but in mind as well. The perils of the Lobe will announce themselves soon enough, and occur more frequently the further we proceed. By travelling through the night, we blend in easily enough to remain invisible to Zürshuck patrols high above. But we must be invisible to more than just eyes."

Sonart scratched his head. "What do you mean?"

"He means, keep your piehole shut as we move," Seolad grumbled before Gjen could voice a more tactful version. "And if it can be helped— do not think of anything either."

"Your essay is partly right, Seolad," Gjen corrected, "But basic thoughts of survival will actually make our geas foolproof: the purpose of moving, the need for food and water, shelter and rest. Do this and we'll stay invisible to any orbs that spy through the magics of the Darkest One. We will appear as nothing more than the fouler, baser denizens of the desert."

Gjen dropped to one knee, bringing all their heads to the same level. He offered them a reassuring smile that drew them into a huddle. "Confront your doubts and rein them in. Dwell not on the obstacles, but the goal beyond, and we shall succeed where others have failed."

Iomi cast her eyes to the ground. "And what of all the Cradle's dwarven—are we to abandon kith and kin?"

Gjen reached out and with a finger gently lifted her chin. His grin never wavered. "Though we seek to escape it, Iomi. There is hope yet for the Cradle. Remember, Grendamaul didn't begin as an evil and cursed land, and its soils have a long memory. You may think they only condemn, but I tell you true, they can also protect."

Seolad had no compunction about spreading his ire as he scowled at Iomi and filled the silence with a tumble of rude noises. But Gjen only chortled and beamed as he gave Seolad's beard a playful tug. Thank the stars, the act did not reignite the blackbeard's fiery tongue.

"Apart from the incantation I utter to create a glamour over our passage, think as I have asked, until I say otherwise," Gjen finished. "Silence in speech, silence in thought. Other than my voice, let peace be our parasol and guard our purpose." With that, the wizard stood and reached for his sceptre. "Let us be off."

When the light in the headpiece winked out, darkness engulfed them. They set out once more, moving across the dunes, quiet as shadows, listening to the sound of Gjen's lullaby, accompanied by the soft drone of the steady night wind. The breeze also shifted the sand, which covered their tracks moments after they passed.

Their first night proved the worst, wearing heavily on Sonart's unaccustomed legs. His muscles ached and harangued for solace. Gjen seemed determined to push them until they dropped.

Sonart disgorged his growing apprehension as Seolad did his bitterness, through the stiffness of their calves, the calluses that taxed their feet, and their grumbling bellies.

Looking down at the boots Gjen had supplied, Sonart shuddered to think how much harder their passage would've been without them.

As for Iomi, she passed much lighter on her feet than he and Seolad combined, almost accustomed to the adverse trek. But as the night waned, her head and arms drooped and she dragged her pads as well.

Only Gjen comported himself without any outward duress, walking with efficiency, obviously honed from experience with the soft unstable terrain. The wizard looked as though he floated over the dunes, but that might have been an illusion born of fatigue.

By the gradual brightening of the sombre clouds overhead, dawn approached at last. The crowded puffs hung like lifeless wraiths in the calm that heralded the day. Like the dwarven plodding beneath them, the clouds seemed stifled to immobility from one bleak horizon to the other.

Gjen guided them onto a stretch of fractured hardpan. One of the cracks spread and deepened before them, until it formed a fissure large enough for the small cadre to slip into. Sonart imagined himself part of a single insect with eight legs, as he followed the others, heaving his weariness into the barren crevice.

As soon as they moved beneath the fissure's slight overhang, Gjen stopped his incantation and announced softly, "It is safe to speak openly again. We will rest here until nightfall."

"What's this *glamour* you invoked with your chanting?" Sonart asked.

Gjen propped his sceptre against the granite hedge and removed his pack. "The psalms I recite shield us from senses that reconnoitre from the realm of magic," he explained. "As the cloaks obscure the visual senses of any onlooker, the chant shrouds us in a similar way. We would appear as small desert animals, our voices: sighs of the wind. It is how Laethan and I made the traverse, and dwelt a spell in Grendamaul undetected."

"Laethan?" Iomi asked.

"My apostate," the wizard said in a tired voice. "With great sorrow, he perished while making our first attempt to liberate Sonart. But that's a tale for another time. In truth, lass, my lids have grown too heavy to further burden my tongue, after so much chanting. Let us sleep—while we may."

Sonart's guilt resurfaced at Gjen's mention of the mysterious paragon. Resolve and a burning need for justice vied for his thoughts as he joined the others.

They laid out their bedding in a row, atop a large swathe of even sand that had infiltrated the cove.

Sleep came easily and quickly for them all.

Stephen Fenech

51: Corner Turns
Brooke

Brooke opened his mouth in stunned silence. Yerik stopped snarling, his canine ire vanishing like a candle snuffed in a gust. The Warang Chief reclined on his haunches and fell reticent, as though nothing had happened.

The rest of the wolves quieted as well. A moment later, they filed out past the line of blank-faced Wrayns, too shocked to notice their departure.

A haughty Lonus broke the silence, snorting moisture back through his nasal passages. "A measure of justice at last." He spat loudly on the ground. "The traitor's stars have finally aligned."

Brooke bristled, stifling the urge to strike the turbulent man with the pommel of his sword. But the damage was already done. More violence would not quell the band's dysfunction. He swallowed his anger while his scabbard swallowed his sword.

Brooke kept both sheathed, choosing to ignore Lonus' belligerence. His eyes sought refuge in the trees, his vehemence ghosting away with every breath.

A chill breeze made the commander shiver. Only then did his near nakedness dawn, clad in naught but his undergarments—exactly as Targin had been when they first met. If only he could match the Vein's control of this rabble.

Suddenly drained, Brooke moved to Gnor until he stood inches from his face. "Explain."

Gnor's tight expression hardened further, his bitterness all too palpable and contagious. But the stout man did not direct his glower at Brooke. "I tried to commune with Yerik the entire time, beseeching him to desist." He met the commander's fiery gaze. "But the Chief shut me out."

"Wonderful," Brooke returned, throwing his hands up. "How could this happen so close to our centre? Lonus says we suffered losses elsewhere in the camp. Do you know the full toll?"

Gnor bit his lip. "Truthfully, I do not, Commander. All communion has been suspended and no Nightwolf, Warang or Wrayn, responds to my calls." He let out a heavy breath. "But I'll investigate immediately."

Brooke remained unsatisfied but he surrendered a curt bow to the old Wrayn.

Gnor turned to go when Brooke raised an arm. "Wait—walk with me.

I'd better get dressed. There'll be no rest for me this night. My heart is crushed."

They moved back to Brooke's tent as the wolves disassembled and the men and women either moved to secure the area or retreated to their own fires and tents. Gnor waited patiently as Brooke pulled up his britches outside the tent and donned the rest of his outer layers and boots.

When he'd finished, Brooke whispered, "This wasn't a random attack, was it?" He already knew the truth but needed to hear it from the Wrayn's lips.

Gnor stole a glance over his shoulder before shaking his head slowly. "You were targeted again."

Brooke raised an eyebrow. "By Val?"

"It would appear so, aye." The Bulldog left something unsaid.

Brooke dug deeper, grasping at the roots of Gnor's unvoiced words. "That doesn't make sense, Gnor. With the lavatrols' attack, I might understand, but why would Val save me from them only to assassinate me here in the wild?"

Gnor splayed his hands. "Stars blacken, I don't know. Val has always been a conundrum—perhaps the *demonica* took him."

Brooke stewed over that possibility for a moment. "What of the Nightwolf, Val slew?"

"The Wrayn had been fully cloaked, so I couldn't tell. I'll examine him now—with your leave." Gnor added in a tired voice.

He took three steps before Brooke stopped him again. "Gnor?"

The bald man paused and wheeled.

"That third arrow, which prevented the second from piercing Val—an arrow aimed at an arrow—how?"

"Closer to the mark, whom?"

"Closest—why?" Brooke grated.

Gnor's chest deflated. "Not all the Nightwolves thought Val the culprit."

The fourth shaft too corroborated as much: shot without an arrowhead—not intended to kill but enough to penetrate the leather and push Val out of harm's way.

Brooke measured the man before him and decided to leave well enough alone for now. "Send some Warangs down there to find Val's body," he instructed. "Though I'm far from convinced that he was the cutthroat, he would've had help—and not just the physical kind. Keep this much to yourself, but tread carefully, eyes turned inwardly as well as out."

"Commander."

Still conflicted, Brooke pulled his brows together. "I want to know how many Warangs and Wrayns we lost tonight. Identify them. See if there are any intruders among the slain. Then muster the Nightwolves and break camp. I will not linger. We ride through the night as soon as we can." He glanced around at the remorseless trees. "This place is evil."

Gnor nodded. "Aye, it is."

Brooke watched Gnor stride away before making his way to the edge of the cliff. He stared down into the chasm's impenetrable shadows. Brapin's words came back to him, *Val's purpose, for good or ill, will be revealed. Where he must go and what he must do is not where the Nightwolves may follow.*

"You lived a mystery, and died one," Brooke whispered to the void. "I can only hope our stars aligned before you took the deepest sleep." *What did you want me to know?*

Only the wind answered him, brushing brisk dampness against his face, leaving yet another puzzle, another failure to his soaring tally.

Brooke lost count of the minutes before he turned and made his way back to the central encampment. He found Alghan awaiting him.

"Commander," the tall man greeted. "Not all Nightwolves have checked in with Gnor, but he has communed a rough estimate of the full reckoning."

"And?" Brooke prompted.

"Five Warangs and three Wrayns, but no infiltrators among them."

"And the one Val dispatched?"

"Gone."

Brooke blinked. "What?"

Alghan inclined his chin, his expression grave. "Gnor examined the others' reports. He's organized search parties, relaying your orders to the pack. When he came back to the main encampment the corpse had vanished."

Brooke dropped his jaw. "But he shed so much blood—I saw it firsthand. It would have left a trail. Are you telling me there's no sign anywhere of the corpse being dragged out?"

As if the air of turmoil and dissension could not sink any lower.

"Aye, seems the way of it." Alghan expunged his lungs. "While we focused on the melee between Val and Lonus, any sign of that Wrayn disappeared."

Which meant the slain figure was the infiltrator, or one of them and…

the collaborators might still lurk among the pack. Brooke's hands went clammy. He watched Alghan's mouth move, the words palpable enough, but he grew deaf to them. Refused to accept them.

Trepidation gave way to alarm. Brooke shifted his gaping eyes to the Wrayns. They all evaded his scrutiny, their resentment plain in the way they perfunctorily packed their gear onto the Warangs' saddles. Cynical irony clung to Brooke like a shadow. At least communion had resumed, and a semblance of order restored.

When the pack signalled their readiness to mobilize for the onward march, the eight dead Nightwolves were placed atop a makeshift pyre, erected over two adjoined fires. In moments, they lay burning on the raised bed of dried branches and brush, cut quickly to grant them a token measure of ceremony and respect.

Brooke chewed the inside of his cheek as he regarded the flames. They greedily licked the fuel, adding to his sense of urgency. Doubt gnawed at him. Had the fallen all perished at the hands of the same mole—the hands of Val? No, the last Wrayn corpse disappeared after Val jumped.

The answer stood right in front of Brooke, but he couldn't see it. Stars eclipse, *think* man.

"Commander!"

Brooke spun.

Gnor raced towards him, tight lines of worry etching his face. The fire's flicker played orange havoc with his wracked features.

And cast Brooke into a deeper abyss of dread.

The closest Nightwolves stopped and stared as the Bulldog sprinted past. Never before had the staunch man looked so fazed. Primal terror had taken root in his wide eyes. It could mean only one thing.

Suddenly heartsick, Brooke grappled Gnor's shoulders. *Vamsah, mercy, don't let it be him.* "Gnolin?"

"Missing!" Gnor admitted between gasps. "The boy is missing."

Past several dry-swallows, Brooke gathered himself and held Gnor's eyes. "We'll find him, Gnor—whole and alive—I swear it." Stars be fucked—folly stacked upon folly. He released the trembling man and bounded three steps past him.

"Nightwolves, we have a missing pup!" he thundered. "Commence a search until Gnolin is found. He is our first priority—our only priority. Now fly!"

His hoarse commands left his throat ragged as the band snapped to it, sprinting away in every direction. *Least I hold sway for this much.* Targin's charge was testing him like never before. But despite the mental and emotional strain, he would weather it. He had to, for Gnolin's sake.

Brooke lurched into a run and skidded to a halt a second later as another thought struck him. "Weet—has he recovered? If anyone knows, he would—those two were inseparable." They'd been together in the tent. If someone had abducted Gnolin or forced him to flee, Weet may know."

"Commander!" Onis called behind him in a voice like a funeral dirge. "Weet too has vanished."

Brooke wound his foot back and kicked a rock. "Stars *eclipse* the fucking damned!"

Gnor clenched his bald head in his hands and sagged to his knees. "First Father, Vamsah, Lightbringer, watch over him—my only blood and heir." His voice faltered into discordant sobs. "...because I can't right now."

Brooke's heart pressed flat, seeing this mighty warrior so distressed, crumpled by despair. His thoughts shot to his own two boys and how he'd feel if he'd lost them.

Brooke had to be a pillar for Gnor. He crouched and braced his hands on the stout man's frame. "We will find your grandson. I swear it on my life—on my family's—I'll see you reunited, both in good health."

Gnor stopped bawling, but when his red-rimmed gaze met Brooke's, they looked unswayed.

Brooke shifted his grip under Gnor's stricken arms and hoisted him up. "Come, do not fence with dire thoughts to validate them. Imagine the lad whole, and whole we will find him. Come, we can add four more eyes to the search."

Dawn drew near as they joined the hunt.

An hour passed.

And another.

The Nightwolves had fanned out, ranging far and wide to complete their steward's task, and still no sign of Weet or Gnolin. Even with their keen senses, the Warangs had failed to pick up anything resembling the scents of the missing lads—as though they'd simply vanished.

For all Brooke's adamance about departing before dawn, one thing, then another had forced the band to linger. At least the light of a new day would expedite their search.

But when dawn arrived, its light limped into the forest, hushed and subdued, revealing a dim ocean of grey overhead. Being on high ground, errant clouds from the central mass filtered through the elms and pines where they searched.

The wafts would sweep in and hover like undecided wraiths as the breeze which impelled them waned and surged from a different direction. The swirling mist clung to the nettle-laden ground as it sifted past, obscuring all but the closest trees.

With Gnor wed to Brooke's side, they marched further out, through a different tract filled with dank cloisters of fog-shrouded underbrush. Stung by the sharp pine needles, nipped by cold and damp, both men shared an equal measure of toil and weariness.

Grim and slim their chances: Brooke knew it, and bet that Gnor had reached the same conclusion. It's what kept them both silent beyond the basic need for search and surveillance—that, and the unsaid portent of their predicament.

The forest appeared a cemetery without the headstones, but Brooke knew the copse kept its dead. And held its secrets.

Eyes scanning the trees, Brooke tried to ignore his nagging apprehension, putting the responsibility he took for Gnolin's disappearance above all other considerations. He would make amends. Conviction fuelled his legs, built a second redoubt to reinforce his sapping strength with bricks of constitution.

But the elusive forest met his efforts, with the adverse, sapping his walls and draining his resolve with an unquenchable fount of asperity, borne of fate's maligned heart.

Brooke had picked this course after Brapin had cajoled him into following it instead of what Alghan suggested. Curse the dotard; now their predicament had worsened tenfold.

The commander exhaled, expunging the pointless conventions of blame and regret. Nothing would be gained by dwelling on the grievous mistakes that brought him here. He was here, and he had to keep moving forward. Had to get the pack out of these damn woods. He would see it set aright, or die try—

A shiver coursed down the centre of Brooke's spine, making him flinch.

A faint presence.

Then nothing.

But the air grew suddenly colder. A sense of ruthlessness escalated, then twice as quick diminished like a passing squall. He couldn't place it, but he sensed its like before.

Brooke raised an arm like a barricade in front of Gnor. "Stop."

Both men turned and faced one another in the dank void.

"Commune with our farthest flanks," Brooke whispered. "Bring them in now."

Gnor swallowed and croaked, "What is it?" By his pained tone he was really asking, *are we abandoning the search?*

Brooke matched his stance. "I felt something just now—something ghoulish, unnatural."

The stout man frowned, but he complied, closing his eyes and falling serene. Brooke waited patiently as the Wrayn's orbs moved from side to side behind his closed lids. He made no other hint of movement.

"The outriders along our flanks report nothing," Gnor began. "Advance patrols—nothing. Likewise, with both lateral thrusts. And the retreat, nothing as—wait."

Another twitch of coldness, more acute this time, and closer. Brooke felt his joints fuse. His muscles tightened to the point of snapping the bones they wrapped.

"Something's afoot, draws near to the rearguard. They report..."

Brooke let out an exasperated breath. "Fuck the report. Call them back to this spot, now, call them *all* back." His eyes darted in every direction, trying to pierce the mist that coalesced beyond the nearest trees—something surreal.

The trees themselves swayed, independent of the wind. The bark of their onyx trunks pulsated up and down.

"Rally the Wolves!" Brooke cried.

Gnor's lids fluttered open. "Flanks and patrols have heard. All storm in to rejoin."

Just as Gnor finished, the trees transformed behind the curtain of fog. Branches became arms, trunks splitting down the middle from the ground up to form legs. They loomed everywhere: hulking black shapes converging on the pair.

"Too late!" Gnor shouted. "Quick Commander, this way!"

Gnor surged forward, leading Brooke past the nearest of the maligned forms. Running an arbitrary course, branches grazing their arms, needles pricking their cheeks, they barely managed to stay clear of the closest abominations.

Brooke tore after Gnor, his body bursting with adrenaline, suppressing fatigue to maintain the Wrayn's insane pace. His thoughts raced back to his fateful decision that brought them to this juncture. Seemed inconsequential at the time. Now it would prove tragic. *Well-chosen—? Fucking hell, I have doomed them all.*

Brooke chanced a glance over his shoulder. Ranks of lessrtrols detached themselves from behind the changing trees, coming at them in big galumphing strides.

Ahead, the start of the escarpment Gnor mentioned came up fast. It sloped down to their left. Not quite vertical, but close enough. They met its edge and traced a manic line along its demarcation, driving their legs like furious pistons.

As the height of the ridge increased, the enemy lines thinned—the trolls' main thrust seemed focused far behind them.

But more than a dozen of the beasts had singled them out. They gave hard chase, bulldozing the ground, ripping it up in their wake. What the trolls lacked in cunning they made up in speed and brute strength.

The gap shrank.

Past Gnor's fleeing form, a massive sinkhole loomed directly before Brooke. It caused a depression in the land and terminated in a V-shaped gully, cutting a furrow into the scarp.

Brooke grimaced as more of the black shapes bore down from the far side of the depression.

"That tears it, Commander!" Gnor bellowed as he darted. The Wrayn launched himself off the ledge. "Deepest sleep take *meeeeeeeeeeeeeeeeeee…*"

The faces of Dayanthi and the children before him, Brooke leapt after Gnor—into oblivion.

The pair plunged, disappearing into the roiling clouds beneath them.

52: Sifting Sand
Sonart

Sonart floats within the aura, willing himself through the tunnels and gates, along an all-too-familiar path into the Cleft Augury. And with cloying certainty, he knows treachery will soon follow.

But he must proceed, even as a wound—unhealed, a storm's orphan. No, that is not right: not orphaned by the storm, forged by it. He brings the storm. Wields the Sword. It glares back brilliantly, chromatic hues flaring brighter, dancing at his command.

'Finish what you began,' the Sword urges. 'What Creation wrought you to do.'

An invasive presence approaches. Sonart feels a ghost of its dark hunger. Something he's encountered before: black beyond all blacks. But there can be no turning away from it as the Sword transfers the Vein's thoughts to its power. The emblem can repel even such uncharted depths of darkness.

Tendrils of shadow grapple filaments of light in a million separate battles. Hordes of Zürshuck crowd around to take its place.

All at once, the dwarven realizes, he is not in the Cleft.

But back in the Hive—in His arena.

Sonart poises the blade against this new assault. The weapon seems an extension of himself, symbiont. Lightning strikes, searing white bolts igniting as the Sword finds its first Zürshuck. And incinerates it.

The blade flashes and consumes a second demon and a third. A fourth winged malefactor blasts into nothingness.

Streaks of ebony light combat Sonart from all directions, trying to prevent him from unleashing a power he cannot fully control or comprehend.

The pressure of the magical melee cannot be contained any longer. It orgasms everywhere. Zürshuck disintegrate in swathes.

Only to be replaced by more Winged Ones and with them, an army of lesser demons, ranks of flaming Colossals at their head.

And above their lines, giant wings aflutter, the Four Siphons appear. The entire host charges.

Sonart forms a wilderen shield, fed by the limitless power of his Sword. It repels them all.

But then, a new adversary enters the arena. Static bursts of voided un-light herald its arrival as it coalesces into a single penumbra above Sonart. Its gloom suffocates the aura.

Beyond horrific, it emerges from its shroud. Gloom incarnate, the ultimate nemesis has come. Sonart cannot fully see it, but its presence permeates ungodly terror, horrible in any nightmare—there can be no doubt, tis the alien adversary returned.

Souleater.

The hyperdemon has blindsided Sonart—goaded him here from the Cleft all along. Did it know the Vein would be completely unprepared for it to confiscate him?

The weight proves too great. Souleater pushes Sonart's defences down. Both the shield and the Sword that fuels it succumb like cracking eggshells. The combined forces will break the Vein...

The Darkest One appears, crowing in sinister mock as the endgame unfolds. Sonart's Sword is wrenched from his hand.

"No!" Sonart cries.

The Raven Enigma gathers itself, rears up, and pounces.

Sonart thinks sideways. Focuses on being... NOT HERE. *The Darkest One's orbs release their hate. And soften—? His visage brightens. Deathwrought's carriage becomes that of a man. Holding the Sword in one hand, he shakes Sonart with the other as the aura dissipates around him.*

The Sword transforms into a staff. And Sonart gleans the truth at last.

It is not the Darkest One who rattles him so briskly, but Gjen—wresting him awake.

Sonart bolted upright, panting so hard, he thought his lungs would burst. Stiffness sapped him so utterly, he felt bruised in every muscle. He grimaced and moaned aloud, dull pain rising like an aftershock from the mental trap he narrowly escaped.

But had he?

When his breathing slowed, his eyes sought Gjen's. By the wizard's glistening skin, slumped brows, and weighted scrutiny, he too survived a taxing journey.

Sonart marked the shift in Gjen's countenance from a twilight of terror, through a night of consternation, easing into a dawn of relief. The wizard exhaled, shoulders slackening as he leaned back and relaxed his grip on his staff.

Sonart's gaze fell upon his dwarven companions, faces blanched and frowning, leaning forward on braced arms.

This was madness. How could Gjen think him capable of such an undertaking? When the first day of the quest brought on the worst attack yet?

Sonart washed down his despair with bitterness as he gripped Gjen's arm. "I had it. I had the Sword, in-my-hand—and," he swallowed hard, his beard dipping to the ground. "And I lost it. Deathwrought has his prize."

The dwarven Vein vanished from the dais an instant before Souleater collided with its stone surface.

And exploded.

Without any of the Blood Scion's wilderen power to resist the hyperdemon's attack, Souleater's puissance recoiled, seeking the path of least resistance.

Before any could react, the blast scoured the entire enclosure, funnelling up and down the length of the Hive, vaporizing demons and Colossals and Zürshuck as it went.

The uppermost reaches of Deathwrought's chapel charred obsidian, melting to glass in spots. The entire tower bucked and cracked in several places all the way down to the Circled River.

Closest to the impact, several large sections of the outer wall blew out, sending a deluge of fragmented ironock and stone hurling down towards the moat. Raining mortar and metal collided with several Winged Ones, unable to veer away in time. Swatted from the sky, they plummeted into the firewater far below.

Up in the desecrated chantry, only Deathwrought, His Four Siphons, and the volatile hyperdemon responsible for the detonation survived.

Gjen braced Sonart's quivering shoulders. "Listen to my voice. Heed my words."

Reluctantly, the dwarven gave Gjen his eyes.

"The Darkest One has nothing." Gaze unflinching, Gjen set his jaw. "If he had reaped your Sword, you would not be here. But you *are* here, in body and mind. And the Sword lies with you still. You claimed it for good when you slew the Zürshuck. Hidden until bidden, the Cleft Sword berths within you—your emblem to keep."

"Then why can't I draw it forth now?" Sonart croaked.

"I cannot be certain of its exact mechanism," Gjen confessed. "That remains yours to discover."

Sonart cursed.

"But take heart. My own emblem strengthened in the Sword's presence. And has not ebbed." The wizard rotated his sceptre, eyes fixed on the turning headpiece. "When you feel the pull of the Sword's sibling emblems, you will grasp the triggers of your own. Perhaps the blade requires you to be in proximity to the other Scions—aye, the emblem *bearers* themselves."

Eyes searching, Sonart splayed his hands. "But I need the Sword now! How can I believe what you say without proof? Seems hopeless."

Gjen raised a finger. "By its very nature, hope buckles down to task when surety sinks lowest. As a vessel of unimaginable power, the Sword can make entire realms quake. But it can work to your detriment if forced. The blade can, and has, cut both ways. It will come to you when hope and life require it. Do not abuse its privilege as a False Vein once did long ago, or like him, you will rain destruction upon Areth and beyond. From what I witnessed, you almost did exactly that."

Sonart knitted his brows. "False Vein?"

"False prophet more accurately," Gjen amended. "Though the man must've fancied himself one, truth be told. Lord Shirdron was his name—a Kazir like me, former king and alchlemage. But he became a spurious clairvoyant. The lord misinterpreted the prophecies in the Kusp, goaded by the Darkest One with lies and lures, to reach wrong conclusions."

Gjen ran a hand through his hair and surveyed each of the dwarven's faces before continuing. "Shirdron panicked. With the Kalibah lodestone in his possession, he inadvertently unleashed a torrent of devastation, instigating the right triggers of the Starbond but at the wrong time. The False Starbond fed on and poisoned itself, looping destruction and tearing the lands from one end of Areth to the other. Our world still feels the effects of that ruinous incident. To this day, his name endures as an object of disdain to all the races."

"Then, you must teach me to know the difference," Sonart said.

"My father told me to blunder fabulously is 'to do Shirdron proud,'" Seolad put in. "Admittedly, I hadn't a fucking clue what he was talking about."

Gjen gave Seolad a thin smile before returning his attention to Sonart. "You already know—*felt* the conflict of purpose. You saw the perilous consequence if you deigned to match power with power at the wrong time, and acted instinctively—well done by the way. Stars illuminate me, I will guide you as best I can, but have faith. Vamsah will light your true path."

Sonart could not shirk his doubt, but he offered the wizard a perfunctory nod.

"Good," Gjen said with conviction. "Now, as your guide, I think we should first take care of your more immediate needs."

"Gjen?" Iomi chimed in. "What is Areth and this *world* you mention?"

The wizard shifted his torso to face her. "Grendamaul—what you call the Cradle—is but one region of a much larger realm that has been kept from your knowledge your entire life. That realm is spherical in shape and we call it Areth."

Iomi's frown deepened. "A sphere?"

"Think of it as a ball thrown in the air, but instead of returning to the earth it stays aloft."

Iomi's eyes widened. "We live—on that?"

"Aye," Gjen confirmed. "And there exist countless globes in the heavens. All stars are spheres as well."

"Your answers only confuse me further," Iomi admitted. "Maybe you can add that to your list of lessons."

"I promise," the wizard said with a glowing smile.

Seolad grumbled something under his breath. Sonart exhaled and looked away. Chastising the foul-mouthed dwarven would only incite more foulness.

After a less-than-desirable meal of dried shrubs, bread, and water, a small flask dropped between Sonart's legs. Startled, his pupils shot up to see Gjen's apologetic grin.

"A salve I brought with me from the Main. Rub it on your legs and it will loosen the knots in your muscles and mind, but use it sparingly. We've completed but the first of many such days, and that flask is all I have left."

Sonart took the bottle in his hand and examined it. "Gjen?"

"Aye?"

"Won't they be alerted to our presence here in the Lobe—our escape?"

"In time, possibly, but not now. Apart from my own glamours, the Sword also armours you against seeking orbs." Gjen gave a faint chuckle. "And with the Hive's upper temple in shambles, they will have more than enough to occupy their minds as they lick their wounds, not barring the fact of how you slipped through their fingers."

"Sideways," Sonart murmured as he rolled up his trouser leg and opened the flask. He poured a dab on his outstretched palm and worked it into his skin. The ointment stung a little at first, but soon, nurturing warmth penetrated his marrow. When a euphoric tune escaped his lips, Seolad and Iomi quickly followed suit.

After their songs ebbed, Gjen stood. "Now that we're all refreshed, time to quiet your minds and move on."

The salve worked miraculously, but as the small cadre set out from the alcove, Sonart still detected a dull remnant from the previous night's strain. After the better part of a league, even that diminished.

Sonart's steps fell into an almost hypnotic cadence with the other three. By their unfaltering pace in the sand, they too had fully reaped the benefit of the balm.

As much as Gjen allowed, Sonart pondered how abruptly he'd acquired his three companions. Shayla had come upon him in a similar fashion—with

417

harrowing results. Would it be the same with Seolad and Gjen? With Iomi?

The maiden looked fair like Shayla. Had Sonart not been committed to silence he would've pressed her with questions. Did Gjen recruit her for some reason other than her ties to her father or her skills as a healer? Past any doubt, the maiden suspected it as well.

Iomi had a strange air about her, which might explain her introversion. She did not speak often, acknowledging them with the meekest of glances and nods. She seemed to ponder her role, her woe, and the most opportune moment to send Sonart into the deepest sleep—as Shayla had plotted.

But as he watched her tresses bounce ahead of him, Sonart chased his dreary thoughts away.

A hand brushed his shoulder. Sonart chanced to look up at Gjen. The wizard continued to face forward, lids shut, chant unbroken, but his thoughts seeped into the dwarven's mind. '*For a desert mouse, you ponder a great deal on matters unbefitting a rodent. Do not let your mind stray from the simple things. Be at one with the Kusp—and the rodent's task.*'

When Gjen's mouth curved into a faint smirk, a wave of chagrin heated Sonart's cheeks. He swung his beard forward, concentrating on the dunes and hardpan ahead. In the dim twilight, the expanse stretched forever, their passage marked only by an endless procession of crags and strewn boulders. The arid breeze filled Sonart's lungs, dried his hands—*paws* and upturned ears and sinewy tail and—

'*Get down!*' Gjen's urgent communion barraged Sonart's mind. Without thinking, he dropped to the sand. Plumes of brown grit attacked his eyes, wedged his lips and teeth. As the others flattened their carriages beside him, adrenaline spiked his blood.

Sonart stifled the air in his throat, suppressing a dire need to sneeze.

thrump, thrump, thrump, thrump.

The sound of numerous wings grew steadily louder until their discordant overture filled Sonart's ears. Winged Ones.

He braced for pain, the rip of a claw, fang, or wing. His suspense protracted. The cacophony continued for half a minute.

And diminished. *Thrump, thrump, thrump thrump.*

Sonart released the breath pent in his lungs. The din petered to a faint utterance lost in the drone of the wind. Only then did he notice that Gjen's chant never broke, maintaining its protective mantra.

Sonart inhaled and exhaled for several moments. In and out. And in. And out. He tilted his beard skyward.

'*Head down,*' Gjen projected harshly.

Sonart shoved his face back into the sand, swallowing the silent reprimand and a handful of granules.

Twenty heartbeats later, the pounding wings returned. By the lower volume and pitch, the demons flew further off and were fewer in number.

This time when the sound faded, he remained prostrate and kept still. Until Gjen reached out with his mind. *'It is safe now. You may rise.'*

They all stood and brushed themselves off. *'The Zürshuck search the Lobe systematically, but blindly. We remain undetected. Let us continue with a little more caution to our thoughts.'* Gjen studied Sonart as he conveyed this. *'Seems Deathwrought has elected to begin his search from afar and draw in.'*

'Could the Darkest One be aware of our intent?' asked Sonart.

"Nay," Gjen communed. *'He counts on... something else.'*

Seolad's gruff voice broke the silence, "What?"

'Something, local, my good dwarven,' Gjen replied, letting the blunt trespass go without reproach. *'If our foes had any inkling, we'd have already been captured.'* His surety silenced any gainsay. Not even Seolad challenged the wizard.

Gjen tilted his staff forward and cocked his head at the three dwarven. *'Now, quickly, let us proceed.'*

The hours in the deepening gloom dragged on until a slash of grey on the horizon whispered the approaching morning. With it, the time for them to seek shelter.

Thankfully, the next two nights followed a similar uneventful course. Sonart took heart, believing Gjen's appraisal of their situation would attest true. For certain, their passage became easier, having grown accustomed to the demands of the terrain.

By the fifth morning, the height of the Innereach had diminished substantially. Distance and dust shrouded its onyx peaks in a grey haze.

Yet with each new dawn, the Outereach grew no closer. The mountains remained visible just above the horizon, no taller than half the width of Sonart's thumb placed sideways. He also kept track of the clouds swirling overhead. So far, stars align, the changing winds presaged no razor storms.

But their food had run low and the frequency of the crevices they'd relied on so crucially thinned out. The notion weighed down more heavily the next day when Gjen informed the party that they'd crossed the point of no return.

Of course, there would be no turning back. Had Bordu and Piskin made it this far? Did his late peers reach the same conclusion before the Zürshuck rained down on them? Sonart quieted the painful memory as he marched on through the sixth night.

When darkness retreated, Gjen halted the company by a tiny outcrop of craggy rocks.

"We have come far enough to resume very limited conversation when we stop," Gjen said. "But never on the march. Also, this will be the last time we can use the terrain itself for shelter. Henceforth the lay grows flatter, sandier, and more exposed. But we will endure."

"The rocks do not give enough height," Seolad muttered. "In the wide-open, even with the cloaks, we will not be mistaken for any desert rodent, because the vermin themselves would not be out in the open."

"You are correct, my friend, but I've anticipated this," the wizard replied. "I carry a sheet spun of an elven cloth from their faraway forest sanctuary, Grenfor Talarben. Once pegged down and covered with trappings of sand, it will appear nothing more than a shift in the terrain to any Winged Ones flying overhead. Even from the ground, it would be extremely difficult to distinguish from its surroundings."

The blackbeard's scowl lost clarity and he dipped his chin, apparently mollified. In this instance, Sonart couldn't blame Rusic's son for his frustration. He shared Seolad's longing to be done with the hazardous trek.

But more than that, Sonart yearned for the chance to open his heart to Iomi, without the other two listening in. He had so much he wanted to tell the taciturn maiden, so much he needed to learn and share and absolve. But for the silence Gjen commanded, it would have to wait.

Sonart let out a resigned breath, scratched his auburn beard, and studied the maiden. At least the fire of hatred no longer burned in her beautiful greys.

What's more, when Iomi caught him staring, she offered a faint smile.

Its warmth and unexpectedness shocked Sonart. And made his long-frozen heart tremble, and begin to thaw.

53: Sand Sifted
Sonart

Rain fell the following evening. Stars align, it had not been conjured by the Scourge, but it did carry a strange mist that blanketed the land. Both mountain ranges were now equally lost even before darkness added its own obscurity.

The downpour wore heavily on the small company as they picked up their gear, rendered sodden as soon as Gjen pulled back the elven sheet.

When they stopped earlier that morning, Seolad added to their woes with his announcement that the healing salve had run out. No one responded to the testy blackbeard's complaint. Like Sonart, they'd grown accustomed to his griping and dismissed it.

Gjen took up the march, followed by Sonart, who chanced his luck walking abreast of Iomi. Seolad brought up the rear.

Through the uncomfortable drizzle, Sonart made out Gjen's steady chanting, except when the wind gusted and keened past, swallowing the wizard's incantations.

The ululating squall turned the rain into lashing nettles as it whipped strands of Sonart's hair against his face. Past his tangled curtain, he kept a covert eye trained on Iomi.

Mouth forming a tight line, the maiden seemed more determined than the wind as she ploughed on, her mane darting across her high blushed cheekbones.

Despite the gloom, Iomi noticed Sonart's reconnoitre for she turned towards him and touched his arm. The maiden pushed her matted hair back to one side of her face, held it there, and smiled openly.

All at once, the weight in Sonart's heart vanished. He grinned back at her, the elements all but forgotten.

Until the rudest grunt sounded behind him. They both spun.

Seolad had caught their silent exchange and glowered at them in obvious distaste.

Let him simmer. Iomi's beam had confirmed something wonderful. No longer would Sonart have to tread helplessly alone. If only he'd known this would come to pass while pining away in the Dunge. That he would tramp away from that doom, on common purpose with three resolute souls—to right so many—

The ground suddenly disappeared beneath Sonart's feet.

Iomi cried out as the entire company sank into fluid earth.

Stung into sharpness by its chill, Sonart seized Iomi's waist and hauled her to him. Even as their legs pushed deeper into the granular ooze, the rank of dead things filled the air.

Gjen's voice pierced the tumult, "Your Sword, dwarven! Call it forth!"

Urgency swatted Sonart into a panic as he strove to repeat what he'd done with the Winged One.

Nothing.

"Stars burn you both, help me!" Seolad snarled behind him.

Joined at the hip with Iomi, Sonart reached back with his free hand to seize Seolad. His digits fell short. To his horror, Rusic's son had sunken much deeper than the rest of them.

Again, Gjen cried over the furore, "Hold together."

Heartsick at his inability to do the wizard's bidding, Sonart's nerves frayed. They would die and he was powerless to prevent it.

A flash staggered his senses, punctuated by a crack that made the air rumble. Tiny flecks of light lingered as the initial burst ghosted away. The pinpoints danced in the darkness, revealing the ironock concentration etching Gjen's face. Lips working soundlessly, the wizard clearly drove some kind of spell.

An incoherent sound escaped Seolad's mouth as his head disappeared beneath the surface.

"Gjen!" Sonart wailed in despair. "We're losing Seolad!"

Another blast of light shot forth and penetrated the earth deep.

Sonart kicked involuntarily.

Something solid resisted his weight. Rocks had formed in clumps like disjointed steps beneath his boots. Gave their soles traction.

With it, he pushed himself and Iomi higher. Then ploughed his fist into the ooze towards the spot where Seolad had disappeared. His fingers found the dwarven's tunic, purchased, and *hhhhhhh-auled* him up, gritting his teeth with the effort.

By slow increments, the fluid sand relented and Seolad's body drew closer, higher. His head broke the surface.

To Sonart's relief, the blackbeard coughed and gagged.

But a moment later, Sonart's elation turned to ash as Seolad lost consciousness and grew still.

"Quickly!" Gjen commanded. "Grab at the solid bits you see forming at the surface."

Iomi, still tightly nestled in the crook of Sonart's arm, reached out and fastened her fingers about Seolad's cloak. She held him fast while Sonart used his unrestricted hand to grapple the closest of the floating rocks.

The piece formed a ledge, anchoring all three dwarven. It expanded, pushing them away from the centre of the pool.

Gjen used the same method with a different sill and soon all four companions knit together. As one group they drifted to the pool's edge.

"You first," Sonart instructed Iomi. "Surrender Seolad's load here. I'll keep him while you ladder over me. Quick, get to solid ground."

With great effort, Iomi clambered up his body and heaved her carriage onto the firmament. Still panting, she spun on all fours, stuck out her hands, and gripped Seolad under his armpits while Sonart did his best to assist her.

But his muscles screamed for solace; their strength sapped.

Abruptly, the burden vanished, relieving Sonart completely of Seolad's weight. A moment later, steady hands hauled Sonart up and deposited him on the drenched but solid patch. He rolled onto his back and faced the ebony heavens. In the last flicker of the magic-born light, Gjen's grim orbs fixed him with his scrutiny.

Sonart's head reeled with dizziness and his lungs eagerly sucked air. His thoughts clouded as a tide of darkness rose about him.

Smack!

Sonart shuddered as Gjen's hand slapped him hard across the face, jolting him back to full alertness.

"No-you-don't," Gjen growled. "We must get away from this snare or our quest ends here." The wizard's trenchant command brooked no argument. Sonart hauled himself unsteadily to his feet.

"It forced me to abandon my concealing chant, and use direct magic," Gjen said, a mix of anger and worry fretting his tone. "With the trap sprung— they may know exactly where we are."

Sonart's alarm mounted when Gjen hefted Seolad over his shoulder. The gruff dwarven didn't move. Had he succumbed? If so, what was the point? Though tough as they came, would Seolad pull through?

Sonart's questions went unvoiced. Without another word, Gjen hastened away, resuming his chant as he strode.

The rain continued unabated as Sonart staggered in procession, struggling to keep pace with the wizard's brisk gait.

Arms folded tightly beneath her breasts, Iomi trailed behind.

Silent as shadows, they moved as fast as they dared, winding a disjointed path around unseen traps. They hopped over certain patches and paused at others while Gjen stretched out his hand, clearly warding their safest course across the precarious swathe.

Sonart's legs became whips of pain, a constant lash unfastening what remained of his resolve. Worsened by the pelting torrent, his apprehension kept his pupils darting in all directions.

Iomi, on the other hand, defied nature: her steps surefooted, her constitution, a marvel, she carried on without complaint. The irony of Seolad's recent protests about her left Sonart disconcerted.

The march seemed interminable, as much for the physical strain as Sonart's mental anguish. He had failed them when they needed him most. And now they paid the penalty for his wilderen ineptitude. He should have—

Gjen broke through Sonart's self-recrimination. '*We are not safe yet,*' the internal voice said. '*Evil plagues this stretch, but for all their prowess in setting such traps, they only know that one has been triggered—not what or who triggered it. And even if they did, they would likely think us consumed by it, drowned or succumbed to the same poison which taints Seolad's body now. Do not fear for him; I have much experience with his affliction.*'

After a few more steps Gjen added '*Trust as well, such snares will never trip me up again.*'

'*Such snares? What of another kind?*" Sonart communed.

'*We will soon be free of all—I swear,*' the wizard offered.

Upon hearing Gjen's assurances, renewed hope washed Sonart clean. With a lighter disposition, the dwarven's steps fell, well not so hard.

Together, they trudged on into the night, over the treacherous terrain. At length, the rain subsided, giving way to a cool breeze. Sodden to the bones, the company halted shortly after.

Sonart noticed Iomi shivering and kindled his arm around her. She gave him an ambivalent look but didn't baulk or flinch at his touch.

"We are safe here," Gjen whispered as he lay Rusic's son down. "Iomi, tend to Seolad while Sonart and I make camp."

Iomi bent over the blackbeard's inert form and set to task, making the unconscious dwarven as comfortable as possible while Sonart helped Gjen erect the canopy right over them.

"Do not blame yourself, Sonart," Gjen said as he propped a support pole, which lifted the shelter's roof. "Seolad is a stout one and he swallowed but a mouthful or two of its filth. He will survive, as will we. Aye, we walked into a trap, but twas I who led us there, not you. I should've been more vigilant instead of pressing you three so hard. The fault lies with me, and I am sorry."

"But if it not for you, all of us would have succumbed," Sonart said as he bound and secured a line to the mast. "The Sword—you said I had it."

"You do." Gjen maintained. "But now that I consider it, perhaps the trap had been set *for* the Sword. Remember, your emblem serves as more than a simple ironock weapon, but a wilderen key and talisman tooled by the Creator for a much higher purpose. I believe the Sword may have acted of its own volition. Sensed that if it intervened, the Darkest One would pilfer it. My staff would work—or *not* work, the same in such straits. Trust that your emblem did not abandon you. The Sword will find you again, and I will assist."

When Gjen and Sonart entered the makeshift shelter, they sealed the flaps behind them and immediately moved to Iomi's side. The wizard held some small plants in his hand.

"Thank you, Iomi," Gjen said. "Go rest—you deserve it. I will tend to Seolad from here."

Gjen took a blue crystal from his cloak and presented it to the two dwarven. "This is a fragment of the Kalibah lodestone and the source of the trapper draw's power. Back up a step. I'll place it on the ground between us and attenuate its magic to our need. It will draw the dampness from your garments much the quicker."

Sonart and Iomi shared a frown as they looked upon the glass fragment. Frowns turned to gasps when Gjen set the crystal on the ground between them and ignited it.

The Kalibah flared, casting azure light over them. Its heat penetrated Sonart to his core. And just as the wizard promised, the gem began to draw moisture from their soaked garments. For several minutes, Sonart could only gape as steam escaped his clothing in skeins, coloured blue by the shard's cool spectrum.

Soon after, the Kalibah rendered the two dwarven comfortable enough to hunker down, huddle together, and fall fast asleep.

54: Moot…
Targin

No matter how many times Targin entered Serenthia's council chamber, the same unbridled joy always welled in his heart. Arguably the most beautiful space in the entire palace. Unlike the majority of halls excavated from solid bedrock by dwarven of a forgotten age, the assembly hall had been placed in a pre-existing cathedral-sized fissure.

Rather than smoothening out the irregular slopes and crevices to give it symmetry, the dwarven chose to add minimal embellishments to flaunt the rugged beauty of the four-hundred-foot-high enclosure: a mark of true craftsmanship. And pure genius.

The chamber had filled with various high-ranking officers and heads of state. Some Targin recognized from Johlarin's small circle but many foreigners as well—dark-skinned men and women from the south, and blond pale folk of northern stock. A few elven stood to one side of the auditorium, speaking quietly among themselves, grim expressions on their angelic faces.

"No surprise there," Targin mumbled, almost relieved to see the lot of them in typical character. Beside him, Lorin nodded.

But then one elven emerged from behind a pair of guards and Targin's heart sank. The newcomer clearly looked highborn, clad in regal finery, which quickly marked his house and station, including a golden tiara encrusted with a large emerald gem in its centre. A forest green cape draped over one shoulder, fastened by a golden brooch in the centre of his boyish chest.

"Not just highborn," Lorin observed. "But a prince."

"Here?" Bile rose in Targin's mouth.

"My Lord?" Both men spun as an usher approached. The fledgling guard, not quite twenty, halted between Targin and Lorin. "His Grace awaits you. This way."

Targin gave the stripling a curt nod and turned to his companion. "You first."

The usher hesitated and swallowed. "Apologies, but I was bidden to collect only you to the inner council."

The Nightwolf clenched his face into a knotted glare, withering the young man until his lips quivered. "Whether Lorin hears counsel from the eagle riders now, or from me later, he will know every detail either way. Details, which might prolong keeping this pretty kingdom and your pretty face intact. Better let him discern which facts are the correct ones—as he has done since before you were a twinkle in your father's eye."

Lorin chuckled. "Leave him be, Targin."

Targin flicked his chin at the guard. "I'd offer this cub the same advice."

The Nightwolf's scathing tone decided the callow retainer as he led them to the centre of the meeting parties where the king awaited.

On either side of the main podium, two separate underground rivers flowed and drained down a series of small chutes. The water gushing over the cataracts coalesced in long narrow pools lining either side of the assembly hall before joining in confluence behind it and down through a tunnel.

The charging torrents freshened the chamber's air while the din of the diminutive cascades had a soothing effect on the ears. Targin likened the auditorium to a sloped karst, rising betwixt girdling rivers fifty feet below.

The seats and stepped podium had been hewn from the stone itself, as were the two bridges connecting the atoll to the entrances across either river. The focal point of the chamber centred on a round granite table. Set atop the middle stage, it measured ten feet in diameter and six inches thick.

For this chamber alone, generations of dwarven revered their ancestors by making pilgrimage. If any midges were present now, they'd gone and hid themselves between the pews and their taller peers.

Small wonder Johlarin chose the venue to hear solemn counsel. It would help ratify negotiations, temper deliberations, and blunt hostilities should they arise during proceedings—all of which were likely to happen today.

Despite his years and the wrinkles that marked them like tree rings around a wizened visage, King Johlarin maintained an air of gentleness beneath his hard and alert exterior. Twenty years earlier, he'd have made a daunting Nightwolf in his own right. A brawny man, Targin's future father-in-law stood proud, his back straight, stomach flat, as formidable in stature as Targin himself.

Johlarin's longish white mane framed a piercingly handsome face, weathered by war and loss. Deep-blue eyes surveyed their surroundings swiftly—and locked onto Targin's green greys. The king's orbs betrayed nothing to those around him, but Targin read a cross between relief and irritation.

His Grace wore a thick grey cloak and cape, embroidered with gold and red filigreed lace over silver chainmail. A deeper grey pelt stretched across the regent's broad shoulders, held in place by a black metallic clasp with a ruby cabochon in the centre of his chest.

The crown on Johlarin's head had been crafted from gold and obsidian, interwoven to resemble a wreath of kraken tentacles. Encrusted with simple garnets, the headpiece occasionally cast a flitting light against the king's snowy hair and beard.

"Lorin," Johlarin greeted as they drew up. His voice rolled off his tongue, deep, rich, authoritative. "The Princess has spoken of your role in securing our borderlands—how did she put it—crucial as ever. You have my thanks, ranger."

Lorin bowed. "Your Grace."

Johlarin turned to Targin and sized him up. "The Queen told me the tale of your return—specifically the state of it."

Targin lifted his shoulders and let out a breath. "Sorry, Highness. I slipped."

"So I've heard." The king's wrinkles deepened, his face graver than usual. "'Tis not mere goblin poison on the quarrels that bit you and your mount. My alchlemage found the wound cursed with the blood lore of dark elven."

"Thorian would be right, for I don't slip up easily. The dark elven's oily—"

"That being the case," Johlarin said, raising his voice over the Nightwolf. "The situation's escalated beyond our worst imagining. War is one thing, but the implication of *their* involvement in the Endstorm, this close to the Starbond—"

"Transcends what's writ in the Kusp," Targin said. "Brapin told me."

Johlarin looked off into the middle distance. "Discord and duplicity." His eyes sought Targin again. "I'm afraid our way of life has come to an end."

Targin adjusted his collar. The damn thing was too tight for his thick neck, or maybe it was the thick air, or the elven 'jury' scrutinizing him now. "Brapin said that too. Referred to the same skew from the Testament's prophecy."

"No doubt." Johlarin blew out his cheeks and rubbed his forehead. "I appreciate your service with the Wolves, and the risks you took to make it here. Strangely, the delay caused by your recovery has brought you to this meeting at the most opportune time. But the efforts our enemy took to prevent you—" he shook his head slowly, "—provides evidence enough."

The king nudged his chin at the elven envoy. "There are greater costs to pay, but pay them we must."

Targin frowned at Johlarin's choice of words. A thunderhead of trepidation swallowed him beneath its shadow and rumbled in his ears.

"I don't know the details of this council," the Nightwolf admitted. "But I came with counsel of my own—might as well kill two foes with one arrow."

Johlarin shot Targin a sideways glance. "Make sure your quarrel flies true, lest you prick more than you bargained for."

Targin's unease at the king's cryptic comments escalated to alarm, but before he could inquire, the jingling chime of small bells announced the start of the moot.

"We'll speak in private later," Johlarin said quietly before he moved off to address the dignitaries and council members. Targin took a seat beside Lorin in the front row. Or sank into it. Thick sage-coloured moss grew on it, affording a natural cushion more comfortable than any royal pillow. Genius.

Targin spotted the monarch's sceptre propped against his throne. Johlarin had no need to wield his emblem in session or anywhere else. His commanding presence asserted his stolid kingship well enough. The regent always regarded the ornament with disdain.

Johlarin raised his arms above his shoulders. When everyone had seated themselves and the last murmurs of conversations petered into silence, he brought them down again and cleared his throat. "Friends and allies, I thank you all for convening on such short notice."

The king studied the assembly with a raptor's focus. "We've come to exchange words, set pieces upon a war board, and face our doom united. The Night we've long awaited hastens to dark fruition. Left unchecked, it will swallow and consume us all."

Several in the congregation nodded and a few shifted in their seats, but all eyes fastened on Johlarin. Only the sound of the rivers' gurgling water filled his pauses and drowned their echoes.

"Great in number and terrible in might our enemies have grown," Johlarin declared as he paced the central rostrum. "The redemption of our world will not be sought on a battlefield alone. Ironock, timeliness, cunning, courage, constitution—we'll need them all in great measure when the fight of our time joins. But to parry Deathwrought's thrust, we've more to consider. As done in the Rennen, his minions seek to subvert and divide us. We cannot let this happen."

The king's fierce pupils found Targin. "The Nightwolves' campaign to stymie the infestation in neighbouring realms has met with success—and sadly, terrible collateral damage. But I maintain that had I not sanctioned the covert strikes, left to their own devices, the subjects of those kingdoms would already be annihilated. Or worse, set to dark purpose by the mad whims of tyrants like Cele. The forsaken shores of Grendamaul prove this well enough."

Johlarin clasped his hands behind his back and took several paces in silence but his attention lingered on Targin. "It proved logical to target their military infrastructures, taking away their ability to wage war with swift decisive action. I regret to say a few like Pathguard and Cillinox still retain that ability. The Nightwolves have only bought us some time to manoeuvre."

Targin's gaze drifted up the slope towards the back of the congregation.

Along the top aisle, he spotted Tasmin, clad in a ranger's attire with riding leathers and boots. The shieldmaiden's arms folded in front of her, legs braced, face unsmiling.

The Nightwolf grinned, tossed his chin at her, and tried to make eye contact, but his efforts went unrewarded. A poet's study in terseness, the princess watched her father intently—definitely Johlarin's daughter.

Disappointed, Targin shifted his attention back to the king.

"Although we hold the threat in check, our hand is slipping," Johlarin said as he resumed his pacing. Every head in the chamber turned to follow him. "All the turmoil can be placed at the feet of one reprehensible puppet master: the necromage, Necatar. He has infected those realms, rotting them from within, beginning with their rulers."

The monarch gripped his beard and slowly moved his head from side to side. "What I authorised the Nightwolves to do was regretful, sinful—aye. But compared to what that fiend Necatar has cooked up, twas the lesser of two evils by far. If we survive this mess, I pledge to offer all aid and resources to help rebuild those countries."

Johlarin lifted a finger as he stepped closer to Targin and handed him a tight smirk. "Even if we kennel such a dangerous wolf and let him off leash from time to time, they'll see the truth of matters ere the twilight. The Scion has found us the right man to accomplish this monumental task."

The king's digit never strayed from the Nightwolf, but his carriage shifted back to the crowd. "Long has this one been branded a brigand across the Main, but stars be damned, his purpose *reflects* our purpose. With little time to organize, more binding allegiances must be forged today."

Johlarin turned to the elven prince, who swept his arm courteously and cast his saintly peepers to the ground at the monarch's feet.

Targin's throat went dry.

"Serenthia endures as a bastion but a beleaguered one." Johlarin steepled his hands. "Hobgoblins, dark elven—and as incredible as it sounds, lavatrols, now ambush our supply chains. Villages along our frontier remain under constant threat. Yet, the shroud of the sprites still pushes unfriendly eyes away and our entry wards keep ever watchful."

The king touched one of the gilded kraken tentacles atop his crown and winked at Targin. "In this fight, we must look for the attack we do not see coming." He gulped and lowered his voice. "I believe we have a spy in our midst—perhaps in this very chamber."

The twin rivers could not quell the troubled murmurs that arose, but Johlarin's speech cut through their tension like a knife. "The Darkest One would have you dwell on such intrigues; make you second guess every decision. If you do, we'll suffer Pathguard's fate. We simply cannot war amongst ourselves."

"A repeat of the Rennen seems inevitable, Johlarin," a noble from Mirningshire called from the back of the assembly. Targin recognized the highborn's raiment and sickle crest from the eastern farming realm. "What then would you have us do?"

Johlarin squared his jaw. "Steel your tempers before you temper your steel, for one. And your wits, for another. Stay vigilant. My heart tells me things are not as they seem."

"The sprites' magic is not infallible," Thorian, the king's alchlemage, added. "We must tread carefully: I fear pitfalls along any path we choose."

The mumbling grew louder, the air of unease rooted deeper. Targin felt it in his bones like a maligned presence seething into the enclosure.

But this time, his adroit king offered no assurances. He stood in stoic silence, evidently waiting for his grim import to berth all harbours.

When the noise of the streams rinsed the dissension away, Johlarin's face brightened. "It heartens me to welcome into our fold, Prince Serion of House Westafr, and his esteemed elven host. He speaks as envoy on behalf of his august sire, most honourable King Westafr of the Three Cities Realm. Eagle riders and Children of Light, Earthen-communed, and sprite peers, may our stars brighten one another in shared counsel. Vamsah willing, we will augur a new allegiance between our two races."

New allegiance? As the leader of the elven stood, Targin blinked and forgot to draw air. *This is far worse than I thought. What impels Johlarin so? Have his thoughts addled? Did Necatar get to him?*

When Serion stepped forward, Targin saw him clearly for the first time. The prince could have been a princess if not for the title, this wiry pale-skinned blond, flaunting a long silvery mane and features too chiselled, too perfect and bright. Maybe the dandy had been snipped true, rodless under all that finespun livery.

"Your Grace," the elven returned in a high-pitched lyrical voice. Stars, he even sounded female as he placed his delicate palms together. "I apologize that my father could not attend this council himself. I will explain the reason soon enough. As for my older brother, Ayr was pressed with other troubles, his health notwithstanding. As matters stand, I am their highest vassal to treat with you."

"You have my ears the same, and those of whom I rule," Johlarin decreed.

"You honour us with your formal salutation. We too recognize men, Freeborn, Last Born, Children of Earth, Hawk Riders. The elven extend our recognition to the Nightwolves, for their unyielding coven and continued protection of Areth," Serion went on, lauding plodding reverence.

"May we all work together for its sanctity and preservation. That the Stardimmer's shroud, which ever seeks to stifle the Heart of Creation, can be annulled, that the Four Veins as Vamsah's Blood Scions meet with victory in the Starbond. So that the seeds of the Twin-Gaia flourish in a new epoch."

Johlarin lowered his head and floated an arm with practised deference for court etiquette. "Stars align, Prince."

"Words unto deeds, effeminate stick-man," Targin grated under his breath.

Lorin flinched beside him. Eyes darkening, he shot Targin a cautionary look. Targin ignored the ranger as he studied the princeling. If the elven or any of his prissy ilk heard his gripe, they revealed nothing.

Serion turned to the assembly and brushed his surcoat from lapel to golden belt twice—like as not to see if his breasts had sprouted yet. "Our histories evince the price of ignoring the signs of prophecy and doom—or worse, acting under feigned pretence. Shirdron's False Starbond spoiled lands and eradicated many races. As did, the genocides in our own Great War, the Eclipsed Dragon Wars and much further back in time, the War of the Elementals, the dispersion and enslavement of the dwarven—a once powerful race unto themselves."

"Here comes the inevitable history lesson," Targin muttered. "Vamsah save us."

Lorin lifted a hand to his mouth, but the Nightwolf caught his shielded snicker.

"Tis well known that doubt still lingers," Serion professed. "The legends and songs in the Kusp's sagas cast shadows across our path. They waylay our attempts to unify the fragments of our allegiance—just as we strive to reunite the lost fragments of the Kalibah."

Targin wasn't sure but he could have sworn the prince eyed him as he mentioned the Starbirth Crystal.

"Once, rampant mistrust prevailed, each side blaming the other for losses incurred. But we must set aside our differences and stand united in solidarity against the coming Endstorm," Serion said.

Targin snorted. *Once?*

The prince raised his arms above his head and faced the flanks of the assemblage. "Aye, men and elven fared better than the dwarven, but both our races have dealt with corruption worming through our lands. Dark elven and goblins controlled by a greater diabolic, have multiplied. Demons too, beyond the calibre of the sprites."

Serion paused and scrubbed a hand over his temple. "The Law of the Octagon, which governs the Veins and Siphons, applies to all races. They struck the freeborn a blow when we lost the Great War."

"Lost?" Targin blurted. "I thought we won—Tragmar saw to that."

"A matter of perspective," Johlarin replied evenly before turning to the prince. "Forgive the interruption, Serion. Pray, continue."

"Time has only made our enemies stronger and better organized," Serion carried on. "Their forces have already mobilized. Very soon, they will make their killing stroke true."

The elven prince dropped his arms to his side, amidst a slew of chin bobs and headshakes. "As His Grace pointed out, victory will not be had on a field of battle alone. Nevertheless, we will fight—that is our combined role, to allow—" Serion glanced at Johlarin, "other tasks to be fulfilled."

Targin sucked in a bellow's worth to quell his dread, heartsick that the princeling could be so deep in Johlarin's confidence. Had the elven been made privy to the Veins' true quest?

"Based on our scouts and loremasters' reconnoitring, the elven have come up with a plan to stem our foes' movements," Serion proclaimed. "Now that we've elected to fight under one banner, King Westafr bade me share it with you—a course my father laid out long ago. For certain, Serenthia can no longer maintain a defensive stance. You must join with the elven." He clenched a fist, winched it up at the elbow, and pumped it. "Strike out in force immediately, ahead of any Merger."

Targin had heard enough. He shot to his feet and brusquely folded his arms beneath his barrel chest. "So, now you'll choose where and when we go, and how?"

Serion blinked.

Targin unfolded his arms and wagged a thick finger like a morningstar pausing before a blow. "Have you gleaned our enemies' direction as well as their intent? Perhaps, Eagle rider, Serenthia can surmise for itself how best to convene and countermove—lead your elven host as *we* see fit."

"Targin, your king does not take kindly to words said out of turn," Johlarin warned, his tone rumbling like distant thunder. "Remember your place."

"With all due respect, Your Grace, how could I forget it?" He shifted his glare back to Serion. "It is by the graves of those who died valorously before me—when the *elven* determined their fate. They decide quickly to use men as fodder in their plans and devices. I ask that Westafr's son remember his place."

Targin twisted his torso to the larger audience, whipping his head about to glean the reactions of any non-elven. "Have we learned nothing from the War of the Rennen? How many sons, brothers, fathers, learned the truth of their place—six feet under?"

His scrutiny seized the elven envoy once again. "They took the deepest sleep so your brethren could pursue the secrets of the world—to arm yourselves against your darker halves. Men died in the crossfire of an elven blood feud. And for what? The dark elven have returned!"

"Silence!" Johlarin boomed. He raised a fist and shook it at the Nightwolf. "I'll not suffer such insolence under my own roof."

Ignoring the king, Targin blazed on, accusation fanning every syllable like wildfire. "And, when the elven achieved their goal, they showed their gratitude by hoarding the lore they reaped."

Targin ripped the collar from his neck, popping the buttons which clattered as they struck the stone floor. "The sprites guide us now, Prince, and we choose a tack that aligns with theirs. They haven't imposed nary the toll you would demand of us—again."

One of the prince's retainers bolted to his feet. "What know you of tolls, *outlaw*?" he seethed, his voice pitching so high it surpassed falsetto. "How much of an ante has your band tallied, laying waste to the cities of the north? How many innocents died at your command, if not directly by your own hand? You seem swift to pass judgement on the elven when there stains as much, if not more blood on your hands, Usurper."

"Florin!" Serion wheeled on the indignant plaintiff, his mouth constricted and trembled. "Do not test me. It does not serve." The elven royal's face reddened to the same crimson that coloured Johlarin's countenance.

"You will show more respect for the Vein of Fire," the prince reprimanded. "Areth's champion—his stars rightly occlude by our past sins. As you well know, we stand sorely in the Strong Helm's debt for hosting this meeting."

The prince turned back to Johlarin. "Pardon the outburst. My Haft is distraught with our recent woes."

Targin's brows furrowed. *Woes?*

Johlarin dismissed Serion's plea with a wave of his hand. "He only answers my own dog's savage bark."

"My Prince," Florin beseeched, his face flushed with rage, his button nose, a ripe fucking turnip. "I do not mean to overstep your authority. But we will be indebted for a lot more if our hosts have their way. We cannot repel the darkness even with this allegiance—as you all know, but dare not say."

Florin stabbed a quivering finger at Targin. "I dub the Nightwolf—" he squeezed his eyes shut. "Pariah! Better deliver him to his rightful master—the Stardimmer—and be done with this farce."

The Haft poured contempt into every utterance. "We needn't die for his cause—enough elven have done so already."

Jaw open, Johlarin gaped at Florin and Serion.

The prince tightened and pulled briskly at his sleeves, his umbrage and chagrin plain. But he recovered a moment later, took a deep breath and released it through his nose. "Florin, you will leave this chamber at once. We will have words later."

A tight-lipped Florin stalked out of the auditorium, scowling at Targin as he did.

The Nightwolf returned the other's glower with a leer. "Officious little twat," he snarled to the elven's departing back.

"Please, forgive the Haft's cutting remarks," Serion said as he furled and unfurled his fingers. "He did not mean them to be taken literally."

Targin scrunched up his face and wrapped his arms about his waist—to hold back a bout of sardonic laughter. "Then, how *must* I take them, Serion?"

"Quietly," Johlarin grated. He pivoted towards the prince, arms extended, face creased apologetically. "I understand, your Haft's words were thoughtlessly said, born of the current turmoil."

"Aye," Serion agreed. "Florin has been overwrought with grief over the recent loss of his kin and the destruction of his home in Arboria. I will keep a shorter rein on him from now on." He gave them a congenial smile, which sent another hot gush of blood to Targin's ears.

"As will I with this short-tempered hell-hound of mine," Johlarin promised. "Lest he wishes to be muzzled, leashed, and kennelled until the Merger."

Orbs casting smouldering daggers at Targin, the king communed, *'Another syllable, and I'll have you removed to my dungeon in irons and flogged with your own toxic tongue.'*

"Pray no, Your Grace," Serion gently interjected. "Let Targin speak his mind. By addressing the mistakes of our past—many of which the elven are solely to blame—we might find reconciliation, to avoid such calamity in the future." He placed his hands together, eyes softening as they settled on Targin. "What say you?"

The entire congregation followed the prince's focus to the Nightwolf.

Teeth clenched, Targin stared back. Until Johlarin cleared his throat like a chimney sweep using a scouring brush.

Targin swallowed his bitterness and inclined his head.

Serion beamed, making his cheeks glow. "Splendid, that pleases me greatly." He licked his lower lip and pondered. "Regarding the Great War, for which the elven have never made proper reparations, our shortcomings proved severe, frequent, and far-reaching. But even they had much deeper roots. Long ago when Areth first formed, the Creator delegated the task of preserving the mechanism of the Starbond to those of his First, the

Highprites responsible for the creation of the elven. In turn, bits and pieces of their lore passed down to us children."

Targin wanted to cover his ears at the elven's dissertation. He craned his neck towards the back of the chamber to gauge Tasmin's reaction, but to his deepening dismay, she had left.

"Yet some among us fled from the light and turned to darkness," Serion went on. "They usurped what parts they gleaned, and bargained them off to the Darkest One. The War that ensued was a conflict of sequestration and attrition, as my forebears sought to stop them. 'Hoarding the lore,' as Targin put it, extends that preservation. Our magic stems from what we've safeguarded. And will culminate in our own emissary, the elven Vein. He is paramount to that end—not merely an elven envoy, but a vassal for all Creation."

Targin swallowed as he conceded the point. Brapin and Gaegungen had said as much of the elven Vein—some direct connection to the Highprites.

Serion's attention drifted to one of the rivers, then the other. By drawing Targin's notice to the water, their gurgling sounded louder.

The prince stepped towards the Nightwolf, making him look up again. "In earnest, Tragmar Son, there are no secrets the elven would keep from this council—or you. If you refer to the lore we've gained from the mystic instruments of the natural world, such knowledge will be made readily available to you. But I mean no insult when I say men cannot grasp the use of its wisdom and power."

Targin arched an eyebrow and tangled his forearms.

"Even if I instructed you step by step," Serion said quickly, "you would not be able to draw it forth, as it was never meant for you. It would be like trying to explain colours to a blind man. The Gaia intended the lore for the elven alone."

Targin rolled his eyes. "How convenient."

Serion splayed his hands. "Stars, Nightwolf, we did not ask for this. The Unnamed Highprite chose us for it. Same as the Creator selected you to be a Vein of Fire, One of the Four Blood Scions, and the merekin, the shepherds of the sea, Granocks, custodians of the forest fair."

The prince let out a weary sigh. "Still, as an act of faith, I'll speak of these learnings, as we've come to understand them."

"By all means do so," Johlarin put in. "Calm my rabid dog."

Despite his mayhem, Targin surrendered a laugh at the king's insult.

Serion grinned faintly. "Essentially, the Starbond is the key to Creation from the nothingness which preceded it—the Void of Obliteration. The newly formed nether-abyss portals the physical Universe, and the spiritual plane that overlaps it. Sprites and all of Vamsah's creations populate our corporeal world, while the demons inhabit the spiritual realm."

Serion sauntered away from Targin along the front row of seated men. "All that is created from the magical realm manifests in the physical. Adversely, a coexistent opposite, births within the spiritual—for they root in the same wilderen fount that manifested both."

Lorin let out a quick cough. "Ah—wasn't that Vamsah's doing?"

The prince stopped midstep and took the scout in. "Yes. When Vamsah, came into being so too did his antithesis, Morgrand. If Vamsah forged the soul of Creation, then Morgrand is the shadow cast by the soul. The Darkest One is in essence a twin entity: Morgrand housed in one of the Highprites, whom he seduced to his cause and supplicated to host his essence. Together, they became a single vessel known as Deathwrought."

Targin regretted sanctioning the elven's ponderous lecture, but with Johlarin fixing him with a dirty look, best to keep quiet.

"Antitheses govern balance," Serion went on. "Sprites to Colossals, elven to dark elven, Vein to Siphon. The Starbirth marked the beginning of Creation as we know it, when our Universe exploded for eons until reaching the Starbalance."

Serion removed his tiara and ran his fingers through his silver-gold mane. "The astral plateau eventually reached equilibrium between Creation and Annihilation. The prophecies of both our races describe this as the Spiral Balance."

The prince reseated his crown and adjusted it with both hands. "Since the Starbirth, the envelope has contained our physical Universe and the spiritual realm. Beyond it resides the Void I mentioned."

Targin grimaced, his palms growing clammy at the recollection of the blighted realm in his visions—and the harrowing entity that dwelt within. The hyperdemon that stalked him still.

"Stars and worlds hasten into confluent aggregation," Serion concluded, "into the Starbond, while we resolve the fate of all realms."

"Creation moves in a circle," Thorian put in as he pinched the bridge of his nose. "It is all based on circles. Time, being one such element of Creation, circles back to its point of origin, the Heart, the Cleft Augury. Areth and the symbiont realm, Otherworld, form the first points on this side of infinity." He meshed his fingers together. "*Knotted* thus since the Starbirth, they shall also mark its terminus in the Starbond. If we derange the circularity in any way, as Shirdron attempted to do, there can be no recovery."

Serion nodded briskly at the alchlemage. "Elven astronomers confirm as much—countless stars aligning to the precession you describe."

"Of late, the tightening orbits of the stars reveal to the naked eye that the Starbond is indeed at hand," Thorian supplied. "Drawn by the limitless power of the Bond, they converge on us here. At present, the vergence of the stars has grown exponentially faster."

"The Starbalance has passed vertex—something any Orbical apprentice would know studying the night sky," said Serion. "But something appears terribly wrong with the stars' realignment that might affect all prophecy forthwith."

Targin adjusted his ruined tunic and cringed as the fabric chafed him. "Maybe the elven got it wrong—wouldn't be the first time."

"It is not elven loremasters who impart the revelation," the prince said. "But the sprites of Etern's Drop and the Timekeepers of Stormhearth."

Johlarin clasped his sceptre and butted it firmly on the floor. A metallic thud sounded. "What were their words?"

"I brought their sealed edict for your perusal and authentication," Serion said. "But before we unfurl it, we have war plans to discuss, if it pleases."

Johlarin exhaled through his nose. "The battles fought throughout the Great War and dare I say the War of the Elementals to maintain this balance will seem but skirmishes compared to the final battle that draws nigh."

"Aye, Your Grace," the prince affirmed before shifting his regard back to Targin. "And there, Nightwolf, sits the limit of elven learnings and lore that we bring to this moot. Creation's circular journey will culminate in the Starbond. Then, all opposites including the Octagon's Four Veins and Four Siphons will face final judgement—Creation versus Obliteration."

Targin scratched the stubble on his chin—he'd forgotten to shave—before a thought occurred to him. He raised a digit. "Who's doing the judging?"

"A great question," Serion vaunted. He sounded impressed by the Nightwolf's intuition. "At rare moments whilst in sleep's twilight, these ethereal beings, these—*observers*—appear in my peripheral and vanish as I train my waking eye. When I pressed my tutors, all they could offer is that we've been observed since the Starbirth, that they judge us impartially, and will continue to do so unto the Starbond."

Targin rubbed a brow and contemplated. "I too have glimpsed them on occasion, quite often actually, as I transitioned from my dreams into consciousness."

Serion's head tilted forward. "I can only imagine that as a Vein, you would draw their attention more readily, cynosure to their observations, garnering more frequent visitations and deeper study. What do you recall?"

"I remember they scared me shitless."

Lorin snorted at Targin's bluntness.

Serion faced the assemblage, his voice rising. "For the Veins to succeed it will be our duty to plough the field, allowing their wilderen seeds to sow the earth, take root in the power of the Twin-Gaia. And replenish the Heart."

The prince laid his palm over his heart like a knight about to swear fealty. "Their way must remain safeguarded. If our own lives must be forfeit… so be it." He paused, looked up at the ceiling, and took two long breaths before continuing. "Alas, the true reason behind my journey here is more than a cumbersome recount of histories and a call to arms."

When Serion's face dropped again his eyebrows kept going, weighted like sagging eaves. "Know that the elven too are in grim stead, which brings me back to the real reason for my father's absence."

A cold sweat trickled down the centre of Targin's back. He detected no facade, no flowery lilt in the way the prince delivered his tidings.

Naked pain fretted the elven's trembling voice. "It cleaves my heart to tell you, the dire fate of Grendamaul's dwarven pales before the travesty visited upon the coastal elven. Our entire realm has been destroyed, our people slaughtered. All Three Cities have been razed to the ground."

55: ...And Mourn
Targin

Hoarfrost crept up Targin's spine. Except for Johlarin, all the men in the assembly gasped and stared, their blanched faces struck by the same verbal lightning bolt. Serion's elven retinues mirrored their prince's distress: hollow grimaces and sunken shoulders, all.

"Deathwrought's war hammer did not swing wildly at the Main. Its barrel struck my people first," the prince said. "And struck us hard. While our watches trained on the sea, forest, and sky, our ears pressed close to the ground, his minions did something we never could have fathomed."

Targin splayed his arms. "What of your armies?"

"Most wards: spur, heel, and wing, had been sent to range our eastern borderlands—after receiving reports of ogre sightings."

Johlarin drew his chin back and narrowed his eyes into slits. "Ogres?" He sought Thorian's reaction. When the gaunt alchlemage shook his head, the king faced Serion. "Those cannibals were eradicated from the Main long before the Eclipsed War. Extinct for thousands of years."

"Save the odd rumour of a glimpse north of the Dead City," Lorin supplied. "And some more encounters in the highest lofts of the Matted Spikes. Admittedly such claims have never been verified—any proof readily erased by the Harrowing before it could."

Serion observed Lorin with wary eyes. For a moment it looked as if he might add something more. But then he veered back to Johlarin. "We thought the same as the most adamant naysayer, Your Grace. Until we found evidence of their passage: footprints matching depictions from our ancient texts. Though no casualties or damage followed them, communion with the forest animals confirmed our suspicions. They witnessed an entire tribe of the beastmen lurk past."

"Perhaps, a false lure to draw out your forces," Lorin pointed out. "I too bridge with animals, and they've never spoken of ogres. Neither have any Granocks." He shifted his regard to Targin and linked thoughts, *'Nor my wizened forest ally.'*

"Paperman—aye," Targin said in the ranger's ear. Over breakfast that morning, their conversation had centred on the eclectic forest hermit. Lorin praised the old one's gifts with wood lore, and the tranquil cabin that served as Paperman's domicile, a day's march or so north of the Strong Helm.

"Why hadn't the animals sent warning ahead of your search?" Lorin asked Serion.

"They tried, but something blocked their communion. My scouts think it may have stemmed from the ogres themselves."

Lorin scratched the back of his ear. "You need a mind for that, and from what my mentor said of the giant berserkers, they understood a single code—to the death."

"Mindless beasts, indentured to the Darkest One—according to what I've read," Thorian added. "So, if indeed it was a shroud, it stands to reason one of his higher minions conjured it."

"And that crony resided in Arboria," Serion said. "One of our own betrayed us."

Mouths agape in stunned silence, Nightwolf, ranger, alchlemage, and king exchanged looks of disbelief.

"Tis true." Serion deflated his lungs and slouched as though crumpled by a rockslide. When he spoke again his voice sounded buried under one. "We did not think to look within our own keep. Legions of lavatrols cracked rents in the foundation of our deepest cellars. They tunnelled to points beneath our wards where caesuras bridged... directly into Infern."

Targin started. "Infern?" He spun on Thorian. "Is that even possible?"

"Aside from the Kusp, ancient texts speak of it, aye" Thorian replied. "Though not since the lost days when Highprites walked the earth."

Targin angled back to Serion. "How do you know this for certain?"

"Hordes of demons in the skin of men poured out, followed by dark elven. As our magics concentrated on repelling the incursion within our walls, a throng of trolls appeared outside our gates while hobgoblins astride crowbats harried our battlements from above. We had enough pointwards and defences to repel and keep them all at bay, but..."

After a vacuous silence, Targin prompted past a gulp, "But?"

Tears welled up in Serion's eyes and streamed down his face. "That's when our horns sounded a different tune—one of hope. The men of the Northern Kingdoms appeared with the soldiers of Pathguard at their vanguard. From the ramparts, their twin tower banners could be seen from afar. A host of spurwards and heelwards and well-equipped pointwards. Thousands ahorse, and more afoot, they marched south along our coastal buttresses."

Thorian's jowls pressed back. "The Northerners' allegiances vary with the changing of the wind—but did they vanquish the besiegers?"

"Aye," the prince confirmed. "They routed all the trolls—cut them down to the last beast. And shot down most of the crowbats with crossbows and ballistae. Four-armed arbalests set atop windlass-mounted wagons they carted with them as well. When they offered to fight the intruders within the city, King Westafr didn't hesitate. He ordered the guards to open the gates. Once inside, the Northern commander hastened to treat with my sire and me in the king's main audience chamber."

Serion's lower lip bulged. "It was quick. A poisoned knife to the heart. In the ensuing chaos, I tried to use my elven magic to obliterate the assassin, but counter-spells cast by dark elven loremasters suppressed my efforts." He buried his head in his hands. "I managed to tear away the glamour concealing their commander's true identity—as he slew the King's Highguard."

The prince's orbs lifted like dead things emerging from a grave. They crawled towards Targin. "Twas the necromage, Necatar. He came for me next. But my defensive spells still worked. I conjured a shield and screen that veiled my escape. Through a secret passage that led to the palace ramparts, I stole, making it as far as the northeast ravelin of the bailey. There, atop the parapets of the cavalier, I could only watch as the northern soldiers turned on the elven and... and joined forces with the demons."

Targin gasped and drew his head back. "No."

Serion's retinues all nodded in answer. "Tis true, Nightwolf," one of them confirmed.

"My magic failed me then and the enemy descried my station." The prince gulped. "As they swarmed the battlements, I climbed to the crown of our loftiest turret. Too high up, nowhere to run, I was trapped and powerless to help my subjects—understand?" he beseeched. "No one answered. No one could."

Presently, Lorin stood. "So, what did you do?" He ambled around the table. "And what of your brother?"

Serion's voice finally cracked, "I don't know Ayr's fate. He rode for Canelgren, two days before. Attempts to commune with him have failed. I can only presume he perished when the city fell."

"How *did* you escape?" asked Targin, his own heart pounded flat.

"I flew," the princeling said. "Several eagle riders returned to thwart my pursuers and lift me to safety. Made all speed to a border waypoint where our wingwards and heelwards had encamped. We sent three eagle riders back to the Tri-Cities to search for survivors."

"And?" Targin probed.

Serion's red-rimmed eyes glistened as they locked onto one of his guards—a captain by raiment and armour. "Tyrsus?"

The captain inclined his head and stood. "When the riders returned, they reported that our three sibling cities had been razed to the ground. The very stone of their castles rendered molten where the lavatrols passed. All their inhabitants lost. They left Arboria, Canelgren, and Galandrium in smoking ruins. The demons have torn asunder the entire lowland between."

"Thank you, Cousin," Serion said. Tyrsus bowed and sat down again.

The prince pivoted back to Targin. "As I said, the hellspawn have rent a rift into their dark spiritual realm. It has widened. Infern remains open, with lavatrols to guard it. Demons can now enter Areth without the need of a magical force—the Summoner has wrought this. Once a pristine fertile realm, our lands have been blighted like the Cradle, corrupted like the Land of Fire."

The prince choked on his last word and cast his eyes to the ground.

Cries of utter shock and dismay reverberated throughout the chamber.

When the uproar diminished, Serion hauled his tortured face to meet their enquiry. "With naught to save or salvage, I turned our host east towards Serenthia, flying ahead with the eagle congress. If nothing else has befallen them, the rest of my wards—spur, point, and heel—should arrive on the morrow."

"Stars blacken all," Johlarin fumed, nostrils flaring like a riled bear. He slammed a fist on the table. The gems of his rings smacked loudly as they struck the granite. "Pathguard and the Northern Kingdoms in collusion with demons and dark elven? Beguiled or not, this isn't mere betrayal. It's treason and sacrilege of the highest, foulest, most reprehensible order!"

With both hands, Johlarin hefted his sceptre across his waist as though about to cast a javelin.

But twice as quick, his temper simmered, glower fading as he tilted his head to the cavern ceiling. "Westafr was both staunch ally and wise regent. Deeply stung and moved, my heart bleeds for your loss, Serion. And your path—to be coronated under such dreadful circumstances." He lowered his gaze to the prince. "But you are the rightful king now."

"Prince will suffice, Your Grace," Serion said, recovering a semblance of calm and fortitude. "My grief yet outweighs any notion of office, formality, line, or legacy. To me, I'd only dishonour the memory of my father and brother."

Targin guzzled air past the rock he uncovered in his throat, forcing it down into his soured belly. Save Serion, every elven in his company had their faces in their hands in shared angst. That, more than anything, vouched the legitimacy of the highborn's appalling tale.

With great effort, the Nightwolf found his voice. "How could Pathguard amass such an army this soon? And take them so far?" He shook his head slowly. "Serion, Vamsah as my witness, I left Cele's war engine in a smouldering heap of rubble—completely dysfunctional. Twas the same with the other Northern Kingdoms."

Serion nodded briskly and snorted back a rushed breath. Despite the canyons under his eyes, the prince straightened his tunic and regained his composure. "Aye, but consider the translation hubs. The dark elven are well versed in their use. One such portal lay in the heart of Galandrium."

Targin's eyebrows sought his hairline. "They must've stormed through there—initially—taken that city from within and then made for the other two centres."

"Necatar put them to it," Serion said, jutting his bladed chin at Targin. "Of late he works closely with dark elven to exploit and undermine our lore. Through his own theurgies, the necromage holds sway over the demons he's summoned."

Thorian turned to Johlarin. "Regardless of blame, Majesty, this recaptured ability to conjure a demon portal at random poses the most dreadful threat."

"My loremasters believe proximity to the translation hub is a requisite for the caesura's manifestation," Serion offered.

"Let us hope so," Thorian replied in a cautious tone. He blew out his cheeks. "On that note, the loss of that particular transport nucleus is cardinal. Its sequester or destruction will greatly limit our options."

"Aye," Johlarin agreed. "A bold and stunning move—one that will put the Four Veins at greater risk."

"At least for the time being," said Thorian, "I believe the path of the Veins and that of our armies must wed."

Johlarin stroked his beard as he studied Thorian's face. "I concur."

Serion sniffled back moisture through his nasal passages once, twice. "I hope that I have answered Targin's second grievance—to his satisfaction."

"Prince Serion?" Targin waited for the highborn's attention. "Condolences. I am not so callous as to be unmoved by your tragedy. I've misjudged you—and your Haft—for that, my humblest apology. When you mentioned earlier in the glaive that Florin's home in Arboria had been destroyed, I took your meaning for a single dwelling, not the entire city."

"My thanks, Nightwolf," Serion said in a dull voice. "Your words offer a kindness not easily rendered."

In the weighted air, the silence grew louder. Anguish reigned.

King Johlarin broke it with a loud cough. He wheeled on the assemblage. "Serenthia will not sit idle while our enemies desecrate our holy lands uncontested. And neither will I."

"Nor I." Targin set his jaw. "Bring forth a map. And the sprites' edict. Let's see what Dras and his order have conceived."

A hunched elderly scribe from Johlarin's small circle unravelled a long scroll across the table and weighted its corners with metal ingots.

The main quorum gathered around.

Johlarin set his sceptre aside and joined them. "We should decide on a waypoint to muster our troops. Allow enough time for our rooks to arrive at each of the freeborn kingdoms—which stand and function, hopefully, ruled by a regent still of sound mind."

"Why not commune and save the trouble?" one of Serion's retainers asked.

"Because, elven," Targin said, "Communion amongst distant untried vassals can be intercepted and twisted into falsehood. Should the same happen to a rook's message, if sealed properly, it vouches safe for itself. If unsecured and attainted, the receiving party will know it for a ruse whence they open it."

"As for the other countries rekindled to our cause," Johlarin went on, "I want two birds per realm, one to the ruler, another to the principal asset we've placed in their ranks. Our scouts will depart before evenfall to scope our path, ahead of the elven host."

Serion produced a small vellum, sealed with a teal wax imprint. The pendant-sized relief depicted a fortress straddling the edge of a cascade. The sprite's emblem of Etern's Drop. "The tactical appraisal I promised." As he extended his hand to the king, Serion faced his aide. "Watch and learn."

Johlarin accepted the parchment. When he broke the seal, it released a puff of silver magic dust that glittered in the chamber's light.

Targin nodded to himself. The powder certified the edict's authenticity, not so much in the visual display, but the familiar wilderen connection the Nightwolf felt.

Even as the sparkles settled, the king unfurled the small scroll. His eyebrows angled down as he read. And arched high when he finished.

Hand lowering to his side, Johlarin turned to Targin. "Says we must keep our wingwards grounded—including your hawkrike. Move our offensive in two stages."

Targin blinked. "What? That's ludicrous."

When the monarch passed him the scroll, Targin had to read it several times to believe his eyes. He gritted his teeth when he looked up again. "Your Grace, without our raptors, we'll be vulnerable. Forget crowbats, the Siphons will have dragons. Their scales are hard, their fire, hot." He handed the scroll to Prince Serion before seeking his king's regard.

"Nevertheless," Johlarin countered, "this directive has an Orbical's mark on it. Strikes me as a higher extension of your pathless path." He exhaled and allowed his broad shoulders to sink. "The sprites would not impart such instruction lightly. If this be their will, then I don't want a single warbird up there unless absolutely necessary. You can commune with the Strong Helm easily enough from the field—"

The elven retinue harrumphed. "I thought—"

"Targin's connection is not untried," Lorin put in, silencing the cortege mid-spate.

"Aye," Johlarin agreed before cornering Targin with his scrutiny. "Send for the wingwards at need, after we've drawn battle lines, seen what enemies we face, and how we must face them. The avians can fly swift enough. I'll not delay here any longer than we absolutely must. We march."

Serion glanced up from the page. "Holding back our raptors presents one boon." All heads tracked the elven. "A reserve force to press our foes with a hidden attack. Marching with so many wingwards aloft, filling the sky above us, makes our intent known to any troll that glances up."

Targin opened his mouth to protest when the king's eyes dropped to the map. "Point taken."

With a bejewelled hand, Johlarin gestured to a tract on the chart, roughly halfway between Serenthia and the Relay. "We'll set camp there. Assemble our van and allow time for our nearest allies to send forth their hosts. The more distant kingdoms will have to direct their troops straight to the battlefront. As the eagle riders' reconnaissance indicates, our enemies will likely launch their assault from the Three Cities, along multiple fronts."

Fingers splayed, Johlarin fanned his hands from the Main's western coast and across the map.

Targin cleared his throat. "Considering all the possibilities, our best bet is the Relay. I propose we gather further north than what you suggest, My

Liege."

Targin reached over and tapped his target three times with his forefinger. "Here, along the broken slopes of the Valley Kobal, we'll control a place of strength and relative safety, adding the ability to track our enemies' movement over greater distance. If we must make do without patrolling hawks and eagles, it will at least give us fair warning of any aerial attack, not to mention the higher ground over any land-based assaults, plus ideal cover from either."

Johlarin scratched his forehead as he studied the map. "The terrain will slow their advances from any front including the skies. Whatever route they choose, we would still retain the option of moving our host ahead of theirs, while undercover."

"Right," Targin said. "Staying on the ground offers a reciprocal advantage: their crowbats will give away any hidden positions. Those birds will not stray far from our foe's ground forces. Unlike our raptors, crowbats must be continually coerced to obey their riders—trust me, I know."

Targin's suggestion garnered many murmurs of approval. The elven prince cocked his temple at him, then the map. "I support this course. Many elven warriors have already taken refuge in adjoining cirques, coombs, and valleys. I'll commune with them to make all haste to that spot, secure it ahead of our arrival. They will add their strength to our forces long before battle is joined."

Encouraged, Targin continued, "If we make our armies visible as they muster along the slopes, the enemy may hold, expecting us to try and draw them towards the forests flanking our frontiers."

"Where we would surely have the advantage," another of Serion's guards ventured.

Targin shook his head. "They've been attacking frontier villages with raiding parties along those very lines. To test the waters, they've brought lavatrols to Serenthia's very doorstep, trying to coax us to move our forces out to protect our most distant parishes." *As they did with your cities.*

The elven soldier blinked. "And?"

"It demonstrates they're wise to the ploy," Targin said, his pupils flitting to the back of the chamber. Though Tasmin was no longer present, he quietly acknowledged her intuition in the matter. He did catch Lorin's smile on the rebound, which sent blood to his cheeks. "We must be ready for the cloaked attack beyond our periphery."

Serion and Johlarin frowned, their faces equally blank.

"The Three Cities—or what's left of them—may yet confirm the true *false lure* now," Targin explained. "Necatar and the dark elven have something else planned—a trap no one in this council chamber can predict. During my many months of covert activities, I've learned something of the Summoner's intrigues of court and military tack." Targin fell into silent contemplation as he swept the faces at the table.

The sound of rushing water filled the lapse, until Johlarin broke it. "We haven't all day, Nightwolf," he complained. "Speak your mind."

"They *saw* Serion escape with news of what transpired," Targin said. "They would know we've convened since their invasion. Like the recent assaults on our own frontier, we'd be led to believe the Tri-Cities marked the false lure."

Targin extended his finger at the Main's western seaboard. "They want us to avoid moving our forces directly against them there on the coast. Stars, I wouldn't doubt if they expect our attack—exactly where I just proposed. We'd be there, sure of the advantages and unwittingly remove the threat we pose guarding Serenthia from a closer vantage."

Targin's hypothetical summary brought confused expressions to every face, except Lorin, who flicked his chin in understanding. Johlarin too seemed to comprehend, biting his lip as he mulled it over.

Serion brought up his index finger as if to make a point, but then wagged it dismissively. "In this, Targin, our stars cross. Keep a token force here, but remember this is the *Hidden* Kingdom. Our foes would have nothing to attack. The elven cities were made vulnerable by the presence of the translation hub. Nothing remotely like that exists within a hundred leagues of here."

The prince took a breath and looked around. "As you know, even if all the forces of the turned kingdoms stormed past, the sprites' enchantments would befuddle them. Allies, the same; I myself and my entire company had to be escorted by Johlarin's sentries."

Many of the bronze-skinned envoys from the southern kingdoms inclined their heads at the elven's appraisal. Lorin and Thorian paid the delegation fleeting looks before turning to gauge Targin's response.

When he did not refute, Serion went on. "A heelward perhaps, no more than two, but after what I saw done to the Three Cities, we'll need every last sword, pike, and bow in a freeborn's hand. Leaving even one heelward from the brewing Endstorm squanders a valuable resource."

Johlarin rubbed sweat-lined palms together. After several tense moments, he sighed heavily. "If it pleases, Serion, tell the council the rest of the sprites' missive."

The prince gave a slight bow before meeting Targin's watch. "I'll spare you the celestial matters discussed earlier. Once we establish our bearing on the slopes of Kobal, as the Vein proposed, the sprites urge us to move swiftly and lightly towards the canyon below the Spires' Crest."

Targin dipped his chin. "We will catch them off-guard. The Relay will force them to separate crowbat riders from their troops on the ground—to bottleneck time and again in its endless chokepoints."

"Precisely," Serion acknowledged. "If you examine the map, you can see how the chasm folds and refolds, forming intermediate barriers against a direct assault. Even if the enemy wishes to avoid entering it, they would still thin their lines to march around its countless obstacles."

The elven brushed his hands across the map, tracing exact references with his digits. "As Targin asserts, in any attack scenario, we can skirt the slopes of the Valley Kobal with advance warning." The prince leaned forward and pressed both palms on the table.

Targin ran his tongue against the inside of his cheek. *Move quickly enough and we may be able to secure Sentinel's Retreat before the enemy— the true objective of the sprites.*

Serion looked up and scanned the faces around him. "Any questions?"

Targin sure had one: was it mere coincidence that the prince's scheme harmonized with his own goal? Apart from that, the Nightwolf noted close to a hundred flaws in the plan.

But he kept his tongue seated. Partly because Serion held sway over Johlarin and the council now. Though mostly because the sprites had made the tactical decree, seconded by Brapin.

Perhaps that's what the old fool meant by it being paramount to reach Sentinel's Retreat on foot. If so, true to form, the Orbical failed to mention that a million more feet would follow his. Targin let out a quiet laugh, imagining Brapin's wizened smile and bird-bone shrug.

Admittedly, Serion's plan held merit, but two heelwards—two hundred infantry—left for Serenthia's safeguard seemed piteous at best. The elven's point about the Hidden Kingdom resonated true enough; even civilians and their supply trains had to pass the thorough inspection of sentries and magical wards before passing the main gate. Farmers hauling wagons of produce, merchants carting their wares, the same.

If an enemy was sighted, easily and quickly done with regular scouting patrols and at least a league of open steppe in all directions, the entrances could all be shut with ample warning. The entire kingdom would go into lockdown, outlasting any siege.

Yet Lorin's caution stuck fast and fresh in Targin's mind. It fed his scepticism. Stars, would that he met with Brapin after and not before this meeting? He could sorely use the Orbical's counsel now... and Gjen's.

Where on Areth was that damnable wizard? If the Kazir had returned from his mission south, the Nightwolf had received no news.

Beyond tired, having added insult to the elven's devastation, Targin did not contest Serion again. He looked to his king.

Johlarin retrieved his sceptre and sat on the moss-covered seat of his throne. Eyes fixed on its gem-laden headpiece, the king brooded from under heavy brows.

Targin floated a palm over the map. "What say you, Your Grace?"

Johlarin clapped his free hand on his knee. "I see merit in the sprites' plan. The advantage of having the Hidden Kingdom is that it remains so. Such was the case during the Rennen. It will be so again. The key to this theatre roots in our initiative—which you all seem eager to embrace."

The regent's tone implied a *but* that lingered like a haunting ghost in the silence. His nose wrinkled and he held up a hand as though banning the wraith. "But I caution vigilance. It will hold the greatest weight at the end of the day."

Johlarin checked himself, his study shifting away to the middle distance. With a deep breath, the king stood and joined Targin. "Where is the band now?"

"In truth, the Nightwolves should have arrived already, but I suspect they'll be here within a week. They prefer to tread the pathless path in silence, in case unfriendly ears might be listening in. So, even if I sought communion, they know enough not to respond."

"Understood," Johlarin said in a resigned tone. "Even if the enemy began their advance yesterday, it would take them at least three times that to reach us here. As Serion pointed out, no portals exist within a hundred leagues, and our foes still don't know where we are."

Targin retained his doubt, but he gave Johlarin the most convincing smile he could feign under the circumstances.

Crow's feet crinkling, Johlarin's lopsided grin indicated he knew exactly how Targin felt. The king shifted his attention to the quorum. "If there are no further objections...?"

They all shook their heads.

"Then, as this moot ordained, we'll send forth our troops to the slopes of Kobal, as soon as we can arm them." The regent's orbs settled on Targin. "I'll retain the Nightwolves when they arrive—they can serve as city watch. A few short days in the interim will make little difference." Adopting an imperative stance, Johlarin planted his sceptre firmly on the ground and lifted his voice, "Muster the troops and call the banners. Scribes take to writ. Henceforth, Serenthia officially declares war against the Darkest One, and the northern hosts who follow him. As King, I command it."

Targin placed a fist over his heart. "Words unto deeds, Highness."

Discussions concerning all the logistics such as routes, supply trains, weapon caches, provisions, and the best mobilization and deployment of wards, dominated the rest of the meeting.

Late afternoon had dimmed the chamber's crystalline striations when the pages and custodians entered to tidy up.

Targin and Lorin were the last to leave the rocky cathedral. They did so in silence and sobriety, listening to the watery torrent of the girdling rivers. The pair took the last echoes of their footfalls with them.

56: Disclosures
Sonart

Sonart awoke to a gruff voice in his ear. He stirred and rose to find Gjen hovering over Seolad. The blackbeard's condition had improved dramatically—not only conscious but complaining.

By Gjen's sunken orbs and sallow cheeks, he'd stayed up all day to nurse the poisoned dwarven back to health and his usual ire.

Sonart's heart went out to the wizard.

"Kind of you to think so, Sonart," Gjen said wearily. "But I am well, and as you can see, so is our companion. Seolad will be ready to travel this eventide, which draws nigh as we speak. Our rations have been sorely depleted after losing Seolad's pack in the sand trap, but we will find other bounties to nourish us—if you know where to look," he added with a wink.

Seolad's expression contained no inkling of gratitude: his face, a crabby mask of etched lines and tight lips. But he didn't aim his curling nose at Gjen or Sonart, it targeted Iomi, making her cower.

"Keep this one well away from me," Seolad grated.

Sonart saw red and flared, "I thought the toxin Iomi helped Gjen rid you of would stay ridden. But it has wormed its way back, finding the perfect niche in your foul trap—or do you rave from some other irritation of the mind?"

"Rave?" the blackbeard baulked. "At your foolishness perhaps, unable to grasp our true plight. You're the one blinded by the trap between her legs."

Gjen let out a long breath. "Out with it, Seolad. What vexes you?"

Seolad's eyes shot daggers at Iomi. "I don't *trust* her."

Teeth on edge, Sonart seethed. "We're in this mess together, stars burn you. Why must you persist in mongering suspicion? You've proven yourself the dysfunctional element here. Iomi pulled your miserable hide out of that vile pool. Helped save your life. If you cannot speak with a civil tongue, then do not speak at all."

"Words unto deeds," Seolad groused. "Choose not to heed mine, and you wed us to Deathwrought's doom, served on this witch's palanquin."

"Be silent," Gjen interposed. "Both of you. This quarrel avails nothing and is counterproductive. Tangle beards if you must, but dispute respectfully, and Vamsah save us, quietly."

A razor storm scoured Seolad's countenance, his reply pure abrasion. "This fool will stay his tongue, but not his eyes. Something befalls us again, I'll run her through."

Fists balled, Sonart thrust his face within inches of the blackbeard's flaring nostrils. "That will be the last thing you do!"

"Enough!" Gjen blazed. He came between the two combatants bristling with anger. "Stars cauterize your stubborn dwarven heads, have you both taken leave of your senses? And forgotten where we are? Save your strength for the journey ahead. You're going to need it—and each other."

Sonart was the first to turn away. His gaze fell upon Iomi. Her eyes were downcast, tears spilling over her cheeks.

Heart wrenching in knots, Sonart placed a hand on her arm to comfort her but she stiffened at his touch.

"The snare's evil lingers and makes us act so," Gjen said to the air. "Let us make haste and be gone from its influences. The morrow will mark the halfway point to our destination."

Not soon enough, the time to set out arrived. Sonart swallowed in dismay when he egressed that evening. Despite Gjen's assurances, the Outereach appeared ever-distant, as though to make mock of their audacity. The mountains only lost their cold ridicule when darkness fell.

A sombre mood hung over them like a pall as they continued their trek across the Lobe's gloomy flat.

With their supplies exhausted, hunger made Sonart's stomach protest more acutely. The belly groans nagged at his thoughts, but they also helped him blot out his terse confrontation with Seolad, and the bruise from Iomi's shunning.

Gjen had surmised their situation accurately enough: morale was floundering and hope had all but vanished. That quickly validated the unseen danger of the Lobe, a menace seeded from within their own hearts. Something more damaging than the threats from the air or those concealed in the land.

With dawn, thank the stars, the pale light revealed the mountains of the Outereach had grown closer at last, clearer, more prominent, gaining more than twice their height since he glimpsed them the previous evening. As well, the four black sentinels of the Innereach had vanished completely below the horizon.

Sonart turned to Gjen. "Will we be able to replenish our rations soon? I would that my cursed stomach gets used to emptiness as my legs have taken to this long march."

"Aye, quite soon," the wizard chuckled. "Now, if we align ourselves to such thoughts, we guise our true motive perfectly and will pass unmolested. All our wounds will heal faster the further we steal away from the Cradle's centre. In this same diametric fashion, my own magic flourishes. Already it grows much more powerful than when we first met."

"Seemed powerful enough then," Sonart observed.

As soon as they'd stopped and erected their tent, Gjen left the shelter in the predawn light. The three dwarven listened intently as the wizard scratched the earth close to their shelter.

Abruptly the sound stopped. "I have located some. All of you, come."

They jumped to their feet and raced outside. Crouched on his knees, Gjen dug through a two-foot hollow, scalloping it from the caked hardpan.

The wizard stabbed at its centre with his staff before loosening the dirt with his fingers. Then, he reached into the hole and pulled out a vine of gnarled roots laden with several bell-shaped tubers.

Gjen beamed as he appraised the purple bouquet of dangling bulbs "The key to our survival out here. *Naocci.* Untainted by Grendamaul's scourge, and mentioned in the Kusp—the true Kusp of the Testament."

"What do we do with it?" Sonart asked.

"Why, you eat it." The wizard's grin connected his ears. "The fruit is medicinal, magical—and quite tasty. Envoys carried the seedlings here long before the corruption of your lands."

"Carried? From where?" Sonart asked.

"I mentioned the distant land before, far away to Areth's north, Grenfor Talarben. If we survive, I will take you all there. The bounty in the Land of Giant Trees is—"

"Can we trust this food?" Seolad interrupted.

Gjen answered the blackbeard's glower by plucking one of the small fruits and stuffing it in his mouth. His face softened and his lips curved into a grin. Proof enough.

Sonart's stomach protested louder.

"Let me try," Seolad said, his hunger clearly outweighing his distrust.

"Take it," Gjen encouraged as he offered the bunch. "There's plenty in this cluster and more to uncover in the immediate patch."

The three dwarven tore off a few bulbs each. The fruit felt smooth to the touch. Sonart put one in his mouth and bit down. A burst of radiant sweetness filled his pallet. He had never tasted anything so delicious, so intense, in his entire life. It soothed him, sating his hunger as he savoured its taste.

Then the true benison of the fruit took hold. The naocci rekindled Sonart's strength, in mind and body, his clarity of purpose, and his verve. The colour returned to Iomi's face. And she smiled, making her face glow. More the miracle, even the canyons of Seolad's scowl shallowed.

"This vaults a hundred blessings—simply—wonderful, Gjen," Sonart extolled between mouthfuls. "My heart's weight has never felt so lifted. In fact, I think it's completely gone."

"How right you are," the wizard returned warmly. "It is a gift of the sprites—nourishment for body and soul. A single bulb can sustain you for a whole day. The hardiest of all plants, infused with so much earthen magic. Even the Darkest One's taint cannot curtail its proliferation. The elven have a saying that 'while naocci yet grows, hope remains.'"

"Sprites? Elven? You mention many names I am unfamiliar with,"

Sonart confessed.

Gjen laughed. "Words do not do justice to either. Your eyes will fit my puzzle pieces together a far *sight* better. But for now, back into the shelter, we must go. Light will soon be upon us, and with it, the perils of the foothills draw closer."

Seolad and Iomi disappeared into the tent, but when Gjen made to follow them, Sonart stopped him with a hand. "A word."

The wizard paused and met his gaze. "Aye?"

"We've returned to good stead with the naocci—and I thank you, but," Sonart chewed his lip, his voice dropping to a whisper. "I cannot help but wonder why we journey as four when we function as three. Why *did* you bring Seolad into our company? He is mean-mouthed, vile—and seems set on disrupting our harmony and purpose."

Gjen hesitated, glancing at the tent before drawing Sonart several paces away. "Vamsah guides my hand in all things, Sonart. Seolad is no different. Laethan and I observed him for a spell before announcing ourselves. From what we gleaned of Rusic's son, he demonstrated unyielding tenacity— likely the most steadfast, honour-bound dwarven you'll ever meet. He will hold the line when it comes to opposing the minions of Deathwrought. Ever-abrasive, Seolad gives new meaning to the word, bellicose. But he will never stray from the path, even should it mean his death."

When Sonart considered his hazardous reunion with Seolad and the blackbeard's fearless attack against the Zürshuck, he saw Gjen's point.

"Seolad's heart is troubled, but incorruptible and ever true it holds," Gjen went on. "As such, his role will be as important as yours and mine. When the darkest times descend, you will be grateful not to scorn such firebrand material. He may not be a Vein, but he was forged in the same fire as you. In time, you will measure his worth above all the ironock in the Cradle."

Sonart remained aloof. "I'm sorry, but I cannot see that, let alone believe it."

"Give him space and time, let him vent as is his wont. He will rally on his own terms. Will you do this for me?"

The dwarven hesitated. "I only wish he wasn't such a bastard. But I will. My trust in you stands implicit. You deliver my only hope, especially after learning I cannot work the Sword to our purpose."

"Never think that," Gjen mildly scolded. "If you trust me, then trust in Vamsah's weapon. It only seems dormant, but make no mistake you have sequestrated it. And will learn to wield it."

"But when I want—need—to draw it, I wield naught but air," Sonart muttered.

Gjen rolled his eyes. "Because you don't trust."

Already exhausted by his trials and travails, the debate spun Sonart in circles. He let it rest. "I just hope it's not too late before I make the discovery. Only now I'm beginning to realize how little I know. This extra burden you place before me seems overwhelming to think on, let alone carry out."

"Do not dwell on it too greatly, for time will bond you to your charge whether you will it or not. As to your father's words, by all means, think on them. But they act as the catalyst to the larger truth we all must face."

Sonart blinked. "And that is?"

"All life is sacrosanct, every individual parcel to and vital towards the survival of Creation's whole. The Cradle's people must be redeemed and freed from their suffering. That includes—" Gjen's voice caught. "—the Kworn. They too must be saved."

"Kworn?" Sonart spat. He spun on the wizard. "They're *savages*—mindless minions of Deathwrought—nothing more."

Gjen blew out his cheeks. "That may seem so, but there was a time before the Great War when you would've held your fury in check."

"An army of larruping goons, the Kworn destroy and pillage. Indentured to the Darkest One, they trample us under their boots. Abominations"

"They are—aye," Gjen agreed. "Under the claw of the Zürshuck, who must answer to the Colossals, who bend the knee to the Four."

Sonart blew out his cheeks and nodded. "That defines the Cradle's cruel hierarchy."

The wizard lifted a finger, his eyebrows following suit. "But it was not always so. A thousand years ago, the Kworn paid a price for losing the Eclipsed War. Beneath their attainted exteriors, lie the souls of men like me. They once fought beside your forebears against the tide of evil when the Darkest One invaded the Cradle. Consumed when the Winged Ones fell upon and befouled them with Deathwrought's power."

Sonart sized up the wizard, trying to draw a comparison to a Kworn in all its ugly perversion, and failed. "Befouled *men?*"

Gjen nodded. "For your skills as builders and miners, the dwarven were spared the same fate, but even that will change."

Sonart made the connection and inhaled. "The Afflicted Ones."

"Deathwrought's evil knows no bounds. Pain and suffering drive His purpose, but tis also his source of true felicity. You've retained your selves, untouched by his witchery—but slaves nonetheless—long enough to complete the Hive. Now that it is done, the Darkest One has no further use for your people, other than making them suffer, to diminish the lifeforce of the Gaia."

Gjen paused and scratched the top of his head as he studied Sonart. "If it's any consolation, the plague of the Afflicted Ones has not become pandemic, and your recent near-miss in the Hive has set our foes back a considerable amount of time. The dwarven still have hope."

"Hooks and Dunge," Sonart cursed, trembling with umbrage. "Our kind would rally if they knew the dire extent of their plight."

"True, they would, but who would be the one to tell them? Under present circumstances, it would fall on deaf or compromised ears."

Sonart knitted his brows. "What do you mean?"

"How do you think they would react? You'd be arrested and revealed to Deathwrought before you uttered a word of warning. Men and dwarven stood as a unified force then, to rally as you say in the Eclipsed War. This is the result. Have faith that despite the loss of the council, the dwarven underground still moves and plots. But real change will only come when the Four Veins unite." Gjen gave Sonart a thin smile. "We're halfway there."

Sonart sighed. "How could my forefathers let this happen?" *How could they have laid this burden upon my shoulders? How could my father?*

"They wouldn't have," Gjen said. "They fought it with their dying breaths. The armies of the Darkest One slew those old enough to pass on their knowledge. Hundreds of children met their end in that black campaign. Only a few, like the stalwart ancestors of your father, slipped past the raking claw to keep the truth alive."

"What of the men? Did that fiend kill their children as well?"

Gjen shook his head. "No, but their women grew barren before they died. Their wombs could no longer be seeded. Within a generation, no more women walked among them. All the surviving men were mutated but kept alive by the same sorcery. They did not die unless slain. Apart from serving a purpose, policing the dwarven undercaste, they would eternally mourn their bereft lives and loves, further wounding the Gaia. The Kworn were not so mindless then. Over the centuries they devolved so. Still, through gut instinct, they retain the capacity to regret."

"Is that the reason behind their Ritual?" Sonart asked.

"Ritual?" Gjen frowned. "I know not of any ritual."

Sonart described the night his father disappeared.

"Strange indeed. Perhaps you are right. I will delve further, when and if we make it out of this mess."

Something danced in Sonart's peripheral and he glanced back at the tent. Iomi watched him from under the flap. Although out of earshot, she seemed to sense what had been said.

Sonart met her gaze, but it only chased her eyes away as she ducked back inside.

57: Outereach
Sonart

Hours into their night march, the terrain began to fold in on itself. The gradual rolls and dips fragmented into a plain filled with scree and boulders, some as large as houses. Sonart grimaced as the gravel played havoc with his footing and the steady incline put extra pressure on his calves. Vapour escaped the redbeard's lips and his sweat grew cold.

"Take heart," Gjen quietly voiced in the darkness. "The slope and temperature drop indicate we've entered the foothills of the Outereach."

With dawn, the mountains loomed ahead, still some distance but much closer than Sonart expected. He fixed his eyes on them as the small company pushed toward the first alcove this side of the Lobe. A welcome discovery, it offered them a natural shelter without the need to erect their own.

Sonart craned his neck up at the closest summit and let out a sigh. "The mountains appear stark this close, but majestic and beautiful as well. Why does the Outereach look so strikingly different than the Inner?"

"They are untainted mountains, my friend," Gjen explained. "Though once, the same could be said of the Innereach spires. Before the Darkest One corrupted the Spikes to mimic the obsidian pallor of his Hive. And yes, I do take into account the smoke from the molten lakes at their bosom. It is no natural accretion that chars their mountainsides but dark magic."

Gjen tripped Sonart's recollect, tempting him to make mention of Souleater—the nefarious entity he'd confronted twice now. But exhaustion left him unsure how to frame his question, and with Iomi and Seolad listening in, he decided it best to let the hyperdemon riddle slide for now. He'd sleep on it and ask Gjen in the morning.

Iomi floated an arm towards the peaks. "What are those white manes draping their crowns?"

"Snow," the wizard replied. "Derived from water, rendered a powdery crystalline form by the colder temperatures at those soaring heights."

Iomi's knitted her brows. "Like the Scourge's ice squalls we sometimes experience in the darker days of winter?"

"Similar but it won't strip the flesh from your bones if you get caught in it. Apart from avalanches, snow is a gentle, innocent substance. Unlike the denizens that infiltrate these surroundings."

Iomi gulped. "They are?"

"Disfavoured among the Zürshuck," said Gjen. "Banished from the Hive. Of these scavengers, we must now be extra vigilant."

"I'll be more careful," Sonart promised. He dipped his beard and glanced at the others. "We all will."

"Good," Gjen said. "For though the brutish lot wield no magic, best to avoid them altogether. Easily done on the terrain before us. And my beak will be able to sniff them out before any chance encounters." The wizard extended a finger between two of the distant peaks. "In three days' time, I hope to get clear to the other side of that chain."

"As do I," Seolad said. He looked around suspiciously, then entered the fissure that would serve as their domicile. Iomi followed on his heels.

Sonart lingered and gaped up at the wizard. "Other side?"

Gjen smiled and nodded.

Something about the notion left a needle of doubt stuck in Sonart's mind. It wasn't anything Gjen said exactly, but something elusive within his own heart. *Mine Eyes Are Your Eyes.*

The wizard cleared his throat. "Past time we get out of sight. In we go."

With an effort, Sonart shirked his unease and followed Gjen into the alcove. Once in the cavern's shelter, he found a morose Iomi sitting on a rock opposite Seolad. The blackbeard busied himself pouring water from Gjen's trapper draw into his own drinking flagon.

No one instigated further conversation, so Sonart laid out his bedroll in silence, curled up into a ball and tried to nod off. Better to bring this last day on the fringe to an end. Begin the final three-day leg refreshed.

But that strange disquiet pricked Sonart again, leaving him anxious and vulnerable. Consciousness finally lost its grip on the troubled dwarven, and he fell into a fitful trance...

En mass, Zürshuck slay Sonart's brethren. The Afflicted Ones succumb to their ailment through death—or devolve into diminutive versions of Kworn.

Then matters worsen.

Zürshuck swarm from the Hive in unfathomable numbers. They fill Sonart's sight with fifty-thousand beating wings. The vision repeats from the moment the demons alight, plays out again and repeats, repeats, repeats.

A visual echo.

Sonart focuses beyond the obvious and finds his answer. The view of the hordes taking wing from their onyx monolith remains constant. But with every iteration, the background itself changes. Each reveals a different domain: plains with vast tracts of green foliage, barren steppe strewn with animals the like of which Sonart has never seen, cities that span the horizon, occupied by immense buildings comparable in size to the Hive. The towers all burn—their flames more voracious than those spewed by the Hive.

The Zürshuck blot out the panorama and the vision replays.

Myriad scenes cycle faster and faster into a dizzying kaleidoscope. Merge into one, drawing Sonart into a cyclone of vertigo. It wrenches him into blackness, but the gloom does not last.

Flashes of other visions appear. A resurgence of his suffering in the Dunge and the Hive. The torment spreads like wildfire across the Cradle, escalating to savage anarchy upon the heads of the lower castes.

Several harrowing images of Winged Ones and Colossals follow as they decimate the dwarven and the Kworn with impunity. Carnage and destruction flash across the blighted dreamscape. Sonart's people forced into hiding, existing in despair and mourning—always mourning.

Citadels fall and burn.

Sonart floats in the centre of it all, trying to prevent it with impotent means.

Countless Afflicted Ones press towards him. They mewl and wheeze, so far gone with leprous limbs and ruined carriages. Each bears the sinister face of Deathwrought like a brand.

They smother Sonart, crush him under their weight. His ultimate undoing. Their masks mesh together into one face, one dwarven face. And that face...

belongs to Mila.

Farkshone Village burns all around her. Mila spins about, desperately calling out Sonart's name, paralyzed amidst the chaos: fleeing dwarven, crumbled buildings, scorched fields.

Tears stream down her soot-marred face.

Abruptly she turns her back to him and stiffens. An inert form lay at her feet. She kneels beside it.

Her backside blocks Sonart's view. He cannot make out who lies on the ground. Until a Zürshuck's spear sails into view and impales his aunt. The impact drives her forward. She collapses across the prostrate body to form a crucifix of appendages.

Sonart reels in horror.

Auckland.

He stares up at the clouds with vacant eyes.

A tenebrous shadow unlike any other passes over the length and breadth of the Cradle. It doesn't merely mute the light, as would a dimming, but causes a full fade into inky blackness.

Complete erasure. Complete obliteration.

Sonart acknowledges his failure. And the death of the Cradle.

Synonymous with its destruction, the annihilation spreads outward, exceeding his scope of knowledge. Unfathomable places: globes revolving around spherical fires in a blackened expanse.

461

The Void?

But then, at the height of his despair, over this greater reality, Sonart finds he is not alone. Three others have joined him, united not only in common purpose, but in common despondency.

*They strengthen one another, greater than the sum of their parts. Synergy, like music. No, not like music, there **is** music, strange and wonderful to Sonart's ears. It infuses him and his three counterparts with hope. Binding them in a preternatural union.*

But then, the music grows discordant. Hope wavers as One among the Four falters. Although Sonart cannot see faces, he discerns two things about the fallen: He is a man, tall like Gjen, younger with angelic features and a long mane of blond hair. He changes into another man, a muscle-bound giant with a bold countenance and a mop of dark curled hair.

The giant braces, stuck in the harrowing scene of a city filled with blazing megaliths. The remaining three compeers are forced to stop. One of them retreats to help. He is...?

The encompassing shadows envelop Sonart and the face is lost, along with the other two.

Together they let out a piercing wail that scales high enough to exceed sound. Their silent howls carry him out of the obliteration and into... snow.

Could it be the stuff Gjen described? All of Sonart's senses assure him that it is. He stands knee-deep in a drift. A freezing blanket. Flurries whip his cloak about him in pounding gusts. He squints. The sheath of white has been stained red. Blood trails away along three separate channels, but all terminate into a single distinct mound a short distance away.

Partially covered by a drift of snow, the three companions he set out with from Bulkforge lay piled on their backs staring up at the veiled sky, empty expressions on their ashen faces. Gjen lies on the bottom with the skewed forms of Seolad and Iomi atop.

All three are pinioned to the snowy ground by the same metallic shaft that dwarfs a Zürshuck's spear or Colossal's blade. Like the latter, it glows red hot, as though fired straight from the forge into its marks. It sizzles. Steam rises, where the snow touches it.

With slow deliberation, Sonart approaches the pyre, trudging through the discoloured snow. Suddenly, a force sweeps him off his feet and floats him through the air to hover above the three corpses. Only then does he understand: tis the Augury Sword impaling his friends.

His Sword.

Sonart tastes blood. Like a dam breaking, it wells up in gurgling founts. And in that moment, a primal truth bites into his mind: He is the Sword that has slain them.

But... wielded by another. Mine Eyes Are Your Eyes.

In a spasm of asphyxia, Sonart burst into consciousness. He sprung into a seated position and raged at the ceiling of the narrow cavern, "*Ahhhhhhhaugh!*"

His three companions jumped up and braced, stung into full wakefulness and fright. Struggling against invisible bonds, Sonart paused long enough to discern that no harm had befallen them. But whatever alarm they voiced was lost on him.

No hope or assurance could quell this monstrous revelation. Sonart's instincts supported the conclusion as surely as his skeleton did his body. Deaf to Gjen's pleading and Seolad's gruff protests, Sonart lurched to his feet and bolted from the alcove.

Once in the open, intense daylight blasted him and forced his eyes to cringe shut. One forearm thrown across his forehead to shield his gaze, he sucked in the frigid air. It burned his lungs.

Somehow, he brought his pulse under control while his throbbing orbs adjusted. All he could do was gape, transfixed by what he beheld. A starker element furthered the Lobe's bleakness. It had been erased white—by snow.

The expanse sprawled beneath their concealed encampment, filling the scree slope and the entire vista as white as the great weltering blanket of clouds above.

Sonart had only dreamt of it a scant moment before. But this scene did not appear even remotely similar: no snowflakes fell from the sky and the ivory tract did not sink knee-deep, only dusted the rocks less than an inch.

Still, the calamity of the foretelling was too traumatic to contain: an inescapable doom that Sonart would let pass. Vamsah had erred, placing the onus of salvation on his shoulders. A coward's shoulders that now shirked their charge and abandoned the destitute to a fate worse than death.

Sonart lumbered forward, carrying his burdens fifty paces across the snow-swept ground. There, he stopped, allowing the icy wind to gnaw at him, penetrating the folds of his cloak.

The dwarven glanced back across the immeasurable distance they had come, awaiting confirmation.

When nothing happened, Sonart allayed his doubts and turned back towards the alcove. As he did, something caught his notice. At the very edge of the horizon, tiny dots appeared. He blinked rapidly to dispel his tears and decide the contest between mind and pupils. His sight crisped.

The dots lingered, multiplied, and grew. Definitive humanoid shapes flew towards him.

Within moments, the thrum of their wings rose above the wind. Stars chase the shadows, that sounded too close—came from—*behind*.

Sonart spun as a second legion of Winged Ones—the exiles—fell from the sky above the closest foothills. Two Zürshuck fronts hemmed his cadre in.

Deathwrought had found him, closing the jaws of his trap.

"Back inside!" Gjen cried from the cavern mouth. "Colossals are upon us!" *Colossals*—!

Sonart surged towards the cave. He managed three steps when a Zürshuck landed hard, directly in front of him to block his retreat.

58: Reaching Out
Sonart

Sonart skidded to a halt, leaving twin trenches in the snow. He drew his blade. Raised it.

The Winged One's torso erupted. Sizzling viscera sprayed Sonart as a smoking cavity gaped in the centre of the demon's chest. Through it, Gjen appeared, bounding towards him.

As the Zürshuck collapsed, Gjen drew up. He seized Sonart by the shoulders, spun him about, and shoved him towards the fissure. "Get—*in there*. Run!"

Sonart raced to the cleft's mouth but did not enter. He turned, anxious to help the wizard.

Gjen faced off against multiple adversaries, alighting all around him. The wizard's powerful voice etched the air as he roared, "We'll have none of this business here, vile and accursed. Begone or be dead—your choice."

They advanced on taloned feet, fanning their razor-tipped wings.

Gjen slammed the butt of his staff on the snow-dusted rock.

Thunder cracked in Sonart's heart as multiple bolts of lightning forked out from the sceptre's crown.

The discharges incinerated the closest ranks into acrid vapour. Those behind were batted away and burned in one fell swoop. The airborne Zürshuck crashed to the ground like throttled stones.

A few cavorted. None arose.

Gjen wielded his staff like a sword as he raced back to the entrance, firing searing bolts in wide arcs. So swift and powerful his defence, the electric web swept aside any stray Zürshuck that survived his initial volley. And dispatched them.

Gjen met Sonart at the cave's mouth and herded him into the alcove. Once inside, the wizard spun on his heel and cast a barrier of blue light over the opening. Its brilliant nimbus routed all shadow from the cleft and turned Sonart's pupils into pinheads.

Gjen wheeled back and nodded briskly. "That will buy us a little time, but Colossals will prove impervious to such a shield. They will be here in moments."

"What can we do?" Sonart asked between pants.

Gjen dropped to a knee and produced his sapphire crystal from the folds of his cloak. "Quickly, all of you gather around."

When the three dwarven huddled in, the wizard sized them up. "Sonart, you and Seolad will take this." He placed the gem in Sonart's palm while a grim Seolad and a wide-eyed Iomi looked on. "No time to explain so you must trust me implicitly. When you hear my command, run as fast as you can up the slope towards the pass. The Kalibah will aid and guide you to my hidden locus."

"What about Iomi and you?" Sonart protested.

"To survive this onslaught, we *must* split up. Iomi will stay by my side—I am more than capable to ward her. The two of you must clasp hands, and run as one. Do not separate. Keep that bond until you are both safely out of harm's way." His tone sharpened. "Do you understand?"

Both dwarven nodded emphatically.

"Like so." Gjen fastened their hands together. "Now, make ready. On my command."

Sonart and Seolad tightened their grip on one another and held their breath.

The wizard rose and faced the entrance. He lifted his staff.

Moments passed eternally as the sound of crunching snow drew closer—with it, a growing electrical hum.

Closer.

Louder.

Closer.

With a mighty shout, Gjen slammed his staff into the cavern floor. The ceiling and walls of the grotto exploded outward in a parasol of detritus. Thunderous cracks split the gutrock beneath the party but left them unharmed.

And suddenly in the open.

Carried on a blustery hot wind, cobalt smoke assaulted Sonart's nose and eyes.

Through the drifting skeins of rock dust, the closest Winged Ones lay buried. Gjen had seared the immediate area into a melted onyx expanse.

An indigo aura of residual magic hung in the air like a pall, engulfing the entire corridor and making the ground throb and shimmer.

But beyond that, a fresh wave of Zürshuck rallied and converged, wings folded as they dove.

Frozen by the sheer scale of the response, Sonart could only stare at the arena of chaos. Until Gjen's voice bellowed behind him, "*Now! Run!*"

Sonart and Seolad lurched into motion. They tore up the snow, atop the abattoir of Zürshuck corpses.

Surprise and power careered through Sonart as the dwarven pair dashed up the grade with unnatural speed.

Ahead, two massive luminescent forms materialized. They bore down on the fleeing dwarven, flaming broadswords in their grasp.

Colossals.

Gjen's crystal flared savagely as the sentinels raced to head them off. The dwarven's speed tripled. Even as the Colossals' blades swooped down, Sonart and Seolad ducked past their cordon and won free.

The dwarven's velocity tripled again. And again.

Sonart looked down and gasped. His legs and those of his cohort no longer penetrated the snow. The pair of them ran on air as if blown forward by the force of a razor storm.

Sonart's sprinting thoughts too skimmed the white powder, capable of one dogged goal.

Escape.

The cloud of destruction fell back. Lost within moments. A league passed, then another. The dwarven pair loped on unhindered, up and through the pass that crossed the Outereach. Charging up one slope, down the next, leaping over impossible chasms. They streaked across the alpine landscape of snow and rock and cloud. The scenery flashed by. Although driven by the gale of their wilderen sprint, the cold had no effect.

But where would the crystal lead them?

Despite Sonart's distrust and the reason for it, their expedited journey proved a fantastic thing to experience. Unless he missed his guess, they put ten unhindered leagues behind them when the light of the crystal began to dim. Their celerity lessened and their footfalls purchased snow once more. With the guttering of power, their hearts took up the unaided tempo of their pumping legs.

A moment later they drew to a stop. Sonart glanced back over his shoulder. Stars align, they remained alone. Beyond the last fifty paces, no footprints impressed the snow. Of course, they weren't followed—Gjen's bold ploy took their enemies at a critical moment unexpected.

In this instance, the wizard seemed to know exactly how events would play out before they happened. Stranger still, Sonart found himself partly aware of the same.

But how?

The trick had worked but at what cost?

A shadow passed over Sonart's reflections as he inspected his raiment, still stained with the dried blood of the hollowed-out Zürshuck Gjen slew. Did the death of the Kalibah's light connote the end of the wizard as well?

Sonart shuddered at the thought, but how could Gjen possibly protect Iomi *and* repel that army—armies—alone? Hooks and Dunge, he'd left the wizard to contend with Colossals. Although Sonart had been faced with dire need, once again the Sword would not come. Twas the wizard's magic that pushed them onward, as fierce and mighty as any Deathwrought wielded.

The dwarven turned his red beard up at the veil of clouds, much closer at this elevation.

"This is all my fault, Gjen," Sonart said to the wind. "I'm so sorry."

"You should be," Seolad said coldly as he unclasped his hand from Sonart's. "That I never finished her."

Acid surged through Sonart's blood. "You really are a bastard."

"By Vamsah's holy scrotum, are you that much a fool, or merely thinking again with your cock? Can't you see? Twas your sacrosanct Iomi who brought this folly upon us. She betrayed us again. And now there will be no escape. I only wish I had the satisfaction of running her through like I did that other cunt—end another Proclaimer, as she has ended us."

Sonart shook with rage. His hand reached for the hilt of his sword, but never made contact.

Seolad didn't miss the gesture. His smile cut like a knife. "Go ahead. Try."

"We should have—" Sonart stopped himself, realizing it would only escalate matters.

"Say it. You wish that I had been left behind." Pain underlined Seolad's ragged voice. But the dark storm in his eyes lingered. "I, who saved your miserable ass—more than once—so you might fulfil your gods-be-damned purpose."

"You rave—the result of a life forged in anger. I wish for our survival—all of us—that includes even you."

"Prove it," Seolad pressed as he simmered. "For at this moment, I feel anything but your trusted companion."

Sonart glowered back, fists clenched, but the moment passed and his shoulders sagged in resignation. He unfurled his fingers, met Seolad's fiery stance. And offered the blackbeard his arm.

Seolad's reluctance was plain in his wavering expression and arm. He clearly weighed the truce before capitulating. Clasping Sonart's elbow in one hand, the blackbeard offered him the elbow of his other arm. Sonart fastened a palm over the blackbeard's joint in the gruff dwarven fashion.

Their grips tightened. Fuelled by a mix of anger, armistice, and resolve they locked eyes and butted heads in a display of solidarity and strength.

"We must not dally—Brother," Sonart croaked with some effort. "Let us away. Else, Gjen's sacrifice will serve nothing."

"Aye," Seolad agreed as he disengaged, his tone and countenance sharing the same grimness. "Words unto deeds."

In silent procession, they slogged up through the skirling white lament of the mountains' higher reaches.

Soon, the snow crusted over and the way became easier, but a shroud of mist began to sift past—no doubt what Gjen had called ice fog. The wisps of cloud crept along the ground, brushing past them like giant wraiths.

Within the ether, two jutting buttresses emerged dead ahead. The pair closed the distance until they filed through a narrow fissure between the two walls.

Neither could be sure if they trekked in the right direction.

Neither knew if they would survive along any path they chose.

Neither really cared.

The fog grew thicker until it swallowed the frozen tract a mere thirty yards ahead. Although Sonart's body generated some heat by trudging on, it was not enough to keep the frigid damp at bay. It seeped into his cloak.

On the heels of their ceasefire, Sonart harboured a lingering regret for the way he had treated Seolad. In his own uncouth way, Rusic's son only sought to protect him—something the Vein could not repay in kind.

Sonart had failed his unlikely companion twice with Vamsah's supposed super sword. Near broken in spirit, his doubts about the weapon crystalized, especially after his last vision.

Either way the blade will cut. Was that what Deathwrought meant by 'the seed not flourishing'? Sonart would be denied his emblem by some hex of the Darkest One until He controlled both Sword and wielder. In all likelihood, he'd never be free of Deathwrought's taint.

Seolad cleared his throat and pointed. "Look."

Sonart followed his mate's outstretched finger. And stared.

The land abruptly ended.

Unsure, Sonart walked to the edge of the drop. And peered down into an undulating swirl of waxing and waning cloud. He felt his jaw drop over the precipice, his heart chasing it down.

The Void of Obliteration.

Sonart's gaze followed the edge left and right to where it disappeared into the mist on either side. Trepidation crawled like a spider up his spine as his focus drifted back to Seolad.

They exchanged frowns in silence.

"This is no glamour," Seolad said. "We must've come the wrong way."

Sonart presented the crystal shard in his fidgeting hand. "But the crystal led us here."

"Perhaps, when the stone's power abated, we veered from the true path. Maybe, we should retrace our steps and find another route."

If they did that, they could search for an eternity, meet a frozen doom lost in the unforgiving domain. But Sonart could offer no other recourse.

He swallowed hard and forced a reluctant nod. "Seems even the corrupted Kusp spoke truly of the Void." He indicated the abyss with his free hand. "We'll find nothing that way except death."

As they turned to go, some distant recall tingled at the base of Sonart's neck. Made him hesitate.

Seolad's eyebrows dovetailed. "What?"

"I—don't know—a premonition grounds me here, something familiar like—" He dithered a moment and then realization took hold. "By the Stars, I think I've been here before."

"The ice fog clouds your mind and muddles your wits," Seolad said with a touch of irritability. "We're the only two dwarven in the history of the Cradle to get here."

"Can you be sure of that?"

The prickly dwarven threw up his hands. "How can it be otherwise?"

"I'm learning to trust my instincts," Sonart declared. "They prove right while everything else goes awry." *All you must do is survive.*

Seolad rolled his eyes but managed to hold his fire back and keep his voice calm. "What then? What *sign* have you been given?"

Sonart weighed his response carefully, but it didn't take a sage to know that Seolad wouldn't like any version. "We must wait," he said at last.

Hearing his own reply triggered something within Sonart. Made him stand straighter and clear his senses.

Before a poleaxed Seolad could frame a fitting rebuke, the wind changed direction, murmuring past the pair from out of the Void. It carried a briny scent.

Realization dawned and Sonart exclaimed, "That's it! Can you smell it?"

Seolad snorted twice, and arched a brow. His scowl formed a question. "Aye, but what is it?"

"Salt, in the air." Sonart stuck out his tongue and smiled around it. "Stars, you can even taste it."

"But, what does it mean?"

"I had a premonition once, whilst captive in the Dunge—a vision within a vision. Then, staring out an antechamber window atop the Hive, I sensed it again, but never so acutely as I do now. I'd been too young to remember. Somehow, I have trodden here before. Of that, I am certain." *The answer will find you.*

"And I'm certain your riddles will be the death of me," Seolad grumbled. "Speak plainly man. Are we going to sit here and play twenty guesses while the Winged Ones search—and dispense their brand of certainty—namely the Hooks and Dunge?"

"Patience," Sonart calmly rebuffed.

"I am but…" Seolad's protest died on his lips as the crystal flared to life, blazing more intensely than ever before. They both gawked. Sonart's soul reignited along with Seolad's beaming face.

The blackbeard firmly clasped Sonart's forearm. "This could mean only one thing."

"Gjen is alive!" Sonart finished for him. Both dwarven rejoiced. "See how it pulses like a heartbeat of power itself."

After their initial shock subsided, they looked around before returning their faces to the Kalibah's sapphire nimbus. They stared at the crystal, biting their lips as its heat imbued them. And stared. And—

Seolad started. "Wait. Move the crystal to the right."

Sonart did so and the light dimmed noticeably along its right facet.

"Now, the left," the blackbeard instructed.

Glory washed through Sonart as the Kalibah shard brightened more intensely on that side. It frizzled with cool energetic light that frothed and excited one facet.

Sonart moved in that direction with Seolad falling in step behind him. Along the very edge of the world, they walked, one eye on the crystal, one eye towards the Void, guided by the reborn beacon of magic and hope.

The way began sloping downward and Sonart had to ease away from the land's end, should he float off or plunge into its infinite fathoms.

As they descended, the crystal blazed more magnificently in the direction he trod. The grey mist appeared to retreat from it, cowering before the brilliant azure gemstone Sonart held firmly before him.

But the incline grew more precarious, angling down at a steeper angle as it tipped towards the Void. Soon, a slope replaced the edge but still disappeared into mist the same. The crystal never wavered however, beckoning them down towards the abyss.

For a moment, Sonart doubted the eccentric plunge, but the prospect of turning back seemed worse. He continued to scale down the slant, leaning heavily into the slope while clutching the stone. One misstep and he would lose traction; tumble into the Void.

"Sonart!" his companion called behind him. "We obviously erred. Abandon this blind trek. If we continue down this way, we'll only stumble and cast ourselves into the Void."

"No!" Sonart shouted behind him, surprised at the authority his voice mustered. "We're getting close—I can feel it."

Seolad stopped.

Sonart continued.

With the blackbeard's legs braced against the slope above him to his left and the drop into the Void ever on his right, Sonart followed the demarcation until a strange opaque expanse appeared out of the shroud directly in front of him.

This grey mountain wall did not retreat with the mists. It would not yield and only reflected the light of the crystal, converging closer until it barred the dwarven's path.

It was a dead end.

59: True Lies
Targin

The hall that led into Johlarin's private quarters served as both gallery and museum: testimony to Areth's great ancestry. Here, the king paid tribute to all the world's historical events and the prolific figures that moved them along.

Targin walked past statues twice the size of a man, pausing at every tapestry and painting that lined the walls of the massive antechamber. Small sculpted dioramas encased in glass boxes depicted several scenes of important battles fought throughout the realm's turbulent history.

When his eyes fell upon a gloomy painting highlighting the last battle fought in the War of the Rennen, he stopped. Lingered. The art piece portrayed a staggering host of men in pitched battle with goblins, trolls, and dark elven. They fought under a sky gone black with storm clouds and raining arrows while legions of hawks and crowbats clashed overhead.

But of course, no eagles—or their elven flyers.

Resentment made Targin lift clenched hands. Regret made him drop them down again. He had been but an infant when that Great War claimed his mother, Amahnia. He reached his eighth year when lingering hostilities in the war's aftermath claimed his father, Stal.

Even the memory made his heart palpitate as Targin reflected. Goblin hellions butchered the other villagers and razed the immediate hamlet when they rampaged through at the behest of dark elven.

He too would've been slain had the dark elven captain spotted him hiding beneath the horse wagon. Couched above the wheel axle, swallowed by moon shadows, he could only watch and despair as the dark elven put his father to the sword.

Immediately after the devils departed, Targin rushed from his hiding place to his father's side. With scant minutes left before he succumbed to his injuries, Stal revealed startling news: he was not Targin's real father.

At the time, a shocked Targin thought the lull of the deepest sleep had affected his sire's last words, but he eventually learned the truth from the sprites, confirmed by Johlarin, Brapin, and Gaegungen. Targin's true father was a rogue and war hero, hearkening to the name of Torin Tragmar—the First Nightwolf.

Stal disclosed how an old crone had brought his adopted son to the steading as a babe in swaddling, having saved him after his true father died in battle. She proved to Stal that Targin would one day rise to become a central figure in the Kusp's prophesized Starbond—that he would be a Vein of Fire. Exactly how she convinced his surrogate father, he did not say.

The crone made Stal and Amahnia swear to shield the babe from others, and never to disclose the truth of his heritage until he became a man grown. She promised the answer would find and prepare Targin for what the fates had in store. Then the old woman left and was never seen or heard from again.

With that, Stal's words slurred into incoherence. His movements grew sluggish. A minute later he died, leaving a distraught Targin cradling his head, staring into his vacant orbs.

Alone in a desecrated settlement with both sets of parents dead, Targin believed Vamsah had abandoned him. His lungs began to heave.

But even as he finished burying his sire, scattered troops of Serenthia found him. At their head strode Thorian, much younger then. He took Targin to the closest orphanage, extolling as gently as he could over the boy's survival—said that his was a charmed life.

Charmed or cursed, bereft either way, Targin brooded. He grew up in the relative peace following the Great War, rising like the Nightwolves had from the ashes of their homeland's scourge.

But even that tale had a few holes, which he admitted to no one.

Targin vowed to one day take up his blood father's mantle—seek out Tragmar's Wolves—if they still existed.

A few years later, he achieved his goal, albeit not in the way he'd expected.

Twas the start of a bitter winter when the migratory birds had long fled south, Targin wandered into the woods. All the trees had been reduced to bare wooden skeletons, cringing in the cold.

A strapping young lad by then, he often went there to escape the orphanage, finding solace in the forest's seclusion. Mind quieted, he could make better sense of the visions, the whispers from the abyss, some light, some dark. But who or what sent them, he could not fathom.

This day, he meandered past his usual haunts, beyond a dark creek that furrowed a dip in the forest. Within the dank recess, he stumbled upon a cadre of goblins. He took the three for spies, trying to slip past Serenthia's nets.

The goblins set upon him with fangs gnashing and blades drawn.

"Dinner!" the largest of them jeered as his cohorts surrounded Targin.

Out of nowhere, a ghostly Warang leapt into the fray. The white-furred canine blindsided the goblins, bowling over the smaller two. Before they could give answer, he snapped their necks with a lightning one-two clamp of his terrible jaws. The wolf made to turn when the remaining goblin brought his rapier up and struck the canine's flanks.

Red smeared white.

A lesser beast might have fled or been felled by that first bite, but this Warang took four slashes, as though toying with his foe—or waiting?

On gut instinct, young Targin picked up one of the dead creature's swords and plunged it into the cavorting goblin's back. Outraged, he spun to deal a killing stroke.

His blade arced high. Came down.

And served Targin a deep slash across his forehead. Targin gagged on pain as metal kissed bone. But there it stopped as the Warang knocked the goblin's feet from under him with a sweep of his paw. Claws pressing the fiend down, the wolf clamped his jaws around the cretin's neck and ripped out his throat.

Targin's vision swam through a stream of blood, certain he would be next. But as the goblin leaked the last of his black fluids, the Warang padded up to the boy and licked his wound with a massive pink tongue.

Targin reached up and gently ran his fingers through the smooth fur beneath the wolf's muzzle. His coat looked more silver than white.

Unbeknownst to Targin at the time, their common purpose had forged a lifelong bond of beast and man. Both had spilled blood. Both had blood spilt. The lad grew up tempered by many desperate events but they always brought him back to the wolf's cunning and resilience in that direst of moments.

Woozy from the gash to his crown, Targin faltered and sank to his knees. The Warang settled on the forest floor, rolled his great head in a circular motion, and nudged the boy with his snout.

Targin shimmied onto the wolf's back, splayed his arms down the canine's flanks and clutched two fistfuls of fur. The Warang rose and raced him back to the glen where the orphanage stood.

Covered in blood, further obscured by the dim light of eventide, the caregivers misunderstood the Warang's motive when he lowered his charge.

They rushed in, loosing a volley of arrows and slingshot rocks.

The wolf bolted for the fence of trees behind him, swallowed by the forest in three heartbeats.

In the days that followed, Targin discovered he could commune with the Warang. He was named Yerik, meaning *Appointed,* chief to a pack of great wolves descended from the *Noirlunen.*

Targin thought that would be the last of Yerik. And for a long time, it was. But then, on a bright spring morning a week short of his eighteenth star-cycle, the white wolf returned. He emerged from a different tract of woodland, beside a small cottage Targin had built.

Busy chopping kindling outside, Targin dropped his axe as he caught sight. But when he beckoned Yerik, the ghostly canine neither approached nor communed.

More wolves emerged behind their chief, in a seemingly endless procession. All the canines—some black, some silver grey, others chestnut, charcoal, or deep brown, flanked their chief. Roughly three hundred in total, the pack formed up and sat back on their haunches.

Bewildered, Targin settled on the ground opposite the fold and joined them in their silent vigil.

Time slowed.

And sped up again, when a band of two hundred shadowy men clad and hooded in midnight black joined the pack—a much younger Gnor and a two-eyed Jaak at their head.

Men and wolves seemed content to stand or sit and wait as though attending service at some outdoor kennel turned convent. Only the sound of clucking chickens and bleating goats, safe in their respective pens, carried on the wind.

So transfixed by the strange congregation, Targin failed to notice the tiny sprite sauntering towards him until he came within a few steps.

Heart pounding, Targin bolted to his feet.

An assuring smile painted the beautiful nymph's face and his words sounded like a youngling's innocent song. "Time to make good on your promise, Targin, Torin son. Though it seems your promise will make good on you. I am Dras by the way, First of the sprites of Etern's Drop."

Targin dry-swallowed. "My stars eclipse, little one. What in blazes do you mean?"

Large rainbow eyes beamed up at Targin. "Didn't your surrogate father, Stal, relay the Kazir's words—that the answer would find you?" The sprite laughed as he swept his tiny arm at the encircling wolves and men. "It has."

When Targin shook his head in confusion, the sprite explained, "Stars align in our common purpose. Join the Nightwolves and you will fulfil the destiny you set for yourself. Continue your father's legacy. And make history."

And so far, Targin realized as he came back to the moment in Johlarin's private hall, they had done exactly that.

Seemed fitting that his eyes should settle on the gallery's largest painting—and as far as he was concerned its greatest piece. It depicted Tragmar, atop a pediment littered with goblin corpses—as he crushed the neck of their king, Rathnonek—a moment before he too was slain.

On either side of the main canvas, other historical paintings depicted more significant conflicts. One showed the dispersion of the firedrakes at the twilight of the Dragon Wars, when the region south of the Ghost Spires, had been rent by their fiery exchanges. Dark magics had further sickened the tract into a wasteland, now known as the Dead Forest.

It revealed nothing of Lord Shirdron's part, even though the alchlemage struck the very flint that curtailed the Dragon Wars. So loathed was he, all of Areth's races expunged his name from their chronicles. Stars, for a false prophet, Shirdron had proven thrice the outlaw than Targin himself.

Small wonder, after the near-fatal wounds inflicted upon the Twin-Gaia. Though, the dwarven had paid the heaviest price of Shirdron's False Starbond. It eviscerated the Main and wiped out their kingdom. Those not turned to ash by fire-rain had their lives left in tatters. The survivors either dispersed into the hills and mountains of the Matted Spikes or set out to sea and made for the ancestral homes of their lost brethren in Grendamaul—the Cradle—by all accounts a fate far worse.

In sharp contrast to all the others, the last canvas illustrated the first moot of the Kings of Old. They stood in the courtyard garden of Cillinox Castle, surrounded by pergolas adorned with brilliant spring flowers of yellow, pink-blue, and purple. On a giant stone table before them stretched a map of the Main.

It ushered in the Age of Renewal when all the kings stood together at last to redraw the map of the continent. Having deemed Areth delivered into an era of everlasting peace, the monarchs annexed lost kingdoms and rebuilt their own, intent on restoring the world.

They ignored the prophecy of the Kusp and the Starbond it foretold; the regents actually believed the freeborn had vanquished Deathwrought for good.

This marked the moment of their greatest bliss and their greatest folly. Hope fuelled their accord. But had they known how generations later, such division would lead to subversion and segregation—that it would devolve into paranoia, subterfuge, betrayal, and ultimately warmongering, they'd have taken that map and burned it to cinders.

Not by coincidence, King Johlarin placed this particular painting last, with a simple metal placard beneath, ironically titled: BEWARE GIFTS.

Twas a baleful prompt that things were never as they seemed. To his credit, His Grace never banked on a fool's hope.

Learn the past. Squeeze the present. Forge the future. With this ethos driving his thoughts, Targin turned to make for the king's chamber when the door to Johlarin's solar opened.

60: And False Truths
Targin

Clad in a casual grey robe of roughspun, Johlarin stood framed in the portcullis. Crownless, his white mane hung loosely over his shoulders.

The regent's eyes softened as they settled on Targin. He offered a half-smile. "It bodes well for you to keep these events in mind while we plan the events yet to pass—something you and I shall effort this night."

Targin frowned. "I thought you had already done that, Your Grace."

"My edicts to the council stand. My instruction to you will be somewhat different. I couldn't make my full intentions known in session—not with the enemy's ear present."

"Plots within plots," Targin mused darkly as he joined his king. "You truly do think like a Nightwolf."

"No, I merely think. You more than anyone should know that things are not always as they seem."

"Yes, of course," said Targin. "What do you wish?"

"I have great fear—its merit validated."

"For Serenthia?"

A shadow crept over Johlarin's face. "For you."

Targin merged his brows all the tighter. "Pray tell."

Johlarin beckoned him into the solar. Once inside, he closed the door and faced the Nightwolf. "You're not the only one to have sittings with the sprites."

"Have you guested them here in my absence or sought their counsel at the Drop?"

"Neither," Johlarin said. "They sought me through visions—strong visions. I don't fully comprehend their meaning, but I have no doubt what I should relay. In sooth, their counsel to you is but preface to what you must confront."

"How can you know what I must confront?" Targin asked, sharper than he intended. "And why didn't they contact me directly—as they have done since I was a boy?"

Johlarin studied him before replying, "The poison combined with the enchantment left you susceptible. Until Thorian had repaired that breach, you may have surrendered some secret in your compromised state."

Targin stared. As always, Serenthia's ruler voiced the hard truth.

"You said it yourself in session," Johlarin pointed out. "The art of communion can just as readily be manipulated by the enemy, especially dark elven. As to why the sprites chose me, perhaps I seem genuine in my guidance of those I rule and swore to protect."

He threw the Nightwolf a sideways glance. "Perhaps for my lenience with you. I opened my heart to them, as you laid plain your distaste towards the elven—which I have not forgiven you for by the way."

Targin raised a hand in defence. "I do not seek your forgiveness in matters where men's lives may teeter on a rigged scale. Nor will I hand truth to those we simply cannot trust—such a foundation riddles with faults. There is too much history with the elven to set aside. And I cannot lead any soul on a campaign I don't fully trust myself."

The king sighed and moved to a small table where a silver tray held a glass decanter filled with purple berry wine and two long-stemmed glasses. He poured the wine into one of the glasses and handed it to Targin. "Though you always seem to forget that I am still your king, I do appreciate your frankness."

Johlarin poured himself a glass and took a sip. "But it's the specifics of your quest I wish to address. You acknowledge that apart from accompanying Areth's forces into battle and shepherding your three counterparts to what end the sprites have intended, there's another task."

Targin sipped the wine, letting his tongue swim through its fruity pool before swallowing. "The Kalibah—yes, I know."

Johlarin dipped his chin. "You're well aware that in the aftermath of the Eclipsed War, the Kalibah shards scattered across the Main. Some of the fragments were recovered and put into safekeeping. Others, entrusted to men or elven, had been found out by one of our many foes and confiscated, their guardian slain. But the largest of the shards—and the most potent has never been found. The Testament points to the northern hinterlands, but not exactly where."

The Nightwolf tilted his head forward. "I have an inkling, but in truth, I'm not entirely sure. Brapin probably knows where but remains elusive."

The king bit his lower lip and pondered. "Questionable though his ways may be, the Orbical's heart is pure, his mind sharp as a honed dirk."

"Stars align, to a cutting and painful fault," Targin agreed, his words ending with a wry chuckle. "But I've found that his riddlesome words have a habit of steering me to the truth and solution therein."

Johlarin nodded in silence and looked away. "You said he was *elusive*." His eyes returned to Targin. "Did he divulge anything?"

Targin took another drink. "Brapin says the key lodestone has resurfaced somewhere close to the caldera of Death."

The king lowered his glass abruptly. "Mount Marwolaeth? In the Land of Fire? It lies a thousand leagues north of here. If the flaming earth doesn't claim you, legions of lavatrols lie between you and it. Serion intends us to plough the field but never considered that it might be a lava field. Besides all that, Serenthia could never march an army up there in time to deal with them."

"We won't need to," Targin said. "If the bulk of the lavatrols be in Tragmar or the elven lands, as the prince claims, they will be diminished in the Land of Fire itself. Incapable of respawning, once slain, Areth has one less abomination to deal with." He let out a dry laugh. "She's got her hands full with me."

Johlarin ignored the jest, his face an impenetrable mask of sternness. "What do you propose?"

"I'll march with you and our troops as planned and once battle joins, steal away to await the Merger. When I retrieve my three companions, we'll leave the Relay and head north."

"And then?"

Targin drained the rest of his glass and poured himself another. "We'll make for Etern's Drop. If anyone knows where the united Veins must go to reclaim the precious Kalibah and replenish the Heart in the Cleft Augury, it would be the sprites. Lucky for us, their stronghold lies more or less on the way to Marwolaeth."

Johlarin knitted his brows, his doubt all too apparent in the quiver of his crow's feet. "Targin, my stars eclipse in this matter."

Targin gently placed his free hand on the monarch's shoulder. "The sprites gifted me with their power for a reason—it will give me advantages."

"I see." Johlarin let out a deep breath as Targin removed his palm. The king set his glass on the table, walked over to the hearth, and braced his hands on the mantle, his back to Targin. "Or should I say, I was shown—a vision. In it, you sought the Kalibah, past an emptied battlefield, across the Ice Wastes, but—" he paused and faced the Nightwolf. "You were alone. The rest seems an unguided quest, set by the whims of a highborn elven with flowery speech."

Targin arched an eyebrow at that, cheekbones buoying higher. He was relieved to hear Johlarin speak openly, his disdain for the elven made plain.

He gave his king a resigned grin. "Unfortunately, Highness, it is precisely that which I must concede. Brapin proved most adamant—and quite annoying on that particular point."

The king strode back to the table, orbs flaring. He raised his index finger. "Concede nothing to Serion!"

Targin shrugged. "That goes without saying. But it's not the elven prince to whom I must concede, but the elven Vein. He's *never* set foot on Areth. Knows nothing of our ways and plight—least not on a conscious level. When he joins the quest, he'll prove my greatest charge."

"Where is he now?"

"Where he's always been—Areth's symbiont realm—beyond the Hinge."

"Yes, Otherworld, through the Eye. It's mentioned several times in the Kusp, but why there?"

"Apparently, for his protection." Targin lifted his shoulders. "Perhaps, so that his command of the wilderen magic could be nurtured and left to develop, unhindered by the enemy."

The king made a sour face, the corners of his mouth pulling down. "Unhindered? I strongly doubt that. The enemy seeks to thwart us on every front, Targin, by any means," he added. "They'll find him there."

"No question," Targin allowed, "Deathwrought himself has made similar attacks against the dwarven Vein already, but this Sonart at least has Gaegungen and Laethan as his wards—he could ask for none better. Stars, the attack on me at Riverside—that too was not random. Spies are everywhere—perhaps even among my Nightwolves. The moles communed with dark creatures of the earth and worst among them, the witchy-bitchy dark elven."

Johlarin scowled. "Do the sprites concur with Brapin? The elven Vein is more important than the Kalibah shard?"

Targin inclined his head.

"Then the war is a front," the king guessed, his eyes narrowing. "The Kalibah—a trap, and for all intents and purposes we must make the enemy believe we've taken the bait, marching for just cause at the elven's side."

Johlarin reached for his glass again and drank more wine. "As to your elven charge," he considered between sips, "if Brapin has said so, then who am I to disagree with the Orbical? Protect the elven Vein at all costs. But stars, how will you know where to meet him?"

"I will know. Again, for his protection, a level of ambiguity seems vital."

"I know his brand of ambiguity—I met Brapin on occasion," Johlarin disclosed with a snicker. "You're beginning to sound just like him."

"That should please him," Targin chortled before adding more seriously, "Everything is linked, Your Grace—my charges, the Kalibah, and the War—do not discount that entirely. We have the dying Gaia to consider. But you are right. If I don't seek the Kalibah while guiding the Veins, if we neglect any part of this three-fold quest, we'll be overwhelmed when the Final Dark falls."

Johlarin's lips trembled, gloom weighing his eyes. "I'm afraid we'll be overwhelmed regardless."

Targin twirled the stem of his glass, making its purple contents dance. "Truthfully, I'm hard-pressed to sanction any edict that keeps our warbirds on the ground, but I wouldn't question the sprites' judgement. They possess spirits incorruptible to evil. That's why the Darkest One is so bent on their destruction; why he can't attack them directly and has tried for years to corrupt the hearts of men—to goad them into alienating or attacking the sprites themselves."

"Thorian mentioned something of this to me," Johlarin said. "A few sprites may be slain, at least in their corporeal forms, but the essence of their collective power endures. The Twin-Gaia fosters them and gives them life. They cannot be ousted directly by the hand of evil, but they're just as vulnerable as the Gaias—*if* the Last Born themselves fall to corruption."

"I won't let that happen," Targin assured as he placed his vessel on the table.

"I hope so." The king exhaled slowly, his brows drooping. "You've never entered a campaign based so firmly on the pathless path and visions. And the lay above Etern's Drop…" He slowly shook his head as his eyes met the Nightwolf's. "Far as I know, it's uncharted."

Targin ran his fingers through his hair. "I'm no Lorin, but I'll do what I can in the forest ranger's stead. I'll look after my counterparts when we begin our search." He deflated his chest. "That said, I do not relish taking them into the wretched haunts above the Drop—admittedly, I'll be just as lost as them."

"That's something I will handle."

Targin wheeled at the sound of Tasmin's voice.

Armed and clad in boiled leathers, the princess stood by the entrance, hands braced on hips, a puckish smile playing on her lips.

61: Annulment
Targin

"Like *fuck* you will!" Targin roared.

"Like fuck, I *will!*" Tasmin fired back, no less trenchant.

Targin was having none of it. Eyes igniting into pinnacles of fury, he spun on the king. "Johlarin, talk sense to the hellion—forbid her. Your daughter cannot be allowed to go."

The king coughed. "I've already tried."

"You—*knew?*"

"She claims it is the will of the sprites, through visions," Johlarin said sheepishly. "And I believe her."

"With respect, don't play that card with me again, Your Grace. It can only hold so much value. She lies and twists your heart until you yield. Trust me, I know."

Hands still fastened to her hips, Tasmin jerked them to one side like a tolling bell. "You know nothing, but let's straighten the twists of your tangled disillusions. Out with them, Dog—I am listening."

Targin balled two fists and worried at them. "As if I don't have enough detractors," he griped. "Warfare is the province of men alone."

Johlarin stared over the Vein's quivering knuckles, a beseeching look creasing his crow's feet into a single fold.

"I'll do what you ask in the manner you wish it done," Targin pressed as he dropped his hands. "But I'll *not* stand by and watch you send this plotting vixen to an untimely death."

Undaunted, Tasmin walked a calculated circle between her father and Targin. As she cornered around her spouse-to-be, her sinuous form brushed against his carriage, a wisp of her silvery mane glanced his nose with a feather's touch.

Targin sniffed her honeyed apple fragrance. And threw his hands up in disgust. "Twats of a thousand aged whores, she's your only daughter!"

"And your future wife," Johlarin pointed out, "but her own person, which you seem to forget. Tasmin follows her own course, Nightwolf—her own pathless path. As does her mother, Atheri." Conviction pressed his lips. "As do you."

The king took a drink of his wine and placed the glass on the table. "Far be it for me to tell you to respect her choices as I esteem the steps of my beloved wife and queen. But even your Orbical would agree that it is wisdom to compromise and reciprocate within your coven."

Johlarin lifted his chin to Tasmin and brought his shoulders back. "My daughter knows the range of those lands a far cry better than any of our scouts, and she's been above the Drop. Tasmin has mastered communion and combat under *Lorin's* guidance. Would you deign to gainsay our best ranger's tutelage?"

Targin stared.

"She's also had tenure with elven quartermasters and loremasters during most of her childhood," the king went on. "Stars, she even speaks their language. As a woman grown, I wouldn't doubt she can best near any man or hobgoblin if put to it."

Tasmin flashed a dagger. Before Targin could react, she pressed its tip under his chin. "And don't you forget it." While the blade glinted in the hearth's light, she handed him an impish grin.

Glowering, Targin brushed the dirk away. "Johlarin, I'll uphold my solemn vows, follow every edict, perform every task. On my oath as Blood Scion, I'll serve as the Veins' forest guide." His neck muscles bulged. "Stars burn her, do not fall for the chicanery of this—wilful Princess of Infern."

"I love the image!" Tasmin laughed wryly. "Please, brute, paint another canvas of my female strength and superiority."

"Targin," Johlarin chastised with a shake of his head. "You said yourself, you do not know all the threads of the tapestry we weave."

Stabbing a finger at Tasmin, Targin seethed, "If her witchcraft is involved, burn it all." A threat trembled on the tip of his tongue, but he checked himself and continued more judiciously. "My Liege, whatever it takes, I'll unite the Veins and lead them north of the Drop. Find this forsaken crystal, reassemble the whole lodestone with our scraps. And use the fucking thing myself!"

The king's eyes widened. "No!" he sputter-croaked, horror close to the surface. "Absolutely not. Targin, that is something you must *never* attempt. Do not even entertain the notion of taking the full Kalibah into your custody."

A shadow of some buried fear crept into the king's blanched features and he quivered noticeably.

It made Targin swallow. "Think me another Shirdron?"

Johlarin did not answer. He shifted his attention to the princess. "Tasmin has convinced me that she's been touched by the sprites in this—"

"Do the sprites tell you when and how to shit as well?" Targin barked.

"—matter—as I hoped to convince you of mine," Johlarin finished in a grating voice. He adopted a rigid stance and scowled. "Do not interrupt me again. My trust in Tasmin's certitude surpasses my love for her. She will go with you. As king—your king, I command it."

"Squander your family as you will, King, for it may supplant *your* love,"

Targin returned. "But it shall never infiltrate mine." He slapped his chest hard. "This heart is not so callow. She will only jeopardize the success of my mission. I cannot watch over her as well as the Veins when we tread such volatile ground."

"There'll be no need to guard me," Tasmin announced. "I won't be travelling with you."

When Targin frowned, she amended, "least not immediately."

Throat raw from shouting, Targin croaked, "Pray, explain your glib tongue."

Tasmin reached behind her back and adjusted the cuff of her left riding boot, then the right. With fierce grace, she walked over to the table where the wine bottle sat. But did not reach for a glass or pour a drop.

She turned and faced Targin. "Though we may arrive in the same vicinity, if not the exact location, my path lies upon a different road than yours. But our purposes entwine. Our goals are shared."

Targin knitted his brows but chose to ignore her latest riddle. His ire simmered as he met the king's eyes. "The only road she should be tramping thread the frontier villages surrounding Serenthia. Do not forget what we risk by rushing to the elven's aid. She's best suited to protect *this* vital stronghold, lest *it* be compromised." He snarled in Tasmin's direction. "But she may have already done so."

Johlarin brusquely waved his hand at the terse quip. He seemed to rise in stature like one of the warrior sculptures warding the hall outside his solar. "Look to the task at hand, Nightwolf. When her time comes, Tasmin will help by setting you on the right path to the Kalibah. She will not guide you to it. As for Serenthia, let me worry about protecting the Strong Helm— which you plainly doubt me capable."

"I've never doubted you, or your rule upon the Kraken Throne. But I do question your personal wisdom of late."

Johlarin's face tightened but he exhaled through his nose.

Targin crossed his arms. "Though I refuse her utterly in this matter, I cannot disallow her to go." His regard veered to Tasmin, sending a blizzard of disdain to match her icy smirk. "But I will not suffer a future spouse of mine to endanger herself and those under my protection, heedless of my wishes, when and where another scout could step in just as well."

The smile fell away from Tasmin's face and her eyes darkened. "What are you saying?" Her body tensed, palm hovering over her sword pommel.

"I think I speak clear enough." Targin's mouth warped into a sneer. "Come, seek the Kalibah, by whatever hell-laden path you choose to trample over my heart. But do so with the knowledge that—that you forfeit our betrothal."

Tasmin's orbs flared like those of a dragon, her lips parting, poised to unleash a fiery torrent.

Daring her to do so, Targin leaned forward and braced, bile rising up his throat like a volcano about to erupt.

Glowers locked, matching strength for strength, fire with fire.

The king opened his mouth, lips working in vexed silence.

The air hushed and stilled. The quiet became deafening.

Tasmin finally broke it. She picked up the bottle of wine and threw it at Targin's head.

He ducked, barely avoiding the swift missile as it sailed overhead to crash against the mantle above the hearth. The bottle shattered in a bouquet of glass shards. It bled purple berry wine down into the fire, making it hiss sharply.

Tasmin fled towards the door, nostrils flaring, fighting for air. Without mercy, the chamber door slammed shut behind her. Its shudder echoed throughout the room, reverberating off the walls and making every piece of chattel tremble.

When the clamour finally ebbed, Targin wheeled on the king, mirroring the stone shield that guarded the regent's face.

Johlarin slowly splayed his hands. "Do not revile her, Targin. Be reasonable."

"That time has come—and passed. When you agreed to send your only child on this suicidal errand."

Johlarin winced, his hurt plain in the deepening furrows of his visage. His eyebrows sagged. "It is the sprites who send her, not me."

"Stars burn us all, you *believe* her? She blasphemes their good name, using it to press her case, and lend her their advantage."

"Advantage? Do you rave?" Johlarin raked his fingers through his white tresses. He opened and closed his hand as he grasped at calm. "What *advantage* can she possibly seek, to put herself in the path of imminent danger? To place me in such grief?"

"I cannot grasp her motives—ever," Targin complained. "Maybe she wishes to assert her worth to you, to me, to herself, to the sodding Areth Gaia. One can never know the depths of a woman's soul, especially one filled with such scorn and firebrand grit as the princess."

"Aye, and forsooth," Johlarin said bitterly. "Sadly, you *don't* know. Consequently, you may have just let go of the truest reasons for undertaking this terrible quest. Clearly, you don't deserve her."

"Now, tis you who speaks the truth," Targin muttered, his voice hoarse. "Another woman would have heeded my decision in this matter, without question. Granted, I spoke harshly, as is my way, but my concern roots only for her safety. You know that."

Johlarin gulped but remained silent. His lids lowered briefly and lifted again.

Targin breathed deep and rubbed the back of his neck, kneading the knots there until he relaxed. "Perhaps extricating myself from her will be the safest thing for both of us. But separating her from you—Your Grace, you did not so much as contest her. Why did you not forbid it?"

Johlarin dropped his shoulders and met Targin's glare with resignation. "Because... I am dying."

Targin blinked. Then started, a sudden weight compressing his chest like petrifying armour. "*Dying*? What do you mean?"

The king unfastened the top three buttons of his robe and revealed a violet welt the size of a plum above his collarbone. Two black scabs haloed by green coronas stood like nipples at the top of the mound. "Bitten, by a very poisonous wasp, enhanced by blood magic. It recently infiltrated the Hidden Kingdom. That is why the centipus attacked you—the sentinel sensed something out of place when you arrived, but could not single it out."

Johlarin rebuttoned his robe. "Thorian has confirmed it. He found the black insect in question, dead, its poison spent but still fresh. The infliction has proven impervious to even his medicine and magic. I'm afraid it is a mortal wound. The wasp's venom will consume me ere long—for a certainty before you join battle."

Targin stammered half-syllables, which made Johlarin chuckle with dry mock. "Had a feeling this ill bit of news would finally make you shut up. Oh well, I don't fear the deepest sleep—when you reach my age you no longer need worry about dying young."

Targin snorted, unamused by the dark jape. "How could this happen? You had sprite wards in place."

"Even wards may be lifted, if one knows their secret mechanism," the king continued more gravely.

"The spy?"

Johlarin nodded. "I suppose when Necatar realized he couldn't subvert my mind, like as not due to my long and fruitful pact with the sprites, he resorted to other means. Fret not, Nightwolf. Old and afflicted as I am, I'm not dead yet. And I still have a kingdom to rule—one on the verge of the last battle of our time. On that note, you must lead our army in my stead."

The king searched Targin's face. "My trust in the sprites knows no measure—that I take with me to the grave. Your silence about my ailment, I ask that you take to yours. Only you and Thorian share this knowledge. Atheri and Tasmin must never know how I died."

It was my fault. Guilt consumed Targin and made his mouth go dry.

"And please, Targin, since we'll never have this opportunity again, I bequeath you keep love and war separate. Your heart can be its own worst enemy. Do not let emotion muddle your focus. Concentrate on that, probably the most monumental of your list of charges. Take heed, for not everything is what it seems."

"Words unto… to live by." Targin bowed his head as if receiving benediction. "Our stars will align in this, Your Grace—I promise."

Johlarin exhaled and his eyes softened. "And as a dying man's last request, please, quell your fury at my daughter and her quest. Like you, highborn or no, she feels justified in her role, carrying out her task as she deems fit. Support her justification. Let it mirror your own. Vamsah guide you, my son."

Targin inclined his chin and made to leave the chamber.

"One more thing," the king said to his back.

Targin stopped short of the entrance and curved around. "Aye?"

Johlarin slid him a sideways look. "That Florin—the elven prince's Haft—watch him with the scrutiny of a hawkrike."

"You forget, Your Grace, I collect malefactors faster than shit collects flies."

The king smiled and waved him off.

Targin left the chamber, closing the door with nary a hush. His mind burst with so many thoughts competing for his consideration. He suppressed all but one.

With that as his compass point, he knew exactly what must be done first.

62: Prisms
Sonart

Sonart craned his neck up at the granite wall blocking his passage. Immense and impervious, full of crags and striations of layered stone, the mountain soared. Like the Hive and the Thorned Spikes surrounding it, this monolith also pierced the swirling mass of clouds not more than a thousand feet above him, its summit lost to sight.

But in contrast, the towering face was a natural structure, cast in neutral grey that matched the indifferent ceiling. A mountainous barricade of ancient making, magnificent yet remorseless as it greeted him and Seolad with the only answer that mattered—no.

As the doctrine of the Kusp ordained, the mighty Outereach sentinels served as the Cradle's first line of defence against the Void of Obliteration. The barrier kept the nothingness beyond from consuming the lands within.

But now it also denied Sonart and Seolad further passage forward. Their only choice: return up the hazardous slope on their left or cast themselves into the Void to their right.

And yet, the crystal's guiding flare insisted they go straight toward the obstruction. Were they meant to scale it?

As impossible as the prospect seemed, the jewel remained absolute. Whenever Sonart turned the blue gem away from the wall, its luminosity dimmed or guttered completely.

But if they could not deviate, where else could they go?

Seolad caught up then, cheeks reddened and puffed by cold, eyebrows knitted, equally baffled over their dilemma.

Sonart envisioned Gjen imploring him to trust. He bit his lower lip in concentration, holding the crystal at arm's length. And advanced towards the wall. He would solve the riddle of the stone, not because he vowed to do so. But because he must.

Snow crunching under his boots, Sonart leaned into the gradient as he marched, Seolad trudging slightly lower on his right side. They drew up to the wall's base. Sonart held the gem inches from the barricade's cold, aged face.

The dwarven pair now stood at the very point of vertex where the wall met the slope, sliding away and down to their right. Sonart examined the gem fastidiously. Its azure glow only brightened the stone beyond it.

Seolad too considered the jewel, studied Sonart, frowned up at the barrier. And cursed.

Sonart stared at the wall.

The wall stared right back, impassive as before.

But the Scion refused to give up.

The crystal's glow began to pulsate, as though coaxing him to try something different, lateral. He tapped the gem itself against the rockface and its light winked out.

Sonart's heart sank.

"Now what?" Seolad groaned.

As Sonart turned to placate his crestfallen companion something caught his notice. Less than a hundred feet down the slope, where its lip merged with the sheer drop of the granite wall, jutted a boulder the size of three large Kworn standing abreast.

Sandwiched between the boulder and the wall, a neat stack of crates and sacks rested, a drift of snow angling two feet up one side of the pile.

Something lateral.

The supplies had been hidden from all angles of the precipice and its sloped warrens. Except for this precise spot. The cache would've otherwise gone undetected had the crystal not led them to this exact place.

Sonart beamed as he met Seolad's clenched face: part grimace, part glower. "And now—that." He pointed over his companion's shoulder drawing his focus to the provisions.

A rare smile spread across the blackbeard's wind-burned mien and his eyes softened.

Sonart handed Seolad the crystal, who dropped it into a side pocket of his cloak.

"We'll need to retreat a few steps to ensure we catch that boulder," Sonart said.

Seolad dipped his beard. "And guarantee the slab catches us—aye."

Sonart took seven measured steps away from the wall until the boulder rested directly below him down the tricky slope. Slowly, methodically, he lowered himself towards the rock. As he neared it, the icy grade grew steeper. It angled near-vertical just beyond his goal. He would have to slide the last twenty feet. If he missed the rock, he'd go over the edge.

Sonart gulped as he lowered his rump to the slant, knees pressed up, boots still purchasing.

With a silent word of prayer to the stars, he lifted his heels.

The sudden lurch forced a gasp from Sonart's mouth.

But he slid straight and true. With a grunt, his boots butted up against the rock and he bent his knees to absorb the impact.

Sonart didn't move for a moment, both hands anchored to the rock's solid surface. After three deep breaths, he rose. Clinging to the frigid relief, he eased around its curve to where the supplies lay.

Sonart found a huge pile of coiled rope, affixed to the jutting boulder with a metal spike. At eighteen-inch intervals, bulbous knots ran the entire length of the thick cord. They would make it possible for the dwarven to rest their weight when they tired.

As Sonart unravelled the braided line, feeding an arm's span over the edge, and another, and another, Seolad appeared.

The blackbeard carefully edged his body around the sarsen, as Sonart had done.

"Almost missed it," he declared past an exhalation. Seolad's crooked smirk indicated he enjoyed the risky slide. It marked the dwarven's second happy signal in one day. Perhaps there was hope for him yet.

"Terrified me as well," Sonart admitted. He tilted his head towards the crates. "See if you can open the stores while I pay this line out."

With a curt nod, Seolad wrestled the pack open and removed its cache of smaller containers.

Sonart fed the last bit of line over the precipice when a grating sound drew his attention to Seolad, prying one of the rectangular boxes open.

The blackbeard brought the splayed container close to his face, sniffed its contents, and bunched up his nose.

Within the box, wrapped in a cloth, nested a bundle of what looked like skinned and dried roots. Seolad lifted one and rubbed it between his fingers. "Strange, it's pliable—not frozen."

"I presume those are for eating," Sonart said.

"Are you mad?" Seolad tsked. "Have you ever seen their like before? We've no idea what effect they will have if we ingest them."

"Like naocci," Sonart pointed out as he joined his cohort. "I hardly think the Kalibah led us to a climbing rope, only to poison us with these roots. Clearly, one was meant for the other."

Before Seolad could object, Sonart snapped the root out of his hand and bit into it.

The vegetable tasted bitter at first, but its effect was certainly not toxic. As bits of the strange frond trickled down the dwarven's throat, a nurturing glow charged his muscles with new vigour. It also sharpened his mind.

Still chewing, Sonart shifted his regard from the root to Seolad. "Eat." He gestured to the length still in his hand. "Trust me, Brother, you'll need it."

Seolad surveyed the chasm below and sighed. "Damn it all, I'd warrant the same." He took a piece from the container, tore off a chunk, and gnawed at it.

Almost immediately the colour returned to Seolad's features, relaxing the troubled ditches lining his mouth and eyes.

After they had consumed several lengths, Seolad set to piling the containers back into the pack and hoisted the entire bundle on his back. "A lifetime's toil in the mines will help here. At least some good came of those cursed pits."

Sonart gave his companion a brief smile as he readied the rope, giving it a hard yank. Satisfied, he measured the span between the rock and the vertical drop.

"I don't know where this will take us," Sonart said as he backed towards oblivion's edge. "I can only hope it proves better than this forlorn pillar."

As he made to begin his descent, Seolad gripped his shoulder. "Let me go first this time."

Sonart arched an eyebrow and studied his compeer for a moment, finding naught but earnest concern in the blackbeard's fierce gaze. With a nod, he handed the line to Seolad and they traded places.

"For the Cradle," Seolad said. "Until we return—to un-fuck it." With that, he descended, his black crown dropping out of sight as he rounded the lip of the shelf.

Sonart waited a few breaths before beginning his own descent. When he reached the same curve, he could see straight down.

Past Seolad's lowering form, wisps of vapour licked the granite cliff face. Further below, the slick wall disappeared completely, swallowed by the shroud.

Sonart concentrated on the next knotted rung, and the next, and the next, casting uncertainty aside as he worked his way down the line.

At every interval, both arms held his weight until he could seat himself on the knot below. In this way, the pair lowered themselves, pausing only momentarily to gauge each other's progress. Neither complained of fatigue.

Hundreds of feet later, relief buoyed Sonart when Seolad called up, "I found a ledge!"

Sonart peered down just as Seolad alighted onto a jut of rock. When his turn came to step onto the narrow tier, he found his companion seated, waiting patiently. "Rest a bit. I found another rope secured over there."

Sonart followed Seolad's outstretched arm to the spiralled mass, longer than the first cord.

"Seems the wizard left the means for our escape after all," Seolad conceded.

"Aye," Sonart replied, too winded to say anything else. But as he plopped himself down beside his peer, he thought a great deal more.

Gjen's assurance sounded moot in the wizard's absence. The harrowing vision of the Cradle's plight, of Auckland and Mila's fate, resurfaced. If the dire foretelling showed true, there'd be nothing left to return to. How would

Sonart unravel this debauched mess without his fellow Vein to guide him? The answer was simple: he could not.

Sonart blew out his cheeks, suppressing the sensation of smallness roiling in his gut. His only course was to go on.

Abruptly, Seolad stood. From the second helical mound, he picked up the rope's weighted end and let it dangle two feet from one hand. Then measured three arm spans into suspended loops, held fast in his other hand.

Seolad windmilled the weighted length, arm ablur as he drew back. With a powerful thrust of his carriage, he flung the entire mass out into the abyss. The rope sailed over the edge. The rest of its length chased it like an uncoiling snake.

Once again, Seolad began the climb down with Sonart following mechanically behind. They moved in tandem hundreds of feet to the next shelf.

Five ledges they passed, all similar to the first. At each landing, they rested a few minutes, ate more of the strange root and pushed on.

There seemed no end to their downward journey.

But something did change. The lower they dropped, the warmer the temperature became and the stronger the scent of brine in the air.

When the visibility increased, he called down to Seolad, "The mists thin!"

Seolad craned his neck up. "Aye, and no wind, nary the stir of a zephyr—another small mercy."

Less than a hundred feet further down, the shroud cleared.

As he emerged, Sonart beheld a staggering view. Five hundred feet below, the vertical wall ended into a billowing leaden plateau that stretched away to the horizon.

Yet, dissimilar to any steppe Sonart had ever seen. Undulating like something alive, the expanse rolled, swelled, and receded in endless procession. The vista mesmerized him with its slow roil. Then it hit him.

Water—a seemingly infinite span of it. Exactly as he had experienced in his dreams while incarcerated in the Dunge.

After another hundred feet, a soothing din arose: water crashing against the base of the cliff wall, girdled in white foam. The sound grew steadily louder as the pair halved the remaining height.

Sonart paused to listen as he followed the rock and water demarcation to distant buttresses, independent of the wall. Ranging between one and two hundred feet high, they impaled the water, frothing white like the main wall.

Terrible and magnificent. Dramatic and alive.

When Sonart looked down again, he started. Seolad was gone. Stars, he couldn't have fallen—he made no cry. He just, disappeared, as though plucked from existence.

Heartsick, Sonart tightened his grip on the rope. He hung there trying to wrap his mind around the impossible.

He glanced back up the line, weighing the slim chances of another ascent when a voice cried out from below, "Hello!"

Sonart flinched, pupils darting back down. And flinched a second time.

Seolad's head protruded from the rock itself, his face half-scowling up at him. "If you're done admiring the view, get your lollygagging rump down here, and hurry up about it. We're losing daylight, and it's already getting dark in here."

Despite the hostility behind the gruff dwarven's complaint, Sonart laughed out loud, relief flooding through him. He should have taken greater stock in Gjen's careful contingencies—that, where the rope finally ended, some new mechanism of escape would begin.

Descending the last rungs, Sonart faced a wide-open cleft. Still dangling from the rope, all he could do was marvel at the wondrous sight within. Beyond a stone rampart, best likened to a window sill, thirty feet in depth and width, a vast natural chamber opened up. From the cave's vaulted ceiling, enormous stalactites hung in multiple rows like fangs in a mouth. They disappeared into the deeper gloom further in.

Connected to the edge of the sill, which faced inward, a rigged network of ropes and pulleys traversed the craggy ceiling, affixed with hooked ironock spikes. A thick line married with two thinner cords formed three points of an inverted triangle to form a suspended rope bridge.

The lower rope provided a stepping line and the higher two functioned as handrails. At regular three-foot intervals, wires connected the stepping line to the other two cables in a V-formation. The entire construct hugged the natural curvature of the cave's roof and ran a gradual course, angling down to its bottom, two hundred feet below, or near enough.

Seolad had seated himself next to the rigging. Knees up, head cradled in both calloused hands with his matted beard draping over them, he waited with obvious impatience.

Sonart's grumpy companion never looked so good.

The Vein alighted onto the ledge, walked to its inner verge, and gazed down. Far below, through another amazing portcullis, water heaved in, churned, and splashed against the cave walls—though with nowhere near the same ferocity as outside.

The turbulent liquid's roar echoed in Sonart's ears as it bounced off the cavern walls, cordoning his high vantage point. Beyond the cave's mouth, the water continued to pitch and roll to infinity, an endless blight of blustery waves.

The smell of salt overpowered Sonart's nose. The taste of it had a refreshing effect as it caressed his lips. He breathed deep.

The temperature had risen considerably too.

Seolad cleared his throat, bringing Sonart out of his trance. "Our destination is at hand—obvious enough," he added with a smirk. "Let's not dally, and be done with it."

Sonart would have liked to rest, if only to admire the strange domain a while longer, but he saw the logic behind Seolad's point: the day had waned. He bowed his head in assent.

The two dwarven eased their way onto the suspended bridge, Seolad taking the lead once more. With his arms affixed to both handrails, he cleared the ledge and began walking. Sonart followed, ever careful, with only one rope separating him from the daunting fall.

Close to the bottom, the roar of the crashing waves deafened them, drowning out their voices as they drew closer to the relentless swells. The rope bridge grew slick as it negotiated a path between two larger stalagmites. Both had moulded their own conic islands.

Beyond their threshold, the angry water calmed its tumult at last, but the echo of its imperious passage amplified. The stalactites and stalagmites appeared smaller here and the water spray clung to the dwarven's outer garments, crusting their cloaks with salt. Small wonder, since the highest wave crest came close enough to touch.

Moments later, Seolad stopped and turned, waiting for his peer to catch up. His voice rose above the hubbub as Sonart neared. "There's something up ahead in the shallows, waiting. Some kind of—monster."

Sonart grimaced, apprehension mounting. "What?"

The blackbeard floated an arm and pointed over his shoulder.

When Sonart reached Seolad and espied what he meant, he gaped. Towards the back of the cave where it narrowed into a grotto like a roughly hewn transept, Seolad's monster came into view.

And indeed, it looked foreboding, but also inanimate. The creature nestled prone, water lapping against its carriage, a curved bird-like head staring forward. More a statue suited for a square's plinth than hiding in this dank cave—if not for its enormous size and the eerie green glow that spilled from its lantern orbs.

What looked like fissures etched the creature's husk. The same light its eyes emitted also emerged from a series of round holes dotting its flanks.

The profile of the behemoth, roughly two hundred feet long, appeared as impassive as the stone surrounding it. Though white in colour, it blended into the grey dullness of the granite, jutting out of the water in front of it.

Three thick poles impaled its husk, each rising nearly sixty feet. Smaller poles crossed the shafts at right angles, forming a trio of giant crucifixes, hitched with ropes and pullies.

Was the monster tethered?

If it had noticed them, it did not react in any way. Unlikely in any case, considering that the suspended walkway led directly onto its flat back.

Despite Seolad's protests, Sonart started forward, shimmying past his disgruntled companion, who begrudgingly followed a moment later.

The two dwarven approached the creature with slow deliberate steps. Since stealth seemed futile at this point, they settled on not riling the leviathan with any sudden movement.

As Sonart passed the last islets and into the final sanctum, the air grew quieter. The waves had spent most of their fury further out. Now they generated a shushing cadence, which pacified the Vein as he drew up beside the beast.

Evenfall finally vanquished the day's last light, but the emerald aura emanating from the juggernaut provided Sonart with more than enough to see. He halted and faced Seolad.

When the blackbeard dipped his chin, Sonart drew a deep breath and stepped onto the monster's back.

Nothing happened.

Seolad joined him. Together the pair surveyed the many oddities on the shelled surface. Strange cavities and ridges looked as though they had been excavated, giving Sonart conflicting impressions of an ironock mine and that of some cottage courtyard.

"Stars eclipse, what is this thing?" Sonart asked the damp air.

"*She*—is called a Chiva," a melodious voice proclaimed behind him.

Both dwarven snapped to attention and wheeled about. In their haste, they collided with one other and tumbled in a heap atop the monster's shell.

Untangling in a flurry, they scrambled to their feet and drew their swords.

Fear and fight surged through Sonart's blood. And twice as quick, froze him where he stood, unprepared for what he beheld.

Not ten feet away, back pressed to the floor, legs spread eagle, a pint-sized shaggy creature held its belly and rocked from side to side, laughing with a youngling's innocence. The sight disarmed both dwarven, leaving them speechless as the imp hopped up to face them.

The creature, no taller than Sonart's arm, resembled a round beakless bird. On closer inspection, what he mistook for an avian's wings were in fact, huge ears. They fanned out near the top of its furry head and flanked a tiny horn, the size of a thumb. Diminutive arms and legs, lined with fur, supported a large circular head. Under a sheaf of long whiskers, a downcast mouth revealed ivory buckteeth—as it giggled hysterically.

But the tiny daemon's enormous eyes gave it unequivocal beauty. Glistening eyes, three times the size of any dwarven's, painted in the most intense melange of green, indigo, and violet.

Set in a sad expression, the runt's colourful orbs filled with kindness and intelligence that drew Sonart in. Whatever manner of creature stood before him, it most certainly had not been Cradle-born.

"Oh-ho," it chaunted. "Stars shine the heavens anon, dwarven will be dwarven—eager to make the small laugh big."

Despite his sore arse, Sonart had to agree with the funny being at how comical his collision with Seolad must have looked.

By the blackbeard's tight expression, he did not share Sonart's opinion.

As if sensing the dwarven's ire, the little rascal piped up in a lyrical voice that warmed the air, "I mean you no harm and less insult, Seolad of Rusic. Forgive my indulgence. It merely tickles me to jest. And laughter is the medicine for the soul. In the troves and treasures of humour and prank, I spend and allow myself to be spent. Vamsah knows, I am one of his funniest-looking creations. So, spend away—I welcome such repayment."

"You—know us?" Seolad asked in a shocked voice.

"Indeed. I've been waiting to offer the Chiva's hospitality—and that of my masters." It hesitated then, large eyes searching left, then right. "Speaking of which, where are Gjen and Laethan?"

The two dwarven exchanged a look before Sonart turned to the creature. "Sadly, my little friend, I have grievous tidings. This Laethan, whom I've never met, has taken the deepest sleep. And the wizard, Gjen, is lost, along with Iomi, the last of our companions. An overwhelming number of enemies ambushed and forced us to separate. I do not know their fate, but considering our dire situation, both may have perished as well."

The creature received Sonart's ill news with equanimity. It did not lose its gentle demeanour, but its joviality ebbed. "Poor Laethan—ever-resourceful, ever kind was he—may his stars brighten in the Great Beyond."

Seolad cocked his beard at the runt. "Who—*what* are you?"

Flecks of orange and yellow sparkled in the imp's pupils. "Vamsah and the Whole of Creation call me a sprite. And my name is Mium." His smile widened. "But no, Sonart of Farkshone, I assure you, Gjengaegungen is very much alive."

Sonart exhaled and his shoulders sagged, suddenly sanguine.

But Seolad pressed his lips into a taut line and fixed the sprite with a dubious look. "How can you be so sure?"

"My Kalibah crystal still lights," Mium replied without hesitation. "It is a vessel imbued with the wizard's magic—his lifeforce sustains it. Only if he crosses the last border will it diminish. Here, I'll show you. Come inside. I'll show you. Come."

The statement baffled Sonart. He glanced around the contours of the cave before regarding the little nymph once more. "Inside? Where?"

"As I said, this glorious creature we stand upon is a Chiva," Mium vaunted. "Her kind has aided seafarers since time out of mind—as a vessel to ply the waters of Areth." He arched an eyebrow. "Did Gjen not explain this to you?"

Blank stares answered Mium's tease. A bemused grin crossed Seolad's lips. Even in such a confused context, that made his third. The sight heartened Sonart as he gave the sprite his attention again.

"No matter, my friends," Mium said. "Your world is about to become much, much larger. With the Chiva's permission, we will reach our destination."

When the two dwarven dawdled, the sprite pressed, "I vouchsafe that like me she intends you no harm. The Chiva lives only beneath the shell on which we now roost. Her outer husk has been tooled and fashioned as the deck of a ship to suit our purposes. Rooms and holds have been dug out of her shell to accommodate us all."

Sonart squished up his face. "That sounds cruel. Does that not cause this," he splayed his arms and tilted his head toward the deck, "this—*Chiva*, pain?"

"The Chiva? Stars no, of course not!" The corners of Mium's mouth worked with what looked like amusement as he danced in a circle and gestured everywhere with outstretched arms. "She carries her derelict capsule as dead matter, like your fingernails or your hair. As such, she feels nothing done to the outer layer of her husk, except relief. Any excavation only lightens the load," the sprite chortled.

Sonart joined Mium in his merriment. "I can relate to that."

Seolad grunted.

Though both dwarven seemed equally daunted and amazed to learn about the fascinating leviathan, more so that their teacher resembled a plump and talkative fowl with boundless energy.

But most of all: they now stood and breathed in the Void, outside the Cradle. Still alive to realize it.

Without further deliberation, they followed the sprite through the closest fissure into the Chiva's husk.

63: Mium
Sonart

The organic contours inside the Chiva's shell matched those on the outside. But had he not seen both with his own eyes, Sonart would have sworn he'd entered the finest room in a king's palace. Well, insofar as what he conjured as a wee lad from his father's bedtime stories.

The interior appeared simple but brightly lit with many wall sconces. Some bore glowing emerald crystals, others narrow tongues of orange-yellow flame. Together, they cast the eggshell walls in a mix of green light tempered with swathes of warmth.

The partitions had been smoothened to a matte finish, rounded where they met the floor—no sharp edges or corners anywhere.

The common room centred on a bold wooden table, surrounded by chairs laden with cushions of textured beige cloth. Shelves filled with stacks of thick books and glass jars adorned almost every wall.

Framed landscape paintings decorated the remaining panels. They portrayed scenes that resembled visions Sonart recalled much earlier. He'd never seen a place boasting such comfort, beauty, and majesty in its appointments.

"Come," Mium beckoned. He led them down a corridor that brought them into a relatively plain chamber. Compared to the rest of the vessel, this enclosure looked strikingly different and more familiar.

Runes and markings engraved the floor, identical to those Sonart had seen in the Darkest One's Hive chantry. But the space reminded him most of the Cleft Augury, instilling the same feeling of reawakening.

Mium padded up to a crystal, set in the stone dais at a juncture where four furrowed lines intersected. He pointed to a scalloped hollow on the opposite side of the glowing rock. "Gjen removed its counterpart before he and Laethan left. Normally, the other sits there. When this one flares, as it does now, it signals that Gjen has accessed his power."

"Did the wizard take only one crystal with him?" Seolad asked.

"Yes. What of it?"

Seolad unslung his pack, reached into his side pocket, and produced the crystal Gjen had entrusted to them.

"He gave this to you?" The sprite sounded more impressed than worried.

"Aye," Seolad confirmed. "Had no choice. As Sonart already told you, the flying vermin ambushed us."

The sprite's demeanour did not change. "Yes, I can feel you speak the truth." He raised his tiny hands and made a placating gesture. "But allay any fears, Rusic son. What you saw and did may seem hopeless, but it bespeaks a lateral tack of Gjen's to befuddle your enemies and help you win free."

Seolad's eyebrows pulled together. "How could you possibly know?"

"I am a sprite," Mium said without hesitation. "Sprites see truth, as animate a thing to me as your honour is to you, Seolad, and your visions are to you, Sonart. Part of the wilderen magic of my kind."

"You must tell us more of your people's ways when the tale merits a better ear—one not so desperate as mine," Sonart said. "But right now, my sole concern is for Gjen and Iomi's safety."

"Right to say. Because of the Darkest One's wards over the Cradle, I have shared your concern over Gjen and poor Laethan for more than six months. Half a star-cycle, in forced silence. But now that you've been successfully collected, I think I can risk a little magic of my own, to arrest your fears."

The sprite pointed to the stone in Seolad's hand. "Place it in the vacant hollow. It will aid my communion efforts with the wizard."

Seolad did as the sprite instructed, stepping back as his crystal reignited, matching luminescence with its brother.

Mium moved into the centre of the dais and tilted his head towards the ceiling. The sprite's lids closed over his enormous orbs and for the first time since Sonart met him, Mium's smile faded. His fur rustled as the nymph made a tremulous sound like that of a purring cat. Though his lips did not so much as quiver. His tiny body grew still.

The smell of ozone permeated the air as the two crystals pulsated with greater radiance, before dimming to their former brightness.

The air hushed.

Sonart held his breath.

At length, Mium opened his eyes, and his grin returned. "Gjen and Iomi will join us shortly."

"T-truly?" Sonart stutter-blurted. His heart leapt at the news, bringing his feet along for the ride.

The sprite's smirk broadened full-blown. "Truly—aye. We set the translation point when Seolad placed the crystal in its home sheath. Gjen's aware of its reactivation. He knows the gate has reopened. And that you've both arrived safely to await him under my protection. When the wizard deems the time ready to make a safe translation, he will come."

Unable to contain his elation, Sonart thrust his fist at the ceiling and cheered in triumph. Then, on sudden impulse, he clasped Seolad about the shoulders and hugged him firmly, red beard pressing black.

"Warms my soul, that does," said Mium, breaking their moment of camaraderie. "And nurtures the Twin-Gaia. But let us not linger here."

When the pair disengaged, Seolad offered Sonart a curt nod, and cast another at the sprite. "Stars align. Where to?"

"The kitchen," Mium replied. "We need to get your livery cleaned and dried and put some healthy grub in your bellies. Oh, and we have plenty of wine," he added with a wink up at Seolad. Only after the sprite pointed it out, did Sonart realize how sodden and stained his person.

"A song to my heart, that is," Seolad said. "And my stomach. Better address the first two, so I can relax with a libation, or several."

Sonart and Mium shared a chuckle at that. Small as he was, the sprite bore such an air of confidence, it imbued both dwarven. Sonart had all but forgotten his earlier anxieties.

Mium led them along a different hallway that ran perpendicular to the main passage and down a stairwell. Once they arrived in the kitchen, the little creature motioned them to a hearth where a barrel-sized pot simmered over a bed of red coals.

Sonart and Seolad removed the first layers of their garments and hung them up to dry on a rack in front of the mantle.

A few stools, too big for the dwarven, lined an oversized table, but they both managed to seat themselves without too much difficulty. The sprite climbed atop the table itself. He gestured towards the pot with one hand, floated his other to the pantry, and brought both hands together in a quick clap.

Two bowls immediately sailed through the air from the storeroom to the pot. The vessel promptly tipped, pouring a healthy measure of its steaming broth into each bowl.

As the crockeries floated to the table and parked before each dwarven, Sonart looked down in delight. After the bitter roots, the savoury vegetable stew made his mouth water when its herb-laden scent found his nose.

Next, a loaf of seed-encrusted bread placed itself on a wooden slab. Cups filled with mead and a set of utensils followed, settling down neatly beside the bowls.

Sonart's wide-eyed marvel at Mium's fantastic display matched his stomach's praise for the sprite's food. The dwarven squirrelled the arboreal stew by the mouthful. It tasted so hearty and delicious, even Seolad's hard eyes eased their grip.

When Sonart had sopped up the last of the broth with his remaining hunk of bread, he drained his mead, glancing at Seolad over the rim of his cup. The blackbeard had beaten him to that finish, dropping his cup to the table and letting out a sonorous belch. "Aye, well and good—that proved." He turned to Mium. "A fine kitchen scullion you make, little one. My compliments and my thanks."

"And my promised wine," Mium said. A flagon of red and a bottle of white flew to the table.

As Seolad reached for the red vintage, Sonart uprooted himself. "Mead's enough for this dwarven. With your leave, Mium, I wish to be there when our companions arrive."

Mium bowed. "Of course."

Sonart retraced his steps back to the room with the crystals, leaving Seolad, the sprite, and their wine, in each other's company.

Once there, he sat on the floor with his back propped up against the wall and stared at the concentric circles, the double-crucifix, and the octagon perimeter that framed the dais.

From his lower vantage, the relief looked like a miniature model of the entire Cradle. Each carved line could be a road or river, the rows of spoked crystals likened to the circular chains forming the Inner and Outereach.

Somewhere atop that forsaken land, Gjen and Iomi lingered and endured, but were they truly safe? Or did they toil still in pitched battle?

Sonart could not allow himself to rest until they returned, unharmed. So many unvoiced thoughts and feelings had passed between him and Iomi. He needed to tell her about Shayla, how the Proclaimer's betrayal had jaded his relationship with everyone.

But most especially with Iomi.

As he pondered, the minutes grew to hours and when those fled, Sonart's eyelids grew heavy. He slumped to the floor trying to fight his body's insistence, but eventually exhaustion and the hearty meal took their toll. His willpower lost its fuel and his head sagged.

Sonart fell into a deep and untroubled sleep.

When Sonart awoke, his head swam, trying to remember where he was. Until the cool floor beneath his back reminded him. Something gently tugged at his beard. He opened bleary eyes to see Mium, upside down, looming over him excitedly.

"It's happening!" the sprite declared. "They're coming through."

Sonart bolted upright. The two crystals flared in tandem as if focusing their power. Narrow beams of light forked out from them and traced a path along the etched canals in the floor. They intensified and branched. Then all at once, they shot to the very centre in one horrendous burst. The conflagration erased all detail of the room in a blinding white light.

An instant later the aura winked out, ghosting back to relative darkness.

The crystals' light ebbed in afterglow, the last trace of their power thinning from the imprinted lines of the rostrum.

But before their light faded completely, the glowing silhouettes of two inert figures materialized in the centre of the dais.

Despite their initial obscurity, the size of their carriages matched Sonart's recall, leaving no doubt: Gjen and Iomi had returned.

Sonart stole a glance at Seolad, standing by the doorway. Wide-eyed incredulity painted his face.

As the arrivals' glow dimmed, crisping the details of their features and colours to normalcy, Sonart scrambled to their side and knelt. Though unconscious, both still drew air. His heart told him the worst was behind them. He gently rustled Gjen's shoulder, then that of Iomi. The wizard stirred. The maiden did not.

Gjen's eyes cringed open and trembled. But then a wan smile crossed his gaunt face. He looked so haggard and worn—his recent ordeal must have taxed him unimaginably. He had aged too: his wrinkles and the amount of grey in his hair and beard appeared to have doubled.

"Stars—align," Gjen whispered as his regard inched towards Sonart. "We are well met." The wizard's gaze drifted languidly about the room before returning to him. "I see, we have all arrived in one piece—or near enough."

Gjen coughed and sputtered as he forced himself into a seated position, leaning back on propped arms. His eyes closed and his lips pressed into a thin line, as though impelling new verve into his blood.

When his eyelids fluttered open, the wizard's voice took on a note of urgency. "We must tend to Iomi. She's taken a grievous wound."

Gjen faced them each in turn. "Mium, see to it. Prepare her a bed and treatment. Sonart, when our sprite is ready, take her to it and assist him. Seolad, help me to my chamber. I need to rest for a spell—no pun intended."

The sprite sprang into action to do Gjen's bidding. A moment later, the wizard limped out of the room, using Seolad as a crutch and leaving Sonart alone with Iomi. He sat beside her and placed a hand on her forehead.

She burned hot to the touch but he had seen much worse in the Dunge. Then his eyes fell upon a dark stain on her lower abdomen and he gasped.

When Mium greeted him beyond the portcullis, Sonart carefully slipped his arms under Iomi's pallid form, hauled her up, and followed the sprite into another room. He gently set her down on the bed Mium had prepared. Dwarven and sprite set to staunching and cleansing her wounds.

At Mium's behest, Sonart held a compress, ready to fasten it to the maiden's right side, while the sprite prepared some kind of ointment with a small mortar and pestle. When Mium finished stirring the bowl, it revealed a thin white jelly, flecked with bits of silvery-green alloy.

"As soon as the unguent touches the wound, be swift with the compress," Mium instructed. "It was fine to touch her skin before, but henceforth, while the balm's magic activates, we must not touch any part of her body directly with our hands, lest we taint the salve's potency. Also, it will prevent the infection from spreading to us."

When Sonart nodded, Mium applied the contents of the bowl into the gaping hole marring Iomi's side. A sizzling sound emanated from the contact, accompanied by an acrid smell of cleaning solvents.

As soon as the tiny ladle left the hole, Sonart promptly plugged the gap, pressing the bandage delicately but firmly. He could feel the wound throb under his touch. Ugly black ichor and yellow puss oozed out around the edge of the compress.

Quick as a whip, Mium rubbed more of the salve directly into the rank substance. Sonart felt something push up through the bandage as if trying to escape and he pressed down harder while the sprite frantically worked the unguent into the murky liquid wrongness.

To Sonart's relief, the wound's corrosive effect diminished. The throbbing and sound abated too and the black and yellow ooze dried up. A few heartbeats later, it became crusty, flaking off like crumbs.

Iomi's breathing grew even and the colour returned to her cheeks.

With a reassuring bob of his crown, Mium announced, "The salve has done its work."

Sonart let out the lungful of air he had seized.

"She has attained safe harbour," the sprite went on. "But we should leave her to rest until morning."

"Nay, my friend," Sonart croaked. "That is something I cannot do. You go on, help Seolad tend to Gjen. I wish to stay by her side and keep vigil."

"I understand," Mium said, giving Sonart's arm a gentle pat. With that, he left, quietly closing the door behind him by simply bringing his tiny hands together.

Sonart pulled up a chair and sat heavily upon it, an island of calm in a sea of grief. Iomi became his solace, his haven. He wanted to close the rift between them—a gap breached not by his own will, but one for which he would answer nonetheless.

As Sonart maintained his silent watch, he vowed to Iomi's unconscious form that he would fix matters between them.

64: Detour
Brooke

Brooke's first impact with the near-vertical slope jarred him like a hammer against softwood. It wrenched the air from his lungs as he tumbled in a bath of dirt and rocks.

He flipped over once, twice, thrice...bounced...

sailed .../ com—plete—ly air—borne \...*smack.* The next collision smote him harder, unhinging his mind from the torture of his tissue. An avalanche of debris trailed, increasing with every second of his fall.

The fault scarp raked his flesh and bent his digits in directions never intended for them to go. His body, a die shaken in a cup—about to die.

Such thoughts raced past the adrenaline and the agony.

Wracked and torn, gravity finally married his flailing carriage to the slope. The jouncing relented.

And the dragging began. Friction and abrasion, chafing anguish, slam, buck—*fuck*—slowing, burning, skidding, drag-g-g-g-i-i-n-ggggg...

Stop.

Brooke reached the bottom of the escarpment, and by some miracle of Vamsah, still breathed—pain's white fire assured him of that. His military training promised more than one sprain, but nothing seemed broken. His fingers felt tender and in places completely numb but all ten aligned straight. And the torn flesh of his body: a Siphon's fork heated by a lavatrol, but still nothing beyond repair.

The commander coughed and sneezed hard. Something chunky discharged. With his frayed sleeve, he wiped his nose and mouth. It came away stained with bloody grit. Cringing as he did, Brooke forced himself to sit up.

It had proven nothing short of a lucky suicide jump, though in Gnor's case, it may have been an unlucky one. Peering into the choking haze, Brooke searched for some sign of his companion. He refrained from calling out his name in the likely chance that one of those vile tree creatures or trolls followed them down. But nothing had crashed after them.

Still, Brooke waited, peered through watery eyes, and listened.

Nothing.

But then... a faint moaning nearby. As the cloud of dust shifted away, he spotted Gnor, face down in the dirt, sandwiched between a thick tangle of brush and a rough-barked tree. The limb appeared to have bowed under the

Nightwolf's impact.

"Gnor," he croaked. "Are you all right?"

Gnor managed to get his hands under him, enough to raise his head and meet Brooke's searching gaze. The Wrayn looked as if he'd been on the losing side of a vicious brawl. A gash adorned his bald crown, and thin lines of blood crisscrossed the Bulldog's face, further marred with abrasions. One eye had been swollen shut and the other bloodied to the pupil like some half-demon.

But Gnor's split lips cracked a smile that made Brooke's shoulders sag. "Aye, still whole." The man paused, glanced around, then sputtered through a grimace. "Praise Vamsah's stars, Targin cannot see this tangle—I'd perish from his endless japes alone."

Brooke understood what Gnor meant: the bent tree was only an illusion created by the scraped-off bark in the brush and the tightness of the man's fit around twin trunks. He had also ploughed a shallow trough in the last stage of his wake.

Despite his own aches and the severity of their situation, Brooke stifled a snicker. "He'll not hear a word from me." He quickly scanned the lay. "No one will, if we don't get out of here."

Brooke rose carefully, wincing as he did, and hobbled to the stout man's prostrate form. "Can you sit up? Here, let me help."

When Gnor nodded, Brooke placed his hands under the Wrayn's armpits and carefully hoisted him into a seated position.

"The brush levied heavy tolls for my passage down," Gnor said. "Pride and person."

"Seems you paid in full," Brooke chortled. He inspected the gashes on his own arms and legs, caked in dust and already scabbing over. "As did I."

Gnor gulped. His crow's feet converged and he flicked his chin beyond Brooke. "All surviving Nightwolves will have gone to ground. They'll tread the pathless path in silence, since communion might alert any adversaries to our location."

Brooke looked up and regarded either side. The black escarpment lifted to the clouds to his right, and a broken maze of stony channels spread out to his left until a fog obscured them. Bracketed by tracts of maples, the mist would help veil their passage but might also hinder their orientation. "Can you figure out where we are?"

Gnor cocked an eyebrow. "As I said, Commander, I know these haunts like the back of my hand, perhaps better."

With a whimper, the old Wrayn climbed to his feet and surveyed their surrounds. "Aye, we move in this direction." He floated an arm to indicate their exact route. "At most, two leagues. Then we can converge with the intended path to a safer waypoint. The other Wolves know enough to do the same—including my grandson."

Before the stout man could take his first step, Brooke raised a hand to stop him.

Gnor paused. "Commander?"

Brooke dry-swallowed. "What of Gnolin? Our search?"

The bald man pressed his lips together, face hardening. "You are right. My son's pup *is* alive. We never found him among the dead. And he vanished long before the tree creatures and trolls attacked. Like his father, he is a resourceful boy. Gnolin will reach the muster point. With a head start, he might even be waiting for us by the time we arrive."

Brooke feigned an encouraging smile to hide his doubt and guilt. He could not believe the courage and fortitude Gnor showed in the face of such calamity. Would that he could glean a measure for himself. He felt fully responsible for their woes, and sure his companion thought the same. He had to say something.

"Gnor, I made the wrong decision at the Plunge. I cannot mask my folly with false bravado. I am failing my charge. Henceforth, you assume the agency. Lead the Wolves."

Gnor shook his head. "No." His abrupt refusal sounded cast in stone. "If you had made the wrong choice, Commander, we'd all be dead. This is what happens when you do something unexpected—something the enemy doesn't like." He paused and gave Brooke a long look.

"The pathless path," Brooke ventured.

"Aye, now you understand," the stout man confirmed. "Our enemies' campaign proved debauched from the start. The lessrtrols waited in ambush—in the other direction. When the attack came, it was staggered, improvised, rushed—because we showed up where we *weren't* supposed to be. You do not wield a true heart, but the truest."

"Truest fool-mind, you mean," Brooke muttered as he met Gnor's stare. "You're the soothsayer."

"Truer Wrayns run with our band than me." Gnor moved his head from side to side. "Even an ogre sensed that about you. So, take Helmdak's accolade as sanction. Take heart, Steward. And stop blaming yourself before I bop you on your thick head."

Gnor sighed as he adjusted his sword belt. "As to leading our rabble after we regroup, with all due respect, you can take your request—and cram it up your ass."

Brooke's smirk joined Gnor's. "Seems Brapin's edge has not been lost on you."

"Stars align," the Bulldog said.

They set out, limping and supporting one other as they slogged on.

Cloaked and hooded, Necatar hovered above the ground. Naught but a depthless shadow emerged from the dark sorcerer's cowl, which rode on top of his broad skeletal shoulders.

His long-established allegiances with the demons of Infern had rendered him so—the blood magic price for the power he wielded over the hellions.

The folds of his cloak undulated rapidly as if caught in a wind, though nary a breath existed. A dead calm prevailed in the air.

And within him.

But whirling around his innermost focal point raged a murderous tempest. Outwardly, Necatar took great pains to appear unhurried as he sidled along the cliff edge. With deliberate grace, he loomed over the heads of the dark elven pair. They in turn cowed and trembled beneath his spectre, keeping their yellow eyes averted.

"Tell me again," Necatar hissed, his voice gliding on a razor blade. "I must have—misheard you."

One of the dark elven captains mustered his courage, craned his neck up, and met Necatar's scrutiny. "The ss-sycophants no longer commune."

"And nobody, not even a Nightwolf, could ss-survive that fall," his companion added fervently.

"I—disagree." the necromage said. The two elven exchanged fearful looks. "I would you ascertain the truth of the matter, before attempting to placate me with what you think you know."

"But how?" the second dark elven asked.

Necatar wrenched him off his feet and flung him headlong over the precipice.

The dark elven who remained could only stare in frozen shock as his companion disappeared into the void, his squeal chasing after him.

"If your peer dies, his theory will confirm the truth. And your worst nightmare. But if he survives that fall, even broken, then so did Brooke."

"I will check," the dark elven stuttered before clarifying, "after I find a ss-safe way down. I will learn how the trolls fared with the Nightwolves."

Necatar swept forward and cornered him. "Why do you think I am here, you feeble-minded fool? Your attack proved clumsy and ineffectual! You struck before the time was ripe—before the signal had been given!"

He served the elven a backhanded blow which sent him sprawling to the ground. "Your misstep nearly cost us the larger trap. What possessed you to send your ilk to do the job single-handedly, only to have them slain instead? You squandered resources, and alerted the Wolves in the process."

Delivering a physical beating excited the necromage, but he held his lusts in check. He needed this one. He would feast on another shortly.

When the clammy elven recovered, rising unsteadily to his feet, Necatar resumed his tirade, "If not for my own magics, your true numbers would've been discovered. Had your worm-king not been placed elsewhere, he would skin you alive for such failure—and rightly so. I shall tell Menagerie what transpired and let *him* deal with you."

"My brethren are ss-still placed!" the dark elven blurted past bloodied teeth. "And the lessrtrols will march obediently unto death if we coerce the mindless brutes—exploit their ss-strength with our lore."

Necatar's bony arm shot out from under his cloak and seized the dark elven by the throat. "But their fury cannot be called to action on a whim! It must be slowly *cooked* into frenzy. Otherwise, we waste their might." *Trolls are useless to me—their hard flesh and middling souls cannot bait demons. But when this one has completed his task...*

"The Nightwolves must all die," Necatar seethed. He tightened his grip until the elven wheezed. "But my target... tis the will of Deathwrought Himself that Commander Brooke be captured. Not killed!"

The dark elven's yellow orbs bulged. Necatar watched with relish, until the cur reached the verge of asphyxia. Only then did he release him. The captain sagged to his knees and doubled over, hands shooting to his throat as he desperately gulped air.

Without meeting his interrogator's glower, the dark elven managed to get his breathing under control. "If he is—an enemy of Deathwrought, Master—ss-surely his removal—?" the elven squeaked between pants.

"His death would eliminate an obstacle to our designs," Necatar allowed, surprised at his own serenity. "But the Darkest One has deeper plans for the commander." *He gives my master pause, as my mole gives me.*

Another clever one—perhaps too clever.

The captain scampered to his feet. "We—I—will not fail you."

"I know." Necatar thrust his pallid face from the shade of his hood so it caught the light. "If you value your wretched soul."

The necromage turned and studied the bed of clouds twenty feet below the ridge. He had not found Brooke's remains down there. The commander evinced uncanny luck—bestowed by the sprites, or mayhap the Lightbringer Himself. *Charmed thus, he persists, and remains hidden from me.*

"Brooke is alive," Necatar revealed as he faced the onyx swine once more. "Bring him before me and all may be forgiven. But if you fail me again, cretin, you fail the Darkest One. And your companion's fate will pale in comparison to what Menagerie and I will do to you. Death will be the least of it."

"I will, Master, I ss-swear it," the captain assured.

"Go then. Recover him. Do not return until you do."

The dark elven surged away along the bluff's lip. The lore of his brethren sped his passage so that his feet barely skimmed the ground.

Despite the steady breeze, the skunky stench of Promo's weed overpowered the pine fragrance wafting past Sin's nose. The closest evergreens rose roughly eighty feet away from his chateau's raised sundeck. Seated in a lounge chair, observing the scrim beyond the deck's wooden rail reminded the singer he'd not quite finished his tale.

Sin glanced over the side table, nestled between him and Promo. "So, where was I?"

"Camping," the guitarist supplied.

Sin nodded. "Right. So, they're camped in this cloud forest, when the trees came... alive! And attacked, but the ninja guys and their wolves escaped mostly—it was brutal. The trees kept coming—the goddam trees!"

"What, like—*cough-cough*—Ants?" Promo asked innocently as he took another drag from his joint. He made a circling gesture with his free hand as smoke jittered from one side of his mouth. "Y'know—those tree guys."

Sin shook his head and looked down at his rock glass, half filled with rum and coke. He swirled the glass making the ice cubes dance in a clunking swirl. "No, not Ents. These things were like monster wraiths—evil demons.

And..."

Sin paused and swallowed, remembering the floating sorcerer with his two ebony-skinned minions. It was the same one, had to be—the same fuck that capsized the boat. And killed his parents.

The singer looked up at his bandmate again, but Promo had shifted his gaze to the sun as it set over the Adirondacks. Between flitting wisps of the guitarist's long black hair, his pupils glinted with pinnacles of orange light.

Sin followed Promo's stare. The sun had turned the mountains into cones of gold, leaving their lower reaches lost in gloom. For a time, they both watched in silence and peace, sharing an appreciation for its natural splendour.

"Bloody grim picture you paint, Brother," Promo said when the sun had dipped behind the slopes. "But what else is new?" He stubbed out his joint in an ashtray, reached for his beer glass, and faced Sin again. "Good thing none of that shit is real."

Feigning a grin, Sin raised his beverage.

The two friends clinked glasses and drank.

Promo sighed as he parked his empty glass on the table. "Argo?" He pointed at the vessel.

"A forstaw—aye," Sin's butler, Argyle replied in his thick Scottish accent. The old man retrieved the glass and placed it on his tray. "Nother pint, comin' up, Peter." With that, he turned and walked back towards the patio entrance.

"Cheers," Promo called over his shoulder. He yawned and faced Sin, offering the singer a half-smile. "If your dream was real, man, sounds like a job for Bear. And a million more just like him."

Stephen Fenech

65: Un-slaved
Sonart

"Gjen!" Sonart exclaimed as the wizard appeared in the kitchen doorway, a long scroll held in one hand. "Stars, you look positively radiant compared to yestereve. So good to see you up and about this morning."

Gjen bowed. "Kind of you to say, Sonart."

"Now that we do, what happened?" Seolad asked, bold as you please.

The wizard sighed, "A lengthy tale, my friends, worthy of more than a piecemeal summary, but I promise to regale you once we are well on our way. Iomi is safe enough to travel, and with my night's rest, I've regained enough strength and faculty for my theurgy. We must sail away post-haste."

The adamance in Gjen's voice could not be plainer as he moved to the kitchen table and spread the crinkled parchment across its surface.

Sonart and Seolad gathered around and climbed opposite stools. Mium floated up and stood atop the table—the sprite could fly! He planted both feet on one edge of the curling vellum to keep it flat, while the two dwarven held the other corners down.

"This sketch illustrates our route north from Grendamaul," Gjen said as he leaned over the detailed map. He traced his index finger over a dotted red line that zig-zagged up the chart from the Cradle and across the Void. Only, the expanse had been named 'Southern Ocean.'

Sonart frowned as he studied the mysterious chart. The whole of the Cradle occupied but one small parcel at its bottom.

"In these haunts, the less magic we use, the better," Gjen said. "And best—none at all. The wilderen spells Mium and I set when we first harboured here still veil the Chiva's presence. They will follow her when she departs. Bolstering her invisibility will be the extent of our magical expenditures if it can be helped."

Gjen's regard lifted from the scroll to Sonart. "You and I will guide the Chiva from her tight berth and out to open sea—steer her clear of the shoals that lay just beneath the surface." He paused and sized up the dwarven. "We must see to a harness for you. The waters keep relatively calm within the grotto but beyond the break, they can prove treacherous."

Sonart nodded, and though terms like *sea, shoals,* and *sail away* struck him unfamiliar, he trusted Gjen would explain their meaning.

The wizard shifted his focus to Seolad. "You and Mium will need to check the integrity of all the deck's chattel. My good sprite knows what is required and will make a proper boatswain of you yet."

Gjen turned to Mium. "Take Seolad below and teach him the vessel's internal mechanisms. We will set out as soon as I have conveyed our intent to the Chiva." With that, he refurled the scroll and left the room, robes fluttering behind, Sonart in tow.

Outside, dawn's chill suffused the damp air of the cavern. It penetrated Sonart's clothing and seeped into his bones.

Gjen led him across a two-foot plank that bridged the Chiva's back with the adjacent outcrop.

"To the leviathan's prow," Gjen announced. "Come."

Sonart grimaced as he followed Gjen to the Chiva's head. The list of foreign terms grew longer every time the damn wizard opened his mouth. Sonart would need to write them all down soon to avoid embarrassment.

As the two companions drew up to the impassive creature's head, she watched them with four-foot-wide orbs. They cast a green ethereal glow against the craggy shoreline and illuminated the gloom of the deeper recesses.

Gjen rested his hands against the sea creature's flank. When the wizard closed his eyes, so did the Chiva. After several moments, both sets of eyelids flickered open.

A smile crossed Gjen's face. "The Chiva assents. She knows our destination and will carry us there."

Amazed, Sonart asked, "What *is* this creature?"

Gjen looked down and met Sonart's stare. "The ancient race of Chiva come from a forgotten age, close to the world's beginning. As old as Areth herself. We are all infants in their eyes, so with reverence, bowing to a long-held and virtuous tradition, we humbly ask before burdening them. Even in the Great War, they were given the choice to cede their service or not. I'll delve deeper into their tale when time allows. For now, the Chiva must clear the shackles mooring her to this berth."

He paused and studied Sonart's measure. "Come, you need to get fitted with a harness and affixed to the deck before we can proceed."

With a firm tug, Sonart tested the inch-thick rope tethering him to the Chiva's back. It chafed his palms a little but otherwise seemed sound.

Next, he checked the fastening rings screwed into the creature's shell, the metal circlets on the leather harness clipped to his chest and girdle, and finally the straps of the bind itself.

Satisfied, he cocked his beard at Gjen. "Secure enough."

"Good," the wizard said. "We only await Mium's essay of the launch."

As if on cue, the sprite opened a door at the other end of the deck. "All is prepared below, Master Gjen. Seolad has proven a quick study—he mans the sail-wheels as we speak. Set and poised for unfurling, the sheets are. We're ready to disembark."

"Well done, Mium," the wizard called back. "May our stars align and guide the Chiva. To the task then!" He turned back to Sonart. "We'll speak again in the meeting room fore long."

When Mium reclosed the door, Gjen shifted his attention to a pair of retasked leadlines firmly grasped in his hands. Focused on the centre of the Chiva's prow, the wizard's face tensed in concentration, wrinkles converging as he pulled the ropes taut. They protested loudly.

Shallow creaking resonated up and down the Chiva's length. A shudder rumbled Sonart's soles, then a forward nudge, as the leviathan broke a few inches free of her mooring.

By small increments, the Chiva advanced, each pull coming smoother than the last. Soon, her bow pitched and yawed slightly as she cleared the fissure's shelf for deeper waters. The jarring pauses gradually abated as her bulk became fully buoyant. She glided forward under her own power—stretching her *fins* as Gjen had called them. By her acceleration, the Chiva seemed eager to move after her six-month hibernation. Sonart could relate, imagining the leviathan's relief.

"A submerged rock approaches," Sonart warned, fanning his arm towards it. "Ten feet off our left flank."

The sea creature shifted right to avoid the obstruction.

"A shoal to starboard—head left," Gjen instructed a moment later.

The Chiva did so.

Under Gjen and Sonart's verbal guidance, the Chiva manoeuvred around the maze of drowned blockages and conical islands, clearing a few of them by less than a foot. Her turns and progress came easier and more fluid, the further she absconded from the hidden anchorage.

Eventually, the Chiva passed all the close-knit obstacles and sailed towards the final breakwater near the giant cave's mouth. The sound of roiling water grew steadily louder and salt spray began coating everything, including Sonart and Gjen.

The rocking motion grew more pronounced in the steady swell as the living seacraft negotiated the widening channel. Around the final granite barrier, she heaved with agility, precision, and mounting speed.

All at once, the Chiva emerged from the shadow of the two-hundred-foot portcullis, into morning light and open water.

Taller waves immediately assaulted her, breaking against her waist and making her decks roll and tilt.

Thrown off-balance, Sonart braced as a sudden wind blasted him with a thousand freezing nettles against his sodden face. Unaccustomed to such movement, he would have pitched overboard if not for the harness Gjen provided.

Erring on the side of caution, Sonart took up the slack of his tether and coiled it around an ironock set of hitches attached to the Chiva's back. When the line tautened and his footing secured, he could relax.

Within minutes, his role as watch seemed superfluous. The Chiva had picked up enough momentum to move on a swift and even 'keel.'

As the living vessel slipped away from the Cradle, white spray burst into vaporous clouds on either side of her. Then, with even greater vigour, the Chiva surged past the last islets, pinnacles, and shoals—to open water.

Still braced to the deck, Sonart could only gape at the surrounding grandeur. If only Auckland or his father could see him now. Wonder coursed through his blood when he tilted his head up to the mist-shrouded Outereach, looming behind the Chiva. The sheer walls of the natural fortress fell into crashing surf, dwarfing the great vessel.

Thicker skeins of vapour obscured the grey cliff face even more. Within minutes it faded away completely as the Chiva drew Sonart away from the dismal realm it contained. When he faced the bow again, his thoughts changed direction to match.

Across an endless expanse that part of him still regarded as the Void of Obliteration, he was escaping, heading towards an undiscovered territory— insofar as his people knew. Sonart knew different, and would learn a great deal more.

For his own eyes now bore witness to the twisted falsehoods of the Kusp—the dwarven's tainted version. If only he could share the experience, open his brethren's minds, and *un-slave* them…

They would condemn him as a heretic.

Sonart inhaled a lungful of the brisk salt air and slowly let it out. One journey at a time, dwarven. This marked but the first step towards an alternative future no one he knew could have possibly fathomed.

Gjen's voice brought him back from his thoughts. "Our work is done here, my friend. Best we go inside."

Sonart unfastened the ironock clips to his harness and carefully followed the wizard into the swaying husk of the powerful creature beneath them.

66: North
Sonart

"She is much better," Gjen confirmed as he strode into the common room. He clutched a flagon of wine in one hand and the stems of three metal goblets in the other. "And before you ask, Sonart, by *she*, I mean both: the Chiva and Iomi."

The wizard placed the items on the table and slumped wearily into a chair across from the two dwarven. A breath escaped him that challenged the frozen gusts outside.

After a moment, Gjen leaned forward and lined up the three cups, uncorked the flagon, and poured a measure of violet wine into each. He passed the first to Seolad and the second to Sonart.

The fruity bouquet of the vintage filled the room.

"Let no one tell you any different, my friends, magic—especially glamourous magic—is hard work." He tipped the goblet to his lips and drank, his crow's feet easing.

"Warrant it is," Seolad said before swallowing a mouthful. "With such a geas over the sea creature, how do we fare?"

Gjen pondered the question. "We haven't been attacked or even noticed yet, so I'd say we fare well. As I explained, the three masts that support the sails are essential for such a long journey."

Seolad dipped his beard. "Aye, the oilcloth sheets catch and harness the wind. They will take most of the burden off the leviathan."

Gjen nodded. "For the better part of an hour, she has been pulled along by the power of the wind, using her strength only to trim our heading."

"Can the Chiva truly guide us to our destination?" Sonart asked.

"She will require some help from time to time, but generally speaking, yes. Don't let the Chiva's impassive demeanour fool you. Her senses are much shrewder than yours or mine," chided Gjen. "And her kind, most resilient, so worry not for her welfare."

"Good, because I *am* worried about Iomi," Sonart confessed.

Gjen raised an eyebrow. "Indeed. Well, you need only trouble yourself with time—allowing enough of it to pass for her convalescence. But she will make a full recovery."

The wizard poured himself another cup of wine and drank. He shot Sonart a sideways look. "Now, if memory serves, I owe your ears the levy of a tale."

Relieved by Gjen's assurances, Sonart straightened in his chair. "And my ears expect full payment."

Gjen tossed his head and laughed from his belly, warming the room with mirth. "Of course, though when I am done, I would hear how it went with you and Seolad. Consider it a trade of tales."

Sonart beamed. "Agreed."

Gjen leaned back in his chair and took another sip of wine. Over the goblet's rim, his gaze drew in both dwarven. "If you recall, our situation turned quite grim when we parted ways. I couldn't afford to have you snatched away by Deathwrought's hordes so close to our finish line. Therefore, with the full power of the Kalibah, I impelled you far and fast from our midst. But also covered your escape with a glamour—like the one that shrouds the Chiva now. Otherwise, the Winged Ones would have tracked you from on high."

Mium entered the room and floated up above the table. His large orbs darted left and right, a comical expression of mock confusion on his face. His impression of a befuddled Zürshuck was not lost on his audience, especially when he began flapping his large ears to mimic wings.

The sprite's grin joined theirs as he settled atop the table beside the wine flagon. Out of thin air, he conjured a cup, no bigger than a thimble and extended the tiny chalice forward. A small measure of red escaped the bottle to pool neatly in the vessel. "If anyone has the ears for long tales, I most certainly fit that bill."

Gjen's smirk broadened as he studied the sprite. "Except for the nearest Colossals, the rest of our enemies believed you had returned to my side, sheltered and pinioned." He slowly shook his head. "To safely thread such a gauntlet, my efforts came frighteningly close to failure. But by dividing the targets, I could focus my magic on protecting Iomi."

Mium padded to the table's edge and sat beside Sonart. Legs dangling, the nymph sipped his wine.

"One of the Colossals ducked past my defences," the wizard revealed in a more sombre tone. "It struck Iomi, but praise Vamsah, I managed to deflect the worst of the burning thrust in time, relieving the sentinel of its flaming sword. I then used the weapon to relieve the Colossal of its head."

The simper on Seolad's face stretched along an absolutely vicious curve.

"Still, inundated we remained," Gjen went on. "Having too many foes to mount a proper safeguard, I had to act quickly and laterally."

Sonart frowned. "My stars eclipse."

"I tricked them," Gjen answered. "Employed an illusion from my early apprenticeship days, a spell somewhat more complicated than the one I used to cover your escape. I mirrored our four images onto an unlucky quartet of Zürshuck. While my targeted demons met the dire fate intended for us—at the claws and spears of their own brood—I stole away with Iomi. At that point, the Colossals considered us dead. Iomi and I were of course long gone when they discovered their error. So, unheeded, we took an arbitrary path, perpendicular to the true course that led to the mountain pass that you two used."

Seolad furrowed his brows. "Where in seven hells did you go?"

Gjen lifted his shoulders. "Why, to another cavern. I blocked the entrance with a special shield. The barrier rendered the fissure indiscernible from the rockface surrounding it."

The wizard took a longer pull from his goblet and sighed. "Within a day, Mium signalled that he'd joined the two brother crystals for a proper translation. My destination now shone like a beacon. In the meantime, I tended to Iomi, placing her in a deep healing sleep to keep the Colossal's succubus from killing her. I expended most of my magics to maintain our concealment—and yours. Unfortunately, I no longer possessed the Kalibah's power to amplify the translation."

Sploosh!

A large swell intercepted the Chiva, tilting the room hard to the left. Everyone braced and waited until it levelled again.

Both dwarven lowered their grimaces to their cups. The same guilt pressing Sonart seemed to weigh heavily upon Seolad—unless it was the sea sickness Mium warned them about.

"Do not blame yourselves for my choice," Gjen soothed. "And I wasn't exactly helpless without the gem. Make no mistake, your flight superseded all other considerations. The let merely delayed me, nothing more."

The dwarven lifted their eyes to Gjen's easy smile.

"So, your translation?" Sonart asked.

"I had to guess at its equation, positioning stars from memory," Gjen said. "With nothing to trace the frame and symbols of a translation gate, I used my blood to auger and draw the correct markings. In place of etched canals, my pseudo cleft served the requisite. When all was ready, I began the incantation, drawing from the synergistic power of the joined Kalibah gems. They secured the bridge and helped pull us in." He clapped his hands together. "And here we are."

Seolad scratched his head. "But how did a simple illusion fool the Colossals? Are they not entities of magic themselves?"

Gjen regarded the tight-faced dwarven for a moment before shifting his focus to Mium.

In the space of an eyeblink, Gjen was no longer Gjen, but Mium, and the sprite had become the wizard, sitting cross-legged on the table. Sonart and Seolad reeled back and nearly fell off their chairs.

Mium—or rather Gjen in Mium's body—spoke with the sprite's voice, "It was not enough to merely project my physical form to deceive such powerful foes, but also a surrogate of my thoughts—and the soul that impels them. Think of the exchange as a reciprocal echo. On that note, as far as our enemies know, my echo led back to the Steppe, invoking translation to do so."

Gjen reversed the spell and Mium became himself once again. The sprite rolled onto his back and fell into another fit of laughter.

"Stars, Gjen, you truly are a master of your craft," Sonart extolled.

The wizard looked off into the middle distance. "Only time will tell who masters whom when the Starbond draws nigh."

After a longer, more vacuous pause, Gjen exhaled and sought Sonart's attention. "Now, tell this old book how the pair of you fared. I'd have that thirst slaked before I consume any more of this heady vintage."

As Sonart told their tale, Gjen lit his pipe and refilled all their cups, while outside, the Chiva's sail-rigged husk knifed through the loneliest waters of oblivion.

The first day of Sonart's true emancipation departed over the horizon in solitude, leaving the sea creature in a ghostly gloom.

But inside her thick shell, the lights burned bright.

Later that night and over the next few days, Sonart renewed his vigil by Iomi's side. He only left her chamber to help Seolad and Mium with the rigging of bulwark lines and the lay of the sails.

Despite his earlier misgivings, Seolad had developed a rapport with Mium, and they debated tirelessly on some point or another.

The sprite clearly sported such activity.

But when the work was done, and his tongue tired of bandying gruff but good-natured banter, Seolad retreated to his own space, often fastening himself to the Chiva's stern rail. He stood alone for long periods in stoic silence, gazing over the strange creature's wake.

The blackbeard's thoughts would never stray far from where they had escaped, and the people they left behind.

Loss and helplessness beleaguering Sonart's own thoughts, he often stared at Seolad's back, empathizing with the quick-tempered dwarven.

A black doom had fallen upon their brethren—kith and kin they'd abandoned to whatever Deathwrought chose to visit upon them. Now that Sonart had disappeared and apparently taken the Darkest One's coveted talisman with him, matters would get worse.

One evenfall, Seolad caught Sonart watching him. To his shock, the blackbeard did not make any grating remark, but rather beckoned Sonart to join him.

As Sonart made his way to Seolad's side, a wall of wind caught him unprepared and he swooned to port as though in his cups. When he finally managed to sidle up, Seolad pointed over the Chiva's railing towards her starboard side.

Sonart followed the outstretched arm and started. Irregular white objects of various size drifted into view, bobbing erratically on the rolling waves, but not all. Some appeared no bigger than a Kworn, but a few looked nearly twice the height of the Chiva's topmast. As the leviathan sailed past, her luminescent eyes cast them in an emerald nimbus.

"Icebergs!" Sonart exclaimed.

Seolad inclined his head. "I see the wizard has used your free time to illuminate you." He cleared his throat and spat a pea-sized glob of spittle over the stern. "Tell me, what else have you learned? In truth, I could use the company."

The dwarven's openness disarmed Sonart, but he didn't hesitate. "The Cradle—Grendamaul—lies on the bottom of the world, which is a sphere, floating in a black void, and circling a star," he began. "According to Gjen, it is possible, without translation, to leave a place in Areth, travel in a straight line, and eventually return to the same spot."

"Such concepts unlock even more conundrums," Seolad mused darkly, "Perhaps we'll complete such a circle and return to our home. Oust those who've reaped it from under us—and take it back."

"Words unto deeds," Sonart agreed.

After a brief summary of his other learnings, some tales of their fathers' friendship, and a bit of small talk concerning their day-to-day work and functions aboard the living vessel, the two dwarven clasped arms.

They shared a bow of mutual companionship. And when Sonart took his leave, late to resume his vigil by Iomi's side, he left heartened by the bridge he finally established with Rusic's son.

Encouraged that it would hold and strengthen, Sonart returned to the maiden's chamber—where he hoped to build another bridge.

There, seated by her bedside, Sonart reflected on his discussion with Seolad, until his eyelids grew heavy.

The gentle rocking of the Chiva lulled him to sleep.

But in his dreams, he faced the greatest mystery of all. Three enigmatic counterparts, each sharing one-fourth the burden towards an unfathomable place beyond the Cleft Augury. For a certainty, Gjen was one, but who were the other two forming this symbiotic link? They would stand as Four Blood

Scions balancing half the Law of the Octagon, fighting an endgame against the Four Siphons. The Veins of Fire complemented and matched the archdemons, paragon to malefactor, soul to anti-soul.

Sonart could not see the faces of his mysterious companions, but together they amassed unfathomable power, bled fire for justice and salvation, each unique in his quarter-part to make the whole of their, of their… fellowship?

In any case, as Gjen described it, their charge was 'simple enough': ebb the tide of desecration and shield Creation against annihilation. Hooks and Dunge, was the wizard fucking mad?

Sonart's trepidation followed him back into consciousness by Iomi's side. He gazed down upon her face as she slept and reflected. The softness and serenity of her angelic countenance instilled him with a sense of fondness and longing.

Sonart vowed there and then that before the Universe saw justice, he would lead his own people out of the tyranny, persecution, and desolation they'd endured for so long.

As if hearing his thoughts, Iomi stirred.

Sonart held his breath as a murmur escaped her lips.

Unable to contain his sudden elation, he leapt to his feet and bolted from the room. The dwarven raced to Gjen's bed chamber and rapped his fist against the door. "Gjen, open up! She's back."

Sonart heard shuffling and the door burst open. Gjen hastily moved past him without a word and strode towards Iomi's room, Sonart hugging his heels.

Iomi's eyes opened languidly as the two Veins took positions on either side of her bed. She tried to speak but words failed her.

Sonart leaned in and brought his ear close to her mouth.

By the way her neck moved, she was working moisture into her throat to speak. Her lips parted and she whispered, "So-nart."

His heart quickened as he prepared to open it to her, something he had rehearsed in his mind so many times during his vigil.

Weakly, her hand brushed his arm and lingered. Her touch felt very fragile at first, but then the trembling fingers steadied and pressed.

Sonart's mind galloped.

In a frail, faltering voice she spoke. "You—destroyed my family. Killed my father, and then—killed my sister—her blood, our blood—is on your hands. Before you can do the same to me, I will see you dead."

67: March to War
Targin

The blue crystalline ceiling scattered daylight all over Johlarin's vast subterranean hall. Strong enough to infuse Targin's muscles with warmth as he climbed a flight of steps sculpted into the angled ledge.

Pointed like a petrified finger towards the heavens, the pinnacle thrust twenty feet up and out from the cavernous wall behind it. A stone pulpit awaited him at the edge of the drop.

From this high vantage, the Nightwolf surveyed the ranks of soldiers, assembled two hundred feet below him.

Targin had seen and endured many intimidating things in his exploits throughout the Main, but from time to time, he still could feel awe.

This was one of those moments.

Thousands of armour-clad men-at-arms formed battalions, divided into companies according to their field of experience. Lines of hawk riders and archers with bows and quivers slung over their backs joined the amassed pikemen, foot-soldiers, and cavalry, astride their warhorses.

Among them stood a token force of some twenty dwarven envoys. Their king and main host currently held a muster point in the Greyn. The dwarven would not march with Johlarin's army on the morrow, but pledged to join their full might with Serenthia and her allies soon enough.

Atop their great eagles, even the small contingent of elven added strength to the stalwart army. And allowed Targin to dampen his distrust of the pussy willows-made-human. Much sooner than the dwarven, the elven heelwards and spurwards would join Serenthia's legions—to fight as one freeborn host, matching any two kingdoms who dared oppose it.

Problem being, more than two kingdoms would join forces and make the attempt—along with whatever dredges Deathwrought chose to throw at them. In all likelihood, every conceivable brand of evil crony.

A hawk let out a piercing screech. Other shrieks joined its call until an overture of avian greetings filled the enclosure. Targin's raptor had come.

Thanks to Lorin, Thrumvedur appeared fully recovered from his afflictions. Long neck held high, the hawkrike moved with stolid grace. Before the front rank of wingwards, he drew to a stop and returned their salutations with a brusque dip of his beak.

When the other birds fell quiet and bowed their heads in reverence, the silence sounded louder than the cacophony that preceded it. Pride surged through Targin. How he yearned to stand beside his hawkrike. Better yet, astride the honourable *Thunderclap*, roaming the heavens far away from this chaos.

Brapin had dubbed the hawkrike a 'steed of flight'—noble, aye, but an understatement, and much too 'flowery-elven' for the fiercest, most valiant of all warbirds. Next time Targin crossed paths with Alghan, he'd defer to the scholar for a worthier title. Or insist Brapin bestow something more virtuous when he found the old seer in the right mood—likely never.

Targin's mild chuckles petered as snippets of the Orbical's grimmer counsel came back to him: *skews have altered the game... must also attain the Kalibah...* A litany of riddles, threats, and warnings—the eternal bane of Brapin's allegiance.

The Nightwolf wouldn't take part in the Strong Helm's campaign— least not long enough to see it through. He sank further as his solemn musings curved round to Johlarin. His Grace would've led this mad charge had not the Darkest One's agents doomed him to die before his time.

Now, Targin would never call Johlarin father-in-law to his face.

Only to his grave.

And the blame for that direst of lets could be placed solely at Targin's feet. Recalling his vow of silence to the king, guilt coursed through the Nightwolf. It made his stomach churn, forcing one more burden up his throat: Tasmin.

Somewhere down there, hidden among the ranks, the headstrong she-wolf glared up at him—undoubtedly dissecting him with her glower and cursing his name as he scoured the sea of faces searching for her.

Why did he bother? The hellion probably hoped he'd misstep and plunge to his death. Perhaps she hid in some higher alcove, arrow nocked to ensure he did.

Targin cursed her back, for her obstinacy. It'd been a struggle to nurture what they had built between them. But she would let it topple in the winds of war.

Damn it, warfare was the province of men alone. He tightened his grip on Fang's hilt to affirm his belief. It only left a greater emptiness in his heart, so he released the sword. And in so doing, managed to unknot her hold over him. For now.

He'd deal with his many laments in their due time, but now was not it.

With a harsh sniffle, he shored up his grief and anger and focused on the army below. They expected some kind of address.

And stars burn him, he would give it.

Targin clasped the Kalibah crystal, set in the amulet about his neck. Johlarin had warned not to attempt the main lodestone, but he said nothing of the Vein's shard. The cobalt gem's warmth infused the flesh of his fingers, giving his conviction the final boost it needed.

Above his head, he raised thick arms clad in leather gauntlets and vambraces. "Serenthia!" His war cry reverberated in every warren and grotto of the chamber, quelling all voices to hushed whispers.

Before the echoes faded, the Nightwolf filled his lungs again. "Allies of the Strong Helm, all of you champion Areth. Long have we awaited this moment. To begin the toughest campaign of our lives."

Targin delivered his speech on the king's behalf, his scrutiny steadfast. But one eye still hunted for his estranged woman.

"Make no mistake," he bellowed. "What begins this day shall decide the fate of everything we know—and what we don't. I look upon you as one heart united—one resolve against the evil oppression that sets its will against us. Forge your hearts in fire, cast them in ironock, and by the stars, we will prevail."

The tempest of cheers and shouts pressed deep into Targin's trunk, galvanizing his bones and making him straighten. "Many will perish in our crusade. But it will not be grovelling under the heels of the Darkest One's minions. We will not allow ourselves to be unmade. Battling to the last, we take this fight to Deathwrought. To the Void with him!"

"To the Void!" the soldiers howled in response. To the Void! To the Void!" The sound scaled up the heights like a tidal wave of sound, so strong it dislodged the odd crystal from the ceiling.

The Nightwolf made an X of his forearms. Fingers splayed like talons, he closed them into fists making the leather tear over his flexing muscles. The studs on the vambraces popped and showered the podium like chimes. To the thousands of soldiers below, his show of brute strength would hopefully remind them of what was possible.

It would not be lost on any of them.

Except one.

One ward at a time, the massive army filed out through a series of wide tunnels branching Serenthia's warrens. Each unit comprised a hundred men led by one warden. Wingwards of elven led their eagles, men guided hawks, spurwards of cavalry astride great destriers, pointwards of archers, and lastly heelwards of infantry and pikemen.

Ahead of them all, Targin rode point, atop Johlarin's giant warhorse, Tsur. The resounding tumult of clopping hooves, marching boots, and avian squawks behind him sounded like music to the Nightwolf's ears.

For the time being, Targin had to assume the High Regent's office in Johlarin's stead—sharing it with Prince Serion.

A High Warden led each division. Masters of their respective disciplines, these veteran field marshals would task their troops according to the High Regent's military directives. Within this hierarchy, the marshal known as the High Spur, represented all the combined spurwards, The High

Point stood for all the pointwards, High Heel, the heelwards, and High Wing marshalled the wingwards. Barring the last, Targin would need and exploit their invaluable experience very soon.

Several arteries connected Serenthia to the rolling plains—easy enough to navigate when one departed. Entering unannounced was another matter. Intruders got turned around or shown the bedchamber of one of the Hidden Kingdom's monster custodians. *Save a lone insignificant wasp.*

For that, more than anything, Targin would exact vengeance from Necatar, see the fiend take his last poisonous breath. Like the Nightwolf's blood-sire had done to the goblin king, Rathnonek, the Vein would crush the necromage into the deepest sleep.

But before Targin could revel in that act, he had *to* act—lead a march to war and a whole other bloody business, seeing the Vein's quest through to its conclusion. All the light chores, curse the stars.

Thankfully, his brooding shadows fled as Tsur trotted past the main portcullis. Onto a sunny, windswept plain, horse and rider emerged. The abrupt wash of noonday light played havoc with Targin's eyes.

Over the meadows, the breeze brought the clean scents of lavender, mint, and sunflower. Swathes of them coloured the grassy slopes, bowing and rising in time with the passing air. Only a few wisps of cloud drifted in the azure sky above.

With a pull of his mount's reins, Targin brought Tsur to a stop. He looked over his shoulder to study the army's procession as they filtered past. Up the sloped passageway and out from its cavernous mouth, they issued onto the open grassland.

Meanwhile, newly arrived elven forces converged on the field to join them. Hoisted above their frontline, Targin counted ten banners bearing the eagle-winged Tri-City sigil of House Westafr, gold on blue. The standards furled listlessly in the wind.

Having boundless space on the headland, the troops could spread themselves far and wide, forming lines respective of their wards. The pointwards came first, followed by the heelwards. Spurwards atop their mighty horses came next. Lastly, the wingwards emerged, taking wing briefly to stretch their feathers before flocking towards the rear of the daunting host.

The sight made Targin's chest swell. Not since the War of the Rennen, had such an army mustered to fight under one banner.

The great warbirds had assembled strictly out of formality to boost the morale of the main host. Raptors and riders, along with two token heelwards, would stay back until called to the battlefront. The risky ploy bespoke move and countermove. Chance and doom.

Holding back the wingwards made perfect sense—to Serion. 'Press their foes with a hidden attack they would not see coming,' the princeling had urged. Targin begged to differ.

Regardless of the sprite's decree, lobbied further by the highborn elven, Targin remained unconvinced. Having raptors enter the fray after the ground troops joined battle seemed an unwise choice.

As if on cue, Thrumvedur appeared at the tunnel entrance. The hawkrike did not join the other raptors. He strode to the Nightwolf's side.

Targin reached into Tsur's saddlebag, produced a small stick of cured meat, and tossed it to Thrum. The warbird caught it in his curved beak and swallowed the morsel in one gulp.

Eyes locked with his raptor's unblinking orbs, Targin pondered. He found some truth in the elven's argument. With the birds kept fresh and well-fed from Serenthia's stores, a coordinated attack would prove lethal against bats, crowbats, and dragons alike. The higher raptor takes the joust. The enemy's avians would likely be exhausted or wounded from the ground battle by the time the eagles and hawks showed up.

Or so the freeborn hoped.

Truth be said, had the dodgy gambit not been sanctioned by the sprites themselves, Targin would have told the council members to fuck themselves. Alas, no one said it would be easy. And despite his bitterness and doubt, a measure of relief trumped all.

His long wait to emerge from the shadows had finally reached its end. If only the Nightwolves had made it here in time—to spearhead this charge.

Targin regretted leaving Serenthia before his Wolves arrived, but the Merger hastened to fruition and the perils of the Endstorm eclipsed all. Though too hazardous to commune, his Wolves would know where to find him. As matters stood, an army this big would be quite easy to track and hard to fight. In time, Vamsah willing, it would only grow in numbers. Warriors all, true believers in the tenets and prophecies of the Kusp.

But would their faith and resolve be enough?

The hosts of the Darkest One would test the company, regardless of how dauntless it appeared. The enemy's numbers would grow in equal measure. Nay, the final battle would not be fought on even ground—a conviction Targin clung to from the outset.

Bugger it all, if the Relay was to serve as both battlefield and the Merger's juncture, getting there first remained paramount—moulding the crucible's cordons to the freeborn's advantage.

Within the hour, the vanguard had assembled in perfect formation, each ward standing or mounted. Every haftguard, made up of the usual ten wards had finished arraying themselves. They only awaited the signal.

A sea of armour glimmered gold in the sunlight.

Targin turned and faced a row of drummers. "Get everyone's attention.

Upon the first arrow, strike Serenthia's war tocsins." He shifted his gaze to his bannermen. "Signal the other wardens to make ready to march. Raise the white sigil."

A flagbearer hoisted a long fluttering standard, depicting the teal kraken ward of Serenthia set on a white background. It flapped and clapped in the stiff midday breeze.

Targin cleared his throat and turned to Kivuk, the High Warden of all pointwards. "No more speeches, High Point. You know the way. You know your archers. Lead them."

Kivuk dipped his chin. "Ready, My Lord. The first arrow awaits."

The Nightwolf smiled. "Then let the first arrow sing."

Kivuk floated his arm high and signalled one of his point wardens. With a curt nod, the master bowman sank the arrowhead of a long shaft into a chalice of burning oil at his feet. When it ignited, he fitted the bolt to a longbow and heaved, pulling the string back taut until the yew creaked. The archer aimed the flaming quarrel up at the sky.

"Loose!" the High Warden commanded.

With a sharp twang, the special arrow soared three hundred feet into the air. It left a fiery trail in its wake.

All eyes followed it. When it reached apogee, the bolt exploded in a burst of light. The resounding thunderclap would be heard if not felt across the entire headland.

Before its final echo diminished, Serenthia's long-silent war drums sounded, reverberating across the steppe with a guttural *one-Two*, *one-Two* cadence. Horns lifted and added trumpet blasts to the beats.

Targin drew strength from their song as the drums' rumble pounded against his breastplate.

With one final bow towards Thrumvedur, he gripped the reins of his horse tightly and spurred him into a full gallop, making for the vanguard.

Under the command of their High Wardens and field marshals, the freeborn company, twenty-thousand strong, started forward. The ground shook with their passage. A moving bulwark in defiance of the Night.

As the speed of Tsur's passage drew wind that ventilated Targin's open helmet and made his loose curls dance, he gritted his teeth, heart surging with satisfaction and purpose.

The final war had begun.

68: Tug of War
Sonart

Sonart shrank back in horror. Emotions reeling from the sting of Iomi's scorn, he couldn't breathe. She had stabbed him at his most vulnerable. Before Gjen could stop him, he fled the room, dour thoughts running ahead of his legs. After what they had survived together, what he had done to help her, he had expected words of healing. What he received was poison. Betrayal whipped him like no scourge ever could.

Sonart raced outside atop the deck, where a wind-driven rain matched his fury with a rant of its own. Soaked and shaking in seconds, he clung white-knuckled to the midship rail, harnessing himself to the Chiva's back.

Legs braced, he stood in defiance of the wind's piercing gait, and Iomi's treason. The gale's force tore through him, uncaring of his feelings.

More powerful and vehement in its flight across the void, the wind scoured his pain indiscriminately, ripping it away in waves. He squinted at the horizon where the icy waters greeted an endless blanket of clouds.

A hand touched his shoulder. He spun, eyes blazing.

Gjen studied him, sorrow written in his knitted brows. "I am so sorry, my friend. Iomi has suffered great wounds."

"What about me?" Sonart cried. "The weight crushes!"

"I understand," Gjen soothed.

Bristling, Sonart clenched, wanting to lash out. But one more look at Gjen steadied him. "What sister?"

"Shayla was her sister."

"That's—impossible. Not *her*." But even as he said it, the truth surfaced and floated before him plain as day. Xoral had admitted losing one daughter to the Proclaimers. Sonart had blinded himself.

"I'm afraid it is the truth," Gjen said. "Give Iomi time to sort out her feelings. You will—"

"Shayla did not die by my hand, not directly, and neither did Xoral," the dwarven wept.

"I know, but in her mind, you—" Gjen broke off.

Sonart followed the wizard's covert glance. And flinched.

A barefoot Iomi walked towards them on unsteady legs, clad only in her thin sleeping gown. Though neither the teetering of the Chiva nor the lament of the harsh wind and rain seemed to deter her.

She fixed Gjen with an expectant look. He inclined his chin and took his leave. Within moments the two dwarven stood alone in the open.

Keeping his eyes trained on the open water, Sonart could feel the chill of her scrutiny upon him. Had she come to resolve their differences as before? If so, he would welcome a dagger's ironock to this soul biter she had plunged deep into him.

But she just stood like his shadow, refusing to speak. Sonart clung to the last vestiges of his resolve, but her nearness twisted the knife.

He turned and faced her.

The hatred in her glare was unmistakable, but he could not look away. She had passed her verdict. Now she would carry out the sentence.

Deathwrought had spawned the terror that seeded her suffering—and Sonart's. Feeling his hackles rise again, he tore his scowl away and peered into the water's depths.

As though summoned by his recollect, a bodiless manifestation of the Darkest One's head suddenly breached the surface, a stone's throw from the Chiva's port beam.

Sonart gasped, "Stars blacken!"

Larger than the iteration that had swallowed him in the Hive—thirty feet tall—the immense head floated ten feet above the ocean's swell, drifting apace of the sea creature. As before, a multitude of horns impaled the head while tendrils snaked like onyx vines reaching for prey. On the tip of each length, a demon head writhed, bewailing the vehemence of Deathwrought's glower.

Iomi blanched and shrank back.

As the enigma reared higher, a liquid mane of water streamed down its horrific visage. Forks of lightning danced from a pair of serpent eyes glowing scarlet in the centre of the facial mess. The shafts struck in every direction, charging the watery gap between the Darkest One and the Chiva. Each clout sent steaming geysers shrieking to the sky.

"Forsake the Cradle, will you?" Deathwrought bellowed. The acid in his roar singed Sonart's mind and crushed his heart. "You only hasten its destruction. Your doom will follow you wherever you flee. Adjunct to the Octagon? You'll never join the Veins. Alone, you *fail*. Mine Eyes are—"

The Darkest One's bane cut off mid-spate, his discharges snuffed as Gjen stormed into view.

Staff brandished high, face clenched like cracking granite, eyes sparking with cobalt fire, Gjen bawled, "Enough!"

A line of searing white light traced the length of the wizard's emblem. It enveloped his whole body in blinding coruscation. Then launched as a single torrent of hellish flame into the godhead.

The head detonated.

Or so it seemed. Everything surrounding the evil icon erased into white ether. The ivory void encompassed all, except the head. It lingered, mouth agape, fangs gnashing, eyes ablaze. Deathwrought coiled and shook like a boulder pushing upstream, trying to focalize a battery of lightning bolts against the Kazir's onslaught.

But Gjen's staff deflected all, sending every fork askew. The swiftness and sheer *power* of the wizard's attack had caught the Darkest One off-guard. It staggered Sonart too as Deathwrought's head pushed away, black energy dithering, teeth grating in rampant ferocity.

The godhead shrank to half its initial size!

While Gjen appeared to grow.

The wizard's whole outline transformed into something ethereal as his wilderen magic intensified. Sonart sensed limitless power unleashed against his foe.

With one last blast, under the full vigour of Gjen's daunting weapon, Deathwrought winked out.

And reality's blurred details crisped back into focus.

The head did not return. The Darkest One had been expunged. Banished.

Before Sonart could croak his relief, the entire Chiva listed sharply to one side. Over the railing, some three hundred monstrous tentacles shot up, water cascading off their slick skin.

Lined with suction cups, the feelers engulfed the entire vessel like rippling albino eels. Corpse white, most of the serpentine appendages measured no more than three inches in girth but some spanned more than two feet thick. All impossibly long.

Sonart and Iomi shared a cry. *Stars be merciful.*

"An Issicle!" Gjen thundered behind them. "Ice Kraken!"

Some of the tendrils detached their hold on the vessel. Loomed high. And crashed down upon Gjen.

At the last moment, the wizard careened out of the way and the tentacles smashed the deck instead.

Gjen raised his staff and renewed his attack, pummelling the Darkest One's monster with an incessant barrage of lightning bolts. Several tendrils recoiled. Several were eviscerated.

Sonart whipped his head around for an escape. Hooks and Dunge, where in blazes were Seolad and Mium?

Gjen rushed to Sonart and Iomi's side, but before the wizard could launch a defence, a giant tendril batted him from behind and cast him into the sea.

Sonart howled in horror as the writhing limbs converged about the Chiva. A chorus of sucking sounds filled the air, suddenly made putrid with the beast's foul rank. The deck lurched, buffeting Iomi off her feet and shoving Sonart hard to the railing.

The impact made his bones crunch and he nearly pitched over the side. But just managed to brace the guardrail.

The vessel plunged.

Face down, Sonart could only watch as the ocean's surface rushed up to meet and swamp him. The entire hull submerged several feet into the churning depths. Water digested the dwarven but he held on.

Abruptly, the downward movement stopped. Through the foaming turmoil of rushing saltwater, his eyes caught sight of the reason. The Chiva lashed out with fins and flippers, aglow with azure light. They swished and batted tendrils. And released blue fire, igniting sluffs of flesh from the kraken's main bulk.

With an upward heave, the Chiva's deck breached the surface again.

As the sea creature struggled to stay afloat, smaller kraken fronds sprang like jumping serpents at Sonart and Iomi—still clinging to a hawser. Both dwarven rolled away from the frenzy, barely evading the strike.

They regained their feet and made to flee when in a bloom of cracking shell fragments, a massive limb punched up through the Chiva's rain-spattered deck and trapped them.

Iomi screamed as a thinner tendril seized her from behind.

Before Sonart could react, it coiled itself around her calf and yanked. She hit the deck with a thud and grunt.

The appendage squelched as it dragged her backwards on her stomach.

Sonart threw himself across her body, grappled her about the waist with one hand, and tried to draw his blade with the other.

But his position proved all wrong.

His eyes darted left and right as he was pulled along with her towards the railing.

Splat-splat-splat-splat.

Running boots came into view.

Seolad!

Blood in his eyes, the blackbeard tore across the bucking deck. Without any regard for his own safety, sword ready above his head, he dove at the tendril. And severed it in one fluid movement.

Seolad landed with a neat tuck and rolled away. Without pause, he spun and hacked off three more tentacles seeking to pin him from the side. The rest retreated.

Seolad joined Sonart and they dragged Iomi away from the edge. The air grew livid. Flashing bolts of power. Dancing tendrils. A pandemonium of snakes, fire, water—all thrashed together in vicious panoply.

The entire deck wrenched and jumped as the Issicle's head surfaced.

Armoured with a spiked crown of ivory horns, the monstrosity pressed against the Chiva's hull, a full third of the vessel's length. And lifted.

Four bulbous pink orbs converged around a gaping maw in the centre of its head. Rows upon rows of pearlescent fangs, the size of broadswords, filled the sickly orifice. The maw thrashed savagely, unleashing hot breath tainted with rot.

Like a colourless spider pouncing on prey, the Issicle saddled the Chiva. Water swamped every surface as the monster drew in, paused briefly before the dwarven, and slammed its bulk down with unbridled fury.

At the last second, the three dwarven separated and the kraken shattered a section of the Chiva's back instead. Shards of shell exploded outward under the horrendous impact.

When the kraken's face rose again, Seolad and Sonart had their blades ready, poised skyward. But the monster ignored them completely.

Its four massive eyes tracked Iomi.

The Issicle lunged—at her.

Sonart and Seolad rushed to waylay it. A limb speared their flank and knocked them aside. The jarring blow ripped Sonart's sword from his hand and cast it overboard. He cried in dismay as the mouth of doom moved in for the kill, gaping open to swallow Iomi whole.

Before it pounced, a blinding burst of energy broadsided the creature's head, jouncing it with titanic force. The god-hammer blow propelled the kraken away from its target, blackening swathes of its rubbery albino flesh.

Sonart wheeled as Gjen darted across the skewed and splintered deck, directly into the core of feelers. Still on the run, the wizard cast aside his robe—leapt—and sailed over the railing, straight into the monster's orifice.

Gjen?

Iomi's wail wrenched Sonart's eyes and legs away as a canopy of fronds ensnared her again. His footfalls pounded the fissured deck, heartsick to get to her in time.

Just as Sonart reached the maiden, the kraken's head returned, apparently unaffected by the wizard's sacrifice. And undeterred in its dogged hunt. A second curtain of feelers flopped vertically behind Sonart, their tips wriggling a foot above the deck, cutting off any escape.

But then, Seolad appeared beyond the undulating row.

"Catch!" he boomed.

The blackbeard spun on his heel and expertly flung his sword so that it flew beneath the barrier of writhing limbs. The blade alighted on the Chiva's slick deck and slid straight towards Sonart. He arrested the weapon with the sole of his boot. Retrieved and brandished it true—a moment before the snaking tentacles attacked.

Driven by desperation, metal met sinew. Under the force of their assault, the arms severed themselves, sheering cleanly off the razor edge of Seolad's sword. The dismembered lengths slumped onto the deck with sick thumps and squirmed. The rest of the limbs withdrew, giving Sonart a window for escape.

Without thinking, Sonart grabbed Iomi's wrist and snatched her away from the corner, scrabbling for the portcullis just ahead.

Too late: the tendrils interceded again. They forced Sonart to hack them back, one by bloody one. Each severed limb gave him another foot of ground, but it also added to the toll of his fatigue. It became clear he wouldn't make it.

Suddenly, the Chiva rose several feet into the air. The Ice Kraken's head bucked. Tentacles convulsed. And the monster let out a harrowing squeal. Through the creature's trachea, a gaping hole exploded. And immediately obscured in burgeoning smoke—but at the centre of the cloud burned a white-hot pinnacle of light.

When the smoke cleared, framed just inside the mortal wound, Gjen materialized, covered in white slime and a milky liquid that must've served as the monster's blood. Staff in hand, the battered and bruised wizard clung tenaciously to the sea monster's face like a human lesion.

Before Sonart could rejoice, a wall of water burst forth in all directions. Gjen's magical blow had fatally deterred the Issicle but somehow it still pressed its fight, coerced by the will of the Darkest One.

Sails tore as the spars and rigging connecting the Chiva's mainmast to her shell crashed down, barely missing the three dwarven.

Sonart reached the doorway. Sanctuary—steps away.

A rogue tentacle, arcing wildly in the Issicle's death throes, cracked him across the back.

Bones snapped as it swatted him off his feet—flung him headlong into Iomi. Both dwarven tumbled as one body through the entryway and down the flight of stairs within. They hammered against the far wall on the lower landing.

Knocked unconscious by the impact, they crumpled to the floor, entwined like sleeping lovers.

69: By the Stars
Sonart

Sonart's mind floated in a sea of pain, but the wreckage of his spirit, not his body, kept him chained to his bed.

As Gjen, Mium, and Seolad faded in and out of his intermittent consciousness, the Vein clung to one prerogative: help Iomi. She had been *struck*! He bolted upright at the thought. The abrupt movement made him swoon with vertigo before Gjen steadied him.

"Be still, my friend," the wizard soothed. "Iomi fares well. A few broken bones have been set and appear on the mend."

"How bad is she?" Sonart croaked.

Gjen hesitated. "In truth, her recovery will be prolonged, not having the same power of healing that a Vein can harness. But take heart. We remain safe. Mium has righted the harm done to her and the Chiva. The sea creature sails true and ever north from the Cradle, even as she and Iomi convalesce."

Sonart saw the truth of that in the gentle sway of the cabin and the sound of foaming saltwater outside the open window. He let his shoulders sag as he met Gjen's gaze. "I thought I'd wake up dead—thought we all would."

The wizard's wrinkles softened. "You can thank our little sprite here for ensuring that was not the case. While we engaged in pitched battle above, Mium executed powerful spells of sprite lore below, amplifying the Chiva's counterblows against the Issicle. Our good nymph strengthened her underbelly and the core of her hull with an immutable shield. Had he not, her shell would've been crushed by our latest adversary. The Chiva would have foundered and we'd have perished."

Sonart looked to Mium with new appreciation. The sprite shrugged and smiled, big orbs blinking. A good moment passed between them before Sonart faced Gjen again. "Thanks are owed to you and Seolad as well." He sought the blackbeard's attention. "I was wrong to have ever doubted you, wrong to judge your ruthlessness. Without your intervention, the monster would've ended us."

Seolad gave him a gruff nod but said nothing.

Sonart exhaled. "Stars eclipse, what was that horror back there?"

"A juggernaut of Areth's deepest, coldest waters," Gjen explained. "But as you correctly sensed, the devilry of Deathwrought impelled the Ice Kraken to the surface, riling it to madness. The leviathan's possession bore a likeness to your own. But the Darkest One himself can tread no more in these waters. And with every league we put behind us, his dominion diminishes further. No longer can he directly thwart our quest."

Sonart's mouth went dry. "What about indirectly?"

A shadow passed over the wizard's features. "That—remains possible, but not likely. His use of the kraken marked that turning point."

Unwilling to press Gjen any further, Sonart changed the subject. "Is there anything I can do to help speed Iomi's recovery?"

Gjen arched an eyebrow. "Recover yourself would be my best advice."

"Duly—noted," Sonart said, wincing as he did. "If I must continue to lie bedridden and we're relatively protected as you say, I have a million hard questions to ask you."

"Stars align," Gjen chuckled. "I wondered when you would get around to cracking those shells." He nudged his chin at Sonart. "What's on your mind?"

"The markings on the dais where you and Iomi translated aboard the Chiva, I have seen them before, in the safehouse in Bulkforge and in the Hive itself."

"I'm sure you have. They initially harboured the means to access the Cleft Augury."

"So, it's more than translation from point to point?" Sonart asked.

"Yes, though by utilizing the same Augury framework of a properly constructed and marked dais, one may expedite translation to any place, on any plane."

Sonart chewed the inside of his cheek. Fear of the answer made him hesitate but something in the dilation of Gjen's pupils indicated he'd already surmised the Vein's next query.

"Before the exorcism," Sonart began, "the Darkest One pressed me with a phrase: *Mine Eyes are Your Eyes.* Ahead of the Issicle's attack, just before you intervened, He repeated those words."

Gjen rubbed the bridge of his nose and blew out his cheeks. "It appears he has subsumed part of your being unto his own. So, I will simply have to try again to expel his maleficence."

"I thought you already did," Sonart said, dread creeping like bitter sap into his tone.

"I was mistaken," Gjen replied without hesitation. "Or rather, he has found some other means to track you, perhaps through the Octagon link with your respective malefactor, the Siphon, Maudlin."

Sonart swallowed. "The Scourge."

Gjen licked his lips and nodded. But then, his face steeled with conviction. "I will find that link—and cut its throat. Mark my words, Sonart, next time there is an attack, you will have more friends than enemies. You will find in the most unlikely places that new allies come to our aid unbidden, to help us surpass the storm. Deathwrought will think twice before sending any minions to assail you as he did with the Issicle."

"No." Sonart shook his head fervently. "The Ice Kraken never targeted me. Twas Iomi the beast tried to kill."

"If so..." Gjen closed his eyelids as he pondered. "He has failed in that as well."

When Sonart emerged onto the Chiva's top deck, he found darkness. A brisk but refreshing salt breeze filled his lungs and drew him to the sea creature's side.

With the damage the Issicle had inflicted three days ago all patched up and sealed, the Chiva had regained enough verve to resume her voyage under full canvas. That same morn, Sonart saw the last of the icebergs shrink behind the stern balustrade and disappear over the horizon.

Above the battered railing, both sky and water shared the same gloom, dim as ironock ore—except for the green swathe cast by the Chiva's lantern eyes. It danced ahead of her prow, rode the crest of her bow wave, and trailed behind in her frothing wake.

The smell of brine and the sound of foaming saltwater along the leviathan's waist eased the tension in Sonart's neck and shoulders. His world had never seemed so right and serene as it did now. Hard thoughts softening, he opened his mind to receive its amity.

"She does care for you."

At the sound of Mium's voice, Sonart stiffened. The sprite flew up to the railing and perched beside him.

Without looking at the tiny creature, Sonart said to the wind, "She cares—for my death."

"No, Sonart, her heart speaks differently," Mium said. "She reviled you openly—aye. But twas her bereavement and pain that fanned the fire of her harsh words. I've gleaned enough of her inner thoughts, and though she may have blamed you at first, that time has passed."

Sonart looked at him doubtfully but kept quiet.

"Iomi knows you have suffered greatly too—as much a victim as she," Mium went on. "Aside from the death of her father and sister, the maiden has taken a more evasive but no less grievous wound to the heart, something she cannot fully identify herself."

The sprite glanced over his shoulder. "That owes in part to the reason behind Gjen's recruitment of her. Both of your paths link in confluence, but she does not understand how, or for that matter the reason why she is here— like your own plight."

"Oh, I know my role," Sonart said sourly. "All too well. I am a pariah, a scapegoat, a sacrifice, the harbinger of my people's end."

He stabbed a finger south towards his home. "I abandoned them back in that hell, Mium. I've been brought to the point of death, but not allowed to escape through its door. The deepest sleep might have granted me absolution." He shook his head. "No, this Vamsah likes his playtoys."

Sonart lifted his palms and slapped them hard against the railing. "Stars burn me to all blackness, I understand my sordid plight."

"You forget something crucial," Mium gently pointed out.

"What?" Sonart griped.

"Despite your torment—you survived intact. Does that not tell enough of your purpose and constitution? Your power? Do not be disheartened—"

"One must have a heart to be disheartened," Sonart returned with a fierce inhalation. "I have no heart. No hope. I have nothing."

"Then Deathwrought has already won—if you let his dire revelations overwhelm you." Mium spoke softly, but fire forged his words. "Let me guess: you had visions of death, of Grendamaul as a land—and those closest to you?"

Sonart blinked. Mium's words caught him off-guard, making his lips quiver. Any further condemnation faltered as he reconsidered the sprite.

"Nothing more than carefully spun lies and half-truths," Mium pressed. "Even after you discover the truth within the truth, you may find matters reciprocate, and in some cases, contradict. Your purpose as Vein is no different. You and the other three Blood Scions are, all of you, paradoxical. The Darkest One wants you to feel cut off and powerless to act, so you will waver ahead of the Merger and disrupt the Octagon equation. You will yield to him before you join the other three. Dare I say before you begin?"

Mium slid a tiny foot back and forth across the railing. He sighed as he regarded the inky ocean. Sonart followed his gaze.

An uncertain moment passed.

"But you have begun," Mium said at last. "Never forget that. Also, remember *words* of Deathwrought are *ploys* of Deathwrought. Ever he seeks to remove hope, so you'll gaze upon the battlefield with dead eyes."

Sonart warmed to Mium's counsel and he turned to face the sprite.

"He who instigated the False Starbond was misled in the same way," Mium went on. "Shirdron despaired and blighted our world in the process. The dwarven need you to cling to hope—the one imperative, to spare all the people of the free lands from the rampage of the demons. Heed me. Only hope will see you through."

Mium reached out and placed his small hand on Sonart's shoulder. "If you submit, the Everdark shall come to pass, and the astral planes will falter, become indeed the Void of Obliteration your brethren have naively labelled this body of water we sail upon."

"I understand," Sonart said as he reaffirmed his hold on the balustrade. "What do you suggest?"

"My advice to you, Sonart, Farkshone Son, is this: move as though you have already won. And think *sideways*. All you must do is survive, but," Mium pressed his twig of a finger against Sonart's chest. "You must believe in here that you will."

The sprite's words resonated with Sonart again. They renewed the counsel of Rusic and Sonart's own sire. For the first time, the dwarven grasped his doom through a different prism. He stood within the Void, and drew air to appreciate it. He was surviving. Indeed, the mere wind against his cheeks and the plane of water on which the Chiva rushed, laid bare Deathwrought's falsehoods and the truth supporting Mium's exactitude.

Sonart cast away his fear at last. He let it sink into the depths beyond the Chiva's waist, where it belonged. Mind broadening like the endless expanse surrounding him, the dwarven dipped his chin at Mium and took a deep breath. "Thank you and, stars align, I believe what you say."

"Good." The sprite's face brightened into a full-blown smile. Sonart's own grin pulled errant strands of his auburn beard as he sought to match it.

And a genuine friendship forged as the stars of sprite and dwarven did indeed align.

For the rest of the night, they stood in comfortable silence, side by side like equal parts to a whole, companion sentries sharing one solitude against the strengthening front of air that filtered past.

The gloom eventually waned, heralding the approach of a new dawn.

With the trials and travails ahead, Sonart had much to contemplate— tests that would make those already endured pale by comparison. Images of his two remaining counterparts occupied his thoughts: whoever they were, wherever they came from, however their purpose coincided with his own.

Sonart would welcome them and fulfil his role by their side, as he had done with Gjen, as he was doing with Mium. It recalled to him Gjen's promise about the future, that he would have more friends than enemies. A single tear, born of a grasped truth, ran down his cheek and into his beard. As a Vein of Fire, that would be his destiny.

At that precise moment, a strange thing happened up in the endless grey cloud cover. Orange, red, and yellow light seeped past widening breaks. The wash of colour spread, coruscating around the veil. The ceiling parted further, revealing hollows above. Through the opening windows in the sky, beams of radiance lanced down to the ocean.

The air warmed with them, as though permeating from the flames of a hearth. With every passing moment, the illumination intensified, until the clouds themselves resembled golden embers upon a pyre.

Sonart's breath caught as the brightness of the heavens chased away the dullness of the sea, infusing it with a radiant aura. Sharper beams of light connected the shifting windows to the water like gilded swords. One found the Chiva and lit her up, cascading over the living vessel's entire length.

The sabre's heat basked Sonart and its brilliance made him squint. But he welcomed it as it suffused his flesh and bones and soul. A rush of emotion filled the dwarven while he lounged in its intense ginger glow. Twas the most beautiful and enigmatic thing he had ever seen or felt.

And its emanations continued to expand, burning away most of the grey void—the only sky Sonart had ever known. The lingering clouds scattered and became puffy white islands across *blue* heavens.

But behind the creature's wake, the dark veil lingered, unchanged, and impenetrable. That shroud would remain uniform, forever fastening itself to the Cradle like a succubus. A dire reminder that however far the dwarven might venture, Grendamaul, his home, would go on, a den of sinful iniquity, a prison cell and bastion infected by Deathwrought's corruption.

Sonart tightened his lip, hardened his resolve, and vowed there and then, that justice and indemnity would be exacted for the full toll bled from the Cradle's dwarven—and its men.

That day would have to wait for now. But Sonart pledged as Blood Scion and Vein of Fire, he would see it dawn. To that effect, he had buckled down to the task ahead.

From behind the last vestige of distant cloud, a blazing circle of light penetrated the sky. Magnificent, glorious, the magical globe's nimbus swept every horizon.

Sonart gasped at its beauty. "By the Stars, Mium, what is that?"

"That, my friend, *is* a star!" Mium laughed. "The Sun of Areth: cynosure of all the lore which drives our purpose. And it is not alone."

Another sphere appeared, dancing like shivering gold on the water's azure surface. Tears of bliss welled up in a never-before-realized part of Sonart's soul. In the confusing play of so many bittersweet emotions, he laughed and cried at the same time, surprising himself at how easily both fit together.

"Look," Sonart cried, pointing at the sun's reflection. "Our star has a counterpart."

"Like us," the sprite said.

"Aye," the dwarven agreed between joyous sobs. "Just like us."

The two companions embraced. And the Chiva, swift and sure, surged forward, heading directly for that star.

GLOSSARY

Aeol: merekin prince only son of Aeolethlan
Aeolethlan: Last Trident of Parmier
Afflicted Ones: dwarven inflicted with an incurable plague
Aften: dwarven shieldmaiden and master archer
Age of Renewal: or Vamsah's Spring—blissful time in Areth's history
Ahzarim: the great geese of the Main of Areth largest of the world's birds
alchlemage: healer who uses crossed disciplines of science and magic
Alghan: tall Wrayn gifted scholarly one
Allia: princess of the Pebblereach Islands, second in line.
Amahnia: Targin's mother
Andover: Northern Kingdom
arbitier: distinct level of tree patch based on height in Grenfor Talarben
Areth: World and one of the Twin-Gaias
Atheri: Queen of Serenthia, Tasmin's mother
Ayr: elven, King Westafr's son, Prince Serion's older sibling
Bah-R: Highprite, demigod of the seas
Bathurian: King of Cillinox
Befoulen: *The Shard,* archdemon, One of the Four
Bessel: dwarven innkeep of the Golan Hob
Black Eye the: dwarven name given to Deathwrought
bladeorang: large boomerang with razor edges fashioned and used by Quiver
blood magic: dark discipline using pain or sacrifice to summon demons
Blood Scion: One of Four descendants of the ancient lines. Veins of Fire
Bluunsai: King Penthor's alchlemage
Bordu: a dwarven
Brapin: the Orbical *the Geezer*
Brax: Val's Warang
Brooke, Aviry: (pron. *B r uu k* like shook) Commander of Pathguard
Bruna: Head nurse in Serenthia
Bulkforge: the only city in the Cradle
Carval: High Warden of Cillinox and heir apparent
Cele: (pron. *Sel*) King of Pathguard
centipus: freshwater kraken
Char: Nightwolf, Spifer's apprentice
Chiva: (pron. *Shee-va*) giant sea creature with a shell tooled into a sailing vessel
Chronograph: Sphere of Time
Cillinox: Northern Kingdom
Clawvale: The Mountain Kingdom
Cleft Augury: the First Circle—ethereal centre of the Universe where Creation began
Clysm the: arcane wraith of the Oceans
Colossals: eight-foot-tall beings of pure energy conjured by Reechabah Siphon

combart: the art of combat perfected by the Nightwolves
communion: mind-to-mind communication without vocalization, near or far
Coran: King Vakk's Captain of Guard
Cradle: dwarven homeland
crowbat: giant avian half-crow, half-bat ridden by hobgoblins
Cwil: (pron. *swil*) Brant Sobrain's mother
Daleon: The Unifier, First wizard, Used magic to restore land after the Grave Wait helped each race, gave them oaths to follow
Dalwhin: elven ranger of Grenfor Talarben
dark elven: evil counterparts to the elven
Dayanthi: Brooke's wife
deathbreath: brimstone
Deathwrought: Carnalahfardum Farill, Shantisan, Lightdimmer, Nitevesel, The Darkest One, the bane of Creation. Stardimmer
deepest sleep: death
demonica: a spell of the mind to bend one's will
Deqlan: elven scout Prince Serion's cousin
diacorn: double-horned witchorses of Scythia
dimming: night
Dire March: the sojourn of the Noirlunen across the Ice Wastes
doom-drums: massive drums played by Kworn during ceremonies and to mark midday or midnight
double-crucifix: symbol of the Law of the Octagon depicted by two intersecting crosses that form an X and represent balance with eight stranded points of the Veins and Siphons
Downdome: extinct lava lake in the far north
Dras: First of the sprites
drear: day
Dunge: Cradle's dungeon where dwarven are imprisoned
dwarven: dwarf singular or dwarves plural
Earth: World and one of the Twin-Gaias
Eclipsed War: also known as the Dragon Wars, distinction refers to the final days of the war
Ellisar King: Elven Forest Fatherer of Grenfor Talarben
elven: elf singular or elves plural
Endstorm: the Starbond Apocalypse
Etern's Drop: The Three Mountains bastion of the sprites
Eternal, *the River*: alpine river that begins in the Ghost Spires and flows over Etern's Drop into the Webbed Sink
Evangel: Sonart's (late) mother
Evershorn: a Highprite
Eye: turbulent abyss surrounding the Hinge
False Starbond: Rending of the World: disastrous invocation by Shirdron. Also known as Xzligtzka, Apocstrum, and The Rending
Fang: Targin's broadsword
Farkshone: Sonart's father. Also, Cradle village which adopted his name

feather tree: white tree with feathery leaves that offer insulation, indigenous to Spires' Crest lowlands
Ferin and Hue: Brooke's sons
fire-gorgons: cherufes, lavatrols
Florin: elven Serion's Haft
Fram: Gnor's Warang
Frazer: Commander of Pathguard
Frenh: elven of Grenfor Talarben
Ganex: garrison of Pathguard
Ganly: High Wing Warden, brother to the Nightwolf, Gauley
Genu: baker from Pathguard
Ghast: a Mopheus
Ghost Spires: barren mountains of the north
Gjengaegungen: (pron. *jen-ḡae-ḡun-ḡin*) Kazir wizard Vein of Fire
Gnail: (pron. *nail*) Gnor's son *deceased*
Gnolin: (pron. *Know-lin*) Gnail's son, Gnor's grandson
Gnor: (pron. *nor*) veteran Wrayn aka Bulldog
Golan Hob: Pub/Pension in Bulkforge
Goodakh: *The Shrill,* archdemon, One of the Four
Granocks: rock creatures, custodians of the forest
Grave Wait: longest chapter in the Kusp encompassing The Scattering, The Dragon Wars, The Age of Renewal
Great Beyond: Afterworld, the afterlife
Great Soarers: tallest trees in Grenfor Talarben
Great War: War of the Rennen
Grendamaul: cursed land Cradle naturally fortressed continent
Grenfor Talarben: Land of Giant Trees, home of the wood elven
Grey Watchmen: guardians of Stormhearth, Timekeepers
Greyn: forest surrounding the Run
Guile the: arcane wraith of the Sancean
Haft: King's highest retainer, political steward
Harrowing the: arcane wraith of the Ice Wastes
hawkrike: mongrel warbird bred of a seed of a hawk and Ahzarim
Helmdak: ogre chieftain
Hidden Kingdom: Serenthia
Highguard: elite guardians of a given potentate
High Guardian: Leader of the Grey Watchmen
Highprites: Elementals Vamsah's First demigods akin to archangels
Hinge: crosspoint between planes of existence
Hive, the: towering bastion of the Zürshuck and the present seat of Deathwrought
hogsweed: main staple crop of the Cradle
Hogwash: a Nightwolf
Hooks: dwarven gallows
hyperdemon: alien demon entity from outside Creation including Infern
Ice Wastes: polar regions crowning Areth

Immersion: *The* conversion of the merekin from bipeds into aquatic beings
Inaris: Princess of Trusdin Run youngest daughter of King Thestian
Infern: Hell
Innereach: inner ring of mountains in the Cradle
Iomi: dwarven daughter of Xoral
ironbark: trees of the Cradle that grow upside down tunnelling into the soil
ironock: metal ore black in colour hard as steel when forged
Issicle: Ice Kraken
Jaeger: (pron. *Yae-ger*) Quiver's Warang
Johlarin: (pron. *Yo-lar-in*) King of Serenthia
Jǫrmungan: (pron. *Your-mun-Gun*) ancient jabberwocky
Kalibah: Heart of Fire crystal formed through the limitless power at the moment of creation.
Kåreoth: Prince of Cornerstone and eldest son of King Penthor
Kazir magical race from the Kaziri realm. Most become wizards of magic
Kaziri: homeworld of the Kazir Gjengaegungen's birthplace, a world of mostly water
King's Throne: Riverside tavern
Kivuk: pointwards' High Warden
Klin: tavern owner of King's Throne in Riverside
kofei: coffee
Kraken Throne: High Seat of Serenthia's Monarch
Krenal: a Mopheus
Kusp of the Testament the bible and history of Areth
Kworn: a race of bestial warriors that police the dwarven
Lakatos: Highprite Morgrand joined with to become Deathwrought
Land of Fire: fiery blight surrounding Mount Marwolaeth
Lang: a sprite
lavatrols: fire-gorgons, cherufes from the Land of Fire
Law of the Octagon: the law which defines the balance of the Four Veins in direct opposition to the Four Siphons but also the balance of creation to obliteration
lessrtrol: forest or cave troll
Lily: King Penthor's wife Queen of Cornerstone
Limbola: an ethereal domain where the Highprites went after the War of the Elementals
Lobe: desert expanse between Innereach and Outereach
loremaster: powerful elven or dark elven magic wielders
Lorin: Ranger of Serenthia, Targin's friend
Malrik: a dwarven, Sonart's cellmate
Matted Spikes: northwestern mountain chain
Maudlin: *The Shadow,* archdemon, One of the Four
Maxan: Brooke's horse
Menagerie: king of the dark elven
merekin: the sea people of Parmier who follow the Highprite, Bah-R
Merger: the prophesized union of the Four Veins

Metiver Dyrow: Highprites' First Orbical who penned the Kusp at Daleon's behest. Added the first aberrations
mid-death: midnight
mid-drear: noon
Midge: nickname for dwarven, slight derogatory play on *midget*
Mistengrave: river flowing south of Skullen Landing and the mired wetland that surrounds it
Mistspires: mountains of the Four (Siphon archdemons)
Mium: Second of the sprites. Custodian of the Chiva
moon-cycle: one month
Mop: a Ghast
Mopheus: sequentially unfettered beastmen
Morgrand: Vamsah's antithesis turned a Highprite to become Deathwrought.
Mount Marwolaeth: Mount Death—volcano in the Land of Fire within the Ice Wastes
naocci: (pron. *nayo-chay*) purple bell-shaped fruit filled with Gaia power and abundant sustenance
Necatar: King Cele's Haft
necromage: dark sorcerers who use blood-magic and human sacrifice to summon demons
Neglect *the*: Deathwrought's campaign to draw out the Blood Scion through depletion and starvation, ended by Farkshone
Night without Dawn: Nightwolf appellation to the Starbond
Nightwolves: insurgent pack comprised of Warangs and Wrayns: those descended from the Noirlunen considered True Blood
Noirland: homeland of the Noirlunen across the Sancean
Noirlunen true blood ancestors of the Nightwolves made the long march across the Ice Wastes
Observers: winterwights white warrens, hyperangels
ocular: small magnification device for seeing over great distances
Olden Mountain: Areth reference to Machu Picchu
One of the Four: appellation to describe one of the four Siphons
Onis: Wrayn, proficient in tending to injuries
Orb: Island and lake of the same name
Orbical: most powerful Seer and interpreter of the Kusp's prophecy
Otherworld: Earth
Outereach: outer circle of mountains framing the Grendamaul continent
Pal Mer: *sea people, name merekin use for themselves*
Paperman: eclectic forest hermit
Parmier: underwater city of the merekin
Pathguard: Northern Kingdom
Penthor: King of Cornerstone
Piskin: a dwarven
Proclaimers: (of the Kusp) dwarven spies and fanatics
Quiver: Wrayn, master bowman, True, Death Dancer
Quorum: Ghast collective

Racine, Solan: Commander in Pathguard's Highguard, brother to Brooke's wife

Ralaus: Warang, Brooke's mount

Rathnonek: Goblin King killed by Torin in the Black Castle in the Dead City

razor storm: a deadly cyclone born of the Scourge's magic

razorfish: flesh-eating freshwater fish

reddenbark: hundred-foot-tall trees with thick red trunks in the Northern Forest

Reechabah: *The Scourge,* archdemon, One of the Four

Relay, the: greatest and deepest canyon of the Main

Relthi: pseudonym for the summoner

Rennen: War of, abbreviated name, mostly in reference to the Second War

Rikor: troglodyte goblin

Riverside: enchanted forest village

Rolever: Northern Kingdom

Roth's Hold: northern coastal city of ill repute, Spifer and Genu's home

Ruin, the: scourged land below the Land of Fire and above the Dead Forest

Rusic: Seolad's father friend and ally to Farkshone

Salin: political envoy of Serenthia

Sancean: Sea of Sand, domain of the arcane wraith, the Guile

Sarana: a merekin

Scattering the: the epoch when the Ahzarim wandered to the most distant corners of Areth

scruff berries: small purple-blue tree fruit of the Northern Forest

Scythia: witch of the Dead City, Lady with Red Wine

sea-song: voice of power over the sea and its denizens

Seena: daughter of Allia

Seething, River: molten river flowing through Bulkforge used to smelt ironock in dwarven foundries

Sentinel's Retreat: pilgrimage site of the Grey Watchmen, atop one of the twin peaks in the Relay

Seolad: (pron. *syo-lad*) dwarven Son of Rusic

Serenthia: the Strong Helm, the Hidden Kingdom

Serion: elven prince

Shakeh Teron: renowned journeyman and cartographer before the Dragon Wars, charted the Whole of Areth

Shayla: dwarven daughter of Xoral

Shindu: woodsman in the Northern Forest

Shirdron, Lord: the desecrator alchlemage sorcerer former King of Pathguard

Shon: Third of the sprites

Sinathor: (born Zach Thornbury) emissary of the elven and Vein of Fire

Singular: merekin name for the Starbond

Siphons: of Fire *One of the Four* archdemons, highest servants to Deathwrought

Sisters' Feud: turbulent waters between the Three Sisters

Skiln: dark elven commander

Skullen Landing: the Dead City former bastion of the goblins
Sobrain Brant: The Wall soldier in Pathguard's Second Tier Heelward
Sonart: dwarven Vein
Sorgon: Sending—a demon of Infern
Souleater: hyperdemon born of the Void of Obliteration
spectre's breath: assassin's poison
Sphere: Time device of the Grey Watchmen, first Chronograph
Spifer: Nightwolf fire master aka Spitfire, 'the Dragon'
Spires' Crest: mountain chain south of the Relay
Spires' Mast: highest mountain on the Main
Springstead: Northern Kingdom
Sprintgale: a horse
Sprites Vamsah's second creation ethereal beings free of the inherent corruption of Highprites' taint.
spritewater: elixir charmed by the sprites
Stal: Targin's surrogate father
standstill: frozen moment where time moves neither forward nor back
Starbalance: temporal equilibrium between Birth and Bond
Starbirth: the moment of Creation
Starbond: prophesized apocalypse, Final Dark, Endstorm
star-cycle: one year
Stars: celestial bodies (dwarven harbour different beliefs)
State, the: separation of one's soul from their corporeal form to travel
Steppe: narrow ring of habitable land in the Cradle where the dwarven dwell
Stormhearth: bastion of the Time Wardens lost in the Ghost Spires
Strong Helm, the: Serenthia, the Hidden Kingdom
Summoner, the: necromage who summons demons of Infern to do his bidding
Swordswathe: mountain chain above Grenfor Talarben
Targin: Chief of the Nightwolves, warlord
Tasmin: Princess, daughter of Johlarin and Atheri, Targin's betrothed
Thestian: King of Trusdin Run
Thorian: Johlarin's alchlemage
Thorned Spikes: the four central mountains of the Innereach
Three Sisters: large islands off the Main's southern seaboard
Timekeepers: Grey Watchmen of Stormhearth, disciples of the Unnamed Highprite
Tragmar, Torin: Targin's Blood Father killed in the War of the Rennen
Tragmar: land named after Torin Tragmar
translation: magical point-to-point conveyance from one spot to another
trapper draw: magical device to extract water from the air, also a heat source
Tree of Fortunes: first tree planted by the Highprite Evershorn
Trusdin Run: Kingdom in the frozen North
Tsur: King Johlarin's warhorse
Tumbling Perpetual: rotating construct warding the Cleft Augury
turn of the dial: one hour
turncape: betrayer traitor

Twin-Gaia: the name applied to the lifeforce of the two sister worlds: Earth and Areth, sometimes referred to individually as Areth Gaia or Earth Gaia.
Tyrsus: elven captain and cousin to Prince Serion
Unnamed The: Highprite who created Time
Vakk: King of Springstead
Val: Wrayn Targin's Second
Vamsah The Creator Lightbringer, also known as Starsmith and First Father
Veins of Fire: or Blood Scions, prophesized paragons descended from the First through the Lines of Blood
Void of Obliteration: nether plane of oblivion and total nullification
War of the Elementals: first war of Areth
War of the Rennen: (Races) name given to two wars that engulfed all of Areth's denizens. The first 250 years earlier, ending twenty years later; the second thirty years ago lasting three years. Also known as the Great War
Warang: giant wolves with superior intelligence over lesser wolves
Webbed Sink: great basin, an extension of Relay where great spiders dwell
Weet: mute orphaned Wrayn pup
Weight the: dwarven vernacular to describe misery and oppression
Westafr: King of coastal elven of the Three Cities, Prince Serion's father
White Capes: King's elite guard
Wil: son of Allia
wilderen magic: wildest magic limitless power of Creation
Wind: Penthor's horse
winterwights: white warrens, hyperangels
witchorse: diacorn double-horned equestrians indentured to Lady Wrenwyn
Wrayn: black-garbed elite fighters who follow the pathless path.
Wrenwyn: Scythia's former name
Wres: Bessel's wife
Wychwood: indentured copse of sentinel trees surrounding Skullen Landing
Xoral: (pron. *Zoral*) a dwarven elder and alchlemage
Yerik: Warang Chief
Zürshuck: the Winged Ones, winged demons, the lowest cast of Infern

Wrayn Nightwolf band members: Scrit Cras Gnor Gnolin Val Tretak Quiver Alghan Hogwash Barget Gauley Spifer Char Jaak Lonus Gnail, Shora (sister to Jaak's wife), Wals, Sejan, Rurk, Jamb, Cash Rish, Craw, Rurk, Quiver, Gard, Gormel, Quarin, Curls, Wornin, Tallicah
Warang members of the Pack: Bor Ethor Ralaus Liina Jaeger, Yerik, Fram, Gefion, Yggn, Drasil, Patch

Characters from Earth

Angus: Sin's uncle
Argyle: Sin's butler
Bear: Bartholomew Brown, Sin's bodyguard
Bobby: Robert, Sinathor's pilot
Bongo: drummer for Sinathor
Fanning: Bertrand, American President
Gary: Sinathor's Manager
Hastings: Steve, Agent Presidential Guard
Isabella: Sin's (late) mother
Jock: keyboardist for Sinathor
Jonson: detective on Scott's team
Pipes: Peter, rhythm guitarist for Sinathor
Prometheus: Promo, Peter Graven lead guitarist for Sinathor
Ray: bass player for Sinathor
Ruth: Sin's aunt
Scott, Ethan: Agent Special Investigator in the NYPD SIU
Shon: sprite ward of Earth
Tristan: Sin's (late) father

Military Terms

Ward: division of one hundred soldiers plus one warden
Pointward: one hundred archers
Spurward: one hundred cavalrymen and their horses
Heelward: one hundred infantrymen
Wingward: one hundred warbirds, plus their riders
__Warden: commander of entire division (*warden* prefixed Point, Spur, Heel, or Wing)
Guard: i.e., haftguard, made up of ten wards or one thousand men-at-arms
High__Warden: Field General of all wards of a given discipline, also referred to as High Point, High Spur, High Heel, and High Wing

About the Author:

The Earth Gaia birthed Stephen Fenech in Toronto Canada, the fourth of five children to Maltese parents. He works full-time in the television industry but spends a great deal of time travelling the planet. So much so, he has visited every country in the world as a photojournalist and award-winning filmmaker. His documentary *Chad Exodus* won various prizes in several festivals, including the Viewer's Choice Award at the 2013 Malta International Film Festival and the Grand Jury Award at the 2013 Yosemite International Film Festival, which qualified it for Oscar contention. His travel book, *Earth: Been there Done that Got the T-shirt, Book One: The Big Kahuna* was published in 2016. It highlights a three-year trip around the planet. Its follow-up: *Book Two: Missing Pieces to the Global Puzzle* was published in 2017. He has also authored a science fiction novel: *Beacon: A Robot's Odyssey*, also published in 2017. When not writing, he enjoys visual art, beach volleyball, windsurfing, scuba diving and playing the guitar. His photography has provided him many opportunities to reach young people by giving presentations to schools on topics that range from World Religions to Climate Change. He was shortlisted for the Mars One Mission, making the top 600 candidates from an initial roster of 203 000 international applicants. A few years ago, he became the surrogate mother for two orphaned baby racoons—the most humbling experience of his life. He currently resides in Toronto, where he leaves daily rations of cat food out for all the neighbourhood strays and occasional marauding racoons. He likes to think they frequent his house to hear him play his guitar but admits the free food might have something to do with it.

www.ingramcontent.com/pod-product-compliance
Lightning Source LLC
Chambersburg PA
CBHW051930020726
47501CB00001B/65